M is for Mali

Sue Grafton has become one of the most popular female writers, both in the UK and in the US. Born in Kentucky in 1940, she began her career as a TV scriptwriter before Kinsey Millhone and the 'alphabet' series took off. She plans to take Kinsey all the way through the alphabet to Z. Sue lives and writes in Montecito, California and Louisville, Kentucky.

Also by Sue Grafton

A is for Alibi
B is for Burglar
C is for Corpse
D is for Deadbeat
E is for Evidence
F is for Fugitive
G is for Gumshoe
H is for Homicide
I is for Innocent
J is for Judgment
K is for Killer
L is for Lawless
O is for Outlaw
P is for Peril
Q is for Quarry
R is for Ricochet
S is for Silence

Keziah Dane
The Lolly Madonna War

Sue Grafton

M is for Malice

&

N is for Noose

PAN BOOKS

M is for Malice first published 1996 by Henry Holt and Co., Inc., New York.
First published in Great Britain 1997 by Macmillan.
First published in paperback 1997 by Pan Books.
N is for Noose first published 1998 by Henry Holt and Co., Inc., New York.
First published in Great Britain 1998 by Macmillan.
First published in paperback 1999 by Pan Books.

This omnibus first published 2008 by Pan Books
an imprint of Pan Macmillan Ltd
Pan Macmillan, 20 New Wharf Road, London N1 9RR
Basingstoke and Oxford
Associated companies throughout the world
www.panmacmillan.com

ISBN 978-0-330-45785-9

1 3 5 7 9 8 6 4 2

A CIP catalogue record for this book is available from
the British Library.

Printed and bound in Great Britain by
Mackays of Chatham plc, Chatham, Kent

M is for Malice

For my good friends . . .
Barbara Brightman Jones and Joe Jones
and
Joanna Barnes and Jack Warner

ONE

Robert Dietz came back into my life on Wednesday, January 8. I remember the date because it was Elvis Presley's birthday and one of the local radio stations had announced it would spend the next twenty-four hours playing every song he'd ever sung. At six A.M. my clock radio blared on, playing "Heartbreak Hotel" at top volume. I smacked the Off button with the flat of my hand and rolled out of bed as usual. I pulled on my sweats in preparation for my morning run. I brushed my teeth, splashed water on my face, and trotted down the spiral stairs. I locked my front door behind me, moved out to the street where I did an obligatory stretch, leaning against the gatepost in front of my apartment. The day was destined to be a strange one, involving as it did a dreaded lunch date with Tasha Howard, one of my recently discovered first cousins. Running was the only way I could think of to quell my uneasiness. I headed for the bike path that parallels the beach.

Ah, January. The holidays had left me feeling restless and the advent of the new year generated one of those lengthy internal discussions about the meaning of life.

I usually don't pay much attention to the passing of time, but this year, for some reason, I was taking a good hard look at myself. Who was I, really, in the scheme of things, and what did it all add up to? For the record, I'm Kinsey Millhone, female, single, thirty-five years old, sole proprietor of Kinsey Millhone Investigations in the southern California town of Santa Teresa. I was trained as a police officer and served a two-year stint with the Santa Teresa Police Department before life intervened, which is another tale altogether and one I don't intend to tell (yet). For the last ten years, I've made a living as a private investigator. Some days I see myself (nobly, I'll admit) battling against evil in the struggle for law and order. Other days, I concede that the dark forces are gaining ground.

Not all of this was conscious. Much of the rumination was simmering at a level I could scarcely discern. It's not as if I spent every day in a state of unremitting angst, wringing my hands and rending my clothes. I suppose what I was experiencing was a mild form of depression, triggered (perhaps) by nothing more complicated than the fact it was winter and the California sunlight was in short supply.

I started my career investigating arson and wrongful-death claims for California Fidelity Insurance. A year ago, my relationship with CFI came to an abrupt and ignominious halt and I'm currently sharing space with the law firm of Kingman and Ives, taking on just about anything to make ends meet. I'm licensed, bonded, and fully insured. I have twenty-five thousand dollars in a savings account, which affords me the luxury of turning down any client who doesn't suit. I haven't refused a case yet, but I was strongly considering it.

Tasha Howard, the aforementioned first cousin, had called to offer me work, though the details of the job hadn't yet been specified. Tasha is an attorney who handles wills and estates, working for a law firm with offices in both San Francisco and Lompoc, which is an hour north of Santa Teresa. I gathered she divided her time just about equally between the two. I'm normally interested in employment, but Tasha and I aren't exactly close and I suspected she was using the lure of business to insinuate herself into my life.

As it happened, her first call came on the day after New Year's, which allowed me to sidestep by claiming I was still on vacation. When she called again on January 7, she caught me off guard. I was at the office in the middle of a serious round of solitaire when the telephone rang.

"Hi, Kinsey. This is Tasha. I thought I'd try you again. Did I catch you at a bad time?"

"This is fine," I said. I crossed my eyes and pretended I was gagging myself with a finger pointed down my throat. Of course, she couldn't see that. I put a red eight on a black nine and turned up the last three cards. No play that I could see. "How are you?" I asked, perhaps a millisecond late.

"Doing well, thanks. How about you?"

"I'm good," I said. "Gee, your timing's uncanny. I was just picking up the phone. I've been making calls all morning and you were next on my list." I often use the word *gee* when I'm lying through my teeth.

"I'm glad to hear that," she said. "I thought you were avoiding me."

I laughed. Ha.Ha.Ha. "Not at all," said I. I was about to elaborate on the denial, but she plowed right on. Having run out of moves, I pushed the cards aside and began to tag my blotter with a little desktop graffiti. I block-printed the word *BARF* and gave each of the letters a three-dimensional cast.

She said, "What's your schedule like tomorrow? Can we get together for an hour? I have to be in Santa Teresa anyway and we could meet for lunch."

"I can probably do that," I said with caution. In this world, lies can only take you so far before the truth catches up. "What sort of work are we talking about?"

"I'd rather discuss it in person. Is twelve o'clock good for you?"

"That sounds fine," I said.

"Perfect. I'll make reservations. Emile's-at-the-Beach. I'll see you there," she said, and with a click she was gone.

I put the phone down, set the ballpoint pen aside, and laid my little head down on my desk. What an idiot I was. Tasha *must* have known I didn't want to see her, but I hadn't had the nerve to say so. She'd come to my rescue a couple of months before and though I'd repaid the money, I still felt I owed her. Maybe I'd listen to her politely before I turned her down. I did have another quick job in the works. I'd been hired to serve two deposition subpoenas in a civil case for an attorney on the second floor of our building.

I went out in the afternoon and spent thirty-five bucks (plus tip) on a legitimate salon haircut. I tend to take a pair of nail scissors to my own unruly mop about every six weeks, my technique being to snip off any tuft of hair that sticks out. I guess I must have been feeling insecure because it wouldn't ordinarily occur to me to pay real bucks for something I can do so handily myself. Of course, I've been told my hairstyle looks exactly like a puppy dog's backside, but what's wrong with that?

The morning of January 8 inevitably arrived and I pounded along the bike path as if pursued by wild dogs. Typically, I use my jog as a way to check in with myself, noting the day and the ongoing nature of life at the water's edge. That morning, I had been all business, nearly punitive in the energy I threw into the exercise. Having finished my run and my morning routine, I skipped the office altogether and hung around my place. I paid some bills, tidied up my desk, did a load of laundry, and chatted briefly with my landlord, Henry Pitts, while I ate three of his freshly baked sticky buns. Not that I was nervous.

As usual, when you're waiting for something unpleasant, the clock seems to leap forward in ten-minute increments. Next thing I knew I was standing at my bathroom mirror applying cut-rate cosmetics, for God's sake, while I emoted along with Elvis, who was singing "It's Now Or Never." The sing-along was taking me back to my high school days, not a terrific association, but amusing nonetheless. I hadn't known any more about makeup in those days than I do now.

I debated about a new outfit, but that's where I drew the line, pulling on my usual blue jeans, turtleneck, tweed blazer, and boots. I own one dress and I didn't want to waste it on an occasion like this. I glanced at the clock. It was 11:55. Emile's wasn't far, all of five minutes on foot. With luck, I'd be hit by a truck as I was crossing the street.

Almost all of the tables at Emile's were occupied by the time I arrived. In Santa Teresa, the beach restaurants do the bulk of their business during the summer tourist season when the motels and bed-and-breakfast establishments near the ocean are fully booked. After Labor Day, the crowds diminish until the town belongs to the residents again. But Emile's-at-the-Beach is a local favorite and doesn't seem to suffer the waxing and waning of the out-of-town trade.

Tasha must have driven down from Lompoc because a sassy red Trans Am bearing a vanity license plate that read TASHA H was parked at the curb. In the detective trade, this is what is known as a clue. Besides, flying down from Lompoc is more trouble than it's worth. I moved into the restaurant and scanned the tables. I had little appetite for the encounter, but I was trying to stay open to the possibilities. Of what, I couldn't say.

I spotted Tasha through one of the interior archways before she spotted me. She was seated in a small area off the main dining room. Emile had placed her by the front window at a table for two. She was staring out at the children's play equipment in the little beach park across the street. The wading pool was closed, emptied for the winter, a circle of blue-painted plaster that looked now like a landing pad for a UFO. Two pre-school-age children were clambering backward up a nearby sliding board anchored in the sand. Their mother sat on the low concrete retaining wall with a cigarette in hand. Beyond her were the bare masts of boats slipped in the harbor. The day was sunny and cool, the blue sky scudding with clouds left behind by a storm that was passing to the south of us.

A waiter approached Tasha and they conferred briefly. She took a menu from him. I could see her indicate that she was waiting for someone else. He withdrew and she began to peruse the lunch choices. I'd never actually laid eyes on Tasha until now, but I'd met her sister Liza the summer before last. I'd been startled because Liza and I looked so much alike. Tasha was cut from the same genetic cloth, though she was three years older and more substantial in her presentation. She wore a gray wool suit with a white silk shell showing in the deep V of the jacket. Her dark hair was streaked with blond, pulled back with a sophisticated black chiffon bow sitting at the nape of her neck. The only jewelry she wore was a pair of oversized gold earrings that glinted when she moved. Since she did estate planning, she probably didn't have much occasion for impassioned courtroom speeches, but she'd look properly intimidating in a skirmish nonetheless. Already I'd decided to get my affairs in order.

She caught sight of me and I saw her expression quicken as she registered the similarities between us. Maybe all the Kinsey girl cousins shared the same features. I raised a hand in greeting and moved through the lunch crowd to her table. I took the seat across from hers, tucking my bag on the floor beneath my chair. "Hello, Tasha."

For a moment, we did a mutual assessment. In high

7

school biology, I'd studied Mendel's purple and white flowering peas; the crossbreeding of colors and the resultant pattern of "offspring." This was the very principle at work. Up close, I could see that her eyes were dark where mine were hazel, and her nose looked like mine had before it was broken twice. Seeing her was like catching a glimpse of myself unexpectedly in a mirror, the image both strange and familiar. Me and not me.

Tasha broke the silence. "This is creepy. Liza told me we looked alike, but I had no idea."

"I guess there's no doubt we're related. What about the other cousins? Do they look like us?"

"Variations on a theme. When Pam and I were growing up, we were often mistaken for each other." Pam was the sister between Tasha and Liza.

"Did Pam have her baby?"

"Months ago. A girl. Big surprise," she said dryly. Her tone was ironic, but I didn't get the joke. She sensed the unspoken question and smiled fleetingly in reply. "All the Kinsey women have girl babies. I thought you knew."

I shook my head.

"Pam named her Cornelia as a way of sucking up to Grand. I'm afraid most of us are guilty of trying to score points with her from time to time."

Cornelia LaGrand was my grandmother Burton Kinsey's maiden name. "Grand" had been her nickname since babyhood. From what I'd been told, she ruled the family like a despot. She was generous with money, but only if you danced to her tune—the reason the family had so pointedly ignored me and my aunt Gin for

8

twenty-nine years. My upbringing had been blue collar, strictly lower middle-class. Aunt Gin, who raised me from the age of five, had worked as a clerk/typist for California Fidelity Insurance, the company that eventually hired (and fired) me. She'd managed on a modest salary, and we'd never had much. We'd always lived in mobile homes—trailers, as they were known then—bastions of tiny space, which I still tend to prefer. At the same time, I recognized even then that other people thought trailers were tacky. Why, I can't say.

Aunt Gin had taught me never to suck up to anyone. What she'd neglected to tell me was there were relatives worth sucking up to.

Tasha, likely aware of the thicket her remarks were leading to, shifted over to the task at hand. "Let's get lunch out of the way and then I can fill you in on the situation."

We dealt with the niceties of ordering and eating lunch, chatting about only the most inconsequential subjects. Once our plates had been removed, she got down to business with an efficient change of tone. "We have some clients here in Santa Teresa caught up in a circumstance I thought might interest you. Do you know the Maleks? They own Malek Construction."

"I don't know them personally, but the name's familiar." I'd seen the company logo on job sites around town, a white octagon, like a stop sign, with the outline of a red cement mixer planted in the middle. All of the company trucks and job-site Porta Potti's were fire engine red and the effect was eye-catching.

Tasha went on. "It's a sand and gravel company. Mr. Malek just died and our firm is representing the estate."

The waiter approached and filled our coffee cups. Tasha picked up a sugar pack, pressing in the edges of the paper rim on all sides before she tore the corner off. "Bader Malek bought a gravel pit in 1943. I'm not sure what he paid at the time, but it's worth a fortune today. Do you know much about gravel?"

"Not a thing," I said.

"I didn't either until this came up. A gravel pit doesn't tend to produce much income from year to year, but it turns out that over the last thirty years environmental regulations and land-use regulations make it very hard to start up a new gravel pit. In this part of California, there simply aren't that many. If you own the gravel pit for your region and construction is booming—which it is at the moment—it goes from being a dog in the forties to a real treasure in the 1980s, depending, of course, on how deep the gravel reserves are and the quality of those reserves. It turns out this one is on a perfect gravel zone, probably good for another hundred and fifty years. Since nobody else is now able to get approvals . . . well, you get the point I'm sure."

"Who'd have thunk?"

"Exactly," she said and then went on. "With gravel, you want to be close to communities where construction is going on because the prime cost is transportation. It's one of those backwater areas of wealth that you don't really know about even if it's yours. Anyway, Bader Malek was a dynamo and managed to maximize his profits by branching out in other directions, all building-related. Malek Construction is now the third-largest construction company in the state. And it's still family owned; one of the few, I might add."

10

"So what's the problem?"

"I'll get to that in a moment, but I need to back up a bit first. Bader and his wife, Rona, had four boys—like a series of stepping-stones, all of them two years apart. Donovan, Guy, Bennet, and Jack. Donovan's currently in his mid-forties and Jack's probably thirty-nine. Donovan's the best of the lot; typical first child, steady, responsible, the big achiever in the bunch. His wife, Christie, and I were college roommates, which is how I got involved in the first place. The second son, Guy, turned out to be the clunker among the boys. The other two are okay. Nothing to write home about, at least from what Christie's said."

"Do they work for the company?"

"No, but Donovan pays all of their bills nonetheless. Bennet fancies himself an 'entrepreneur,' which is to say he loses great whacks of money annually in bad business deals. He's currently venturing into the restaurant business. He and a couple of partners are opening a place down on Granita. Talk about a way to lose money. The man has to be nuts. Jack's busy playing golf. I gather he's got sufficient talent to hit the pro circuit, but probably not enough to earn a living at it.

"At any rate, back in the sixties, Guy was the one who smoked dope and raised hell. He thought his father was a materialistic, capitalistic son of a bitch and told him so every chance he could. I guess Guy got caught in some pretty bad scrapes—we're talking criminal behavior—and Bader finally cut him off. According to Donovan, his father gave Guy a lump sum, ten grand in cash, his portion of the then-modest family fortune. Bader told the kid to hit the road and not come back.

Guy Malek disappeared and he hasn't been seen since. This was March 1968. He was twenty-six then, which would make him forty-three now. I guess no one really cared much when he left. It was probably a relief after what he'd put the family through. Rona had died two months before, in January that same year, and Bader went to his attorney with the intention of rewriting his will. You know how that goes: 'The reason I have made no provision for my son Guy in this will is not due to any lack of love or affection on my part, but simply because I have provided for him during my lifetime and feel that those provisions are more than adequate— blah, blah, blah.' The truth was, Guy had cost him plenty and he was sick of it.

"So. Fade out, fade in. In 1981, Bader's attorney died of a heart attack and all of his legal files were returned to him."

I interrupted. "Excuse me. Is that common practice? I'd assume all the files would be kept by the attorney's estate."

"Depends on the attorney. Maybe Bader insisted. I'm not really sure. I gather he was a force to be reckoned with. He was already ill by then with the cancer that finally claimed him. He'd also suffered a debilitating stroke brought on by all the chemo. Sick as he was, he probably didn't want to go through the hassle of finding a new attorney. Apparently, from his perspective, his affairs were in order and what he did with his money was nobody else's business."

I said, "Oh, boy." I didn't know what was coming, but it didn't sound good.

" 'Oh, boy' is right. When Bader died two weeks ago,

Donovan went through his papers. The only will he found was the one Bader and Rona signed back in 1965."

"What happened to the later will?"

"Nobody knows. Maybe the attorney drew it up and Bader took it home for review. He might have changed his mind. Or maybe he signed the will as written and decided to destroy it later. The fact is, it's gone."

"So he died intestate?"

"No, no. We still have the earlier will—the one drawn up in 1965, before Guy was flung into the Outer Darkness. It's properly signed and fully executed, which means that, barring an objection, Guy Malek is a devisee, entitled to a quarter of his father's estate."

"Will Donovan object?"

"He's not the one I'm concerned about. The 1965 will gives him voting control of the family business so he winds up sitting in the catbird seat regardless. Bennet's the one making noises about filing an objection, but he really has no proof the later will exists. This could all be for naught in any case. If Guy Malek was hit by a truck or died of an overdose years ago, then there's no problem—as long as he doesn't have any kids of his own."

"Gets complicated," I said. "How much money are we talking about?"

"We're still working on that. The estate is currently assessed at about forty million bucks. The government's entitled to a big chunk, of course. The estate tax rate is fifty to fifty-five percent. Fortunately, thanks to Bader, the company has very little debt, so Donovan will have some ability to borrow. Also, the estate can defer

13

payment of estate taxes under Internal Revenue Service code section 6166, since Malek Construction, as a closely held company, represents more than thirty-five percent of the adjusted gross estate. We'll probably look for appraisers who'll come up with a low value and then hope the IRS doesn't argue too hard for a higher value on audit. To answer your question, the boys will probably take home five million bucks apiece. Guy's a very lucky fellow."

"Only nobody knows where he is," I said.

Tasha pointed at me. "That's correct."

I thought about it briefly. "It must have come as a shock to the brothers to find out Guy stands to inherit an equal share of the estate."

Tasha shrugged. "I've only had occasion to chat with Donovan and he seems sanguine at this point. He'll be acting as administrator. On Friday, I'm submitting the will to the probate court. In essence, all that does is place the will on record. Donovan's asked me not to file the petition for another week or so in deference to Bennet, who's still convinced the later will will surface. In the meantime, it makes sense to see if we can determine Guy Malek's whereabouts. I thought we'd hire you to do the search, if you're interested."

"Sure," I said promptly. So much for playing hard to get. The truth is, I love missing-persons' cases, and the circumstances were intriguing. Often when I'm on the trail of a skip, I hold out the prospect of sudden riches from some recently deceased relative. Given the greediness of human nature, it often produces results. In this case, the reality of five million dollars should make my job easier. "What information do you have about Guy?" I asked.

"You'll have to talk to the Maleks. They'll fill you in." She scribbled something on the back of a business card, which she held out to me. "This is Donovan's number at work. I wrote the home address and home phone number on the back. Except for Guy, of course, the 'boys' are all still living together on the Malek estate."

I studied the back of the card, not recognizing the address. "Is this city or county? I never heard of this."

"It's in the city limits. In the foothills above town."

"I'll call them this afternoon."

TWO

I walked home along Cabana Boulevard. The skies had cleared and the air temperature hovered in the mid-fifties. This was technically the dead of winter and the brazen California sunshine was not as warm as it seemed. Sunbathers littered the sand like the flotsam left behind by the high tide. Their striped umbrellas spoke of summer, yet the new year was just a week old. The sun was brittle along the water's edge, fragmenting where the swells broke against the pilings under the wharf. The surf must have been dead cold, the salt water eye-stinging where children splashed through the waves and submerged themselves in the churning depths. I could hear their thin screams rising above the thunder of the surf, like thrill seekers on a roller-coaster, plunging into icy terror. On the beach, a wet dog barked at them and shook the water from his coat. Even from a distance I could see where his rough hair had separated into layers.

I turned left onto Bay Street. Against the backdrop of evergreens, the profusion of bright pink and orange geraniums clashed with the magenta bougainvillea that tumbled across the fences in my neighborhood. Idly, I wondered where to begin the search for Guy Malek. He'd been gone for eighteen years and the prospects of running him to ground didn't seem that rosy. A job of this kind requires ingenuity, patience, and systematic routine, but success sometimes hinges on pure luck and a touch of magic. Try billing a client on the basis of *that*.

As soon as I got home, I washed off my makeup, I changed into Reeboks, and traded my blazer for a red sweatshirt. Downstairs in the kitchenette, I turned on the radio and tuned the station to the Elvis marathon, which was moving right along. I lip-synched the lyrics to "Jailhouse Rock," doing a bump and grind around the living room. I pulled out a city map and spread it on my kitchen counter. I leaned on my elbows, backside still dancing while I located the street where the Maleks lived. Verdugo was a narrow lane tucked between two parallel roads descending from the mountains. This was not an area I knew well. I laid Donovan's business card on the counter beside the map, reached for the wall phone, and dialed the number printed on the front.

I was routed through the company receptionist to a secretary who told me Malek was out in the field but due back at the office momentarily. I gave my name and phone number, along with a brief explanation of my business with him. She said she'd have him return the call. I'd just hung up when I heard a knock at the door. I opened the porthole and found myself face-to-face with Robert Dietz.

I opened the front door. "Well, look who's here," I said. "It's only been two years, four months, and ten days."

17

"Has it really been that long?" he asked mildly. "I just drove up from Los Angeles. Mind if I come in?"

I stepped back and he moved past me. Elvis had launched into "Always On My Mind," which, frankly, I didn't need to hear just then. I reached over and turned off the radio. Dietz wore the same blue jeans, same cowboy boots, the same tweed sportscoat. I'd first seen him in this outfit, leaning against the wall in a hospital room where I was under observation after a hit man ran me off the road. He was two years older now, which probably put him at an even fifty, not a bad age for a man. His birthday was in November, a triple Scorpio for those who set any store by these things. We'd spent the last three months of our relationship in bed together when we weren't up at the firing range doing Mozambique pistol drills. Romance between private eyes is a strange and wondrous thing. He looked slightly heavier, but that was because he'd quit smoking—assuming he was still off cigarettes.

"You want some coffee?" I asked.

"I'd love some. How are you? You look good. I like the haircut."

"Forty bucks. What a waste. I should have done it myself." I put a pot of coffee together, using the homey activity to assess my emotional state. By and large, I didn't feel much. I was happy to see him in the same way I'd be happy to see any friend of long standing, but aside from mild curiosity, there was no great rush of sexual chemistry. I felt no strong joy at his arrival or rage that he'd shown up unannounced. He was a man of impulse: impatient, restless, abrupt, reticent. He looked tired and his hair seemed much grayer, nearly ashen along his ears. He perched on one of my kitchen stools and leaned his forearms on the counter.

I flipped on the coffeepot and put the bag of ground coffee back in the freezer. "How was Germany?"

Dietz was a private eye from Carson City, Nevada, who'd developed an expertise in personal security. He left to go to Germany to run antiterrorist training exercises for overseas military bases. He said, "Good while it lasted. Then the funding dried up. These days, Uncle Sam doesn't want to spend the bucks that way. I was bored with it anyway; middle-aged man crawling through the underbrush. I didn't have to get out there with 'em, but I couldn't resist."

"So what brings you back? Are you working a case?"

"I'm on my way up the coast to see the boys in Santa Cruz." Dietz had two sons with a common-law wife, a woman named Naomi who had steadfastly refused to marry him. His older son, Nick, was probably twenty by now. I wasn't sure how old the younger boy was.

"Ah. And how are they?"

"Terrific. They've got papers due this week so I said I'd hold off until Saturday and then drive up. If they can get a few days off, I thought we'd take a little trip somewhere."

"I notice you're limping. What's that about?"

He gave a pat to his left thigh. "Got a bum knee," he said. "Tore the meniscus during night maneuvers, stumbling on a pothole. That's the second time I've injured it and the docs say I need to have a knee replacement. I'm not interested in surgery, but I agreed to give the knee a rest. Besides, I'm in burnout. I need a change of scene."

"You were burned out before you left."

"Not burnout. I was bored. I guess neither one is cured by doing more of the same." Dietz's gray eyes were clear. He was a good-looking man in a very non-standard way. "I thought I might stay on your couch for four days if you don't object. I'm supposed to stay off my feet and put ice on my knee."

"Oh, really. That's nice. You drop out of my life for two years and then you show up because you need a nurse? Forget that."

"I'm not asking you to make a fuss," he said. "I figure you're busy so you'll be off at work all day. I'll sit here and read or watch TV, minding my own business. I even brought my own ice bags to stick in the freezer. I don't want anyone hovering. You won't have to lift a finger."

"Don't you think this is a tiny bit *manipulative*, springing it on me like this?"

"It's not manipulative as long as you have the option of saying no."

"Oh, right. And feel guilty? I don't think so," I said.

"Why would you feel guilty? Turn me down if it doesn't suit. What's the matter with you? If we can't tell the truth then what's the point in a relationship? Do as you please. I can find a motel or I can drive on up the coast tonight. I thought it'd be nice to spend a little time together, but it's not compulsory."

I regarded him warily. "I'll think about it." There was no point in telling him—since I was barely willing to admit it to myself—how flat the light had seemed in the days after he left, how anxiety had stirred every time I came home to the empty apartment, how music had seemed to whisper secret messages to me. Dance or decline. It didn't seem to make any difference. I'd imagined his return a hundred times, but never this way. Now the flatness of it was inside and all of my past feelings for him had shifted from passionate involvement to mild interest, if that.

Dietz had been watching me and his squint showed he was perplexed. "Are you *mad* about something?"

"Not at all," I said.

"Yes, you are."

"No, I'm not."

"What are you so mad about?"

"Would you *stop* that? I'm not mad."

He studied me for a moment and then his expression cleared. He said, "Ohhh, I get it. You're mad because I left."

I could feel my cheeks brighten and I broke off eye contact. I lined up the salt and pepper shakers so their bases just touched. "I'm not mad because you *left*. I'm mad because you came back. I finally got used to being by myself and here you are again. So where does that put me?"

"You said you *liked* to be alone."

"That's right. What I don't like is being taken up and then abandoned. I'm not a pet you can put in a kennel and retrieve at your convenience."

His smile faded. " 'Abandoned'? You weren't *abandoned*. What's that supposed to mean?"

Just then the telephone rang, saving us from any further debate. Donovan Malek's secretary said, "Miss Millhone? I have Mr. Malek on the line for you. Can you hold?"

21

I said, "Sure."

Dietz mouthed *Did not.*

I stuck my tongue out at him. I'm very mature that way.

Donovan Malek came on the line and introduced himself. "Good afternoon, Miss Millhone . . ."

"Call me Kinsey if you would."

"Thanks. It's Donovan Malek here. I just spoke to Tasha Howard and she said she talked to you at lunch. I take it she filled you in on the situation."

"For the most part," I said. "Is there some way we can get together? Tasha wants to get moving as soon as possible."

"My attitude exactly. Listen, I've got about an hour before I have to be somewhere else. I can give you some basic information—Guy's date of birth, his Social Security number, and a photograph if that would help," he said. "You want to pop on out here?"

"Sure, I can do that," I said. "What about your brothers? Is there some way I can talk to them, too?"

"Of course. Bennet said he'd be home around four this afternoon. I'll call Myrna—she's the housekeeper—and leave word you want to talk to him. I'm not sure about Jack. He's a little harder to catch, but we can work something out. What you don't get from me, you can pick up from them. You know where I am? On Dolores out in Colgate. You take the Peterson off-ramp and turn back across the freeway. Second street on the right."

"Sounds good. I'll see you shortly."

When I hung up the phone, Dietz was checking his watch. "You're off and running. I've got to touch base with an old friend so I'll be out for a while. Are you free later on?"

"Not until six or so. Depends on my appointment. I'm trying to track down a guy who's been gone eighteen years and I'm hoping to pick up some background from his family."

"I'll buy you dinner if you haven't eaten, or we can go out and have a drink. I really don't want to be a burden."

"We can talk about it later. In the meantime, you'll need a key."

"That'd be great. I can grab a shower before I take off and lock up when I leave."

I opened the kitchen junk drawer and found the extra house key on a ring of its own. I passed it across the counter.

"Are you okay with this? I know you don't like to feel crowded. I can find a little place on Cabana if you'd prefer peace and quiet."

"This is fine for now. If it's too much, I'll say so. Let's just play it by ear," I said. "I hope you like your coffee black. There's no milk and no sugar. Cups are up there."

He put the key in his pocket. "I know where the cups are. I'll see you later."

Malek Construction consisted of a series of linked trailers, arranged like dominoes, located in the cul-de-sac of an industrial park. Behind the offices, a vast asphalt yard was filled with red trucks: pickups, concrete mixers, skip loaders, and pavers, all bearing the white-and-red company logo. A two-story corrugated metal garage stretched across the backside of the property, apparently filled with maintenance and service equipment for the countless company vehicles. Gas pumps stood at the ready. To one side, against a tangle of shrubs, I could see six bright yellow Caterpillars and a couple of John Deere crawler dozers. Men in hard hats and red coveralls went about their business. The quiet was undercut by the rumble of approaching trucks, an occasional shrill whistle, and the steady *peep-peep-peep* signal as a vehicle backed up.

I parked in the side lot in a space marked VISITOR beside a line of Jeeps, Cherokee Rangers, and battered pickups. On the short walk to the entrance, I could hear the nearby freeway traffic and the high hum of a small plane heading for the airport to the west. The interior of the office suggested a sensible combination of good taste and practicality: glossy walnut paneling, steel blue wall-to-wall carpet, dark blue file cabinets, and a lot of matching dark red tweed furniture. Among the male employees, the standard attire seemed to be ties, dress shirts, and slacks without suit coats or sports jackets. Shoes looked suitable for hiking across sand and gravel. The dress code for the women seemed less codified. The atmosphere was one of genial productivity. Police stations have the same air about them; everyone committed to the work at hand.

In the reception area where I waited, all the magazines were work-related, copies of *Pit & Quarry*, *Rock Products*, *Concrete Journal*, and the *Asphalt Contractor*. A quick glance was sufficient to convince me that there were issues at stake here I never dreamed about. I read briefly about oval-hole void forms and multiproperty admixtures, powered telescopic concrete chutes, and portable concrete recycling systems. My, my, my. Sometimes I marveled at the depths of my ignorance.

"Kinsey? Donovan Malek," he said.

I looked up, setting the magazine aside as I rose to shake hands with him. "Is it Don or Donovan?"

"I prefer Donovan, if you don't mind. My wife shortens it to Don sometimes, but I make a rare exception for her. Thanks for being so prompt. Come on back to my office and we can chat." Malek was fair-haired and clean shaven, with a square, creased face and chocolate brown eyes behind tortoiseshell glasses. I judged him to be six feet tall, maybe two hundred twenty pounds. He wore chinos and his short-sleeved dress shirt was the color of cafe au lait. He had loosened his tie and opened his collar button in the manner of a man who disliked restrictions and was subject to chronic overheating. I followed him out a rear door and across a wooden deck that connected a grid of double-wide trailers. The air conditioner in his office was humming steadily when we walked in.

The trailer he occupied had been subdivided into three offices of equal size, extending shotgun style from the front of the structure to the back. Long fluorescent bulbs cast a cold light across the white Formica surfaces of desks and drafting tables. Wide counters were littered with technical manuals, project reports, specs, and blueprints. Sturdy metal bookshelves lined the walls in most places, crammed with binders. Donovan didn't seem to have a private secretary within range of him and I had to guess that one of several women up front fielded his calls and helped him out with paperwork.

He motioned me into a seat and then settled into the high-back leather chair behind his desk. He leaned sideways toward a bookshelf and removed a Santa Teresa high school annual, which he opened at a page marked by a paper clip. He held out the annual, passing it across the desk. "Guy, age sixteen. Who knows what he looks like these days." He leaned back and watched for my reaction.

The kid looking out of the photograph could have been one of my high school classmates, though he preceded me by some years. The two-by-two-inch black-and-white head shot showed light curly hair worn long. Braces on his teeth gleaming through partly opened lips. He had a bumpy complexion, unruly eyebrows, and long, fair sideburns. His shirt fabric was a wild floral pattern. I would have bet money on bell-bottom trousers and a wide leather belt, though neither were visible in the photograph. In my opinion, all high school annuals should be taken out and burned. No wonder we all suffered from insecurity and low self-esteem. What a bunch of weirdos we were. I said, "He looks about like I did at his age. What year did he graduate?"

"He didn't. He got suspended six times and finally dropped out. As far as I know, he never even picked up his GED. He spent more time in Juvie than he did at home."

"Tasha mentioned criminal behavior. Can you tell me about that?"

"Sure, if I can think where to start. Remember the rumor that you could get high off aspirin and Coca-

Cola? He went straight out and tried it. Kid was disappointed when it had no effect. He was in the eighth grade at that point. Discounting all the so-called 'harmless pranks' he pulled back then, I'd say his first serious transgressions dated back to high school when he was busted twice for possession of marijuana. He was into dope big time—grass, speed, uppers, downers. What did they call 'em back then? Reds and yellow jackets and something called soapers. LSD and hallucinogens came in about the same time. Teenagers didn't do heroin or cocaine in those days, and nobody'd ever heard of crack. I guess that's been a more recent development. For a while he sniffed glue, but said he didn't like the effect. Kid's a connoisseur of good highs," he said derisively. "To pay for the stuff, he'd rip off anything that wasn't nailed down. He stole cars. He stole heavy equipment from Dad's construction sites. You get the picture, I'm sure."

"This may sound like an odd question, but was he popular?"

"Actually, he was. You can't tell much from the photograph, but he was a good-looking kid. He was incorrigible, but he had a sort of goofy sweetness that people seemed to find appealing, especially the girls."

"Why? Because he was dangerous?"

"I really can't explain. He was this shy, tragic figure, like he couldn't help himself. He only had one buddy, fellow named Paul Trasatti."

"Is he still around somewhere?"

"Sure. He and Jack are golfing buddies. Bennet pals around with him, too. You can ask when you talk to him. I don't remember any other friends offhand."

"You didn't hang out with Guy yourself?"

"Not if I could help it," he said. "I was busy keeping as much distance between us as possible. It got so I had to lock the door to my room so he wouldn't walk off with everything. You name it, he'd boost it. Stereos and jewelry. Some stuff he did for profit and some was just plain raising hell. After he turned eighteen, he got kind of crafty because the stakes went up. Dad finally flat told him he'd hang him out to dry if he fucked up again. Excuse my bad language, but I still get hot when I think about this stuff."

"Is that when he took off?"

"That was when he shifted gears. On the surface, he cleaned up and got a job out here, working in the maintenance shed. He was clever, I must say. Good with his hands and he had a good head on his shoulders. He must have seen this place as the answer to his prayers. He forged checks on Dad's accounts. He used the company credit card to charge stuff and then sold the goods. Dad, God bless him, was still covering. I begged him to blow the whistle, but he just couldn't bring himself to do it. Guy strung him along, telling lie after lie.

"What can I tell you? Dad wanted to believe him. He'd talk tough. I mean, he'd act like he was really cracking down this time, but when it came right down to it, he always gave in and offered him 'one more chance.' Jesus, I got sick of his saying that. I did what I could to close the loopholes, but I could only do so much." Donovan tapped his temple. "Kid had a screw loose. He was really missing some essential sprocket in the morals department. Anyway, the last stunt he pulled—and this didn't come out until he'd been gone a couple months—was a scam where he cheated some 'poor old widder woman' of her nest egg. That was the last straw. Dad had already kicked his ass out, but we were still stuck with the mess."

"Where were you at that time? I take it you were working for your father."

"Oh, yeah. I'd graduated by then. I'd been in and out of Vietnam, and I was working here as a mining engineer. I got my degree at Colorado School of Mines. My dad's degree was civil engineering. He started Malek Construction back in 1940, the year I was born, and bought his first gravel pit in forty-three. We were a construction outfit first and ended up owning all our aggregate sources. In fact, we built the business around that because it gives us a competitive edge. There's a lot of companies around here that do construction that don't own their aggregate sources and they end up buying from us. I'm the only one of the kids who went into the family business. I didn't get married till I was thirty-five."

"I understand your mother died the year Guy left," I said.

"That's right. She'd been diagnosed with lung cancer maybe ten years before. Fought like an alley cat, but she finally went under. I'm sure the uproar didn't help. Dad never remarried. He didn't seem to have the heart for it. All he cared about was the company, which is why I was so surprised about the will. Even in 1965, I can't believe he wanted Guy getting so much as a nickel from his estate."

"Maybe someone will come across the second will."

"I'd like to think so, but so far I've turned the house upside down. There was nothing like it in the safe deposit box. I hate to consider what's going to happen if Guy shows up again."

"Meaning what?"

"He'll cause trouble of some kind. I can guarantee it."

I shrugged. "He might have changed. People sometimes straighten out."

Donovan gestured impatiently. "Sure, and sometimes you win the lottery, but the odds are against. That's how it is and I guess we'll have to live with it."

"You have any idea where he might be?"

"No. And I don't lie awake at night trying to figure it out either. Frankly, it makes me crazy to think of him coming home to roost. I understand that by law he's entitled to his fair share of the estate, but I think he ought to be a brick about it and keep his hands to himself." He picked up a piece of paper and slid it in my direction. "Date of birth and his Social Security number. His middle name is David. What else can I tell you?"

"What about your mother's maiden name?"

"Patton. Is that for ID purposes?"

"Right. If I find him, I'd like to have a way to confirm it's really Guy we're dealing with."

"You're picturing an impostor? That's hard to imagine," he said. "Who'd want to be a stand-in for a loser like him?"

I smiled. "It's not that far-fetched. The chances are remote, but it's been done before. You don't want to end up turning money over to a stranger."

"You got that right. I'm not all that thrilled to give the money to *him*. Unfortunately, it's not up to me. The law's the law," he said. "At any rate, I leave this to you. He was a hard-livin', hard-drinkin' kid before the age of twenty-one. As to his current whereabouts, your guess is as good as mine. You need anything else?"

"This should do for the time being. I'll talk to your brothers and then we'll see where we stand." I got to my feet and we shook hands across the desk. "I appreciate your time."

Donovan came around the desk, walking me to the door.

I said, "I'm sure Tasha will have the proper notices published in the local paper. Guy may get wind of it, if he hasn't already."

"How so?"

"He might still be in touch with someone living here."

"Well. That is possible, I suppose. I don't know how much more we're obliged to do. If he never turns up, I guess his share of the estate gets placed in an escrow account for some period of time. After that, who knows? The point is, Tasha insists we get it settled and you don't want to mess with *her*."

"I should think not," I said. "Besides, closure is always nice."

"Depends on what kind you're discussing."

31

THREE

I stopped by the office and opened a file on the case, recording the data Donovan had given me. It didn't look like much, the merest scrap of information, but the date of birth and Social Security number would be invaluable as personal identifiers. If pressed, I could always check with Guy Malek's former high school classmates to see if anybody'd heard from him in the years since he left. Given his history of bad behavior, he didn't seem like a kid others would have known well or perhaps cared to have known at all, but he might have had confederates. I made a note of the name Donovan had given me. Paul Trasatti might provide a lead. It was possible Guy had turned respectable in the last decade and a half and might well have come back to his reunions from time to time. Often the biggest "losers" in high school are the most eager to flaunt their later successes.

If I had to make an educated guess about his original destination on the road to exile, I'd have to say San Francisco, which was only six hours north by car, or an hour by plane. Guy left Santa Teresa when the Haight-Ashbury was at its peak. Any flower child who wasn't already brain-dead from drugs had gravitated to the Haight in those days. It was the party to end all parties, and with ten grand in his pocket his invitation would have been engraved.

At three-thirty, I locked up my office and went down to the second floor to pick up instructions for service on the two deposition subpoenas. I retrieved my car and headed to the Maleks' place. The house was at the end of a narrow lane, the fifteen-acre property surrounded by an eight-foot wall intersected by an occasional wooden gate. I'd grown up in this town and I thought I knew every corner of it, but this was new to me, prime Santa Teresa real estate dating back to the thirties. The Maleks must lay claim to the last section of flat land for miles. The rear portions of the property must have tilted straight uphill because the face of the Santa Ynez Mountains loomed above me, looking close enough to touch. From the road, I could pick out individual patches of purple sage and coyote brush.

The iron gates at the entrance to the property stood open. I followed the long, curved driveway past a cracked and neglected tennis court into a cobblestone turnaround tucked into the L of the main residence. Both the house and the wall that encompassed the grounds were faced with dusky terra-cotta stucco, an odd shade of red halfway between brick and dusty rose. Massive evergreens towered above the grounds and a forest of live oaks stretched out to the right of the house as far as the eye could see. Sunlight scarcely penetrated the canopy of branches. Near the front of the house, the pine trees had dropped a blanket of needles that must have turned the soil to acid. There was little if any grass and the damp smell of bare earth was pervasive. Here and there, a shaggy palm tree asserted its spare presence. I could see several outbuildings to the right—a bungalow, a gardener's shed, a greenhouse—and on the left, a long line of garages. The driveway apparently continued on around the rear of the house. A Harley-Davidson was parked on a gravel pad to one side. There were flowerbeds, but even the occasional suggestion of color failed to soften the somber gloom of the mansion and the deep shade surrounding it.

The architectural style of the house was Mediterranean. All of the windows were flanked with shutters. A series of balustrades punctuated the stark lines of the facade and a lovers' stairway curved up along the left to a second-story veranda. All the trim was done in dark green, the paint color chalky with age. The roof was composed of old red tile, mottled with soft green algae. The poured concrete urns on either side of the front door were planted with perennials that had died back to sticks. The door itself looked like something that had been lifted from one of the early California missions. When I pressed the bell, I could hear a single resonating note strike within, tolling my presence to the occupants.

In due course, the door was opened by a white woman of indeterminant age in a gray cotton uniform. She was of medium height, thick through the middle, her shoulders and breasts slumping toward a waist that had expanded to accommodate the gradual accumulation of weight. I pegged her in her early forties, but I couldn't be sure.

"Yes?" Her eyebrows needed plucking and her blond

hair showed dark roots mixed with gray. This was a woman who apparently whacked at her own hair with some kind of dull instrument, a not unfamiliar concept. Her bangs had been cut slightly too short, curling across her forehead unbecomingly. Maybe forty dollars for a haircut wasn't too much to pay.

I handed her my business card. "Are you Myrna?"

"That's right."

"I'm Kinsey Millhone," I said. "I believe Donovan called to say I'd be stopping by this afternoon. Is Bennet at home?"

Her expression didn't change, but she seemed to know what I was talking about. She was plain, her nose maybe half a size too big for her face. Her lips were antiqued with the remnants of dark lipstick, probably eaten off at lunch or imprinted on the edge of her coffee cup. Now that I'd become an aficionada of drugstore cosmetics, I was acting like an expert. What a laugh, I thought.

"He just got in. He said to put you in the library if you arrived before he came down. Would you like to follow me?"

I said, "Sure." I loved the idea of being "put" in the library, like a potted plant.

I followed her across the foyer, toward a room on the right. I took in my surroundings surreptitiously, trying not to look like a mouth breather in the process. In the homes of the rich, it doesn't do to gape. The floor was dark parquet, a complicated herringbone pattern with the polished wooden chevrons blending together seamlessly. The entrance hall was two stories high, but little if any light filtered down from above.

Tapestries were hung along the walls at intervals, faded depictions of women with high waists and faces shaped like hard-boiled eggs. Gents in cloaks rode on horse-back, trailed by hunting dogs on chains. Behind them, a merry band of woodcutters toted a dead stag that had spears sticking out of its torso like Saint Sebastian. I could tell right away that theirs was a world devoid of animal-rights activists.

The library had the look of a private men's club, or what I imagine such a place would look like if women were allowed in. Several large red Oriental carpets had been laid side by side to form a continuous floor covering. One wall was paneled in dark walnut and there were floor-to-ceiling bookshelves on the other three. The windows were tall and narrow, diamonds of leaded glass admitting more chill air than afternoon light. There were three groupings of ripped red-leather club chairs and an enormous gray stone fireplace with a gas starter, its inner hearth blackened by countless fires. The room smelled of charred oak and book mold and suggested the kind of dampness associated with poorly laid foundations. For a family that had amassed a fortune in the construction business, they really ought to think about pumping money into the place. Failing major home improvements, a quick trip to Pier I would have done wonders.

For once, left to my own devices, I didn't bother to snoop. Guy Malek had been gone for eighteen years. I wasn't going to find a copy of his outbound bus schedule or a drawer filled with personal diaries he'd kept as a lad. I heard someone walking on the second floor, the ceiling creaking as the steps passed from one side to the other of the room above. I circled the library, glancing out of every window I passed. The room was a good thirty feet long. At the far end, a solarium looked out on the rear lawn, a large expanse of dormant grass with a murky-looking koi pond in the center. The surface of the water was choked with lily pads.

I moved back toward the door and heard someone come down the stairs and traverse the hall. The door opened and Bennet Malek came in. He was four years younger than Donovan with the same fair hair. Where Donovan's was glossy, Bennet's was coarse, and he kept it cut short to discourage a visible tendency to curl. He'd apparently given up his battle to stay clean shaven and a blond beard and mustache now defined the lower portion of his face. He was heavyset, looking beefy across the shoulders and thick through the chest. He wore jeans and a navy sweatshirt with the sleeves pushed up along forearms densely matted with hair. Tasha had tagged him as a man who invested and lost sums of money on various faulty commercial ventures. I wondered how I might have responded to him if I hadn't been told in advance of his poor business sense. As it was, I found myself disregarding the hearty confidence he was at pains to project. Belatedly, I noticed that he carried the last half inch of a drink in his right hand, gin or vodka over ice with a twist. He set the drink on the end table closest to him.

He held out his hand and shook mine with unnecessary strength. We weren't about to arm wrestle so what was the point? His fingertips were icy and faintly moist to the touch. "Bennet Malek, Miss Millhone. Nice to meet you. Don said you'd be coming.

Can I offer you a drink?" He had a big booming voice and made solid eye contact. Very manly, I thought.

"Thanks, but I'm fine. I don't want to take any more time than I have to. I know you're busy."

"Fair enough. Why don't you have a seat?" he said. His attentiveness seemed feigned, a salesman's maneuver for putting the customer at ease. I'd been in this man's company thirty seconds or less and I'd already developed an aversion to him.

I perched on the edge of a club chair with a wide, sunken seat. The leather surface was slippery and I had to fight a tendency to skid backward into the depths. As a child, I used to polish the trailer park sliding board to lightning-fast speeds by vigorous rubbings with sheets of Cut-Rite waxed paper. The glossy leather cushion had the same slick feel to it. To avoid losing traction, I had to keep my weight pitched forward, feet together and flat on the floor.

Bennet settled into the chair to my left with a series of creakings. "I understand you're a private investigator," he said.

"That's right. I've been licensed for ten years. I was a police officer before that. What about you? What sort of work do you do?"

"I'm into venture capital. I look for promising little companies with cash-flow problems."

And drain them dry, no doubt. "Sounds like fun," I remarked.

"It's gratifying. Let's put it that way." His voice had dropped into a confidential tone. "I take it you met with Don?"

"That's right. I talked to him earlier this afternoon."

He shook his head almost imperceptibly. "Did he mention the missing will?"

"Tasha told me about that when she was briefing me at lunch," I said. Vaguely, I wondered why he was raising the subject. The existence of a second will was really not my concern. "I guess your brother lucked out," I said.

He snorted. "I'll tell you what bugs me. I remember when Dad signed the second will. I can picture the day just as clear as I'm sitting here. Dad's attorney and two witnesses came out to the house."

"Well, that's interesting. Do you remember who they were?"

"The witnesses? Two women. I remember that much. I assumed they worked for the attorney, but I may have made that up. They weren't personal friends of Dad's as far as I know. The four of them came in here and emerged maybe half an hour later."

"Have you told Tasha about this?"

"I mentioned I was here the day the second will was signed. I can't remember now if I mentioned witnesses or not."

"I'd tell her, if I were you. She may find a way to determine who they were. From what I've heard, no one disputes the fact that a second will was drawn up, but was it signed in your presence? Were you apprised of the provisions?"

"Well, I wasn't in the room with him if that's what you're getting at. Dad referred to it later, but he never spelled it out. The question is, what happened to it?"

I shrugged. "Your father could have changed his mind. He could have torn it up and tossed it out."

Bennet stirred restlessly. "So everyone says, though I'm not convinced. It's an interesting issue, if you think about it. I mean, look at the facts. The will comes up missing and the black sheep of the family makes out like a bandit. Dad signed it in March and Guy left within days."

"You're saying your brother stole it?"

"I'm saying, why not? I wouldn't put it past him. He stole everything else."

"But what good would that do? Even if he snitched a copy, the attorney probably kept the original. Once Guy was gone, he had no way of knowing your father wasn't going to turn around and make another will just like it. Or write a third will altogether. From what Donovan's told me, your father was good at talking tough and not so good when it came to follow-through."

He shook his head and his expression was patronizing. "True enough. That's why I'm going back through all of Dad's personal papers. It's not that we want to deny Guy any monies he may be entitled to, but this is bullshit in my opinion. He collected his share once. Dad had the second will drawn up with every intention of eliminating Guy's claim. That's why he gave him the cash to begin with—to pay him off in full. I heard him allude to it many times over the years. As far as he was concerned, the ten grand he gave my brother was the end of it."

"Well, I wish I could help, but this is really not my turf. Tasha's the expert. I suggest you sit down and talk to her."

"What about my father's deal with Guy?" he went

on argumentatively. "It was a verbal agreement, but doesn't that count for anything?"

"Hey, you're asking the wrong person. I have no idea. No one knows where Guy is, let alone what kind of bargain he made the day he left."

His smile flickered and I could see him curb a desire to continue arguing the point. "You're right, of course," he said. "So what can I tell you about Guy?"

"Let's start with the obvious. Did he say anything to you about his plans before he left?"

"I'm afraid Guy wasn't in the habit of discussing anything with me."

I shifted the subject slightly. "Could he have headed up to San Francisco? Donovan says he was into drugs in those days and the Haight might have been a draw."

"It's always possible. If that's where he went, he never said a word to me. I should probably warn you, the two of us weren't close. I don't mean to seem uncooperative, but I don't have much to offer in the way of information."

"Did you ever hear him mention a possible career? Did he have any personal passions?"

Bennet's smile was thin. "He made a career out of doing as little as possible. His passion was getting into trouble, making life miserable for everyone else."

"What about his employment? What kind of jobs did he have?"

"None significant. When he was still in his teens, he worked in a pizza place until he got caught skimming cash. He also got a job doing telephone sales. That lasted two days. I don't remember his ever doing much else until he started working for Dad. He pumped gas

41

for a while so I suppose he might have become a career gas station attendant."

"What kind of car did he drive?"

"He drove the family Chevy until he was involved in a hit-and-run accident and his license was suspended. After that, Dad refused to let him use any of the family vehicles."

"Do you know if his license was ever reinstated?"

"If it wasn't, he probably drove without. He never cared much about life's petty little rules and regulations."

"Did he have any hobbies?"

"Not unless you count smoking dope and getting laid."

"What about his personal interests? Did he hunt, or fish? Did he skydive?" I was floundering, casting about in an attempt to develop a sense of direction.

Bennet shook his head. "He was a vegetarian. He said nothing should ever have to die so that he could eat. He was petrified of heights so I doubt he ever jumped out of airplanes or climbed mountains or bungee-jumped."

"Well, at least we can eliminate that," I said. "Did he have medical problems?"

"Medical problems? Like what?"

"I don't know. I'm just trying to find ways to get a bead on him. Was he diabetic? Did he have allergies or any chronic illnesses?"

"Oh. I see what you're getting at. No. As far as I know, his health was good—for someone so heavily into drink and drugs."

"Donovan says he had one good friend. Somebody named Paul?"

"You're talking about Paul Trasatti. I can give you his telephone number. He hasn't gone anywhere."

"I'd appreciate that."

He recited the number off the top of his head and I made a quick note in the little spiral-bound notebook I carry.

I tried to think about the areas I hadn't covered yet. "Was he a draft dodger? Did he protest the war in Vietnam?"

"He didn't have to. The army wouldn't take him. He had bad feet. Lucky him. He never gave a shit about politics. He never even voted as far as I know."

"What about religion? Did he do Yoga? Meditate? Chant? Walk on hot coals?" This was like pulling teeth.

He shook his head again. "None of the above."

"What about bank accounts?"

"Nope. At least he didn't have any back then."

"Did he own any stocks or bonds?"

Bennet shook his head again. He was beginning to seem amused at my persistence, which I found irritating.

"He must have cared about something," I said.

"He was a fuckup, pure and simple. He never lifted a finger for anyone except himself. Typical narcissist. The girls couldn't get enough of him. You figure it out."

"Look, Bennet. I understand your hostility, but I can do without the editorializing. You must have cared about him once."

"Of course," he said blandly, averting his gaze. "But that was before he became such a pain in the ass to all of us. Besides, he's been gone for years. I suppose at some level I have some kind of family feeling, but it's hard to sustain given his long absence."

"Once he left, none of you ever heard from him?"

His eyes came back to mine. "I can only speak for myself. He never called me or wrote. If he was in touch with anyone else, I wasn't told about it. Maybe Paul knows something."

"What sort of work does he do?"

"He's a rare-book dealer. He buys and sells autographs, letters, manuscripts. Things like that." He closed his mouth and smiled faintly, volunteering nothing unless I asked point-blank.

I wasn't getting anywhere and it was probably time to move on. "What about Jack? Could Guy have confided in him?"

"You can ask him yourself. He's right out there," Bennet said. He gestured toward the windows and I followed his gaze. I caught a glimpse of Jack as he crossed the back lawn, heading away from the house toward a slope to the left. The rear of the property picked up just enough sun to foster a mix of coarse, patchy grasses, some of which were dormant at this time of year. He had a couple of golf clubs tucked carelessly under one arm and he carried a bucket and a net in a blue plastic frame.

By the time we caught up with him and Bennet had introduced us, Jack was using a sand wedge to smack golf balls at the net he'd set up twenty yards away. Bennet withdrew and left me to watch Jack practice his chipping shots. He'd swing and I could hear the thin whistle as the club cut through the air. There'd be a whack and the ball would arc toward the net, with an unerring accuracy. Occasionally, a shot would hit the grass nearby, landing with a short bounce, but most of the time he nailed the target he was aiming for.

He wore a visor with PEBBLE BEACH imprinted on the rim. His hair was light brown, a shock of it protruding from the Velcro-secured opening at the back. He wore chinos and a golf shirt with the emblem for St. Andrew's stitched on the front like a badge. He was leaner than his two brothers and his face and arms were tanned. I could see him measure the trajectory of the ball as it sailed through the air. He said, "I hope this doesn't seem rude, but I've got a tournament coming up."

I murmured politely, not wanting to break his concentration.

Whistle. Whack. "You've been hired to find Guy," he said when the ball landed. He frowned to himself and adjusted his stance. "How's it coming?"

I smiled briefly. "So far all I have are his date of birth and his Social Security number."

"Why did Donovan tell you to talk to me?"

"Why wouldn't I talk to you?"

He ignored me for the moment. I watched as he walked out to the net and leaned down, gathering the countless balls which he tossed in his plastic bucket. He came back to the spot where I was standing and started all over again. His swing looked exactly the same—time after time, without variation. Swing, whack, in the net. He'd put the next ball down. Swing, whack, in the net. He shook his head at one shot, responding to my comment belatedly. "Donovan doesn't have much use for me. He's a Puritan at heart. It's all work, work,

work with him. You have to be productive—get the job done. All that rah-rah-rah stuff. As far as he's concerned, golf isn't worthy of serious consideration unless it nets you an annual income of half a million bucks." He paused to look at me, leaning lightly on his golf club, as if it were a cane. "I don't have any idea where Guy went, if that's what you're here to ask. I was finishing my senior year at Wake Forest, so I heard about it by phone. Dad called and said he'd told Guy to hit the road. They'd had a quarrel about something and off he went."

"When was the last time you saw him?"

"When I was home for Mother's funeral in January. When I came home again for spring break, he'd been gone maybe three days. I figured the whole thing would blow over, but it never did. By the time I graduated and came home in June, the subject was never mentioned. It's not like we were forbidden to refer to him. We just didn't, I guess out of consideration for Dad."

"You never heard from Guy at all? Not a call or a postcard in all these years?"

Jack shook his head.

"Didn't that bother you?"

"Of course. I adored him. I saw him as a rebel, a true individual. I hated school and I was miserable. I did poorly in most classes. All I wanted was to play golf and I didn't see why I had to have a college education. I would have gone off with Guy in a heartbeat if he'd told me what was going on. What can I tell you? He never called. He never wrote. He never gave any indication he gave a shit about me. Such is life."

"And nobody outside the family ever reported running into him?"

"Like at a convention or something? You're really scraping the bottom of the barrel on that one."

"You think you'd have heard *something*."

"Why? I mean, what's the big deal? People probably pull this shit all the time. Go off, and nobody ever hears from them again. There's no law says you have to stay in touch with people just because you're related."

"Well, true," I said, thinking of my own avoidance of relatives. "Do you know of anyone else who might help? Did he have a girlfriend?"

Jack smiled mockingly. "Guy was the kind of fellow mothers warn their little girls about."

"Donovan told me women found him attractive, but I don't get it. What was the appeal?"

"They weren't women. They were girls. Melodrama is seductive when you're seventeen."

I thought about it briefly, but this seemed like another dead end. "Well. If you have any ideas, could you get in touch?" I took a card from my handbag and passed it over to him.

Jack glanced at my name. "How's the last name pronounced?"

"*Mill*-hone," I said. "Accent on the first syllable. The last rhymes with bone."

He nodded. "Fair enough. You won't hear from me, of course, but at least you can say you tried." He smiled. "I'm sure Don was way too cool to mention this," he said mildly, "but we're all hoping you won't find him. That way we can file a petition asking the court to declare him dead and his share can be divided among the three of us."

"That's what 'diligent search' is all about, isn't it? Tell Donovan I'll call him in a day or two," I said.

I walked back across the grass toward the house. What a bunch, I thought. Behind me, I could hear the whistle of Jack's swing and the sound of the clubhead on impact. I could have knocked at the front door again and asked the housekeeper if Donovan's wife, Christie, was at home. As an old college chum of Tasha's, she might at least be gracious. On the other hand, she wasn't married to Donovan at the point when Guy departed, and I couldn't believe she'd have anything of substance to contribute. So where did that leave me?

I got in my car and started the engine, shifting into first. I eased down the long drive toward the street beyond. At the front gate, I paused, shifting into neutral and letting the car idle while I considered the possibilities. As nearly as I could tell, Guy Malek hadn't been a property owner in Santa Teresa County, so there wasn't any point in checking the tax rolls or real property records. From what his brothers had indicated, he'd never even rented his own apartment, which meant I couldn't consult with a past landlord, or query the water, gas, electric, or phone companies for a forwarding address. Most of those records aren't kept for eighteen years anyway. What else? At the time he'd left Santa Teresa, he had no job and no significant employment history, so there wasn't any point in checking with the local labor unions or with Social Security. He didn't vote, own a car or a gun, didn't hunt or fish, which probably meant he didn't have any permits or licenses on record. He'd probably acquired a driver's license and a vehicle by now. Also, using past behavior as a future indicator, he probably had a criminal history in the system somewhere, certainly with the National Crime Information Center. Unfortunately, I didn't have access to that information and, offhand, I couldn't think of anyone who'd be willing to run a computer check. A law enforcement officer with proper authorization has all sorts of databases available that I couldn't tap into as a licensed private eye.

I put the VW in first gear, hung a left, and drove over to the Department of Motor Vehicles. It was just shy of closing time and the place was clearing out. I filled out a form, asking for a records' search. Often, DMV records will be out of date. People move, but the change of address won't show up in the DMV computers until a driver's license or a vehicle registration is renewed. In this case, if Guy Malek had left the state, all the data might well be years out of date, if it showed up at all. At the moment, however, it seemed like the quickest way to get a preliminary fix on the situation. Since I didn't have his driver's license number, I picked up an ANI Multiple Record Request Form, filling in his full name and date of birth. The Automated Name Index file would either show no record for the criteria given, or would show a match for last name, first name, middle initial, and birthdate. As soon as I got back to the office, I'd put the form in the mail and ship it off to Sacramento. With luck, I could at least pick up his mailing address.

In the meantime, since the office was nearly empty, I

asked one of the DMV clerks to check the name through her computer.

She turned and gave me her full attention. "Are you nuts? I could get fired for doing that," she said. She turned the monitor on its swivel so I couldn't peek at the screen.

"I'm a PI," I said.

"You could be the Pope for all I care. You'll have to wait to hear from Sacramento. You get nothing from me."

"It was worth a try," I said. I tried a winsome smile, but it didn't get me far.

"You got a nerve," she said. She turned away with a reproving shake of her head and began to pack away her desk.

So much for my powers of persuasion.

FOUR

I returned to the office, typed up the envelope, wrote a check to the state, attached it to the form, affixed a stamp, and stuck the packet in the box for outgoing mail. Then I picked up the phone and called Darcy Pascoe, the secretary/receptionist at California Fidelity Insurance. We chatted briefly about the old days and I caught up on minor matters before making the same request to her that I'd made to the DMV clerk. Insurance companies are always running DMV checks. Darcy wasn't actually authorized to inquire, but she knew how to bend the rules with the best of them. I said, "All I need is a mailing address."

"What's your time frame?"

"I don't know. How about first thing tomorrow?"

"I can probably do that, but it'll cost you. What's this kid's name again?"

When I got home, lights were on in the apartment, but Dietz was still out someplace. He'd brought in a soft-sided suitcase that he'd placed beside the couch. A quick check in the closet showed a hanging garment bag. In

51

the downstairs bathroom, his Dopp kit was sitting on the lid to the toilet tank. The room smelled of soap and there was a damp towel hung across the shower rod. I went back to the kitchen and turned on the radio. Elvis was singing the final chorus of "Can't Help Falling In Love."

"Spare me," I said crossly and turned the thing off. I went up the spiral stairs to the loft where I kicked off my Reeboks and stretched out on the bed. I stared up at the skylight. It was well after five o'clock and the dark had fallen on us like a wool blanket, a dense, leaden gray. Through the Plexiglas dome, I couldn't even see the night sky because of the overcast. I was tired and hungry and strangely out of sorts. Being single can be confusing. On the one hand, you sometimes yearn for the simple comfort of companionship; someone to discuss your day with, someone with whom you can celebrate a raise or tax refund, someone who'll commiserate when you're down with a cold. On the other hand, once you get used to being alone (in other words, having everything your way), you have to wonder why you'd ever take on the aggravation of a relationship. Other human beings have all these hotly held *opinions*, habits, and mannerisms, bad art and peculiar taste in music, not to mention mood disorders, food preferences, passions, hobbies, allergies, emotional fixations, and attitudes that in no way coincide with the correct ones, namely yours. Not that I was thinking seriously of Robert Dietz in this way, but I'd noticed, walking into the apartment, an unnerving awareness of the "otherness" of him. It's not that he was intrusive, obnoxious, or untidy. He was just *there*, and his presence acted on me like an irritant. I mean, where was this going? Nowhere that I could tell. I'd no more than get used to him than he'd hit the road again. So why bother to adjust when his company wasn't permanent? Personally, I don't consider flexibility that desirable a trait.

I heard a key turn in the lock and I realized, with a start, I'd drifted off to sleep. I sat up, blinking fuzzily. Below me, Dietz was turning on additional lights. I could hear the crackle of paper. I got up and moved over to the railing, looking down at him. He turned on the radio. I put my fingers in my ears so I wouldn't have to listen to Elvis sing soulfully about love. Who needs that shit? Dietz was a big country music fan and I was hoping he'd flip the station to find something more twangy and a lot less to the point. He sensed my presence and tilted his face in my direction. "Good. You're home. I didn't see your car outside," he said. "I picked up some groceries. You want to help me unload?"

"I'll be there in a minute." I made a quick detour to the bathroom, where I ran a comb through my hair, brushed my teeth, and availed myself of the facilities. I'd forgotten how domesticated Dietz could be. When I thought about the man, it was his personal-security expertise that came foremost to mind. I padded down the stairs in my sock feet. "How'd you know what we needed?"

"I checked. Surprise, surprise. The cupboards were bare." He had the refrigerator open, placing eggs, bacon, butter, lunch meats, and various other high-fat, high-cholesterol items in the bins. On the counter was a six-pack of beer, two bottles of Chardonnay, extra-crunchy peanut butter, canned goods and assorted condiments, along with a loaf of bread. He'd even remembered paper napkins, paper towels, toilet paper, and liquid detergent. I put the canned goods in the cabinet and turned off the radio. If Dietz noticed, he said nothing.

Over his shoulder, he said, "How'd the interview go?"

I said, "Fine. I haven't made a lick of progress, but you have to start someplace."

"What's the next move?"

"I'm having Darcy run a DMV check through the insurance company I used to work for. She hopes to have something early tomorrow morning. Then we'll see what's what. I have other lines of pursuit, but she's my best bet so far."

"You're not working for California Fidelity these days?"

"Actually, I'm not. I got my ass fired because I wouldn't kiss someone else's. I rent an office in a law firm. It works out better that way."

I could see him toy with other questions, but he must have decided that the less said the better.

He changed the subject. "Can I talk you into eating out?"

"What'd you have in mind?"

"Something in walking distance where we don't have to dress."

I looked at him for a moment, feeling strangely unwilling to cooperate. "How's the old friend?"

Dietz suppressed a smile. "He's fine. Is that what's bothering you?"

"No. I don't know. I think I've been depressed for weeks and just now got in touch with it. I'm also nervous about the job. I'm working for my cousin Tasha, which I probably shouldn't be doing."

"A cousin? That's a new one. Where did she come from?"

"God, you *are* out of date."

"Grab a jacket and let's go. You can talk about it over dinner and bring me up to speed."

We walked from my apartment to a restaurant on the breakwater, three long blocks during which little was said. The night was very chilly and the lights strung out along the harbor were like leftover Christmas decorations. Over the softly tumbling surf, I could hear the tinkle of a buoy, the tinny sound mixing with the gentle lapping of water against the boats in the marina. Many vessels were alight and the occasional glimpses of the live-aboards reminded me of a trailer park, a community of small spaces, looking cozy from outside. Dietz's pace was rapid. He had his head bent, his hands in his pockets, heels clicking on the pavement. I kept up with him, my mind running back over what I knew of him.

His upbringing had been a strange one. He'd told me he was born in a van on the road outside Detroit. His mother was in labor and his father was too impatient to find an emergency room. His father was a brawler and a bully who worked the oil rigs, moving his family from one town to the next as the mood struck. Dietz's granny, his mother's mother, traveled with them in the vehicle of the moment—a truck, a van, or a station wagon, all secondhand and subject to breakdown or quick sale if the money ran low. Dietz had been educated out of an assortment of old textbooks while his mother and granny drank beers and threw the cans out the window onto the highway. His dislike of formal schooling was an attribute we shared. Because he'd had so little experience with institutions, he was fiercely insubordinate. He didn't so much go against regulations as ignore them, operating on the assumption that the rules simply didn't apply to him. I liked his rebelliousness. At the same time, I was wary. I was into caution and control. He was into anarchy.

We reached the restaurant, the Tramp Steamer, a cramped and overheated gray-frame establishment located up a narrow flight of wooden stairs. A modest effort had been made to give the place a nautical feel, but its real attraction was the fare: raw oysters, fried shrimp, peppery chowder, and homemade bread. There was a full bar near the entrance, but most of the clientele preferred beer. The air was saturated with the smell of hops and cigarette smoke. Between the honky-tonk jukebox, the raucous laughter, and conversations, the noise was palpable. Dietz scanned the room for seating, then pushed through a side door and found us a table on the deck, overlooking the marina. Outside, it was quieter and the chill air was offset by the red glow of wall-mounted propane heaters. The briny scent of the ocean seemed stronger up here than it had down below. I took a deep breath, sucking it into my lungs like ether. It had the same sedative effect and I could feel myself unwind.

"You want Chardonnay?" he asked.

"I'd love it."

I sat at the table while he moved back inside to the bar. I watched him through the window in conversation with the bartender. As he waited for the order, his gaze moved restlessly across the crowd. He crossed to the jukebox and studied the selections. Dietz was the sort of man who paced and tapped his fingers, subterranean energy constantly bubbling to the surface. I seldom saw him read a book because he couldn't sit still that long. When he did read, he was out of commission, utterly absorbed until he was finished. He liked competition. He liked guns. He liked machines. He liked tools. He liked climbing rocks. His basic attitude was "What are you saving yourself for?" My basic attitude was "Let's not jump right into things."

Dietz wandered back to the bar and stood there jiggling the change in his pocket. The bartender set a mug of beer and a glass of wine on the counter. Dietz peeled off some bills and returned to the deck, trailing the smell of cigarette smoke like a strange aftershave. He said, "Service is slow. I hope the food's good." We touched glasses before we drank, though I wasn't sure what we were drinking to.

I opened a menu and let my eyes trace the choices. I wasn't really that hungry. Maybe a salad or soup. I usually don't eat much at night.

"I called the boys," he remarked.

"And how are they?" I asked. I'd never met his two sons, but he spoke of them with affection.

"They're fine. The boys are great," he said. "Nick turns twenty-one on the fourteenth. He's a senior at

Santa Cruz, but he just changed his major so he'll probably be there another year. Graham's nineteen and a sophomore. They're sharing an apartment with a bunch of guys this year. They're smart kids. They like school and seem to be motivated. More than I ever was. Naomi's done a good job, without a lot of help from me. I support 'em, but I can't say I ever spent much time on the scene. I feel bad about that, but you know how I am. I'm a rolling stone. I can't help it. I could never settle down and buy a house and work nine to five. I can't behave myself in a situation like that."

"Where's Naomi?"

"San Francisco. She got a law degree. I paid her tuition—I'm good about that end—but all the hard work was hers. The boys say she's getting married to some attorney up there."

"Good for her."

"How about you? What have you been up to?"

"Not a lot. Mostly work. I don't take vacations so I haven't been anywhere that didn't somehow involve a stakeout or a background check. I'm a bundle of laughs."

"You should learn how to play."

"I should learn how to do a lot of things."

The waitress approached, moving toward us from a table in the angle of the deck. "You two ready to order?" She was probably in her late twenties, a honey blond with her hair in a boy-cut and braces on her teeth. She wore matching black shorts and tank top as if it were August instead of January 8.

"Give us a minute," Dietz said.

We ended up splitting a big bowl of steamed mussels,

nestled in a spicy tomato broth. For entrees, Dietz had a rare steak and I had a Caesar salad. We both ate as though we were racing against the clock. We used to make love the same way, like some contest to see who could get there first.

"Tell me about the depression," he said when he had pushed his plate aside.

I gestured dismissively. "Forget it. I don't like to sit around feeling sorry for myself."

"Go ahead. You're allowed."

"I know I'm allowed, but what's the point?" I said. "I can't even tell you what it's about. Maybe my serotonin levels are off."

"No doubt, but what's the rest of it?"

"The usual, I guess. I mean, some days I don't get it, what we're doing on the planet. I read the paper and it's hopeless. Poverty and disease, all the bullshit from politicians who'd tell you anything to get elected. Then you have the hole in the ozone and the destruction of the rain forests. What am I supposed to do with this stuff? I know it's not up to me to solve the world's problems, but I'd like to believe there's a hidden order somewhere."

"Good luck."

"Yeah, good luck. Anyway, I'm struggling for answers. Most of the time, I take life for granted. I do what I do and it seems to make sense. Once in a while I lose track of where I fit. I know it sounds lame, but it's the truth."

"What makes you think there are any answers?" he said. "You do the best you can."

"Whatever that consists of," I remarked.

"Therein lies the rub." He smiled. "What about the job? What scares you about that?"

"I always get amped on the eve of a big one. One of these days I'm going to fail and I don't like the thought. It's stage fright."

"Where'd the cousin come from? I thought you didn't have any family."

"Don't I wish," I said. "Turns out I have a bunch of cousins up in Lompoc, all girls. I'd prefer not to have anything to do with them, but they keep popping up. I'm too old to cope with 'togetherness.' "

"Such a liar," he said fondly, but he let it pass.

The waitress came by. We declined dessert and coffee. Dietz asked for the check, which she produced from a sheaf tucked in the small of her back, taking a few seconds to total it out. Her yellow socks and black high-tops really gave the outfit some class. She placed the bill facedown on the table slightly closer to Dietz's side than to mine. This was probably her tactic for playing it safe in case we were a twosome whose roles were reversed.

She said, "I can take that anytime you want." She moved off to deliver ketchup to another table. She must have the metabolism of a bird. The cold wasn't even producing goose bumps.

Dietz glanced at the check briefly, recalculating the total in the blink of an eye. He leaned sideways to extract his wallet and pulled out a pair of bills that he slid under his plate. "Ready?"

"Whenever you are."

We took the long way home. It seemed easier talking in the dark without looking at each other. The conversation was superficial. I'm an expert at using words to keep other people at bay. When we got home, I made sure Dietz had everything he needed—sheets, two pillows, an extra blanket, a small alarm clock, and a fresh towel—all of life's little amenities, except me.

I left him below and headed up the spiral stairs. When I got to the top, I leaned over the rail. "With your bum knee, I take it you won't be jogging with me in the morning."

"Afraid not. I'm sorry. It's something I miss."

"I'll try not to wake you. Thanks for dinner."

"You're welcome. Sleep well."

"Use your ice pack."

"Yes ma'am."

As it turned out, I slept a lot sooner than he did. Dietz was a night owl. I'm not sure how he occupied himself. Maybe he polished his boots or cleaned his handgun. He might have watched late-night television with the sound turned down. I sure never heard him. Once in a while, in turning over, I realized the light was still on in the living room. There was something so parental about his being on the premises. One thing about being single, you don't often feel protected. You tend to sleep with your mental shoes on, ready to leap up and arm yourself at the least little noise. With Dietz on guard duty, I got to cruise through a couple of rounds of REM, dreaming right up to the split second before the alarm went off. I opened my eyes, reached out, and caught it just before it blared.

I did my morning ablutions behind closed doors so the sound of running water wouldn't carry. Shoes in hand, I crept down the stairs in my stocking feet and tiptoed out the front door without waking him. I laced up, did a quick stretch, and set off at a fast walk to get warmed up. The night had shifted from pitch black to charcoal gray and by the time I reached Cabana, the darkness was beginning to lift. Dawn painted the early-morning sky in pale watercolor hues. The ocean was silver blue, the sky washing up from a smoky mauve to soft peach. The oil derricks dotted the horizon like clusters of iridescent sequins. I love the sound of the surf at that hour, the squawk of seagulls, the soft cooing of the pigeons already strutting along the path. A platinum blond and a black standard poodle were heading in my direction, a pair I saw most of the mornings I was out.

The run was good. Often three miles just feels like a pain in the ass, something I do because I know I must. For once, here I was feeling grateful to be physically fit. I wouldn't do well with an injury like Dietz's that prevented exercise. I'll never be any kind of champ, but for lifting a depression there's really nothing better. I did the turn at East Beach and started back, picking up my pace a bit. The sun was coming up behind me, sloshing rivulets of yellow light across the sky. Walking home again, winded and sweating, my mood was light and I was feeling good.

Dietz was in the shower when I got in. He'd brought in the paper and set it on the kitchen counter. He'd tidied the bedcovers and folded up the sofa bed, tucking the pillows out of sight somewhere. I put on a pot of coffee and then went upstairs, waiting until I heard him turn off his shower before I started mine. By 8:35, I was dressed, I'd finished breakfast, and I was gathering up my jacket and my car keys. Dietz was still sitting at the kitchen counter with his second cup of coffee and the morning paper spread out before him.

"See you later," I said.

"Have a good one," he replied.

On the way downtown, I stopped off at a nearby condominium with the two subpoenas in hand. I served both without incident, though the fellow and his girl-friend were hardly happy with me. Occasionally, I'll have someone who goes to absurd lengths to avoid service, but for the most part people seem resigned to their fates. If someone protests or turns ugly, my response is usually the same: "Sorry, pal, but I'm like a waitress. I don't cook up the trouble, I just serve it. Have a nice day," I say.

For a change, I parked in the public lot across from the courthouse and walked the two blocks to work. My current office is the former conference room for the law firm of Kingman and Ives, located in downtown Santa Teresa. From my apartment, the drive takes about ten minutes, given the usual traffic conditions. The Kingman building appears to be a three-story stucco structure, but the ground floor is an illusion. Behind a fieldstone facade, complete with barred and shuttered windows, there's actually a small parking lot, with twelve assigned spaces. Most of the office staff and the lesser tenants in the building are forced to scrounge parking elsewhere. The surrounding blocks aren't metered, but parking is restricted to ninety minutes max and most of us receive at least one ticket a month. Some mornings, it's comical watching us pass and repass, trying to beat one another to the available spaces.

I climbed the two flights of stairs, forgoing the pleasures of the elevator, which is small and takes forever, often giving the impression it's on the verge of getting stuck. Once in the office, I exchanged pleasantries with the receptionist, Alison, and Lonnie Kingman's secretary, Ida Ruth. I seldom see Lonnie, who's either in court or working doggedly behind closed doors. I let myself into my office, where I paused to make a note of the date, time, and a brief physical description of the couple to whom I'd served the subpoenas. I typed up a quick invoice, then picked up the telephone, leaning back in my swivel chair as I tossed the paperwork in my out box. California Fidelity didn't open until nine, but Darcy usually came in early.

"Hey, Darcy. It's me," I said when she answered on her end.

"Oh hi, Kinsey. Hang on a minute. I'm not at my desk." She put me on hold and I listened to leftover Christmas carols while I waited, feeling mildy optimistic. I figured if she hadn't found anything she'd have said so.

Half a minute passed and then she clicked back in. "Okay. Guy David Malek doesn't have a current driver's license in the state of California. His was surrendered in 1968 and apparently it's never been reissued."

"Well, shit," I said.

Darcy laughed. "Would you just *wait*? You're always jumping to conclusions. All I said was he doesn't drive. He has a California identification card, which is where I picked up the information. His mailing address is Route 1, Box 600, Marcella, California, 93456. That's probably the same as his residence. Sounds like a ranch or a farm. You want to see the picture?"

"You have a current *picture* of him? This is great. I don't believe it. You're a wizard."

"Hey, you're dealing with a pro," she said. "What's your fax number?"

I gave her Lonnie's fax number while I reached for the telephone book. "Are you sure he's in Marcella? That's less than a hundred miles away."

"According to DMV records. That should make your job easy."

"Ain't that the truth. What do I owe you?"

"Don't worry about it. I had to fake out some forms to make the request look legitimate, but nobody's going to check. Took less than a minute."

"You're a doll. Thanks so much. I'll be in touch and we'll have lunch. I'll pay."

Darcy laughed. "I'll take you up on that."

I put the phone down and paged through the telephone book, looking up the area code for Marcella, California. It was actually in the 805 area, the same as Santa Teresa. I tried directory assistance, giving the operator Guy Malek's name. There was no telephone listed at the address I'd been given. "You have any other listing for Guy Malek in the area? G. Malek? Any kind of Malek?"

"No ma'am."

"All right. Thanks."

I trotted down the hall to the fax machine just in time to see a copy of Guy Malek's photo ID slide out. The black-and-white reproduction had a splotchy quality, but it did establish Guy David Malek's SEX:

M; HAIR: BLND; EYES: GRN; HT: 5–08; WT: 155; DOB: 03-02-42. He looked ever so much better than he had in his high school annual. Three cheers for him. I confess I felt smug as I sat down at my desk, the little show-off in my nature patting herself on the back.

I called Tasha's office and identified myself to her secretary when she picked up. She said, "Tasha's in a meeting, but let me tell her it's you. She can probably take a quick call if it's important."

"Trust me, it is."

"Can you hold?"

"Sure." While I waited, I laid out a hand of solitaire. One card up and six cards down. In some ways, I was sorry everything had come together so fast. I didn't want Donovan to think he was paying for something he could have done himself—though in truth, he was. There's a lot of information available as a matter of public record. Most people simply don't have the time or the interest in doing the grunt work. They're all too happy to have a PI do it for them, so in the end everybody benefits. Still, this one was almost too easy, especially since I wasn't sure the family would believe their real interests had been served by my discovery. I turned the next card up on the second pile and placed another five cards down.

Tasha clicked on, sounding terse and distracted. "Hi, Kinsey. What's up? I hope this is important because I'm up to my ass in work."

"I have an address for Guy Malek. I thought I'd better let you know first thing."

There was half a second's silence while she processed the information. "That was fast. How'd you manage?"

I smiled at her tone, which was the perfect blend of surprise and respect. "I have my little ways," I said. Ah, how seductive the satisfaction when we think we've impressed others with our cleverness. It's one of the perversities of human nature that we're more interested in the admiration of our enemies than the approbation of our friends. "You have a pencil?"

"Of course. Where's he living?"

"Not far." I gave her the address. "There's no telephone listed. Either he doesn't have phone service or it's in someone else's name."

"Amazing," she said. "Let me pass this along to Donovan and see what he wants to do next. He'll be delighted, I'm sure."

"I doubt that. I got the impression they'd all be happier if Guy turned up dead."

"Nonsense. This is family. I'm sure things will work out. I'll have him give you a call."

Within fifteen minutes, my phone rang. Donovan Malek was on the line. "Nice work," he said. "I'm surprised how quick it was. I thought the search would take weeks."

"It's not always this easy. We got lucky," I said. "You need anything else?"

"Tasha and I just had a chat about that. I suggested we have you go up there in person. She could contact him by letter, but people sometimes react oddly getting mail from an attorney. You feel threatened before you even open the envelope. We don't want to set the wrong tone."

"Sure, I can talk to him," I said, feeling puzzled what the right tone would be.

"I'd like a firsthand report about Guy's current circumstances. Are you free sometime in the next two days?"

I checked my calendar. "I can go this afternoon if you like."

"The sooner the better. I want this handled with kid gloves. I have no idea if he's heard about Dad's death, but even with the estrangement, he could be upset. Besides, the money's a touchy issue. Who knows how he'll react."

"You want me to tell him about the will?"

"I don't see why not. He's bound to find out eventually."

FIVE

I glanced at my watch. Since there was nothing on my schedule, I thought I might as well hit the road. It was just now nine-thirty. A round-trip to Marcella would take a little more than an hour each way. If I allowed myself an hour to track down Guy Malek, I'd still have plenty of time left to grab a quick lunch and be back mid-afternoon. I opened my bottom desk drawer and took out my map of California. According to the legend, Marcella was maybe eighty miles north, with a population of less than fifteen hundred souls. I didn't think it would take even an hour to locate him once I hit town, assuming he was still there. The conversation itself probably wouldn't take more than thirty minutes, which meant I might get this whole job wrapped up by the end of the day.

I put a call through to Dietz and let him know what was going on. I could hear the television in the background, one of those perpetual news broadcasts riddled with commercials. At the end of the hour, you know more about dog food than you do about world events. Dietz indicated he had no particular plans. I wasn't sure if he was angling for an invitation to accompany me, but since he didn't ask the question, I didn't answer it. I didn't want to feel responsible for his entertainment anyway. I told him I expected to be back by three and would bypass the office and come straight home. We could figure out what to do about dinner when I finally rolled in.

I gassed up my VW and headed north on 101. The sunshine was short-lived. Where the highway hugged the coastline, the fog had rolled in and the sky was now milky white with clouds turning thick at the edge. Along the road, the evergreens stood out against the horizon in a variety of dark shapes. Traffic moved steadily, mostly single-passenger cars with an occasional horse van, probably heading to the Santa Ynez valley just north of us. We hadn't had much rain and the hills looked like dull hay-colored mounds with an occasional oil rig genuflecting in a series of obsequious bows toward the earth.

The road turned inland and within the hour, the clouds had burned off again, fading back into a sky of pale blue, streaked with a residual haze as wispy as goose down. Just outside Santa Maria, I took 166 east and drove for ten miles on the two-lane road that paralleled the Cuyama River. The heat from the January sun was thin up here. Through the valleys and canyons, the earth smelled dry and a string of bald brown hills rose up in front of me. Rain had been promised, but the weather seemed to flirt, teasing us with high clouds and a hint of a breeze.

The town of Marcella was situated in the shadow of the Los Coches Mountain. Driving, I was aware of the unseen presence of the great San Andreas Fault, the 750-

mile fracture that snakes up the California coastline from the Mexican border to the triple junction near Mendocino, the Pacific and North American plates grinding against each other since time began. Under the thin layers of granite and marine sediment, the crust of the earth was as cracked as a skull. In this area, the San Andreas Fault was intersected by the Santa Ynez Fault with the White Wolf and the Garlock not far away. It's speculated that the mountains in this part of the state once ran north-south like other mountains along the coast. According to theory, the southern tip of this chain was snagged by the Pacific plate many millions of years ago and dragged sideways as it passed, thus shifting the range to its current east-west orientation. I'd been driving my car once during a minor quake and it felt like the VW had suddenly been passed by a fast-moving eighteen-wheeler. There was a lurch to the right, as if the car had been sucked into a sudden vacuum. In California, where the weather seems to change so little, we look to earthquakes for the drama that tornadoes and hurricanes provide elsewhere.

At the junction of two roads, I caught sight of a discreet sign and turned southward into the town of Marcella. The streets were six lanes wide and sparsely traveled. An occasional palm or juniper had been planted near the curb. There were no buildings over two stories high and the structures I saw consisted of a general store with iron bars across the front windows, a hotel, three motels, a real estate office, and a large Victorian house surrounded by scaffolding. The only bar was located in a building that looked like it might have been a post office once, stripped now of any official function. A Budweiser sign was hanging in a window. What did the citizens of Marcella do for a living, and why settle here? There wasn't another town for miles and the businesses in this one seemed weighted toward drinking beer and going to bed soon afterward. If you wanted fast food or auto parts, if you needed a prescription filled, a movie, a fitness center, or a wedding gown, you'd have to drive into Santa Maria or farther north on 101 to Atascadero and Paso Robles. The land surrounding the town seemed barren. I hadn't seen anything that even halfway resembled a citrus orchard or a plowed field. Maybe the countryside was devoted to ranches or mines or stock-car races. Maybe people lived here to escape the hurly-burly of San Luis Obispo.

I found a gas station on a side street and stopped for directions. The youth who emerged was about seventeen. He was skinny, had pale eyes, hair shaved very close up to his ears, and a tangle of teeth, all reminiscent of someone in an early episode of *The Twilight Zone*. I said, "Hi. I'm looking for a friend of mine named Guy Malek. I think he lives on Route 1 somewhere, but he didn't give me directions." Well, okay. I was fudging, but I didn't outright *lie*. I *would* be Guy's friend when he heard the news about the five million bucks.

The youth said nothing, but he pointed a trembling finger like the Ghost of Christmas Past.

I glanced over my shoulder. "Back that way?"

"That's the house."

I turned to stare with astonishment. The property was enclosed by chain-link fencing. Beyond a rolling chicken wire gate, I could see a small house, a shed, a large barn with corrugated metal siding curling away from the seams, an old yellow school bus, a single gas pump, and a sign too faded to read at any distance. The gate was open. "Oh. Well, thanks. Do you know if he's home?"

"No."

"He's not?"

"No, I don't know. I didn't see him today."

"Ah. Well, I guess I'll go knock."

"You could do that," he said.

I pulled out of the station and drove across the road. I nosed the VW through the open gate and parked on a length of raw dirt that I took for a driveway. I got out. The surface of the yard was white sand with a rim of brown grass around the edge. The house was frame, painted once-upon-a-time white, one story with a wooden porch built across the front. A trellis that shielded the windows on the left sported only one bare vine, which twisted through the latticework like a boa constrictor. A matching trellis on the right had collapsed under its burden of dry, brown vegetation. Various wires extended from the roofline, connecting the occupants to telephone, cable, and electricity.

I climbed the wooden stairs and knocked on the dilapidated screen. The front door was shut and there were no signs of life. There was a fine dusting of soot everywhere, as if the structure were downwind of a smelting plant. The porch floor began to tremble in a way that suggested that someone was traversing the wooden floor inside of the house. The door was opened and I found myself face-to-face with the man I took to be Guy Malek. Aside from a three-day growth of beard, he didn't look anywhere near his age. His hair looked darker and straighter than it had in his high school yearbook, but his features were still boyish: khaki green eyes fringed with dark lashes; a small, straight nose; and a generous mouth. His complexion was clear and his color was good. Age had sketched in fine lines around his eyes and the flesh along his jaw was beginning to sag, but I'd have pegged him in his mid-thirties. At fifty and sixty, he'd no doubt look just the same, the years making only moderate adjustments to his good looks. He wore denim overalls on top of what looked like a union suit. He was in the process of putting on a blue jeans jacket when he answered the door, and he paused to straighten the collar in the back before he said, "Hey."

As an adolescent, Guy Malek had been as dorky looking as the rest of us. He was the bad kid, lawless and self-destructive, one of life's lost souls. He must have been appealing because he was so in need of rescue. Women can't resist a man who needs saving. Now his good angel had apparently taken up residence, bestowing on his countenance the look of serenity. It seemed odd that his brothers had matured so differently. Already, I liked this man better than his siblings. Aside from the scruffiness, he didn't look like he was snorting, sniffing, or mainlining illegal substances.

"Are you Guy Malek?"

His smile was hesitant, as though I might be someone he had met before whose name he wished he remembered. "Yes."

"My name is Kinsey Millhone. I'm a private investigator from Santa Teresa." I gave him a business card. He studied the card, but didn't offer to shake hands.

His were as soiled as an auto mechanic's. I could see a muscle work in his jaw.

His eyes came up to mine and his entire body became still. The smile faded. "My family hired you?"

"Well, yes," I said. I was about to launch into a diplomatic account of his father's death when I saw tears rise in his eyes, blurring the clear green of his gaze. He looked upward, blinking, and took a deep breath before he brought his attention back to mine. He dashed at his cheeks, laughing with embarrassment.

He said, "Whoa," pinching at his eyes with the fingers of one hand. He shook his head, trying to compose himself. "Sorry. You caught me by surprise. I never thought it would matter, but I guess it does. I always wished they'd send someone, but I'd about given up hope. How'd you find me?"

"It wasn't that hard. I ran a DMV check and came up with your California identification card. I tried directory assistance, but they didn't have you listed. I take it you don't have a phone."

"Can't afford one," he said. "You want to come in?" His manner was awkward and he seemed unsure of himself. His gaze fell away from mine and then came back again.

"I'd like that," I said.

He stepped back to allow me entrance and I passed into a room that was about what you'd expect. The interior construction was crude and featured wide, unfinished floorboards and windows that didn't quite shut. Various pieces of old furniture had been moved into the space, probably cadged from the city dump . . . if there was one in this town. Every surface was piled high with soiled clothes and books and magazines and utensils, pots and pans and canned goods and tools. There were also what looked like farm implements whose functions were unclear. There was a tower of used tires in one corner of the room and a toilet that didn't seem connected to much of anything. Guy caught my puzzlement. "I'm holding that for a fellow. I have a real bathroom in there," he said, smiling shyly.

"Glad to hear that," I said and smiled back at him.

"You want a cup of coffee? It's instant, but it's not bad."

"No, thanks. Were you on your way out?"

"What? Oh, yeah, but don't worry about that. I have to be someplace shortly. Have a seat." He pulled out a handkerchief and paused to blow his nose. I could feel anxiety stir in my chest. There was something touching about his openness. He gestured toward a frayed, lumpy couch with a spring sticking through the cushion. I perched on the edge, hoping not to do serious damage to my private parts. My discomfort was related to the fact that Guy Malek apparently thought his family had hired me to conduct the search out of sentiment. I knew their real attitude, which was actually hostile if the truth be known. I did a quick debate with myself and decided I'd better level with him. Whatever the outcome of our conversation, it would be too humiliating for him if I let him harbor the wrong impression.

He pulled up a wooden chair and sat facing me directly, occasionally mopping at his eyes. He didn't apologize for the tears that continued to spill down his cheeks. "You don't know how hard I prayed for this," he said, mouth trembling. He looked down at his hands and began to fold the handkerchief in on itself. "The pastor of my church . . . he swore up and down it would come to pass if it was meant to be. No point in praying if it isn't God's will, he said. And I kept saying, 'Man, it seems like they'd have found me by now if they cared enough, you know?' "

I was struck by the fact that his circumstances were oddly reminiscent of mine, both of us trying to assimilate fractured family connections. At least he welcomed his, though he'd misunderstood the purpose of my visit. I felt like a dog having to set him straight. "Guy, as a matter of fact, it's more complicated. I have some bad news," I said.

"My father died?"

"Two weeks ago. I'm not sure of the date. I gather he'd had a stroke and he was also struggling with cancer. He'd been through a lot and I guess his body just gave up on him."

He was silent for a moment, staring off into space. "Well. I guess I'm not surprised," he said. "Did he . . . do you know if he was the one who asked for me?"

"I have no idea. I wasn't hired until yesterday. The probate attorney is getting the process underway. By law, you're required to be notified since you're one of the beneficiaries."

He turned to me, suddenly getting it. "Ah. You're here on official business and that's all it is, right?"

"More or less."

I watched as the color rose slowly in his cheeks. "Silly me," he said. "And here I thought you were sent by someone who actually gave a shit."

"I'm sorry."

"Not your fault," he said. "What else?"

"What else?"

"I'm wondering if you have any other news to impart."

"Not really." If he'd picked up on the fact that he was due to inherit money, he gave no indication.

"I don't suppose there's any chance my father asked for me."

"I wish I could help, but I wasn't given any details. It's possible, I'm sure, but you may never know. You can ask the attorney when you talk to her. She knows a lot more than I do about the circumstances of his death."

He smiled fleetingly. "Dad hired a woman? That doesn't sound like him."

"Donovan hired her. She went to school with his wife."

"What about Bennet and Jack? Are they married?" He said the names as if the sounds hadn't been uttered for years.

"No. Just Donovan. I don't think he and Christie have any kids as yet. He runs the company, which I understand is now the third-largest construction firm in the state."

"Good for him. Donnie was always obsessed with the business," he said. "Did you talk to the other two?"

"Briefly."

The character of his expression had completely changed as we spoke. What had started out as happiness had shifted to painful enlightenment. "Correct me if I'm wrong, but I get the impression they're not really interested in me. The attorney said they had to do this

78

so they're doing it. Is that it? I mean, the three of them aren't burdened by a lot of warm, gooey feelings where I'm concerned."

"That's true, but it probably stems from the situation when you left. I was told you were in a lot of trouble, so their memories of you aren't that flattering."

"I suppose not. Nor mine of them if it comes right down to it."

"Besides, nobody really believed I'd find you. It's been what, eighteen years?"

"About that. Not long enough, apparently, from their perspective."

"Where'd you go when you left? Do you mind if I ask?"

"Why would I mind? It doesn't amount to much. I went out to the highway to hitch a ride. I was heading for San Francisco, zonked out of my head on acid. The fellow who picked me up was a preacher, who'd been hired by a church about a mile from here. He took me in. I was tripped out so bad I didn't even know where I was at."

"And you've been here all this time?"

"Not quite," he said. "It wasn't like I cleaned up and got straight, just like that. I screwed up more than once. I'd backslide . . . you know, get drunk and take off . . . but Pete and his wife always found me and brought me back. Finally, I realized I wasn't going to shake 'em off. Didn't matter what I did. They were sticking to me like glue. That's when I took a stand and found Jesus in my heart. It really turned my life around."

"And you never got in touch with your family?" I said.

He shook his head, his smile bitter. "They haven't exactly been clamoring for me, either."

"Maybe that will change when I talk to them. What else can I tell them? Do you work?"

"Sure, I work. I do maintenance at the church and, you know, general handyman jobs around town. Painting and repairs, plumbing, electrical. About anything you need. Mostly minimum wage, but I'm the only one does it, so I stay busy."

"Sounds like you've done all right for yourself."

He looked around him. "Well, I don't have much, but I don't need much either. Place isn't mine," he said. "The church provides my housing, but I make enough to take care of the basics. Food and utilities, that sort of thing. I don't drive, but I have a bike and that gets me most places in a town this size."

"You've changed quite a lot."

"I'd be dead otherwise." He glanced at his watch. "Listen, I don't mean to rush you, but I probably ought to get myself on over to the church."

"I won't keep you then. I appreciate your time. Can I give you a lift?"

"Sure. We can talk on the way."

Once in the car, he directed me back to the highway. We turned right onto 166, heading east again. We drove for a while in companionable silence. He slid a look in my direction. "So what's your assignment? Find me and report back?"

"That's about it," I said. "Now that we have a current address, Tasha Howard, the attorney, will be sending you notice of the probate."

"Oh, that's right. I forgot. I'm a beneficiary, you said." His tone had turned light and nearly mocking.

"That doesn't interest you?"

"Not particularly. I thought I needed something from those people, but as it turns out, I don't." He pointed at an upcoming junction and I took a right-hand turn onto a small side road. The roadbed had been down-graded from blacktop to loose gravel, and I could see the plumes of white dust swirling up in my rear window as we drove. The church was situated at the edge of a pasture about a half mile down. The sign said: JUBILEE EVANGELICAL CHURCH.

"You can pull up right here," he said. "You want to come in and see the place? If you're paid by the hour, you might as well have the full tour. I'm sure Donnie can afford it."

I hesitated slightly. "All right."

He cocked his head. "You don't have to worry. I won't try to convert you."

I parked and the two of us got out. He didn't issue a proclamation, but I could tell from his manner that he was proud of the place. He took out a ring of keys and let us in.

The church was small, a frame building, little more than one room. There was something about its plain appearance that spoke of goodness. The stained glass windows were not elaborate. Each was divided into six simple panels of pale gold with a scripture written across the bottom. There was an unadorned wood pulpit at the front, positioned to the left of a raised and carpeted platform. On the right, there was an organ and three rows of folding chairs for the choir. Last

Sunday's flowers consisted of a spray of white gladioli. "Place was destroyed by fire about ten years back. Congregation rebuilt everything from the ground right on up."

I said, "How'd you get on track? That must have been hard."

He sat down in one of the front pews and I could see him look around, perhaps seeing the place as I saw it. "I give credit to the Lord, though Pete always says I did the work myself," he said. "I grew up without much guidance, without values of any kind. I'm not blaming anybody. That's just how it was. My parents were good people. They didn't drink or beat me or anything like that, but they never talked about God or faith or their religious beliefs, assuming they had any, which I don't guess they did. My brothers and I . . . even when we were little kids . . . never went to Sunday school or church.

"My parents disliked 'organized religion.' I don't know what that phrase meant to them or what their perception was, but they took pride in making sure none of us were ever exposed to it. Like a disease of some kind. I remember they had a book by this guy named Philip Wylie. *Generation of Vipers*. He equated the church teachings with intellectual corruption, the stunting of young minds."

"Some people feel that way," I said.

"Yeah, I know. I don't get it, but it's something I run into out there in the world. It's like people think just because you go to church you're not all that bright. I mean, just because I'm born-again doesn't mean I lost IQ points."

"I'm sure you didn't."

"Thing is, I was raised without a moral compass. I couldn't get a sense of what the rules were so I just kept pushing. I kept crossing the line, waiting for somebody to tell me where the boundaries were."

"But you were getting into trouble with the law from what I heard. You must have known the rules because every time you broke one, you ended up in court. Donovan says you spent more time in Juvenile Hall than you did at home."

His smile was sheepish. "That's true, but here's what's weird. I didn't mind Juvie all that much. At least I could be with kids as screwed up as I was. Man, I was out of control. I ran wild. I was a maniac, freaked out about everything. It's hard to think about that now. I have trouble relating to myself and who I was back then. I know what happened. I mean, I know what I did, but I can't imagine doing it. I wanted to feel good. I've thought about this a lot and that's the best explanation I've been able to come up with. I felt bad and I wanted to feel better. Seemed to me dope was the quickest way to get there. I haven't touched drugs or hard liquor for more than fifteen years. I might have a beer now and then, but I don't smoke, don't play cards, don't ballroom dance. Don't take the Lord's name in vain and don't cuss . . . all that much. Stub my toe and I can turn the air blue, but most of the time, I avoid swear words."

"Well, that's good."

"For me, it is. Back then, I was always teetering on the brink. I think I was hoping my parents would finally draw the line and mean it. That they'd say, 'Here, this is it. You've finally gone and done it this time.' But you know what? My dad was too soft. He waffled on everything. Even when he kicked my ass from here to next Tuesday, even when he threw me out of the house, he was saying, 'Give this some thought, son. You can come back when you've figured it out.' But like what? Figured what out? I didn't have a clue. I was rudderless. I was like a boat going full throttle but without any real direction, roaring around in big circles. Know what I mean?"

"Sure I do. In high school, I was a screwup myself. I ended up as a cop before I did this.".

He smiled. "No kidding? You drank and smoked dope?"

"Among other things," I said, modestly.

"Come on. Like what?" .

"I don't know. Kids in my class were all clean-cut, but not me. I was a wild thing. I ditched school. I hung out with some low-life dudes and I liked that. I liked *them*," I said. "I was the odd one out and so were they, I guess."

"Where'd you go to high school?"

"Santa Teresa High."

He laughed. "You were a low-waller?"

"Absolutely," I said. Low-wallers were the kids who quite literally perched on a low wall that ran along the back of the school property. Much smoking of cigarettes, funky clothes, and peroxided hair.

Guy laughed. "Well, that's great."

"I don't know how great it was, but it's what I did."

"How'd *you* get on track?"

"Who says I am?"

He got to his feet as if he'd come to a decision.

"Come on out to the parsonage and meet Peter and Winnie," he said. "They'll be in the kitchen at this hour setting up supper for the Thursday night Bible study."

I followed him up the center aisle and through a door at the rear. I could feel the first stirrings of resistance. I didn't want anyone pushing me to convert. Too much virtue is just as worrisome as wickedness in my book.

SIX

The parsonage was situated on the property adjacent to the church and consisted of a rambling white frame farmhouse, two stories tall, with green shutters and a shabby green shingled roof broken up with dormers. Across one end was a wide screened-in porch distinctly tilted, as though an earthquake had pulled the concrete foundation loose. Behind the house, I could see a big red barn with a dilapidated one-car garage attached. Both the house and the barn were in need of a fresh coat of paint, and I noticed sunlight slanting through the barn roof where it was pierced with holes. Metal lawn chairs were arranged in a semicircle in the yard under a massive live oak tree. A weathered picnic table flanked with benches was set up close by where I pictured Sunday school classes and church suppers during the summer months.

I followed Guy across the yard. We went up the back steps and into the kitchen. The air was scented with sauteed onions and celery. Peter was a man in his sixties, balding, with a wreath of white hair that grew down into sideburns and wrapped around his jaw in a closely trimmed beard linked to a matching mustache. Pale sunlight coming through the window illuminated a feathery white fuzz across his pate. He wore a red turtle-neck with a ribbed green sweater over it. He was just in the process of rolling out biscuit dough. The baking sheets to his right were lined with rows of perfect disks of dough ready for the oven. He looked up with pleasure as the two of us came in. "Oh, Guy. Good, it's you. I was just wondering if you were here yet. The furnace over at the church has been acting up again. First it clicks on, then it clicks off. On then off."

"Probably the electronic ignition. I'll take a look." Guy's posture was self-conscious. He rubbed his nose and then stuck his hands in his overall pockets as if to warm them. "This is Kinsey Millhone. She's a private detective from Santa Teresa." He turned and looked at me, tilting his head at the minister and his wife as he made the introductions. "This is Peter Antle and his wife, Winnie."

Peter's complexion was ruddy. His blue eyes smiled out at me from under ragged white brows. "Nice to meet you. I'd offer to shake hands, but I don't think you'd like it. How are you at homemade biscuits? Can I put you to work?"

"Better not," I said. "My domestic skills leave some-thing to be desired."

He was on the verge of pursuing the point when his wife said, "Now, Pete . . ." and gave him a look. Winnie Antle appeared to be in her late forties with short brown hair combed away from her face. She was brown-eyed, slightly heavy, with a wide smile and very white teeth. She wore a man's shirt over jeans with a long knit vest that covered her wide hips and ample derriere. She was chopping vegetables for soup, a mountain of carrot coins piled up on the counter next to her. I could see two bunches of celery and assorted bell peppers awaiting her flashing knife. She was simultaneously tending a stock-pot filled with vegetable cuttings boiling merrily. "Hello, Kinsey. Don't mind him. He's always trying to pass the work off onto the unsuspecting," she said, sending me a quick smile. "What brings you up this way?"

Peter looked at Guy. "You're not in trouble, I hope. You have to watch this man." His smile was teasing and it was clear he had no real expectation of trouble where Guy was concerned.

Guy murmured the explanation, apparently embarrassed to be the recipient of such bad news. "My father died. Probate attorney asked her to track me down."

Peter and Winnie both turned their full attention on Guy, whose earlier emotions were well under control. Peter said, "Is that the truth. Well, I'm sorry to hear that." He glanced over at me. "We've often talked about his trying for a reconciliation. It's been years since he had any contact with his dad."

Guy shifted his weight, leaning against the counter with his arms crossed in front of him. He seemed to be directing his comments at me, his tone wistful. "I don't know how many letters I wrote, but none of them got sent. Every time I tried to explain, it just came out sounding . . . you know, wrong, or dumb. I finally let it be till I could work out what it was I wanted to say. I kept thinking I had time. Mean, he wasn't old, by any stretch."

"It must have been his time. You can't argue with that," Peter said.

Winnie spoke up. "If you don't feel like work today, you go ahead and take off. We can manage just fine."

"I'm all right," Guy responded, again with discomfort at being the center of attention.

We spent a few minutes going through an exchange of information; how I'd managed to locate Guy and what I knew of his family, which wasn't much.

Peter was shaking his head, clearly regretful at the news I was bringing. "We think of Guy as one of our own. First time I ever saw this boy, he's a sorry sight. His eyeballs were bright red, sort of rolling around in his head like hot marbles. Winnie and me, we'd been called to this church and we'd driven all the way out to California from Fort Scott, Kansas. We'd heard all sorts of things about hippies and potheads and acid freaks, I think they called 'em. Kids with their eyes burned out from staring at the sun completely stoned. And there stood Guy by the side of the road with a sign that said 'San Francisco.' He was trying to be 'cool,' but he just looked pitiful to me. Winnie didn't want me to stop. We had the two kids in the backseat and she thought sure we'd be turned into homicide statistics."

"It's been a lot of years since then," Winnie said.

Pete looked over at Guy. "What are you thinking to do now, Guy, go back to Santa Teresa? This might be time to sit down with your brothers and talk about the past, maybe clean up some old business."

"I don't know. I suppose. If they're willing to sit down with me," Guy said. "I guess I'm not quite ready to make a decision about that." He glanced at me. "I know they didn't send you up here begging me to come back, but it seems like I might have *some* say in the matter. Would it be all right if I called you in a day or two?"

"No problem. In the meantime, I need to head home," I said. "You've got my card. If I'm not in the office, try that second number and the call will be forwarded automatically." I took out a second business card and jotted down Tasha Howard's name. "This is the attorney. I don't remember her phone number offhand. She has an office in Lompoc. You can call directory assistance and get the information from them. She's not that far away. If nothing else, you might make an appointment to have a chat with her. You'll need advice from an attorney of your own. I hope everything works out."

"I do, too. I appreciate the fact you made the trip," Guy said. "It's a lot more personal."

I shook hands with him, uttered polite noises in the direction of Peter and Winnie Antle, and made my getaway. I cruised down the main street of Marcella again, trying to get a feel for the place. Small and quiet. Unpretentious. I circled the block, driving along the few residential streets. The houses were small, built from identical plans, one-story stucco structures with flat rooflines. The exteriors were painted in pastel shades, pale Easter egg colors nestled in winter grass as dry as paper shreds. Most of the houses seemed shabby and dispirited. I saw only an occasional occupant.

As I swung past the general store, heading out to the main road, I spotted a sign in the window advertising fresh sandwiches. On an impulse, I parked the car and went in and ordered a tuna salad on rye from the woman at the deli counter in the rear. We chatted idly while she busied herself with the sandwich preparations, wrapping my dill pickle in a square of waxed paper so it wouldn't make the bread all mushy, she said. Behind me, two or three other customers went about their business, guiding small grocery carts up and down the aisles. No one turned to stare at me or paid me the slightest attention.

I let her know I'd just been over at the church. She exhibited little curiosity about who I was or why I was visiting the pastor and his wife. Mention of Guy Malek produced no uneasy silences nor any unsolicited confidences about his past history or his character.

"This seems like a nice town," I said as she passed my lunch across the counter. I handed her a ten, which she rang into the cash register.

"If you like this kind of place," she remarked. "Too quiet for my taste, but my husband was born here and insisted we come back. I like to kick up my heels, but about the best we can manage is a rummage sale now and then. Whooee." She fanned herself comically as if the excitement of used clothing was almost more than she could bear. "You want a receipt?" she said, counting out seven ones and change.

"I'd appreciate it."

She tore off the register receipt and handed it to me. "You take care of yourself."

"Thanks. You, too," I said.

I ate while I drove, steering with one hand as I alternated bites of dill pickle and tuna sandwich. The price had included a bag of potato chips, and I munched on those, too, figuring I'd cover all the necessary food groups. I'd forgotten to ask Guy his mother's maiden name, but the truth was, I had no doubt he was who he said he was. He reminded me of Jack, whose coloring and features were quite similar. Donovan and Bennet must have favored one parent while Guy and Jack looked more like the other. As cynical as I was, I found myself taking at face value both the reformation of Guy Malek and his current association with Jubilee Evangelical. It was always possible, I supposed, that he and the minister were singularly crafty frauds, who'd cooked up a cover story for any stranger who came calling, but for the life of me I didn't see it and I didn't believe anything sinister was afoot. If bucolic Marcella was the headquarters for some cult of neo-Nazis, Satanists, or motorcycle outlaws, it had sure escaped my notice.

It was not until I had passed Santa Maria, heading south on 101, that I realized Guy Malek had never asked how much his share of the estate would be. I probably should have volunteered the information. I could have at least given him a ballpark figure, but the question had never come up and I'd been too busy trying to evaluate his status for my report to Donovan. His emotional focus was on his father's death and the loss of his opportunity to make amends. Any profit was apparently beside the point as far as he was concerned. Oh, well. I figured Tasha would be in touch with him and she could give him the particulars.

I arrived in Santa Teresa without incident at two P.M. Since I was home earlier than I'd thought, I went into the office, typed up my notes, and stuck them in the file. I left two phone messages, one for Tasha at her office and one on the Maleks' home machine. I calculated my hours, the mileage, and miscellaneous expenses, and typed an invoice for my services to which I affixed the receipt for the tuna sandwich. Tomorrow, I'd include it with the typed report of my findings, send a copy to Tasha and one to Donovan. End of story, I thought.

I retrieved my car, unticketed, from an illegal space and drove home, feeling generally satisfied with life. Dietz fixed supper that night, a skilletful of fried onions, fried potatoes, and fried sausages with liberal doses of garlic and red pepper flakes, all served with a side of drab, grainy mustard that set your tongue aflame. Only two confirmed single people could eat a meal like that and imagine it was somehow nutritious. I handled the cleanup process, washing plates, flatware, and glasses, scrubbing out the frying pan while Dietz read the evening paper. Is this what couples did any given night of the week? In my twice-married life, it was the drama and grief I remembered most clearly, not the day-to-day stuff. This was entirely too domestic . . . not unpleasant, but certainly unsettling to someone un-accustomed to company.

At eight, we walked up to Rosie's and settled into a back booth together. Rosie's restaurant is poorly lighted, a tacky neighborhood establishment that's been there for twenty-five years, sandwiched between a Laund-romat and an appliance repair shop. The chrome-and-Formica tables are of thrift-shop vintage and the booths lining the walls are made of construction-grade plywood, stained dark, complete with crude hand-gouged messages and splinters. It's an act of reckless abandon to slide across the seats unless your tetanus shots are current. Over the years, the number of California smokers has steadily diminished, so the air quality has improved while the clientele has not. Rosie's used to be a refuge for local drinkers who liked to start early in the day and stay until closing time. Now the tavern has become popular with assorted amateur sports teams, who descend en masse after every big game, filling the air with loud talk, raucous laughter, and much stomping about. The regulars, all four bleary-eyed imbibers, have been driven to other places. I rather missed their slurred conversation, which was never intrusive.

Rosie was apparently gone for the night and the bartender was someone I'd never seen before. Dietz drank a couple of beers while I had a couple of glasses of Rosie's best screw-top Chardonnay, a puckering rendition of a California varietal she probably bought by the keg.

I freely confess it was the alcohol that got me into trouble that night. I was feeling mellow and relaxed, somewhat less inhibited than usual, which is to say, ready to flap my mouth. Robert Dietz was beginning to look good to me, and I wasn't really sure how I felt about that. His face was chiseled in shadow and his gaze crossed the room in restless assessment while we chatted about nothing in particular. Idly, I told him about William and Rosie's wedding and my adventures on the road, and he filled in details about his stay in Germany. Along with the attraction, I experienced a low-grade sorrow, so like a fever that I wondered if I were coming down with the flu. At one point, I shivered and he looked over at me. "You okay?" he asked.

I stretched my hand out on the table and he covered it with his, lacing his fingers through mine. "What are we doing?" I asked.

"Good question. Why don't we talk about that? You go first."

I laughed, but the issue wasn't really funny and we both knew it. "Why'd you have to come back and stir things up? I was doing fine."

"What have I stirred up? We haven't done anything. We eat dinner. We have drinks. I sleep down. You sleep up. My knee's so bad, you're in no danger of unwanted advances. I couldn't make it up those stairs if my life depended on it."

"Is that the good news or the bad?"

"I don't know. You tell me," he said.

"I don't want to get used to you."

"A lot of women can't get used to me. You're one of the few who seems remotely interested," he said, smiling slightly.

Here's a word to the wise: In the midst of a tender discussion with one woman, don't mention another one—especially in the plural. It's bad policy. The minute he said it, I had this sudden vision of a long line of females with me standing not even close to the front of the pack. I could feel my smile fade and I retreated into silence like a turtle encountering a dog.

His look became cautious. "What's wrong?"

"Nothing. I'm fine. What makes you think there's anything wrong?"

"Let's don't talk at cross-purposes," he said. "You obviously have something to say, so why don't you say it?"

"I don't want to. It doesn't matter."

"Kinsey."

"What?"

"Come on. Just say it. There's no penalty for being honest."

"I don't know how to say it. You're here for four days and what am I supposed to do with that? I'm not good at being left. It's the story of my life. Why get enmeshed when all it means is I get to have my heart ripped out?"

He lifted his eyebrows, shrugging with his face. "I don't know what to tell you. I can't promise to stay. I've never stayed in one place for more than six months max. Why can't we live in the present? Why does everything have to have a guarantee attached?"

"I'm not talking about guarantees."

"I think you are," he said. "You want a lien against the future, when the fact is you don't know any more than I do about what's coming next."

"Well, that's true and I'm not arguing that. All I'm saying is I don't want to get involved in an on-again-off-again relationship, which is what this is."

Dietz's expression was pained. "I won't lie. I can't pretend I'll stay when I know I won't. What good would that do?"

I could feel my frustration rise. "I don't want you to pretend and I'm not asking you to promise. I'm just trying to be honest."

"About what?"

"About everything. People have rejected me all my life. Sometimes it's death or desertion. Infidelity, betrayal. You name it. I've experienced every form of emotional treachery there is. Well, big deal. Everybody's suffered something in life and so what? I'm not sitting around feeling sorry for myself, but I'd have to be a fool to lay myself open to that shit again."

"I understand that. I hear you and believe me, I don't want to be the one to cause you pain. This is not about you. It's about me. I'm restless by nature. I hate to feel trapped. That's how I am. Pen me in and I'll tear the place apart trying to get out," he said. "My people were nomads. We were always on the move. Always on the road. We lived out of suitcases. To me, being in one spot is oppressive. You want to talk about death. It's the worst. When I was growing up, if we stayed in one town for long, my old man would get busted. He'd end up in county jail or in the hospital or the local drunk tank. Any school I attended, I was always the new kid and I'd have to fight my way across the school yard just to stay alive. The happiest day of my life was the day we hit the road again."

"Free at last," I interjected.

"That's right. It's not that I might not want to stay. It's that I'm incapable of it."

"Oh, right. 'Incapable.' Well, that explains it. You're excused," I said.

"Don't be so touchy. You know what I mean. God almighty, I'm not proud of myself. I don't relish the fact that I'm a rolling stone. I just don't want to kid myself and I don't want to kid you."

"Thank you. That's great. In the meantime, I'm sure you have ways of amusing yourself."

He squinted. "Where did that come from?"

"This is hopeless," I said. "I don't know why we even

bother with this. You're addicted to wandering and I'm rooted in place. You can't stay and I can't leave because I love where I am. This is your biennial interlude and I'm here for the duration, which means I'm probably doomed to a lifetime of guys like you."

" 'Guys like *me*?' That's nice. What does that mean?"

"Just what it says. Emotionally claustrophobic. You're a basket case. So as long as I'm attracted to guys like you, I can bypass my own—" I stopped short, feeling like one of those cartoon dogs, skidding on a cartoon floor.

"Your own what?"

"None of your business," I said. "Let's drop the conversation. I should have kept my mouth shut. I end up sounding like a whiner, which is not what I intend."

"You're always so worried about sounding like a whiner," he said. "Who cares if you whine? Be my guest."

"Oh, *now* you say that."

"Say what?" he said, exasperated.

I assumed an attitude of patience that I scarcely felt. "One of the first things you ever said to me was that you wanted—how did you phrase it—'obedience without whining.' You said very few women ever mastered that."

"*I* said that?"

"Yes, you did. I've tried very hard ever since not to whine in your presence."

"Don't be ridiculous. I didn't mean it that way," he said. "I don't even remember saying it, but I was probably talking about something else. Anyway, don't change the subject. I don't want to leave it on this note. As long as the issue's on the table, let's get it settled."

"What's to settle? We can't settle anything. There's no way to resolve it, so let's drop the whole business. I'm sorry I brought it up. I've already got this ongoing family nonsense. Maybe I'm upset about that."

"What nonsense? You're related to these people, so what's the problem?"

"I don't want to get into it. Aside from whining, I hate to feel like I'm repeating myself."

"How can you repeat yourself when you never told me to begin with?"

I ran a hand through my hair and stared down at the tabletop. I'd been hoping to avoid the subject, but the topic did seem safer than discussing our relationship, whatever that consisted of. I couldn't come up with any rational defense of my reluctance to engage with this newfound family of mine. I just didn't want to do it. Finally, I said, "I guess I don't like to be pressured. They're so busy trying to make up for lost time. Why can't they just mind their own business? I'm not comfortable with all this buddy-buddy stuff. You know how stubborn I get when I'm pushed."

"Why did you agree to work for that attorney then? Isn't she your cousin?"

"Well, yes, but I didn't *intend* to agree. I intended to turn her down, but then greed and curiosity got the better of me. I have a living to earn and I didn't want to refuse out of perversity. I know I'll regret it, but I'm into it now so there's no sense beating myself up."

"Sounds harmless enough on the face of it."

"It's not harmless. It's annoying. And besides, that isn't the point. The point is, I'd like for them to respect my boundaries."

"What boundaries? She hired you to do a job. As long as you get paid, that's the end of it."

"Let's hope. Besides, it's not her so much as the other two. Liza and Pam. If I give an inch, they'll invade my space."

"Oh, bullshit. That's California psychobabble. You can't live your life like a radio talk show."

"What do you know? I don't notice you all cozied up to your family."

I could see him flinch. His expression shifted abruptly to one of injury and irritation. "Low blow. What I say about my kids, I don't want you throwing back in my face."

"You're right. I'm sorry. I withdraw the remark."

"Withdraw the knife and the wound's still there," he snapped. "What's the matter with you? You're so bristly these days. You're doing everything you can to keep me at arm's length."

"I am not," I said, and then I stared at him, squinting. "Is that true?"

"Well, look at your behavior. I haven't even been here two days and we're already fighting. What's that about? I didn't travel all this way to pick a fight with you. I wanted to see you. I was excited we'd have time together. Hell. If I'd wanted to fight, I could have stayed with Naomi."

"Why didn't you? I don't mean the question in a mean-hearted way, but I'm curious. What happened?"

"Oh, who knows? I have my version, she has hers. Sometimes I think relationships have a natural lifespan. Ours ran out. That's all it was. The explanations come afterwards when you try to make sense of it. Let's get back to you. What's going on in your head?"

"I'd rather fight than feel nothing."

"Those are your only two options?"

"That's what it feels like, but I couldn't say for sure."

He reached out and gave my hair a tug. "What am I going to do with you?"

"What am I going to do with *you?*" I replied.

SEVEN

When we returned to the apartment at ten-fifteen, Henry's kitchen light was on. Dietz said his knee was killing him, so he let himself into the apartment where he intended to take a couple of pain pills, prop his feet up, and put his ice pack to work. I said I'd be along momentarily. Our conversation at Rosie's hadn't really gone anywhere. I couldn't bear to continue and I couldn't bear behaving as though the subject hadn't been broached. I didn't know what I wanted from him and I wasn't sure how to say it anyway, so I just ended up sounding needy. My general policy is this: If your mind isn't open, keep your mouth shut, too.

I knocked on Henry's backdoor, waving at him through the window when he looked up at me. He was sitting in his rocking chair with the evening paper and his glass of Jack Daniel's. He smiled and waved back, setting the paper aside so he could let me in. He had the heat turned up and the inside air was not only warm, but deliciously scented with yesterday's cinnamon rolls.

"This feels great. It's really cold out there," I said. The kitchen table was covered with old black-and-white photographs sorted into piles. I glanced at them briefly

as I pulled out a kitchen chair and turned my attention
to him. From my point of view, Henry Pitts is perfec-
tion—smart, good-natured, and responsible—with the
cutest legs I've ever seen. He's been my landlord for five
years, since the day I spotted the ad for the apartment
in a Laundromat. Henry was looking for a long-term
tenant who was clean and quiet; no children, loud
parties, or small, yapping dogs. As a lifelong mobile-
home inhabitant, I was addicted to compact spaces,
but ready to limit contact with a lot of close, unruly
neighbors. Trailer-park life, for all its virtues, entails
an intimate acquaintance with other people's private
business. Since I make a living as a snoop, I'd just as
soon keep my personal affairs to myself. The converted
single-car garage Henry was offering was better than
my fantasies and affordable as well. Since then, the
place had been bombed and rebuilt, the interior fitted
out in teak and as cleverly designed as a ship's.

From the outset, Henry and I established just enough
of a relationship to suit us both. Over the years, he's
managed to civilize me to some extent and I'm certainly
more agreeable now than I was back then. Little by
little, we forged the bond between us until now I consider him the exemplary mix of friend and generic
family member.

"You want a cup of tea?" he asked.

"No, thanks. I just stopped to say hi before I hit the
sack. Are these family pictures?" I asked, picking one
at random.

"That's the claim," he said. "Nell sent me those. She
came across two boxes of old family photographs, but
none are labeled. No names, no dates. She hasn't any

103

idea who these people are and neither do the other sibs. What a mess. Take my word for it. You should mark all your photographs, even if it's just a quick note on the back. You might know who's who, but nobody else will."

"Do they look familiar to you?"

"A few." He took the print I was looking at and squinted as he held it to the light. I peered over his shoulder. The woman in the picture must have been in her twenties, with a broad, bland face and hair drawn back in a bun. She wore a white middy blouse, with a calf-length skirt, dark stockings, and flat, dark shoes with a bow across the instep. Standing beside her was a glum-faced girl of eight with a drop-waist sailor dress and ankle-high lace-up shoes. "I believe this is a picture of my mother's younger sister, Augusta, taken in Topeka, Kansas, back in 1915. The child's name was Rebecca Rose, if memory serves. She and her mother both died in the big influenza epidemic of 1918." He picked up another one. "This is my mother with my grandfather Tilmann. I'm surprised Nell didn't recognize them except her eyesight's fading. Now that I think of it, I'm not sure why it matters. None of us have children, so once we're gone, it won't make any difference who these people are."

"Well, that seems sad. Why don't you put 'em in an album and pass them on to me? I'll pretend they're mine. What was his first name?"

"Klaus. My mother's name was Gudrun." The man staring fixedly at the camera must have been in his late seventies, the daughter beside him in her fifties by the look of her. I said, "What's the name Tilmann? Is that

German? I somehow imagined you were all Swedes or Finns."

"Oh no, we're not Scandinavian. They're gloomy sorts, in my opinion. The Tilmanns were good German stock. Headstrong, autocratic, vigorous, and exacting. Some would say impossible, but that's a matter of interpretation. Longevity is genetic and don't ever let anybody tell you otherwise. I read those articles about folks who live to be a hundred. They all try to take credit, claim it's because they smoke or don't smoke, eat yogurt, take vitamins, or a tablespoon of vinegar a day. What nonsense. War and accidents excepted, you live a long time because you come from other people who live a long time. You have to take responsibility. You can't subject yourself to any kind of gross mistreatment. My mother lived to be a hundred and three and I imagine the remaining five of us will live that long as well."

"You certainly seem to be in good shape. Nell's what, ninety-six? And you have your eighty-sixth birthday coming up on Valentine's Day."

Henry nodded, making a motion as if to knock on wood. "We're healthy, in the main, though we're all shrinking down to some extent. We've talked about this and it's our contention that the shrinkage is nature's way of assuring you don't take up so much space in your coffin. You lighten up, too. Feels like taking air into your bones. Makes it easy on the pallbearers. And, of course, your faculties shut down. You get blind as a bat and your hearing fades. Charlie says it sounds like he's got a pillow on his head all the time these days. Get old, you might as well not worry about your dignity.

Anybody talks about dignity for old folks has never been around one as far as I can tell. You can keep your spunk, but you have to give up your vanity early on. We're all in diapers. Well, I'm not, but then I'm the baby in the family. The rest of them leak any time they cough or laugh too hard.

"Nell says one reason she misses William so much now he's moved out here is because they can't play bridge like they used to. Have to play three-handed, which isn't as much fun. Lewis was thinking about asking a cousin to move in, but Nell won't tolerate another woman in the house. She says she's had her brothers to herself now for sixty years and she's not about to change. Nell says once she 'goes' they can do anything they want, depending on who's left."

"I can't believe they're still willing to endure the winters in Michigan. Why don't they all move out here? You could play all the bridge you want."

"There's talk of that. We'll just have to see. Nell has her ladies' luncheon group and she hates to leave them." Henry put the photo down and took his seat again. "Now then, how are you? I had a nice chat with your friend Dietz. He says you picked up some work."

"Actually, I finished it. One of those quickies you remember fondly when the tough ones come along," I said. I took a few minutes to fill him in on the search for Guy Malek.

Henry shook his head. "What's going to happen? Do you think he'll get his share of the estate?"

"Who knows? I don't always hear the end of it, but Tasha thinks they'll be able to work something out."

106

"How long will Dietz be here? I thought I'd have the two of you over for supper one night."

"Probably not long. He's on his way up to Santa Cruz to see his sons," I said.

"Well, let me know if he's still going to be here Saturday and I'll cook something special. We'll invite William and Rosie and Moza Lowenstein, if she's free."

By the time I let myself into my place, Dietz had fallen asleep in his underwear, slouched down in his chair, snoring lightly. The television set was on, the volume low, the channel tuned to a nature show about underwater shark attacks. Dietz had his leg propped up on the edge of the sofa bed, a blanket pulled up across his chest and shoulders. The partially melted ice pack had toppled to the floor. I put that ice pack in the freezer and took out a second one, laying it carefully across his knee without waking him. His kneecap was swollen, the bare flesh looking pale and vulnerable. I left him as he was, knowing he'd wake long before morning. He sleeps in fits and starts like an animal in the wild, and I knew from past experience he seldom manages to make it through the night without getting up at least twice.

I eased off my shoes and made my way up the spiral stairs. From above, I stared down at him. His lined face looked alien in sleep, as if sculptured in clay. I seldom saw him at ease. He was restless by nature, perpetually in motion, his features animated by the sheer force of his nervous energy. Even as I watched, he stirred himself awake, jerking upright with a look of disorientation. I could see him wince, reaching for the ice pack balanced on his distended joint. I stepped away from the loft rail and went into the bathroom, where I washed my face and brushed my teeth. It was no doubt the proximity to all that testosterone, but I could feel the murmur of sexuality at the base of my spine. I grabbed an oversized T-shirt from a hook on the bathroom door. I usually sleep in the nude, but it seemed like a bad idea.

Once ready for bed, I turned out the light and slipped under the quilt. I reached out and set my alarm, watching the digital clock flip from 11:04 to 11:05. Below, I could hear Dietz get up and move into the kitchen. The refrigerator door opened and closed. He took down a glass and poured himself a drink—wine, orange juice, or milk—something liquid at any rate. I heard him pull out a kitchen stool, followed by the rustle of newspaper. I wondered what he was thinking, wondered what would happen if I heard him climbing the stairs. Maybe I should have pulled on a robe and gone down to join him, thrown caution to the wind and to hell with the consequences, but it was not in my nature. Being single for so long had made me cautious about men. I stared up at the Plexiglas skylight above my bed, thinking about the risks involved in reaching out to him. Passion never lasts, but then what does? If you could have it all, but only briefly, would the rush of love be worth the price in pain? I could feel myself sinking into sleep as though weighted down with stones. I didn't rise again until 5:59 A.M.

I pulled on my sweats, preparing for my run as usual. Dietz was in the shower when I left the house, but I noticed with a pang he was in the process of packing. He'd laid the soft-sided suitcase open on the floor near the sofa bed, which he'd folded away. The blanket had been refolded and placed across one end. He'd piled the sheets he'd used near the washer. Maybe he felt his exodus would address my issues with him, minimizing the chances of my forming an attachment. What I noticed, perversely, was that, having felt nothing on his arrival, I was now afflicted with a stinging sense of loss at his departure. He'd been with me for two days and I was already suffering, so maybe I'd been smart not to take things any further. I'd been celibate for so long, what was another year without sex? I made an involuntary sound that might have been a whimper if I allowed myself such things.

I closed the door quietly behind me, breathing deeply as though the damp morning air might ease the fire in my chest. Having passed through the front gate, I paused while I stretched, keeping my mind a blank. In the last several years as a private investigator, I've developed a neat trick for shutting off my feelings. Like others who work in the "helping" professions—doctors and nurses, police officers, social workers, paramedics— emotional disconnection is sometimes the only way to function in the face of death with all its tacky variations. Originally, my detachment took several minutes of concentrated effort, but now I make the shift in the blink of an eye. Mental-health enthusiasts are quick to assure us that our psychological well-being is best served by staying in touch with our feelings, but *surely* they're not referring to the icky, unpleasant ones.

The run itself was unsatisfactory. The dawn was overcast, the sky a brooding gray unrelieved by any visible sunrise. Gradually, daylight overtook the lowering dark, but the whole of it had the bleached look of an old black-and-white photograph. My gait felt choppy and I never really hit my stride. The air was so chilly I couldn't even generate a decent sweat. I dutifully counted off the miles, feeling gratified to be doing it in spite of myself. Some days the discipline is an end in itself, a way of asserting the will in the face of life's little setbacks. I walked the half block home, carefully brushing aside any slovenly sentiment.

Dietz was sitting at the counter when I got in. He'd put on a pot of coffee and set out my cereal bowl. His bowl was already washed, rinsed, and drying in the dish rack. His suitcase, fully zipped, was waiting by the door along with his garment bag. Through the open bathroom door, I could see he'd tidied the basin of all his personal possessions. The scent of soap mingled with his aftershave, a damp male perfume permeating everything.

"I thought it might be easier if I took off," he said.

"Sure, no problem. I hope you're not doing it on my account."

"No, no. You know me. I'm not that good at staying put," he said. "Anyway, you probably have a lot of work to do."

"Oh, tons," I said. "You're heading up to Santa Cruz?"

"Eventually, yes. I'll drive on up the coast, maybe spend a day in Cambria. With this knee, I have to break up the trip, anyway. You know, get out and stretch every hour or so. Keep it warm and loose. Otherwise, it locks up."

"What time are you taking off?"

"Whenever you leave for work."

"Well, great. I'll just grab a shower then and you can hit the road."

"Take your time. I'm in no hurry," he said.

"I can see that," I remarked, as I headed up to the loft. This time he didn't ask if I was mad. This was good because, in truth, I was furious. Under the fury was the old familiar pain. Why does everyone end up leaving me? What did I ever do to them? I went through my morning routine as efficiently as possible, flung on my clothes, and ate my cereal without pausing to read the paper. To demonstrate my indifference to his abrupt departure, I took out fresh sheets and asked him to help me remake the sofa bed. I hoped the implication was that some other guy was lined up for bed space as soon as he left. Neither of us said much and what we said was transactional. "Where's the other pillowcase?" About like that.

Once the sofa was redone, he took his suitcase to the car and came back for the garment bag. I walked him out to the curb and we exchanged one of those insincere kisses with the sound effects attached. *Mmch!* He fired up his Porsche and I dutifully waved as he roared off down the street. You little shit, I thought.

I went into the office, ignoring a faint tendency to tear up for no reason. The day yawned in front of me like a sinkhole in the street. This was just what it felt like when he left before. Now how does this happen to someone of my rare spunk and independence? I played a few rounds of solitaire, paid some bills, and balanced my checkbook. Anxiety whispered in my gut like a stomachache. When the phone finally rang just before lunch, I snatched up the receiver, absurdly grateful at the interruption.

"Kinsey. This is Donovan. How are you?"

"Gee, I'm just fine. How are you?"

"Well enough. Uh, listen, we got your message and we'd like to compliment you on a job well done. Tasha had to fly back to San Francisco this morning, but she said she didn't think you'd mind giving us the information firsthand. Could you stop by the house for a drink late this afternoon?"

"Well, sure. I could do that. I was going to type up my report and put it in the mail, but I can give you a rundown in person if you'd prefer."

"I'd appreciate that. I expect Jack and Bennet will want to be there as well. That way, if they have questions, you can fill us all in at the same time and save yourself the repetition. Would five-thirty be convenient?"

"Fine with me," I said.

"Good. We'll look forward to seeing you."

After I hung up, I could feel myself shrug. I had nothing against an informal report as long as I didn't somehow get sucked into the family drama. Aside from Guy, I wasn't crazy about the Malek brothers. I happened to believe Guy had changed his wicked ways, so maybe I could do him a service and convince the others. Not that it was any of my business how the monies were distributed, but if there were any lingering questions about his "worthiness," I certainly had an opinion. Besides, with Dietz now gone, I didn't have anything better to do.

I skipped lunch and spent the afternoon cleaning my

office. Lonnie Kingman had a maintenance crew that serviced the premises weekly on Friday afternoons, but it felt therapeutic to get in there and scrub. I even spent twenty minutes dusting the artificial ficus plant someone had once mistaken for real. The space I occupied had originally been a conference room with a full "executive" bathroom attached. I found a plastic bucket, sponges, cleansers, a toilet brush, and mop and entertained myself mightily killing imaginary germs. My method of coping with depression is to take on chores so obnoxious and disgusting that reality seems pleasant by comparison. By three o'clock, I smelled of sweat and household bleach and I'd forgotten what I was so unhappy about. Well, actually, I remembered, but I didn't give a shit.

Having sanitized the suite, I locked the door, stripped off my clothes, hopped in the executive shower, and scrubbed myself. I dressed again in the same jeans, pulling on a fresh turtleneck from the ready supply I keep handy for sudden travel. What's life without a toothbrush and clean underpants? I typed up the official version of my encounter with Guy Malek, tucking one copy in my office files, another in my handbag. The third I addressed to Tasha Howard at her San Francisco office. The end. Finito. Done, done, done. This was the last job I'd ever take from her.

By 5:25, dressed in my best (and only) wool tweed blazer, I drove through the entrance to the Malek estate. It was close to dark by then, the winter-shortened days still characterized by early twilights. My headlights swept in a forlorn arc across the stucco wall surrounding the fifteen-acre property. Along the rim of the wall, three strands of rusted barbed wire had been strung years ago, broken now in places and looking singularly ineffective. Who knows what intruders were anticipated back then? A chilly wind had picked up and the darkened treetops swayed and shivered, whispering together about things unseen. There were lights on in the house, two upstairs windows illuminated in pale yellow where much of the first floor was dark.

The housekeeper had neglected to turn on the outside lights. I parked in the turnaround and picked my way across the cobblestone courtyard to the shadowy portico that sheltered the entranceway in front. I rang the bell and waited, crossing my arms for warmth. The porch light was finally flipped on and Myrna opened the door a crack.

"Hi, Myrna. Kinsey Millhone. I was here the other day. Donovan invited me for drinks."

Myrna didn't exactly break into song at the news. Apparently, advanced classes in Housekeeper's Training School cautioned the students not to give expression to sudden bursts of joy. In the two days since I'd seen her last, she'd renewed the dye job on her hair and the whole of it was now a white blond that looked like it would be cold to the touch. Her uniform consisted of a gray top worn over matching gray pants. I would have bet money the waistband was unbuttoned underneath the tunic. "This way," she said. Her crepe-soled shoes squeaked slightly on the polished parquet floor.

A woman called down from somewhere above our heads. "Myrna? Was that the front door? We're expecting someone for drinks." I glanced up, following the sound of her voice. A brunette in her late thirties was leaning on the stair rail above our heads. She caught sight of me and brightened. "Oh, hi. You must be Kinsey. You want to come on up?"

Myrna veered off without another word, disappearing into the rear of the house as I climbed the stairs.

Christie held out her hand when I reached the upper landing. "I'm Christie Malek. Nice to meet you," she said as we shook hands. "I take it you've met Myrna."

"More or less," I said. I took her in at a glance, like an instant Polaroid. She was a fine-featured brunette with shiny dark hair, worn shoulder length. She was very slender, wearing jeans and a bulky black-ribbed sweater that came down almost to her knees. She had the sleeves rolled back and her wrists were thin, her fingers long and cool. Her eyes were small, a dark penetrating blue, beneath a lightly feathered brow. Her teeth were as perfect as a mouthwash ad's. The absence of eye makeup gave her a recessive, slightly anxious air, though her manner was friendly and her smile was warm enough. "Donovan called to say he'd be a few minutes late. Jack's on his way home and Bennet's around some place. I'm just going through Bader's papers and I'd love some company."

Still talking to me, she turned and moved toward the master bedroom, which I could see through an open doorway. "We're still looking for the missing will, among other things. Ever hopeful," she added wryly.

"I thought Bennet was going to do that."

"This is how Bennet does things. He loves to delegate."

I hoped there was a touch of irony in her tone. I couldn't be sure so I kept my mouth shut.

The suite we entered was enormous; two substantial rooms separated by a pair of doors that had been pushed into their respective wall pockets. We passed through the outer room, which had been furnished as a bedroom. The walls were padded fabric, covered in rose-colored silk with a watered sheen to the finish. The carpet was off-white, a dense, cut pile. Pale, heavy drapes had been pulled back to reveal the leaded glass windows that looked out onto the cobblestone entrance at the front of the house. There was a marble fireplace on the wall to the left. Two matching sofas were arranged on either side of it, plump, upholstered pieces covered in a subdued floral chintz. The four-poster bed had been flawlessly made, not a ripple or a wrinkle in the snowy-white silk coverlet. The surface of the bed table seemed unnaturally bare, as if once-personal items had now been hidden from sight. It might have been my imagination, but the room seemed to harbor the lingering scent of sickness. I could see that closets were being emptied, the contents—suits and dress shirts—packed into large cardboard boxes supplied by the local Thrift Store Industries downtown.

"This is gorgeous," I said.

"Isn't it?"

Beyond the sliding doors, a home office had been set up, with a large walnut desk and antique wooden file cabinets. The ceilings in both rooms were twelve feet high, but this was by far the cozier of the two. A fire had been laid in a second marble fireplace and Christie paused to add a log to an already snapping blaze. The walls here were paneled in walnut as dark and glossy as fudge. I could see a copier, a fax machine, computer, and a printer arranged on the built-in shelves on either side of the fireplace. A paper shredder stood on one side of the desk, its green On button lighted. I could see printed acknowledgments stacked up waiting to be addressed to those who'd sent flowers to the funeral.

Christie returned to the desk where she'd emptied the contents of two drawers into banker's boxes that she'd labeled with a black marker. There were two big plastic garbage bags bulging with discarded papers. Thick files were stacked on the desktop and a number of empty file folders were strewn across the carpet. This was the kind of task I knew well, classifying the odds and ends left behind by the dead. Below, in the court-yard, we could hear a motorcycle cruise in, the engine being revved once more before it was silenced.

Christie cocked her head. "I hear the Harley. Sounds like Jack's home."

"How's it going so far?"

Her expression was a wry mix of skepticism and despair. "Bader was supremely organized for the most part, but he must have lost his enthusiasm for jobs like this. Look at all this stuff. I swear, if I'm ever diagnosed as terminal, I'm going to clean out my files before I get too sick to care. What if you kept pornographic pictures or something like that? I'd hate to think of someone sorting through my private affairs."

"Nothing in my life is that interesting," I said. "You want help?"

"Not really, but I could use the moral support," she said. "I've been in here for hours. I have to look at every single piece of paper and figure out if it's worth saving, though most aren't as far as I can tell. I mean, what do I know? Anything I'm not sure about, I put in one pile. The really junky stuff, I go ahead and shove in a garbage bag. I don't dare shred a thing and I'm afraid to toss much. I know Bennet. As sure as I pitch something, he tears in here and wants to know where it is. He's done that to me twice and it was just dumb luck the trash hadn't been picked up. I'm out there in the dark, like a bag lady, pulling crumpled papers out of the garbage can. This third pile is everything that looks important. For instance, here's something you might like." She picked up a file from the stack on top of the desk and handed it to me. "Bader must have put this together back in the early sixties."

A quick glance inside revealed a collection of newspaper clippings related to Guy's past misbehavior. I read one at random, an article dating back to 1956 detailing the arrest of two juveniles, boys aged fourteen and thirteen, who were believed to be responsible for a spree of graffiti vandalism. One of the teens was booked into Juvenile Hall, the other released to his parents. There must have been twenty-five such snippets. In some cases, the authorities withheld the names because the boy or boys arrested were still minors. In other articles, Guy Malek was identified by name.

"I wonder why Bader kept clippings. It seems odd," I said.

"Maybe to remind himself why he disinherited the kid. I figure Bennet will want 'em for ammunition if it comes down to that. It's exhausting just trying to make these decisions."

"Quite a job," I said and then shifted the subject matter. "You know, it occurred to me that since the two wills were drawn up only three years apart, the two witnesses for the first might have been witnesses for the second will, too. Especially if they were paralegals or law clerks working in the attorney's office."

She looked at me with interest. "Good point. You'll have to mention that to Donovan. None of us are anxious to see five million bucks flying out the window."

There was a tap at the door and we both turned to see that Myrna had reappeared. "Donovan's home. He asked me to serve the hors d'oeuvres in the living room."

"Tell him we'll be down in a second, as soon as I wash my hands. Oh, and see if you can round up the other two."

Myrna took in the request, murmured something inaudible, and withdrew from the room.

Christie shook her head, lowering her voice a notch. "She may be on the glum side, but she's the only person in the house who doesn't argue with everyone."

EIGHT

Lights were on and Donovan was in the living room when Christie and I came downstairs. He'd changed out of his work clothes, pulling on a heavy cream-colored knit sweater over casual pants. He'd exchanged his dress shoes for a pair of sheepskin slippers that made his feet look huge. A fire had been laid and he was poking at the logs, turning a bulky wedge of oak so that its uppermost side would catch. Donovan picked up another piece of wood and thunked it on top. A shower of sparks flew up the chimney. He replaced the fire screen and wiped his hands on his handkerchief, glancing over at me. "I see you've met Christie. We appreciate your coming over. Keeps it simpler all around. Can I make you a drink? We've got just about anything you'd want."

"A glass of Chardonnay would be fine."

"I'll get it," Christie said promptly. She moved over to a sideboard crowded with liquor bottles. A bottle of Chardonnay had been chilling in a cooler beside a clear Lucite ice bucket and an assortment of glasses. She began to peel the foil from the neck of the wine bottle, with a look at Donovan. "You having wine?"

120

"Probably with dinner. I think I'll have a martini first. Gin is Bennet's winter drink," he added as an aside to me.

Ah, the seasonal alcoholic. What a nice idea. Gin in the winter, maybe vodka in spring. Summer would be tequila and he could round out the autumn with a little bourbon or scotch. While she opened the wine, I took a momentary survey.

Like the bedroom above, this room was immense. The twelve-foot ceiling was rimmed with ten-inch crown molding, the walls papered in a narrow blue-and-cream stripe that had faded with the years. The pale Oriental carpet had to be seventeen feet wide and probably twenty-five feet long. The furniture had been arranged in two groupings. At the far end of the room, four wing chairs faced one another near the front windows. Closer to the center of the room, three large sofas formed a U in front of the fireplace. All of the side pieces—an armoire, an escritoire, and two carved and inlaid wooden tables—were the sort I'd seen in antique stores, heavy, faintly fussy, with price tags that made you squint because you thought you'd read them wrong.

Christie returned with two glasses of wine and handed one to me. She took a seat on one of the sofas and I sat down across from her with a murmured "thanks." The blue floral pattern was faded to a soft white, the fabric threadbare along the arms and the cushion fronts. There was a large brass bowl filled with fresh flowers and several copies of *Architectural Digest* lined up on the square glass coffee table in the crook of the U. There was also an untidy stack of what looked like condolence cards. While I was thinking about it, I took out my typed report and placed it on the table in front of me. I'd leave it for Donovan so he'd have a copy for his files.

I heard footsteps in the hall and the sound of voices. Jack and Bennet came into the living room together. Whatever they'd been discussing, their expressions were now neutral, conveying nothing but benign interest at the sight of me. Bennet wore a running suit of some silky material that rustled when he walked. Jack looked as if he'd just come in off the golf course, his hair still disheveled from the imprint of his visor. He wore a bright orange sweater vest over a pink short-sleeved golf shirt and his gait tended to a lilt as if he were still wearing cleats. Jack poured himself a scotch and water as dark as iced tea while Bennet made a pitcher of martinis that he stirred with a long glass wand. I made note of his vermouth-to-gin ratio—roughly two parts per million. He poured one for himself and one for Donovan, adding olives to both. He brought the martini pitcher over to the coffee table and set it down within range.

While drinks were being poured, various pleasantries were exchanged, none of them heartfelt. As with tobacco, the rituals of alcohol seemed to be a stalling technique until those assembled could get themselves psychologically situated. I had an odd sensation in my chest, the same itch of anxiety I'd felt before a third-grade dance recital in which I played a bunny, not a specialty of mine. My aunt Gin was ill and unable to attend, so I'd been forced to do my hippy-hopping in front of countless alien adults, who didn't seem to find me winsome. My legs were too skinny and my fake ears wouldn't stand up. The brothers Malek watched me with about the same enthusiasm. Donovan took a seat next to Christie on the couch across from me while Jack sat facing the fireplace with Bennet on his left.

It was interesting to see the three brothers in the same room together. Despite the similarities in their coloring, their faces were very different, Bennet's the more so because of his beard and mustache. Donovan and Jack were built along finer lines though neither was as appealing as their errant brother, Guy. Jack leaned forward and began to sift idly through the sympathy cards.

I thought Donovan was on the verge of asking for my report when Myrna came into the room with assorted edibles on a serving tray. The tray itself was the size of a manhole cover, very plain, probably sterling silver, and distinctly tarnished along the edges. The hors d'oeuvres, in addition to what looked like Cheez Whiz on saltines, consisted of a bowl of peanuts and a bowl of unpitted green olives in brine. No one said a word until she'd departed, closing the door behind her.

Jack leaned forward. "What the fuck is this?"

Bennet laughed at the very moment he was swallowing a mouthful of martini. He made a snorting sound as he choked and I saw gin dribble out his nose. He coughed into his handkerchief while Jack shot a smile in his direction. I bet as children they'd paused in the midst of dinner, opening their mouths to one another to exhibit masticated food.

Christie flashed them a look of disapproval. "It's Enid's night off. Would you quit with the criticism?

Myrna's a nurse. She was hired to look after Dad, not to wait on the two of you. We're lucky she stayed on and you bloody well know it. Nobody else lifts a finger around here except me."

"Thanks for setting the record straight, Christie. You're a fuckin' peach," Jack said.

"Knock it off," Donovan said. "Could we hold off on this until we hear from her?" He grabbed a handful of peanuts, eating one at a time as his focus returned to me. "You want to fill us in?"

I took a few minutes to detail the means by which I'd managed to locate Guy Malek. Without mentioning Darcy Pascoe or California Fidelity Insurance, I played out the steps that led to the information on his identification card. I'll admit I stretched it out, making it sound more problematic than it had actually been. "As nearly as I can tell, your brother's cleaned up his act. He's working as the custodian for the Jubilee Evangelical Church. I gather he doubles as a handyman for various people in Marcella. He says he's the only one in town doing home maintenance, so he earns decent money, by his standards. His lifestyle is simple, but he's doing okay."

Donovan said, "Is he married?"

"I didn't ask if he was married, but he didn't seem to be. He never mentioned a wife. His housing's provided by the church in exchange for his services. The place is pretty funky, but he seems to manage all right. I grant you these are superficial judgments, but I didn't really stop to investigate."

Bennet shaved an olive with his teeth and placed the

pit on a paper napkin. "Why Marcella? That's a dirt bucket of a place."

"The pastor of this fundamentalist church picked him up hitchhiking out on 101 the day he left home. Essentially, he's been in Marcella ever since. The church he joined seems pretty strict. No dancing, card playing, things like that. He did say he had a beer now and then, but no drugs. That's been for the better part of fifteen years."

"If you can believe him," Bennet said. "I don't know how much you could tell from the brief time you spent. You were there for what, an hour?"

"About that," I said. "I'm not exactly an amateur. I've dealt with addicts in the past and believe me, he didn't look like one. I can spot a liar, too."

"No offense," he said. "I'm skeptical by nature when it comes to him. He always put on a good show." He finished his martini, holding the glass by the stem. The last vestiges of the gin formed a distinct scallop along the rim. He reached for the pitcher and poured himself another drink.

"Who else did you talk to?" Donovan asked, reasserting his presence. He was clearly running the show and wanted to make sure Bennet remained aware of it. For his part, Bennet seemed more interested in his martini than the conversation. I could see the lines of tension in his face smooth out. His questions were meant to demonstrate his control of himself.

I shrugged. "I made one stop in town and mentioned Guy in passing to the woman who runs the general store. There couldn't be more than five or six hundred residents and I figure everyone there knows everybody else's business. She didn't bat an eye and had no comment about him one way or the other. The pastor and his wife seemed genuinely fond of him and spoke with some pride of the distance he's come. They could have been lying, putting on a show, but I doubt it. Most people aren't that good at improvising."

Jack picked up a cracker and lifted the dollop of Cheez Whiz off the surface like he was licking the filling from an Oreo. "So what's the deal? Is he born-again? Has he been baptized? Do you think he's accepted our Lord Jesus in his heart?" His sarcasm was offensive.

I turned to stare at him. "You have a problem with that?"

"Why would I have a problem? It's his life," Jack said.

Donovan shifted in his seat. "Anybody else have a question?"

Jack popped the cracker in his mouth and wiped his fingers on a napkin while he munched. "I think it's great. I mean, maybe he won't want the money. If he's such a good Christian, maybe he'll opt for the spiritual over the materialistic."

Bennet snorted with annoyance. "His being a Christian has nothing to do with it. He's penniless. You heard her. He's got nothing. He's flat broke."

"I don't know that he's broke. I never said that," I interjected.

Now it was Bennet's turn to stare. "You seriously think he's going to turn down a great big whack of dough?"

Donovan looked at me. "Good question," he said. "What's your feeling on the subject?"

"He never asked about the money. At the time I think he was more interested in the idea that you'd hired someone to find him. He seemed touched at first and then embarrassed when he realized he'd misunderstood."

"Misunderstood what?" Christie said.

"He thought I'd been asked to locate him because of family interest or concern. It became obvious pretty quickly that the point of the visit was to notify him of his father's death and advise him he was a possible beneficiary under the terms of Bader's will."

"Maybe if he thinks we're all kissy-kissy, he'll give up the money and opt for love instead," Jack suggested.

Donovan ignored him. "Did he say anything about talking to an attorney?"

"Not really. I told him to get in touch with Tasha, but she's the attorney for the estate and she's not going to advise him about that aspect of the situation. If he calls her, she'll refer him to a lawyer unless he already has one."

Donovan said, "In other words, what you're saying is we don't have any idea what he'll do."

Bennet spoke up. "Of course we do. There's no mystery. He wants the *money*. He's not a fool."

"How do you know what Guy wants?" Christie responded with a flash of irritation.

Bennet went right on. "Kinsey should have asked for his signature on a quitclaim. Get him signed off. Make a settlement before he has a chance to think too much."

Donovan said, "I asked Tasha about that. I suggested we draw up a disclaimer, thinking Kinsey could take it with her. Tasha nixed that. She said a disclaimer would be meaningless because he could always maintain later he wasn't properly represented or he was unduly influenced, overcome by the emotions of the moment, shit like that, which would make it useless. I thought her point was well taken. Tell the man his father's dead and then whip out a quitclaim? It's like waving a red flag in front of a bull."

Christie spoke up again, saying, "Kinsey had a good idea. She pointed out that since the two wills were drawn up just three years apart the witnesses for the second will might have been the same as the ones for the first. If we can track down the witnesses, it's always possible one of them was aware of the provisions."

"Like a secretary or a paralegal?" Donovan asked.

"It's possible. Or maybe the clerk/typist acted as a witness. *Somebody* had to be involved in the preparation of that document," I said.

"If there was one," Jack said.

Donovan's mouth pulled down as he considered the point. "Worth a try."

"To what end?" Jack asked. "I'm not saying we shouldn't make the effort, but it probably won't do any good. You can be a witness to a will without being aware of what's in it. Besides, what if the second will left everything to Guy? Then we'd really be screwed."

Bennet was impatient. "Oh come on, Jack. Whose side are you on? At least the witnesses could testify the second will was signed. I heard Dad say half a dozen times Guy wasn't getting a thing—we all heard him say that—so wouldn't that make a difference?"

"Why should it? Dad had the will. He kept it in a file right upstairs. How do you know he didn't revoke it in the end? Suppose he tore it up before he died? He had notice enough. He knew his days were numbered."

"He would have told us," Bennet said.

"Not necessarily."

"Jesus, Jack. I'm telling you, he said Guy would get nothing. We've been over this a hundred times and he was adamant."

"It doesn't matter what he said. You know how he was when it came to Guy. He never stuck to his guns. *We* might have been forced to toe the mark, but not him."

Donovan cleared his throat and set his glass down with a sharp tap. "All right. Knock it off, you two. This is getting us nowhere. We've been through enough of this. Let's just see what Guy does. We might not have a problem. We don't know at this point. Tasha said she'd contact him if he doesn't get in touch with her first. I might drop him a note myself and we'll take it from there."

Bennet sat up straight. "Wait a minute. Who put you in charge? Why can't we discuss this? It concerns all of us."

"You want to discuss this? Fine. Go ahead," Donovan said. "We all know your opinion. You think Guy's a slimeball. You're completely antagonistic and with *that* attitude, you'll be pushing him right to the wall."

"You don't know any more about him than I do," Bennet said.

"I'm not talking about him. I'm talking about you. What makes you so sure he wants the money?"

"Because he hated us. That's why he left in the first

place, isn't it? He'd do anything to get back at us and what better way than this?"

"You don't know that," Donovan said. "You don't know what went on back then. He may not harbor any ill will toward us at all. You go in there punching and he's going to go on the offensive."

"I never did anything to Guy. Why would he hate me?" Jack said blithely. He seemed amused at the fireworks between his two brothers and I wondered if he didn't habitually goad them.

Bennet snorted again and he and Jack locked eyes. Something flashed between them but I wasn't sure what.

Donovan intervened again with a warning look at both. "Could we stick to the subject? Anybody have something new to contribute?"

"Donovan runs the family. He's the king," Bennet said. He looked at me with the slightly liquid eyes of someone who's had too much to drink. I'd seen him suck down two martinis in less than fifteen minutes and who knew what he'd consumed before he entered the room? "The man thinks I'm a dick. He may pretend to be supportive, but he doesn't mean a word of it. He and my father never actually gave me enough money to succeed at anything. And then when I failed—when a business went under—they were quick to point out how I'd mismanaged it. Dad always undercut me and the notion that Guy can come along now and insist on his share is just more of the same as far as I'm concerned. Who's looking out for our interests? It ain't *him*," he said, jerking a thumb at Donovan.

"Wait a minute. Hold it! Where's that coming from?"

"I've never really stood up and asked for what's

mine," Bennet said. "I should have insisted a long time ago, but I bought into the program, the story you and Dad cooked up. 'Here, Bennet, you can have this pittance. Do the best you can with this pathetic sum of money. Make something of yourself and there'll be more where that came from. You can't expect us to underwrite the whole venture.' Blah blah blah. That's all I ever heard."

Donovan squinted at him, shaking his head. "I don't believe this. Dad gave you hundreds of thousands of dollars and you pissed it all away. How many chances do you think you get? There isn't a bank in this town that would have given you the first *dime*—"

"Bullshit! That's bullshit. I've worked like a dog and you know it. Hell, Dad had a lot of business failures and so have you. Now suddenly I have to sit here and fuckin' justify every move I make—just to get a little seed money."

Donovan looked at him with disbelief. "Where's all the money your partners put in? You blew that, too. You're so busy playing big shot, you're not tending to business. Half of what you do is outright fraudulent and you know it. Or if you don't, more's the pity because you'll end up in jail."

Bennet pointed a finger, poking the air repeatedly as if it were an elevator button. "Hey, I'm the one taking risks. I'm the one with my ass on the line. You never put yourself out there on the firing line. You played it safe. You were Daddy's little boy, the little piggy who stayed home and did exactly what Daddy said. And now you want credit for being such an all-fired success. Well, fuck that. To hell with you."

"Watch the *f* word. Ladies present," Jack said in a singsong tone.

"Shut up, you little piss. No one's talking to you!"

Christie cast a look in my direction and then raised a hand, saying, "Hey, fellas. Couldn't we postpone this until later? Kinsey doesn't want to sit here and listen to this. We asked her to have a drink, not a ringside seat."

I took my cue from her and used the opportunity to get to my feet. "I think I should leave you alone to discuss this, but I really don't think you need to worry about Guy. He seems like a nice man. That's the bottom line from my perspective. I hope everything works out."

A paragraph of awkward verbiage ensued: apologies for the outburst, hasty explanations of the strain everyone was under in the wake of Bader's death. Personally, I thought they were a bunch of ill-mannered louts and if my bill had been paid I might have told them as much. As it was, they assured me no offense was intended and I assured them, in turn, that none had been taken. I can fib with the best of them when there's money at stake. We shook hands all around. I was thanked for my time. I thanked them for the drink and took my leave of them.

"I'll walk out with you," Christie said.

There was a moment of quiet as we left the living room. I hadn't realized I was holding my breath until the door closed behind us and I could suck in some fresh air.

"Let me grab a jacket," Christie said as we crossed the foyer. She made a detour to the closet, pulling on a dark wool car coat as we passed into the night air.

The temperature had dropped and a dampness seemed to rise up from the cobblestones. The exterior lights were now on, but the illumination was poor. I could see the dim shape of my car, parked on the far side of the courtyard, and we headed in that direction. The lighted front windows threw truncated panels of yellow on the driveway in front of us. In the living room, the three Malek brothers were more than likely engaged in fisticuffs by now.

"Thanks for getting me out of there."

"I'm sorry you had to see that. What a zoo," she said. She shoved her hands in her pockets. "That goes on all the time and it drives me insane. It's like living in the middle of a giant preschool free-for-all. They're all three years old. They're still slugging it out over the same toy truck. The tension in this house is unreal half the time."

"Bennet's drinking doesn't help."

"It's not just that. I came into the marriage thinking I was going to be part of a loving family. I never had any brothers and I thought the idea was keen. They seemed close at first. I mean, they sure fooled me. I guess I should have figured out that three grown men still living together under Daddy's roof didn't exactly speak of mental health, but what did I know? My family's so screwed up, I wouldn't know a healthy one if it leapt up and bit me. I wanted kids. Looks like I got 'em," she remarked in a wry aside. "I hate sitting around watching these 'boys' bicker and connive. You ought to see them operate. They fight over absolutely everything. Anything that comes up, they all instantly take the most disparate positions possible. Then they all take sides and form these temporary coalitions. It'll be Donovan and Jack against Bennet one day. The next day, Bennet and Jack form a team against Donovan. The allegiances vary according to the subject matter, but there's never accord. There's never any sense of all for one and one for all. Everybody wants to be right—morally superior—and at the same time, everybody feels completely misunderstood."

"Makes me glad to be an orphan."

"I'm with you on *that* one." She paused with a smile. "Or maybe I'm just annoyed because none of them are ever on my side. I live with a perpetual stomachache."

"You don't have any kids?"

"Not yet. I keep trying, but of course I can't seem to get pregnant in this atmosphere. I'm coming up on forty so if something doesn't happen soon, it's going to be too late."

"I thought women were having babies into their fifties these days."

"Not me. Forget it. Life's hard enough as it is. I mean, what kid would volunteer to come into a house like *this*? It's disgusting."

"Why do you stay?"

"Who says I'll stay? I told Donovan last fall, I said, 'One more round, buddy, and I'm outta here.' So what happens next? Bader up and dies. I don't feel I can walk out when things are such a mess. Also, I suppose I still harbor the dim hope that things'll work out somehow."

"I'm sure my finding Guy couldn't be a help," I said.

"I don't know about that. At least now maybe the three of them will gang up against *him*. In the end, that might be the only issue they agree on."

I glanced toward the lighted windows of the living room. "You call *that* 'agreement'?"

"Oh, they'll get around to it. There's nothing like the common enemy to unify the troops. The truth is, Guy's the one I feel sorry for. They'll take him to the cleaners if they have half a chance and from what you say, he's the best of the lot."

"Donovan seems okay," I said.

"Ha. That's what I thought, too. He puts up a good front, but that's all that is. He's learned how to function in the business world so he's got a little more polish. I'm sure nobody said so, but I know they were impressed with the job you did."

"Well, I appreciate that, but at this point, these people don't need a PI—"

"They need a referee," she laughed. "Tasha didn't do you any favors when she got you involved in this. I'm sorry you had to see 'em at their worst. Then again, at least you can appreciate what I have to live with."

"Don't worry about it. It's finished business," I said.

We said our good-nights and I slid in behind the wheel, taking a few minutes to get my car warmed up. The residual tension had left me feeling icy cold and I drove home with the VW heater level pulled to maximum effect. This consisted of a thin tongue of warm air licking at the bottoms of my shoes. The rest of me was freezing, a cotton turtleneck and wool blazer providing little in the way of insulation. As I turned onto my street, I gave brief consideration to having dinner up at Rosie's. I hadn't managed to eat so much as an unpitted olive at the Maleks' during the cocktail hour. I'd pictured sumptuous canapes that I could chow down instead of dinner, but the uproar had made even the Cheez Whiz seem less than appetizing. At the back of my mind, I knew I was avoiding the idea of going home to an empty apartment. Better now than later. It was only going to get worse.

I parked my car close to the corner and hoofed my way back to Henry's driveway. A dense fog had begun to blow in from the beach and I was heartened by the fact that I'd left a light on in my living room. At least letting myself in wouldn't feel so much like breaking and entering. I passed through the squeaky gate with my house key at the ready, unlocked my door, and tossed my handbag on the kitchen counter. I heard the downstair's toilet flush and a thrill of fear washed over me. Then the bathroom door opened and Robert Dietz walked out, looking as startled as I was. "I didn't hear you come in," he said. "I forgot to give back your key."

"What are you doing here? I thought you left."

"I got as far as Santa Maria and had to come back. I was halfway down the street and I missed you like crazy. I don't want us leaving each other on a bad note."

I felt a pain in my chest, something fragile and sharp that made me take a deep breath. "I don't see a way to resolve our basic differences."

"We can be friends without resolution. I mean, can't we?"

"How do I know?" I tried to shut down, but I couldn't quite manage it. I had an inexplicable urge to weep about something. Usually good-byes do that, tender partings in movies accompanied by music guaranteed to rip your heart out. The silence between us was just as painful to me.

"Have you had dinner?"

"I hadn't decided about that yet. I just had drinks with the Maleks," I said faintly. The words sounded odd and I wanted to pat myself on the chest as a way of consoling myself. I could have handled the situation if only he hadn't come back. The day had been hard, but I'd survived it.

"You want to talk?"

I shook my head, not trusting my voice.

"Then what? You decide. I'll do anything you want."

I looked away from him, thinking about the fearful risks of intimacy, the potential for loss, the tender pain implicit in any bond between two creatures—human or beast, what difference did it make? In me, the instinct for survival and the need for love had been at war for years. My caution was like a wall I'd built to keep me safe. But safety is an illusion and the danger of feeling too much is no worse than the danger of being numb. I looked back at him and saw my pain mirrored in his eyes.

He said, "Come here." He made a gesture with his hand, coaxing me to move closer.

I crossed the room. Dietz leaned into me like a ladder left behind by a thief.

NINE

Dietz's knee was so swollen and painful he couldn't make it up the stairs, so we unfolded the sofa bed. I brought the duvet down from the loft. We turned off the lamp and crawled naked beneath the comforter's downy weight like polar bears in a cave. We made love in the puffy igloo of the quilt while around us streetlights streamed through the porthole window like moonlight on snow. For a long time, I simply drank in the musky scent of him, hair and skin, feeling my way blindly across all his textured surfaces. The heat from his body thawed my cold limbs. I felt like a snake curling up in a patch of sunlight, warmed to the depths after a long unforgiving winter. I remembered his ways from our three months together—the look on his face, the hapless sounds he made. What I'd forgotten was the smoldering response he awakened in me.

There was a brief time in my youth when my behavior was both reckless and promiscuous. Those were the days when there seemed to be no consequence to sex that wasn't easily cured. In the current marketplace, you'd have to be a fool—or suicidal—to risk the casual encounter without a lot of straight talk and doctors' certificates changing hands. For my purposes, celibacy is my habitual state. I suppose it's a lot like living in times of famine. Without hope of satiation, hunger diminishes and the appetite fades. With Dietz, I could feel all my physical senses quicken, the yearning for contact overcoming my natural reticence. Dietz's injury required patience and ingenuity, but somehow we managed. The process entailed considerable laughter at our contortions and quiet concentration during the moments between.

Finally, at ten, I flung the covers aside, exposing our sweaty bodies to the arctic temperatures surrounding us. "I don't know about you, but I'm starving," I said. "If we don't stop and eat soon, I'll be dead before morning."

Thirty minutes later, showered and dressed, we found ourselves sitting up at Rosie's in my favorite booth. She and William were both working, he behind the bar and Rosie out waiting tables. Ordinarily, the kitchen closed down at ten, and I could see she was just on the verge of saying as much when she noticed the whisker burn that had set my cheeks aflame. I put my chin in my palm, but not before she caught sight of my sex rash. The woman may be close to seventy, but she's not unperceptive. She seemed to take in at a glance both the source of our satisfaction and our avid interest in food. I thought the application of my makeup had successfully disguised my chafed flesh, but she was visibly smirking as she recited the meal she intended to prepare for us. With Rosie, there's no point in even pretending to order. You eat what she decides will be perfect for the occasion. In honor of Dietz's return, I noticed her English was marginally improved.

She parked herself sideways to the table, wiggling slightly in place, refusing to look directly at either of us after that first sly glance. "Now. Here's what you gonna get and don't make with the usual face—like this—while I'm telling you." She pulled her mouth down, eyes rolling, to show Dietz my usual enthusiasm for her choices. "I'm fixing Korhelyleves, is also called Souse's Soup. Is taking couple pounds of sauerkraut, paprika, smoked sausage, and some sour cream. Is guaranteed to perk up tired senses of which you look like you got a lot. Then, I'm roasting you little cheeken that I'm serve with mushroom pudding—is very good—and for efter, is hazelnut torte, but no coffee. You need sleep. I'm bringing wine in a minute. Don't go way."

We didn't leave until midnight. We didn't sleep until one, wound together on the narrow width of the sofa bed. I'm not accustomed to sleeping with someone else and I can't say it netted me any restful results. Because of his knee, Dietz was forced to lie on his back with a pillow supporting his left leg. This gave me two choices: I could lie pressed against him with my head resting on his chest, or flat on my back with our bodies touching along their lengths.

I tried one and then the other, tossing relentlessly as the hours ticked away. Half the time, I could feel the sofa's metal mechanism cut across my back, but if I switched to the other position with my head on his chest, I suffered from heatstroke, a dead arm, and a canned left ear. Sometimes I could feel the exhalation of his breath on my cheek and the effect drove me mad.

I found myself counting as he breathed, in and out, in and out. In moments, the rhythm changed and there'd be a long pause in which I wondered if he were in the process of dropping dead. Dietz slept like a soldier under combat conditions. His snores were gentle snuffles, just loud enough to keep me on sentry duty, but not quite loud enough to draw enemy fire.

I slept finally—amazingly—and woke at seven energized. Dietz had made coffee and he was reading the paper, dressed, his hair damp, a pair of half-glasses sitting low on his nose. I watched him for a few minutes until his gaze came up to mine.

"I didn't know you wore glasses."

"I was too vain before this. The minute you were out the door, I put 'em on," he said with that crooked smile of his.

I turned on my side, folding my right arm under my cheek. "What time will the boys be expecting you?"

"Early afternoon. I have motel reservations at a place close by. If they want to spend the night, I'll have room."

"I'll bet you look forward to seeing them."

"Yes, but I'm nervous about it, too. I haven't seen them for two years—since I left for Germany. I'm never quite sure what to talk about with them."

"What do you talk to anyone about? Mostly bullshit."

"Even bullshit requires a context. It gets awkward for them, too. Sometimes we end up going to the movies just to have something to talk about later. I'm not exactly a fount of paternal advice. Once I quiz them about girlfriends and classes, I'm about out of conversation."

"You'll do fine."

"I hope. What about you? What's your day looking like?"

"I don't know. This is Saturday, so I don't have to work. I'll probably nap. Starting soon."

"You want company?"

"Dietz," I said, outraged, "if you get in this bed again, I won't be able to walk."

"You're an amateur."

"I am. I'm not used to this stuff."

"How about some coffee?"

"Let me brush my teeth first."

After breakfast, we went down to the beach. The day was cloudy, the marine layer holding in the heat like foam insulation. The temperature was close to seventy and the air soft and fruity, with a tropical scent. Santa Teresa winters are filled with such contradictions. One day will feel icy while the next day feels mild. The ocean had a slick sheen, reflecting the uniform white of the sky. We took off our shoes and carried them, scuffling along the water's edge with the frothy play of waves rolling across our bare feet. Seagulls hovered overhead, screeching, while two dogs leaped in unison, snapping at the birds as if they were low-flying Frisbees.

Dietz took off at nine, holding me crushed against him before he got in the car. I leaned on the hood and we kissed for a while. Finally, he pulled back and studied my face. "If I come back in a couple of weeks, will you be here?"

"Where else would I go?"

"I'll see you then," he said.

"Don't worry about me. Any old day will do," I remarked, waving, as his car receded down the block. Dietz hated to be specific about dates because it made him feel trapped. Of course, the effect of his vagueness was to keep me feeling hooked. I shook my head to myself as I returned to my place. How did I end up with a man like him?

I spent the rest of the morning getting my apartment tidied up. It didn't really take much work, but it was satisfying nonetheless. This time I wasn't really feeling depressed. I knew Dietz would be coming back, so my virtuous activity had more to do with reestablishing my boundaries than warding off the blues. Since he'd done the grocery shopping, my cupboard was full and my refrigerator stocked, a state that always contributes to my sense of security. As long as you have sufficient toilet paper, how far wrong can life go?

At lunchtime I spotted Henry sitting in the backyard at a little round picnic table he'd picked up in a garage sale the previous fall. He'd spread out some graph paper, his reference books, and a crossword key. As a pastime, Henry constructs and sells crossword puzzles for those wee yellow books sold near grocery store checkout lanes. I made a peanut-butter-and-pickle sandwich and joined him in the sunshine.

"You want one?" I asked, holding out my plate.

"Thanks, but I just had lunch," he said. "Where'd Dietz disappear to? I thought he intended to stick around."

I filled him in on the "romance" and we chatted idly while I ate my sandwich. The texture of the peanut butter was a sublime contrast to the crunch of the bread-

and-butter pickles. The diagonal cut exposed more filling than a vertical cut would and I savored the ratio of saltiness to tart. This ranked right up there with sex without taking off any clothes. I made a sort of low moan, nearly swooning with pleasure, and Henry glanced up at me. "Give me a bite of that."

I let him have the plump center portion, keeping my fingers positioned so he couldn't take too much.

He chewed for a moment, clearly relishing the intense blend of flavors. "Very weird, but not bad." This is what he always says when he samples this culinary marvel.

I tried another bite myself, pointing to the puzzle he was working on. "How's this one coming? You've never really told me how you go about your business." Henry was a crossword fanatic, subscribing to the *New York Times* so he could do the daily puzzle, which he completed in ink. Sometimes, to amuse himself, he left every other letter blank, or filled in the outer borders first in a spiral moving toward the center. The puzzles he wrote himself seemed very difficult to me, though he claimed they were easy. I'd watched him construct dozens without understanding the strategy.

"I've actually upgraded my technique. My approach used to be haphazard. I'm better organized these days. This is a small one, only fifteen by fifteen. This is the pattern I'm using," he said, indicating a template with the gridwork of black squares already laid in.

"You don't devise the format as well?"

"Usually not. I've used this one several times and it suits my purposes. They're all symmetrical and if you'll notice, no area is closed off. The rules say the black squares can't exceed more than one sixth of the total number. There are a few other rules tossed in. For example, you can't use any words of fewer than three letters, stuff like that. The good ones have a theme around which the answers are organized."

I picked up one of his reference books and turned it over in my hand. "What's this?"

"That book lists words in alphabetical order from three through fifteen letters. And that one's a crossword finisher that lists words in a complicated alphabetical order up through seven letters."

I smiled at the enthusiasm that had crept into his voice. "How'd you get into this?"

He waved dismissively. "Do enough of 'em and you can't help it. You have to have a go at it yourself, just to see what it's like. They even have crossword championships, which started in 1980. You ought to see those puppies go. The puzzles are projected on an overhead screen. A real whiz can answer sixty-four questions in under eight minutes."

"Are you ever tempted to enter?"

He shook his head, penciling in a clue. "I'm too slow and much too easily rattled. Besides, it's a serious business, like bridge tournaments." His head came up. "That's your phone," he said.

"It is? Your hearing must be better than mine." I hopped up from the table and made a beeline for my place, picking up the receiver just as my answering machine did. I reached for the Off button as my voice completed its request for messages. "Hello, hello. It's me. I'm really home," I sang.

"Hey," a man's voice said mildly. "This is Guy. Hope you don't mind my calling on a weekend."

"Not at all. What's up?"

"Nothing much," he said. "Donovan called me at the church. I guess last night the three of them—him and Bennet and Jack—had a meeting. He says they want me to come down for a few days so we can talk about the will."

I felt my whole body go quiet. "Really. That's interesting. You going to do it?"

"I think so. I might, but I'm not really sure. I had a long talk with Peter and Winnie. Peter thinks it's time to open up a dialogue. He's got a prayer meeting in Santa Teresa tomorrow, so it works out pretty good. They can bring me down after church, but he thought it'd be smart to talk to you about it first."

I was silent for a moment. "You want the truth?"

"Well, yeah. That's why I called."

"I wouldn't do it if I were you. I was over there last night and it all seems very tense. It's nothing you'd want to be exposed to."

"How so?"

"Feelings are running high and your showing up at this point is only going to make things worse."

"That was my first reaction, but then I got to thinking. I mean, Donovan called me. I didn't call him," he said. "Seems to me if the three of them are offering a truce, I should at least be willing to meet 'em halfway. It can't hurt."

I suppressed an urge to start shrieking at him. Shrieking, I've discovered, is really not a sound method for persuading other people to your point of view. I'd

seen his brothers in action and Guy was no match. I
wouldn't trust those three under any circumstances.
Given Guy's emotional state, I could see why he'd be
tempted, but he'd be a fool to go into that house without
counsel. "Maybe it's a truce and maybe not. Bader's
death has brought up all kinds of issues," I said. "You
go in unprepared and you'll end up taking on a whole
raft of shit. You'd be walking into a nightmare."

"I understand."

"I don't think so," I said. "Not to criticize your
brothers, but these are not nice fellows, at least where
you're concerned. There's a lot of friction between them
and your appearance is only going to add fuel to the
fire. I mean, honestly. You can't imagine the dynamic."
I noticed the pitch and volume of my voice going up.

"I have to try," he said.

"Maybe so, but not *that* way."

"Meaning what?"

"You're going to find yourself in exactly the same
position you were in when you left. You'll be the fall
guy, the scapegoat for all their hostility."

I could hear him shrug. He said, "Maybe we need to
talk about that then. Get it out in the open and deal
with it."

"It's out in the open. Those three aren't shy about
anything. The conflicts are all right out there in front
of God and everyone and believe me, you don't want
their venom directed at you."

"Donovan doesn't seem to bear me any ill will and
from what he says, Bennet and Jack don't either. The
truth is, I've changed and they need to see that. How
else can I persuade 'em if it isn't face-to-face?"

I could feel my eyes cross while I tried controlling my impatience. I knew I'd be smarter to keep my mouth shut, but I've never been good at keeping my opinions to myself. "Look, Guy, I don't want to stand here and try to tell you your business, but this isn't about you. This is about their relationship to each other. It's about your father and whatever's been going on in the years since you left. You'll end up being the target for all the anger they've stored up. And why put yourself through that?"

"Because I want to be connected again. I screwed up. I admit that and I want to make it up to them. Peter says there can't be any healing unless we sit down together."

"That's all well and good, but there's a lot more at stake. What if the subject of the money comes up?"

"I don't care about the money."

"Bullshit. That's bull. Do you have any idea how much money we're talking about?"

"Doesn't make any difference. The money doesn't matter to me. I don't need money. I'm happy as I am."

"That's what you say now, but how do you know that won't change? Why create problems for yourself later on? Have you talked to Tasha? What's she say about this?"

"I never talked to her. I called the office in Lompoc, but she'd already left for San Francisco and after that, the secretary said she was taking off for Utah on a ten-day ski trip."

"So call her in Utah. They have phones up there."

"I tried that. They wouldn't give me her number. They said if she called in, they'd give her my name and number and she'd call if she could."

148

"Then try someone else. Call another attorney. I don't want you talking to your brothers without legal advice."

"It's not about legalities. It's about mending the breach."

"Which is exactly what's going to make you a sitting duck. Your agenda has nothing to do with theirs. They don't give a shit about forgiveness, if you'll pardon my French."

"I don't see it that way."

"I know you don't. That's why we're having this argument," I shrieked. "Suppose they try to pressure you into making a decision?"

"About what?"

"About anything! You don't even know what's in your best interest. If your sole aim is to make peace, you're only going to get screwed."

"How can I get screwed if I don't want anything? They can keep the money if that's the only thing standing between us."

"Well, if *you* don't want the money, why not give it to the church?" The minute I said it, I wanted to bite my tongue. His motives were clean. Why introduce the complication?

He was silent for a moment. "I hadn't thought about that. That's a good point."

"Forget it. Just skip that. All I'm saying is don't go in there alone. Get help so you don't do something you'll regret."

"Why don't you go?"

I groaned and he laughed in response. Going with him was the last thing I wanted to do. He needed protection, but I didn't think it was appropriate for me to step in. What did I have to offer in the way of assistance? "Because it's not my place. I'm not objective. I don't know the law and I don't have any idea what your legal position is. You'd be foolish to come down here and have a conversation with them. Just wait for ten days until Tasha gets back. Don't do anything yet. There's no reason you have to hop-to the minute Donovan whistles. You should be doing this on your terms, not his."

I could hear his reluctance to accept what I was saying. Like most of us, he'd made up his mind before he asked. "You know something? This is the truth," he said. "I prayed about this. I asked God for guidance and this was the answer I got."

"Well, try Him again. Maybe you misunderstood the message."

He laughed. "I did that in a way. I opened my Bible and put my finger on the page. Know what the passage was?"

"I can't imagine," I said dryly.

" 'Be it known unto you therefore, men *and* brethren, that through this man is preached unto you the forgiveness of sins: And by him all that believe are justified from all things, from which ye could not be justified by the law of Moses.' ' Like many of the faithful, he could recite Bible verses like song lyrics.

This time the silence was mine. "I can't argue that. I don't even know what it means. Look, if you're determined to do this, you'll do it, I'm sure. I'm just urging you to take someone with you."

"I just did. I asked you."

"I'm not talking about me! What about Peter and

Winnie? I'm sure they'd be willing to help if you asked and they'd do a much better job. I don't know the first thing about counseling or mediation or anything else. Aside from that, all this family-related stuff gives me the willies."

I could hear Guy smile and his tone was affectionate. "Strange you should say that because somehow it feels like you're part of this. I don't know how, but it sure seems like that to me. Don't you have some kind of issue around family yourself?"

I held the phone away from me and squinted at the handset. "Who, me? Absolutely not. Why would you say that?"

Guy laughed. "I don't know. It just came to me in a flash. Maybe I'm wrong, but it feels like you're connected."

"My only connection is professional. I was hired to do a job. That's the only link I see." I kept my tone casual to demonstrate my nonchalance, but I was forced to put a hand against the small of my back, where an inexplicable drop of sweat was trickling down into my underpants. "Why don't you have a talk with Peter again? I know you're eager to make amends, but I don't want you walking into the lions' den. We all know how the lions and the Christians came out."

He was silent for a moment and then seemed to change the subject. "Where's your apartment?"

"What makes you ask?" I was unwilling to be specific until I knew where he was headed.

"How about this? Maybe we can do this another way. Donovan says everyone's gone tomorrow until five o'clock. Peter'll give me a lift into town, but his schedule's too tight to do much more than that. If he drops me off at your place, could you give me a ride the rest of the way? You don't have to stay. I understand you don't want to be involved and that's fine with me."

"I don't really see how that addresses the point."

"It doesn't. I'm just asking for a ride. I can handle everything else if you can get me over there."

"You're not going to listen to me, are you?" I said.

"I did listen. The problem is I disagree."

I hesitated, but really couldn't see any reason to refuse. I was already feeling churlish because I'd put up such resistance. "That sounds all right. Sure. I can do that," I said. "What time would you get here?"

"Three? Somewhere around then. I don't mean to be a bother. Peter's meeting is downtown, at that church on the corner of State and Michaelson. Is that anywhere close? Because I could walk over to your place and we could go from there."

"Close enough," I said, feeling crabby and resigned. "Look, why don't you give me a call when you get in. I'll swing by the church and pick you up."

"That'd be good. That's great. Are you sure this is okay?"

"No, but don't press your luck. I'm willing to do this much, but don't go asking for reassurance on top of it."

He laughed. "I'm sorry. You're right. I'll see you then," he said. He disconnected on his end.

As I hung up the phone, I was already having doubts. Amazing how quickly someone else's problems become yours. Trouble creates a vacuum into which the rest of us get sucked.

I found myself pacing the living room, inwardly refuting his ridiculous claim about the relevance of his situation to mine. His conflict about family had *nothing* to do with me. I sat down at my desk and made some notes to myself. In case Tasha asked, I thought it might be wise to keep a record of the discussion we'd just had. I hoped he wasn't going to get a bug up his butt about giving all his money to the church. That was really going to cause a problem if he got greedy on behalf of Jubilee Evangelical. I omitted any reference to a charitable donation, thinking if I didn't write it down, the subject wouldn't exist.

I picked up the phone again and put a call through to the Maleks. Myrna picked up and I asked to speak to Christie. I waited, listening as Myrna crossed the foyer and bellowed up the stairs to Christie. When Christie finally picked up the phone on her end, I filled her in briefly on my conversation with Guy. "Will you keep me informed about what's going on?" I asked. "I'll drop him off, but after that he's on his own. I think he needs protection, but I don't want to get into my rescue costume. He's a big boy and this is really none of my business. I'd feel better if I knew there was someone in your camp keeping an eye on him."

"Oh, right. And leave the rescue to me," she said, her tone of voice wry.

I laughed. "Not to get trivial, but he *is* cute," I said.

"Really? Well, that's good. I'm a big fan of cute. In fact, that's how I vote for a presidential candidate," she said. "Personally, I don't think you have anything to worry about. After you left last night, the three of them talked long and hard. Once they got done ripping each other apart, they settled down into some meaningful conversation."

"I'm glad to hear that. I was actually a bit puzzled why Donovan had called him. What's their inclination? Do you mind if I ask?"

"I guess it depends on what he says to them. Ultimately, of course, this is probably something for the lawyers to discuss. I think they want to be honorable. On the other hand, five million dollars might distort anyone's notion of what's fair."

"Ain't that the truth."

TEN

I pulled over to the curb in front of the Faith Evangelical Church the next afternoon at three. Guy had called me at 2:45 and I'd left the apartment shortly thereafter, taking a few minutes to put gas in my car. The sun was out again and the day felt like summer. I wore the usual jeans and a T-shirt, but I'd traded my Reeboks and sweat socks for a pair of openwork sandals in honor of the sudden heat. The grass on the church lawn had been recently cut and the sidewalk was littered with fine green at the edge. The turf itself featured a pale dun-colored haze where the cut blades had browned in the sun. A number of gullible daffodils had taken these balmy temperatures as an invitation to pop their green shafts into view.

There was no sign of Peter, but Guy was standing on the corner with a backpack at his feet. He spotted my car and pretended to hitchhike, holding his thumb out with a smile on his face. I confess when I saw him I could feel my heart break. He'd had his hair cut and his face was so freshly shaved he still sported a dot of toilet paper where he'd nicked himself. He wore a navy blue suit that didn't fit well. The pants were baggy in the butt and slightly too long, the backs of his trouser cuffs brushing the sidewalk. The jacket was wide across the chest, which made the shoulder pads look as exaggerated as a 1940s' zoot suit. The garment had probably been donated to a church rummage sale or maybe he'd bought it from someone weighing forty pounds more. Whatever the explanation, he wore his finery with a self-conscious air, clearly unaccustomed to the dress shirt and tie. I wondered if my own vulnerability had been as apparent during my lunch with Tasha. I'd approached my personal grooming with the same insecurity, perhaps netting myself the same sorry results.

Guy reached for his canvas backpack, clearly happy to see me. He seemed as innocent as a pup. There was a softness about him, something guileless and unformed, as if his association with Jubilee Evangelical had isolated him from worldly influences all these years. The reckless element in his nature was now tamed to a gentleness I'd rarely seen in a man.

He slid into the front seat. "Hey, Kinsey. How are you?" He held his backpack on his lap like a kid on his way to day camp.

I smiled in his direction. "You're all spiffed up."

"I didn't want my brothers to think I'd forgotten how to dress. What do you think of the suit?"

"The color's good on you."

"Thanks," he said, smiling with pleasure. "Oh. By the way, Winnie says hi."

"Hi to her," I said. "What's the deal on your return? When are you planning to go back to Marcella?"

Guy looked away from me out the car window on his side, the casualness of his tone belying its content.

"Depends on what happens at the house. Donovan invited me to stay for a couple of days and I wouldn't mind that if everything works out all right. I guess if it doesn't work, it won't make any difference. I got money in my pocket. When I'm ready to leave, someone can give me a ride to the bus."

I was on the verge of volunteering my services and then thought better of it. I glanced over at him, making a covert study of his face in profile. In some lights, he looked every one of his forty-three years. In other moments his boyishness seemed a permanent part of his character. It was as if his development had been arrested at the age of sixteen, maybe twenty at the outside. He was scanning the streets, taking in the sights as if he were in a foreign country.

"I take it you don't get down here that often," I said.

He shook his head. "I don't have much occasion. When you live in Marcella, Santa Teresa seems too big and too far away. We go to Santa Maria or San Luis if we need anything." He looked over at me. "Can we do a quick tour? I'd like to see what's going on."

"I can do that. Why not? We have time."

I circled the block, coming back out onto State Street. I turned left, heading downtown, a short three blocks away. The business district wasn't much more than twenty blocks long and three or four blocks wide, terminating at Cabana Boulevard, which parallels the beach. For many years, the stores along upper State attracted the bulk of the downtown shoppers. Lower State was considered the less desirable end of town, the street lined with thrift stores, third-rate eateries, a movie theater that smelled of urine, and half a dozen noisy bars and run-down transient hotels. Lately, the area had undergone a resurrection, and the classy businesses had begun to migrate southward along the thoroughfare. Now it was upper State that featured deserted storefronts while lower State had captured all the tourist trade. In warm weather, pedestrians drifted up from the beach, a ragtag parade of sightseers in shorts, licking ice-cream cones.

"It's grown," he remarked.

With a population of eighty-five thousand, Santa Teresa wasn't big, but the town had been flourishing. I tried to see it as he did, cataloging in my mind all the changes that had taken place in the last twenty years. Time-lapse photography would have shown tree trunks elongating, branches stretching out like rubber, some buildings erected while others vanished in a puff of smoke. Storefronts would flicker through a hundred variations: awnings, signs, and window displays, the liquidation sales of one business flashing across the plate glass before the next enterprise took its place. New structures would appear like apparitions, filling in the empty spaces until no gaps remained. I could remember when the downtown sidewalks were made wider, State Street narrowing to accommodate the planting of trees imported from Bolivia. Spanish-style benches and telephone booths had been added. Decorative fountains had appeared, looking like they'd been there for years. A fire had taken out two commercial establishments while an earthquake had rendered others unfit for use. Santa Teresa was one of the few towns that looked more elegant as time passed. The strict regulations of the Architectural Board of Review imposed an air of refinement that in other towns was wiped out by gaudy neon, oversized signage, and a hodgepodge of building styles and materials. As much as the local residents complained about the lengthy approval process, the result was a mix of simplicity and grace.

At Cabana, I drove out along the wharf, wheels thumping along the length. I turned at the end until we were headed back toward town. I motored north on State, seeing the same sights again from the reverse perspective. At Olive Grove, I turned right, driving past the Santa Teresa Mission and from there into the foothills where the Malek estate was tucked. I could sense Guy's interest quicken as the road angled upward. Much of the terrain in this area was undeveloped, the landscape littered with enormous sandstone boulders and prickly cactus with leaves as large as fleshy ping-pong paddles.

The Malek estate sat close to the borders of the backcountry, an oasis of dark green in a region dense with pale chaparral. At irregular intervals, fires had swept across the foothills in spectacular conflagrations, the blaze advancing from peak to peak, sucking up houses and trees, consuming every shred of vegetation. In the wake of these burns, species of native plants known as fire followers appeared, dainty beauties emerging from the ashes of the charred and the dead. I could still see the occasional black, twisted branches of the manzanitas, though it had been five or six years since the last big fire.

Once again, the iron gates at the entrance stood open, the long driveway disappearing around a shaded curve ahead. Somehow the Maleks' evergreens and palms looked alien set against the backdrop of raw mountains. Entering the estate, I sensed how the years of careful cultivation and the introduction of exotic plants had altered the very air that permeated the grounds.

"You nervous?" I asked.

"Scared to death."

"You can still back out."

"It's too late for that. Feels like a wedding where the invitations have gone out—you know, it's still possible to cancel, but it's easier to go through with it than make a fuss for everyone else."

"Don't turn all noble on me."

"It's not about 'noble.' I guess I'm curious."

I pulled into the courtyard and eased the VW around to the left. The garages at the end of the drive were all closed. The house itself looked deserted. All the windows were dark and most of the draperies were drawn. The visage was scarcely welcoming. The silence was broken only by the idling of my engine. "Well. This is it, I guess. Call if you need me. I wish you luck."

Guy glanced at me uneasily. "You have to leave already?"

"I really should," I said, though the truth was I had nothing else to do that afternoon.

"Don't you want to see the place? Why don't you stay a few minutes and let me show you around?"

"I was just here for drinks. It hasn't changed since Friday night."

"I don't want to go inside. I have to work up my nerve. Why don't I show you the place? We could walk around outside. It's really beautiful," he said. He reached out impulsively and touched my bare arm. "Please?"

His fingers were cold and his apprehension was contagious. I didn't have the heart to leave him. "All right," I said reluctantly, "but I can't stay long."

"Great. That's great. I really appreciate this."

I turned off the engine. Guy left his backpack on the front seat and the two of us got out. We slammed the car doors in two quick, overlapping reports, like guns going off. At the last moment, I opened my door again and tossed my handbag in the back before I locked the car. As we crossed the courtyard, Myrna opened the front door and came out on the porch. She was wearing a semblance of uniform; a shapeless white polyester skirt with a matching overblouse, some vague cross between nursiness and household help.

I said, "Hi, Myrna. How are you? I didn't think anyone was here. This is Guy. I'm sorry. I don't remember anyone ever mentioning your last name."

"Sweetzer," she said.

Guy extended his hand, which flustered her to some extent. She allowed him one of those handshakes without cartilage or bone. His good looks probably had the same effect on her that they had on me. "Nice to meet you," he said.

"Nice to meet you, too," she replied by rote. "The family's back around five. You're to have the run of the house. I imagine you remember where your room is if you want to take your things on up."

"Thanks. I'll do that in a bit. I thought I'd show her the grounds first if that's okay with you."

"Suit yourself," she said. "The front door will be

open if you want to come in that way. Dinner's at seven." She turned to me. "Will you be staying on as well?"

"I appreciate the invitation, but I don't think I should. The family needs time to get reacquainted. Maybe another time," I said. "I do have a question. Guy was asking about his father and it just occurred to me that you might know as much as anyone else. Weren't you his nurse?"

"One of them," she said. "I was his primary caregiver the last eight months. I stayed on as housekeeper at your brothers' request," she said, looking at Guy. Her delivery was staunch, as if we'd challenged her right to remain on the premises. From what I'd seen of her, she tended to be humorless, but with Guy she'd now added a grace note of resentment, reflecting the family's general attitude.

Guy's smile was sweet. "I'd like to talk to you about my dad sometime."

"Yes sir. He was a good man and I was fond of him."

There was an awkward moment, none of us knowing how to terminate the conversation. Myrna was the one who finally managed, saying, "Well, now. I'll let you go on about your business. I'll be in the kitchen if you should need anything. The cook's name is Enid, if you can't find me."

"I remember Enid," he said. "Thanks."

As soon as the door closed behind her, Guy touched my elbow and steered me off to the right. We crossed the courtyard together, heat drifting up from the sunbaked cobblestones. "Thanks for staying," he said.

"You're full of thanks," I remarked.

"I am. I feel blessed. I never expected to see the house again. Come on. We'll go this way."

We cut around the south side of the house, moving from hot, patchy sunlight into shade. To me, it felt like another sudden shift in seasons. In the space of fifty feet, we'd left summer behind. In the gloom of heavy shadow, the drop in air temperature was distinct and unwelcome, as if the months were rolling backward into winter again. Vestiges of the hot dry winds blew down the mountainside behind us, tossing restlessly across the treetops above our heads. We rambled beneath a canopy of shaggy-smelling juniper and pine. A carpet of fallen needles dampened our footsteps to a silence.

Near the house, I could see evidence of the gardeners—raked paths, the trimmed shape of bushes, a profusion of ferns ringed with small perfect stones—but the larger portion of the property was close to wilderness. Many of the plants had been allowed to grow unchecked. A violet-colored lantana tumbled along the terrace wall. A salmon-pink bougainvillea climbed across a tangled stretch of brush. To our right, a solid wash of nasturtiums blanketed the banks of an empty creek bed. In the areas of bright sun, where the dry breezes riffled across the blossoms, several scents arose and mingled in an earthy cologne.

Guy seemed to scrutinize every square foot we traversed. "Everything looks so much bigger. I remember when some of these trees were just planted. Saplings were this tall and now look at them."

"Your memories sound happy. That surprises me somehow."

"This was a great spot to grow up. Mom and Dad bought the place when I was three years old. Donovan was five and the two of us thought we'd died and gone to heaven. It was like one great big playground. We could go anywhere we wanted and no one ever had to worry. We made forts and tree houses. We had sword fights with sticks. We played cowboys and Indians and went on jungle expeditions in the wilds of the sticker bushes. When Bennet was a little guy, we used to tie him to a stake and he'd wail like a banshee. We'd tell him we were going to burn him if he didn't shut up. He was younger than us and he was fair game."

"Nice."

"Boy-type fun," he said. "I guess girls don't do that."

"How could your parents afford a place like this? I thought your father made his money later, in the years since you left."

"Mom had some money from a trust fund. The down payment was hers. Actually, it wasn't that much money even for the time. The house was a white elephant. It was on the market for nearly ten years and it was empty all that time. The story we heard was that the previous owner had been murdered. It's not like the house was haunted, but it did seem tainted. Nobody could make a deal work. We were told it fell out of escrow five or six times before my parents came along and bought it. It was big and neglected. The wiring was bad and the plumbing was shot. Daylight was showing through big holes in the roof. Tree rats ran everywhere and there was a family of raccoons living in the attic. It took 'em years to pull it all together. In the meantime, Dad's plan was to buy adjacent properties if they came up for sale."

"What is it now, fifteen acres?"

"Is that right? The original parcel was six. There probably isn't a lot more land available in this area."

"Is this city land or county?"

"We're right at the upper edges of the city limits. Lot of what you're looking at up there is part of the Los Padres National Forest." The term *forest* was a misnomer. The arching mountain range above us was overgrown with nettle, ceanothus, pyracantha, and coastal sage scrub, the soil too poor to support many trees. In the higher elevations, a few pines might remain if the wildfires hadn't reached them.

We passed the tennis court, its surface cracked and weedy along the edges. A tennis racket had been tossed to one side, exposed to the elements long enough to warp, its nylon strings sprung. Beyond the tennis court, there was a glass-enclosed structure I hadn't seen from the drive. The lines of the building were low and straight, with a red-tile roof that had altered with time until its color was the burnt brown of old bricks.

"What's that?"

"The pool house. We have an indoor pool. Want to see it?"

"Might as well," I said. I trailed after him as he approached a covered flagstone patio. He crossed to the building's darkened windows and peered in. He moved to the door and tried the knob. The door was unlocked, but the frame was jammed and required a substantial push before it opened with the kind of scrape that set my teeth on edge.

"You really want to do this?" I asked.

"Hey, it's part of the tour."

To me, it felt like breaking and entering, a sport I prefer to get paid for. The sense of trespass was unmistakable, nearly sexual in tone, despite the fact that we'd been given permission to roam. We entered an anteroom that was used to store an assortment of play equipment: badminton rackets, golf clubs, baseball bats, a rack lined with a full set of croquet mallets and balls, Styrofoam kickboards for the pool, and a line of fiberglass surfboards that looked as if they'd been propped against the wall for years. The gardener was currently keeping his leaf blower and a riding mower in the space to one side. While I didn't see any spiders, the place had a spidery atmosphere. I wanted to brush my clothes hurriedly in case something had dropped down and landed on me unseen.

The pool was half-filled and something about the water looked really nasty. The decking around the pool was paved with a gritty-looking gray slate, not the sort of surface you'd want to feel under your bare feet. At one end of the room was an alcove furnished in rattan, though the cushions were missing from the sofa and matching chairs. The air was gloomy and I could hear the sound of dripping water. Any hint of chlorine had evaporated long ago and several unclassified life-forms had begun to ferment in the depths.

"Looks like it's time to fire the pool guy," I remarked.

"The gardener probably does the pool when he remembers," Guy said. "When we were kids this was great."

"What'd you and Donovan do to Bennet down here? Drown him? Hang him off the diving board? I can just imagine the fun you must have had."

Guy smiled, his thoughts somewhere else. "I broke up with a girl once down here. That's what sticks in my mind. Place was like a country club. Swimming, tennis, softball, croquet. We'd invite dates over for a swim and then we'd end up making out like crazy. Girl in a bathing suit isn't that hard to seduce. Jack was the all-time champ. He was randy as a rabbit and he'd go after anyone."

"Why'd you break up with her?"

"I don't remember exactly. Some rare moment of virtue and self-sacrifice. I liked her too much. I was a bad boy back then and she was too special to screw around with like the other ones. Or maybe odd's the better word. A little nutsy, too needy. I knew she was fragile and I didn't want to take the chance. I preferred the wild ones. No responsibility, no regrets, no holds barred."

"Were your parents aware of what was going on down here?"

"Who knows? I'm not sure. They were proponents of the 'boys will be boys' school of moral instruction. Any girl who gave in to us deserved what she got. They never said so explicitly, but that's the attitude. My mother was more interested in being everybody's pal. Set limits on a kid and you might have to take a stand at some point. She was into unconditional love, which to her meant the absence of prohibitions of any kind. It was easier to be permissive, you know what I mean? This was all part of the sixties' feel-good bullshit. Looking back, I can see how much she must have been affected by her illness. She didn't want to be the stern, disapproving parent. She must have known her days

167

were numbered, even though she survived a lot longer than most. In those days, they did chemo and radiation, but it was all so crudely calibrated they probably killed more people than they cured. They just didn't have the technology or the sophisticated choice of treatments. It's different today where you got a real shot at survival. For her, the last couple of years were pure hell."

"It must have been hard on you."

"Pure agony," he said. "I was the child most identified with her. Don't ask me why, but Donovan and Bennet and Jack were linked to Dad while I was my mother's favorite. It drove me wild to see her fail. She was faltering and in pain, going downhill on what I knew would be her final journey."

"Were you with her when she died?"

"Yes. I was. The rest of 'em were gone. I forget now where they were. I sat in her room with her for hours that day. Most of the time she slept. She was so doped up on morphine, she could hardly stay awake. I was exhausted myself and laid my head on the bed. At one point, she reached out and put her hand on my neck. I touched her fingers and she was gone, just like that. So quiet. I didn't move for an hour.

"I just sat by the bed, leaning forward, with my head turned away from her and my face buried in the sheets. I thought maybe if I didn't look, she might come back again, like she was hovering someplace close and might return to her body as long as no one noticed she'd left. I didn't want to break faith."

"What happened to the girl you broke up with?"

"Patty? I have no idea. I wrote to her once, but never heard back. I've thought of her often, but who knows where she is now or what's happened to her. It might be the best thing I ever did, especially back then. What a bastard I was. I have a hard time connecting. It's like somebody else was doing it."

"But you're a good person now."

He shook his head. "I don't think of myself as good, but sometimes I think I come close to being real."

We left the pool house behind, moving temporarily onto the sunny stretch of lawn where I'd watched Jack hit golf balls. We were on the terrace below the house, shadows slanting toward us as we crossed the grass.

"How do you feel? You seem relaxed," I said.

"I'll be fine once they get here. You know how it is. Your fantasies are always stranger than reality."

"What do you picture?"

He smiled briefly. "I have no idea."

"Well, whatever it is, I hope you get what you need."

"Me, too, but in the long run, what difference does it make? You can't hide from God and that's the point," he said. "For a long time, I was walkin' down the wrong road, but now I've turned myself around and I'm goin' back the other way. At some point, I'll meet up with my past and make peace."

We had, by then, reached the front of the house again. "I better scoot," I said. "Let me know how it goes."

"I'll be fine."

"No doubt, but I'll be curious."

As I got into my car and turned the key in the ignition, I watched him head toward the front door with his backpack. I waved as I passed and then watched him in my rearview mirror as I eased down the drive. I rounded the curve and he was gone from view. It's painful to think of this in retrospect. Guy Malek was doomed and I delivered him into the hands of the enemy. As I pulled through the gates, I could see a car approach. Bennet was driving. My smile was polite and I waved at him. He stared at me briefly and then glanced away.

ELEVEN

At ten o'clock Monday morning I received a call that should have served as a warning. Looking back, I can see that from that moment on, troubles began to accumulate at an unsettling rate. I'd gotten a late start and I was just closing the front gate behind me when I heard the muffled tone of the telephone ringing in my apartment. I did a quick reverse, trotting down the walkway and around the corner. I unlocked the front door and flung it open in haste, tossing my jacket and bag aside. I snatched up the receiver on the fourth ring, half expecting a wrong number or a market survey now that I'd made the effort. "Hello?"

"Kinsey. This is Donovan."

"Well, hi. How are you? Whew! Excuse the heavy breathing. I was already out the door and had to run for the phone."

Apparently, he wasn't in the mood for cheery chit-chat. He got straight to the point. "Did you contact the press?"

It was not a subject I expected the man to broach at this hour or any other. I could feel a fuzzy question mark forming over my head while I pondered what he could possibly be talking about. "Of course not. About what?"

"We got a call from the *Dispatch* about an hour ago. Somebody tipped off a reporter about Guy's return."

"Really? That's odd. What's the point?" I knew the *Santa Teresa Dispatch* occasionally struggled to find noteworthy items for the Local section, but Guy's homecoming hardly seemed like a big-time news event. Aside from the family, who'd give a shit?

"They're playing it for human interest. Rags to riches. You know the tack, I'm sure. A lowly maintenance worker in Marcella, California, suddenly finds out he's a millionaire and comes home to collect. It's better than the lottery given Guy's personal history, as you well know."

"What do you mean, as *I* well know? I never said a word to the press. I wouldn't do that."

"Who else knew about it? No one in the family would leak a story like that. This is a sensitive issue. The last thing we need is *publicity*. Here we are trying to hammer out some kind of understanding between us and the phone hasn't stopped ringing since the first call came through."

"I don't follow. Who's been calling?"

"Who hasn't?" he said, exasperated. "The local paper for starters and then the L.A. *Times*. I guess one of the radio stations got wind of it. It'll go out on the wire services next thing you know and we'll have six friggin' camera crews camped in the driveway."

"Donovan, I swear. If there was a leak, it didn't come from me."

"Well, someone spilled the beans and you're the only one who stands to benefit."

"Me? That makes no sense. How would I benefit from a story about Guy?"

"The reporter who called mentioned you by name. He knew you'd been hired and he was interested in how you'd gone about finding Guy after all these years. He as good as told me he intended to play that angle: 'Local PI locates heir missing eighteen years.' It's better than an advertisement for all the work you'll get."

"Donovan, stop it. That's ridiculous. I'd never blab client business under any circumstance. I don't need more work. I have plenty." This was not entirely true, but he didn't need to know that. The bottom line was, I'd never give client information to the media. I had a reputation to protect. Aside from ethical considerations, this was not a profession where you wanted to be recognized. Most working investigators keep a very low profile. Anonymity is always preferable, especially when you're inclined, as I am, to use the occasional ruse. If you're posing as a meter reader or a florist delivery person, you don't want the public to be aware of your true identity. "I mean, think about it, Donovan. If I'd actually given him the story, why would he be quizzing you about my methods? He'd know that already so why would he ask you?"

"Well, you might have a point there, unless he was looking for confirmation."

"Oh, knock it off. You're really stretching for that one."

"I just think it's damn suspicious that you got a plug."

"Who's the reporter? Did you ask where he got his information?"

"He never gave me the chance."

"Well, let me put in a call to him. Why don't we just ask him? It might be something simple or obvious once you hear. You remember his name?"

"Katzensomething, but I don't think it's smart for you to talk to him."

"Katzenbach. I know Jeffrey. He's a nice man."

Donovan plowed on, not wanting to yield his ground. "I'm telling you, lay off. I don't want you talking to him about anything. Enough is enough. If I find out you're behind this, I'll sue your ass from here to next Tuesday," he said and banged down the receiver on his end.

The "screw *you*" I offered snappishly came half a second too late, which was just as well.

The minute he'd broken the connection my adrenaline shot up. My mouth was dry and I could feel my heart begin to pound in my ears. I wanted to protest, but I could see how it looked from his perspective. He was right about the fact that I was the only one outside the family who knew what was going on. More or less, I thought, pausing to correct myself. Myrna could have tipped the paper, but it was hard to see why she'd do such a thing. And of course, Peter and Winnie knew what was going on, but again why would either one of them want to make the matter known? I had a strong impulse to pick up the phone and call Katzenbach, but Donovan's admonition was still ringing in my ears. Once in touch, I was worried the reporter would start pumping me for information. Any comment I made might be quoted in a follow-up and then my credibility would be shot for sure.

Dimly, I wondered if Guy could have tipped off the paper himself. It seemed unlikely, but not impossible and I could see a certain canny logic if the move was his. If the issue of his inheritance became public knowledge, his brothers would have a hell of a time trying to screw him out of it. The problem with that notion was that Guy had never demonstrated much interest in the money and he certainly hadn't seemed concerned about protecting his share. Could he be as devious and manipulative as his family claimed?

I snagged my jacket and my handbag and headed out again. I tried to shake off my anxiety as I walked the short distance to my car, which was parked half a block down. There was no way to convince the Maleks of my innocence. Accused of the breach, I found myself feeling apologetic, as if I'd actually been guilty of violating the family's trust. Poor Guy. In the wake of my denial, they'd probably turn on *him*.

By the time I reached the downtown area, I'd managed to distract myself, wondering if I'd find a parking space within a reasonable radius of Lonnie Kingman's building. I tried the spiral approach, like a crime scene investigation, starting at the inner point and working outward. If nothing opened up, I could always use the public parking lot, which was three blocks away.

The second time I circled, I saw a van pull into the stretch of red-painted curb in front of the building. The door on the passenger side slid back and a fellow with a camcorder swung himself out on the walk. The slim blond who anchored the six o'clock news hopped down from the front seat and scanned the numbers on the building, verifying the address from a note on her pad. Coming up from behind, I couldn't see the logo on the side of the van, but it had an aerial on top that looked fierce enough to receive messages from outer space. Oh, shit. As I passed the van, I could see KEST-TV painted on the side. I resisted the urge to speed away as the woman threw a glance in my direction. I peered to my left, turning toward the building across the street. I waved merrily at someone emerging from the Dean Witter office. Maybe the press would mistake me for a cruising mogul with some money to invest. I kept driving, eyes pinned on my rearview mirror as the cameraman and his companion went into the entranceway.

Now what? I didn't like the idea of skulking in the bushes like a renegade. Maybe I was being paranoid and the crew was on its way to cover something else. I drove several blocks before I spotted a pay phone on the corner. I left my car at the curb, dropped a quarter in the slot, and dialed Lonnie's private line. He must have been in court because Ida Ruth picked up, thinking it was him. "Yessir?"

"Ida Ruth, this is Kinsey. Did a TV crew show up looking for me?"

"I don't think so, but I'm back here at my desk. Let me check with Alison up front." She put me on hold for a moment and then clicked back in. "I stand corrected. They're waiting for you in reception. What's going on?"

"It's too complicated to explain. Can you get rid of them?"

"Well, we can get 'em out of here, but there's no way

we can keep them from hanging around on the street outside. What did you do, if I may be so bold?"

"Nothing, I swear. I'm completely innocent."

"Right, dear. Good for you. Stick to that," she said.

"Ida Ruth, I'm serious. Here's the deal," I said. I filled her in briefly and heard her cluck in response. "My, oh my. If I were you, I'd lay low. They can't stay long. If you tell me how to reach you, I'll call you when they're gone."

"I'm not sure where I'll be. I'll check back in a bit." I put the receiver down and scanned the street corner opposite. There was a bar on the corner that appeared to be opening. I could see a neon light in the window blink on. As I watched, a fellow in an apron opened the front door and kicked the doorstop into place. I could always hang out in there, drinking beer and sniffing secondhand smoke while I figured out what to do next. On the other hand, come to think of it, I hadn't *done* anything so why was I behaving like a fugitive? I fished around in the bottom of my bag and came up with a second coin. I put a call through to the *Dispatch* and asked for Jeffrey Katzenbach. I didn't know him well, but I'd dealt with him on a couple of occasions in the past. He was a man in his fifties, whose career had been stalled by his appetite for cocaine and Percocet. He'd always been sharp if you caught him early in the day, but as the afternoon progressed, he became harder to deal with. By nightfall, he could still function, but his judgment was sometimes faulty and he didn't always remember the promises he'd made. Two years ago, his wife had left him and the last I'd heard, he'd finally straightened up his act with the help of Narcotics

Anonymous. Guy Malek wasn't the only one who'd undergone personal transformation.

When I got through to Katzenbach, I identified myself and we exchanged the usual pleasantries before getting down to business. "Jeffrey, this is strictly off the record. The Maleks are my clients and I can't afford to be quoted."

"Why? What's the problem?"

"There isn't any problem. Donovan's pissed off because he thinks I called you and spoiled the family reunion."

"Sorry to hear that."

"How'd you get wind of it? Or is this a 'confidential source'?"

"Nothing confidential about it. There was a letter on my desk when I got in last night. We've always encouraged our subscribers to get in touch if they think there's a story we might not've heard about. Sometimes it's just trivia or crank stuff, but this one grabbed my attention."

"Who sent the letter?"

"Some fellow named Max Outhwaite with an address on Connecticut out in Colgate. He thought it was an item worth bringing to our attention."

"How'd he hear about it?"

"Beats me. He talked like he'd known 'em all for years. Basically, the letter says a search was conducted and Bader Malek's son Guy was located after an absence of eighteen years. That's correct, isn't it? I mean, tell me I'm wrong and I'll eat my jockey shorts."

"You're correct, but so what?"

"So nothing. Like he says, here's this fellow working as a janitor in some backwater town, finds out he's inheriting five million bucks. How often does that happen? He thought the community would be interested. I thought it sounded like a winner so I put a call in to the Maleks. The number's in the book, it didn't require any red-hot detective work. I talked to Mrs. Malek—what's her name, Christie—who confirmed the story before I even got to Donovan. Sure enough, that's the deal unless there's something I missed."

"And I was mentioned by name?"

"You bet. It's one of the reasons I figured it was on the up-and-up. I tried to reach you last night, but all I got was your answering machine. I didn't bother to leave a message. I figured you were on your way over there to help 'em celebrate. How'd you find the guy? Outhwaite's letter says you got a lead on him through the DMV."

"I don't believe this. Who is this man and where's he getting his information?"

"How do I know? He acted like he was maybe a friend of the family. You never talked to him yourself?"

"Jeffrey, knock it off. I didn't call so you could pump me. I'm trying to persuade the Maleks I didn't leak this thing."

"Too bad you didn't. You could have filled in the details. I went back to check with Outhwaite and the guy doesn't exist. There's no Outhwaite in the phone book and no such house number anywhere on Connecticut Avenue. I tried a couple of other possibilities and I came up with blanks. Not that it matters as long as the story's legitimate. I got confirmation from the family."

"What about the L.A. *Times*? How did they get wind of it?"

"Same way we did. Outhwaite dropped 'em a note—almost like a press release. It's been a slow week for news and we're always on the lookout for human-interest stuff. This was better than a little lost kitty-cat trapped in a well. I thought it was worth pursuing, especially when I saw you were involved."

"I wish you'd done some fact checking with me along the way."

"Why? What's the problem?"

"There isn't any *problem*," I said, irritably. "I just think the family might appreciate a little privacy before the whole world rushes in. By the way, Jeffrey, I've heard you tippy-tapping on your keyboard ever since we started this conversation. I told you this is off the record."

"What for? It's a nice story. It's a great fantasy. What's the deal with the Maleks? Why're they so pissed with the coverage? We did front page, second section when Bader Malek died. He was an important figure in the community and they were happy to have the tribute. What's so hush-hush about Guy? Are they trying to cut him out of his inheritance or something?"

I rolled my eyes skyward. The man couldn't help but press for information. "Listen, buddy, I'm as clueless as you. What about the letter? What happened to it?"

"It's sitting right here."

"You mind if I have a copy? It would go a long way toward restoring my credibility. I feel like a fool having to defend myself, but I have a reputation to maintain."

"Sure. I can do that. I don't see why not. We're interested in Guy's perspective if you can talk him into it."

"I'm not trading—but I'll do what I can."

"Terrific. What's your fax number?"

I gave him the number of Lonnie Kingman's machine and he said he'd fax the letter over. If I located Max Outhwaite, Jeffrey wanted to talk to him. Fair enough. I said I'd do what I could. It didn't cost me anything to profess my conditional cooperation. I tried not to be too profuse in my thanks. It's not like I planned to take the letter straight to Donovan, but I was curious about the contents and thought it made sense to have a copy for my files. At some point, Katzenbach would extract something from me in return, but for now, I was fine. I didn't believe Guy would agree to an interview, but maybe he'd surprise me.

I got back in my car and drove over to the public parking lot. From there, I hoofed it to the office on foot. There was no sign of the KEST-TV van out front. I took the stairs two at a time and entered Kingman and Ives through an unmarked door around the corner from the main entrance. In the back of my mind, I was mulling over the possibility that maybe Bennet or Jack had taken the letter to the *Dispatch*. I couldn't see what it would net either of them, but *someone* had an interest in seeing Guy's homecoming splashed across the news and it was someone who knew more than I was comfortable with. Again, I could feel the faint nudge of uneasiness. Darcy Pascoe's computer search had been a bit of a fudge. I hoped she wasn't going to find herself in trouble as a result of my request. I checked the fax machine in Lonnie's office and found the copy of Max Outhwaite's letter sitting in the slot as promised. I went to my office, reading as I went.

Dear Mr. Katzenbach,

Thought you'd be interested in a Modern-Day "Cinderfella" story taking place right here in Santa Teresa! As I recall, your the reporter, who wrote about Bader Malek's death last month. Now, word around town has it that his Probate Attorney hired a Private Investigater (a "Female" no less) to locate his missing son, Guy. If you've been around town as long as me, you'll remember that as a youngster, Guy Malek was caught in a number of scrapes, and finally disappeared from the local scene, nearly twenty years ago. You'd think finding someone like that after all this time would prove daunting, but Milhone (the aforementioned "Female" Detective) ran a DMV check, and turned him up in less than two days!! Seems he's been up in Marcella ever since he left, and he's working as a <u>janiter</u> in a church up there! He's one of those "Born-Agains," who probably didn't have two nickles to rub together, but his father's death has turned him into an instant millionnaire!! I think people would be heartened to hear how he's managed to turn his life around, threw his Christian Faith. Folks might also enjoy hearing what he's planning to do with his new-found riches. With all the bad news that besieges us from day to day, wouldn't this story give everyone a nice lift? I think it would be a

wonderfull inspiration to the Community! Let's
hope Guy Malek is willing to share the story of
his "good fortune" with us. I look forward to
reading such an article and know you'd do a fine
job of writing it! Best of luck and God Bless!

> Sincerely yours,
> Max Outhwaite
> 2905 Connecticut Ave.
> Colgate, CA

I noticed I held the letter by the corners, as if to avoid
smudging prints, a ridiculous precaution given the fact
that it wasn't even the original. The note was neatly
typed, with no visible corrections and no words XXX'd
out. Granted, there were spelling errors (including my
name), an excessive use of commas, a tendency toward
the emphatic, and a bit of Unnecessary Capitalization!
but otherwise the intentions of the sender seemed
benign. Aside from alerting the press to something that
was nobody else's business, I couldn't see any particular
attempt to meddle in Guy Malek's life. Maximilian (or
perhaps Maxine) Outhwaite apparently thought subscribers to the *Santa Teresa Dispatch* would be warmed
by this story of a Bad Boy Turned Good and the
Resultant Rewards! Outhwaite didn't seem to have an
ax to grind and there was no hint of malice to undercut
his (or her) enthusiasm for the tale. So what was going
on?

I set the letter aside, swiveling in my swivel chair
while I studied it covertly out of the corner of my eye.
As a "Female" Detective, I found myself vaguely

bothered by the damn thing. I didn't like the intimate acquaintance with the details and I couldn't help but wonder at the motivation. The tone was ingenuous, but the maneuver had been effective. Suddenly, Guy Malek's private business had been given a public audience.

I placed the letter in the Malek file, turning it over to my psyche for further consideration.

I spent the rest of the morning at the courthouse, taking care of other business. As a rule, I'm working fifteen to twenty cases concurrently. Not all of them are pressing and not all demand my attention at the same time. I do a number of background checks for a research and development firm out in Colgate. I also do pre-employment investigations, as well as skip traces for a couple of small businesses in the area. Periodically, I'm involved in some fairly routine snooping for a divorce attorney down the street. Even in a no-fault state, a spouse might hide assets or conceal the whereabouts of communal items, like cars, boats, planes, and minor children. There's something restful about a morning spent cruising through the marriage licenses and death records in pursuit of genealogical connections, or an afternoon picking through probated wills, property transfers, and tax and mechanics' liens at the county offices. Sometimes I can't believe my good fortune, working in a business where I'm paid to uncover matters people would prefer to keep under wraps. Paper stalking doesn't require a PI to slip into a Kevlar vest, but the results can be just as dangerous as a gun battle or a high-speed chase.

My assignment that Monday morning was to probe

the financial claims detailed in a company prospectus. A local businessman had been approached to invest fifty thousand dollars in what looked like a promising merchandising plan. Within an hour, I'd found out that one of the two partners had filed for personal bankruptcy and the other had a total of six lawsuits pending against him. While I was about it, I did a preliminary search for Max Outhwaite, starting with voter registration and working my way through local tax rolls. I crossed the street to the public library and tried the reference department. Under that spelling, there were no Outhwaites listed in the local phone books and none in the city directories going back six years. This meant nothing in particular as far as I could see. It did suggest that "Max Outhwaite" was a nom de plume, but under certain circumstances, I could relate to the maneuver. If I wanted to call an issue to the attention of the local paper, I might conceivably use a fake name and a phony address. I might be a prominent person, reluctant to have myself associated with the subject in question. I might be a family member, eager to get Guy in trouble, but unwilling to take responsibility. Writing such a letter was hardly a crime, but I might feel guilty nonetheless and not want the consequences blowing back on me.

For lunch I bought a sandwich and a soft drink from a vending machine and sat on a stretch of lawn out behind the courthouse. The day was hot, the treetops buffeted by dry winds coming off the desert. The branches of the big evergreens planted close to the street seemed to shimmer in the breeze, giving off the scent of pitch. I leaned back on my elbows and turned my face up to the sun. I can't say I slept, but I gave a good impression of it. At one o'clock, I roused myself and went back to the office where I began to type up my findings for the cases I'd worked. Such is the life of a PI these days. I spend more time practicing my skills with a Smith-Corona than a Smith & Wesson.

TWELVE

My run that morning had been unsatisfactory. I'd done what needed doing, dutifully jogging a mile and a half down the bike path and a mile and a half back, but I'd never developed any rhythm and the much-sought-after endorphin rush had failed to materialize. I've noticed on days when the run isn't good, I'm left with an emotional itch that feels like anxiety, in this case compounded by mild depression. Short of drink and drugs, sometimes the only remedy is to exercise again. I swear this is not a compulsion on my part so much as a craving for relief. I drove over to Harley's Beach and found a parking spot in the shelter of the hill. The lot was nearly empty, which surprised me somehow. Usually, there's an assortment of tourists and beach-combers, joggers, lovers, barking dogs, and parents with small children. Today, all I spotted was a family of feral cats sunning themselves on the hillside above the beach.

I staggered across an expanse of loose, dry sand until I reached the hard pack at the water's edge. I would have pulled off my shoes and socks, rolling up my pant legs so I could jog in the surf; however someone had recently given me a small book about tide pools.

I'd leafed through with interest, imagining myself in the role of inquisitive naturalist, poking among the rocks for tiny crabs and starfish (though their undersides are completely disgusting and gross). Until I read this colorful, informative pamphlet, I'd had no idea what strange, ugly beasties existed close to shore. I'm not the kind of person who sentimentalizes nature. The outdoors, as far as I can see, is made up almost entirely of copulating creatures who eat one another afterward. To this end, almost every known animal has developed a strategy for luring others within range. Among life-forms in the sea—some quite minuscule—the tactic involves thorny parts or pincers or tiny three-jawed mouths or trailing stingers or vicious suckers with which they latch on to one another, causing painful death and dismemberment, all in the name of nourishment. Sometimes the juice is slurped out of the victim long before death occurs. The starfish actually takes out its own stomach, enfolds its live prey, and digests it outside its body. How would you like to put your bare foot down on that?

I ran in my shoes, splashing through the surf when the waves came close. Soon my wet jeans clung to my legs, the heavy fabric cold against my shins. My feet were weighted as though with stones and I could feel the sweat begin to soak through my shirt from the labor of the run. Despite the damp breeze coming off the ocean, the air felt oppressive. For the third day in a row, Santa Ana winds were blasting in from the desert, blowing down the local canyons, pulling moisture from the atmosphere. The mounting heat collected, degree by degree, like a wall of bricks going up. My progress felt slow and I forced myself to focus on the sand shimmering ahead of me. Since I had no way to measure distance, I ran for time, jogging thirty minutes north before I turned and jogged back. By the time I reached Harley's Beach again, my breathing was ragged and the muscles in my thighs were on fire. I slowed to a trot and then geared down to a walk as I returned to my car. For a moment, I leaned panting against the hood. Better. That was better. Pain was better than anxiety any day of the week and sweat was better than depression.

Home again, I left my soggy running shoes on the front steps. I padded upstairs, peeling out of my damp clothes as I ascended. I took a hot shower and then slipped into a pair of sandals, a T-shirt, and a short cotton skirt. It was now close to four and there was no point returning to the office. I brought in the mail and checked for phone messages. There were five: two hang-ups; two reporters who left numbers, asking me to get back to them; and a call from Peter Antle, the pastor of Guy's church. I dialed the number he'd left and he picked up so fast I had to guess he'd been waiting by the phone.

"Peter. I got your message. This is Kinsey in Santa Teresa."

"Kinsey. Thanks for being so prompt. Winnie's been trying to call Guy, but she can't seem to get through. The Maleks have the answering machine on and nobody's picking up. I don't know what Guy's plans are, but we thought we'd better warn him. There are reporters camped out at the gas station across from his place. We have people knocking on the church door and a pile of messages for him."

"Already?"

"That was my reaction. Frankly, I don't understand how this got out in the first place."

"Long story. I'm still in the process of looking into it. I know the family was contacted by the local newspaper first thing this morning. The reporter here had had a letter delivered to him at the paper. I guess something similar was sent to the L.A. *Times*. I haven't seen the news yet, but I have a feeling it's going to get bigger before it goes away."

"It's even worse up here. The town's so small, none of us can manage to avoid the press. Do you have a way to get in touch with Guy? We're here for him if he needs us. We don't want him to lose his footing in the stress of the situation."

"Let me see if I can find a way to get through. I guess this is his fifteen minutes of fame, though frankly, I can't understand why the story's generating so much attention. Why should anyone give a fat rat's . . . aa . . . ah . . . ear? He doesn't even have the money yet and who knows if he'll ever see one red cent."

I could almost see Peter's grin. "Everyone wants to believe in something. For most people, a big windfall would literally be the answer to all their prayers."

"I suppose so," I said. "At any rate, if I reach him, I'll have him give you a call."

"I'd appreciate that."

After we hung up, I flipped on the TV set and tuned in to KEST. The evening news wouldn't air for an hour, but the station often ran quick promos for the show coming up. I suffered through six commercials and caught the clip I'd suspected would be there. The blond anchorwoman smiled at the camera, saying, "Not all news is bad news. Sometimes even the darkest cloud has a silver lining. After nearly twenty years of poverty, a Marcella maintenance man has just learned he'll be inheriting five million dollars. We'll have that story for you at five." Behind her, the camera showed a glimpse of a haggard-looking Guy Malek, staring impassively from the car window as Donovan's BMW swung through the gates of the Malek estate. I felt a pang of guilt, wishing I'd talked him out of coming down. Given his bleak expression, the homecoming wasn't a success. I picked up the phone again and tried the Maleks' number. The line was busy.

I called the number every ten minutes for an hour. The Maleks had probably taken the phone off the hook, or maybe their message tape was full. In either event, who knew when I'd get through to him.

I debated with myself briefly and then drove over to the house. The gate was now closed and there were six vehicles parked along the berm. Reporters loitered, some leaning against their car fenders, two chatting together in the middle of the road. Both men were smoking and held big Styrofoam coffee cups. Three camera units had been set up on tripods and it looked as if the troops were prepared to stay. The late-afternoon sun slanted between the eucalyptus trees across from the Malek property, dividing the pavement into alternating sections of light and shadow.

I parked behind the last car and went on foot as far as the call box near the front gate. All activity behind me ceased and I could feel the attention focus on my back. No one answered my ring. Like the others, I was going to have to hang around out here, hoping to catch sight of one of the Maleks exiting or entering the grounds. I tried one more time, but my ringing was greeted with dead silence from inside the house.

I returned to my car and turned the key in the ignition. Already, a dark-haired woman reporter was ambling in my direction. She was probably in her forties, with oversized sunglasses and bright red lips. As I watched, she fumbled in her shoulder bag and pulled out a cigarette. She was tall and slender, decked out in slacks and a shortcropped cotton sweater. I marveled she could bear it with the heat sitting where it was. Gold earrings. Gold bracelets. A daunting pair of four-inch heels. For my taste, walking in high heels is like trying to learn to ice-skate. The human ankle does not take readily to such requirements. I admired her balance, though I realized when she reached me that in bare feet she'd probably be shorter than I. She made a circling motion, asking me to roll down my car window.

"Hi. How are you?" she said. She held up the cigarette. "You have a light for this?"

"Sorry. I don't smoke. Why don't you ask one of them?"

She turned, her gaze sliding back to the two men standing in the road. Her voice was husky and her tone was dismissive. "Oh, them. That's the boys' club," she remarked. "Those two won't even give you the time of day unless you have something to trade." Her eyes flicked back to me. "What about you? You don't look like a reporter. What are you, family friend? An old sweetheart?"

I had to admire the placid way she eased right into

it, casual, unconcerned. She was probably wetting her pants, hoping I'd provide a little tidbit so she could scoop her competition. I started rolling up my window. Quickly, she raised her handbag and turned it sideways, inserting it into the space so the window wouldn't close all the way. There was now a seven-inch gap where her leather bag was wedged.

"No offense," she said, "but I'm curious. Aren't you that private investigator we've heard so much about?"

I turned the key in the ignition. "Please remove your bag." I cranked the window down about an inch, hoping she'd pull the bag free so I could be on my way.

"Don't be in such a hurry. What's the rush? The public has a right to know these things. I'm going to get the information anyway so why not make sure it's accurate? I heard the kid spent a lot of time in jail. Was that here or up north?"

I cranked the window up a notch and put the car in gear. I pushed my foot down lightly on the gas pedal and eased away from the berm. She held on to the bag by its strap, walking beside the car, continuing the conversation. I guess she was accustomed to having the driver at her mercy once she used the old handbag trick. I increased my speed sufficiently to force her into a trot. She yanked the strap, yelling "Hey!" as I began to accelerate. I couldn't have been driving more than two miles an hour, but that's a tough pace to maintain when you're wearing heels that high. I inched my foot down on the gas. She released the bag and stopped where she was, watching with consternation as I pulled away. I passed the two guys in the road who seemed to enjoy the rude comment she was yelling after me. I couldn't hear the words, but I got the drift. In the rearview mirror, I saw her flip me the bird.

She removed a high heel and flung it at my rear window. I heard a mild thump on impact and saw the shoe bounce off behind me as I picked up speed. The long strap of the handbag dangled and flapped against the car door. About a hundred yards down the road, I paused long enough to roll down my window and give the bag a shove. I left it there in the road, curled like a possum, and drove to my apartment.

There were two newspapers on the sidewalk when I got home. I picked up both and left one on Henry's back doorstep before I let myself in. I turned on some lights and poured myself a glass of wine, then sat at the kitchen counter and spread the paper out in front of me. The story was in the second section and the tone was odd. I'd expected a fairy-tale version of Guy's life to date, his estrangement from the family and his subsequent spiritual transformation. Instead, Jeff Katzenbach had patched together, in excruciating detail, an inventory of all the sins from Guy's youth: countless episodes of reckless driving, vandalism, drunk and disorderly conduct, assault and battery. Some charges dated back to his juvenile record and should have been purged or remained sealed by the courts. Where had Katzenbach gotten his information? Some of it, of course, was a matter of public record, but I wondered how he'd known to look. He'd obviously been tipped off by Max Outhwaite's reference to Guy's earlier scrapes. I thought back uneasily to the file of news clippings Bader Malek had kept. Was there any way he could have seen that? This would have been a second leak of sorts. The first was the fact of Guy's return; the second, this detailed criminal history. I noticed Katzenbach had couched his revelations in typical journalistic fudgings. The word *alleged* appeared about six times, along with *confidential sources, informants close to the family, former associates,* and *friends of the Maleks who asked to remain anonymous.* Far from celebrating Guy's good fortune, the public was going to end up resenting his sudden wealth. Reading between the lines, you could tell Katzenbach considered Guy Malek an undeserving scoundrel. Somehow his current church affiliation looked self-serving and insincere, the convenient refuge of a culprit hoping to make himself look good in the eyes of the parole board.

For supper, I made myself a hot hard-boiled egg sandwich with lots of mayonnaise and salt and perched at the counter eating while I scanned the rest of the paper. I must have been more absorbed than I thought because when the telephone shrilled, I flung my sandwich sideways in response. I snatched up the receiver, heart thumping as though a gun had just been fired in my ear. If this turned out to be a reporter, I was going to hang up. "Yes."

"Hey."

"Oh shit. Guy, is that you? You scared the hell out of me." I leaned down and gathered up the remains of my sandwich, popping the crust in my mouth while I licked at my fingers. There was mayonnaise on the floor, but I could tend to that later.

"Yeah, it's me. How are you?" he said. "I tried calling a while ago, but you were out, I guess."

"Thank God you called. I was just over at the house,

but I couldn't get anyone to answer my ring. What's happening?"

"We just finished dinner. Have you seen the news?"

"I have the paper in front of me."

"Not so good, huh."

"It's not that bad," I said, hoping to cheer him up. "It does look like somebody's really got it in for you."

"That's my assumption," he said lightly.

"Are you all right? Peter called earlier. He's been trying to get in touch, but all he's managed so far is the answering machine. Did you get his message?"

"No, but why would I? Everybody here is pissed at me. They think I notified the paper, trying to get attention. There's a powwow on for later, after Donovan gets home. He's got a meeting until nine. The delay's making me sick. Reminds me of that old business, 'You wait until your father gets home and he'll give you the what for.' "

I found myself smiling. "You want me to come get you? I can be there in fifteen minutes."

"Yes—no—I don't know what I want. I'd like to get out of here, but I don't dare take off with things as they are."

"Why not? The damage is done. Whoever spilled the beans, made it look as bad as they could. If *you'd* leaked the news, you'd have put a different spin on it."

"How would I manage that? You can't put a different spin on the truth."

"Of course you can. It's called politics."

"Yeah, but I did all those things. This is just payback time. I told you I was bad. At least, now you know the worst."

"Oh stop that. I don't care about that stuff. All I care about is getting you out of there."

"You want to come for a visit? I could sneak out for a few minutes. Jack and Bennet are downstairs and Christie's in the office, going through some of Dad's old papers."

"Sure. I can pop back over there. What do you want me to do? Shall I ring from the gate?"

"No, don't do that. I'll meet you out on Wolf Run Road," he said. "If the side gate's locked, I can scale the wall. I'm an expert at getting out. When I was a kid I used to do it all the time. That's how I managed to get in so much trouble back then."

"Why don't you bring your backpack and let me spirit you away," I said. "I'll drive you to Marcella and you can hire an attorney to handle your interests from here on."

"Don't tempt me. Right now, all I need is civilized conversation. Park in that little grove of trees just across from the gate. I'll be out there in fifteen minutes."

I took a few minutes to tidy up the kitchen and then I changed into jeans, a dark shirt, and my Reeboks. The evening air felt uncharacteristically warm, but I wanted to be prepared for night maneuvers if need be. Once at the Maleks', I took a quick swing by the front gate. There were now two more news crews and the gathering had taken on the feel of a vigil outside a prison. Portable lights had been turned on and a man with a microphone spoke directly to a camera, making gestures toward the house. I saw the dark-haired reporter, but she didn't see me. She seemed to be bumming a light for her cigarette from a poor un-suspecting "source."

I followed the wall, circling the property as I turned left on Wolf Run. I spotted the gate, a dark blot in an otherwise unbroken expanse of wall. I pulled off onto the berm across the road, gravel crackling under my wheels. I shut down the engine and sat there, listening to the tick of hot metal and the murmur of the wind. There weren't any street lamps along this section of the road. The high night sky was clear, but the moon had been reduced to the merest sliver, a frail curve of silver in a sky pale with stars. The dust in the air was as fine as mist. In the ambient light, the pavement was a dull, luminous gray. The stucco wall enclosing the Malek property had been robbed of its pink luster and stretched now like a ghostly band of drab white. June and July were traditionally dry and I associated the Santa Ana winds with the end of summer—late August, early September, when the fire danger was extreme. For years, January had been the rainy season, two weeks of rain that we hoped would fill our annual quota. Yet here we were with the dry wind tossing in the treetops. The bend and sway of tree boughs set up a hushed night music, accompanied by the rustling percussion of dry palm fronds, the occasional snap of tree limbs. By morning, the streets would be littered with dead leaves and the small withered skeletons of broken branches.

The gate opened without a sound and Guy emerged, head down. He wore a dark-colored jacket, his fists shoved into his pockets as though he were cold. I leaned over and unlocked the door on the passenger side. He slid into the seat and then pulled the door shut without slamming it. He said, "Hey. Thanks for coming. I thought I'd go crazy without a friendly face. I'd have called you before, but they were watching me like a hawk."

"No problem. I don't know why you don't break and run while you can."

"I will. Tomorrow. Or maybe the day after that. I told you we're supposed to have another meeting tonight just to talk about some things."

"I thought you already talked."

"Well, we did. We do. Every time I turn around, we have another chat."

"That's because you haven't knuckled under yet," I interjected.

"I guess that's it." He smiled in spite of himself. His tension was contagious and I could have sworn I smelled alcohol on his breath. I found myself with my arms crossed, one leg wound around the other as if to protect myself.

"I feel like we're having an affair," I said.

"Me, too. I used to meet girls out here in the old days when I was grounded. I'd slip over the wall and we'd screw in the backseat of a car. There was something about the danger set me on fire, and them, too. Made most of 'em seem more interesting than they were."

"I know this is none of my business, but have you been drinking?" I asked.

He turned and looked out the passenger window, shrugging. "I had a couple of drinks last night before all this shit came down. I don't know what got into me. Don't get me wrong—they were being nice at that point, but you could tell they were nervous and so was I. I'm ashamed to say this, but the alcohol did help. It mellowed us out and smoothed the conversation. Tonight was pretty much the same except everybody's mood was different. Cocktail hour comes along and those guys really hit it."

"Bennet and his martinis."

"You bet. I figure that's the only way I'll get through. Peter wouldn't be too happy with me, but I can't help it. I can feel myself sliding back to my old ways."

"What'd you think of Christie?"

"She was nice. I liked her. I was surprised at Bennet—at the weight he'd put on, but Jack seemed the same, still nuts about golf. And Donovan hasn't changed."

"What've they said to you so far?"

"Well, we talked some about the money, what else? I mean, the subject does come up. It's like Donovan says, we can't just ignore the issue. It's like this big dark cloud hanging over us. I think we were all uncomfortable at first."

"Have you resolved anything?"

"Well, no. Nothing much. At first, I think they were wondering, you know, generally, about my attitude. Now, anything I say and everybody jumps right on in. Tell you the truth, I'd forgotten what they're like."

"How do they seem to you?"

"Angry. Underneath it all, they're pissed. I keep feeling the anger coming up inside me, too. It's all I can do to keep a lid on it."

"Why bother? Why not blow? The three of them certainly don't hesitate."

"I know, but if I flip my lid that's only going to make

matters worse. I'm trying to show 'em I've changed and then I find myself feeling like I always did. Like I want to smash lamps, throw a chair through a window, get stoned or drunk or something bad like that."

"That must be a trial."

"I'll say. I mean, literally. All I can think about is maybe this is some kind of test of my faith."

"Oh, it is *not*," I said. "It may be a test of your patience, but not your faith in God."

He shook his head, pressing his hands down between his knees. "Let's talk about something else. This is making me so tense I could fart."

I laughed and changed the subject. For a while we chatted about inconsequential matters. Hunched there in the front seat, I was reminded of the occasional dates I had in high school where the only hope of privacy was remaining closed away in some kid's car. On chilly evenings, the front windshield would fog up even if all we did was talk. On warm nights like this, we'd sit with the windows rolled down, radio tuned to some rock and roll station. It was Elvis or the Beatles, clumsy moves and sexual tension. I don't even remember now what we talked about, those lads and I. Probably nothing. Probably we drank purloined beer, smoked dope, and thought about the incredible majesty of life.

"So what else's going on? Aside from interminable meetings?" I asked. Like a rough place on a fingernail, I couldn't resist going back to it. Apparently, Guy couldn't resist it either because we fell right into the subject again.

This time he smiled and his tone seemed lighter. "It's nice to see the house. I found some letters of my mother's and I read those today. She's the only one I ever missed. The rest of 'em are a waste."

"I don't want to say I told you so, but I did predict this."

"I know, I know. I thought we could just sit down like grown-ups and clean up some old business, but it doesn't really happen like that. I mean, I keep wondering if there isn't some kind of defect in me because everything I do just seems to come out wrong. Whatever I say seems 'off,' you know? They look at me like I'm speaking in tongues and then I see them exchange these looks."

"Oh, I know that one. Jack and Bennet are big on flicking looks back and forth."

"That's the easy part, but there's worse."

"Like what?"

"I don't even know how to describe it. Something under the surface. Something slides right by and no one owns up to it, so then I start questioning my own thought process. Maybe I'm nuts and it's not them after all."

"Give me an example."

"Like when I told 'em I'd like to give something to the church? I honestly don't want the money for me. I mean that. But Jubilee Evangelical saved my life and I want to give something back. To me, that doesn't seem so wrong. Does it seem wrong to you?"

"No, not at all."

"So, I say that and all of a sudden we're in the middle of a power play. Bennet's saying how it really doesn't seem fair. You know how he talks with that slightly pompous air of his. 'Our family's never been religious.

Dad worked for the good of us all, not for the benefit of some church he never heard of.' He says it all in this completely rational tone and pretty soon I wonder if what I want to do is right after all. Maybe they have a point and *my* values are screwed up."

"Sure they have a point. They want you to relinquish all claim so they can divide up your portion among themselves. They know perfectly well you're entitled to a quarter of his estate. What you do with your share is none of their business."

"But how come I end up the magnet for all that rage?"

"Guy, stop. Don't do that. That's the third time you've said that. Don't get into self-blame. The games-manship has obviously been going on for years. That's got to be why you left in the first place, to get away from that stuff. I swear they were behaving the same way before you showed up."

"You think I should leave?"

"Well, of course I do! I've said it all along. You shouldn't take their abuse. I think you should get the hell out while you have the chance."

"I wouldn't call it 'abuse.' "

"Because you're used to it," I said. "And don't get sidetracked. Your brothers aren't going to change. If anybody goes down for the count, it's going to be you."

"Maybe so," he said. "I don't know. I just feel like I have to stay since I've come this far. If I cut and run, we're never going to find a way to work this through."

"I can tell you're not listening, but please, *please*, don't agree to anything without talking to an attorney first."

"Okay."

"Promise me."

"I will. I swear. Well, I gotta go before somebody figures out I've escaped."

"Guy, you're not sixteen. You're forty-three years old. Sit here if you want. You can stay out all night. Big whoop-dee-do. You're an adult."

He laughed. "I *feel* like I'm sixteen. And you're cute."

He leaned over quickly and brushed my cheek with his lips. I could feel the soft scratch of his whiskers against my face and I caught a whiff of his aftershave.

He said, "Bye-bye and thanks." Before I could respond, he was out of the car, shoulders hunched up against the wind as he moved to the gate. He turned and waved and then he was swallowed up by the dark.

I never saw him again.

THIRTEEN

Guy Malek was killed sometime Tuesday night, though I didn't actually hear about it until Wednesday afternoon. I'd spent most of the day over at the courthouse sitting in on the trial of a man accused of embezzlement. I hadn't been associated with the case—undercover cops had nailed him after seven months of hard work—but some years before, I'd done surveillance on him briefly at the request of his wife. She suspected he was cheating, but she wasn't sure with whom. Turned out he was having an affair with her sister and she broke off relations with both. The man was dishonest to the core and I confess I found it entertaining to watch the legal system grind away at him. As often as I complain about the shortage of justice in this world, I find it infinitely satisfying when the process finally works as it should.

When I got back to the office after court adjourned, there was a message from Tasha waiting on my machine. I noticed, in passing, it was the Maleks' number she'd left. I called, expecting to have Myrna pick up. Instead Tasha answered as if she'd been manning the phones. The minute I heard her, I realized how irritated I was that she'd gone out of town just as Guy arrived. If she'd been doing her job, she might have steered the family off their campaign of pressure and harassment.

Smart mouth that I am, I launched right in. "At long last," I said, "it's about time you got back. All hell's broken loose. Have you heard what's going on? Well, obviously you have or you wouldn't be there. Honestly, I adore Guy, but I can't stand the rest of 'em—"

Tasha cut in, her voice flat. "Kinsey, that's why I called. I cut my trip short and flew back from Utah this afternoon. Guy is dead."

I was silent for a beat, trying to parse the sentence. I knew the subject . . . *Guy* . . . but the predicate . . . *is dead* . . . made no immediate sense. "You're kidding. What happened? He can't be *dead*. When I saw him on Monday he was fine."

"He was murdered last night. Somebody smashed his skull with a blunt instrument. Christie found him in bed this morning when he didn't come down for breakfast. The police took one look at the crime scene and got a warrant to search the premises. The house has been swarming with cops ever since. They haven't found the murder weapon, but they suspect it's here. They're still combing the property."

I kept getting hung up about two sentences back. "Somebody killed him in bed? While he *slept?*"

"It looks that way."

"That's disgusting. That's awful. You can't be serious."

"I'm sorry to spring it on you, but there isn't any nice way to put it. It *is* disgusting. It's terrible. We're all numb."

"Has anybody been arrested?"

"Not at this point," she said. "The family's doing what they can to cooperate, but it doesn't look good."

"Tasha, I don't believe this. I'm sick."

"I am, too. A colleague called me in Utah this morning after Donovan called him. I left everything behind and got myself on a plane."

"Who do they suspect?"

"I have no idea. From what I've heard, Jack and Bennet were both out last night. Christie went to bed early and Donovan was watching TV upstairs in their sitting room. Myrna's apartment is off the kitchen in back, but she says she was dead to the world and didn't hear anything. She's currently down at the station being interviewed. Christie came in a little while ago. She says the detectives are still talking to Donovan. Hang on."

She put a hand across the mouthpiece and I heard her in a muffled discussion with someone in the background. She came back on the line, saying, "Great. I just talked to the homicide detective in charge of things here. He wants to keep the phone line open, but says if you want to come over he'll tell the guys at the gate to let you in. I told him he ought to talk to you since you were the one who found Guy in the first place. I told him you might have something to contribute."

"I doubt that, but who knows? I'll be there in fifteen minutes. Do you need anything?"

"We're fine for the moment. If no one's at the gate, the code is 1–9–2–4. Just punch the number in at the call box beside the drive. See you shortly," she said.

I grabbed my blazer and my handbag and went out to my car. The day had been mild. The high winds had moved on, taking with them the unseasonable heat.

The light was waning and as soon as the sun set, the temperatures would drop. I was already chilled and I shrugged into my blazer before I slid beneath the wheel. Earlier in the day, I'd tried to use my wipers and washer fluid to clean the dust off my windshield and now it was streaked in a series of rising half moons. The hood of my car was covered with the same fine layer of dust, as pale as powder, and just as soft by the look of it. Even the seat upholstery had a gritty feel to it.

I put my hands together on the steering wheel and leaned my forehead against them. I had absolutely no feeling. My interior process was held in suspended animation, as if the Pause button had been pushed on some remote control. How was it possible Guy Malek was gone? For the past week, he'd been such a presence in my life. He'd been both lost and found. He'd occupied my thoughts, triggering reactions of sympathy and exasperation. Now I couldn't quite remember his face—only a flash here and there, the sound of his "Hey," the whiskery brush of his chin on my cheek. He was already as insubstantial as a ghost, all form without content, a series of fragmented images without permanence.

What seemed so odd was that life just went *on*. I could see traffic passing along Cabana Boulevard. Two doors away, my neighbor raked brittle leaves into a pile on his lawn. If I turned on the car radio, there'd be intervals of music, public service announcements, commercials, and news broadcasts. Guy Malek might not even be mentioned on some stations. I'd lived my entire day without any intuition that Guy had been murdered, no tremor whatsoever in my subterranean landscape. So what's life about? Are people not really dead until we've been irrefutably informed? It felt that way to me, as though Guy had, just this moment, been jettisoned out of this world and into the next.

I turned the key in the ignition. Every ordinary act seemed fraught with novelty. My perceptions had changed, and with them many of my assumptions about my personal safety. If Guy could be murdered, why not Henry, or me? I drove on automatic pilot while the street scenes slid past. Familiar neighborhoods looked odd and there was a moment when I couldn't recall with any certainty what town I was in.

Approaching the Maleks', I could see that traffic had increased. Cars filled with the curious cruised by the estate. Heads were turned almost comically in the same direction. There were cars parked on both sides of the road out front. Tires had chewed into the grass, plowing down bushes and crushing the stray saplings. As each new car appeared, the assembled crowd would turn, craning and peering to see if it was someone of note.

My car didn't seem to generate a lot of interest at first. I guess nobody could believe the Maleks would drive a VW bug, especially one like mine, with its dust and assorted dings. It was only when I pulled up at the gate and gave my name to the guard that the reporters surged forward, trying to catch a glimpse of me. They seemed to be fresh troops. I didn't recognize anyone from my earlier trip over.

Somehow the national media had already managed to get camera crews assembled, and I knew that by seven the next morning, someone closely associated with the Maleks would be seen in a three-minute interview. I don't know how the major networks make arrangements so quickly. It was one of the miracles of technology that less than twenty-four hours after Guy Malek's death, somebody would do a close-up of a tear-stained face, maybe Christie's or Myrna's or even Enid's, the cook I'd yet to meet.

There was a black-and-white patrol car parked to one side, along with a vehicle from a private firm. I spotted the security guard pacing along the road, trying to keep the crowd from moving in too close. A uniformed police officer checked my name on his clipboard and waved me in. The gate swung inward by degrees and I idled the engine until the gap was sufficient to ease through. In that brief interval, there were strangers knocking on my car window, yelling questions in my direction. With their various handheld mikes extended, they might have been offering gimcracks for sale. I kept my eyes straight ahead. When I pulled forward through the gate, two male reporters continued to trot alongside me like cut-rate Secret Service agents. The security guard and the cop both converged, cutting off their progress. In my rearview mirror, I could see them begin to argue with the officer, probably reciting their moral, legal, and Constitutional rights.

My heart rate picked up as I eased up the driveway toward the house. I could see five or six uniformed officers prowling across the property, eyes on the ground as if hunting for four-leaved clovers. Light tended to fade rapidly at this hour of the day. Shadows were already collecting beneath the trees. Soon they'd need flashlights to continue the search. There was a second uniformed officer posted at the front door, his face impassive. He walked out to meet my car and I rolled down my window. I gave him my name and watched him scan both his list and my face. Apparently satisfied, he stepped away from the car. In the courtyard to my left, there were already numerous cars jammed into the cobblestone turnaround. "Any place in here all right?"

"You can park in the rear. Then come around and use the front door to go in," he said, and motioned me on.

"Thanks."

I pulled around to the left and parked my car at the far end of the three-car garage. In the diminishing light, a cluster of three floods, activated by motion sensors, flashed on to signal my presence. Except for the kitchen on this end of the house and the library on the other, most of the windows along the front of the house were dark. Around the front, the exterior lighting seemed purely decorative, too pale to provide a welcome in the accumulating gloom.

The uniformed police officer opened the door for me and I passed into the foyer. The library door was ajar and a shaft of light defined one pie-shaped wedge of the wood parquet floor. Given the quiet in the house, I was guessing the technicians were gone—fingerprint experts, the photographer, the crime scene artist, coroner, and paramedics. Tasha appeared in the doorway. "I saw you pull in. How're you doing?"

I said "Fine" in a tone that encouraged her to keep her distance from me. I noticed I was feeling churlish, as much with her as with circumstance. Homicide makes me angry with its sly tricks and disguises. I wanted Guy Malek back and with some convoluted emotional logic, I blamed her for what had happened. If she hadn't been my cousin, she wouldn't have hired me in the first place. If I hadn't been hired, I wouldn't have found him, wouldn't even have known who he was, wouldn't have cared, and would have felt no loss. She knew this as well as I did and the flicker of guilt that crossed her face was a mirror to mine.

For someone who'd flown back from her vacation in haste, Tasha was flawlessly turned out. She wore a black gabardine pantsuit with a jacket cropped at the waist. The slim, uncuffed trousers had a wide waistband and inverted pleats in front. The jacket had brass buttons and the sleeves were trimmed with a thin gold braid. Somehow the outfit suggested something more than fashion. She looked crisp, authoritative, and diminutive, the dainty MP of lawyers here to keep matters straight.

I followed her into the library with its clusters of dark red cracked leather chairs. The red Oriental carpets looked drab at this hour. The tall leaded glass windows were tinted with the gray cast of twilight, as chilly as frost. Tasha paused to turn on table lamps as she crossed the room. Even the luster of the dark wood paneling failed to lend coziness to the cold stone hearth. The room was shabby and smelled as musty as I remembered it. I'd first met Bennet here just a week ago.

I left my handbag beside a club chair and circled the room restlessly. "Who's the chief investigator? You said there was someone here."

"Lieutenant Robb."

"Jonah? Oh, terrific. How perfect."

"You know him?"

"I know Jonah," I said. When I'd met him, he was

working Missing Persons, but the Santa Teresa Police Department has a mandatory rotation system and detectives get moved around. With Lieutenant Dolan's retirement, there was an opening for a homicide investigator. I'd had a short-lived affair with Jonah once when he was separated from his wife, a frequent occurrence in the course of their stormy relationship. They'd been sweethearts since seventh grade and were no doubt destined to be together for life, like owls, except for the intervals of virulent estrangement coming every ten months. I suppose the pattern should have been evident, but I was smitten with him. Later, not surprisingly, she crooked her little finger and he went back to her. Occasionally now, the three of us crossed paths out in public and I'd become an expert at pretending I'd never dallied with him between my Wonder Woman sheets. This probably accounted for his willingness to have me on the scene. He knew he could trust me to keep my mouth shut.

"What's the story?" she asked.

"Nothing. Just skip it. I feel bitchy, I guess, but I shouldn't take it out on you."

I heard footsteps on the stairs and looked up as Christie came in. She wore bulky running shoes and a warm-up suit in some silky material, the blue of the fabric setting off the blue in her eyes. She wore scarcely any makeup and I wondered if this was the outfit she was wearing when Guy's body was discovered. The library, like the living room, was equipped with a wet bar: a small brass sink, a mini-refrigerator, an ice bucket, and a tray of assorted liquor bottles. She moved over to the fridge and removed a chilled bottle of white wine. "Anybody want a glass of wine? What about you, Kinsey?"

I said, "Alcohol won't help."

"Don't be absurd. Of course it will. So does Valium. It doesn't change reality, but it improves your attitude. Tasha? Can I interest you in a glass of Chardonnay? This is top of the line." She turned the bottle so she could peer at the price tag on the side. "Nice. This is $36.95."

"I'll have some in a bit. Not just yet," Tasha said.

Mutely, the two of us watched while Christie cut the foil cap from a wine bottle and used a corkscrew. "If I smoked, I'd have a ciggie, but I don't," she said. She poured herself some wine, the bottle clinking clumsily on the rim of the Waterford crystal. "Shit!" she said, pausing to inspect the damage. A jagged crack ran down the side. She dumped the contents in the sink and tossed the glass in the trash. She picked up a second glass and poured again. "We need a fire in here. I wish Donovan were home."

"I can do that," I said. I moved over to the hearth and removed the fire screen. There were six or seven hefty pieces of firewood in a brass carrier. I picked up one and chunked it onto the grate.

"Make sure you don't destroy any evidence," she said.

I looked up at her blankly.

"Ted Bundy killed one of his victims with a hunk of wood," she said, and then shrugged with embarrassment. "Never mind. Not funny. What a day," she said. "I can't figure out how to handle it. I've felt drunk since this morning, completely out of control."

I stacked two more logs on the grate while she and Tasha talked. It was a relief to be involved in a task that was basic and inconsequential. The wood was beautifully seasoned oak. Most of the heat would go straight up the chimney, but it would be a comfort nonetheless. I flicked on the electric match, turned the key in the gas starter, and listened to the comforting *whunk* as the jets ignited. I replaced the fire screen, pausing to adjust the height of the flame. Belatedly, I tuned into their conversation.

Tasha was saying, "Did you ask to have an attorney present?"

"Of course I didn't ask for an attorney. I didn't *do* anything. This was just routine," Christie said irritably. She remained standing behind the bar, leaning against its leather surface. "Sorry. What's the matter with me? I'm completely frazzled."

"Don't worry about it. Who's still down there?"

"Jack and Bennet, I think. They kept everybody separated like they did here. So absurd. What do they think, Donovan and I aren't going to discuss it in detail the minute we can put our heads together?"

"They don't want to risk your influencing one another," I said. "Memory's fragile. It's easily contaminated."

"None of us have anything much to report," she said. "I drank too much at dinner and fell asleep by nine. Donovan was watching TV in the sitting room off our bedroom."

"What about Guy?"

"He went up to bed about the same time I did. He was drunk as all get-out thanks to Bennet's martinis."

She caught sight of her fingertips and frowned to herself. She turned away from us and ran water in the sink. "They took prints for comparison."

Tasha directed a brief comment to me. "After the body was removed and the fingerprint techs were finished, the homicide investigator had one of the Maleks' housecleaning crew come over and walk through Guy's room with him describing the usual position of furniture, lamps, ashtrays, that sort of thing."

"Did they find anything?"

"I have no idea. I'm sure she was cautioned to keep her mouth shut. I know they tagged and bagged a bunch of items, but I don't know exactly what or why they were significant. Now they've brought in additional officers and started a grid search of the grounds. Apparently, they spent a lot of time down in the pool house earlier."

Christie broke in. "I could see them from up in my room checking perimeter gates, any point of entrance or exit."

"They're still out there on the property. I noticed that when I came in. But why check the exterior? It almost had to be someone in the house."

Christie bristled. "Not necessarily. What makes you say that? We have people all over. Maybe fifteen a week, with the gardeners and the car washers, housecleaners, and the woman who takes care of the plants. We have no idea where those people come from. For all we know, they're convicted felons or escapees from a mental institution."

I wasn't going to speak to her flight of fancy. If the notion gave her comfort, let her hang on to it. "It's always possible," I said, "but I'm assuming none of them have access to the house at night. I thought you had an alarm system."

"Well, we do. The police were interested in the system as well, but that's the problem," she said. "With all the high winds we've had here the past couple of days, windows were blowing open and the alarm kept going off. It happened twice Monday night after we'd all gone to bed. Scared the shit out of me. We finally turned it off so it wouldn't happen again. Last night, the system wasn't on at all."

"When do they think Guy was killed?" I asked.

"Around ten, I gather. Between ten and eleven. The detective didn't actually say that, but I noticed that was the period that seemed to interest him. Bennet and Jack were both out until late."

A woman in a housekeeper's uniform, with an apron tied over it, peered in at the door. She was short and round, and looked like someone whose eating habits had long ago outstripped any fat-burning activities. She was probably in her mid-forties, with dark hair pulled back neatly under a red-and-white bandanna she'd wrapped around her head. I wasn't sure if the purpose was ornamental or meant to keep falling hair from seasoning the food. "Excuse me. I'm sorry to interrupt, but I'm wondering what time you want dinner served."

Christie made a face. "My fault, Enid. I should have talked to you. Donovan's not back yet and I'm not really sure about Jack and Bennet. What are we having? Will it hold?"

"Baked chicken breasts. I stopped off at the market on my way in to work. I went ahead and changed the menu, so there's plenty if you're having extra people. I did up some oven-roasted potatoes and a casserole of sweet-and-sour cabbage. I can wait and serve if you like." Somehow she managed to indicate without a word that waiting around to serve dinner was the last choice on her list.

"No, no, no. I don't want you to do that. Just leave things in the oven and we can help ourselves. As soon as you're ready, go ahead and take off. I know you were in early."

"Yes, ma'am. Myrna called me. I came as soon as I heard."

"Have the police talked to you? I'm assuming they have. They talked to everyone else."

Enid picked at her apron uncomfortably. "I talked to Lieutenant Bower shortly before you did, I believe. Do you want me tomorrow at the usual time?"

"I don't know yet. Call me in the morning and we'll see what's going on. I may want you here early if that's all right with you."

"Of course."

As soon as she withdrew, Christie said, "Sorry for the interruption. That's Enid Pressman. She's the cook. I guess I could have introduced you. I didn't mean to be rude. Tasha's met her before."

"That's perfectly all right," I said. I made a quick mental note to have a chat with Enid at some point. She'd neatly avoided relating much in the way of information.

Tasha said, "Maybe I will have that drink. Here, let me get it. You look exhausted. We need to sit."

Christie had put the wine bottle in a cooler and now

grabbed two more glasses. Tasha moved over to the bar and took the cooler from her, setting it down on a table between two chairs. Christie quizzed me with a gesture, asking if I was ready to have wine.

"I'm fine for now, but go ahead," I said.

Christie curled up in one of the leather chairs. She tucked her legs under her and crossed her arms.

I took the chair closest to the fireplace while Tasha perched on the arm of the chair next to Christie's. Tasha said, "What about Bennet? Where was he last night?"

"I'm not really sure. You'd have to ask him about that."

"And Jack?"

"Over at the country club with a hundred other fellows. There's a pro-am tournament coming up this weekend. Practice rounds start on Thursday. He went to the pairings' party with a friend of his."

"That should be easy enough to verify," Tasha said.

"Would you quit talking like that? He didn't kill Guy and neither did I."

"Christie, I'm not accusing you. I'm trying to analyze your position here. Given the situation, suspicion's bound to fall on one of you. I don't mean you specifically, so don't take offense. Other people may have access to the property, but who'd have a better motive than the family? There's a lot of money at stake."

"But Tasha, that's ridiculous. If one of us were going to kill him, why do it here? Why not somewhere else? Make it look like an accident or random violence."

I raised my hand like a student. "Think of the

convenience. If you kill a man in his sleep, you don't have to worry about him putting up a fight."

Jonah Robb appeared in the doorway, his gaze fixed on Christie. "We'll be taking off shortly. The bedroom's still sealed pending the coroner's report. It's strictly off-limits until you hear from us. We'll be here early tomorrow morning to finish things up."

"Of course. Will there be anything else?"

"I understand your brother-in-law received some mail . . ."

"We gave that to the other detective, Lieutenant Bower."

Jonah nodded. "Fine. I'll check with her."

"Do you have any idea what time we can expect my husband? When I left the station, he was still being interviewed."

"I'll have him call if he's there when I get back to the station. With luck, he'll be done and on his way home."

"Thanks."

Jonah's gaze came to rest on mine and he tilted his head. "Can I see you out here?"

I got up and crossed the room. He held the door open and we went into the hall.

He said, "Donovan tells us you were the one who located Guy on behalf of the estate."

"That's right."

"We're going to want to talk to you in the morning, picking up background information."

"Of course. Glad to help. I can stop by at nine on my way into work," I said. "What's this business about the mail?"

"I haven't seen it yet," he said obliquely, meaning *none-of-your-beeswax*. We looked at each other for perhaps half a moment longer than was absolutely essential. I'd always thought Jonah was good-looking. Black Irish, I think they call them. Blue eyes, coal-black hair. He looked worn-out and tense, his eyes surrounded by a lacework of fine lines, his skin looking coarser than I remembered. Perhaps as a side effect of my renewed sexuality, I found myself sizing up the men in my life. With Jonah, there was a dark radiance in the air. I felt like a fruit fly, wondering if the pheromones were mine or his.

"How's Camilla?"

"She's pregnant."

"Congratulations."

"It's not mine."

"Ah."

"What about you? You involved with anyone these days?"

"Could be. It's hard to know."

His smile was brief. "See you in the morning."

That you will, I thought.

FOURTEEN

Once Jonah was gone, I found myself reluctant to return to the library. I could hear Christie and Tasha talking together companionably, their voices light, the conversation interspersed with nervous laughter. The subject had obviously changed. The ego is ill-prepared to deal with death for long. Even at a wake or a funeral, the topic tends to drift to safer ground whenever possible. I scanned the empty foyer, trying to get my bearings. Across from the library was the living room. I'd been in there, but I'd never seen the rest of the ground floor.

I passed under the stairs to an intersecting corridor that branched off in both directions. I caught a glimpse of a powder room across the hall. I saw two doors on the right, but both were closed. Under the circumstances, I thought it unwise to snoop indiscriminately. In the unlikely event I encountered a cop, I was roaming in the guise of someone looking for the kitchen so I could offer my help.

Before, the house had felt comfortable despite the touches of shabbiness that appeared throughout. Now I was acutely aware of the imprint of Guy's murder.

The very air seemed heavy, the gloom as languorous as a dense fog drifting through the rooms.

I took a left, moving toward the unhappy scent of cooked cabbage at the end of the hall. In a sudden glimpse of the future, I could envision the day when this house would be sold to a private boys' school and the smell of cruciform vegetables would overpower all else. Young lads in hard shoes would clatter through the halls between classes. The room where Guy had been bludgeoned to death would be turned into a dormitory where adolescent boys would abuse themselves surreptitiously after lights out. Always, there would be rumors about the pale apparition gliding down the corridor, hovering on the landing at the turn of the stairs. I found myself walking quickly, anxious for human company.

Beyond the dining room and butler's pantry, the swinging door to the kitchen stood open. The room looked vast to me, but then my entire culinary kingdom would fit in the rear of a moderately priced station wagon. The floors were pale, glossy pegged oak planks stretching out in all directions. The custom cupboards were dark cherry and the counters were topped with mottled green marble. There were sufficient cookbooks, utensils, and small appliances in view to furnish one small section of a Williams-Sonoma retail outlet. The stove top looked bigger than the double bed in my loft and the refrigerator had clear doors with all the contents on view. To the right, there was the equivalent of a little sitting area; and beyond, there was a glassed-in porch that extended the entire length of the room. Here the lush scent of roast chicken and garlic overrode the odor of cooked cabbage. Why does someone else's cooking always smell so much better than your own?

Myrna had come back from the police station. She and Enid were standing together near one of the two kitchen sinks. Myrna's face looked puffy and the prickle of red around her eyes suggested she'd been crying, not within the last few minutes, but perhaps earlier in the day. Enid had pulled on a poplin raincoat and the yards of tan fabric gave her the hapless form and shape of a baked potato. She'd removed her bandanna. Bareheaded, she had a wiry bird's nest of hair that was dark strands streaked with gray. Tea mugs in hand, they must have been having a few last words about the murder because both looked up guiltily as I came in. Given their proximity to events, the two of them must have been privy to just about everything. Certainly, the family wasn't shy about airing their conflicts. God knows they'd squabbled in front of me. Enid and Myrna must have picked up on plenty and probably compared notes.

Enid said, "Can I help you?" She was using the same tone museum guards take when they think you're about to reach out and touch something on the far side of the rope.

"That's what I came to ask," I said. "Can I do anything to help?" Little Miss Goody Two-shoes working on a Girl Scout merit badge.

"Thanks, but everything's under control," she said. She emptied her mug in the sink, opened the dishwasher, and set it in the top rack. "I better go while I can," she murmured.

Myrna said, "I can walk you out if you want."

"I'll be fine," Enid replied. "I can turn on the lights

in back." And then with a look at me, "Can I fix you a cup of tea? The water's hot. I'm just on my way out, but it won't take but a minute."

"I'd like that," I said. I'm not that fond of tea, but I had hoped to prolong the contact.

"I can do it," Myrna said. "You go on."

"Are you sure?"

"Absolutely. We'll see you tomorrow."

Enid reached out and patted Myrna on the arm. "Well. Bye-bye. I want you to talk to my chiropractor about that bursitis and you call if you need me. I'll be home all evening." Enid took up a wide canvas tote and disappeared through the utility room, moving toward the backdoor.

I watched Myrna plug in the electric tea kettle. She opened a cabinet nearby and took down a mug. Wincing, she reached for a canister and removed a tea bag that she placed in the mug. Meanwhile, outside, I could hear a car door slam shut and moments later, the sound of Enid starting her car.

I moved over to the counter and perched on a wooden stool. "How're you doing, Myrna? You look tired," I said.

"That's my bursitis flaring up. It's been bothering me for days," she said.

"The stress probably contributes."

Myrna pursed her lips. "That's what my doctor says. I thought I'd seen everything. I'm used to death. In my job, I see a lot of it, but this . . ." She paused to shake her head.

"It must have been hellish around here today. I could

225

hardly believe it when Tasha told me," I said. "You've worked for the Maleks, what . . . eight months?"

"About that. Since last April. The family asked me to stay on after Mr. Malek died. Somebody had to take responsibility for running the house. Enid was tired of doing it and I didn't mind. I've managed many a household, some of 'em a lot bigger than this."

"Couldn't you be making a lot more money as a private-duty nurse?"

She took down a sugar bowl and found a creamer that she filled from a carton of half-and-half in the refrigerator. "Well, yes, but I needed some relief from all the terminal illness. I become attached to my patients and where does that leave me when they pass? I was living like a gypsy, moving from job to job. Here I have a small apartment of my own and the duties are largely supervisory. I do light cooking occasionally on Enid's nights off, but that's about it. Of course, they complain. They're hard to please sometimes, but I don't let it bother me. In some ways, I'm used to it. The sick are often difficult and it doesn't mean anything. I let it roll right off me."

"I take it you were here last night."

The tea kettle began a hoarse whisper that rapidly turned into a shriek. She paused to unplug it and the shrill sound subsided as though with relief. I waited while she filled the mug and brought it over to me. "Thanks."

I could see her hesitate, apparently debating with herself about her next comment. "Is something bothering you?" I asked.

"I'm not sure what I'm allowed to say," she hesitated. "The lieutenant asked us not to talk to the press . . ."

"Not surprising," I said. "Have you seen 'em out there?"

"Like vultures," she remarked. "When I came back from the station, they were all yelling and vying for my attention, pushing microphones in my direction. Made me want to pull my jacket right up over my face. I felt like one of those criminals you see on the television."

"It's probably only going to get worse. This started out as a minor human-interest story. Now it's big news."

"I'm afraid so," she said. "But to answer your question, yes, I was here, but I didn't hear anything. I've had trouble sleeping lately with this arm of mine. Ordinary analgesics don't begin to touch the pain, so I'd taken a Tylenol with codeine and a prescription sleeping pill. I don't do that often because I dislike the effect. Leaves me feeling logy the next morning, like I never quite wake up. Also, I find the sleep so deep it's almost not restful. I went to bed about eight-thirty and didn't stir until nearly nine this morning."

"Who discovered the body?"

"I believe it was Christie."

"What time was this?"

"Shortly after ten. I'd made myself a cup of coffee and I was back here in the kitchen, watching the morning news on that little TV set. I heard all the commotion. They were supposed to meet for breakfast to talk about the will, and when Guy didn't come down, I guess Bennet got furious. He thought Guy was playing games, at least that's what Christie told me later. Bennet sent her upstairs to fetch him. Next thing I knew they'd dialed 9–1–1, but I still wasn't sure what was going on. I was just on my way out there when Donovan came in. He looked awful. He'd lost all his color and was white as a sheet."

"Did you see the body?"

"I did, yes. He asked if I'd go up. He thought there might be something I could do, but of course there wasn't. Guy must have been dead several hours by then."

"There's no doubt?"

"Oh, none. Absolutely. He was cold to the touch and his skin was waxen. His skull had been crushed and there was blood everywhere, most of it dried or congealed. Given his injuries, I'd say death must have been quick, if not instantaneous. Also, messy. I know the police have been puzzled by that aspect of the murder."

"Which aspect?"

"What the killer did with his own clothes. Not to be gross about it, but there would have been quite an area of splatter. Blood and brain material. There's no way you could leave the premises without attracting attention. The detectives were interested in a number of articles of clothing. They asked for my help since I take items to the cleaners."

"Did they find anything significant?"

"I don't know. I gave them everything that was going out today. They talked to Enid at length, but I'm not sure what they wanted with her."

"You have any idea what the weapon was?"

"I wouldn't hazard a guess. That's not an area where I feel qualified to comment. There was nothing in the room, at least as far as I could see. I did hear one of the detectives say the autopsy was scheduled first thing tomorrow morning. I imagine the medical examiner will have an opinion," she said. "Have you been hired by the family to investigate?"

I could feel the lie form, but then thought better of it. I said, "Not yet. Let's hope it doesn't come to that. I can't believe anybody in the family is going to turn out to be responsible."

I expected her to pipe up with protests and reassurances, but the quiet that followed was significant. I could sense a desire to confide, but I couldn't imagine what. I let my gaze rest on hers with an expression I hoped appeared trustworthy and encouraging. I could almost feel my head tilt like a dog trying to decipher the direction of a high-pitched whistle.

She'd become aware of a dried speck on the counter and she worked at it with her fingernail, not looking at me. "This is really none of my business. I had only respect for Mr. Malek . . ."

"Absolutely."

"I wouldn't want anyone to think badly of me, but I can't help but hear things while I'm going about my business. I'm paid well and God knows, I enjoy the work. Or at least I did."

"I'm sure you're only trying to help," I said, wondering where she was going with this.

"You know, Bennet never agreed to share the money. He wasn't convinced that was Bader's intention and neither was Jack. Of course, Jack sided with Bennet in just about everything."

"Well, maybe they weren't convinced, but given the

missing will, I don't know what choice they had, short of court action. I gather nothing was settled."

"Not at all. If they'd settled their business, Guy would have gone home. He was miserable here. I could see it in his face."

"Well, that's true. When I talked to him on Monday, he admitted he'd been drinking."

"Oh, especially last night. They started with cocktails and went through four or five bottles of wine with dinner. And then, port and liqueurs. It was still going on when I went off to bed. I helped Enid with the dishes and she could see how exhausted I was. Both of us heard them quarreling."

"Bennet and Guy quarreled?"

She shook her head, lips moving.

I cupped a hand to my ear. "Excuse me. I didn't hear that."

She cleared her throat and raised her voice half a notch. "Jack. Guy and Jack quarreled before Jack went off to his country club. I told the lieutenant about it and now I'm wondering if I should have kept my mouth shut."

"The truth is the truth. If that's what you heard, you had to tell the police."

"You don't think he'll be mad?" Her tone was anxious, her expression almost childlike in its apprehension.

I suspected the entire family would have fits when they heard, but we all had an obligation to cooperate with the police investigation. "Maybe so, but you can't worry about that. Guy was *murdered* last night. It's not up to you to protect anyone."

She nodded mutely, but I could see she remained unconvinced.

"Myrna, I mean this. Whatever happens, I don't think you should feel responsible."

"But I didn't have to volunteer the information. I like Jack. I can't believe he'd hurt anyone."

"Listen, you think I'm not going to end up in the same position? The cops are going to talk to me, too. I have to go down there tomorrow and I'm going to end up doing exactly what you did."

"You are?"

"Of course. I heard them quarrel the night I came here for drinks. Bennet and Donovan were going at it hammer and tongs. Christie was the one who told me they did it all the time. That doesn't make 'em killers, but it's not up to us to interpret the facts. You have to tell the cops what you heard. I'm sure Enid will back you up. Nobody's going to be arrested on that basis anyway. It's not like you saw Jack coming out of Guy's room with a bloody two-by-four."

"Not at all. Of course not." I could see some of the tension begin to leave her face. "I hope you're right. I mean, I can see what you're saying. The truth is the truth. All I heard was a quarrel. I never heard Jack threaten him."

"Exactly," I said, with a glance at my watch. It was nearly six by then. "If you're through for the night, I better let you go. I probably ought to get on out of here myself, but first I want to have a little chat with Christie."

Anxiety flickered in her eyes. "You won't mention our conversation?"

"Would you quit *worrying?* I won't say a word and I don't want you saying anything either."

"I appreciate that. I believe I would like to go wash my face."

I waited until Myrna had disappeared through the utility room, moving toward her apartment. My tea was untouched. I emptied my cup and left it in the sink. Despite Enid's good example, I've never owned a dishwasher and don't know the first thing about loading one. I pictured one false move and every dish would go flying, crashing in a heap of rubble. I returned to the library. Christie and Tasha had turned on the television set. Christie held the remote and she was switching from channel to channel to see if she could catch the news. She pressed the Mute button when I came in, turning to look at me. "Oh, there you are. Come in and join us. Tasha thought you were gone."

"I'm on my way," I said. "I went out to the kitchen to see if I could help out there. Could I ask you a question before I take off? I heard you mention the mail when you were talking to Lieutenant Robb. Can I ask what that was?"

"Sure. Uhm, let's see. I guess late Monday afternoon someone put an unsigned letter in the mailbox. The envelope had Guy's name on it, but there was no return address. He left it on the hall table when he went to bed last night. I thought the police might want to take a look."

"Was it typed or handwritten?"

"The envelope was typed."

"Did you read the letter?"

"Of course not, but I know it bothered Guy. He

didn't say what it was, but I gather it was something unpleasant."

"Did he ever mention a Max Outhwaite? Does the name mean anything to you?"

"Not that I remember." She turned to Tasha. "Does it ring a bell with you?"

Tasha shook her head. "What's the connection?"

"That's how the reporter first heard Guy was back. Someone named Max Outhwaite dropped off a letter at the *Dispatch*, but when Katzenbach checked it out, there was no one by that name and no such address. I double-checked as well and came up blank."

"Never heard of him," Christie said. "Is there any chance he's connected to one of Guy's old sprees? Maybe Outhwaite was somebody Guy mistreated back then."

"Possible," I said. "Do you mind if I check Bader's file upstairs?"

"What file?" Tasha asked.

Christie answered before I did. "Bader kept a folder of newspaper clippings about Guy's various arrests and his scrapes with the law. It goes back quite a way."

"I'll tell you something else crossed my mind," I said. "This Outhwaite, whoever he is, certainly put Jeff Katzenbach on the trail of Guy's criminal history. I'm not sure Jeff would have known about it otherwise. The minute I saw the letter, I remember wondering if it was really Bennet or Jack who tipped him off somehow."

"Using Outhwaite's name?"

"It seems possible," I said.

"But why would either of them do that? What's the point?"

"That's the problem. I don't know. Anyway, I could be off base on this one," I said. "I do like the idea that Outhwaite's someone Guy sinned against in the old days."

"Take the file if you want. It was still on the desk in Bader's office last I saw."

"Let me pop upstairs and grab it. I'll be right back."

I moved out of the library and crossed the foyer. Maybe when I talked to Jonah, he'd level with me about the letter. I went up the steps two at a time, studiously avoiding a look down the hall. I had no idea which room Guy had been in, but I didn't want to go near it. I took a hard left at the head of the stairs and went straight to Bader's room, where I opened the door and flipped on the overhead light. Everything seemed to be in order. The room was cold and smelled slightly musty from disuse. The overhead illumination was dim and the pale colors in the room looked flat. I passed through to the office beyond, hitting switches as I went. Bader's life force was being systematically erased. Closets had been emptied, all the personal items removed from his desktop.

I surveyed the surrounding area. I spotted the folder with all the newspaper articles about Guy's past behavior, relieved that the cops hadn't swept through and taken it. On the other hand, the search warrant probably wasn't that broad. The list of property to be seized might have been directed only toward the murder weapon itself. I leafed through the clippings, speed-reading for content, looking for the name *Outhwaite* or anything close. There was nothing. I checked through some of the stray folders on the desk, but found nothing else that seemed relevant. One more dead end, though the idea was sound—someone with a grudge making Guy's life difficult. I pressed the file under my arm and left the room, turning off the lights as I went.

I pulled the door shut behind me, pausing in the hallway outside the master suite. Something felt wrong. My first urge was to scurry down the stairs toward the lighted rooms below, but I found myself slowing. I could hear a crackling sound and I peered to my left. The far end of the corridor was enveloped in shadow, except for an X of crime scene tape across three doorways. As I watched, the tape seemed to become nearly luminous, vibrating audibly as if rattled by wind. I thought for a moment the tape would break free, clicking and snapping as though a current were moving through it. The air on the landing was chilly and there was the faint scent of something animal—wet dog or old fur. For the first time, I allowed myself to experience the horror of Guy's death.

I began to descend, one hand on the railing, the other clutching the file. I pivoted, reluctant to turn my back on the darkness behind me. For a moment, I scrutinized the stretch of corridor I could see. Something hovered in my peripheral vision. I turned my head slowly, nearly moaning with fear. I could see sparkles of light, almost like dust motes materializing in the stillness. I felt a sudden flush of heat and I could hear ringing in my ears, a sound I associated with childhood fainting spells. My phobia about needles had often inspired such episodes. When I was young, I was often subjected to a typhoid inoculation, a tine test for tuberculosis, or a periodic tetanus injection. While the nurse took the time to pooh-pooh my fears, assuring me "big girls" didn't put up the fuss I did, the ringing would begin, building to a high pitch and then silence. My vision would shrink, the light spiraling inward to a tiny point. The cold would rush up and the next thing I'd know, there'd be anxious faces bending over me and the sharp scent of smelling salts held under my nose.

I leaned back against the wall. My mouth flooded with something that tasted like blood. I closed my eyes tightly, conscious of the thudding of my heart and the clamminess in my palms. While Guy Malek slept, someone had crept along this hallway in the darkness last night, toting a blunt object of sufficient brute matter to extinguish his life. Less than a day ago. Less than a night. Perhaps it had taken one blow, perhaps several. What troubled me was the notion of that first bone-crushing crack as his skull shattered and collapsed. Poor Guy. I hoped he hadn't wakened before the first blow fell. Better he slept on before the last sleep became final.

The ringing in my ears went on, mounting in intensity like the howling of wind. I was weighted with dread. Occasionally in nightmares, I suffer from this effect— an overpowering urge to run without the ability to move. I struggled to make a sound. I would have sworn there was a presence, someone or something, that hovered and then passed. I tried to open my eyes, almost convinced I'd see Guy Malek's killer passing down the stairs. My heartbeat accelerated to a life-threatening pitch, thrumming in my ears like the sound of running feet. I opened my eyes. The sound ceased abruptly. Nothing. No one. The ordinary noises of the house reasserted themselves. The scene before me was blank.

Polished floor. Empty hall. Incandescent light from the chandelier. Glancing back down the corridor, I could see that the X of crime scene tape was simply tape again. I sank down on the stairs. The whole of the experience had surely taken less than a minute, but the rush of adrenaline had left my hands shaking.

Finally, I roused myself from the step where I'd been sitting for God knows how long. From somewhere downstairs, I could hear a mix of male and female voices, and I knew without question that Donovan, Bennet, and Jack had returned from the police station, arriving while I was still in Bader's office. Below me, the library door stood open. Tasha and Christie must have gone to join them. Faintly, from the direction of the kitchen, I could hear the clatter of ice cubes and the clink of bottles. Drink time again. Everybody in the house seemed to need alcohol along with extended psychiatric care.

I completed my descent, anxious to avoid encountering the family. I returned to the library, peering in with caution, relieved to see the room empty. I grabbed up my handbag and shoved the file down in the outside pocket, then headed for the front door, heart still pounding. I pulled the door shut behind me, careful to soften the sound of the latch clicking into place. Somehow it seemed important to slip away undetected. After my experience on the stairs—whatever it was—I was incapable of making superficial conversation. It didn't seem unreasonable to suppose that someone in this household had murdered Guy Malek and I'd be damned if I'd make nice until I knew who it was.

FIFTEEN

Back in my neighborhood, parking spaces were at a premium and I was forced to leave my VW almost a block away. I locked the car and trotted to my apartment. It was fully dark by then and a chill shivered in the trees like wind. I crossed my arms for warmth, clutching the strap of my handbag as it bumped against my side. I used to carry a handgun as a matter of course, but I've given up that practice. I moved through the gate, which gave its usual welcoming squeak. My place was dark, but I could see the lights on in Henry's kitchen. I didn't want to be alone. I headed for his backdoor and rapped on the glass.

He emerged moments later from the living room. He gave a half wave when he saw me and crossed to let me in. "I was just watching the news. The murder's on all channels. Sounds bad."

"Awful. It's vile."

"Have a seat and get warmed up. It's gotten nippy out there."

I said, "Don't let me interrupt. I'll be fine sitting here."

"Don't be silly. You look cold."

"I'm freezing."

"Well, wrap up."

I put my bag down and grabbed his afghan, folding its weight around me like a shawl as I slid into his rocking chair. "Thanks. This is great. I'll be warmer in a minute. It's mostly tension."

"I'm not surprised. Have you eaten supper yet?"

"I think I had lunch, but I can't remember what I ate."

"I've got beef stew if you want. I was just about to have a bowl myself."

"Please." I watched as Henry adjusted the flame under the stew. He took out a loaf of homemade bread, sliced it thickly, and placed it in a basket with a napkin folded over it. He assembled bowls and spoons, napkins, and wine glasses, moving around the kitchen with his usual ease and efficiency. Moments later, he set bowls of stew on the table. I left his rocking chair and shuffled over to the kitchen table still wrapped in his afghan. He pushed the butter in my direction as he settled in his chair. "So tell me the story. I know the basic details. They've been blasting that across the TV screen all afternoon."

I began to eat as I talked, realizing how hungry I was. "You may know more than I do. I'm too smart to stick my nose in the middle of a homicide investigation. These days it's hard enough to put a case together without an outsider interfering."

"You're not exactly an amateur."

"I'm not an expert either. Let the techs and forensic specialists give it their best shot. I'll keep my distance unless I'm told otherwise. My stake's personal, but it's really not my business. I liked Guy. He was nice. His brothers piss me off. This is great stew."

"You have a theory about the murder?"

"Let's put it this way. This is not a case where some stranger broke in and killed Guy in the middle of a robbery. The poor man was asleep. From what I heard, everybody'd been drinking, so he more than likely passed out. He wasn't used to hard liquor, especially in massive quantities, which is how the Maleks go at it. Somebody knew where his room was and probably knew he was in no condition to defend himself. I tell you, with the possible exception of Christie, I've developed such an aversion to that family I can hardly bear to be under the same roof with them. I feel guilty about Guy. I feel guilty about finding him and guilty he came back. I don't know what else I could have done, but I wish I'd left him in Marcella where he was safe."

"You didn't encourage him to return."

"No, but I didn't argue that strenuously either. I should have been more explicit. I should have detailed their attitude. I thought the danger was emotional. I didn't think anyone would go after him and bludgeon him to death."

"You think it was one of his brothers?"

"I'm tempted by the idea," I said reluctantly. "It's a dangerous assumption and I know I shouldn't jump to conclusions, but it's always easier to pin suspicion on someone you dislike."

By eight-thirty that night, I was back in my apartment with the door locked. I sat at the kitchen counter for what felt like an hour before I worked up the courage to call Peter and Winnie Antle, who'd been following the story on the Santa Maria news station. The entire church congregation had come together earlier that evening, shocked and saddened by the murder. I hoped to cushion their loss, though in reality their faith provided them more comfort than I was able to offer. I told them I'd do what I could to keep in touch, and I broke the connection feeling little or no solace. Once the lights were turned out, I lay in my bed with a stack of quilts piled over me, trying to get warm, trying to make sense of what had happened that day. I was weighted with dread. Guy's death had generated something far worse than grief. What I experienced was not sorrow, but a heavy regret that was wedged in my chest like an undigested lump of hot meat. I didn't sleep well. My eyes seemed to come open every twenty minutes or so. I changed positions and adjusted the covers. First I was too hot, then too cold. I kept thinking the next arrangement of limbs would offer sufficient comfort to lure me to sleep. I lay on my stomach with my arms shoved under my pillow, turned on my back with my shoulders uncovered. I tried my left side, knees pulled up, arms tucked under, switched to my right side with one foot sticking out. I must have set the alarm without thinking about it because the next thing I knew, the damn thing was going off in my ear, bringing me straight up out of the only decent sleep I'd managed all night. I turned off the alarm. I refused to run. There was no way I was budging from the chrysalis of heat-generating quilts. Next thing I knew, it was nine-fifteen and I felt compelled to drag myself out of bed. I had a date with

Jonah Robb down at the police station. I checked my reflection in the bathroom mirror. Nice. My color was bad and I had bags under my eyes.

As it turned out, it wasn't Jonah I spoke to but Lieutenant Bower. She kept me waiting for fifteen minutes, sitting on a little two-person bench in what I suppose would be referred to as the lobby at the police station. Under the watchful gaze of the officer at the desk, I shifted in my seat and stared at the rack of crime prevention pamphlets. I also eavesdropped shamelessly while six whining drivers came to complain about their traffic tickets. Finally, Lieutenant Bower peered around the door from the Investigative Division. "Miss Millhone?"

I'd never met Betsy Bower, but I'd been curious about her. The name suggested someone perky and blond, a former varsity cheer-leader with terrific thighs and no brains. To my dismay, Lieutenant Bower was the least perky woman I'd had the pleasure to meet. She was the police equivalent of an Amazon: statuesque, eight inches taller than I, and probably fifty pounds heavier. She had dark hair that she wore skinned straight back, and little round, gold-rimmed glasses. She had a flawless complexion. If she wore makeup at all, it was artfully done. When she spoke, I caught sight of endearingly crooked teeth, which I realized later might have explained her reluctance to smile. It was also possible she didn't like me and longed to squash me like a bug.

I followed her into a small cubicle with two wooden chairs and a scratched wooden table that had a tendency to wobble if you tried to rest your arm on it, pretending to be relaxed. She had nothing with her—no pen, no legal pad, no file, no notes. She looked directly at me, offering a few brisk sentences after which it was my turn. Somehow I had the feeling she'd remember every word I said. More likely our conversation was being recorded surreptitiously. I would have done a furtive feel-check for wiring along the underside of the table, but I was worried about the wads of old chewing gum and dried boogers parked there.

She said, "We appreciate your coming in. I understand you were hired by the estate to locate Guy Malek. Can you tell me how you went about that?" Her gaze was watchful, her manner subdued.

The question caught me by surprise. I felt a sudden flash of fear, color rising in my cheeks as if I'd just emerged from a tanning booth. I stalled like a little airplane with a tank full of bad fuel. Too late, I realized I should have prepared for this. Ordinarily, I don't lie to police officers because that would be very naughty, wouldn't it? At heart, I'm a law-and-order type. I believe in my country, the flag, paying taxes and parking tickets, returning library books on time, and crossing the street with the light. Also, I'm inclined to get tears in my eyes every time I hear the National Anthem sung by somebody who really knows how to belt it out. Right then, however, I knew I was going to have to do a little verbal tap dance because how I "went about" finding Guy Malek wasn't exactly legitimate. Neither Darcy Pascoe nor I had any business dipping into CFI's computer system to do a DMV check on a matter completely unrelated to an insurance claim. I'd probably violated some kind of civil ordinance or penal code number something-something. At the very least, the two of us were in serious breach of company policy, department regulations, common decency, and proper etiquette. This might well go down on my permanent record, something my elementary school principal had threatened me with every time I fled school with Jimmy Tait in the fifth and sixth grades. I didn't think what I'd done was a jailable offense, but I was, after all, sitting at the police station and I did have my private investigator's license to protect. Since I'd now hesitated a conspicuous five seconds, I thought it was wise to launch in on *something*.

I said, "Ah. Well. I met with Donovan, Bennet, and Jack Malek last Wednesday. In the course of those conversations, I was given Guy Malek's date of birth and his Social Security number. So late in the day on Thursday, I went over to the DMV offices and asked the clerk if there was any record of a driver's license in Guy Malek's name. The information that came back was that his license had been surrendered in 1968, but that he'd been issued a California identification card. His mailing address was listed in Marcella, California. I reported that to Tasha Howard, the attorney for the estate, and to Donovan Malek, who authorized me to drive up to Marcella to verify the address. Marcella's a small town. I wasn't there ten minutes before I got a line on Guy. Frankly, I didn't think he should come down here."

"Why is that?"

Hey, as long as my butt wasn't on the line, I didn't care who I ratted out here. "His brothers were upset at having to give him a share of their father's estate. They felt he'd been paid all the monies he was entitled to. There was the issue of a second will, which came up missing when the old man died. Bennet was convinced his father had disinherited Guy, but since that will was never found, the prior will was the one being entered into probate." I did a little detour at that point, giving Lieutenant Bower the gist of the business about Max Outhwaite, whose letter to the *Dispatch* had set all the adverse publicity in motion. She didn't leap up with excitement, but it did serve to distract her (I hoped) from the issue of my illegal computer access.

She took me through a series of questions related to the Maleks' attitude toward Guy, which I characterized as hostile. I told her about the outburst I'd witnessed between Donovan and Bennet. She asked me a number of pointed questions about Jack's statements regarding Guy, but I honestly couldn't think of anything he'd said that suggested a homicidal bent. In our initial conversation, he'd expressed bitterness at Guy's defection, but that had been almost eighteen years ago, so I wasn't convinced it was relevant. Though I didn't say so to her, I'd pegged Jack as the family mascot, someone harmless and doglike, trained to distract others with his antics. I didn't feature him as a prime player in any ongoing domestic drama.

"When did you last talk to Guy?" she asked.

"He called Monday night. He needed a break so I drove over to the house and met him near the side gate. I was glad to hear from him. I'd been worried because I knew the media had picked up the story. Peter Antle, the pastor of his church up north, had been trying to get in touch with him. The house was literally under siege and it wasn't possible to get a call through. I'd driven over there once before, hoping to make contact, and I'd just about given up."

"Why were you so interested in talking to him?"

"Largely, because Peter and his wife, Winnie, were concerned."

"Aside from that."

I stared at her, wondering what she had in mind. Did she think I was *romantically* involved? "You never met Guy," I said, stating it as fact and not a question.

"No." Her face was without animation. Her curiosity was professional and had an analytic cast to it. That was her job, of course, but I found myself struggling to articulate his appeal.

"Guy Malek was a beautiful man," I said in a voice suddenly fragile. Inexplicably, I found myself pricked by grief. My eyes stung with tears. I could feel my face get puffy and my nose turn hot. It seemed odd that in Henry's company I'd felt nothing while there, but in the face of Betsy Bowers's cold authority, all my unprocessed sorrow was surfacing. I took a deep breath, trying to cover my emotions. I was avoiding her eyes, but she must have picked up on my distress because she produced a tissue from somewhere that suddenly appeared in my field of vision. I took it with gratitude, feeling vulnerable and exposed.

Within moments, I was fine. I have strong self-control and managed to get my emotions back in the box again. "Sorry. I'm not sure where that came from. I really haven't felt much sorrow since I heard about his death. I should have guessed it was down there. He was a good person and I'm really sorry he's gone."

"I can understand that," she said. "Would you care for some water?"

"I'll be fine," I said. "It's funny—I really only saw him three times. We talked on the phone, but we weren't exactly best friends. He seemed boyish, a young soul. I must have a weakness for guys who never quite manage to grow up. I'd already given Donovan an invoice and I figured my job was done. Then Guy called on Saturday. Donovan had called him, urging him to come down so they could talk about the will. Personally, I didn't think the visit was such a hot idea, but Guy was determined."

"Did he say why?"

"He had emotional accounts to pay. At the time he left home, he was messed up on drugs. He'd been in a lot of trouble and alienated just about everyone. Once he was settled in Marcella, he cleaned up his act, but he'd left a lot of unfinished business. He said he wanted to make his peace."

"When you last spoke to him, did he mention contact with other people from his past?"

"No. I know a letter was delivered—Christie mentioned it last night—but that came on Monday and Guy never said a word about it when I saw him. As far as I know, there was nothing else. Was it significant?"

"We'd rather not discuss the content until we check it out."

"Who wrote it? Or would you rather not discuss that either?"

"Right."

"Was it typed?"

"Why do you ask?"

"Because of the letter to the *Dispatch* that generated

all the hype. If the papers hadn't been tipped off, no one would have known he was back in town."

"I see what you're saying. We'll follow up."

"Can I ask about the autopsy?"

"Dr. Yee hasn't finished yet. Lieutenant Robb is there now. We'll know more when he gets back."

"What about the murder weapon?"

Her face went blank again. I was wasting my breath, but I couldn't seem to let go. "You have a suspect?" I asked.

"We're pursuing some possibilities. We're doing backgrounds on a number of people associated with the family. We're also checking everybody's whereabouts to see if all the stories add up."

"In other words, you won't say."

Chilly smile. "That's correct."

"Well. I'll do what I can to help."

"We'd appreciate that."

She made no move to close, which was puzzling. From my perspective, we'd pretty much wound up our chat. She'd asked all her questions and I'd told her what I knew. In the unspoken structure of a police interview, Detective Bower was in charge and I'd have to dance to her tune. In the unexpected pause, I could see that it was suddenly her turn to stall.

She said, "Rumor has it you're involved with Lieutenant Robb."

I squinted at her in disbelief. "*He* told you that?"

"Someone else. I'm afraid this is a small town, even smaller when it comes to law enforcement. So it's not true?"

"Well, I *was* involved, but I'm not now," I said. "What makes you ask?"

The look on her face underwent a remarkable alteration. The careful neutrality fell away and in one split second, she went from blank to blushing.

I sat back in my chair, taking a new look at her. "Are you *smitten* with him?"

"I've been out with him twice," she said cautiously.

"Ohhh, I see. Now I get it," I said. "Listen, I'm fond of Jonah, but it's strictly over between us. I'm the least of your worries. It's the dread Camilla you'd better be concerned about."

Detective Betsy Bower had abandoned any pose of professionalism. "But she's living with some guy and she's *pregnant*."

I raised a hand. "Trust me. In the continuing saga of Jonah and Camilla, the mere fact of this infant has no bearing on their relationship. He may act like he's cured, but he isn't, believe me. Camilla and Jonah are so enmeshed with each other I don't know what it would take to split up their act. Actually, now that I think about it, you probably have as good a shot at it as any."

"You really think so?"

"Why not? I was always too caught up in my own abandonment issues. I hated being a minor player in their little theater production. We're talking seventh-grade bonding. Junior high school romance. I couldn't compete. I lack the emotional strength. You look like you could tackle it. You have self-esteem issues? Are you a nail biter? Bed wetter? Jealous or insecure?"

She shook her head. "Not a bit."

"What about confrontation?"

"I like a good fight," she said.

"Well, you better get ready then because in my experience, she's indifferent to him until someone else comes along. And for God's sake, don't play fair. Camilla goes for broke."

"Thanks. I'll remember. We'll be in touch."

"I can't wait."

On the street again, I felt as if I was emerging from a darkened tunnel. The sunlight was harsh and all the colors seemed too bright. Nine black-and-white patrol cars were lined up along the curb. Across the street, a row of small California bungalows were painted in discordant pastel shades. Flowering annuals in fuchsia, orange, and magenta stood out in bold relief against the vibrant green of new foliage. I left my car in the public parking lot and walked the remaining blocks to work.

I entered Kingman and Ives by the unmarked side door. I unlocked my office and let myself in, glancing down at the floor. On the carpet, there was a plain white business-size envelope with my name and address typed across the front. The postmark was Santa Teresa, dated Monday P.M. Distracted, I set my bag on the desk, took out Bader's file, and set it on top of the file cabinet. I went back to the letter and picked it up with care. I centered it on my desk, touching only the corners while I lifted the handset and dialed Alison in reception.

"Hi, Alison. This is Kinsey. You know anything about this letter that was slipped under my door?"

"It was delivered yesterday afternoon. I held on to it up here, thinking you'd be back, and finally decided

250

it was better to go ahead and stick it under your door. Why, did I do something wrong?"

"You did fine. I was just curious."

I put the phone down and stared at the envelope. I'd picked up a fingerprint kit at a trade show recently and for a moment I debated about dusting for latents. Seemed pointless to tell the truth. Alison had clearly handled it and even if I brought up a set of prints, what was I to do with them? I couldn't picture the cops running them on the basis of my say-so. Still, I decided to be cautious. I took out a letter opener and slit the flap of the envelope, using the tip to slide the note onto my desk. The paper was cheap bond, folded twice, with no date and no signature. I used a pencil eraser to open the paper, anchoring opposite corners with the letter opener and the edge of my appointment book.

Dear Miss Milhone,

I thought I should take a moment to inlighten you on the subject of Guy Malek. I wonder if you rilly know who your dealing with. He is a liar and a thief. I find it sickning that he could get a second chance in life threw the acquisition of Sudden Riches. Why should he get the benefitt of five million dollars when he never urned one red cent? I don't think we can count on him making amens for his passed crimes. You better be carefull your not tared with the same brush.

I found a transparent plastic sleeve and slid the letter inside, then opened my desk drawer and took out the copy of the letter Max Outhwaite had written to Jeffrey

Katzenbach, placing the two side by side for comparison. On superficial examination, the typefont looked the same. As before, my name was misspelled. Thanks, it's two *l*'s, please. The sender seemed to have a problem distinguishing *your* from *you're* and consistently reversed the two. The use of *threw* for *through* was the same, but there were other oddities of note. My letter was less than half the length of the one to Katzenbach, yet it had more spelling mistakes. To my untutored eye, the two sets of errors were curiously inconsistent. If the writer were relying strictly on phonetics, why would words like *acquisition*, *aforementioned*, and *besieges* be spelled right? Certainly in my letter, there were far fewer commas, exclamation points, and Capitalizations! It was possible there was a certain level of carelessness at work, but I also had to wonder if the writer weren't simply *pretending* to use language badly. There was something vaguely amusing about the use of the word *amens* instead of *amends*, especially in the context of a born-again.

From another angle, why affix the name *Max Outhwaite* to the first letter, tacking on the embellishment of a phony address, and leave mine unsigned? I had to guess that *Outhwaite* imagined (quite correctly, as it turned out) that an unsigned letter to the *Dispatch* would get thrown in the trash. It was also likely the sender had no idea I'd end up with both. While I understood the reasoning behind the letter to the *Dispatch*, why this one to me? What was Outhwaite's intent?

I took out my magnifying glass and cranked up my three-way bulb to maximum illumination. Under magnification, other similarities became apparent. In both documents, the letter *a* was twisted on its axis, leaning slightly to the left, and on the lowercase *i* a portion of the serif was broken off along the bottom. Additionally, the lowercase *e, o, a,* and *d* were dirty and tended to print as filled dots instead of circles, suggestive of an old-fashioned fabric ribbon. On my portable Smith-Corona, I'd been known to use a straight pin to clean the clogged typewriter keys.

I left the letters on my desk and took a walk around the room. Then I sat down in my swivel chair, opened my pencil drawer, and pulled out a pack of index cards. It took me fifteen minutes to jot down the facts as I remembered them, one piece of information per card until I'd exhausted my store. I laid them out on my desk, rearranging the order, shuffling them into columns, looking for connections I hadn't seen before. It didn't amount to much from my perspective, but there'd soon be more information available. The autopsy was done by now and the medical examiner would have a concrete opinion about the manner and cause of death. We were all assuming Guy died from blunt-force trauma to the head, but there might be some underlying pathology. Maybe he'd died of a heart attack, maybe he'd been poisoned, expiring in his sleep before the first blow was struck. I couldn't help but wonder what difference any of it made. Guy would be laid to rest, his body probably taken back to Marcella for burial up there. The various forensic experts would go on sifting through the evidence until the case was resolved. Eventually, the story would be told in its entirety and maybe I'd understand then how everything fit. In the meantime, I was left with all the unrelated fragments and a sick feeling in my stomach.

I took the letters down the hall, the one still encased in its plastic sleeve. At the Xerox machine, I made a copy of each so that I now had two sets. The copies I placed in my briefcase, along with the notes I'd made on my index cards. The originals I locked away carefully in my bottom drawer. When the phone rang, I let the answering machine pick up. "Kinsey, this is Christie Malek. Listen, the police were just here with a warrant for Jack's arrest—"

I snatched up the receiver. "Christie? It's me. What's going on?"

"Oh, Kinsey. Thank God. I'm sorry to bother you, but I didn't know what else to do. I put a call through to Donovan, but he's out in the field. I don't know where Bennet's gone. He left about nine, without a word to anyone. Do you know the name of a good bail bondsman? Jack told me to get him one, but I've looked in the Yellow Pages and can't tell one from the other."

"Are you sure he's in custody? They didn't just take him to the station for another interview?"

"Kinsey, they put him in *handcuffs*. They read him his rights and took him off in the back of an unmarked car. We were both in shock. I don't have any money— less than a hundred bucks in cash—but if I knew who to call . . ."

"Forget about the bondsman. If Jack's being charged with murder, it's a no-bail warrant. What he needs is a good criminal attorney and the sooner the better."

"I don't know any attorneys, except Tasha!" she

shrieked. "What am I supposed to do, pick a name out of a *hat?*"

"Wait a minute, Christie. Just calm down."

"I don't want to calm down. I'm scared. I want help."

"I know that. I know. Just wait a minute," I said. "I have a suggestion. Lonnie Kingman's office is right next door to mine. You want me to go see if he's in? You can't do better than Lonnie. He's a champ."

She was silent for an instant. "All right, yes. I've heard of him. That sounds good."

"Give me a few minutes and we'll see what we can do."

SIXTEEN

I caught Lonnie's secretary, Ida Ruth, on her way back from the kitchen with a coffeepot in hand. I hooked a thumb in the direction of Lonnie's door. "Is he in there?"

"He's eating breakfast. Help yourself."

I tapped on the door and then opened it, peering in. Lonnie was sitting at his desk with an oversized plastic container of some kind of chalky-looking protein drink. I could see bubbles of dried powder floating on the surface and the barest suggestion of a milky mustache on Lonnie's upper lip. From assorted bottles, he'd emptied out a pile of vitamins and nutritional supplements, and he was popping down pills between sips of a shake so thick it might have been melted ice cream. One of the gel caps was the size and the color of a stone in a topaz dinner ring. He swallowed it as though he were doing a magic trick.

Lonnie more nearly resembles a bouncer than an attorney. He's short and stocky—five feet four, two hundred four pounds—bulging with muscles from his twenty years of power lifting. He's got one of those revved-up metabolisms that burns calories like crazy and he radiates high energy along with body heat. His speech is staccato and he's generally amped up on coffee, anxiety, or lack of sleep. I've heard people claim he's on the sauce—shooting anabolic steroids in concert with all the iron he pumps. Personally, I doubt it. He's been manic for the whole nine years of our acquaintance and I've never seen him exhibit any of the rage or aggression allegedly generated by extended steroid use. He's married to a woman with a black belt in karate and she's never once complained about testicles shriveled to the size of raisins, another unhappy side effect of steroid abuse.

His usually shaggy hair had been trimmed and subdued. His dress shirt was pulled tightly across his shoulders and biceps. I don't know his neck size, but he claims a tie makes him feel he's on the brink of being hanged. The one he was wearing was pulled askew, his collar unbuttoned, and his suit jacket off. He'd hung it neatly from a hanger hooked through the handle of a file drawer. His shirt was spanking white, but badly wrinkled, and he had rolled up the sleeves. Sometimes he wears a vest to conceal his rumpled state, but not today. He swallowed the last of a palmful of pills, holding up a hand to indicate that he was aware of me. He chugged off the balance of his protein drink and shook his head with satisfaction. "Whew, that's good."

"Are you tied up at the moment?"

"Not at all. Come on in."

I entered the office and closed the door behind me. "I just got a call from Christie Malek. Have you been following that story?"

"The murder? Who hasn't? Sit, sit, sit. I'm not due in court until two P.M. What's up?"

"Jack Malek's been arrested and needs to talk to an attorney. I told Christie I'd see if you were interested." I took a seat in one of two black leather client chairs.

"When was he picked up?"

"Fifteen or twenty minutes ago, I'd guess."

Lonnie began to screw the lids back on the motley collection of bottles sitting on his desk. "What's the deal? Fill me in."

I brought him up to speed on the case as succinctly as possible. This was our first conversation about the murder and I wanted him to have as thorough an understanding as I could muster on short notice. As I spoke, I could see Lonnie's gears engage and the wheels start to turn. I was saying, "Last I heard—this was from the housekeeper—Guy and Jack quarreled after hours of heavy drinking and Jack went off to a pairings' party at the country club."

"I wonder how the cops are gonna bust that one. You'd think at least half a dozen people would have seen him there." Lonnie shot a glance at his watch and began to roll his sleeves down. "I'll pop on over to the station house and see what's going on. I hope Jack has sense enough to keep his mouth shut until I get there."

He pushed away from his desk and took his suit jacket from the hanger. He shrugged himself into it, secured his collar button, and slid his tie into place. Now he looked more like a lawyer, albeit a short, beefy one. "By the way, where does Jack fit? He the oldest or the youngest?"

"The youngest. Donovan's the oldest. He runs the company. Bennet's in the middle. I wouldn't rule him out if you're looking to divert suspicion. He was the most vocal in his opposition to Guy's claim on the estate. You want me to do anything before you get back?"

"Tell Christie I'll be in touch as soon as I've talked to him. In the meantime, go on over to the house. Let's put together a list of witnesses who can confirm Tuesday night. The cops find the murder weapon?"

"They must have. I know they did a grid search of the property because I saw 'em doing it. And Christie says they carted off all kinds of things."

"Once I finish with Jack, I'll have a chat with the cops and find out why they think he's good for this. It'd be nice to have some idea what we're up against."

"Am I officially on the clock?"

He looked at his watch. "Go."

"The usual rates?"

"Sure. Unless you want to work for free. Of course, it's always possible Jack won't hire me."

"Don't be silly. The man's desperate," I said. I caught Lonnie's look and amended my claim. "Well, you know what I mean. He's not hiring you because he's desperate—"

"Get out of here," Lonnie said, smiling.

Briefcase in hand, I hiked back over to the public parking lot, where I retrieved my car. My attitude toward Jack Malek had already undergone a shift. Whether Jack was guilty or innocent, Lonnie would hustle up every shred of exculpatory evidence and plot, plan, maneuver, and strategize to establish his defense. I was no particular fan of Jack's, but working for Lonnie Kingman I'd be kept in the loop.

*

As I approached the Maleks', I was relieved to see that the roadway on either side of the estate was virtually deserted. The shoulder was churned with tire prints, the ground strewn with cigarette stubs, empty cups, crumpled paper napkins, and fast-food containers. The area outside the gate had the look of abandonment, as if a traveling circus had packed up and crept away at first light. The press had all but disappeared, following the patrol car taking Jack to County Jail. For Jack, it was the beginning of a process in which he'd be photographed, frisked, booked, fingerprinted, and placed in a holding cell. I'd been through the process myself about a year ago and the sense of contamination was still vivid. The facility itself is clean and freshly painted, but institutional nonetheless; no-frills linoleum and government-issue furniture built to endure hard wear. In my brush with them, the jail officers were civil, pleasant, and businesslike, but I'd felt diminished by every aspect of the procedure, from the surrender of my personal possessions to the subsequent confinement in the drunk tank. I can still remember the musky smell in the air, mixing with the odors of stale mattresses, dirty armpits, and bourbon fumes being exhaled. As far as I knew, Jack had never been arrested and I suspected he'd feel as demoralized as I had.

As I drove the VW up to the gate, a hired security guard stepped forward, blocking my progress until I identified myself. He waved me on and I eased up the driveway into the cobblestone courtyard. The house was bathed in sunlight, the grounds dappled with shade. The old, sprawling oak trees stretched away on all sides, creating a hazy landscape as if done in watercolors.

Tones of green and gray seemed to bleed into one another with the occasional spare sapling providing sharp contrast. I could see two gardeners at work; one with a leaf blower, one with a rake. The sounds of machinery suggested that branches were being trimmed somewhere out of sight. The air smelled of mulch and eucalyptus. There was no sign of the search team and no uniformed officer posted at the front door. To all intents and purposes, life had reverted to normal.

Christie must have been watching, perhaps hoping for Donovan. Before I was even out of the car, she'd come onto the porch and down the steps, walking in my direction. She wore a white T-shirt and dark blue wraparound skirt, her arms folded in front of her as though for comfort. The sheen in her dark hair had faded to a dull patina, like cheap floor wax on hardwood. Her face showed little of her emotions except for a thin crease, like a hairline crack, that had appeared between her eyes. "I heard the car on the drive and thought it might be Bennet or Donovan. Lord, I'm glad to see you. I've been going crazy here by myself."

"You still haven't gotten through to Donovan?"

"I left word at the office, saying it was urgent. I didn't want to blab all our business to his secretary. I've been waiting by the phone, but so far I haven't heard a word from him. Who knows where Bennet is? What about Lonnie Kingman? Did you talk to him?"

I filled her in on Lonnie's intentions. "Have the police unsealed the bedroom?"

"Not yet. I meant to ask about that when they showed up this morning. I thought they came to *do* something up there. Take photographs or measure or move the furniture. I never imagined they were here to arrest anyone. I wish you could have seen Jack. He was scared to death."

"I'm not surprised. What about you? How are you holding up?"

"I'm antsy. And feel my fingers. They're as cold as ice. I catch myself pacing, half the time jabbering away. This is all so unreal. We may have problems, but we don't kill one another. It's ridiculous. I don't understand what's going on. Everything was fine and now this." She seemed to shudder, not from cold, but from tension and anxiety. In the wake of Jack's arrest, she'd clearly erased all her earlier complaints.

I followed her around the front and into the house. The foyer felt chilly and again I was struck by the shabbiness. A wall sconce hung awry. In the hanging chandelier, several flame-shaped bulbs were missing and some were tilted like crooked teeth. The tapestries along the wall were genuine, faded and worn, depicting acts of debauchery and cruelty picked out in thread. I felt my gaze pulled irresistibly toward the stairs, but the landing above was empty and there was no unusual sound to set my teeth on edge. The house was curiously quiet, given events of the past few days. These people didn't seem to have friends rushing in with offers of help. I wasn't aware of anyone bringing food or calling to ask if there was anything to be done. Maybe the Maleks were the sort who didn't invite such familiarities. Whatever the reason, it looked like they were coping without the comfort of friends.

Christie was still chatting, processing Jack's arrest. I've noticed that people tend to drone on and on when they're unnerved. "When I saw Detective Robb on the doorstep, I honestly thought they were coming with information and then they asked if Jack was in and I still didn't think anything about it. I don't even know what's supposed to happen next."

We moved into the library, where I sank into a club chair and Christie paced the floor. I said, "I guess it depends on what he's charged with and if bail's been set. Once he's booked in, the DA has twenty-four hours to file his case. Jack has to be arraigned within forty-eight hours, excluding Sundays and holidays, of course. So this is what, Thursday? They'll probably take him before a magistrate today or tomorrow."

"What's arraignment? What does that mean? I don't know the first thing. I've never known anyone who's been arrested, let alone charged with *murder*."

"Arraignment's the process by which he's formally charged. They'll take him into court and identify him as the person named in the warrant. He'll be told the nature of the charges against him and he'll be asked to plead guilty, not guilty, or no contest."

"And then what?"

"That's up to Lonnie. If he thinks the evidence is weak, he'll demand a preliminary hearing without waiving time. That means within ten court days—two weeks—they'll have to have him in there for a prelim. For that, the prosecuting attorney's present, the defendant and his counsel, the clerk, and the investigating officer, blah, blah, blah. Witnesses are sworn in and testimony's taken. At the end of it, if it appears either that no public offense has been committed or that there's not sufficient cause to believe the defendant's guilty, then he's discharged. On the other hand, if there's sufficient evidence to show the offense has been committed and sufficient cause to believe the defendant's guilty, then he's held to answer. An information's filed—that's a formal, written accusation—in Superior Court, he enters a plea, and the matter's set for trial. There's usually a lot of bullshit thrown in, but that's essentially what happens."

She paused in her pacing and turned to stare at me, aghast. "And Jack's in *jail* all this time?"

"He's not allowed to post bail on a homicide."

"Oh my God."

"Christie, I've been in jail myself. It's not the end of the world. The company's not that great and the food's off the charts when it comes to fat content—hey, no wonder I liked it," I added in an aside.

"It isn't funny."

"Who's being funny? It's the truth," I said. "There are worse things in life. Jack might not like it, but he'll survive."

She reached out and placed a hand on the mantelpiece to steady herself. "Sorry. I'm really sorry. I didn't mean to snap at you."

"You better have a seat."

She did as I suggested, perching on the edge of the chair next to mine. "You must have come for some reason. I never even asked what it was."

"Lonnie was hoping you'd know who was at the club that night. We need someone who can verify Jack's presence at the pairings' party."

"That shouldn't be too hard. I guess the police are already talking to people at the country club. I'm not sure what the deal is on that. I've gotten two calls this morning, one from Paul Trasatti, who says he needs to talk to Jack, like pronto."

"Were they together Tuesday night?"

"Yes. Jack picked him up and took him to the club. I'm sure they sat at the same table. Paul can give you the names of the other eight sitting with them. This is all so crazy. How can they possibly think Jack's guilty of anything? There must have been tons of people there that night."

"What's Paul's number?"

"I don't know. It's got to be in the book. I'll go look it up."

"Don't worry about it. I can check that out in a bit. Once he confirms Jack's alibi, it should go a long way."

Christie made a face. " 'Alibi.' God, I can't stand the word. Alibi implies you're guilty and you've cooked up some story to cover your ass."

"Can I use your phone?"

"I'd prefer it if you'd wait until Donovan or Bennet check in. I want to keep the line free until I hear from them. I hope you don't mind."

"Not at all," I said. "You mentioned the police picking up some items. Do you have any idea what they took?"

She leaned her elbows on her knees and put her hands across her eyes. "They left a copy of the warrant and a list of items seized. I know it's around here somewhere, but I haven't seen it yet. Donovan went down to the pool house as soon as they left. He says they took a lot of sports equipment—golf clubs and baseball bats."

I winced, thinking of the impact of such items on the human skull. Switching the subject, I asked, "What about Bennet? Where was he that night?"

"He went back to the restaurant he's remodeling, to see what the workers had done that day. Construction's been a nightmare and he spends a lot of time down there."

"Did anybody see him?"

"You'd have to ask him," she said. "Donovan and I were here. We'd had quite a lot to drink at dinner and I went straight to bed." There was a marked tremor in the hand Christie was running through her hair.

"Have you had anything to eat?"

"I couldn't touch a bite. I'm too anxious."

"Well, you ought to have *something*. Is Enid here yet?"

"I think so."

"Let me check in the kitchen and have her make you a cup of tea. You should have a cookie or a piece of fruit. You look awful."

"I feel awful," she said.

I left her in the library and headed down the hall. I couldn't believe I'd put myself on tea detail again, but simply being in the house made me tense. Any activity helped. Besides, I didn't want to pass up the chance to talk to Enid if she was on the premises.

"Me again," I said when I entered the kitchen.

She was standing at the island with a cutting board in front of her, smashing garlic with the blade of a Chinese cleaver. She was wrapped in a white apron with a white cotton scarf around her head, looking as round and as squeezable as a roll of toilet paper. While I watched, she laid down assorted sizes of unpeeled cloves, placed the wide blade on top of them, and pounded once with her fist. I could feel myself flinch. If the blade were angled incorrectly, she was going to end up whacking down on it with the outer aspect of her own hand, hacking straight to the bone. I stopped in my tracks. With her eyes pinned on me politely, she repeated the process, fist smashing down. She lifted the blade. Under it, the hapless garlic had been crushed like albino cockroaches, the peel sliding off with the flick of a knife tip.

"I thought I'd fix Christie a cup of tea," I said. "She needs something in her system—do you have a piece of fruit?"

Enid pointed at the refrigerator. "There are grapes in there. Tea bags up in the cabinet. I'd do it myself, but I'm trying to get this sauce under way. If you set up a tray, I'll take it in to her."

"No problem. You go right ahead."

She leaned to her left and slid open a compartment in which the trays were stored, pulling out a teak server with a rim around the edge. She placed it on the marble counter next to six big cans of crushed tomatoes, two cans of tomato paste, a basket of yellow onions, and a can of olive oil. On the stove top, I noticed a stainless steel stockpot.

I moved over to the cabinet and removed a mug, pausing to fill the electric kettle as I'd seen Myrna do. I glanced at Enid casually. "You have paper napkins somewhere?"

"Third drawer on the right."

I found the napkins and placed one, along with a

teaspoon, on the tray. "I take it you heard about Jack's arrest."

She nodded assent. "I was coming in the gate just as they were taking him away. I wish you could have seen the look on his face."

I shook my head regretfully, as if I gave a shit. "Poor thing," I said. "It seems so unfair." I hoped I hadn't laid it on too thick, but I needn't have worried.

"The police were asking about his running shoes," she said. "Something about a pattern on the soles—so there must have been bloody footprints in the bedroom where Guy was killed."

"Really," I replied, trying to disguise my startlement. Apparently, she felt no reluctance about discussing the family's business. I'd thought I'd have to be cunning, but she didn't seem to share Myrna's reservations about tattling. "They picked up the shoes yesterday?"

"No. They called me this morning at home. Before I left for work."

"Lieutenant Robb?"

"The other one. The woman. She's a cold fish, I must say. I hope she's not a friend of yours."

"I only met her this morning when I went in to be interviewed."

She flicked me a look as if taking my measure. "Myrna tells me you're a detective. I've seen 'em on the TV of course, but I never met one in real life."

"Now you have," I said. "In fact, I work in the same firm as Jack's attorney, Lonnie Kingman. He's on his way over to the station house to talk to Jack." I was anxious to press her on the matter of the shoes, but worried she would clam up if I seemed too intent.

She dropped her eyes to her work. She was tapping the Chinese cleaver in a rapid little dance that reduced all the garlic to the size of rice grains. "They searched for the shoes all day yesterday. You've never seen anything like it. Going through all the closets and trash cans, digging in the flowerbeds."

I made a little mouth noise of interest. It was clear Enid had an avid interest in all the trappings of police work.

She said, "They told me I was actually the one who put 'em on the right track. Of course, I had no idea the shoes would turn out to be Jack's. I feel terrible about that. Myrna's beside herself. She feels so guilty about mentioning the quarrel."

"It must have been a shock about the shoes," I prodded.

"Jack's my favorite among the boys. I came to work here twenty-five years ago. This was my first job and I didn't expect to stay long."

"You were hired as a nanny?"

"The boys were too old for that. I was more like a companion for Mrs. Malek," she said. "I never trained as a cook. I simply learned as I went along. Mrs. Malek—Rona—was beginning to fail and she was in and out of the hospital all the time back then. Mr. Malek needed someone to run the house in her absence. Jack was in junior high school and he was pretty much at loose ends. He used to sit out in the kitchen with me, hardly saying a word. I'd bake a batch of cookies and he'd eat a whole plate just as fast as he could. He was really like a little kid. I knew what he was hungry for was his mother's praise and attention, but she was much too sick. I did what I could, but it nearly broke my heart."

"And Guy was how old?"

She shrugged. "Eighteen, nineteen. He'd already given them years of aggravation and grief. I never saw anything like him for the trouble he made. It was one scrape after another."

"How did he and Jack get along?"

"I think Jack admired and romanticized him. They didn't pal around together, but there was always a certain amount of hero worship. Jack thought Guy was like James Dean, rebellious and tragic, you know, misunderstood. They never had all that much to do with one another, but I can remember how Jack used to look at him. Now, Bennet and Jack, they were close. The two younger boys tended to gravitate to one another. I never had much use for Bennet. Something sneaky about him."

"What about Donovan?"

"He was the smartest of the four. Even then he had a good head for business, always calculating the odds. When I first came to work, he'd already been off to college and was planning to come back and work for his dad full-time. Donovan loves that company more than any man alive. As for Guy, he was the troublemaker. That seemed to be his role."

"You really think Jack might have been involved in Guy's death?"

"I hate to believe it but I know he felt Guy broke faith with him. Jack's a fanatic about loyalty. He always was."

"Well, that's interesting," I said. "Because the first

time I was here, he said much the same thing. He was off at college when Guy left, wasn't he?"

Enid was shaking her head. "That wouldn't have mattered. Not to him. Somehow, in Jack's mind, when Guy went off on his great adventure, he should have taken him along."

"So he saw Guy's departure as betrayal."

"Well, of course he did. Jack's terribly dependent. He's never had a job. He's never even had a girl. He has no self-esteem to speak of and for that, I blame his dad. Bader never took the time to teach them they were worth anything. I mean, look at the reality. None of them has ever left home."

"It couldn't be healthy."

"It's disgraceful. Grown men?" She opened the can of olive oil and poured a short stream in the stockpot while she turned up the flame. She moved the cutting board from the counter and balanced the edge of it on the pot, sliding garlic across the surface. The sound of sizzling arose, followed moments later by a cloud of garlic-scented steam.

"What's the story on the shoes? Where did they turn up?"

She paused to adjust the flame and then returned the board to the counter, where she picked up an onion. The peeling was as fragile as paper, crackling slightly as she worked. "At the bottom of a box. You remember the cartons of Bader's clothing Christie packed away? They were sitting on the front porch. The Thrift Store Industries truck stopped by for an early-morning pickup first thing yesterday."

"Before the body was discovered?"

"Before anyone was even up. I don't know how I connected it. I saw the receipt lying on the counter and didn't think much about it. Later, it occurred to me—if the shoes weren't on the premises, they must be somewhere else."

"How'd you figure out where they were?"

"Well, that's just it. I was loading the dishwasher, you know, humming a little tune and boom, I just knew."

"I've done the same thing. It's almost like the mind makes an independent leap."

Enid flashed me a look. "Exactly. He must have realized he left a shoe print on the carpeting upstairs."

"Did you see it yourself?"

"No, but Myrna says she saw it when she went in Guy's room." She paused, shaking her head. "I don't want to think he did it."

"It *is* hard to believe," I said. "I mean, in essence, he must have killed Guy, seen the footprint, slipped off his shoes and shoved them in the box on his way out of the house. He was lucky—or thought he was."

"You don't sound convinced."

"I just have trouble with the notion. Jack doesn't strike me as that decisive or quick. Doesn't that bother you?"

She thought about that briefly and then gave a shrug of dismissal. "A killer would have to depend on luck, I guess. You can't plan for everything. You'd have to ad-lib."

"Well, it backfired in this case."

"If he did it," she said. She picked up a can and tilted it into the electric opener. She pressed a lever and watched as the can went round and round, rotating blades neatly separating the lid from the can. Kitchens are dangerous, I thought idly as I looked on. What an arsenal—knives and fire and all that kitchen twine, skewers, meat pounders, and rolling pins. The average woman must spend a fair portion of her time happily contemplating the tools of her trade: devices that crush, pulverize, grind, and puree; utensils that pierce, slice, dissect, and debone; not to mention the household products that, once ingested, are capable of eradicating human life along with germs.

Her eyes came up to mine. "Do you believe in ghosts?"

"No, of course not. What makes you ask?"

She glanced toward the corner of the kitchen where I noticed, for the first time, a staircase. "Yesterday I went upstairs to put some linens away. There was a Presence in the hall. I wondered if you believed in them."

I shook my head in the negative, remembering the chill in the air and the roaring in my ears.

"This one smells of animal, something damp and unclean. It's very strange," she said.

SEVENTEEN

I left the Maleks' shortly after one o'clock. Driving home, I spotted a pay phone at a corner gas station. I pulled in and parked. Outside the service bay, a group of kids from the local alternative high school had organized a car wash. According to the hand-lettered sign, the price was $5.00 and proceeds were being used to pay f-- a trip to San Francisco. There was not a customer in sight. Buckets of soapy water waited at the ready and the kids milled around in a manner that suggested they were about to spray one another down with hoses. With luck, I wouldn't end up in the line of fire.

I looked up Paul Trasatti in the telephone book. There were two numbers listed; one a residence on Hopper Road, the other—with no address—simply said Paul Trasatti, Rare Books. I found a handful of loose change at the bottom of my handbag and fed coins into the slots. I dialed the business number first, thinking it more likely I'd catch him at his desk. Trasatti answered before the phone on his end had finished ringing the first time.

"Trasatti," he said, tersely. He sounded like a man

who'd been waiting for a call regarding drop-off instructions for the ransom money.

"Mr. Trasatti, my name is Kinsey Millhone. I'm a private investigator, working with Jack Malek's attorney. You knew he'd been arrested?"

"I heard about that this morning. I called to talk to Jack and his sister-in-law told me they'd just taken him away. Did she tell you to call?"

"Well, no. Not really. I—"

"How'd you get my number?"

"I looked you up in the telephone book. I need information and I thought maybe you could help."

"What kind of information?"

"I'll be talking to Lonnie Kingman and I know he'll want to hear about Jack's activities that night."

"Why can't he ask Jack?"

"I'm sure he will," I said, "but we're going to need someone who can verify Jack's claims. Christie says he drove you over to the country club Tuesday evening. Is that true?"

There was a fractional hesitation. "That's right. He picked me up after dinner. Truth is, I ended up trading places with him, so I was the one driving. He was too tipsy. This is strictly off the record, right?"

"I'm not a journalist, but sure. We can keep it off the record, at least for now," I said. "Tipsy, meaning drunk?"

"Let's just say I was the designated driver in this case."

I closed my eyes, listening for the subtext, while cars passed back and forth on the street behind me. "Were you seated at the same table?"

"Tables were reserved. We had assigned seats," he said. He was being as cagey as a politician. What was going on here?

"That's not what I asked. I'm wondering if you can verify his presence at the pairings' party."

A brief, most curious silence ensued. "Can I ask you a question?" he said.

"What's that?"

"If you're working for this attorney . . . what'd you say his name was?"

"Lonnie Kingman."

"Okay, this Kingman fellow. I know he can't repeat anything said between him and Jack, but what about you? Does the same thing apply to you?"

"Our conversation isn't privileged, if that's what you want to know. Anything relevant to Jack's defense, I'll be reporting to Lonnie. That's my job. I *can* be trusted with information. Otherwise, I'd be out of business by now," I said. "Were you sitting with Jack?"

"See, that's what the police have been asking me," he said. His mouth must have been dry because I could practically hear him lick his lips before he spoke. "Jack's a good friend and I don't want to get him in any more trouble than he's in. I've done everything I could short of telling lies."

"You don't want to lie to the cops," I said. Maybe the line was tapped and they were checking my attitude.

"Well, no, I wouldn't. And that's just it," he said. "I didn't come right out and say so, but there was a stretch when Jack was, you know, uhm, off somewhere. What I mean is, I couldn't say he was right there in my line of sight."

"Uhn-hun. How long a stretch?"

"Might have been as much as an hour and a half. I didn't think anything of it at the time, but you know, later—like when this other business came up—I did wonder about the time frame. I wouldn't want to be quoted, but just between us."

"Do you know where he was?"

"I know where he *said* he was. Out walking the tenth hole."

"In the *dark*?"

"That's not as odd as it sounds. I've done the same thing myself. Smokers go outside to have a cigarette sometimes. Most club members know the course by heart so it's not as if you're likely to get lost or fall down a hole."

"But why would he do that in the middle of a pairings' party?"

"He was upset—I'd say real upset—when he came to pick me up. That's another reason I insisted on driving. Jack tends to be careless about things like that."

"Did he say what upset him?" I waited. "I can keep it to myself," I said.

"He said him and Guy got into an argument."

"About what?"

"Probably the money. I'd say the money."

"You're talking about the money Guy was due to inherit."

"That's right."

"So Jack was drunk and upset and when the two of you arrived at the club, he disappeared."

"Uhn-hun."

"Did you believe him?"

"About taking a walk? More or less. I mean, it makes sense—you know, if he was trying to sober up and cool off."

"And *did* he seem cooler when he got back?"

For a moment, I thought the line went dead. "Mr. Trasatti?"

"I'm here. See, the thing is, he didn't actually get back in time to give me a ride. I had to find someone else."

"And that's what you told the police?"

"Well, I had to. I felt bad, but they were real persistent and it's like you said, I couldn't *lie.*"

"Was his car still there?"

"I think so. I couldn't swear to it. I thought I saw it in the parking lot when I was set to go, but I might have been mistaken."

"But you're sure there was no sign of Jack?"

"That's right. A friend of mine said he saw him take off across the fairway at the first hole. Then this other fellow ended up giving me a ride home."

"Can I have both those names?" I cocked one shoulder, anchoring the handset against my ear while I fumbled in my bag for a pen and a scrap of paper. I made a note of the names, neither of which rang a bell. "And how did you find out where Jack had been?"

"He called first thing the next morning to apologize and that's when he explained."

"He called Wednesday morning?"

"I just said that."

"I wanted to make sure I understood you correctly. Do you remember what time he called?"

"About eight, I guess."

"So this was before anyone knew Guy Malek was dead."

"Must've been. I know Jack never mentioned it. You'd think if he knew he'd have spoken up."

"Is there anything else you remember from your conversation with him?"

"Not that I can think of. I probably got him in enough trouble as it is. I hope you won't tell him I told you all this."

"I doubt I'll have occasion to talk to Jack," I said. "I appreciate your help. You may hear from Lonnie Kingman or me again on this." You're certainly going to end up on the witness stand, I thought.

"I guess it can't be helped," he said glumly, as if reading my mind. He disconnected before I could press him for anything else.

I checked the pile of change I'd laid on the shelf near the coin box. I dropped more coins in the slot and dialed Lonnie's private line. He picked up on his end without identifying himself.

"This is Kinsey," I said. "How'd it go?"

"Don't let me handle any sharps. I might open a vein."

"You heard about the shoes?"

"Did I ever," he said. "Lieutenant Robb delivered the happy news with glee."

"I take it the pattern on the sole matched the print at the scene."

"Oh, sure. And to make things even better, he says the lab found bits and pieces of Guy Malek's brain spattered on the instep. I mean, Jesus, how's Jack going to explain a fleck of brain matter buried in the eyelet of his shoes? This is not like 'Oh gee fellas, Guy-accidentally-cut-himself-and-must-have-bled-on-me.' "

"What'd Jack have to say?"

"I haven't had a chance to ask. Once he invoked, the cops hustled him out to County Jail for booking. I'm going out there later and have a long chat with him. He'll probably tell me the shoes were stolen. Oh yeah, right."

"What about the murder weapon?"

"They found a baseball bat shoved in with a bunch of sports equipment down at the pool house. Somebody'd made a clumsy attempt to wipe it clean, but traces of blood were still on the hitting area. At least there were no prints, so we can thank God for small favors. What about his alibi? I hope you're going to tell me a hundred club members had an eye on him at all times."

"No such luck," I said. I laid out the sequence of events as Paul Trasatti had reported them.

I could hear Lonnie sigh. "Too bad Jack wasn't out there screwing somebody's wife. You have a theory, I'm sure."

"He could have left the club on foot. There are half a dozen places near the road where he could've climbed the fence."

"And then what?" Lonnie said. "The country club is miles from the Malek estate. How's he going to get from there to the house again without somebody seeing him?"

"Lonnie, I hate to tell you this, but the man has a Harley-Davidson. He could have hidden his motorcycle earlier. The house might be an hour away on foot, but it's only ten minutes by car."

"But so what? Where was Bennet that night? And what about Donovan? He was right there on the premises when the murder occurred."

"I can talk to Bennet this afternoon."

"Did anybody see Jack climb the fence? I doubt it. Anybody see the Harley during the period we're discussing?"

"I can check it out," I said.

"I know the line the cops are taking. They're saying Jack's room adjoined Guy's. All he had to do was slip from one room to the other, bash his brains out, and slip back again."

"Not that simple," I said. "Don't forget he's got to hide the shoes at the bottom of the thrift box, wipe the blood off the bat, and return it to the pool house before he hightails it back to the country club."

"Good point. Is there a guardhouse at the club? Someone might have noted what time he left."

"I'll pop over there and check. I can also clock the time it takes to get from there to the house and back."

"Hold off on that. We'll get to that eventually. For now, let's focus on finding someone else to blame."

"That shouldn't be too hard. I mean, Jack's not the only one with access to Guy's room. Anybody in the house could have entered the same way. The cops have the murder weapon, but from what you've said, they don't have Jack's fingerprints."

"Yeah, they can't find anybody else's either."

"So how are they going to prove Jack was wielding the damn thing? Maybe he was framed."

Lonnie snorted in my ear. "Somebody'd have to take a pair of forceps and fuckin' *tweeze* up brain material,

281

then tiptoe into Jack's room, find the shoes in the closet, and deposit all the little brainy bits."

"It's always possible, though, isn't it?"

"It's possible Santa Claus came down the chimney and did the deed himself. Stinks. The whole thing stinks."

"I like the idea about eyewitnesses. So far it doesn't sound like there's anyone who can place him at the murder scene."

"Not so far, no, but I'm sure the cops are out scouring the neighborhood."

"Well, then we'll scour some, too."

"You're such an optimist," he said.

I laughed. "Actually, I can't believe I'm standing here defending him. I don't even like Jack."

"We're not paid to like him. We're being paid to get him out of this," Lonnie said.

"I'll do what I can."

"I know you will."

Before I left the service station, I paused long enough to pull up to the pump so I could fill my gas tank. On the hood of my car, the early-morning dew had now combined with the dust from Monday's Santa Ana winds. My former VW was dingy beige and never showed dirt. With this snappy 1974 model, the streaks were more conspicuous, rivulets of pale blue cutting through a speckled patina of soot. A bird had passed its judgment on the hood as well. I paid for the gas and then turned the key in the ignition, peered over my right shoulder, and backed up into the area where the car wash was being held. The kids began to whistle and clap, and I found myself smiling at their enthusiasm.

I stood to one side while one of them crawled inside with a bottle of window cleaner. Another fired up the Shop-Vac and began to suck grit off the floor mats. A crew of three were sudsing down the outside, all of them towering over the vehicle. The kid with the Shop-Vac finished cleaning the interior and I watched him approach from the far side of the car with an envelope in hand. He held it out to me. "Have you been looking for this?"

"Where did that come from?"

"I found it beside the passenger seat in front. Looks like it slipped down in the crevice."

"Thanks." I took the envelope, half expecting to see the now-familiar typeface. Instead, my name was scrawled across the front in ballpoint pen. I waited until the kid had moved away and then I opened the envelope and removed the single sheet of paper. The message was handwritten in black ink; the penmanship distinct, a peculiar blend of cursive and printing. I flicked a glance at the signature. *Guy Malek*. I could feel ice crystals forming between my shoulder blades.

Monday night. Waiting for you to show.

Hey K . . .

Sure hope I have the nerve to pass you this note. I guess I must have if you're reading it. I haven't asked a girl on a date since I was fifteen years old and that didn't work out so hot. I got a big zit on my chin and spent the whole evening trying to think up excuses to keep my face turned the other way.

Anyway, here goes.

Once this family mess is settled, would you like to take off for a day and go to Disneyland with me? We could eat snowcones and do Pirates of the Caribbean and then take the boat ride through Small World singing that song you can't get out of your head for six months afterward. I could use some silliness in my life and so could you.

Think on't and let me know so I can stock up on Clearasil.

Guy Malek

P.S. Just for the record, if anything should happen to me, make sure my share of Dad's estate goes to Jubilee Evangelical Church. I really love those folk.

By the time I finished reading, my eyes had filled with tears. This was like a message from the dead. I stared off across the street, blinking rapidly. I could feel pain in my chest and my facial features were instantly defined by heat as my nasal passages seized up. I wondered if grief had the capacity to suffocate. In conjunction with the sorrow came a rush of pure rage. I sent Guy my thoughts across the Ether. I'm going to find out who killed you and I'm going to find out why. I swear I will do this. I swear it.

"Miss? Your car's ready."

I took a deep breath. "Thanks. It looks great." I gave

the kid ten bucks and took off with the radio cranked up full blast.

When I got home, I spotted Robert Dietz's little red Porsche parked out in front of my apartment. I set my briefcase on the pavement while I stood at the curb and studied it, afraid to believe. He'd told me he was going to be gone two weeks. This was just coming up on one. I circled the car and checked the license plate, which read DIETZ. I picked up my briefcase and let myself in the gate. I rounded the corner and unlocked my door. Dietz's suitcase was sitting beside the couch. His garment bag was hooked across the top of the bathroom door.

I said, "Dietz?"

No response.

I left my handbag and the briefcase on the counter and crossed the patio to Henry's, where I peered in the kitchen window. Dietz was sitting in Henry's rocking chair, his pant leg pulled up to expose his injured knee. The swelling had visibly diminished and from various gestures he was making, it seemed safe to guess he'd had the fluid drained out of it. Even his pantomime of a hypodermic needle being stuck into his flesh made my palms start to sweat. At first he didn't see me. It was like watching a silent movie, the two men earnestly engrossed in medical matters. Henry, at eighty-five, was so familiar to me—handsome, good-hearted, lean, intelligent. Dietz was constructed along sturdier lines—solid, tough, stubborn, impulsive, just as smart as Henry, but more streetwise than intellectual. I found myself smiling at the two of them. Where Henry was mild, Dietz was restless and rough, without artifice. I valued his honesty, distrusted his concern, resented his wanderlust, and yearned for definition in our relationship. In the midst of all the heaviness I felt, Dietz was leavening.

He glanced up, spotting me. He raised a hand in greeting without rising from the chair.

Henry crossed to the door and let me in. Dietz lowered his pant leg with a brief aside to me about a walk-in medical clinic up in Santa Cruz. Henry offered coffee, but Dietz declined. I don't even remember now what the three of us talked about. In the course of idle chitchat, Dietz put his hand on my elbow, setting off a surge of heat. Out of the corner of my eye, I caught his quizzical look. Whatever I was feeling must have been transmitted through the wires to him. I must have been buzzing like a power line because even Henry's easy flow of conversation seemed to falter and fade. Dietz glanced at his watch, making a startled sound as if late for an appointment. We made our hasty excuses, moving out of Henry's backdoor and across to my place without exchanging a word.

The door closed behind us. The apartment felt cool. Pale sunlight filtered through the shuttered windows in a series of horizontal lines. The interior had the look and the feel of a sailboat: compact, simple, with royal blue canvas chairs, walls of polished teak and oak. Dietz undid the bed in the window bay, easing out of his shoes. I slipped my clothes off, aware of flickering desire as each garment was removed. Dietz's clothes joined mine in a heap on the floor. We sank together, in a rolling motion. The sheets were chill at first, as blue as the sea, warming at contact with our bare limbs. His skin was luminous, as polished as the surface of an abalone shell. Something about the play of shadows infused the air with a watery element, bathing us both in its transparent glow. It felt as if we were swimming in the shallows, as smooth and graceful as a pair of sea otters tumbling through the surf. Our lovemaking played out in silence, except for a humming in his throat now and then. I don't often think of sex as an antidote to pain, but that's what this was and I fully confess—I used intimacy with the one man to offset the loss of the other. It was the only means I could think of to console myself. Even in the moment, what seemed odd to me was the flicker of confusion about which man I betrayed.

Later, I said to Dietz, "Are you hungry? I'm starving."

"I am, too," he said. Gentleman that he was, he'd padded over to the refrigerator where he stood buck naked in a shaft of hot light, contemplating the interior. "How could we be out of food? Don't you eat when I'm gone?"

"There's food," I said defensively.

"A jar of bread-and-butter pickles."

"I can make sandwiches. There's bread in the freezer and half a jar of peanut butter in the cupboard up there."

He gave me a look like I'd suggested cooking up a mess of garden slugs. He closed the refrigerator door and opened the freezer compartment, poking through some cellophane-wrapped packages of meat products covered in ice crystals and suffering from freezer burn. He closed the freezer, returned to the sofa bed, and got under the sheets. "I'm not going to last long. We have to eat," he said.

"I couldn't believe you came back. I thought you were taking the boys off on a trip."

"Turns out they had plans to go camping with friends in Yosemite and didn't know how to tell me. When I read about the murder in the Santa Cruz papers, I told them I needed to drive back. I felt guilty as hell, but they were thrilled to death. Given the perversity of human nature, it pissed me off somehow. They could hardly get me in the car fast enough. I pull away and I'm looking in the rearview mirror. They don't even stop to wave. They're galloping up the outside stairs to grab their sleeping bags."

"You had a few days together."

"And that was good. I enjoyed them," he said. "So tell me about you and what's been happening down here."

Having been through the drill with Lonnie, I laid out events with remarkable efficiency, faltering only slightly in my account of Guy. Even the sound of his name touched a well of sorrow in me.

"You need a game plan," he said, briskly.

I waggled my hand, maybe-so-maybe-not. "Jack will probably be arraigned tomorrow if he hasn't been already."

"Will Lonnie waive time?"

"I have no idea. Probably not."

"Which means he'll insist on a prelim within ten court days. That doesn't give us much time. What about this business of Max Outhwaite? We could try chasing that down."

I noted the "we," but let it sit there unacknowledged. Was he seriously proposing help? "What's to chase?" I asked. "I tried the hall of records and voter registration. Also the city directories. The name's as phony as the address."

"What about the crisscross?"

"I did that."

"Old telephone books?"

"Yeah, I did that, too."

"How far back?"

"Six years."

"Why six? Why not take it all the way back to the year Guy Malek left? Even before that. Max Outhwaite could be the victim of a rip-off during his teen crime years."

"If the name's a fake, it's not going to matter how far back I go."

"In other words, you were too lazy," he said, mildly.

"Right," I said, without taking offense.

"What about the letters themselves?"

"One's a fax. The other's typed on ordinary white bond. No distinguishing marks. I could have dusted for prints, but there didn't seem to be much point. We've got no way to run them and nothing for comparison even if a latent turned up. I did put the one letter in a plastic sleeve to protect it to some extent. Then I made copies of both letters. I left one set at the office, locked away in my desk. I get paranoid about these things."

"You have the other set here?"

"In my briefcase."

"Let's take a look."

I pushed the sheet back and got up. I retrieved my

briefcase from the kitchen counter and sorted through the contents, returning to the sofa bed with my pack of index cards and the two letters. I slid between the sheets again and handed him the paperwork, turning over on my side so I could watch him work. He put his glasses on. "This is really romantic, you know that, Dietz?"

"We can't screw around all day. I'm fifty. I'm old. I have to save my strength."

"Yeah, right."

We propped up the pillows and settled in side by side while Dietz read the two letters and thumbed through my index cards. "What do you think?" I asked.

"I think Outhwaite's a good bet. Seems like the object of the exercise is to find another candidate, divert attention from Jack if nothing else."

"Lonnie said the same thing. The evidence looks damning, but it's all circumstantial. Lonnie's hoping we can find someone else to point a finger at. I think he favors Donovan or Bennet."

"The more the merrier. If the cops think Jack's motivation was Guy's share of the inheritance, then the same case could be made for the other two. It would have been just as easy for one of them to slip into Guy's room." He was thumbing through the index cards. He held a card up. "What's this mean? What kind of scam are you referring to?"

I took the card and studied it. The note said: *widow cheated out of nest egg.* "Oh. I'm not sure. I wrote down everything I could remember from my first interview with Donovan. He was talking about the scrapes Guy'd been in over the years. Most sounded petty— acts of vandalism, joyriding, stuff like that—but he was also involved in a swindle of some kind. I didn't ask at the time because I was just starting my search and I was focusing on ways to track him down. I didn't care what he'd done unless it somehow pertained."

"Might be worth it to take a good hard look at his past. People knew he was back. Maybe somebody had a score to settle."

"That crossed my mind, too. I mean, why else would Max Outhwaite notify the paper?" I said. "I've also toyed with the idea that one of Guy's brothers might have written the letters."

"Why?"

"To make it look like he had enemies, someone outside the family who might have wanted him dead. By the way, Bader kept a file of newspaper clippings, detailing Guy's escapades."

Dietz turned and looked at me. "Anything of interest?"

"Well, nothing jumps right out. I've got it at the office, if you want to see for yourself. Christie offered to let me take it when I was at the house."

"Let's do that. It sounds good. It might help us develop another lead." He went back to the two letters, analyzing them closely. "What about the third one? What did Guy's letter say?"

"I have no idea. Lieutenant Bower wouldn't tell me and I couldn't get much out of her. But I'd bet money it's the same person in all three cases."

"Cops probably have their forensic experts doing comparisons."

"Maybe. They may not care about Max Outhwaite

now that Jack's in custody. If they're convinced he's good for it, why worry about someone else?"

"You want some help with the grunt work?"

"I'd love it."

EIGHTEEN

I dropped Dietz at the public library while I drove out the freeway to Malek Construction. I hadn't expected to be gone long, but as I turned into the parking lot, I spotted Donovan getting into a company truck. I called his name and gave a quick wave, pulling into a visitor's space two spots away from his. He waited while I approached and then leaned over and rolled down the window on the passenger side.

Donovan's face creased with a smile, his dark eyes all but invisible behind dark sunglasses. "How are you?" he asked. He slid his glasses up on top of his head.

"Fine. I can see I caught you on your way out. Will you be gone long? I have some questions."

"I've got some business at the quarry. I'll only be gone about an hour if you want to come along with me."

I thought about it briefly. "Might as well," I said.

He moved his hard hat from the passenger seat to the floor, then opened the truck door for me. I hopped in. He wore blue jeans and a jean vest over a blue plaid sportshirt with the sleeves rolled up. His feet were shod in heavy-duty work boots with soles as waffled as tire treads.

"Where's the quarry?"

"Up the pass." He fired up the pickup and pulled out of the parking lot. "What's the latest word from Jack?"

"I haven't talked to him, but Lonnie Kingman had a meeting with him before they took him off to jail. You talked to Christie?"

"I took a late lunch," he said. "I must have gotten home about ten minutes after you left. I had no idea this stuff was going on. How's it looking at this point?"

"Hard to say. Lonnie's in the process of working out his strategy. I'll probably take a run over to the country club later to start canvassing members who were there on Tuesday. We'd love to find someone who could place Jack at the club between nine-thirty and eleven-thirty."

"Shouldn't be too hard."

"You'd be surprised," I said.

I'm about as perky as an infant when it comes to riding in trucks. Before we'd even reached the narrow highway that snaked up the pass, I could feel the tension seeping out of me. There's something lulling being a passenger in a moving vehicle. In Donovan's pickup, the combination of low grinding sound and gentle bumping nearly put me to sleep. I was tired of thinking about murder, though I'd have to bring the subject around to it eventually. In the meantime, I asked him about the business and took inordinate pleasure in the length of his reply. Donovan steered with one hand, talking over the rattle of the truck.

"We've gotten into recycle crushing where we take broken concrete and asphalt. We have a yard in Colgate where we collect it and we have a portable plant—well, we have two portable plants now—one in Monterey and one in Stockton. I think we were one of the first in this area to do that. We're able to crush the materials into road base that meets the specifications. It costs more to haul the materials here than it does the material itself, so you have a cost advantage in the haul."

He went on in this vein while I wondered idly if it might be worthwhile to verify his claims about the company's solvency. When I turned back in, he was saying, "Right now, we produce about the same quantity out at the rock quarry as we do out at the sand and gravel mine. By far the majority of the sand and gravel operation goes into the production of asphalt concrete. We're the closest asphalt concrete plant to Santa Teresa. We used to have one in Santa Teresa where we hauled in the sand and the gravel and the liquid asphalt and we made it there, but again, it was more economical to make the product here and haul it into Santa Teresa. I'm probably the only man alive who rhapsodizes about road base and Portland Cement. You want to talk about Jack."

"I'd rather talk about Guy."

"Well, I can tell you Jack didn't kill him because it makes no sense. The first thing the cops are going to look at is the three of us. I'm surprised Bennet and I aren't under scrutiny."

"You probably are, though at the moment, all the evidence seems to point to Jack." I told him about the running shoes and the baseball bat. "You have any idea where the Harley-Davidson was that night?"

"Home in the garage, I'd guess. The Harley's Jack's

baby, not mine. I really didn't have occasion to see it that night. I was upstairs watching TV."

We headed up the pass on a winding road bordered by chaparral. The air was still, lying across the mountains in a hush of hot sun. The woody shrubs were as dry as tinder. Farther up the rocky slopes, weeds and ornamental grasses—ripgut and woodland brome, foxtail fescue and ryegrass—had spread across the landscape in a golden haze that softened the stony ridges. Scarcely a breeze stirred outside, but late in the day, the warm descending air would begin to blow down the mountainside. Relative humidity would drop. The wind, squeezing through the canyons, would start picking up speed. Any tiny flame from a campfire, burning cigarette, or the inadvertent spark from weed abatement equipment, might be whipped up in minutes to a major burn. The big fires usually struck in August and September after months under high-pressure areas. However, lately the weather had been moody and unpredictable and there was no way to calculate the course it might take. Below us and at a distance, the Pacific Ocean stretched away to the horizon in a haze of blue. I could see the irregularities of the coastline as it curved to the north.

Donovan was saying, "I didn't see Jack that night once he left for the club so I can't help you there. Aside from his whereabouts, I guess I'm not really sure what you're looking for."

"We can either prove Jack didn't do it or suggest someone else who did. Where was Bennet that night? Can he account for his time?"

"You'd have to ask him. He wasn't home, I know that much. He didn't come in until late."

"The first time we met you told me about some of Guy's bouts with the law. Couldn't someone have a grudge?"

"You want to go back as far as his days in Juvenile Hall?"

"Maybe. And later, too. You mentioned a 'widder' woman he cheated out of money."

Donovan shook his head. "Forget it. That's a dead end."

"How so?"

"Because the whole family's gone."

"They left town?"

"They're all dead."

"Tell me anyway."

"The widow was a Mrs. Maddison. Guy was gone by then and when the old man heard what Guy'd done, he refused to make good. It was one of the few times he got tough. I guess he'd finally gotten sick of cleaning up after him. He told the woman to file charges, but I'm sure she never got around to it. Some people are like that. They don't take action even when they should."

"So what's the story?"

We reached the summit and the road opened out to a view I love, a caramel-colored valley dotted with dark green mounds of live oak. Ranches and campgrounds were woven into the land, but most were invisible from up here. The two-lane highway widened into four and we sped across the span of the Cold Spring Bridge. "Guy got involved with a girl named Patty Maddison.

That's two *d*'s in Maddison. She had an older sister named Claire."

I heard a dim clang of recognition, but couldn't place the name. I must have made some kind of sound because Donovan turned and gave me a quick look. "You know her?" he asked.

"The name's familiar. Go on with the story. It'll come to me."

"Their old man never had a dime, but he'd somehow acquired some rare documents—letters of some kind—worth a big chunk of change. He'd been sick and the deal was, when he died the mother was supposed to sell 'em to pay for the girls' educations. The older sister had graduated from a college back East and she was waiting around to go to medical school. Some of the money was earmarked for her and some for Patty's college.

"The Christmas before he took off, Guy knocks on this woman's door. He says he's a friend of Patty's and presents himself as an appraiser of rare documents. He tells her there's some question about the authenticity of the letters. Rumor has it, says he, these are fakes and he's been hired by the father to take a look at them."

"This was while the father was still alive?"

He shook his head. "He'd been dead a month by then. He died at Thanksgiving time. Mom's feeling very nervous because the letters are really all she has. She doesn't know beans about an appraiser being hired, but it all sounds legitimate—like something her husband would have done toward the end—so she hands the letters over to Guy and he takes them away."

"Just like that?" I asked. "She didn't ask for ID or credentials?"

"Apparently not. He had some business cards done up and he handed her one, which she took at face value. You have to understand, this was all pieced together months afterward. What the hell did she know? She needs an appraisal done anyway in preparation for selling."

"I can't believe people are so trusting."

"That's what keeps con artists in business," he said. "Go on."

"Well, Guy keeps the letters for two weeks. He claims he's subjecting them to a number of scientific tests, but what he's really doing is making copies, elaborate forgeries. Or, not so elaborate as it turns out. At any rate, he's putting together a set of fakes good enough to pass superficial inspection. After two weeks, he takes the copies back and gives her the bad news. 'Golly, gee, Mrs. Maddison, these really *are* fakes,' he says, 'and they're not worth a *dime*.' He tells her to ask any expert and they'll tell her the same. She nearly drops dead from shock. She takes 'em straight to another expert and he confirms what Guy's said. Sure enough, the letters are completely worthless. So here's this lady whose husband's dead and she suddenly has nothing. Next thing you know, she's knocking on Dad's door demanding restitution."

"How'd she figure out it was Guy?"

"He'd been seeing Patty Maddison . . ."

I said, "Ohhh. That Patty. I get it. Guy told me about her the day we walked the property. He said he'd broken up with her. Sorry to interrupt, but I just remembered where I'd heard the name. So how'd they know it was him? Did Patty point a finger?"

Donovan shook his head. "Far from it. Patty tried to protect him, but Guy had just taken off and Mrs. Maddison put two and two together."

"Mrs. Maddison hadn't met him?"

"Only the one time when he showed up for the appraisal. Obviously, he didn't use his own name."

Donovan slowed and turned left off the main highway. We followed a two-lane paved road for a mile until it turned to gravel, small rocks popping as the truck bounced upward. Ahead, I could see white dust, like smoke, drifting across the road as it curved around to the left where it widened to reveal the quarry site. Massive benches of raw soil and rock had been cut into the hillside. There were no trees and no vegetation in the area. The din of heavy machinery filled the still mountain air. Much of the area was a flat, chalky gray contrasting sharply with the surrounding gray-green hills and a sky of pale blue. The mountains beyond were cloaked in dark green vegetation interspersed with the gold of short dry grassy patches. Tiers had been cut into the side of the hill. Everywhere there were steep piles of earth and gravel, shale and sandstone, eroding raw earth and rock. Conveyor belts trundled rock upward toward the crusher, where rocks as big as my head were being shaken down into vibrating jaws that reduced them to rubble. Rugged horizontal and inclined screens and feeders sorted the crushed rock into various sizes.

Donovan pulled up close to a trailer, turned off the ignition, and set the hand brake. "Let me take care of business and I can finish the story on the way back.

There's a hard hat in the back if you want to take a walk around."

"You go ahead. I'll be fine."

Donovan left me in the pickup while he conferred with a man in coveralls and a hard hat. The two disappeared into the trailer while I waited. From a distance, the machinery was the size of Matchbox toys. I watched as a conveyor belt moved loose rock in a steady stream that poured off the end into a cascading pile. I lifted my chin, shifting my sights to the countryside stretched out in a pristine canvas of hazy mountain and low-growing dark green. I let my gaze drift across the site, trying to make sense out of what Donovan had said. As nearly as I remembered Guy's passing reference to Patty, he saw his discretion with her as his one decent act. He'd described her as unstable, emotionally fragile, something along those lines. It was hard to believe he'd try to convince me of his honor when he'd gone to such lengths to rip her mother off. In truth, he'd ripped Patty off too since the money from the letters was supposed to go to her.

The sun was beating down on the cab of the pickup. Donovan had left the windows open so I wouldn't cook to death. White dust clouded the air and the growling of heavy equipment battled the quiet. I could hear the clank of metal, the high whine of shifting gears as a wheel loader grumbled across flat ground as barren as a moonscape. I unsnapped my seat belt and slouched down on my spine with my knees propped on the dashboard. I didn't want Guy to be guilty of a crime of this magnitude. What was done was done, but this was bad, bad, bad. I was prepared for pranks, willing to accept minor acts of mischief, but grand larceny was tough to overlook, even at this remove.

I didn't realize I'd been dozing until I heard the crunch of work boots and Donovan opened the truck door on the driver's side. I awoke with a start. He kicked the sides of his boots against the floor frame, knocking gravel loose before he slid in beneath the steering wheel. I sat up and refastened my seat belt.

"Sorry it took so long," he said.

"Don't worry about it. I was just resting my eyes," I said dryly.

He slammed the door, clicked his seat belt into place, and turned the key in the ignition. Within moments, we were bouncing down the road toward the highway again. "Where was I?" he asked.

"Guy switched a set of forged letters for the real ones and then disappeared. You were saying your father refused to make good."

"I'll say. The letters were worth something close to fifty thousand dollars. In those days, Dad didn't have that kind of money and wouldn't have paid anyway."

"What happened to the letters? Did Guy sell them?"

"He must have, because as far as I know, they were never seen again. Paul Trasatti could tell you more. His father was the appraiser brought in once the switch was made."

"So he was the one who confirmed the bad news to Mrs. Maddison?"

"Right."

"What happened to her?"

"She was a lush to begin with and she'd been popping

pills for years. She didn't last long. Between the alcohol and cigarettes, she was dead in five years."

"And Patty?"

"That was unfortunate. In May of that year—this was two months after Guy left—Patty turned up pregnant. She was seventeen years old and didn't want anyone to know. She'd had a lot of mental problems and I think she was worried they'd put her away, which they probably would have. At any rate, she had an illegal abortion and died of septicemia."

"What?"

"You heard me right. She had what they referred to as a 'backroom' abortion, which was more common than you'd think. Procedure wasn't sterile—just some hack down in San Diego. She developed blood poisoning and she died."

"You're kidding."

"It's the truth," he said. "We weren't down on Guy for nothing. I know you think we're nothing but a bunch of hostile jerks, but this is what we've had to live with and it hasn't been easy."

"Why wasn't something said before now?"

"In what context? The subject never came up. We all knew what happened. We discussed it among ourselves, but we don't run around airing our dirty laundry in front of other people. You think we like owning up to his part in it?"

I brooded about it, staring out at the passing roadside. "I'm really having trouble believing this."

"I'm not surprised. You don't want to think Guy would do a thing like that."

"No, I don't," I said. "Guy told me Patty was hung

up on him. He considered it his one decent act that he didn't seduce her when he had the chance. Now why would he say that?"

"He was hoping to impress you. Stands to reason," he said.

"But there wasn't any context. This was passing conversation, something he brought up. He didn't go into any detail. What's to be impressed about?"

"Guy was a liar. He couldn't help himself."

"He might have been a liar back then, but why lie about the girl all these years later? I didn't know her. I wasn't pressing for information. Why bother to lie when he had nothing to gain?"

"Look, I know you liked him. Most women did. You start feeling sorry for him. You feel protective. You don't want to accept the fact he was twisted as they come. This is the kind of shit he pulled."

"It isn't that," I said, offended. "He'd undergone a lot of soul-searching. He'd committed his life to God. There wasn't any point fabricating some tall tale about Patty Maddison."

"He was busy revising history. It's something we all do. You repent your sins and then in memory, you start cleaning up your past. Pretty soon, you're convinced you weren't nearly as bad as everyone said. The other guy was a jerk, but you had good reason for anything you did. It's all bunk, of course, but which of us can stand to take a look at ourselves? We whitewash. It's human nature."

"You're talking about the Guy Malek of the old days. Not the one I met. All I know is, I have a hard time picturing Guy doing this."

"You knew him less than a week and believed everything he said. He was a bad egg."

"But Donovan, look at the nature of his crimes. None of them were like this," I said. "As a kid, he was into vandalism. Later, he stole cars and stereos to pay for drugs. Forgery's too sophisticated a scheme for someone who spent his days getting high. Trust me. I've been high. You think you're profound but you're barely functional."

"Guy was a bright boy. He learned fast."

"I better talk to Paul," I said, unwilling to concede.

"He'll tell you the same thing. In fact, that's probably what put the idea in Guy's head in the first place. You have a good friend whose dad deals in rare documents, it doesn't take any great leap to figure it out when you've got access to something valuable."

"I hear what you're saying, but it isn't sitting right."

"You know anything about liars?" Donovan asked.

"Sure, I think I can say so. What about 'em?"

"A liar—a truly dedicated liar—lies because he can, because he's good at it. He lies for the pure pleasure, because he loves getting away with it. That's how Guy was. If he could tell you some lie—even if it meant nothing, even if there was nothing to be gained—he couldn't resist."

"You're telling me he was a pathological liar," I said, restating his claim in a tone of skepticism.

"I'm saying he enjoyed lying. He couldn't help himself."

"I don't believe that," I said. "I happen to think I'm a pretty good judge of liars."

"You know when some people lie, but not all."

"What makes you such an expert?" I said, beginning to take offense. Donovan was just as annoyed with me.

He made a dismissive gesture. I suspected he wasn't used to having women argue with him. "Forget it. Have it your way," he said. "I can tell I'm not going to persuade you of anything."

"Nor I you," I said tartly. "What happened to the older sister?"

Donovan grimaced with exasperation. "Are you going to take my word for it or is this an excuse for another round of arguments?"

"I'm arguing about Guy, not the Maddisons, okay?"

"Okay. Claire—the older one—abandoned her plans for med school. She had no money and her mom was sinking like a stone. For a while she came back to take care of her. That was maybe six months or so. Once mom was gone, she went back to the East Coast—Rhode Island or some place. Might have been Connecticut. She got married to some fellow, but it didn't work out. Then about a year ago, she offed herself. Or so I heard."

"She committed suicide?"

"Why not? Her whole family was gone. She had no one. The family was a bit dicey to begin with—bunch of manic-depressives. I guess something must have finally pushed her over the edge."

"What'd she do, jump off a building?"

"I don't know how she did it. I wasn't being literal. There was a notice in the local paper. It happened back east somewhere."

I was silent again. "So maybe one of the Maddisons killed Guy. Wouldn't that make sense?"

"You're fishing. I just told you, they're all gone."

"But how do you know there isn't someone left? Cousins, for instance? Aunts and uncles? Patty's best friend?"

"Come on. Would you really murder someone who wronged a relative of yours? A sibling, maybe. But a cousin or a niece?"

"Well, no, but I'm not close to my relatives. Suppose something like that happened to your family."

"Something did happen to my family. Guy was killed," he said.

"Don't you want revenge?"

"Enough to kill someone? Absolutely not. Besides, if I cared enough to kill, I wouldn't wait this long. You're talking eighteen years."

"But Guy was missing all that time. You notice, once he came home, he was dead within days."

"True enough," he said.

"Does the name Max or Maximilian Outhwaite figure into this in any way? It could even be Maxine. I can't swear to gender."

Donovan turned and looked at me with surprise. "Where'd you come up with that one?"

"You know the name?"

"Well, sure. Maxwell Outhwaite's the name Guy used on the business cards he made to cheat Mrs. Maddison."

I squinted at him. "Are you sure?"

"That isn't something I'd forget," he said. "How'd you come across it?"

" 'Max Outhwaite' was the one who wrote the letters to the *Dispatch* and the L.A. *Times*. That's how the press knew Guy was home."

NINETEEN

Once back at Malek Construction, I left Donovan in the parking lot and picked up my car. I was feeling anxious and confused. This Max Outhwaite business made no sense at all. Maybe Dietz had come up with a line on him. Throw the Maddisons into the mix and what did it add up to? I glanced at my watch, wincing when I saw how late it was. The trip up the pass had taken more than an hour and a half.

Dietz was waiting in front of the public library. I pulled over to the curb and he slid into the passenger seat. "Sorry I'm late," I said.

"Don't worry about it. I got news for you. Outhwaite's a myth. I checked the city directories for the last twenty-five years and then went across the street and checked the County Clerk's office. No one by that name was ever listed in the phone book or anywhere else. No marriages, no deaths, no real property, building permits, lawsuits, you name it. Everybody alive leaves a trail of some kind. The name has to be phony unless we're missing a bet."

"There *is* a connection, but it's not what you'd expect," I said. I filled him in on my conversation with

Donovan while we headed for home. I'd forgotten how nice it was to have someone to consult. I told him about the Maddisons and Guy's alleged involvement in the family's downfall. "Maxwell Outhwaite was the name used by the fictitious appraiser who stole fifty thousand dollars' worth of rare documents. I'm not convinced it was Guy, but Donovan seems to take it for granted. Now, honestly," I said. "If you'd known about the Maddisons, wouldn't you have told someone?"

"Namely you?"

"Well, yes, me," I said. "Donovan could have *mentioned* it. Same with Max Outhwaite. The name pops up again years later—why didn't he tell someone?"

"Maybe Katzenbach never told him there was a letter and that Outhwaite was the name of the sender."

"Oh. I see what you're saying. I guess it's possible," I said. "It still annoys me no end. I wish we could find the typewriter. That would be a coup."

"Forget it. There's no way."

"What makes you say that? It has to be around here somewhere. Someone typed both those letters on the same machine."

"So what? If I were writing poison-pen notes, I'd hardly sit at my desk and use my own IBM. I'm too paranoid for that. I'd use one of the rental typewriters at the public library. Or maybe find a place selling typewriters and use one of theirs."

"This machine isn't new. The typeface has an old-fashioned look to it and a lot of the letters are clogged. It's probably got a fabric ribbon instead of carbon film."

"Those typewriters at the library aren't exactly hot off the assembly line."

"Pick me up some samples and we'll do a comparison. There are a couple of typeface defects that should help us pin it down. I'm sure a document expert could find others. I've only eyeballed it."

"The clogged letters don't mean much. Go after 'em with cleaning fluid and poof, those are gone."

"Sure, but don't you think the majority of people who write anonymous letters assume they're safe from discovery?"

"They might assume they're safe, but they're not," Dietz said. "The FBI maintains extensive files of anonymous letters. Plus, they have samples of type from most known machines. Post Office does, too, and so does the Treasury Department. They can determine the make and model of almost any machine. That's how they nail cranks, especially people who send threatening letters to public officials. The only way to play it safe is to dismantle the machine."

"Yeah, but who's going to trash a typewriter? If you thought you were safe enough to use your own machine, you wouldn't turn around and toss it in the garbage afterward. And in this case, why bother? Those letters were a nuisance, but hardly actionable."

Dietz smiled. "What, you picture it sitting out on someone's desk?"

"Maybe. It's possible."

"Keep an eye out."

"I know you're just saying that to humor me," I said.

"What else did Donovan have to say about the Maddisons?"

"Not much. He claims they're all gone, but I don't think we should take his word for it."

"It's worth pursuing," Dietz said. "As stories go, it's not bad."

"What do you mean, 'it's not bad'? I think it's fabulous. I mean, talk about a motive for murder. It's the best lead we've had—"

"The only lead," he pointed out.

I ignored the obvious. "On top of that, we have Outhwaite, who seems to tie right back to them."

"Shouldn't be too hard to track down the name Maddison with two *d*'s. Even if they're not local, they had to come from somewhere."

"Donovan says the father died around Thanksgiving of 1967 and Patty followed, probably in May or June of 1968. The mother died five years later, but that's as much as I know. You may not find Claire at all. He says she moved back to the East Coast and married. He does remember reading about her death in the local paper, so there must have been a notice in the *Dispatch*. Maybe she kept her maiden name?"

"I'll get on it first thing."

"You will? I can't believe you're volunteering. I thought you hated doing this stuff."

"Good practice. It's nice to keep a hand in. This way I know I haven't lost my touch," he said. "We might try the newspaper morgue if we can get Katzenbach's cooperation. They might have old clips on the Maddisons along with the obits."

"That's a sexy suggestion."

"I'm a sexy guy," he said.

When we got home, I changed into my sweats in preparation for jogging. I had slept through my usual six A.M. run and I was feeling the effects. I left Dietz in the living room with his leg propped up, icing his bum knee while he flipped from channel to channel, alternately watching CNN, talk shows, and obscure sporting events. I headed out the front door, thankful for the opportunity to spend time alone.

There was scarcely any breeze coming off the ocean. The late-afternoon sun had begun to fade, but the daylong baked beach was still throwing off heat saturated by the smell of kelp and brine. The fronds of the palm trees looked like construction paper cutouts, flat dark shapes against the flat blue sky. I lengthened my stride, running at a pace that felt good. The stiffness and fatigue gradually gave way to ease. My muscles became liquid and sweat trickled down my face. Even the burning in my chest felt good as my body was flooded with oxygen. At the end of the run, I flung myself down on the grass, where I lay panting. My mind was a blank and my bones were washed clean. Finally, my breathing slowed and the run-generated heat in my body seeped out. I did a series of stretches and then roused myself. As I headed for home, I could feel the return of the Santa Ana winds lufting down the mountainside. I showered and changed clothes, throwing on a T-shirt and jeans.

Dietz and I had dinner up at Rosie's. William was working behind the bar again. At the age of eighty-seven, this was like a whole new career for him. Since their marriage, the two of them had settled into a comfortable routine. More and more, Rosie seemed to be turning management over to him. She'd always maintained tight control of the day-to-day operation, but

William had persuaded her to pay decent wages and as a consequence, she'd been able to hire better employees. And she'd begun to delegate responsibility, which gave her more time to spend with him. William had given up some of his imaginary illnesses and she'd surrendered some of her authoritarianism. Their affection for each other was obvious and their occasional spats seemed to blow over without incident. Dietz was talking to William about Germany, but I was only half attentive, wondering if the two of us would ever reach an accommodation. I pictured Dietz at eighty-seven, me a comparatively youthful seventy-two; retired from the stresses of private-eye work, riddled with arthritis, bereft of our teeth. What would we do, open a private-detective school?

"What are you thinking? You look odd," he said.

"Nothing. Retirement."

"I'd rather eat my gun."

At bedtime, Dietz offered to hobble up the spiral stairs. "My knee's killing me again so I'm probably not much good except for company," he said.

"You're better off downstairs. My bed's not big enough, especially with that knee of yours. I'd just lie there worrying I'd bump you wrong."

I left him below opening up the sofa bed while I ambled up the stairs, talking to him over the rail.

"Last chance," he said, smiling up at me.

"I'm not sure it's smart getting used to you."

"You should take advantage while you can."

I paused, looking down. "That's the difference between us in a nutshell, Dietz."

"Because I live in the moment?"
"Because for you that's enough."

First thing Friday morning, Dietz took his car and headed over to the *Santa Teresa Dispatch* offices while I drove to Paul Trasatti's house. Hopper Road was located midway between the Maleks' and the country club. The neighborhood was small, the street lined with elm trees and dappled with shade. The house was built in the style of an English country cottage, the sort you'd see pictured on a deck of playing cards; gray stone with a thatched roof that undulated like an ocean wave where the gables appeared. The windows were small-paned, leaded glass, the wood trim and the shutters painted white. Two narrow stone chimneys bracketed the house like a pair of matching bookends. The yard was enclosed with a white picket fence, pink and red hollyhocks planted along the front. The small yard was immaculate, thick grass bordered in dark ivy with small flowerbeds along the brick walk leading to the door. Birds twittered in the young oak growing at the corner of the property.

I'd called the night before, of course, wanting to be certain Trasatti would be home. Even on the porch, I could smell bacon and eggs and the scent of maple syrup. My whimper probably wasn't audible above the sound of the mower two doors down. In response to my ring, Trasatti came to the door with his napkin in hand. He was tall and thin, as bald as a lightbulb. He had a large nose, thick glasses, and a jutting chin. His chest was narrow, slightly sunken, swelling to a thickened waistline. He wore a white dress shirt and a pair of stovepipe pants. He frowned at me, looking at his watch with surprise. "You said nine."

"It is nine."

"This says eight." He held his watch to his ear. "Shit. Come on in. You caught me at breakfast. Have a seat in here. I'll be back in a second. You want coffee?"

"I'm fine. Take your time," I said.

The living room was small and perfectly appointed, more like a doctor's office than a place to put your feet up. The furniture had a vaguely Victorian air, though to my untutored eye, it didn't appear to be the real thing. The chairs were small and fussy, rimmed with carved wooden fruit. There were three dark wood tables topped with pink-veined marble slabs, an array of Sotheby's catalogs neatly lined up on one. The carpeting was a short-cut wool pile, pale blue with a border of Chinese dragons and chrysanthemums. Two cloisonne vases were filled with artificial pink and blue flowers of some generic sort. A clock on the mantel had a second hand that clicked distinctly as it inched its way around. I leafed through a Sotheby's catalog, but didn't see much of interest except a letter from the Marquis de Sade, which was being offered at two thousand dollars. The passage quoted was in French and seemed petulant. There was also a pretty little greeting from Erik Satie to Mme Ravel with "decorated borders and raised blind relief heading showing in colour two hands held in front of a rose..." Lots of talk about *jolies fleurs* and *respecteusements.* My thoughts exactly. I've often said as much.

I strolled the perimeter, taking in numerous framed

letters and autographs. Laurence Sterne, Franz Liszt, William Henry Harrison, Jacob Broom (whoever he was), Juan Jose Flores (ditto). There was a long, incomprehensible letter bearing the signature S. T. Coleridge, and some kind of receipt or order blank signed by George Washington. There was another letter written in a crabbed hand, dated August 1710, fraught with brown ink and cross-outs and looking crumpled and stained. Who'd had the presence of mind to save all this litter? Were there people with foresight going through the dustbins back then?

Across the hall, I could see what must have been a dining room done up as an office. There were bookshelves on every wall, some extending across the windows, which greatly diminished the incoming light. Every surface was stacked ten deep, including tables, chairs, and floors. No typewriter on the premises as far as I could see. I had no reason to think Trasatti was involved, but it would have been nice to have a piece of the puzzle fall into place. The air smelled of old dust and book mold, glue, aging paper, and dust mites. A large tortoiseshell cat picked its way daintily across a desk piled with books. This creature had only a stump for a tail and looked like it might be searching out a place to pee.

"Making yourself at home?" came the voice behind me.

I started, making ever so slight a leap.

"I was admiring this enormous cat," I said casually.

"Sorry if I startled you. That's Lady Chatterley."

"What happened to her tail?"

"She's a Manx."

"She looks like a character," I said. Animal people seem to love it when you say things like this. Trasatti didn't seem to warm to it. He gestured me into the office, where he took a seat at his desk, pushing aside an irregular stack of hardback books.

"No secretary?" I asked.

"Business isn't big enough for clerical help. Anything I need done, I use the Mac upstairs. Go ahead and make a space for yourself," he said, indicating the only chair in the room.

"Thanks." I placed some books, a briefcase, and a pile of newspapers on the floor, and sat down.

"Now what can I help you with? I really can't add to what I've already given you in regard to Jack," he said.

"This was in regard to something else," I said while the fifteen-pound cat hopped onto my lap and settled between my knees. Up close, Lady Chatterley smelled like a pair of damp two-week-old socks. I scratched that little spot just above the base of its tail which made the back end of the cat rise up until its rosebud was staring me in the face. I pushed the back end down. I peppered my preface with lots of reassuring phrases—"off the record," "just between us," and other felicitous expressions of confidentiality—before getting down to business. "I'm wondering what you can tell me about the Maddisons—Patty and her sister, Claire."

He seemed to take the question in stride. "What would you like to know?"

"Anything you care to tell," I said.

Paul straightened the stack of books in front of him, making sure all the edges were aligned and the top right-hand corners matched. "I didn't know the sister. She was older than we were. She was off at college by the time the family moved into the area and Patty started hanging out with Guy."

"The Maddisons were new in town?"

"Well no, not really. They'd been living out in Colgate and bought a house closer in. They never had the kind of money we did, the rest of us—not that we were wealthy," he added. "Bader Malek did well back in those days, but he wasn't what you'd call rich."

"Tell me about Patty."

"She was pretty. Dark." He put his hand at eye level, indicating bangs. "Hair down to here," he said. "She'd kind of peer out like this. She was strange, lots of phobias and nervous mannerisms. Bad posture, big tits. She chewed her nails to the quick and liked to stick herself with things." Trasatti put his hands in his lap, trying not to touch the items on his desk.

"She stuck herself? With what?"

"Needles. Pencils. Safety pins. I saw her burn herself one time. She put a lighted cigarette on her hand—casually, like it was happening to someone else. She never even flinched, but I could smell cooked flesh."

"Was Guy serious about her?" I pushed the cat's hind end down again and it began to work its claws into the knees of my jeans.

"She was serious about him. I have no idea what he thought of her."

"What about the others? Donovan and Bennet."

"What about them?"

"I just wondered what they were up to during this period."

"Donovan was working for his dad, as I remember. He was always working for his dad, so that's a safe bet. Jack was back at school by then, so he was only home on occasion. Christmas and spring break."

"And his mother's funeral," I said. I extracted the cat's claws from my knee and held its right paw between my fingers. I could feel its claws protrude and retract, but the cat seemed content, probably thinking about mice. "What about Bennet? Where was he?"

"Here in town. He and I were both finishing at UCST."

"Majoring in what?"

"My major was art history. His was economics or business, maybe public finance. He switched around some. I forget."

"Did it surprise you when Patty turned up pregnant?"

Trasatti snorted, shaking his head. "Patty would screw anyone. She was desperate for attention and we were happy to oblige."

"Really," I said. "Donovan never said she was promiscuous."

"She wasn't the only one. There was lots of screwing in those days. Free love, we called it. We were all smoking dope. Bunch of small-town hippies, or as close as we could get. We were always horny and hungry. Half the girls we hung out with were as fat as pigs. Except for Patty, of course, who was gorgeous, but whacked out."

"Nice of you boys to help yourselves to a minor," I said. "Given her loose ways, how'd you know the baby was Guy's?"

"Because she said it was."

"She could have lied. If she was crazy and stoned, she might have made things up. How do you know the baby wasn't yours?"

Trasatti shifted uncomfortably. "I had no money to speak of. Where's the benefit in claiming it's mine? The Maleks had class. She might have been crazy, but she wasn't stupid. It's like the old joke—"

"I know the old joke," I said. "Was there ever any proof? Did anybody run blood tests to establish paternity?"

"I hardly think so. I'm sure they didn't. This was sixty-eight."

"How do you know Guy wasn't blamed because it was convenient? He was gone by then. Who better to accuse than a chronic screwup like him?"

Trasatti picked up a pencil and then put it down. His expression had gone blank. "What does this have to do with Jack? I thought you were working to try to get him off."

"That's what I'm doing."

"Doesn't sound like that to me."

"Donovan told me about Patty yesterday. I thought the story might pertain, so I'm following up. Did you ever see the letters Guy allegedly forged?"

"Why put it that way? It's what he did."

"Did you actually see him do it?"

"No, of course not."

"Then it's all supposition. Did you ever see the letters?"

"Why would I?"

"Your father did the appraisal when the forgeries were discovered. I thought he might have showed you the copies, if he was training you to follow in his footsteps."

"Who told you that?"

"He handed the business over to you, didn't he?"

Trasatti smiled at me, blinking. "I don't understand where you intend to go with this. Are you accusing me of something?"

"Not at all," I said.

"Because if you are, you're out of line."

"That wasn't an accusation. I never said you did anything. I'm saying Guy Malek didn't. I'm saying someone else did it all and blamed him. What about 'Max Outhwaite'? How does he fit in?"

"Outhwaite?"

"Come on, Trasatti. That's the name Guy supposedly used on his fake business cards."

"Right, right, right. I remember now. Sure thing. I knew it sounded familiar. What's the link?"

"That's why I'm asking you. I don't know," I said. "I think the story of Patty Maddison ties in somehow. Her death, the forged letters. I'm just fishing around."

"You better try something else. The family's gone."

"What makes you so sure?"

Paul Trasatti was silent. He began to arrange a row of paper clips on the side of a magnetized holder on his desk. Each one had to be exactly the same distance from the one above it and the one below.

"Come on. Just between us," I said.

"I tried to find them once."

"When was this?"

"About ten years ago."

"Really," I said, trying not to seem interested. "What was that about?"

"I was curious. I thought there might be other rare documents. You know, passed down to other members of the family."

"How'd you go about it?"

"I hired a genealogist. I said I was trying to find some long-lost relatives. This gal did a search. She took months. She traced the name back to England, but on this end—the California branch—there weren't any male heirs and the line died out."

"What about aunts, uncles, cousins . . .?"

"The parents were both the only children of only children. There was no one left."

"What happened to the copies of the documents?"

"The forgeries were destroyed."

"And the originals?"

"No one's ever seen them again. Well, I haven't in any case. They've never come up for sale in all the years I've done business."

"Do you know what they were?"

"I have the itemized list. My dad kept meticulous records. You want to see it?"

"I'd love to."

Trasatti got up and crossed to a closet. I caught a glimpse of a wall safe and four gray metal file cabinets. Above them, on shelves, there was a series of old-fashioned card files. "I'm going to get all this on computer one of these days." He seemed to know right where he was going and I wondered if this was something he'd done recently. He extracted a card, glanced at it briefly, and then closed the drawer again. He left the closet door ajar and returned to his desk, handing me the card as he passed my chair. The cat had gone to sleep, lying across my knees like a fifteen-pound bag of hot sand.

The list detailed six documents: a framed Society of Boston Membership Certificate and a personal letter, both signed by George Washington and valued at $11,500 and $9,500, respectively; a judicial writ signed by Abraham Lincoln, dated December 1847, valued at $6,500; a wartime document signed by John Hancock, valued at $5,500; a ten-page fragment from an original manuscript by Arthur Conan Doyle valued at $7,500; and a letter signed by John Adams, valued at $9,000.

"I'm impressed," I said. "I don't know beans about rare documents, but these seem fabulous."

"They are. Those prices you're looking at are twenty years out of date. They'd be worth more today."

"How did Patty Maddison's father get his hands on items like these?"

"Nobody really knows. He was an amateur collector. He picked some up at auction and the rest, who knows? He might have stolen them for all I know. My father'd heard about 'em, but Francis—Mr. Maddison—would never let him examine them."

"His widow must have been an idiot to hand 'em over the way she did."

Trasatti made no comment.

"How did Guy hear about the letters?" I asked.

"Patty probably told him."

"Why would she do that?"

"How do I know? Showing off. She was nuts. She did all kinds of weird things."

I saw him glance at his watch. "You have an appointment?" I asked.

"As a matter of fact, I'm hoping we can wrap this up. I have work to do."

"Five minutes more and I'll be on my way."

Trasatti shifted restlessly, but motioned me on.

"Let me try out a little theory. None of this came to light until after Guy took off, right?"

Trasatti stared at me, without offering encouragement.

I was forced to go on, feeling like Perry Mason in a courtroom confrontation, only this wasn't going as well as his always did. "So maybe Jack was the one who got Patty knocked up. I heard Jack was the randy one. According to Guy, he screwed anything that moved."

"I told you he was off at college. He wasn't even here," Trasatti said.

"He came back for his mother's funeral and again for spring break. That was March, wasn't it?"

"I really don't remember."

"As I understand it, Guy had hit the road by then. Jack felt betrayed. He was crushed that Guy'd left without him so maybe he turned to Patty for consolation. At that point, she must have needed comfort as much as he did."

Trasatti kept his face expressionless, his fingers laced together on the desk. "You're never going to get me to say anything about this."

"Jack could have forged the letters. You two were buddies. Your father was an appraiser. You could have cooked up the scheme yourself and showed Jack how to do it."

"I'm finding this offensive. It's pure speculation. It doesn't mean a thing."

I let that one slide, though what he said was true. "Everything was cool until Guy came home again."

"What difference would that make?"

"In the old days, Guy took the blame for everybody's sins, so it just stands to reason everyone felt safe until he showed up again."

"I'm not following."

"Maybe the motive for Guy's murder was never money," I said. "Maybe Jack was just trying to protect himself."

"From what? I don't get it. There's really nothing at stake. The theft was eighteen years ago. The statute of limitations has run out. There's no crime on the books. Even if your guess is correct, Jack's the one who ends up with his ass in a sling. You said you were here to help, but it's blowing right back on him."

"You know what? Here's the truth. I don't really give a shit what blows back on him. If he's guilty, so be it. That isn't my concern."

"Well, that's nice. You want me to pick up the phone and call Lonnie Kingman? He's going to love your attitude and so will Jack. As far as I know, he's the one paying your bills."

"You go right ahead. Lonnie can always fire me if he doesn't like what I'm doing."

TWENTY

I stopped at a pay phone and put a call through to Lonnie, who had the good grace to laugh when he heard my account of the conversation with Paul Trasatti. "Forget it. The guy's a prick. He was just on the phone to me, whining and complaining about harassment. What a jerk."

"Why's he so worried about Jack?"

"Forget Jack for now. I'll take care of him. You better go talk to Bennet; I couldn't get to him. According to the grapevine, he's talking to an attorney in case the hairy eyeball of the law falls on him next. He's still got no alibi, as far as I've heard."

"Well, that's interesting."

"Yeah, people are getting nervous. That's a good sign," he said. He gave me the address of Bennet's restaurant, which was located downtown on a side street off State. The neighborhood itself was marked by a tire store, a minimart, a video rental shop, and a billiard parlor where fights erupted without much provocation beyond excess beer. Parking didn't seem to be readily available and it was hard to picture where the restaurant trade would be coming from.

Apparently, the place had once been a retail store, part of a chain that had filed for bankruptcy. The old sign was still out, but the interior had been gutted. The space was cavernous and shadowy, the floor bare concrete, the ceiling high. Heating ducts and steel girders were exposed to view, along with all of the electrical conduit. Toward the rear, an office had been roughed in: a desk, file cabinets, and office equipment arranged in a bare-framed cubicle. The back wall was solid and through a narrow doorway, I could see a toilet and a small sink with a medicine cabinet above it. It was going to take a lot of money to complete construction and get the business on its feet. No wonder Bennet had been so eager to get his hands on the second will. If Guy's share was divided among his brothers, each would be richer by more than a million, which he could clearly use.

To the right, a huge rolling metal door had been opened onto a weedy vacant lot. Outside, the sun was harsh, sparkling on the broken bottles while its heat baked a variety of doggy turds. There was not a soul in sight, but the building was wide open and I kept thinking Bennet, or a construction worker, would show up before long. While I waited, I wandered into the office area and took a seat at Bennet's desk. The secretarial chair was rickety and I imagined he made his phone calls upright with his hip resting on the desk, which seemed sturdier. Everything in the office had an air of having been borrowed or picked up on the cheap. The calculator tape showed a long series of numbers that didn't add up to anything. I could have checked in the drawers, but I was too polite. Besides, my recent clash with Paul Trasatti had chastened me some. I didn't want Lonnie getting two complaints in a single day.

There was a manual typewriter sitting on a rolling cart. My gaze slid across it idly and then came back. It was an ancient black Underwood with round yellowed keys that looked like they'd be hard to press. The ribbon was so worn it was thin in the middle. I looked over at the rolling door and then surveyed the whole of the empty restaurant space. Still no one. My bad angel was hovering to my left. It was she who pointed out the open packet of typing paper sitting right there in plain sight.

I pulled out a sheet and rolled it into the machine, settling myself on the wobbly typing chair. I typed my name. I typed that old standby: *The quick brown fox jumps over the lazy dog.* I typed the name *Max Outhwaite.* I typed *Dear Miss Milhone.* I peered closely. The vowels didn't appear to be clogged, which (as Dietz had pointed out) didn't mean that much. This could still be the typewriter used for the notes. Maybe Bennet had simply made a point of cleaning his keys. I pulled the paper out and folded it, then stood up and slipped it in the pocket of my jeans. When I got back to the office, I'd see if the defective *a* and *i* were visible under magnification. I still hadn't seen the anonymous letter Guy had received the Monday before he died, but maybe Betsy Bower would relent and let me pirate a copy.

The telephone rang.

I stared at it briefly and then lifted my head, listening for footsteps heading in my direction. Nothing. The phone rang again. I was tempted to answer, but I really didn't need to because the answering machine kicked in. Bennet's voice message was brief and very business-like. So was the caller.

"Bennet. Paul here. Give me a call as soon as possible."

The machine clicked off. The message light blinked off and on. My bad angel tapped me on the shoulder and pointed. I reached out and pressed DELETE. A dis-embodied male voice told me the message had been erased. I headed for the front door, breaking into a trot when I reached the street. Trasatti was a busy boy, calling everyone.

A Harley-Davidson rumbled into view. Shit. Bennet was back just when I thought I'd escaped. I slowed my pace, as if I had all the time in the world. Bennet rolled Jack's motorcycle up to the curb less than ten feet away. He killed the engine and popped the kickstand into place. He peeled off his helmet and cradled it under his arm. I noticed his hair was tightly frizzed and matted with sweat. Despite the heat, he was wearing a black leather jacket, probably protection in case he flipped the bike and skidded. "Working again?"

"I'm always working," I said.

"Did you want to talk to me?" His jacket creaked when he walked. He headed into the restaurant.

I followed. "How goes construction? It's looking pretty good," I said. It looked like a bomb crater, but I was kissing butt. Our footsteps echoed as we crossed the raw concrete floor.

"Construction's slow."

I said, "Ah. What's your target for opening?"

"April, if we're lucky. We have a lot of work to do."

"What kind of restaurant?"

"Cajun and Caribbean. We'll have salads and burgers, too, very reasonably priced. Maybe jazz two nights a week. We're really aiming for the singles' market."

"Like a pickup bar?"

"With class," he said. "This town doesn't have a lot going on at night. Get some dance music in here weekends, I think we're filling a niche. A chef from New Orleans and all the hot local bands. We should pull crowds from as far away as San Luis Obispo."

"That sounds rowdy," I said. We'd reached the office by then and I saw him flick a glance at his answering machine. I was only half listening, trying to think how to keep the conversation afloat. "Any problem with parking?"

"Not at all," he said. "We'll pave the lot next door. We're in negotiations at the moment. There's room for thirty cars there and another ten on the street."

"Sounds good," I said. He had an answer for everything. Mr. Slick, I thought.

"I'll comp you some tickets for the grand opening. You like to dance?"

"No, not really."

"Don't worry about it. We'll get you in and you can cut loose. Forget your inhibitions and get down," he said. He snapped his fingers, dipping his knees in a move meant to be oh so hip.

My least favorite thing in life is some guy encouraging me to "cut loose" and "get down." The smile I offered him was paper-thin. "I hope this business with Jack has been resolved by then."

"Absolutely," he said smoothly, his expression sobering appropriately. "How's it looking so far?"

"He can't account for his time, which doesn't help," I said. "The cops are claiming they found a bloody print from his shoe on the carpet up in Guy's room. I won't bore you with details. Lonnie wanted me to ask where you were."

"The night of the murder? I was club-hopping down in L.A."

"You drove to Los Angeles and back?"

"I do it all the time. It's nothing. Ninety minutes each way," he said. "That night, some of the time I was on the road."

"Did you have a date?"

"This was strictly business. I'm trying to get a feel for what works and what doesn't, sampling menus. You know, listening to some of the L.A. bands."

"I'm assuming you have credit card receipts to back you up."

A fleeting change of expression suggested I'd caught him out on that one. "I might have a few. I'll have to look and see what I've got. I paid cash in the main. It's easier that way."

"What time did you get in?"

"Close to three," he said. "You want to come in the back? I've got some beer in a cooler. We could have a drink."

"Thanks. It's a bit early."

"Where you going?"

"Back to the office. I have a meeting," I said.

*

On the way back to the office, I stopped off at a deli and picked up some soft drinks and sandwiches. Dietz had said he'd be joining me as soon as he'd finished his research. I stashed the soft drinks in the little refrigerator in my office and dumped my handbag on the floor beside my chair. I put the sack of sandwiches on the file cabinet and grabbed the folder full of clippings, which I tossed on my desk. I sat down in my swivel chair and assembled my index cards, the typewritten letters, and the sample I'd just taken from Bennet's machine, lining everything up in an orderly fashion. In the absence of definitive answers, it's good to look organized.

I turned on the desk lamp and pulled out my magnifying glass. The type was no match. I was disappointed, but I wasn't surprised. I took Guy's last letter from my handbag and read the contents again. Aside from his invitation to Disneyland, which I'd have accepted in a flash, I realized that what I was looking at, in essence, was a holographic will. The letter was written entirely by hand and he'd specified in the postscript what he'd wanted done with his share of his father's estate. I didn't know all the technicalities associated with a holographic will, but I thought this might qualify. The handwriting would have to be verified, but Peter Antle could do that when I saw him next. I knew Guy had received a disturbing letter late that Monday afternoon, and whatever its contents, he must have been sufficiently alarmed to want to make his wishes clear. I got up and left the office, taking his letter with me to the copy room. I ran a Xerox and then locked the originals with the others in my bottom drawer. The copy I slid in the outer pocket of my handbag.

I tried to picture Guy, but his face had already faded in my mind's eye. What remained was his sweetness, the sound of his "Hey," the feeling of his whiskers when he'd brushed my cheek with his lips. If he'd lived, I'm not sure we would have had a very strong relationship. Kinsey Millhone and a born-again was probably not a combination that would have gone anywhere. But we might have been friends. We might have gone to Disneyland once a year to experience some silliness.

I went back to my index cards and began to make notes. Every investigation has a nature of its own, but there are certain shared characteristics, namely the painstaking accumulation of information and the patience required. Here's what you hope for: a chance remark from the former neighbor on a skip-trace, a penciled notation on the corner of a document, an exspouse with a grudge, the number on an account, an item overlooked at the scene of a crime. Here's what you expect: the dead ends, bureaucratic bullheadedness, the cul-de-sacs, trails that go nowhere or simply fade into thin air, denials, prevarications, the blank-eyed stares from all the hostile witnesses. Here's what you know: that you've done it before and you have the toughness and determination to pull it off again. Here's what you want: justice. Here's what you'll settle for: something equivalent, the quid pro quo.

I glanced down at my desk, catching sight of the label on the file of clippings. The label had been neatly typed: *Guy Malek, Dispatch Clippings*. The two letters from Outhwaite were lined up with the label itself, which is what made me notice for the first time that the lowercase *a* and the lowercase *i* were both defective on all three documents. Was that true? I peered closely, picking up my magnifying glass again and scrutinizing the relevant characters. It would take a document expert to prove it, but to me it looked like the letters had been typed on the same machine.

I reached for the phone and called the Maleks. In the tiny interval between punching in the number and waiting for it to ring, I was scrambling around in my imagination, trying to conjure up a reason for the call I was making. Shit, shit, shit. Christie picked up on her end, greeting me coolly when I identified myself. I figured she'd talked to Paul Trasatti, but I didn't dare ask.

I said, "I was just looking for Bennet. Is he home, by any chance? I stopped by the restaurant, but he was out somewhere."

"He should be here in a bit. I think he said he was coming home for lunch. You want him to call you?"

"I'm not sure he'll be able to reach me. I'm down at the office, but I've got some errands to run. I'll call back later."

"I'll pass the message along." She was using her good-bye tone.

I had to launch in with something to keep the conversation afloat. "I talked to Paul this morning. What an odd duck he is. Is he still on medication?"

I could hear her focus her attention. "Paul's on medication? Who told you that? I never heard that," she said.

I let a beat pass. "Uhh, sorry. I didn't mean to breach anybody's confidence. Forget I said anything. I just assumed you knew."

"Why bring it up at all? Is there a problem?"

"Well, nothing *huge*. He's just so paranoid about Jack. He actually sat there and accused me of undermining Jack's credibility, which couldn't be further from the truth. Lonnie and I are working our butts off for him."

"Really."

"Then he turned around and called Lonnie. I think he's probably on another phone rampage, hounding everyone he knows with those wild stories of his. Ah, well. It doesn't matter. I'm sure he means well, but he's not doing anybody any favors."

"Is that what you wanted to talk to Bennet about?"

"No, that was something different. Lonnie wanted me to verify Bennet's whereabouts Tuesday night."

"I'm sure he'll be happy to talk to you. I know he's told the police and they seem satisfied. I can leave him a note."

"Perfect. I'd appreciate that. Can I ask you about something? You remember the file I borrowed?"

"With all the clippings?"

"Exactly. I wondered about the label. Did you type that yourself?"

"Not me. I never took typing. My mother warned me about that. Bader probably typed the label or he gave it to his secretary. He thought typing was restful. Shows how much he knew."

"That must have been a while ago. I don't remember seeing a typewriter in his office when I was there."

"He got himself a personal computer a couple of years ago."

"What happened to the typewriter?"

"He passed it on to Bennet, I think."

I closed my eyes and stilled my breathing. Christie's attitude had changed and she was sounding friendly again. I didn't want to alert her to the importance of the information. "What'd Bennet do with it? That's not the one he's using at the restaurant, is it?"

"Nuhn-uhn. I doubt it. It's probably in his room. What's this about?"

"Nothing much. No big deal. Just a little theory of mine, but I'd love to see it sometime. Would it be all right with you if I stopped by to take a look?"

"Well, it's all right with me, but Bennet might object unless he's here, of course. His room is like the inner sanctum. Nobody goes in there except him. We're just on our way out. We have an appointment at eleven. Why don't you ask Bennet when you talk to him?"

"I can do that. No problem. That's a good idea," I said. "And one more quick question. The night of the murder, could you really see Donovan? Or did you just assume he was watching television because the set was turned on in the other room?"

Christie put the phone down without another word.

The minute I hung up, I wrote a hasty note to Dietz, put a couple of pieces of blank paper in the file, and shoved it in my handbag. I headed out the side door and took the stairs down to the street, skipping two at a time. I wasn't sure which "we" had an appointment at eleven, but I was hoping it was Christie and Donovan. If I could get to the Maleks' before Bennet came home, I could probably bullshit my way upstairs and take a look at the machine. It had occurred to me more than once that Jack or Bennet might be behind the letters and the leak to the press. I couldn't pinpoint the motivation, but getting a lock on the typewriter would go a long way toward shoring up the connection. I was also thinking tee-hee on you, Dietz, because I'd told him whoever wrote the letters wouldn't trash the machine. It's the same way with guns. Someone will use a handgun in the commission of a crime and instead of disposing of the weapon, he'll keep it in his closet at home or shove it under the bed. Better to pitch it in the ocean.

I reached the Maleks' in record time, burning up the route I'd driven so many times before. As I approached the estate, I could see the front gates swing open and the nose of a car just appearing around the curve in the drive. I slammed on my brakes and slid into the nearest driveway, fishtailing slightly, my eyes pinned on my rear-view mirror for a moment until the BMW sped past. Donovan was driving, his gaze fixed on the road ahead. I thought I caught sight of Christie, but I couldn't be sure. I heard a car horn toot and looked out through my windshield. The Maleks' neighbor, in a dark blue station wagon, was waiting patiently for me to get out of his driveway. I made lots of sheepish gestures as I put my car in reverse. I backed out of the driveway and pulled over to let him pass. I mouthed the word *Sorry* as he turned to look at me. He smiled and waved, and I waved back at him. Once he was out of sight, I pulled out, crossing the road to the Maleks' entrance gates.

The security guard had been relieved of his duties. I leaned out toward the call box and punched in the gate code Tasha had given me. There was a happy peeping signal. The gates gave a little wiggle and then swung open to admit me. I eased up the driveway and around the curve. Vaguely, it occurred to me that Christie might have stayed home. I'd have to think of a whopper to account for my arrival. Oh, well. Often the best lies are the ones you think up in a pinch.

There were no cars in the courtyard, a good sign I thought. Two of the three garages were standing open and both were empty. I had to leave my vehicle out front, but there didn't seem to be any way around that. If my purpose was legitimate, why would I bother to conceal my car? If the Maleks returned, I'd find a way to fake it. I bypassed the front door and hiked around to the kitchen, pulling the file from my handbag as I rounded the house. Enid was visible through the bay window, standing at the sink. She spotted me and waved, moving toward the backdoor to let me in. She was still drying her hands on a towel when she stepped back, allowing me to precede her into the room.

I said, "Hi, Enid. How are you?"

"Fine," she said. "What are you doing coming to the backdoor? You just missed Christie and Donovan going out the front." She was wearing a big white apron over jeans and a T-shirt and her hair was neatly tucked under a crocheted cap.

"Really? I didn't see them. I rang the front doorbell twice. I guess you couldn't hear me so I thought I'd come around. I can't believe I missed them. My timing's off," I said.

I could see the ingredients for a baking project laid out on the counter: two sticks of butter with the paper removed, a sixteen-ounce measuring cup filled with granulated sugar, a tin of baking powder, and a quart container of whole milk. The oven was preheating and a large springform pan had already been buttered and floured.

She returned to the counter where she picked up her sifter and began sifting cake flour into a mountain that had a perfect point on top. While I watched, she used a spatula to scoop more flour. I seldom bake anything and when I do, I tend to assemble the items as needed, not realizing I'm missing some essential ingredient until I get to the critical moment in the recipe. "Quickly fold in whipped egg whites and finely minced fresh ginger . . ." Enid was methodical, washing up as she went along. I knew she wouldn't bake anything from mixes and her cakes would never fall.

"Where'd everybody go? I didn't see any cars in the garages," I said.

"Myrna's lying down. I imagine she'll be up in a bit."

"What's wrong with her? Is she ill?"

"I don't know. She seems worried and I don't think she's been sleeping that well."

"Maybe I should talk to her. Where's everyone else?"

"Christie says Bennet's coming home at lunchtime. She and Donovan went over to the funeral home. The coroner's office called. The body's being released this afternoon and they've gone to pick out a casket."

"When's the funeral? Has anybody said?"

"They're talking about Monday, just for family and close friends. It won't be open to the public."

"I should think not. I'm sure they've had their fill of media attention."

"Can I help you with anything?"

"Not really. I talked to Christie a while ago and told

her I'd be returning this file. She said to stick it in Bader's office. I can let myself out the front door when I'm done."

"Help yourself," she said. "Take the back stairs if you want. You know how to find the office?"

"Sure. I've been up there before. What are you making?"

"Lemon pound cake."

"Sounds good," I said.

I trotted up the back stairs, folder in hand, slowing my pace when I reached the top landing. The back hall was utilitarian, floors uncarpeted, windows bare. This mansion was built in an era when the wealthy had live-in servants who occupied nooks and crannies squeezed into wings at the rear of the house, or wedged into attic spaces that were broken up into many small rooms. Cautiously, I opened a door on my left. A narrow stairway ascended into the shadows above. I eased the door shut and moved on, checking into a large linen closet and a cubicle with an ancient commode. The corridor took a ninety-degree turn to the right, opening into the main hall through an archway concealed by heavy damask drapes on a wrought-iron rod.

I could see the polished rail of the main stair at the midpoint in the hall. Beyond the stair landing, there was another wing of the house that mirrored the one I was now in. A wide Oriental runner stretched the length of the gloomy hall. At the far end, damask drapes suggested an archway and yet another set of stairs. The wall-paper was subdued, a soft floral pattern repeated endlessly. At intervals, tulip-shaped crystal fixtures were mounted on the walls. They'd probably been installed when the house was built and converted at some point from gas to electricity.

There were three doors on my left, each sealed with an enormous X of crime scene tape. I had to guess that one door led to Guy's bedroom, one to Jack's, and one to the bathroom that connected the two. On the right, there were two more doors. I knew the second was Bader's suite: bedroom, bath, and home office. The door closest to me was closed. I flicked a look behind me, making sure Enid hadn't followed. The whole house was silent. I put my hand on the knob and turned it with care. Locked.

Well, now what? The lock was the simple old-fashioned type requiring a skeleton key that probably fit every door up here. I scanned the hall in both directions. I didn't have time to waste. Bader's suite was closest. I did a racewalk to his bedroom and tried the knob. This room was unlocked. I peered around the door. There was a key protruding neatly from the keyhole on the other side. I extracted it and hurried back to Bennet's room. I jammed the key in the lock and tried turning it. I could feel the key hang, but there was some tolerance to the lock. I applied steady pressure while I jiggled the door gently. It took close to thirty seconds, but the key gave way suddenly and I was in.

TWENTY-ONE

I scanned the room quickly, taking in as much as I could. Two table lamps had been left on. This had to be Bennet's bedroom. He was still in possession of all the paraphernalia from his boyhood hobbies. Model airplanes, model cars, stacks of vintage comic books, early issues of *MAD* magazine, Little League trophies. He'd framed a paint-by-numbers likeness of Jimmy Durante and a color snapshot of himself at the age of thirteen wearing spiffy black dress pants, a pink dress shirt, and a black bolo tie. His bulletin board was still hanging on the back of his closet door. Tacked to the cork were various newspaper headlines about the assassinations of Martin Luther King, Jr., and Bobby Kennedy. There were photographs of the *Apollo 8* spacecraft the day it was launched from Cape Kennedy. A framed movie poster from *The Odd Couple* still hung above his unmade bed. It wasn't hard to pinpoint the peak year in his life. There was no memorabilia beyond 1968.

I flicked on the overhead light and crossed the room, placing my handbag on the floor near my feet. His desk was built-in and ran along the front wall from one side of the room to the other, punctuated by two windows. Bookshelves had been hung on the wall above the desk. Most of the books looked dated, the titles suggestive of textbooks accumulated over the years. I let my gaze skip across the spines. *Ring of Bright Water*, Maxwell; *No Room in the Ark*, Moorehead; *Stalking the Edible Life*, Gibbons; *The Sea Around Us*, Carson. Little or no fiction. Not surprising somehow. Bennet didn't strike me as intellectual or imaginative. A personal computer occupied his desk at center stage, complete with an oversized printer. The machine had been shut down and the glassy gray screen of the monitor reflected distorted slices of the light from the hall door. Everything was a jumble; bills, loose papers, invoices, and stacks of unopened mail everywhere. I spotted the typewriter to the left, covered with a black plastic typewriter "cozy" complete with dust. A stack of books had been placed on top.

I backed up and stuck my head out into the hallway. I did a quick survey, seeing no one, and then closed myself into Bennet's room. If I were caught, there was no way I was going to explain my presence. I went back to the desk, lifted the stack of books from the typewriter, and removed the cover. The machine was an old black high-shouldered Remington with a manual return. Bader must have hung on to the damn thing for forty years. I reached into my bag and removed a piece of blank paper from the folder. I rolled it into the machine, typing precisely the phrases and sentences I'd typed before. *The quick brown fox jumps over the lazy dog.* The typewriter made a racket that seemed remarkably noisy, but it couldn't be helped. With the door to the hall closed, I thought I was safe. *Dear Miss Milhone.* *Max Outhwaite.* Even at a glance, I knew I was in business. The *a* and the *i* were both askew. This was the machine I'd been looking for. I rolled the paper from the machine, folded it, and slipped it in my pocket. Out of the corner of my eye, the name Outhwaite suddenly popped into view. Was I seeing things? I checked the line of textbooks again, squinting as I pulled out the two books that caught my attention. *Ring of Bright Water*, Gavin Maxwell, was the first in that row. In the middle, about six books down, was *Atlantic: History of an Ocean.* The author was Leonard Outhwaite. I stared, feeling rooted in place. Gavin Maxwell and Leonard Outhwaite. *Maxwell Outhwaite.*

I slipped the cover over the typewriter and put the stack of books back in place. I heard a low rumble, like thunder. I paused. Empty coat hangers began to ring, tinkling together in the closet like wind chimes. All the joints in the house began to squeak quietly and the window glass gave a sharp rattle where the putty had shrunk away from the panes. Nails and wood screws chirped. I put a hand on the bookshelf to steady myself. Under me, the whole house shifted back and forth, perhaps no more than an inch, but with a movement that felt like a sudden gust of strong wind or a train rocking on a track. I didn't feel any fear, but I was alert, wondering if I'd have time to clear the premises. An old house like this must have survived many a temblor, but you never quite knew what was coming with these things. So far, I pegged it in the three- or four-point range. As long as it didn't go on and on, it shouldn't do much damage. Lights flickered faintly as if wires were loose and touching one another intermittently. The strobe effect sparked a series of jerky pale blue images, in the midst of which a dark shape appeared across the room. I peered, blinking, trying to see clearly as the shadow moved toward one corner and then blended into the wall.

I made a small sound in my throat, paralyzed. The trembling gradually ceased and the lights stabilized. I clung to the bookshelf and leaned my head weakly on my arm, trying to shake off the frosty feeling that was creeping down my spine. Any minute, I expected to hear Enid calling from the kitchen stairs. I pictured Myrna on her feet, the three of us comparing notes about the earthquake. I didn't want either one of them coming up to search for me. I snagged my handbag and crossed the room. I moved out into the hall, looking quickly in both directions. I locked the door behind me, cranking the key in the lock so hard it nearly bent under my hand.

I ran down the hall on tiptoe, making a hasty detour into Bader's room. I put the key back in the door where I'd found it, then crossed swiftly into his home office. I opened a file cabinet and shoved the folder between two unrelated files where I could find it later. I crossed the room again and went out into the corridor. I walked quickly toward the heavy drapes at the end of the hall, pushed my way through the arch, and hurried along the back corridor. I clattered down the stairs and into the kitchen. There was no sign of Myrna. Enid was calmly pouring a thick yellow batter into the springform pan.

I put my hand on my chest to still my breathing. "Jesus. That was something. I thought for a minute there we were really in for it."

She looked up at me blankly. I could tell she didn't have the faintest idea what I was talking about.

I stopped in my tracks. "The temblor," I said.

"I wasn't aware of any temblor. When was this?"

"Enid, you're kidding. Don't do this to me. It must have been at least four points on the Richter scale. Didn't the lights flicker down here?"

"Not that I noticed." I watched her use a rubber spatula to sweep the last of the batter from the bowl into the pan.

"The whole house was shifting. Didn't you feel *anything?*"

She was silent for a moment, her gaze dropping to her bowl. "You hang on to people, don't you?"

"What?"

"You have trouble letting go."

"I do not. That's not a bit true. People tell me I'm too independent for my own good."

She was shaking her head before I reached the end of the sentence. "Independence has nothing to do with hanging on," she said.

"What are you talking about?"

"Ghosts don't haunt us. That's not how it works. They're present among us because we won't let go of *them.*"

"I don't believe in ghosts," I said, faintly.

"Some people can't see the color red. That doesn't mean it isn't there," she replied.

*

When I reached the office, Dietz was sitting in my swivel chair with his feet up on the desk. One of the sandwich packets had been opened and he was munching on a BLT. I still hadn't eaten lunch so I reached for the other sandwich. I removed a soft drink from the refrigerator and sat down across from him.

"How'd you do at the *Dispatch*?"

He laid the four Maddison obituaries on the desk so I could study them. "I had Jeff Katzenbach dig through the files. Mother's maiden name was Bangham, so I went over to the library and checked the city directory for other Banghams in the area. None. Three of those obits I've verified at the Hall of Records, checking death certificates. Claire's still a question mark."

"How so?" I popped the top on my soda can and began to pick at the cellophane and plastic packet in which my sandwich was sealed.

Dietz was saying, "There's no suggestion how she died. I'd be interested in seeing if we can get the suicide confirmed just to put that one to bed. I got the name of a PI in Bridgeport, Connecticut, and left a lengthy message with her service. I'm hoping someone will return my call."

"What difference does it make how she died?" I tried biting the seal on the cellophane. Was this kiddie-proof, like poison? Dietz held his hand out for the wrapped sandwich and I passed it across the desk to him.

"Suppose she was murdered? Suppose she was the victim of a hit-and-run accident?" He freed the sandwich and gave it back to me.

"You've got a point," I said. I paused to eat while I reread the information. The obits were in date order,

starting with the father's death in late November 1967.
Dietz had had all four of them copied onto one page.

MADDISON, Francis M., 53,
departed suddenly on Tuesday, November 21.
Loving, adored husband of 25 years to Caroline
B. Maddison; beloved father to daughters, Claire
and Patricia. He was a service manager at Colgate
Automotive Center and a member of the
Community Christian Church. He was much loved
and will be missed by family and friends. Funeral:
11:30 A.M. Friday. In lieu of flowers, donations to
the American Heart Association would be
appreciated.

I glanced up at him and said, "Fifty-three. That's
young."

"They were all young," Dietz said.

MADDISON, Patricia Anne, 17,
died Thursday, May 9, at Santa Teresa Hospital.
She is survived by her loving mother, Caroline B.
Maddison, and a devoted sister, Claire Maddison.
At the family's request, services will be private.

MADDISON, Caroline B., 58,
died Tuesday, August 29, at her home after a
lengthy illness. She was born on January 22 to
Helen and John Bangham, in Indianapolis, Indiana,
graduating from Indiana University with a degree
in home economics. Caroline was a devoted wife,
mother, a homemaker, and a Christian. Preceded

in death by her husband, Francis M. Maddison,
and her daughter Patricia Anne Maddison.
Survived by loving daughter Claire Maddison of
Bridgeport, Connecticut. No services are planned.
Contributions may be made to Hospice of Santa
Teresa.

MADDISON, Claire, 39,
formerly of Santa Teresa, died Saturday, March 2,
in Bridgeport, Connecticut. Daughter of the late
Francis M. and Caroline B. Maddison, Claire was
preceded in death by her only sister, Patricia. Claire
graduated from Santa Teresa High School in 1963
and the University of Connecticut in 1967. She
pursued her secondary teaching credential and MA
in Romance Languages at Boston College. She
taught French and Italian at a private girls' academy
in Bridgeport, Connecticut. Service, Tuesday in the
Memorial Park Chapel.

I read Claire's death notice twice. "This was just last
year."

"Thank goodness she'd gone back to her maiden
name," he said. "I don't know how we'd have found
her if she'd been using her ex-hubby's moniker."

"Whoever he was," I said. "She'd probably been
divorced for ages. There wasn't much family to speak
of. You watch the names of the survivors diminish until
there's no one left. It's depressing, isn't it?"

"I thought the mother might have surviving family
members in Indiana, but I can't seem to get a line
on them," Dietz said. "I tried directory assistance in

Indianapolis. There weren't any Banghams listed, so at least on the face of it, we're not talking about a large close-knit clan. Just to be on the safe side, I checked the CALI Directory and put a call through to an Indianapolis private investigator. I asked him to check Caroline Bangham's birth records to see if that nets us anything. We might not glean much, but he said he'd get back to us."

I made a face. "You know what? I think we're spinning our wheels on this one. I just don't buy the idea that some distraught family member would seek revenge eighteen years later."

"Maybe not," he said. "If it weren't for Bader's death, there wouldn't have been a reason to look for Guy at all. He might have gone on living in Marcella for the rest of his days."

"It wasn't strictly Bader's death. It was the will," I said.

"Which brings us back to the five million."

"I guess it does," I said. "I'll tell you what hurts. I feel like I was part of what happened to Guy."

"Because you found him."

"Exactly. I didn't cause his death, in any strict sense of the word, but if it hadn't been for me, he'd be safe the way I see it."

"Hey, come on. That's not true. Tasha would have hired herself some other detective. Maybe not as good as you . . ."

"Don't suck up."

"Look, someone would have found him. It just happened to be you."

"I suppose," I said. "It still feels like shit."

"I'm sure it does."

The phone rang. Dietz answered and then handed me the handset, mouthing the name *Enid*.

I nodded and took the phone. "Hi, Enid. This is Kinsey. How are you?"

"Not so good," she said, fretfully. "Did Myrna call you?"

"Not as far as I know. Let me check my messages." I put a hand across the mouthpiece. "Did the Maleks' housekeeper call or leave a message for me?"

Dietz shook his head and I went back to Enid. "No, there's nothing here."

"Well, that's odd. She swore she was going to call you. I made her promise she would. I went to the supermarket and I was only gone fifteen or twenty minutes. She said she'd be here when I got back, but she's gone and there's no sign of her. I thought you might have asked her to come in."

"Sorry. I never heard from her. What's she want to talk to me about?"

"I'm not sure. I know something's been bothering her, but she wouldn't be specific. Her car's still out back. That's what's so strange," she said.

"Could she have gone to the doctor's? If she really wasn't feeling well, she might have called a cab."

"It's always possible, but you'd think she would have waited to have me take her. This is just so unlike her. She told me she'd help me with dinner. I have a meeting at seven and I have to be out of here early. We discussed it in detail."

"Maybe she's out walking somewhere on the property."

"I thought of that," she said. "I went out there myself, calling, but she's disappeared."

"Enid, let's be realistic. I don't think being gone less than an hour constitutes a disappearance."

"I'm worried something's happened."

"Like what?"

"I don't know. That's why I called you. Because I'm scared."

"What's the rest?"

"That's it."

"No, it's not. You're leaving something out. I mean, so far this doesn't make sense. Do you think she's been abducted by aliens, or what?"

I could hear her hesitation. "I got the impression she knew something about the murder."

"Really? She said that?"

"She hinted as much. She was too nervous to say more. I think she saw something she wasn't supposed to see that night."

"She told me she was sleeping."

"Well, she was. She'd taken some pain medication and a sleeping pill. She slept like the dead, but then she remembered later that she woke up at one point to find someone standing at the foot of her bed."

"Wait a minute, Enid. You're not talking about this woo-woo stuff . . ."

"Not at all. I promise. This is what she said. She said she thought she'd been dreaming, but the more she thought about it, the more convinced she was that it was real."

"What was?"

"The person she saw."

"I gathered that, Enid. Who?"

"She wouldn't tell me. She felt guilty she hadn't said anything before now."

"Myrna feels guilty about everything," I said.

"I know," Enid said. "But I think she was also worried about the consequences. She thought she'd be in danger if she opened her mouth. I told her to tell the police, in that case, but she was afraid to do that. She said she'd rather talk to you first and then she'd talk to them. It's not like her to go off without a word."

"You did check her room?"

"That's the first thing I did. And that's the other thing that bothers me. Something doesn't seem right. Myrna's very fussy. Everything has to be just so with her. I don't mean to criticize, but it's the truth."

"Her room is messed up?"

"It's not exactly messed up, but it doesn't look right."

"Who else is there? Is anybody home besides you?"

"Bennet was here, but I think he's gone. He came in for lunch. I fixed him a sandwich and he took it up to his room. He must have left again while I was at the market. Christie and Donovan are due back any minute. I don't mean to be a bother, but I don't feel right about this."

Dietz was giving me an inquisitive look. Having eavesdropped on my end of the conversation with her, he was suitably mystified. "Hang on a second." I put a palm across the mouthpiece. "How long will you be here?"

"At least an hour," he said. "If you'd ever get off the phone, I might get this call from the East Coast that I've been waiting for. What's the problem?"

"It's Myrna. I'll tell you in a minute." I went back to Enid. "Why don't I come over there," I said. "She might have mentioned something to Christie before they left for the funeral home. You're sure she didn't leave a note?"

"Positive."

"I'll be there in fifteen minutes."

"I don't want you to go to any trouble."

"It's no trouble."

I took my sandwich and soda with me, driving with one hand while I finished my lunch. I kept the chilled soda can between my thighs. Shifting gears is a pain in the ass when you're trying to dine in style. At least I knew the route. I could have done it with my eyes shut.

Enid had left the gate open for me. I pulled into the courtyard and left my car in a spot I was beginning to think should be reserved for me. Donovan's pickup truck was parked to one side of the garage. At first, I thought he was back, but then I remembered that he'd been driving the BMW when he left. Both the open garages were still empty. The driveway angled up along the house on the left. For the first time, I noticed a separate parking pad nearby with spaces for three vehicles. Currently, I could see a bright yellow VW convertible and what looked like a Toyota, a pale metallic blue, maybe three or four years old.

Enid had the backdoor ajar and was standing in the opening. She'd taken off her apron to do the marketing and she now wore a jacket as though chilled by circumstance.

I moved into the utility room. "Still no sign of her?" I asked, following Enid through a door that opened into a rear hall.

"Not a peep," she said. "I'm sorry to be a bother. I'm probably being silly."

"Don't worry about it. You've had a murder in the house. Everybody's nerves are on edge. Is one of those cars out there hers?"

"The Toyota," she said. She paused in front of a door at the end of the hall. "This is hers."

"Have you tried knocking on her door since we talked?"

Enid shook her head. "I think I scared myself. I didn't want to do anything until you arrived."

"Geez, Enid. You're scaring me," I said. I knocked on the door, my head tilted against the panel, listening for sounds that might indicate Myrna was back. I was reluctant to barge right in. She might be napping or naked, just out of the shower. I didn't want to catch her with her dentures out or her wooden leg unstrapped. I tapped again with one knuckle. "Myrna?"

Dead silence.

I tried the knob, which turned easily. I opened the door a crack and peered around the frame. The sitting room was empty. Across from me, the door to the bedroom was standing open and the room appeared to be empty. "Myrna, you in here? It's Kinsey Millhone," I said. I waited a moment and then crossed the room. In passing, I put my hand on the television set, but the housing was cold.

"I told you she wasn't here," Enid said.

I looked into the bedroom. I could see why Enid

felt something was wrong. On the surface, both rooms seemed tidy and untouched, but there was something amiss. It was the little things, the minutiae. The bed was made, but the coverlet was not quite smooth. A picture on the wall was ever so slightly tilted.

"When was the last time you actually saw her?" I leaned down and peeked under the bed, feeling like an idiot. There was nothing under there except an old pair of bedroom slippers.

"Must have been noon."

"Was Bennet here at that point?"

"I don't remember. He was gone when I got back from the market. That's all I know."

In the sitting room, the shade on the floor lamp was askew and it was clear from the dents in the carpet the base had been moved from its usual place. Had there been a struggle of some kind? I looked in the closet. Enid followed me like a kid, about three steps back, possibly feeling the same eerie sense of intrusion that I felt.

"Can you tell if all her clothes are here? Anything missing? Shoes? Coat?"

Enid studied the rack. "I think everything's here," she said and then pointed. "That's her suitcase and her garment bag."

"What about her handbag?"

"It's in the kitchen. I knew you'd ask so I opened it. Her wallet's in there, driver's license, cash, all that stuff."

I moved into the bathroom. I heard a little pop under my shoe, followed by the kind of scratching sound that makes you think of broken glass on ceramic floor tile.

I looked down. There was a touch of dry soil, as from the bottom of a shoe, and two tiny pieces of gravel. "Be careful. I don't want us to disturb that," I said to Enid, who was crowding into the room on my heels.

"Was someone in here?"

"I don't know yet. It could be."

"It looks like someone tried to straighten up and didn't do a very good job of it," she said. "Myrna always left notes if she was going somewhere. She wouldn't just walk out."

"Don't start babbling. I'm trying to concentrate."

I checked the medicine cabinet. All the obvious toiletries were still sitting on the shelf: toothbrush, toothpaste, deodorant, odds and ends of makeup, prescription bottles. The shower curtain was bone-dry, but a dark blue washcloth had been draped over the rim of the basin and it had been recently used. I peered closely at the basin. There was a trace of water around the small brass ring fixture for the outflow valve. Unless my eyes were deceiving me, the water was ever so faintly pink. I lifted the washcloth and squeezed out some of the excess water. There was a splash of bright red against the white of the basin. "You better call 9–1–1. This is blood," I said.

While Enid went off to call the police, I closed the door to Myrna's apartment and I retraced my steps through the utility room to the backdoor. In the kitchen, I could hear Enid on the phone, sounding shaken and slightly shrill. Someone must have been waiting to catch Myrna alone. Outside, I crossed the small back patio and took a right at the driveway. Myrna's car was locked, but I circled the exterior, peering in at the front seats and back seats. Both were empty. Nothing on the dashboard. I was curious if the trunk was locked, but I didn't want to touch it. Let the cops do that. To the right, the driveway formed a dead end with space for three more cars. Beyond that, I saw a long line of drab pink stucco wall and a tangle of woods. Suppose she'd been killed in haste? What would you do with the body?

I headed back toward the garages. Donovan's pickup was parked much closer to the front of the house than the back. There was something about the traces of gravel and dried soil that bothered me. I put a hand out. The hood of the pickup was warm. I walked around the truck, hands behind my back as I scrutinized the exterior. The bed liner was littered with gravel and dead leaves. I peered over the tailgate, looking closely at the liner. There was what looked like a dark smear on one edge. I left that alone. Whatever had happened, they couldn't blame Jack this time.

In the distance, I heard the rumble of a motorcycle and moments later, I looked up to see Bennet roaring down the drive on Jack's Harley-Davidson. I moved away from the truck, watching as he went through his parking ritual. His black leather gloves looked as clumsy as oven mitts. He pulled them off and laid them on the seat, placing his helmet on top. He didn't seem that thrilled to see me. "What are you doing here?"

"Enid called about Myrna. When did you last see her?"

"I saw her at breakfast. I didn't see her at lunch. Enid told me she wasn't feeling well. What's going on?"

"I have no idea. Apparently, she's disappeared. Enid called the police. They'll be here shortly, I'd imagine."

"The police? What for?"

"Why don't you save the bullshit for the cops," I said.

"Wait a minute. 'Bullshit'? What's the matter with you? I'm tired of being treated like a creep," he said.

I started walking away.

"Where are you going?"

"What difference does it make? If I stand here another minute, I'll just end up insulting you."

Bennet walked alongside me. "That wouldn't be a first. I heard about your meeting with Paul. He was pissed as hell."

"So what?" I said.

"I know you think we did something."

"Of course I do!"

He touched my arm. "Look. Hang on a minute and let's talk about this."

"Go ahead and talk, Bennet. I'd love to hear what you have to say."

"All right. Okay. I might as well level with you because the truth isn't nearly as bad as you think."

"How do you know what I think? I think you cheated the Maddisons out of fifty thousand dollars' worth of rare documents."

"Now wait a minute. Now wait. We didn't mean any harm. It was just a prank. We wanted to go to Vegas, but we were broke. We didn't have a dime between us. All we wanted was a few bucks. We were only kids," he said.

"Kids? You weren't kids. You were twenty-three years old. You committed a felony. Is that your rationalization, calling it a prank? You should have gone to prison."

"I know. I'm sorry. It got out of hand. We never thought we could pull it off and by the time we realized how serious it was, we didn't have the courage to admit what we'd done."

"It didn't seem to bother you to blame Guy," I said.

"Listen, he was gone. And he'd done all that other stuff. The family was down on him and Dad just assumed. We were assholes. I know that. We were wrong. I've never felt right about it since."

"Well, that absolves you," I said. "What happened to the letters? Where are they?"

"Paul has them at his place. I told him to destroy them, but he couldn't bear to do it. He's been afraid to put them in circulation."

I could feel my mouth pull down with disgust. "So you didn't even get the money? You are a creep," I said. "Let's talk about Patty."

"The baby wasn't mine. I swear. I never screwed her."

"Paul did, didn't he? And so did Jack."

"A lot of fellas screwed her. She didn't care."

"Not Guy. He never laid a hand on her," I said.

"Not Guy," he repeated. "I guess that's true."

"So whose baby was it?"

"Probably Jack's," Bennet said. "But that doesn't mean he killed Guy. I didn't either. I wouldn't do that," he said.

"Oh, come on. Grow up. You never accepted any responsibility for what happened, the whole lot of you. You let Guy take the blame for everything you did.

Even when he came back, you never let him off the hook."

"What was I supposed to say? It was too late by then."

"Not for him, Bennet. Guy was still alive at that point. *Now*, it's too late."

I looked up to see Enid standing by the hedge. I had no idea how much she'd overheard. She said, "Your partner's on the phone. The police are on the way."

I moved past Enid and walked down the short flight of stairs, crossing the patio to the kitchen door. I found the handset on the counter and I picked it up. "It's me. What's going on?"

"Are you all right? You sound bad."

"I can't stop to tell you. It would take too long. I should have fallen on Bennet and beat the man to death."

"Catch this. I just had a chat with the private investigator in Bridgeport, Connecticut. This gal was at the courthouse when she called in to pick up messages. She went right to the clerk and filled out a request for Claire Maddison's death certificate."

"What was the cause of death?"

"There wasn't one," he said. "As long as she was at it, she made a couple more phone calls and got her last known address. According to the utility company, Claire was living in Bridgeport until last March."

"How did the *Dispatch* end up printing her obituary?"

"Because she sent them one. No one ever asked for proof. I called the *Dispatch* myself and verified the whole procedure. They take down the information and they print it as given."

"She made the whole thing up?"

"I'm sure she did," he said.

"So where did she go?"

"I'm just getting to that. This PI in Bridgeport picked up one more little item. Claire never worked as a teacher. She was a private-duty nurse."

"Shit."

"That's what I said. I'm coming over. Don't do anything until I get there," he said.

"What's to do? I can't move."

How long did I stand at the kitchen counter with the phone in my hand? In a flash, I could see how all the pieces fit. I was missing a few answers, but the rest of them finally fell into place. Somehow Claire Maddison heard about Bader's terminal illness. She shipped the *Dispatch* an obituary just to close that door. She turned herself into Myrna Sweetzer, packed her personal belongings, and headed back to Santa Teresa. Bader was difficult. As a patient, he was probably close to impossible. He must have gone through a number of private-duty nurses, so it was only a matter of Myrna's biding her time. Once she was in the house, the family was hers. She had waited a long time, but the chance to wreak havoc must have been something she savored.

I tried to put myself in her place. Where was she now? She'd accomplished much of her mission, so it was time to fade. She'd left her car, her handbag, and all her clothes. What would I do if I were Claire Maddison? The whole psychodrama of the missing Myrna was just a cover for her escape. She must have pictured the cops digging up the property, looking for a body that was never there. To have the disappearance play out properly, she had to make an exit without being seen, which ruled out a taxicab. She might steal a car, but that was risky on the face of it. And how would she leave town? Would she hitchhike? A motorist passing through might never be aware that anyone was missing or presumed dead. Plane, train, or bus?

She might have a confederate, but much of what she'd done to date required a solitary cunning. She'd been gone more than an hour—plenty of time to walk through the back of the property to the road. I lifted my head. I could hear voices in the foyer. The cops had probably arrived. I didn't want to go through this whole rigmarole. Enid was saying, "It was just so unlike her so I called . . ."

I slipped out the backdoor, racewalking across the patio and out to the driveway. I got in my car and turned the key in the ignition. My brain was clicking along, trying to make sense of circumstances. Claire Maddison was alive and had been living in Santa Teresa since last spring. I wasn't really sure how she'd managed the setup, but I was relatively certain she was responsible for Guy's death. She'd also gone to some lengths to implicate the others, setting it up so that Jack looked guilty, with Bennet as the backup in case the evidence of Jack's culpability failed to persuade the police.

The gate swung open in front of me. I reached the road and turned left, trying to picture the way the property was laid out in relation to the surrounding terrain. I didn't imagine she'd head into the Los Padres National Forest. The mountain was too steep and too inhospitable. It was possible, of course, that in the last eighteen years, Claire Maddison had become an expert at living in the wild. Maybe she planned to make a new home for herself among the scrub oaks and chaparral, feasting on wild berries, sucking moisture from cactus pads. More likely, she'd simply crossed the few acres of undeveloped land that lay between the Maleks' and the road. Bader had purchased everything within range, so it was possible she was still trudging across acreage he owned.

I tried to think what she'd do once she hit the main artery. She could choose left or right, setting out in either direction on foot. She could have hidden a bicycle somewhere in the brush. She might depend on her ability to thumb a ride. Maybe she'd called a taxicab and had it waiting when she emerged on the road. Again, I dismissed that option because I didn't really think she'd take the risk. She wouldn't want to have anyone who could identify or describe her later. She might have purchased another vehicle and parked on a side street, gassed up and ready to be driven away. I tried to remember what I knew of her and realized just how little it was. She was approaching forty. She was overweight. She made no effort to enhance her personal appearance. Given cultural standards, she'd made herself invisible. Ours is a society in which slimness and beauty are equated with status, where youth and charm are rewarded and remembered with admiration. Let a woman be drab or slightly overweight and the collective eye slides right by, forgetting afterward. Claire Maddison had achieved the ultimate disguise because, aside from the physical, she'd adopted the persona of the servant class. Who knows what conversations she'd been privy to straightening the bed pillows, changing the sheets. She'd run the household, served canapes, and freshened the drinks while the lords and ladies of the house had talked on and on, oblivious to her presence because she wasn't one of them. For Claire, it had been perfect. Their dismissal of her would have fueled her bitterness and hardened her determination to take revenge. Why should this family, largely made up of fakes, enjoy the privileges of money while she had nothing? Because of them, she'd been cheated of her family, her medical career. She'd been robbed, violated, and abused, and for this she blamed Guy.

I was now on the two-lane road that I was guessing defined the Malek property along its southernmost boundary. I found a city map in my glove compartment and flapped it open as I drove. I made a clumsy fold and propped it up against the steering wheel, searching for routes while I tried not to ram into telephone poles. I started with the obvious, turning off at the first street, driving in a grid. I should have waited for Dietz. One of us could have been watching for pedestrians while the other drove. How far could she get?

I returned to the main road and drove on for maybe half a mile. I spotted her tramping along a hundred yards ahead of me. She was wearing jeans and good walking shoes, toting a backpack, no hat. I rolled down the window on the passenger side. As soon as she heard the rattle of my VW, she glanced once in my direction and then stared doggedly at the pavement in front of her.

"Myrna, I want to talk to you."

"Well, I don't want to talk to you."

I idled alongside her while cars coming up behind me honked impatiently. I motioned them around, keeping an eye fixed on Myrna who trudged on, tears running down her face. I gunned the engine, speeding off, pulling into the berm well ahead of her. I turned the engine off and got out, walking back to meet her.

"Come on, Myrna. Slow down. It's finally over," I said.

"No, it's not. It's never over until they pay up."

"Yeah, but how much? Listen, I understand how you feel. They took everything you had."

"The bastards," she said.

"Myrna . . ."

"My name is Claire."

"All right, Claire then. Here's the truth. You killed the wrong man. Guy never did anything to you or to your family. He's the only one who ever treated Patty well."

"Liar. You're lying. You made that up."

I shook my head. "Patty slept around. You know she had problems. Those were wild times. Dope and free love. We were all goofy with goodwill, with the notion of world peace. Remember? She was a flower child, an innocent—"

"She was schizophrenic," Claire spat.

"Okay. I'll take your word for it. She probably did LSD. She ate mushrooms. She stuck herself with things. And all the fellows took advantage of her, except Guy. I promise. He really cared about her. He told me about her and he was wistful and loving. He'd tried to get in touch. He wrote to her once, but she was dead by then. He had no idea. All he knew was he never heard from her and he felt bad about that."

"He was a turd."

"All right. He was a turd. He did a lot of shitty things back then, but at heart, he was a good man. Better than his brothers. They took advantage of him. Patty probably wished the baby was his, but it wasn't."

"Whose then?"

"Jack's. Paul Trasatti's. I'm not really sure how many men she slept with. Guy didn't forge the letters, either. That was Bennet and Paul, a little scheme they cooked up to earn some money that spring."

"They took everything away from me. Everything."

"I know. And now you've taken something away from them."

"What?" she said, her eyes blazing with disdain.

"You took the only decent man who ever bore the Malek name."

"Bader was decent."

"But he never made good. Your mother asked him for the money and he refused to pay."

"I didn't blame him for that."

"Too bad. You blamed Guy instead and he was innocent."

"Fuck off," she said.

"What else? What's the rest? I know there's more to this," I said. "You wrote the anonymous letter to Guy, the one the cops have, right?"

"Of course. Don't be dumb. I wrote all the letters up on Bennet's machine. For Guy's letter, I used the Bible.

I thought he'd like that . . . a message from Deuteronomy . . . 'And thy life shall hang in doubt before thee; and thou shalt fear day and night, and shalt have none assurance of thy life.' You like that?"

"Very apt. A good choice," I said.

"That's not all, doll. You missed the best part . . . the obvious . . . you and that fancy-pants probate attorney. I found both wills months ago when I first started working here. I searched through Bader's files every chance I had. I tore up the second will so someone would have to go out looking for Guy. You did all the work for me. I appreciate that."

"What about the blood in your bathroom? Where did that come from?"

She held her thumb up. "I used a lancet. I left a couple drops on the patio and another in the truck. There's a shovel behind the toolshed. That's got blood on it, too."

"What about the dirt and gravel on the bathroom floor?"

"I thought Donovan should have a turn in the barrel. Didn't you think of him when you saw it?"

"Actually he did cross my mind. I'd have gone after him if I hadn't figured out what was going on. But what now? None of this is going to work. The whole plan's caving in. Trying to hike out was dumb. You weren't that hard to find."

"So what? I'm out of here. I'm tired. Get away from me," she said.

"Myrna . . ." I said, patiently.

"It's Claire," she snapped. "What do you *want*?"

"I want the killing to stop. I want the dying to end. I want Guy Malek to rest easy wherever he is."

"I don't care about Guy," she said. Her voice quaked with emotion and her face looked drawn and tense.

"What about Patty? Don't you think she'd care?"

"I don't know. I've lost track. I thought I'd feel better, but I don't." She walked on down the road with me trotting after her. "There aren't any happy endings. You have to take what you get."

"There may not be a happy ending, but there are some that satisfy."

"Name one."

"Come back. Own up to what you did. Turn and face your demons before they eat you alive."

She was weeping freely, and in some curious way, she seemed very beautiful, touched with grace. She turned and started walking backward, her arm out, hand turned up, as though thumbing a ride. I was walking at the same pace, the two of us face-to-face. She caught my eye and smiled, shot a look over her shoulder to check for traffic coming the other way.

We had reached an intersection. There was a wide curve in the road ahead. The stoplight had changed and cars had surged forward, picking up speed. Even now, I'm not certain what she meant to do. For a moment, she looked at me fully and then she made a dash for it, flinging herself into the line of traffic like a diver plunging off a board. I thought she might escape destruction because the first vehicle missed her and a second car seemed to bump her without injury or harm. The drivers in both lanes were slamming on their brakes, swerving to avoid her. She ran on, stumbling as she entered the far lane. An oncoming car caught her and she sailed overhead, as limp as a rag doll, as joyous as a bird.

EPILOGUE

Peter and Winnie Antle came down for Guy's funeral service, which Peter conducted Monday afternoon. I thought the Maleks might object, but they seemed to think better of it. Tasha agreed to submit Guy's holographic will for probate and eventually his portion of the estate will be passed on to Jubilee Evangelical Church. I said nothing of Claire's destruction of the second will. Guy deserved his fair share and I don't think the family will make a fuss about his final wishes.

Last night, Guy Malek came to me in a dream. I don't remember now what the dream was about. It was a dream like any other, set in a landscape only half familiar, filled with events that didn't quite make sense. I remember feeling such relief. He was alive and whole and so very like himself. Somehow in the dream, I knew he'd come to say good-bye. I'd never had a chance to tell him how much he'd meant to me. I hadn't known him long, but some people simply affect us that way. Their sojourn is brief, but their influence is profound.

I clung to him. He didn't speak. He never said a word, but I knew he wanted me to let him go. He was far too polite to chide me for my reluctance. He didn't hurry me along, but he let me know what he needed. In the dream, I remember weeping. I thought if I refused, he would be mine to keep. I thought he could be with me forever, but it doesn't work that way. His time on earth was done. He had other places to go.

In the end, I set him free, not in sorrow, but in love. It wasn't for me. It was something I did for him. When I woke, I knew that he was truly gone. The tears I wept for him then were the same tears I'd wept for everyone I'd ever loved. My parents, my aunt. I had never said good-bye to them, either, but it was time to take care of it. I said a prayer for the dead, opening the door so all the ghosts could move on. I gathered them up like the petals of a flower and released them to the wind. What's done is done. What is written is written. Their work is finished. Ours is yet to do.

N is for Noose

FOR STEVEN,
who makes my life possible.

The author wishes to acknowledge the invaluable assistance of the following people: Steven Humphrey; Eric S. H. Ching; Shelly Dumas and Sergeant Dick Wood, Inyo County Sheriff's Department; Leon Brune, Inyo County Coroner; Donna Milovich, Spellbinder Books; Robert Failing, M.D.; Dennis Prescott, Supervisor (retired), and Larry Gillespie, Senior Investigator, Santa Barbara County Coroner's Office; Deputy Eric Raney, Commander Bill Crook, and Commander Terry Bunn, Santa Barbara County Sheriff's Department; Captain Ed Aasted, Santa Barbara Police Department; Bruce Bennet; Sheila Millington, Automobile Club of Southern California; Sylvia Stallings; Joe Peus, M.D.; B. J. Seebol; and John Hunt, CompuVision, for saving chapter 22.

ONE

Sometimes I think about how odd it would be to catch a glimpse of the future, a quick view of events lying in store for us at some undisclosed date. Suppose we could peer through a tiny peep-hole in Time and chance upon a flash of what was coming up in the years ahead. Some moments we saw would make no sense at all and some, I suspect, would frighten us beyond endurance. If we knew what was looming, we'd avoid certain choices, select option B instead of A at the fork in the road: the job, the marriage, the move to a new state, childbirth, the first drink, the elective medical procedure, that long-anticipated ski trip that seemed like such fun until the dark rumble of the avalanche. If we understood the consequences of any given action, we could exercise discretion, thus restructuring our fate. Time, of course, only runs in one direction, and it seems to do so in an orderly progression. Here in the blank and stony present, we're shielded from the knowledge of the dangers that await us, protected from future horrors through blind innocence.

Take the case in point. I was winding my way through the mountains in a cut-rate rental car, heading

3

south on 395 toward the town of Nota Lake, California, where I was going to interview a potential client. The roadway was dry and the view was unobstructed, weather conditions clear. The client's business was unremarkable, at least as far as I could see. I had no idea there was any jeopardy waiting or I'd have done something else.

I'd left Dietz in Carson City, where I'd spent the last two weeks playing nurse/companion while he recovered from surgery. He'd been scheduled for a knee replacement and I'd volunteered to drive him back to Nevada in his snazzy little red Porsche. I make no claims to nurturing, but I'm a practical person and the nine-hour journey seemed the obvious solution to the problem of how to get his car back to his home state. I'm a no-nonsense driver and he knew he could count on me to get us to Carson City without any unnecessary side trips and no irrelevant conversation. He'd been staying in my apartment for the two previous months and since our separation was approaching, we tended to avoid discussing anything personal.

For the record, my last name is Millhone, first name Kinsey. I'm female, twice divorced, seven weeks shy of thirty-six, and reasonably fit. I'm a licensed private detective, currently residing in Santa Teresa, California, to which I'm attached like a tetherball on a very short cord. Occasionally, business will swing me out to other parts of the country, but I'm basically a small-town shamus and likely to remain so for life.

Dietz's surgery, which was scheduled for the first Monday in March, proceeded uneventfully, so we can skip that part. Afterward, I returned to his condo-

minium and toured the premises with interest. I'd been
startled by the place when I first laid eyes on it, as it
was more lavish and much better appointed than my
poor digs back in Santa Teresa. Dietz was a nomad
and I'd never pictured his having much in the way
of material possessions. While I was closeted in a
converted single-car garage (recently remodeled to
accommodate a sleeping loft and a second bathroom
upstairs), Dietz maintained a three-bedroom penthouse
that probably encompassed three thousand square feet
of living space, including a roof patio and garden with
an honest-to-god greenhouse. Granted, the seven-story
building was located in a commercial district, but the
views were astounding and the privacy profound.

I'd been too polite to pry while he was standing right
there beside me, but once he was safely ensconced in
the orthopedic ward at Carson/Tahoe Hospital, I felt
comfortable scrutinizing everything in my immediate
range, which necessitated dragging a chair around and
standing on it in some cases. I checked closets and files
and boxes and papers and drawers, pockets and suitcases, feeling equal parts relief and disappointment that
he had nothing in particular to hide. I mean, what's the
point of snooping if you can't uncover something good?
I did have the chance to study a photograph of his ex-
wife, Naomi, who was certainly a lot prettier than he'd
ever indicated. Aside from that, his finances appeared
to be in order, his medicine cabinet contained no sinister
pharmaceutical revelations, and his private correspondence consisted almost entirely of assorted misspelled
letters from his two college-aged sons. Lest you think
I'm intrusive, I can assure you Dietz had searched my

apartment just as thoroughly during the time he was in residence. I know this because I'd left a few booby traps, one of which he'd missed when he was picking open my locked desk drawers. His license might have lapsed, but (most of) his operating skills were still current. Neither of us had ever mentioned his invasion of my privacy, but I vowed I'd do likewise when the opportunity arose. Between working detectives, this is known as professional courtesy. You toss my place and I'll toss yours.

He was out of the hospital by Friday morning of that week. The ensuing recovery involved a lot of sitting around with his knee wrapped in bandages as thick as a bolster. We watched trash television, played gin rummy, and worked a jigsaw puzzle with a picture depicting a roiling nest of earthworms so lifelike I nearly went off my feed. The first three days I did all the cooking, which is to say I made sandwiches, alternating between my famous peanut-butter-and-pickle extravaganza and my much beloved, sliced hot-hard-boiled-egg confection, with tons of Hellmann's mayonnaise and salt. After that, Dietz seemed eager to get back into the kitchen and our menus expanded to include pizza, take-out Chinese, and Campbell's soup—tomato or asparagus, depending on our mood.

By the end of two weeks Dietz could pretty well fend for himself. His stitches were out and he was hobbling around with a cane between bouts of physical therapy. He had a long way to go, but he could drive to his sessions and otherwise seemed able to tend to his own needs. By then, I thought it entirely possible I'd go mad from trailing after him. It was time to hit the road before our togetherness began to chafe. I enjoyed being with him, but I knew my limitations. I kept my farewells perfunctory; lots of airy okay-fine-thanks-a-lot-I'll-see-you-laters. It was my way of minimizing the painful lump in my throat, staving off the embarrassing boo-hoos I thought were best left unexpressed. Don't ask me to reconcile the misery I felt with the nearly giddy sense of relief. Nobody ever said emotions made any sense.

So there I was, barreling down the highway in search of employment and not at all fussy about what kind of work I'd take. I wanted distraction. I wanted money, escape, anything to keep my mind off the subject of Robert Dietz. I'm not good at good-byes. I've suffered way too many in my day and I don't like the sensation. On the other hand, I'm not that good at relationships. Get close to someone and next thing you know, you've given them the power to wound, betray, irritate, abandon you, or bore you senseless. My general policy is to keep my distance, thus avoiding a lot of unruly emotion. In psychiatric circles, there are names for people like me.

I flipped on the car radio, picking up a scratchy station from Los Angeles, three hundred miles to the south. Gradually, I began to tune in to the surrounding landscape. Highway 395 cuts south out of Carson City, through Minden and Gardnerville. Just north of Topaz, I had crossed the state line into eastern California. The backbone of the state is the towering Sierra Nevada Range, the uptilted edge of a huge fault block, gouged out later by a series of glaciers. To my left was Mono Lake, shrinking at the rate of two feet a year, increasingly saline, supporting little in the way of marine life beyond brine shrimp and the attendant feasting of the birds. Somewhere to my right, through a dark green forest of Jeffrey pines, was Yosemite National Park, with its towering peaks and rugged canyons, lakes, and thundering waterfalls. Meadows, powdered now in light snow, were once the bottom of a Pleistocene lake. Later in the spring, these same meadows would be dense with wildflowers. In the higher ranges, the winter snowpack hadn't yet melted, but the passes were open. It was the kind of scenery described as "breathtaking" by those who are easily winded. I'm not a big fan of the outdoors, but even I was sufficiently impressed to murmur "wow" speeding past a scenic vista point at seventy miles an hour.

The prospective client I was traveling to meet was a woman named Selma Newquist, whose husband, I was told, had died sometime within the past few weeks. Dietz had done work for this woman in the past, helping her extricate herself from an unsavory first marriage. I didn't get all the details, but he alluded to the fact that the financial "goods" he'd gotten on the husband had given Selma enough leverage to free herself from the relationship. There'd been a subsequent marriage and it was this second husband whose death had apparently generated questions his wife wanted answered. She'd called to hire Dietz, but since he was temporarily out of commission, he suggested me. Under ordinary circumstances, I doubted Mrs. Newquist would have considered a P.I. from the far side of the state, but my trip home was imminent and I was heading in her direction. As it turned out, my connection to Santa

Teresa was more pertinent than it first appeared. Dietz had vouched for my integrity and, by the same token, he'd assured me that she'd be conscientious about payment for services rendered. It made sense to stop long enough to hear what the woman had to say. If she didn't want to hire me, all I'd be out was a thirty-minute break in the journey.

I reached Nota Lake (pop. 2,356, elevation 4,312) in slightly more than three hours. The town didn't look like much, though the setting was spectacular. Mountains towered on three sides, snow still painting the peaks in thick white against a sky heaped with clouds. On the shady side of the road, I could see leftover patches of snow, ice boulders wedged up against the leafless trees. The air smelled of pine, with an underlying scent that was faintly sweet. The chill vapor I breathed was like sticking my face down in a half-empty gallon of vanilla ice cream, drinking in the sugary perfume. The lake itself was no more than two miles long and a mile across. The surface was glassy, reflecting granite spires and the smattering of white firs and incense cedars that grew on the slopes. I stopped at a service station and picked up a one-page map of the town, which was shaped like a smudge on the eastern edge of Nota Lake.

The prime businesses seemed to be clustered along the main street in a five-block radius. I did a cursory driving tour, counting ten gas stations and twenty-two motels. Nota Lake offered low-end accommodations for the ski crowd at Mammoth Lakes. The town also boasted an equal number of fast-food restaurants, including Burger King, Carl's Jr., Jack in the Box, Kentucky Fried Chicken, Pizza Hut, a Waffle House, an

International House of Pancakes, a House of Donuts, a Sizzler, a Subway, a Taco Bell, and my personal favorite, McDonald's. Additional restaurants of the sit-down variety were divided equally between Mexican, Bar-B-Que, and "Family" dining, which meant lots of screaming toddlers and no hard liquor on the premises.

The address I'd been given was on the outskirts of town, two blocks off the main highway in a cluster of houses that looked like they'd been built by the same developer. The streets in the area were named for various Indian tribes: Shawnee, Iroquois, Cherokee, Modoc, Crow, Chippewa. Selma Newquist lived on a cul-de-sac called Pawnee Way, the house a replica of its neighbors: frame siding, a shake roof, with a screened-in porch on one end and a two-car garage on the other. I parked in the driveway beside a dark Ford sedan. I locked the car from habit, climbed the two porch steps, and rang the bell—*ding dong*—like the local Avon representative. I waited several minutes and then tried again.

The woman who came to the door was in her late forties, with a small compact body, brown eyes, and short dark tousled hair. She was wearing a red-blue-and-yellow plaid blouse over a yellow pleated skirt.

"Hi, I'm Kinsey Millhone. Are you Selma?"

"No, I'm not. I'm her sister-in-law, Phyllis. My husband, Macon, was Tom's younger brother. We live two doors down. Can I help you?"

"I'm supposed to meet with Selma. I should have called first. Is she here?"

"Oh, sorry. I remember now. She's lying down at the moment, but she told me she thought you'd be stopping

10

by. You're that friend of the detective she called in Carson City."

"Exactly," I said. "How's she doing?"

"Selma has her bad days and I'm afraid this is one. Tom passed away six weeks ago today and she called me in tears. I came over as quick as I could. She was shaking and upset. Poor thing looks like she hasn't slept in days. I gave her a Valium."

"I can come back later if you think that's best."

"No, no. I'm sure she's awake and I know she wants to see you. Why don't you come on in?"

"Thanks."

I followed Phyllis across the entrance and down a carpeted hallway to the master bedroom. In passing, I allowed myself a quick glance into doorways on either side of the hall, garnering an impression of wildly over-decorated rooms. In the living room, the drapes and upholstery fabrics were coordinated to match a pink-and-green wallpaper that depicted floral bouquets, connected by loops of pink ribbon. On the coffee table, there was a lavish arrangement of pink silk flowers. The cut-pile wall-to-wall carpeting was pale green and had the strong chemical scent that suggested it had been only recently laid. In the dining room, the furniture was formal, lots of dark glossy wood with what looked like one too many pieces for the available space. There were storm windows in place everywhere and a white film of condensation had gathered between the panes. The smell of cigarette smoke and coffee formed a musky domestic incense.

Phyllis knocked on the door. "Selma, hon? It's Phyllis."

I heard a muffled response and Phyllis opened the door a crack, peering around the frame. "You've got company. Are you decent? It's this lady detective from Carson City."

I started to correct her and then thought better of it. I wasn't from Carson City and I certainly wasn't a lady, but then what difference did it make? Through the opening I caught a brief impression of the woman in the bed; a pile of platinum blond hair framed by the uprights on a four-poster.

Apparently, I'd been invited in because Phyllis stepped back, murmuring to me as I passed, "I have to get on home, but you're welcome to call me if you need anything."

I nodded my thanks as I moved into the bedroom and closed the door behind me. The curtains were closed and the light was subdued. Throw pillows, like boulders, had tumbled onto the carpet. There was a surplus of ruffles, bold multicolored prints covering walls, windows, and puffy custom bedding. The motif seemed to be roses exploding on impact.

I said, "Sorry to disturb you, but Phyllis said it would be okay. I'm Kinsey Millhone."

Selma Newquist, in a faded flannel nightie, pulled herself into a sitting position and straightened the covers, reminding me of an invalid ready to accept a bedtray. I estimated her age on the high side of fifty, judging by the backs of her hands, which were freckled with liver spots and ropy with veins. Her skin tones suggested dark coloring, but her hair was a confection of white-blond curls, like a cloud of cotton candy. At the moment, the entire cone was listing sideways and looked sticky with hair spray. She'd drawn in her eyebrows with a red-brown pencil, but any eyeliner or eye shadow had long since vanished. Through the streaks in her pancake makeup, I could see the blotchy complexion that suggested too much sun exposure. She reached for her cigarettes, groping on the bed table until she had both the cigarette pack and lighter. Her hand trembled slightly as she lit her cigarette. "Why don't you come over here," she said. She gestured toward a chair. "Push that off of there and sit down where I can see you better."

I moved her quilted robe from the chair and placed it on the bed, pulling the chair in close before I took a seat.

She stared at me, puffy-eyed, a thin stream of smoke escaping as she spoke. "I'm sorry you had to see me this way. Ordinarily I'm up and about at this hour, but this has been a hard day."

"I understand," I said. Smoke began to settle over me like the fine spray from someone's sneeze.

"Did Phyllis offer you coffee?"

"Please don't trouble. She's on her way back to her place and I'm fine anyway. I don't want to take any more time than I have to."

She stared at me vaguely. "Doesn't matter," she said. "I don't know if you've ever lost anyone close, but there are days when you feel like you're coming down with the flu. Your whole body aches and your head feels so stuffy you can't think properly. I'm glad to have company. You learn to appreciate any distraction. You can't avoid your feelings, but it helps to have momentary relief." She tended, in speaking, to keep a hand up

13

against her mouth, apparently self-conscious about the discoloration on her two front teeth, which I could now see were markedly gray. Perhaps she'd fallen as a child or taken medication as an infant that tinted the surface with dark. "How do you know Robert Dietz?" she asked.

"I hired him myself a couple of years ago to handle my personal security. Someone threatened my life and Dietz ended up working for me as a bodyguard."

"How's his knee doing? I was sorry to hear he was laid up."

"He'll be fine. He's tough. He's already up and around."

"Did he tell you about Tom?"

"Only that you were recently widowed. That's as much as I know."

"I'll fill you in then, though I'm really not sure where to start. You may think I'm crazy, but I assure you I'm not." She took a puff of her cigarette and sighed a mouthful of smoke. I expected tears in the telling, but the story emerged in a Valium-induced calm. "Tom had a heart attack. He was out on the road . . . about seven miles out of town. This was ten o'clock at night. He must have had sufficient warning to pull over to the side. A CHP officer—a friend of ours, James Tennyson—recognized Tom's truck with the hazard lights on and stopped to see if he needed help. Tom was slumped at the wheel. I'd been to a meeting at church and came home to find two patrol cars sitting in my drive. You knew Tom was a detective with the county sheriff's?"

"I wasn't aware of that."

"I used to worry he'd be killed in the line of duty. I

14

never imagined he'd go like he did." She paused, drawing on her cigarette, using smoke as a form of punctuation.

"It must have been difficult."

"It was awful," she said. Up went the hand again, resting against her mouth as the tears began to well in her eyes. "I still can't think about it. I mean, as far as I know, he never had any symptoms. Or let's put it this way: If he did, he never told me. He did have high blood pressure and the doctor'd been on him to quit smoking and start exercising. You know how men are. He waved it all aside and went right on doing as he pleased." She set the cigarette aside so she could blow her nose. Why do people always peek in their hankies to see what the honking noseblow has just netted them?

"How old was he?"

"Close to retirement. Sixty-three," she said. "But he never took good care of himself. I guess the only time he was ever in shape was in the army and right after, when he went through the academy and was hired on as a deputy. After that, it was all caffeine and junk food during work hours, bourbon when he got home. He wasn't an alcoholic—don't get me wrong—but he did like to have a cocktail at the end of the day. Lately, he wasn't sleeping well. He'd prowl around the house. I'd hear him up at two, three, five in the morning, doing god knows what. His weight had begun to drop in the last few months. The man hardly ate, just smoked and drank coffee and stared out the window at the snow. There were times when I thought he was going to snap, but that might have been my imagination. He really never said a word."

"Sounds like he was under some kind of strain."

"Exactly. That was my thought. Tom was clearly stressed, but I don't know why and it's driving me nuts." She picked up her cigarette and took a deep drag and then tapped the ash off in a ceramic ashtray shaped like a hand. "Anyway, that's why I called Dietz. I feel I'm entitled to know."

"I don't want to sound rude, but does it really make any difference? Whatever it was, it's too late to change, isn't it?"

She glanced away from me briefly. "I've thought of that myself. Sometimes I think I never really knew him at all. We got along well enough and he always provided, but he wasn't the kind of man who felt he should account for himself. His last couple of weeks, he'd be gone sometimes for hours and come back without a word. I didn't ask where he went. I could have, I guess, but there was something about him . . . he would bristle if I pressed him, so I learned to back off. I don't think I should have to wonder for the rest of my life. I don't even know where he was going that night. He told me he was staying home, but something must have come up."

"He didn't leave you a note?"

"Nothing." She placed her cigarette on the ashtray and reached for a compact concealed under her pillow. She opened the lid and checked her face in the mirror. She touched at her front teeth as though to remove a fleck. "I look dreadful," she said.

"Don't worry about it. You look fine."

Her smile was tentative. "I guess there's no point in

being vain. With Tom gone, nobody cares, including me if you want to know the truth."

"Can I ask you a question?"

"Please."

"I don't mean to pry, but were you happily married?"

A little burble of embarrassed laughter escaped as she closed the compact and tucked it back in its hiding place. "I certainly was. I don't know about him. He wasn't one to complain. He more or less took life as it came. I was married before . . . to someone physically abusive. I have a boy from that marriage. His name is Brant."

"Ah. And how old is he?"

"Twenty-five. Brant was ten when I met Tom, so essentially Tom raised him."

"And where is he?"

"Here in Nota Lake. He works for the fire department as a paramedic. He's been staying with me since the funeral though he has a place of his own in town," she said. "I told him I was thinking about hiring someone. It's pointless in his opinion, but I'm sure he'll do whatever he can to help." Her nose reddened briefly, but she seemed to gain control of herself.

"You and Tom were married for, what, fourteen years?"

"Coming up on twelve. After my divorce, I didn't want to rush into anything. We were fine for most of it, but recently things began to change for the worse. I mean, he did what he was supposed to, but his heart wasn't in it. Lately, I felt he was secretive. I don't know, so . . . tight-lipped or something. Why was he out on the highway that night? I mean, what was he doing? What was so precious that he couldn't tell me?"

"Could it have been a case he was working on?"

"It could have been, I suppose." She thought about the possibility while she stubbed out her cigarette. "I mean, it might have been job-related. Tom seldom said a word about work. Other men—some of the deputies—would swap stories in social situations, but not him. He took his job very seriously, almost to a fault."

"Someone in the department must have taken over his workload. Have you talked to them?"

"You say 'department' like it was some kind of big-city place. Nota Lake's the county seat, but that still isn't saying much. There were only two investigators, Tom and his partner, Rafer. I did talk to him—not that I got anything to speak of. He was nice. Rafer's always nice enough on the surface," she said, "but for all of the chit-chat, he managed to say very little."

I studied her for a moment, running the conversation through my bullshit meter to see what would register. Nothing struck me as off but I was having trouble understanding what she wanted. "Do you think there's something suspicious about Tom's death?"

She seemed startled by the question. "Not at all," she said, "but he was brooding about something and I want to know what it was. I know it sounds vague, but it upsets me to think he was withholding something when it clearly bothered him so much. I was a good wife to him and I won't be kept in the dark now he's gone."

"What about his personal effects? Have you been through his things?"

"The coroner returned the items he had on him when

18

he died, but they were just what you'd expect. His watch, his wallet, the change in his pocket, and his wedding ring."

"What about his desk? Did he have an office here at the house?"

"Well, yes, but I wouldn't even know where to begin with that. His desk is a mess. Papers piled up everywhere. It could be staring me in the face, whatever it is. I can't bring myself to look and I can't bear to let go. That's what I'd like you to do . . . see if you can find out what was troubling him."

I hesitated. "I could certainly try. It would help if you could be more specific. You haven't given me much."

Selma's eyes filled with tears. "I've been racking my brain and I have no idea. Please just do *something*. I can't even walk in his den without falling apart."

Oh boy, just what I needed—a job that was not only vague, but felt hopeless as well. I should have bagged it right then, but I didn't, of course. More's the pity as it turned out.

TWO

Toward the end of my visit with her, the Valium seemed to kick in and she rallied. Somehow she managed to pull herself together in a remarkably short period of time. I waited in the living room while she showered and dressed. When she emerged thirty minutes later, she said she was feeling almost like her old self again. I was amazed at the transformation. With her makeup in place, she seemed more confident, though she still tended to speak with a hand lifted to conceal her mouth.

For the next twenty minutes, we discussed business, finally reaching an agreement about how to proceed. It was clear by then that Selma Newquist was capable of holding her own. She reached for the phone and in the space of one call not only booked my accommodation but insisted on a ten percent discount on what was already the off-season rate.

I left Selma's at 2:00, stopping off in town long enough to flesh out my standard junk food diet with some Capt'n Jack's fish and chips and a large Coke. After that, it was time to check into the motel. Obviously, I wouldn't be leaving Nota Lake for another day yet, at the very least. The motel she'd booked was the

Nota Lake Cabins, which consisted of ten rustic cottages set in a wooded area just off the main highway about six miles out of town. Tom's widowed sister, Cecilia Boden, owned and managed the place. When I pulled into the parking lot, I could see that the area was a bit too remote for my taste. I'm a city girl at heart and generally happiest close to restaurants, banks, liquor stores, and movie theaters, preferably bug free. Since Selma was paying, I didn't think I should argue the point, and in truth the rough-hewn log exteriors did look more interesting than the motels in town. Silly me.

Cecilia was on the telephone when I stepped into the office. I pegged her at sixty, as small and shapeless as a girl of ten. She wore a red plaid flannel shirt tucked into dark stiff blue jeans. She had no butt to speak of, just a flat plain in the rear. I was already wishing she'd quit perming the life out of her short cropped hair. I also wondered what would happen if she allowed the natural gray to emerge from under the uniform brown dye with which she'd doused it.

The reception area was compact, a pine-paneled cubbyhole hardly large enough for one small upholstered chair and the rack of pamphlets touting the countless recreational diversions available. A side door marked MANAGER probably led to her private apartment. The reception desk was formed by a twelve-inch writing surface mounted on the lower half of the Dutch door that separated the miniature lobby from the office where I could see the usual equipment: desk, file cabinets, typewriter, cash register, Rolodex, receipt ledger, and the big reservations book she was consulting in response to her caller's inquiry. She seemed ever so faintly annoyed with the questions she was being asked. "I got rooms on the Twenty-fourth, but nothing the day after . . . You want fish cleaning and freezing, try the Elms or the Mountain View . . . Uh-huh . . . I see . . . Well, that's the best I can do . . ." She smiled to herself, enjoying some kind of private joke. "Nope . . . No room service, no weight room, and the sauna's broke . . ."

While I waited for her to finish, I pulled out several pamphlets at random, reading about midweek ski lift and lodging packages closer to Mammoth Lakes and Mammoth Summit. I checked the local calendar of events. I'd missed the big annual trout derby, which had taken place the week before. I was also too late to attend February's big fishing show. Well, dang. I noticed the festivities in April included another fishing show, the trout opener press reception, the official trout opener, and a fish club display, with a Mule Days Celebration and a 30K run coming up in May. It did look like it might be possible to hike, backpack, or mulepack my way into the Eastern Sierras, where I imagined a roving assortment of hungry wildlife lunging and snapping at us as we picked our way down perilously narrow trails with rocks rattling off the mountainside into the yawning abyss.

I looked up to find Cecilia Boden staring at me with a flinty expression. "Yes, ma'am," she said. She kept her hands braced on the Dutch door as if defying me to enter.

I told her who I was and she waved aside my offer of a credit card. Mouth pursed, she said, "Selma said to send her the bill direct. I got two cottages available. You can take your pick." She took a bunch of keys from a hook and opened the lower half of the Dutch door, leaving me to follow as she headed through the front door and down a path packed with cedar chips. The air outside was damp and smelled of loam and pine resin. I could hear the wind moving in the trees and the chattering of squirrels. I left my car where I'd parked it and we proceeded on foot. The narrow lane leading to the cabins was barred by a chain strung between two posts. "I won't have cars back in this part of the camp. The ground gets too tore up when the weather's bad," she said, as if in answer to my question.

"Really," I murmured, for lack of anything better.

"We're close to full up," she remarked. "Unusual for March."

This was small talk in her book and I made appropriate mouth noises in response. Ahead of us, the cabins were spaced about seventy-five feet apart, separated by bare maples and dogwoods, and sufficient Douglas firs to resemble a cut-your-own Christmas tree farm. "Why do they call it Nota Lake? Is that Indian?"

Cecilia shook her head. "Nope. Ancient times, nota was a mark burned into a criminal's skin to brand him a lawbreaker. That way you always knew who the evildoers were. Bunch of desperadoes ended up over in this area; scoundrels deported to this country from England back in the mid-seventeen hundreds. Some reason all of them were branded; killers and thieves, pickpockets, fornicators—the worst of the worst. Once their indenture'd been served, they became free men and disappeared into the west, landing hereabouts. Their descendants went to work for the railroad, doing manual labor along with assorted coolies and coloreds.

Half the people in this town are related to those convicts. Must have been a randy bunch, though where they found women no one seems to know. Ordered 'em by mail, if my guess is correct."

We'd reached the first of the cabins and she continued in much the same tone, her delivery flat and without much inflection. "This is Willow. I give 'em names instead of numbers. It's nicer in my opinion." She inserted her key. "Each one is different. Up to you."

Willow was spacious, a pine-paneled room maybe twenty feet by twenty with a fireplace made up of big knobby boulders. The inner hearth was black with soot, with wood neatly stacked in the grate. The room was pungent with the scent of countless hardwood fires. Against one wall was a brass bedstead with a mattress shaped like a hillock. The quilt was a crazy patch and looked as if it smelled of mildew. There was a bed table lamp and a digital alarm clock. The rug was an oval of braided rags, bleached of all color, thoroughly flattened by age.

Cecilia opened a door on the left. "This here's the bath and your hanging closet. We got all the amenities. Unless you fish," she added, in a small aside to herself. "Iron, ironing board, coffeemaker, soap."

"Very nice," I said.

"The other cabin's Hemlock. Located over near the pine grove by the creek. Got a kitchenette, but no fireplace. I can take you back there if you like." For the most part, she spoke without making eye contact, addressing remarks to a spot about six feet to my left.

"This is fine. I'll take this one."

"Suit yourself," she said, handing me a key. "Cars

stay in the lot. There's more wood around the side. Watch for black widder spiders if you fetch more logs. Pay phone outside the office. Saves me the hassle of settling up for calls. We got a cafe down the road about fifty yards in that direction. You can't miss it. Breakfast, lunch, and dinner. Open six o'clock in the morning until nine-thirty at night."

"Thanks."

After she left, I waited a suitable interval, allowing her time to reach the office ahead of me. I returned to the parking lot and retrieved my duffel, along with the portable typewriter I'd stashed in the rental car. I'd spent my off-hours at Dietz's catching up on my paperwork. My wardrobe, in the main, consists of blue jeans and turtlenecks, which makes packing a breeze once you toss in the fistful of underpants.

In the cabin again, I set the typewriter by the bed and put my few articles of clothing in a crudely made chest of drawers. I unloaded my shampoo and placed my toothbrush and toothpaste on the edge of the sink, looking around me with satisfaction. Home sweet home, barring the black widders. I tried the toilet, which worked, and then inspected the shower, artfully concealed behind a length of white monk's cloth hanging from a metal rod. The shower pan looked clean, but was constructed of the sort of material that made me want to walk on tiptoe. Outings at the community pool in my youth had taught me to be cautious, bare feet still recoiling instinctively from the clots of soggy tissues and rusted bobby pins. There were none here in evidence, but I sensed the ghostly presence of some old-fashioned crud. I could smell the same chlorine tinged with someone else's shampoo. I checked the coffee-maker, but the plug seemed to be missing one prong and there were no complimentary packets of coffee grounds, sugar, or non-dairy coffee whitener. So much for the amenities. I was grateful for the soap.

I returned to the main room and did a quick survey. Under the side window, a wooden table and two chairs had been arranged with an eye to a view of the woods. I hauled out the typewriter and set it up on the tabletop. I'd have to run into town and find a ream of bond and a copy shop. These days, most P.I.s use computers, but I can't seem to get the hang of 'em. With my sturdy Smith-Corona, I don't require an electrical outlet and I don't have to worry about head crashes or lost data. I pulled a chair up to the table and stared out the window at the spindly stand of trees. Even the ever-greens had a threadbare look. Through a lacework of pine needles, I could see a line of fencing that separated Cecilia's property from the one behind. This part of town seemed to be ranchland, mixed with large undevel-oped tracts that might have been farmed at one point. I pulled out a tatty legal pad and made myself some notes, mostly doodles if you really want to know.

Essentially, Selma Newquist had hired me to recon-struct the last four to six weeks of her late husband's life on the theory that whatever had troubled him prob-ably took place within that time frame. I don't generally favor spouses spying on one another—especially when one of the parties is dead—but she seemed convinced the answers would give her closure. I had my doubts. Maybe Tom Newquist was simply worried about finances, or brooding about how to occupy his time during his retirement.

I'd agreed to give her a verbal report every two to three days, supplemented by a written account. Selma had demurred at first, saying verbal reports would be perfectly adequate, but I told her I preferred the written, in part to detail whatever information I collected. Productive or not, I wanted her to see what ground I was covering. It was just as important for her to be aware of the information I *couldn't* verify as it was for her to have a record of the facts I picked up along the way. With verbal reports, much of the data gets lost in translation. Most people aren't trained to listen. Given the complexity of our mental processes, the recipient tunes out, blocks, forgets, or misinterprets eighty percent of what's been said. Take any fifteen minutes' worth of conversation and try to reconstruct it later and you'll see what I mean. If the communication has any emotional content whatever, the quality of the information retained degrades even further. A written report was for my benefit, too. Let a week pass and I can hardly remember the difference between Monday and Tuesday, let alone what stops I made and in what order I made them. I've noticed that clients are confident about your abilities until payment comes due and then, suddenly, the total seems outrageous and they stand there wondering exactly what you've done to earn it. It's better to submit an invoice with a chronology attached. I like to cite chapter and verse with all the proper punctuation laid in. If nothing else, it's a demonstration of both your IQ and your writing skills. How can you trust someone who doesn't bother to spell correctly and/ or can't manage to lay out a simple declarative sentence?

The other issue we'd discussed was the nature of my fees. As a lone operator, I really didn't have any hard-and-fast rules about billing, particularly in a case like this where I was working out of town. Sometimes I charge a flat fee that includes all my expenses. Sometimes I charge an hourly rate and add expenses on top of that. Selma had assured me she had money to burn, but frankly, I felt guilty about eating into Tom's estate. On the other hand, she'd survived him and I thought she had a point. Why should she live the rest of her life wondering if her husband was hiding something from her? Grief is enough of an affront without additional regrets about unfinished business. Selma was already struggling to come to terms with Tom's death. She needed to know the truth and wanted me to supply it. Fair enough. I hoped I could provide her with an answer that would satisfy.

Until I got a sense of how long the job would take, we'd agreed on four hundred bucks a day. From Dietz, I'd borrowed a boilerplate contract. I'd penned in the date and details of what I'd been hired to do and she'd written me a check for fifteen hundred dollars. I'd run that by the bank to make sure it cleared before I got down to business. I'm sorry to confess that while I sympathize with all the widows, orphans, and under-dogs in the world, I think it's wise to make sure sufficient funds are in place before you rush to someone's rescue.

I closed the cabin and locked it, hiked back to my rental car, and drove the six miles into town. The highway was sparsely strung with assorted businesses: tractor sales, a car lot, trailer park, country store, and a service station. The fields in between were gold with dried grass and tufted with weeds. The wide sweep of sky had turned from strong blue to gray, a thick haze of white obscuring the mountain tops. Away to the west, a torn pattern of clouds lay without motion. All the near hills were a scruffy red brown, polka-dotted with white. Wind rattled in the trees. I adjusted the heater in the car, flipping on the fan until tropical breezes blew against my legs.

For my stay in Carson City, I'd packed my tweed blazer for dress up and a blue denim jacket for casual wear. Both were too light and insubstantial for this area. I cruised the streets downtown until I spotted a thrift store. I nosed the rental car into a diagonal parking space out front. The window was crowded with kitchenware and minor items of furniture: a bookcase, a footstool, stacks of mismatched dishes, five lamps, a tricycle, a meat grinder, an old Philco radio, and some red Burma-Shave signs bound together with wire. The top one in the pile read DOES YOUR HUSBAND. What, I thought. Does your husband what? Burma-Shave signs had first appeared in the 1920s and many persisted even into my childhood, always with variations of that tricky, bumping lilt. *Does your husband . . . have a beard? . . . Is he really very weird? . . . If he's living in a cave . . . Offer him some . . . Burma-Shave.* Or words to that effect.

The interior of the store smelled like discarded shoes. I made my way down aisles densely crowded with hanging clothes. I could see rack after rack of items that must have been purchased with an eye to function and festivity. Prom gowns, cocktail dresses, women's suits, acrylic sweaters, blouses, and Hawaiian shirts. The woolens seemed dispirited and the cottons were tired, the colors subdued from too many rounds in the wash. Toward the rear, there was a rod sagging under the burden of winter jackets and coats.

I shrugged into a bulky brown leather bomber jacket. The weight of it felt like one of those lead aprons the technician places across your body while taking dental X-rays from the safety of another room. The jacket lining was fleece, minimally matted, and the pockets sported diagonal zippers, one of which was broken. I checked the inside of the collar. The size was a medium, big enough to accommodate a heavy sweater if I needed one. The price tag was pinned to the brown knit ribbing on the cuff. Forty bucks. What a deal. *Does your husband belch and rut? Does he scratch his hairy butt? If you want to see him bathe . . . tame the beast with Burma-Shave.* I tucked the jacket over my arm while I moved up and down the aisles. I found a faded blue flannel shirt and a pair of hiking boots. On my way out, I stopped and untwisted the wire connecting the Burma-Shave signs, reading them one by one.

DOES YOUR HUSBAND

MISBEHAVE?

GRUNT AND GRUMBLE

RANT AND RAVE?

SHOOT THE BRUTE SOME

BURMA-SHAVE.

30

I smiled to myself. I wasn't half-bad at that stuff. I went out to the street again with my purchases in hand. Let's hear it for the good old days. Lately, Americans have been losing their sense of humor.

I spotted an office supply store across the street. I crossed, stocked up on paper supplies, including a couple of packs of blank index cards. Two doors down, I found a branch of Selma's bank and came out with a wad of twenties in my shoulder bag. I retrieved my car and pulled out, circling the block until I was headed in the right direction. The town already felt familiar, neatly laid out and clean. Main Street was four lanes wide. The buildings on either side were generally one to two stories high, sharing no particular style. The atmosphere was vaguely Western. At each intersection, I caught sight of a wedge of mountains, the snow-capped peaks forming a scrim that ran the length of the town. Traffic was light and I noticed most of the vehicles were practical: pickups and utility vans with ski racks across the tops.

When I arrived back at Selma's, the garage door was open. The parking space on the left was empty. On the right, I spotted a late-model blue pickup truck. As I got out of my car, I noticed a uniformed deputy emerging from a house two doors down. He crossed the two lawns between us, walking in my direction. I waited, assuming this was Tom's younger brother, Macon. At first glance, I couldn't tell how much younger he was. I placed him in his late forties, but his age might have been deceptive. He had dark hair, dark brows, and a pleasant, unremarkable face. He was close to six feet tall, compactly built. He wore a heavy jacket, cropped at the waist to allow ready access to the heavy leather holster on his right hip. The wide belt and the weapon gave him a look of heft and bulk that I'm not sure would have been evident if he'd been stripped of his gear.

"Are you Macon?" I asked.

He offered me his hand and we shook. "That's right. I saw you pull up and thought I'd come on over and introduce myself. You met my wife, Phyllis, a little earlier."

"I'm sorry about your brother."

"Thank you. It's been a rough one, I can tell you," he said. He hooked a thumb toward the house. "Selma's not home. I believe she went off to the market a little while ago. You need in? Door's open most times, but you're welcome to come to our place. It sure beats setting out in the cold."

"I should be fine. I expect she'll be home in a bit and if not, I can find ways to amuse myself. I would like to talk to you sometime in the next day or two."

"Absolutely. No problem. I'll tell you anything you want, though I admit we're baffled as to Selma's purpose. What in the world is she worried about? Phyllis and I can't understand what she wants with a private detective, of all things. With all due respect, it seems ridiculous."

"Maybe you should talk to her about that," I said.

"I can tell you right now what you're going to learn about Tom. He's as decent a fellow as you'd ever hope to meet. Everybody in town looked up to him, including me."

"This may turn out to be a short stay, in that case."

"Where'd Selma put you? Some place nice, I hope."

"Nota Lake Cabins. Cecilia Boden's your sister, as I understand it. You have other siblings?"

Macon shook his head. "Just three of us," he said. "I'm the baby in the family. Tom's three years older than Cecilia and close to fifteen years my senior. I've been trailing after them two ever since I can remember. I ended up in the sheriff's department years after Tom hired on. Like that in school, too. Always following in somebody else's footsteps." His eyes strayed to the street as Selma's car approached and slowed, pulling into the driveway. "Here she is now so I'll leave you two be. You let me know what I can do to help. You can give us a call or come knocking on our door. It's that green house with white trim."

Selma had pulled into the garage by then. She got out of the car. She and Macon greeted each other with an almost imperceptible coolness. While she opened the trunk of her sedan, Macon and I parted company, exchanging the kind of chitchat that signals the end of a conversation. Selma lifted out a brown paper sack of groceries and two cleaner's bags, and slammed the trunk lid down. Under her fur coat, she wore smartly pressed charcoal slacks and a long-sleeved shirt of cherry-colored silk.

As Macon walked back to his house, I moved into the garage. "Let me give you a hand with that," I said, reaching for the bag of groceries, which she relinquished to me.

"I hope you haven't been out here long," she said. "I decided I'd spent enough time feeling sorry for myself. Best to keep busy."

"Whose pickup truck? Was that Tom's?" I asked.

Selma nodded as she unlocked the door leading from the garage into the house. "I had a fellow from the garage tow it the day after he died. The officer who found him took the keys out and left it locked up where it was. I can't bring myself to drive it. I guess eventually I'll sell it or pass it along to Brant." She pressed a button and the garage door descended with a rumble.

"You met Macon, I see."

"He came over to introduce himself," I said as I followed her into the house. "One thing I ought to mention. I'm going to be talking to a lot of people around town and I really don't know yet what approach I'll take. Whatever you hear, just go along with it."

She put her keys back in her purse, moving into the utility room with me close behind. She closed the door after us. "Why not tell the truth?"

"I will where I can, but I gather Tom was a highly respected member of the community. If I start asking about his personal business, nobody's going to say a word. I may try another tack. It won't be far off, but I may bend the facts a bit."

"What about Cecilia? What will you say to her?"

"I don't know yet. I'll think of something."

"She'll fill your ear. She's never really liked me. Whatever Tom's problems, she'll blame me if she can. Same with his brother. Macon was always coming after Tom for something—a loan, advice, good word in the department, you name it. If I hadn't stepped in, he'd have sucked Tom dry. You can do me a favor: Take anything they say with a grain of salt."

The disgruntled are good. They'll tell you anything, I thought.

Once in the kitchen, Selma hung her fur coat on the back of a chair. I watched while she unloaded the groceries and put items away. I would have helped, but she waved aside the offer, saying it was quicker if she did it herself. The kitchen walls were painted bright yellow, the floor a spatter of seamless white-and-yellow linoleum. A chrome-and-yellow-plastic upholstered dinette set filled an alcove with a bump-out window crowded with . . . I peered closer . . . artificial plants. She indicated a seat across the table from hers as she folded the bag neatly and put it in a rack bulging with other grocery bags.

She moved to the refrigerator and opened the door. "What do you take in your coffee? I've got hazelnut coffee creamer or a little half-and-half." She took out a small carton and gave the pouring spout an experimental sniff. She made a face to herself and set the carton in the sink.

"Black's fine."

"You sure?"

"Really. It's no problem. I'm not particular," I said. I took off my jacket and hung it on the back of my chair while Selma rounded up two coffee mugs, the sugar bowl, and a spoon for herself.

She poured coffee and replaced the glass carafe on the heating element of the coffee machine, heels *tap-tap-tapping* on the floor as she crossed and recrossed the room. Her energy was ever so faintly tinged with nervousness. She sat down again and immediately flicked a small gold Dunhill to light a fresh cigarette. She inhaled deeply. "Where will you begin?"

"I thought I'd start in Tom's den. Maybe the answer's easy, sitting right up on the surface."

THREE

I spent the rest of the afternoon working my way through Tom Newquist's insufferably disorganized home office. I'm going to bypass the tedious list of documents I inspected, the files I sorted, the drawers I emptied, the receipts I scrutinized in search of *some* evidence of his angst. In reporting to Selma, I did (slightly) exaggerate the extent of my efforts so she'd appreciate what fifty bucks an hour was buying in the current market place. In the space of three hours, I managed to go through about half the mess. Up to that point, whatever Tom was fretting about, he'd left precious little in the way of clues.

He was apparently compulsive about saving every scrap of paper, but whatever organizational principle he employed, the accumulation he left behind was chaotic at best. His desk was a jumble of folders, correspondence, bills paid and unpaid, income tax forms, newspaper articles, and case files he was working on. The layers were twelve to fifteen inches deep, some stacks toppling sideways into the adjacent piles. My guess was he knew how to put his hands on just about anything he needed, but the task I faced was daunting.

Maybe he imagined that any minute he'd have the clutter sorted and subdued. Like most disorganized people, he probably thought the confusion was temporary, that he was just on the verge of having all his papers tidied up. Unfortunately, death had taken him by surprise and now the cleanup was mine. I made a mental note to myself to straighten out my underwear the minute I got home. In the bottom drawer of his desk, I found some of his equipment—handcuffs, nightstick, the flashlight he must have carried. Maybe his brother, Macon, would like them. I'd have to remember to ask Selma later.

I went through two big leaf bags of junk, taking it upon myself to throw away paid utility stubs from ten years back. I kept a random sampling in case Selma wanted to sell the house and needed to average her household expenses for prospective buyers. I kept the office door open, conducting an ongoing conversation with Selma in the kitchen while I winnowed and pitched. "I'd like to have a picture of Tom."

"What for?"

"Not sure yet. It just seems like a good idea."

"Take one of those from the wall by the window."

I glanced over my shoulder, spotting several black-and-white photographs of him in various settings. "Right," I said. I set aside the lapful of papers I was sorting and crossed to the closest grouping. In the largest frame, an unsmiling Tom Newquist and the sheriff, Bob Staffer, were pictured together at what looked to be a banquet. There were several couples seated at a table, which was decorated with a handsome centerpiece and the number 2 on a placard in the middle. Staffer had signed the photograph in the lower right-hand corner: "To the best damn detective in the business! As Ever, Bob Staffer." The date was April of the preceding year. I lifted the framed photo from the hook and held it up to the fading light coming in the window.

Tom Newquist was a youthful sixty-three years old with small eyes, a round bland face, and dark thinning hair trimmed close to his head. His expression was one I'd seen on cops ever since time began—neutral, watchful, intelligent. It was a face that gave away nothing of the man within. If you were being interrogated as a suspect, make no mistake about it, this man would ask tough questions and there would be no hint from him about which replies might relieve you of his attention. Make a joke and his smile in response would be thin. Presume on his goodwill and his temper would flash in a surprising display of heat. If you were questioned as a witness, you might see another side of him—careful, compassionate, patient, conscientious. If he was like the other law enforcement officers of my acquaintance, he was capable of being implacable, sarcastic, and relentless, all in the interest of getting at the truth. Regardless of the context, the words "impulsive" and "passionate" would scarcely spring to mind. On a personal level, he might be very different, and part of my job here was determining just what those differences might consist of. I wondered what he'd seen in Selma. She seemed too brassy and emotional for a man skilled at camouflage.

I glanced up to find her standing in the doorway, watching me. Despite the fact that her clothes looked expensive, there was something indescribably cheap about her appearance. Her hair had been bleached to the texture of a doll's wig, and I wondered if up close I could see individual clumps like the plugs of a hair transplant. I held up the picture. "Is this one okay? I'd like to have it cropped and copies made. If I'm backtracking his activities for the past couple of months, the face could trigger something where a name might not."

"All right. I might like to have one myself. That's nice of him."

"He didn't smile much?"

"Not often. Especially in social situations. Around his buddies, he relaxed . . . the other deputies. How's it coming?"

I shrugged. "So far there's nothing but junk." I went back to the masses of paper in front of me. "Too bad you weren't in charge of the bills," I remarked.

"I'm not good with numbers. I hated high school math," she said. And then after a moment, "I'm beginning to feel guilty having you snoop through his things."

"Don't worry about it. I do this for a living. I'm a diagnostician, like a gynecologist when you have your feet in the stirrups and your fanny in the air. My interest isn't personal. I simply look to see what's there."

"He was a good man. I know that."

"I'm sure he was," I said. "This may net us nothing and if so, you'll feel better. You're entitled to peace."

"Do you need help?"

"Not really. At this point, I'm still picking my way through. Anyway, I'm about to wrap it up for this afternoon. I'll come back tomorrow and take another run at it." I jammed a fistful of catalogs and advertising fliers in the trash bag. I glanced up again, aware that she was still standing in the door.

"Could you join me for supper? Brant's going to be working so it would just be the two of us."

"I better not, but thanks. Maybe tomorrow. I have some phone calls to make and then I thought I'd grab a quick bite and make an early night of it. I should finish this in the morning. At some point, we'll have telephone records to go through. That's a big under-taking and I'm saving it for last. We'll sit side by side and see how many phone numbers you can recognize."

"Well," she said, reluctantly, "I'll let you get back to work."

When I had finished for the day, Selma gave me a house key, though she assured me she generally left the doors unlocked. She told me she was often gone, but she wanted me to have the run of the place in her absence. I told her I'd want to look through Tom's personal effects and she had no objections. I didn't want her walking in one day to find me poking through his clothes.

It was fully dark when I left and the streetlights did little to dispel the sense of isolation. The traffic through town was lively. People were going home to dinner, businesses were shutting down. Restaurants were getting busy, the bar doors standing open to release the excess noise and cigarette smoke. A few hardy joggers had hit the sidewalks along with assorted dog owners whose charges were seeking relief against the shrubs.

Once I was out on the highway, I became aware of

the vast tracts of land that bore no evidence of human habitation. By day, the fences and the odd outbuildings created the impression the countryside had been civilized. At night, the mountain ranges were as black as jet and the pale slice of moon scarcely brushed the snowy peaks with silver. The temperature had dropped and I could smell the inky damp of the lake. I felt a flicker of longing to see Santa Teresa with its red-tile roofs, palm trees, and the thundering Pacific.

I slowed when I saw the sign for Nota Lake Cabins. Maybe a crackling fire and a hot shower would cheer me up. I parked my car in the small lot near the motel office. Cecilia Boden had provided a few low-voltage lights along the path to the cabins, small mushroom shapes that cast a circle of dim yellow on the cedar chips. There was a small lighted lamp mounted by the cabin door. I hadn't left any lights on for myself, sensing (perhaps) that the management would frown on such extravagance. I unlocked the door and let myself in, feeling for the light switch. The overhead bulb came on with its flat forty-watt wash of light. I crossed to the bed and clicked on the table lamp, which offered forty watts more. The digital alarm was flashing 12:00 repeatedly, which suggested a minor power outage earlier. I checked my watch and corrected the time to its current state: 6:22.

The room felt drab and chilly. There was a strong smell of old wood fires and moisture seeping through the floorboards from underneath the cabin. I checked the wood in the grate. There was a stack of newspapers close by meant for kindling. Of course, there was no gas starter and I suspected the fire would take more time to light than I had time to enjoy. I went around the room, closing cotton curtains across the windowpanes. Then I peeled off my clothes and stepped into the shower. I'm not one to waste water, but even so, the hot began to diminish before my four minutes were up. I rinsed the last of the shampoo from my hair a split second before the cold water descended full force. This was beginning to feel like a wilderness experience.

Dressed again, I locked the cabin and headed back toward the road, walking briskly along the berm until I reached the restaurant. The Rainbow Cafe was about the size of a double-wide trailer, with a Formica counter with eight stools running down its length and eight red Naugahyde booths arranged along two walls. There was one waitperson (female), one short-order cook (also female), and a boy busperson in evidence. I ordered breakfast for dinner. There's nothing so comforting as scrambled eggs at night; soft cheery yellow, bright with butter, flecked with pepper. I had three strips of crisp bacon, a pile of hash browns sautéed with onion, and two pieces of rye toast, drenched in butter and dripping with jam. I nearly crooned aloud as the flavors blended in my mouth.

On the way back to my cabin, I paused to use the pay phone outside the office. This consisted of an old-fashioned glass-and-metal phone booth missing the original bifold door. I used my credit card to call Dietz. "Hey, babe. How's the patient?" I said when he answered.

"Dandy. How are you?"

"Not bad. Now on retainer."

"In Nota Lake?"

43

"Where else? Standing in a phone booth in the piney woods," I said.

"How's it going?"

"I'm just getting started so it's hard to tell. I'm assuming Selma talked to you about Tom."

"Only that she thought he had something on his mind. Sounds vague."

"Extremely. Did you ever meet him yourself?"

"Nope. In fact, I haven't even seen her for over fifteen years. How's she holding up?"

"She's in good shape. Upset, as who wouldn't be in her shoes."

"What's the game plan?" he asked.

"The usual. I spent time today going through his desk. Tomorrow I'll start talking to his friends and acquaintances and we'll see what develops. I'll give it until Thursday and then see where we stand. I'd love to be home by the weekend if this job doesn't pan out. How's the knee?"

"Much better. The PT's a bitch, but I'm getting used to it. I miss your sandwiches."

"Liar."

"No, I'm serious. As soon as you finish there, I think you ought to head back in this direction."

"Uh-unh. No thanks. I want to sleep in my own bed. I haven't seen Henry for a month." Henry Pitts was my landlord, eighty-six years old. His would be the cover photo if the AARP ever did a calendar of octogenarian hunks.

"Well, think on it," Dietz said.

"Oh, right. Listen, my Florence Nightingale days are

over. I have a business to run. Anyway, I better go. It's friggin' cold out here."

"I'll let you go then. Take care."

"Same to you," I said.

I put a call through to Henry and caught him on his way out the door. "Where you off to?" I asked.

"I'm on my way to Rosie's. She and William need help with the dinner crowd tonight," he said. Rosie ran the tavern half a block from my apartment. She and Henry's older brother William had been married the previous Thanksgiving and now William was rapidly becoming a restaurateur.

"What about you? Where're you calling from?"

I repeated my tale, filling him in on my current situation. I gave him both Selma's home number and that of the office at the Nota Lake Cabins in case he had to reach me. We continued to chat briefly before he had to go. Once he rang off, I placed a call to Lonnie's office and left a message for Ida Ruth, again giving her my location and Selma's number if she should have to reach me for some reason. I couldn't think of any other way to feel connected. After I hung up, I stuck my hands in my jacket pockets, vainly hoping for shelter from the wind. The notion of spending the evening in the cabin seemed depressing. With only two forty-watt light bulbs for illumination, even reading would be a chore. I pictured myself huddled, squinting, under that damp-looking quilt, spiders creeping from the wood pile the minute I relaxed my vigilance. It was a sorry prospect, given that all I had with me was a book on identifying tire tracks and tread marks.

I crossed to the motel office and peered in through

the glass door. A light was on, but there was no sign of Cecilia. A hand-lettered sign said RING FOR MGR. I let myself in. I bypassed the desk bell and knocked on the door marked MANAGER. After a moment, Cecilia appeared in a pink chenille bathrobe and fluffy pink slippers. "Yes?"

"Hi, Cecilia. Could I have a word with you?"

"Something wrong with the room?"

"Not at all. Everything's fine. More or less. I was wondering if you could spare a few minutes to talk about your brother."

"What about him?"

"Has Selma said anything about why I'm here in Nota Lake?"

"Said she hired you is all. I don't even know what you do for a living."

"Ah. Well, actually, I'm a field investigator with California Fidelity Insurance. Selma's concerned about the liability in Tom's death."

"Liability for what?"

"Good question. Of course, I'm not at liberty to discuss this in any detail. You know, *officially* he wasn't working, but she thinks he might have been pursuing departmental business the night he died. If so, it's always possible she can file a claim." I didn't mention that Tom Newquist wasn't represented by CFI or that the company had fired me approximately eighteen months before. I was prepared to flash the laminated picture ID I still had in my possession. The CFI logo was emblazoned on the front, along with a photograph of me that looked like something the border patrol might keep posted for ready reference.

She stared at me blankly and for one heart-stopping moment I wondered if she was recently retired from some obscure branch of county government. She appeared to be mulling over all the rules and regulations, trying to decide which were in effect on the night in question. I was tempted to embellish, but decided I might be getting in too deep. With lies, it's best to skip across the surface like a dragonfly. The more said at the outset, the more there is to retract later if it turns out you really put your foot in it. She held the door open to admit me. "You better come on in. I don't mind telling you the subject's painful."

"I can imagine it is and I'm sorry to intrude. I met Macon earlier."

"He's useless," she remarked. "No love lost between us. Of course, I never thought of Selma as family either and I'm sure it's ditto from her perspective."

Cecilia Boden's apartment was on a par with my cabin, which is to say, drab, poorly lighted, and faintly shabby. The prime difference was that my place was icy cold where she seemed to keep her room temperature somewhere around "pre-heat." The floor cover was linoleum made to look like wood parquet. She had pine-paneled walls, overstuffed furniture covered with violent-colored crocheted throws. A large television set dominated one corner, with all the furniture oriented in that direction. Cecilia's reading glasses were perched on the arm of the sofa nearest the set. I could see that she was in the process of filling out the crossword puzzle in the local paper. She did this in ballpoint pen without any visible corrections. I revised my estimate of her upwards. I couldn't perform such a feat with a gun to my head.

We took a few minutes to get settled in the living room. While my story sounded plausible, it didn't give me much room to inquire into Tom's character. In any event, why would I imagine Cecilia would have information about what he was doing the night he died? As it turned out, she didn't question my purpose and the longer we chatted, the clearer it became that she was perfectly comfortable discussing Tom and his wife, their marriage, and anything else I cared to ask about.

"Selma says Tom was preoccupied with something in the past few weeks. Do you have any idea what it might have been?"

Cecilia narrowed her eyes at the section of floor she was studying.

"What makes her think there was anything wrong with him?"

"Well, I'm not sure. She said he seemed tense, smoking more than usual, and she thought he was losing weight. She said he slept poorly and disappeared without explanation. I take it this wasn't typical. Did he say anything to you?"

"He didn't confide anything specific," she said, cautiously. "You'll have to talk to Macon about that. They were a lot closer to each other than either one of them was to me."

"But what was your impression? Did you feel he was under some kind of strain?"

"Possibly."

Too bad I wasn't taking notes, what with the wealth of data pouring out. "Did you ever ask him about it?"

"I didn't feel it was my place. That wasn't the nature of our relationship. He went about his business and I went about mine."

"Any *hunches* about what was going on?"

She hesitated for a moment. "I think Tom was unhappy. He never said as much to me, but that's my belief."

I made a sort of *mmm* sound, verbal filler accompanied by what I hoped was a sympathetic look.

She took this for encouragement and launched into her analysis. "Far be it from me to criticize Selma. *He* married her. I didn't. It's possible there was more to her than meets the eye. We'd certainly have to hope so. If you want my opinion, my brother could have done a lot better for himself. Selma's a snob, if you want to know the truth."

This time I murmured, "Really."

Her gaze brushed my face and then drifted off again. "You look like a good judge of character, so I don't feel I'm telling tales out of school when I say this. She has no spiritual foundation even if she does go to church. She's a mite materialistic. She seems to think she can use acquisitions to fill the void in her life, but it won't do."

"For example," I said.

"You saw the new carpet in the living room?"

"Yes, I saw that."

Cecilia shot me a glance filled with satisfaction. "She had that installed about ten days ago. I thought it was in poor taste, doing it so soon, but Selma never asked me. Selma's also confided she's considering having those two front teeth capped, which is not only vain, but completely trivial. Talk about a waste of money. I guess now she's a widder, she can do anything she likes."

What I thought was, what's wrong with vanity? Given the range of human failings, self-absorption is harmless compared to some I could name. Why not do whatever you deem relevant to feeling better about yourself—within reason, of course. If Selma wanted to get her teeth capped, why should Cecilia give a shit? What I said was, "I got the impression she was devoted to Tom."

"As well she should have been. And he to her, I might add. Tom spent his life trying to satisfy the woman. If it wasn't one thing, it was another. First, she had to have a house. Then she wanted something bigger in a better neighborhood. Then they had to join the country club. And on and on it went. Anytime she didn't get what she wanted? Well, she pouted and sulked until he broke down and got it for her. It was pitiful in my opinion. Tom did everything he could, but there wasn't any way to make her happy."

I said, "My goodness." This is the way I talk in situations like this. I could not, for the life of me, think where to go from here. "He was a nice-looking man. I saw a picture of him at the house," I said, vamping.

"He was downright handsome. Why he married Selma was a mystery to me. And that son of hers?" Cecilia pulled her lips together like a drawstring purse. "Brant was a pain in the grits from the first time I ever laid eyes on the boy. He had a mouth on him like a trucker and he was bratty to boot. Back talk and sass? You never heard the like. Did poorly in school, too. Problems with his temper and what they call his impulse control. Of course, Selma thought he was a saint. She wouldn't tolerate a word of criticism regardless of what he did. Poor Tom nearly tore his hair out. I guess he finally managed to get the boy squared away, but it was no thanks to her."

"She mentioned Brant worked as a paramedic. That's a responsible job."

"Well, that's true enough," she conceded grudgingly. "About time he took hold. You can credit Tom for that."

"Do you happen to know where Tom was going that night? I understand he was found somewhere on the outskirts of town."

"A mile north of here."

"He didn't drop in to see you?"

"I wish he had," she said. "I was visiting a friend down in Independence and didn't get back here until shortly after ten fifteen or so. I saw the ambulance pass, but I had no idea it was meant for him."

FOUR

Tuesday morning at nine, I stopped by the offices of the Nota County Coroner. I hadn't slept well the night before. The cabin was poorly insulated and the night air was frigid. I'd moved the thermostat up to 70, but all it did was click off and on ineffectually. I'd crawled into bed wearing my sweats, a turtleneck, and a pair of heavy socks. The mattress was as turgid as a trough of mud. I curled up under a comforter, a quilt, and a wool blanket, with my heavy leather jacket piled on top for the weight. Just about the time I got warm, my bladder announced that it was filled to capacity and required my immediate attention or a bout of bed-wetting would ensue. I tried to ignore the discomfort and then realized I'd never sleep a wink until I'd heeded the message. By the time I got back under the covers, all the ambient heat had been dispelled and I was forced to suffer through the cold again until I drifted off to sleep.

When I woke up at seven, my nose felt like a Popsicle and my breath was visible in puffs against the wan morning light. I showered in tepid water, dried myself shivering, and dressed in haste. Then I dog trotted down the road to the Rainbow Cafe where I stoked up on another breakfast, sucking down orange juice, coffee, sausages, and pancakes saturated with butter and syrup. I told myself I needed all the sugar and fat to refuel my depleted reserves, but the truth was I felt sorry for myself and the food was the simplest form of consolation.

The coroner's office was located on a side street in the heart of the downtown. In Nota County, the coroner is a four-year elected official, who in this case doubled as the funeral director for the county's only mortuary. Nota County is small, less than two thousand square miles, tucked like an afterthought between Inyo and Mono counties. The coroner, Wilton Kirchner III, generally referred to as Trey, had occupied the position for the past ten years. Since there was no requirement for formal training in forensic medicine, all coroner's cases were autopsied by a forensic pathologist under contract to the county.

In the event of a homicide in the county, the Nota County Coroner handles the on-scene investigation, in conjunction with the Sheriff's Department's investigator and an investigator from the Nota County District Attorney's office. The forensic autopsy is then conducted in the "big city" by a pathologist who does several homicide autopsies per month and is called to court numerous times during the year to testify. Since Nota County only has one homicide every two years or so, the coroner prefers that an outside agency provide its expertise, in both autopsy services and testimony.

Kirchner & Sons Mortuary appeared to have been a private residence at one time, probably built in the early twenties with the town growing up around it. The architectural style was Tudor with a façade of pale red brick trimmed in dark-painted timbers. Thin cold sunlight glittered against the leaded glass windows. The surrounding lawns were dormant, the grass as drab and brittle as brown plastic. Only the holly bushes lent any color to the landscape. I could imagine a time when the house might have sat on a sizeable piece of land, but now the property had shrunk and the lots on either side sported commercial establishments: a real estate office and a modest medical complex.

Trey Kirchner came out to the reception area when he heard I was there, extending a hand in greeting as he introduced himself. "Trey Kirchner," he said. "Selma called and said you'd be in here today. Nice to meet you, Miss Millhone. Come on back to my office and let's find out what you need."

Kirchner was in his mid-fifties, tall, broad-shouldered, with a waistline only slightly softer than it might have been ten years before. His hair was a clean gray, parted on the side and trimmed short around his ears. His smile was pleasant, creating concentric creases on either side of his mouth. He wore glasses with large lenses and thin metal frames. The corners of his eyes drooped slightly, somehow creating an expression of immense sympathy. His suit was close-fitting, well pressed, and the dress shirt he wore looked freshly starched. His tie was conservative, but not somber. Altogether, he presented an air of comforting competence. There was something solid about him; a man who, by nature, looked like he could absorb all the sorrow, confusion, and rage generated by death.

I followed him down a long corridor and into his office, which had served as the dining room when the house was first built. The carpet was pale, the wood floors pickled to the color of milk-washed pine. The drapes were beige, silk or shantung, some fabric with a touch of sheen. The mortuary decor leaned to wainscoting, topped with wallpaper murals showing soft mountain landscapes, forests of ever-greens with paths meandering through the woods. This was a watercolor world; pastel skies piled with clouds, the faintest suggestion of a breeze touching the tips of the wallpaper trees. On either side of the corridor at intervals, wide sliding doors had been pushed back to reveal the slumber rooms, empty of inhabitants, bare except for the ranks of gray metal folding chairs and a few potted ferns. The air was cool, underheated, spiced with the scent of carnations though none were in view. Perhaps it was some weird form of mortuary air freshener wafting through the vents. The entire environment seemed geared to somnambulistic calm.

The office we entered seemed designed for the public, not a book, a file, or a piece of paper in sight. I suspected somewhere in the building Trey Kirchner had an office where the real work was done. Somewhere out of sight, too, was the autopsy paraphernalia: cameras, X-ray equipment, stainless steel table, Stryker saw, scalpels, hanging scale. The room where we sat was as bland as a pudding—no smell of formalin, no murky Mason jars filled with snippets of organs—giving no indication of the mechanics of the body's preparation for cremation or burial.

"Have a seat," he said, indicating two matching

upholstered chairs arranged on either side of a small side table. His manner was relaxed, pleasant, friendly, curiously impersonal. "I take it you're here about Tom's death." He reached over and opened the drawer, pulling out a flat manila folder containing a five-page report. "I ran a copy of the autopsy report in case you're interested."

I took the folder. "Thanks. I thought I might have to talk you into this."

He smiled. "It's public record. I could have popped it in the mail and saved you a trip if Selma'd asked for it sooner."

"Tom's death was classified as a coroner's case?"

"Of necessity," he said. "You know he died out on Highway 395 with no witnesses and probably not much warning. He hadn't seen his doctor in close to a year. We figured it was his heart, but you never really know about these things until the post. Could have been an aneurysm. Anyway, Calvin Burkey did the autopsy. He's the forensic pathologist for Nota and Mono counties. Couple of us in attendance. Nothing remarkable showed up. No surprises, nothing unexpected. Tom died of a massive acute myocardial infarction due to severe arteriosclerosis. You'll see it. It's all there. Sections of the coronary artery confirmed ninety-five percent to one hundred percent occlusion. Sixty-three years old. Really, it's amazing he lasted as long as he did."

"Nothing else came to light?"

"In the way of abnormalities? Nope. Liver, gall-bladder, spleen, kidneys were all unremarkable. Lungs looked bad. He'd been smoking all his life, but there was no indication of invasive disease. He'd eaten recently.

According to our report, he'd stopped off at a cafe for a bite of supper. No pills or capsules in his digestive system and the toxin report was clear. What makes you ask?"

"Selma said he'd been losing weight. I wondered if he knew something he wasn't telling her."

"No ma'am. No cancer, if that's what you mean. No tumors, no blood clots, and no hemorrhaging, aside from the myocardium," he said. "Doc said there were signs of a minor heart attack sometime in the past."

I thought about it. "So maybe he knew his days were numbered. That would give him reason to brood."

"Could be," he said. "Tom wasn't in the peak of health, I can assure you of that. The absence of pathology doesn't necessarily mean you feel all that good. I knew him for years and never heard him complain, but he was sixty pounds overweight. Smoked like a chimney, drank like a fish, just to cover both clichés. He was a hell of an investigator, I can tell you that. What's Selma's worry?"

"It's hard to say. I think she feels he was holding out on her, keeping secrets of some kind. She didn't press him for answers so now it's unfinished business and it bothers her a lot."

"And she has no idea what it was?"

"It might not be anything, which is where I come in. Do you have any theories?"

"I don't think you'll turn up anything scandalous. Tom was churchgoing, a good soul. Well liked, well thought-of in the community, generous with his time. If he had any faults, I'd have to say he was straitlaced, too rigid. He saw the world in terms of all black or all white with not a lot in between. I guess he could see the gray, but he never knew what to do with it. He didn't believe in bending the rules, though I've seen him do it from time to time. He was a real straight-ahead guy, but that's good in my opinion. We could use a few more like him. We're going to miss him around here."

"Did you spend any time with him in the past few weeks?"

"Nothing to speak of. Mostly, I saw him in the context of his job. Not surprisingly, the county sheriff's department and the coroner's office are just like that," he said, crossing his fingers. "I'd run into him around town. Played pool with him once. Sucked back a few beers. Bunch of us did a weekend fishing trip last fall, but it's not like we laid around at night baring our souls. Fellow you ought to talk to is his partner, Rafe."

"Selma mentioned him. What's his last name?"

"LaMott."

I sat in the rental car in the Kirchner & Sons parking lot, leafing through Tom Newquist's autopsy report, his death certificate spelling out the particulars of his passing. Age, date of birth, Social Security number, and his usual address; the place and cause of his death and the disposition of his remains. He'd arrived at Nota County Hospital ER as a DOA, autopsied a day later, buried the day after that. On paper, his progression to the grave seemed all too swift, but in truth, once death occurs, the human body is just a big piece of meat quickly going sour. There was something flat and abrupt in the details . . . Tom Newquist deceased . . . his life neatly packaged; beginning, middle, and end. Under the death certificate was a copy of a hand-scrawled note that I gathered had been written by the CHP officer who found him in his truck.

At appx 21 50   ⅔   Ambulance call to roadside 7.2 mi. out Hiway 395.   Subj in pick-up, removed to side of road.   CRP started @ 22 00.   EMT from Nota Lake taking over @ appx. 22 15. Subj DOA on arrival at Nota Lake ER. Coroner notified.

The notation was signed "J. Tennyson." The autopsy report followed; three typewritten pages detailing the facts as Trey Kirchner had indicated.

I'd been hoping the explanation was obvious, that Tom Newquist was caught in the grip of some terminal disease, his preoccupation as simple as an intimation of his mortality. This was not the case. If Selma's perceptions were correct and he was brooding about something, the subject wasn't an immediate threat to his health or well-being. It was always possible he'd been experiencing heart problems—angina pain, arrhythmia, shortness of breath on exertion. If so, he might have been weighing the severity of his symptoms against the consequences of consulting his physician. Tom Newquist might have seen enough death to view the process philosophically. He might have been more fearful of medical intervention than the possibility of dying.

I set the folder on the seat beside me and started the car. I wasn't sure where to go next, but I suspected the logical move would be to talk to Tom's partner,

Rafer LaMott. I checked my map of Nota Lake and spotted the sheriff's substation, which was part of the Civic Center on Benoit about six blocks west. The sun had been climbing through a thin layer of clouds. The air was chilly, but there was something lovely about the light. Along the main thoroughfare, the buildings were constructed of stucco and wood with corrugated metal roofs: gas stations, a drugstore, a sporting goods shop, and hair salon. Rimming the town was the untouched beauty of distant mountains. The digital thermometer on the bank sign showed that it was 42 degrees.

I parked across the street from the Nota Lake Civic Center, which also included the police station, the county courthouse, and assorted community services. The complex of administrative offices was housed in a building that had once been an elementary school. I know this because the words "Nota Lake Grammar School" were carved in block letters on the architrave. I could have sworn I could still see the faint imprint of construction paper witches and pumpkins where they'd been affixed to the windows with cellophane tape, the ghosts of Halloweens past. Personally, I hated grade school, having been cursed with a curious combination of timidity and rebellion. School was a minefield of unwritten rules that everyone but me seemed to sense and accept. My parents had died in a car crash when I was five, so school felt like a continuation of the same villainy and betrayal. I was inclined to upchuck without provocation, which didn't endear me to the janitor or classmates sitting in my vicinity. I can still remember the sensation of recently erupted hot juices collecting in my lap while students on either side of me flocked away in distaste. Far from experiencing shame, I felt a sly satisfaction, the power of the victim wreaking digestive revenge. I'd be sent down to the school nurse where I could lie on a cot until my Aunt Gin came to fetch me. Often at lunchtime . . . (before I learned to barf at will) . . . I'd beg to go home, swearing to look both ways when I was crossing the street, promising not to talk to strangers even if they offered sweets. My teachers rebuffed every plaintive request, so I was doomed to remain; fearful and anxious, undersized, fighting back tears. By the time I was eight, I learned to quit asking. I simply left when it suited me and suffered the consequences later. What were they going to do, shoot me down in cold blood?

The entrance to the Civic Center opened into a wide corridor that served as a lobby, currently undergoing renovations. File cabinets and storage units had been moved into the uncarpeted space. The walls were lined with panels of some unidentified wood. The ceiling was a low gridwork of acoustical tiles. Portions of the hallway were marked off with traffic cones strung together with tape, hand-lettered signs pointing to the current locations of several displaced departments.

I found the sheriff's substation, which was small and consisted of several interconnecting offices that looked like the "Before" photos in a magazine spread. Fluourescent lighting did little to improve the ambience, which was made up of a hodgepodge of technical manuals, wall plaques, glossy paneling, office machines, wire baskets, and notices taped to all the flat surfaces. The civilian clerk was a woman in her thirties who wore running shoes, jeans, and an M.I.T. sweatshirt over a white turtleneck. Her name tag identified her as Margaret Brine. She had chopped-off black hair, oval glasses with black frames, and a dusting of freckles under her powder and blush. Her teeth were big and square with visible spaces between.

I took out a business card and placed it on the counter. "I wonder if I might talk to Rafer LaMott."

She picked up my card, giving it a cursory look. "Will he know what this is about?"

"The coroner suggested I talk to him about Tom Newquist."

Her gaze lifted to mine. "Just a minute," she said. She disappeared through a door in the rear that I assumed led into other offices. I could hear a murmur, and moments later Rafer LaMott appeared, shrugging himself into a charcoal brown sport coat. He was an African American in his forties, probably six feet tall, with a caramel complexion, closely cropped black hair, and startling hazel eyes. His mustache was sparse, and he was otherwise clean-shaven. The lines in his forehead resembled parallel seams in a fine-grained leather. The sports coat he wore over black gabardine pants looked like cashmere. His shirt was pale beige, his tie a mild brown with a pattern of black paperclips arranged in diagonal lines up and down the length.

He had my card in his hand, reading out the information in a slightly cocky tone. "Kinsey Millhone, P.I. from Santa Teresa, California. What can I help you with?"

I could feel a prickly sensation at the back of my neck. His expression was non-committal. Technically, he wasn't rude, but he certainly wasn't friendly and I sensed from his manner he was not going to be much help. I tried a public smile, nothing with any sincerity or warmth. "Selma Newquist hired me. She has some questions about Tom."

He regarded me briefly and then moved through the gate at one end of the counter. "I have to be some place, but you can follow me out. What questions?"

I had no choice but to trot along beside him as he headed down the hall toward a rear entrance. "She says he was upset about something. She wants to know what it was."

He pushed the door open and passed through, picking up his pace in a manner that suggested mounting agitation. I caught the door as it swung shut and passed through right after him. I had to two-step to keep up. He pulled his car keys from his pocket as he descended the steps. He walked briskly across the parking lot and slowed when he reached a nondescript, white compact car, which he proceeded to unlock. As he opened the car door, he turned to look at me. "Listen, here's the truth and no disrespect intended. Selma was always trying to pry into Tom's business, always pressing him for something just in case the poor guy had a fleeting thought of his own. The woman comes equipped with emotional radar, forever scanning her environment, trying to pick up matters of no concern to her. Repeat that and I'll deny it so you can save your breath."

"I have no intention of repeating it. I appreciate your candor—"

"Then you can appreciate this," he said. "Tom never said a word against her, but I can tell you from experience, she's exhausting to be around. Tom was a good guy, but now that he's gone, it's a relief not to have to see her. My wife and I never really wanted to spend time with Selma. We socialized when we had to out of our affection for him. If that sounds spiteful, I'm sorry, but that's the bottom line. My best advice to you is leave the man in peace. He's barely cold in his grave and she's trying to dig him up again."

"Could he have been worried about a case?"

He glanced away from me then with a quick smile of disbelief that I'd pursued the point. I could see him rein himself in, struggling to be patient in hopes of getting rid of me. "He had as many as ten, fifteen files on his desk when he died. And no, you can't see them so don't even ask."

"But nothing particularly distressing?"

"I'm afraid I can't tell you what distressed Tom and what didn't."

"Who's taken over his workload?"

"I took some files. A new guy just hired on and he's taking the rest. None of that information is for public consumption. I don't intend to compromise any ongoing investigation to satisfy Selma's morbid curiosity so you can bag that idea."

"Do you think Tom had personal problems he didn't want her to know?"

"Ask somebody else. I don't want to say anything more about Tom."

"What's the big deal? If you'd give me some help, I'd be out of here," I said.

By way of an answer, he got into the car and pulled the door shut. He turned the key in the ignition, pressing a button in the console. The car window slid down with a mild whir. When he spoke again, his tone was more pleasant. "Hey, this may sound rude, but do yourself a favor and let it drop, okay? Selma's a narcissist. She thinks everything's about her."

"And this isn't?"

He pressed the button again and the window slid back into place. End of subject. End of Q&A. He put the car in reverse and backed out of the space, taking off with a little chirp as he threw the gear into first. I could only stare after him. Belatedly, I sensed a stinging heat rise in my face. I raised a hand to my cheek as though I'd been slapped.

FIVE

I got in my car and headed back to Selma's, still completely unenlightened. I couldn't tell if Rafer knew something or if he was simply annoyed at Selma's hiring a private detective. Oddly enough, I found his rudeness more inspirational than daunting. Tom had died without much warning, out on the highway with no opportunity to clean up his business. For the moment, I was operating on the assumption that Selma's intuition was correct.

I left my car out in front and crossed the lawn to the porch. Selma'd left a note taped to the door saying she'd be over at the church until noon. I tried the door, which was unlocked, so I didn't need the key she'd given me the night before. I let myself in, calling a hello as I entered in case Brant was on the premises. There was no call in response, though several lights in the house were on. I took a few minutes to move through the empty rooms. The house was one story and most of the living space was laid out on one floor. Just off the kitchen, I found a set of stairs leading down to the basement.

I flipped on the light and descended halfway, peering

over the rail. I could see woodworking equipment, a washer and dryer, a hot-water heater, and various odds and ends of furniture, including a portable barbecue and lawn chairs. A half-open door on the far wall led to the furnace room. There appeared to be ample storage. I'd nose around later, going through the cardboard boxes and built-in cabinets.

I returned to Tom's office and sat down at his desk, wondering what secrets he might have kept from view. What I was looking for—if, indeed, there was any-thing—didn't have to be related to Tom's work. It could have been anything: drink, drugs, pornography, gam-bling, an affair, an affinity for young boys, a tendency to cross-dress. Most of us have something we'd prefer to keep to ourselves. Or maybe there was nothing. I didn't like to admit it, but Rafer's attitude toward Selma was already having an effect. I'd resisted his view, but a small touch of doubt was beginning to stir.

I abandoned Tom's desk, feeling restless and bored. So far, I hadn't turned up one significant scrap of paper. Maybe Selma was nuts and I was wasting my time. I went out to the kitchen and poured myself a glass of water. I opened the refrigerator and stared at the con-tents while I pretended to quench my thirst. I closed the refrigerator door and checked the pantry. All the stuff she'd brought back from the store looked alarming; artificial and imitation products of the Miracle Whip variety. There was a plate of what looked like raisin-oatmeal cookies on the counter, with a note that said "Help yourself." I ate several. I left the glass in the drainboard and wandered into the hall. The phone seemed to ring every fifteen minutes, but I let the machine pick up messages. Selma was much in demand, but it was all charity-related work—the church bazaar, a fund-raising auction for the new Sunday school wing.

I turned my attention to the master bedroom. Tom's clothes were still hanging in his half of the closet. I began to go through his pockets. I checked the top shelf, his shoe boxes, dresser drawers, his change caddy. I found a loaded Colt .357 Magnum in one bed table drawer, but there was nothing else of importance. The remaining content of the drawer was that embarrassing assortment of junk everyone seems to keep somewhere: ticket stubs, match books, expired credit cards, shoelaces. No dirty magazines, no sex toys. I looked under the bed, slid a hand along under the mattress, peeked behind picture frames, tapped with a knuckle across the walls in the closet, pulled up a corner of the rug, looking for hidden panels in the floor.

In the master bath, I checked the medicine cabinet, the linen closet, and the hamper. Nothing leaped out at me. Nothing seemed out of place. For a while, in despair, I stretched out on the master bedroom floor, breathing in carpet fumes and wondering how soon I could decently quit.

I went back into the den, where I finished going through the remaining junk on his shelves. Aside from feeling virtuous for cleaning out his desk drawers, I'd acquired absolutely no insights about Tom Newquist's life. I checked his credit card receipts for the past twelve months, but neither his Visa nor his MasterCard showed anything unusual. Most activity on the card could easily be matched to his desk calendar. For instance, a series of hotel and restaurant charges the previous February were related to a seminar he'd attended in Redding, California. The man was systematic. I gave him points for that. Any work-related charges to his telephone bill were later invoiced to his work and reimbursed accordingly. He didn't pad his account by so much as a penny. There was no pattern of outlandish expenses and nothing to suggest any significant or unexplained outlay of cash.

I heard a car pull into the drive. If this was Selma coming in, I'd tell her I was quitting so she wouldn't waste any more of Tom's hard-earned money. The front door opened and closed. I called a "Hello" and waited for a response. "Selma, is that you?" I waited again. "The Booger Man?"

This time I got a manly "Yo!" in response, and Selma's son, Brant, appeared in the doorway. He was wearing a red knit cap, a red sweatsuit, and pristine white leather Reeboks, with a white towel wrapped around his neck. Brant, at twenty-five, was the kind of kid matronly housewives in the supermarket turned around and checked out in passing. He had dark hair and fierce brows over serious brown eyes. His complexion was flawless. His jaw was boxy, his cheeks as honed as if his face had been molded and shaped in clay first and then carved out of flesh. His mouth was fleshy and his color was good; a strong winter tan overlaid with the ruddy burn of snow glare and wind. His posture was impeccable: square shoulders, flat stomach, skinny through the hips. If I were younger, I might have whimpered at the sight of him. As it is, I tend to disqualify any guy that much younger than me, especially in the course of work. I've had to learn the hard way (as it were) not to mix pleasure with business.

"My mom's not here yet?" he asked, pulling the towel from around his neck. He removed his knit cap at the same time and I could see that his hair was curling slightly with the sweaty dampness of his workout. His smile showed straight white teeth.

"Should be any minute. I'm Kinsey. Are you Brant?"

"Yes ma'am. I'm sorry. I should have introduced myself." I shook hands with him across the littered expanse of his father's desk. His palm was an odd gray. When he saw that I noticed, he smiled sheepishly. "That's from weightlifting gloves. I just came from the gym," he said. "I saw the car out front and figured you were here. How's it going so far?"

"Well enough, I guess."

"I better let you get back to it. Mom comes, tell her I'm in the shower."

"Sure thing."

"See you in a bit," he said.

Selma got home at 12:15. I heard the garage door grumble up and then down. Within minutes, she'd let herself in the door that led from the garage into the kitchen. Soon afterward, I could hear the clattering of dishes, the refrigerator door opening and shutting, then the chink of flatware. She appeared in the den doorway, wearing a cotton pinafore-style apron over slacks and a matching sweater. "I'm making chicken salad sandwiches if you'd like to join us. You met Brant?"

"I did. Chicken salad sounds great. You need help?"

"No, no, but come on out and we can talk while I finish up."

I followed her to the kitchen where I washed my hands. "You know what I haven't come across yet is Tom's notebook. Didn't he take field notes when he was working an investigation?"

Surprised, Selma turned from the counter where she was putting together sandwiches. "Absolutely. It was a little loose-leaf notebook with a black leather cover, about the size of an index card, maybe a little bigger, but not much more than that. It must be around here some place. He always had it with him." She began to cut sandwiches in half, placing them on a platter with sprigs of parsley around the edge. Every time I buy parsley, it turns to slime. "Are you sure it's not there?" she asked.

"I haven't come across it. I checked his desk drawers and his coat pockets."

"What about his truck? Sometimes he left it in the glove compartment or the side pocket."

"Good suggestion. I should have thought of that myself."

I opened the connecting door and moved into the garage. I skirted Selma's car and opened the door to the pickup on the driver's side. The interior smelled heavily of cigarette smoke. The ashtray bulged with cigarette butts buried in a shallow bed of ash. The glove compartment was tidy, bearing only a batch of road maps, the owner's manual, registration, proof of insurance, and gasoline receipts. I looked in the side pockets in both doors, looked behind the visors, leaned over and scanned the space under the bucket seats. I checked the area behind the seats, but there was only a small tool kit for emergencies. Aside from that, the interior revealed nothing. I slammed the driver's side door shut, glancing idly along the garage shelves in passing. I don't know what I thought I'd see, but there was no little black notebook within range.

I returned to the kitchen. "Scratch that," I said. "Any other ideas?"

"I'll have a look myself later on today. He could have left the notebook at work, though he seldom did that. I'll call Rafer and ask him."

"Won't he claim the notes are department property?"

"Oh, I'm sure not," she said. "He told me he'd do anything he could to help. He was Tom's best friend, you know."

But not yours, I thought. "One thing I'm curious about," I said tentatively. "The night he died . . . if he'd had any warning . . . he could have called for help if he'd had a radio. Why no CB in his truck? Why no pager? I know a lot of guys in law enforcement who have radios installed in their personal vehicles."

"Oh, I know. He meant to do that, but hadn't gotten around to it. He was always busy. I couldn't get him to take the time to drop it off and get it done. That's the sort of thing you tend to remember when there's no way to deal with it."

Brant reappeared, wearing the blue uniform that identified him as an emergency medical technician for the local ambulance service. B. NEWQUIST was embroidered on the left. His skin radiated the scent of soap and his hair was now shower-damp and smelled of Ivory shampoo. I allowed myself one small inaudible whine of the sort only heard by dogs; neither Brant nor his mother seemed to pick up on it. I sat at the kitchen table, just across from him, politely eating my sandwich while I listened to them chat. Midway through lunch, the telephone rang again. Selma got up. "You two go ahead. I'll pick that up in Tom's den."

Brant finished his sandwich without saying much and I realized it was going to be my job to initiate conversation.

"I take it Tom adopted you."

"When I was thirteen," Brant said. "My . . . I guess you'd call him a birth father . . . hadn't been in touch for years, since my mom and him divorced. When she married Tom, he petitioned the court. I'd consider him my real dad whether he adopted me or not."

"You must have had a good relationship."

He reached for the plate of cookies on the counter and we took turns eating them while we continued our conversation. "The last couple of years we did. Before that, we didn't get along all that great. Mom's always been easygoing, but Tom was strict. He'd been in the army and he came down real hard on the side of obeying rules. He encouraged me to get involved with Boy Scouts—which I hated—karate, and track, stuff like that. I wasn't used to having restrictions laid on me so I fought back at first. I guess I did just about anything I could think of to challenge his authority. Eventually he shaped up," he said, smiling slightly.

"How long have you been a paramedic?"

"Three years. Before that, I didn't do much of anything. Went to school for a while, though I wasn't any great shakes as a student back then."

"Did Tom talk to you about his cases?"

"Sometimes. Not lately."

"Any idea why?"

Brant shrugged. "Maybe what he was working on wasn't that interesting."

"What about the last six weeks or so?"

"He didn't mention anything in particular."

"What about his field notes? Have you seen those?"

A frown crossed his face. "His field notes?"

"The notes he kept—"

Brant interrupted. "I know what field notes are, but I don't understand the question. His are missing?"

"I think so. Or put it this way, I haven't been able to lay hands on his notebook."

"That's weird. When it wasn't in his pocket, he kept it in his desk drawer or his truck. All his old notes, he bound up in rubber bands and stored in boxes in the basement. Have you asked his partner? Might be at the office."

"I talked to Rafer once but I didn't ask about the notebook because at that point, I hadn't even thought to look."

"Can't help you on that one. I'll keep an eye out around here."

After lunch, both Selma and Brant took off. Brant had errands to run before he reported for work and Selma was involved in her endless series of volunteer positions. She'd posted a calendar on the refrigerator and the squares were filled with scribbles for most days of the week. A silence settled on the house and I felt a mild ripple of anxiety climb my frame. I was running out of things to do. I went back to the den and pulled the phone book out of Tom's top drawer. Given the size of the town, the directory was no bigger than a magazine. I looked up James Tennyson, the CHP officer who'd found Tom that night. There was only one Tennyson, a James W., listed on Iroquois Drive in this same development. I checked my city map, grabbed my jacket and my handbag, and headed out to the car.

Iroquois Drive was a winding roadway lined with two-story houses and an abundance of evergreens. Residents were apparently encouraged to keep their garage doors closed. Backyards in this section were fully fenced or surrounded by hedges and I could see swing sets and jungle gyms as well as above-ground swimming pools, still covered for the winter. The Tennysons lived at the end of the street in a yellow stucco house with dark green shutters and a dark green roof. I parked out in front, snagging the morning paper from the lawn as I passed. I pushed the doorbell, but heard no reassuring *ding dong* inside. I waited a few minutes and then tried a modest knock.

The door was opened by a young woman in jeans with a sleeping baby propped against her shoulder. The child might have been six months old; sparse golden curls, flushed cheeks, flannel sleepers with feet, and a big diapered butt.

"Mrs. Tennyson?"

"That's right."

"My name is Kinsey Millhone. I was hoping to have a word with your husband. I take it he's the one who works for the CHP."

"That's right."

"Is he at work?"

"No, he's here. He works nights and sleeps late. That's why the doorbell's turned off. You want to come in and wait? I just heard him banging around so it shouldn't be long."

"If you don't mind." I held up the newspaper. "I brought this in. I trust it's yours."

"Oh, thanks. I don't even bother until he's up. The baby gets into it and tears the whole thing to pieces if I'm not looking. Cat does the same thing. Sits there and bites on it just daring me to get mad."

She moved aside to admit me and I stepped into the entrance. Like Selma's, this house seemed overheated, but I may have been reacting to the contrast with the outside cold. She closed the door behind me. "By the way, I'm Jo. Your name's Kimmy?"

"Kinsey," I corrected. "It was my mother's maiden name."

"That's cute," she said, flashing me a smile. "This is Brittany. Poor baby. We call her Bugsy for some reason. Don't know how that got started, but she'll never live it down." Jo Tennyson was trim, with a ponytail and bangs, her hair a slightly darker version of her daughter's. She couldn't have been much more than twenty-one and may have become a mother before she could legally drink. The baby never stirred as we proceeded to the kitchen. Jo put the newspaper on the kitchen table, indicating a seat. She moved around the room, setting up her husband's breakfast one-handed while the baby slept on. I watched with fascination as she opened a fresh cereal box, shook some of the contents in a bowl, and fetched a spoon from the drawer, which she closed with one hip. She retrieved the milk carton from the refrigerator, poured coffee into three mugs, and pushed one in my direction. "You're not in sales, I hope."

I shook my head and then murmured a thank you for the coffee, which smelled great. "I'm a private investigator. I have some questions for your husband about Tom Newquist's death."

"Oh, sorry. I didn't realize it was business or I could have called him first thing. He's just fooling around. He likes to take his time in the morning because the rest of his day's so hectic. Let me see where he's at. If you want any more coffee, help yourself. I'll be right back."

During her absence, I took the opportunity to engage in a little sit-down observation. The house was untidy— I'd seen that in passing—but the kitchen was particularly disorganized. Counters were cluttered, the cabinet doors hung open, the sink piled with dishes from the last several meals. I thought the vinyl floor tile was gray with a dark mottled pattern, but on closer inspection it turned out to be white overlaid with an assortment of sooty footprints. I straightened up as she returned.

"He'll be right here. I didn't peg you for a detective. Are you local?"

"I'm from Santa Teresa."

"I didn't think you looked familiar. You should talk to Tom's wife. She lives in this subdivision, over in that direction about six blocks, on Pawnee. The snooty street we call it."

"She's the one who hired me. You know her?"

"Uh-unh. We go to the same church. She's in charge of the altar flowers and I help when I can. She's really good-hearted. She's the one who gave Bugsy her little christening dress. Here's James. I'll leave the two of you alone so you can talk."

I got to my feet as he entered the kitchen. James Tennyson was fair-haired, clean-cut, and slender, the kind of earnest young man you want assisting you on the highway when your fan belt goes funny or your rear tire's blown. He was dressed in civilian clothes: jeans, a sweatshirt, and a pair of sheepskin slippers. "James Tennyson. Nice to meet you."

"Kinsey Millhone," I said as the two of us shook hands. "I'm sorry to bother you at home, but I was over at the Newquists and it seemed so close. I saw your name on a report I picked up from the coroner and looked you up in the book."

"Not a problem. Sit down."

"Thanks. Go ahead with your breakfast. I didn't mean to intrude."

He smiled. "I guess I will if you don't mind. What can I do for you?"

While James ate his cereal, I laid out Selma's concerns. "I take it you knew him personally?"

"Yeah, I knew Tom. Mean, we weren't real good friends . . . him and Selma were older and ran with a different crowd . . . but everybody in Nota Lake knew Tom. I tell you, his death shook me. I know he's kind of old, but he was like a fixture around here."

"Can you tell me how you found him? I know he had a heart attack. I'm just trying to get a feel for what happened."

"Well, this was . . . what . . . five, six weeks ago . . . and really nothing unusual. I was cruising 395 when I spotted this vehicle off to the side of the road. Hazard lights were on and the engine was running so I pulled in behind. I recognized Tom's pickup. You know he lives here in the neighborhood so I see the truck all the time. At first I thought he might be having engine problems or something like that. Both the doors were locked, but once I got close I could see him slumped over. I tapped on the window, thinking he'd pulled over and fell asleep at the wheel. I figured the heater was running because the windshield was covered with condensation, windows all cloudy."

"How'd you get in?"

"Well, the window on the driver's side was open a crack. I had a wire in my car and popped the lock up with that. I could see he's in trouble. He looked awful, his eyes open, muck in the corners of his mouth."

"Was he still alive at that point?"

"I'm pretty sure he was gone, but I did what I could. I tell you my hands were shaking so bad, I couldn't make 'em do right. I nearly busted the window and would have if I hadn't managed to snag the lock when I did. I hauled him down out of the truck onto the side of the road and did CPR right there. I couldn't pick up a heartbeat. His skin was cool to the touch, or at least it seemed like that to me. It was freezing outside and even with the heater turned on, temperature inside the truck had dropped. You know how it does. I radioed for help . . . got an ambulance out there as fast as I could, but there was nothing for it. Doc in ER declared him dead on arrival."

"You think he knew what was happening and pulled over to the side?"

"That'd be my guess. He must have had some kind of chest pain, maybe shortness of breath."

"Did you happen to see Tom's notebook? Black leather, about this big?"

He thought back for a moment, shaking his head slowly. "No ma'am. I don't believe so. Of course, I wasn't looking for it. It was in his truck for sure?"

"Well, no, but Selma says he kept it with him and it hasn't turned up yet. I thought maybe you spotted it and turned it into the department."

"I'da probably done that if I'd seen it. I wouldn't want my notes circulating. A lot of it looks like gibberish, but you need 'em when you type up your reports and if you're called on to testify in court. Wasn't among his personal items? The coroner's office would've returned all his clothes and anything he had on him. You know, his watch, contents of his pockets, and like that."

"I asked Selma the same thing and she hasn't seen it. Anyway, we'll keep looking. I appreciate your time. If anything comes to mind, you can reach me through her."

"I can't imagine there's anything to investigate about him. You couldn't meet a nicer fellow. He's the best. A good man and a good cop."

"So I gather."

I went back to the motel. I couldn't face another minute of sitting in Tom's den. For all we knew, Tom might have been suffering from a chemical depression. We'd been assuming his problem was situational, but it might not have been. *My* problem was situational. I was home-sick and wanted out.

I let myself into the cabin, noting with approval that the room had been done up. The bed was made and the bathroom had been scrubbed, the toilet paper left with a point folded in the first sheet. I sat down at the table and rolled a piece of paper in my Smith-Corona. I began to type out an account of the last day's activities. Selma Newquist was just going to have to make her peace with Tom's passing. Death always leaves unfinished business in its wake, mysteries beyond fathoming, countless unanswered questions amid the detritus of life. All the stories are forgotten, the memories lost. Hire anyone you want and you're still never going to find out what a human being is made of. I could sit here and type 'til I was blue in the face. Tom Newquist was gone and I suspected no one would ever know what his final moments had been.

SIX

I found myself that night in a place called Tiny's Tavern, one of those shit-kicking bars so many small towns seem to spawn. Cecilia had indicated this was a popular hangout for off-duty law enforcement and I was there trolling as much as anything. I was also avoiding the cabin, with its frigid inside temperatures and depressive lighting. Tiny's had rough plank walls, sawdust on the floor, and a bar with a brass footrail that stretched the length of the room. As in an old Western saloon, there was a long mirror behind the bar with a glittering double image of all the liquor bottles on display. The place was gray with cigarette smoke. The air was overheated and smelled of spilled beer, faulty plumbing, failed deodorant, and cheap cologne. The jukebox was gaudy green and yellow with tubes of bubbles running up the sides and stocked with a strange mix of gospel tunes interspersed with country music, the latter dominant. Occasionally, a couple would clomp around mechanically on the ten-by-ten dance floor while the other patrons looked on, calling out encouragement in terms I thought rude.

I wasn't sure about the unspoken assumptions in a

place like this. A woman alone might look like an easy mark for any guy on the loose. For a week night, there seemed to be a fair number of unattached fellows in the place, but after an hour on the premises no one seemed to take any particular notice of me. So much for my fantasy of being accosted by cads. I perched on a bar-stool, sipping bad beer and shelling peanuts from a brass bowl that might have enjoyed a previous life as a spittoon. There was something satisfactory about tossing shells on the floor, though sometimes I ate the shells too, figuring the fiber was healthy in a diet like mine, burdened as it is with all that cholesterol and fat.

The bartender was a guy in his twenties with a shaved head, a dark mustache and beard, and a tattoo of a scorpion on the back of his right hand. I flirted with him mildly just to occupy my time. He seemed to understand there was no serious chance of a wild sexual encounter in his immediate future. I put some quarters in the jukebox. I chatted with the waitress named Alice, who had bright orange hair. I made trips to the ladies' room. I practised a little balancing trick with a fork and a burnt match. If there were any off-duty cops on the premises, I realized I wouldn't recognize them in their off-duty clothes.

At ten, Macon Newquist came in. He was in uniform, moving through the bar at a leisurely pace, checking the crowd for drunks, minors, and any other form of trouble in the making. He spoke to me in passing, but didn't seem inclined to make small talk. Shortly after he left, my idleness paid off when I spotted the civilian clerk from the sheriff's substation. I couldn't for the life of me remember her name. She came in as a part of a foursome with a fellow I assumed to be her husband and another couple, all of them roughly the same age. The four were dressed in a combination of cowboy and ski attire: boots, jeans, Western-cut shirts, down parkas, ski mittens, and knit caps. They found an empty table on the far side of the room. I stared at the clerk with her dark hair cropped short above her ears, dark brown eyes glinting behind her small oval glasses. The other woman was auburn-haired, top-heavy, and pretty, probably plagued with unwanted suggestions about breast-reduction surgery. The clerk's hubby held a consultation and then headed in my direction, pausing at the far end of the bar where he ordered a pitcher of beer and four oversized mugs. In the meantime, the women shed their jackets, took up their purses, and left the table, heading toward the ladies' room. I signaled for another beer just to hold my place and then made a beeline for the facilities myself. My path intersected theirs and the three of us reached the door at just about the same time. I slowed my pace and allowed the two of them to enter first.

The clerk was saying, "Oh, honey. Billie's taken up with that trashy fellow from the video store. You know the one with the attitude? I don't know what she sees in him unless it's you-know-what. I told her she ought to think a little more of herself . . ."

The two continued to talk as they passed through the door and into the first two out of three toilet stalls. I entered the third and eavesdropped my tiny heart out while the three of us peed in a merry chorus. What the hell was her name? She and her companion discussed Billie's son, Seb, who suffered from genital warts so persistent his penis looked like a pink fleshy pickle according to someone named Candy who'd dumped him forthwith. Three toilets were flushed in succession and we reassembled at the sinks so we could wash our hands. The other woman skipped her personal cleanliness and moved on to the ritual of combing her hair and adjusting her makeup. I was tempted to point out the sign on the wall, urging us to curb the spread of disease, but I realized the warning was intended for tavern employees. Apparently, the rest of us were at liberty to contaminate anyone we touched. I tried to set a good example, lathering like a surgeon on the brink of an operation, but the woman didn't follow suit.

Miraculously, just then, my brain supplied the clerk's name in a satisfying mental burp. I caught her eye in the mirror and flashed her a smile as she was pulling out a paper towel so she could dry her hands. "Aren't you Margaret?"

She looked at me blankly and then said "Oh hi" without warmth. I couldn't tell if she'd forgotten me, or remembered and simply didn't want to be engaged in conversation. Probably the latter. She crumpled the paper towel and pushed it down in the wastebasket.

"Kinsey Millhone," I prompted, as if she'd recently inquired. "We met this morning at the office when I was talking to Detective LaMott." I held out my hand and she was too polite to decline a handshake.

She said, "Nice seeing you again."

"I thought I recognized you the minute you came in, but I couldn't remember where I knew you from." I turned and gave a little wave to the other woman.

"Hi. How are you? Kinsey Millhone," I said. "And you're . . .?"

She seemed to hesitate, glancing at Margaret. "Earlene." She held her hand out and I had no choice but to take it, germs and all.

"My best friend," Margaret interjected.

"Well, isn't that nice," I said. Earlene's handshake consisted of laying her fingers passively across mine. It was like having a half pound of cooked linguini placed in your palm for safekeeping. She had a round pretty face with a button nose and plump lips, a mutant body that was all breasts, with diminishing hips and legs that petered out into tiny feet. She flicked another look at Margaret, clearly picking up on her lack of enthusiasm. I was acting like a salesperson, forcing chitchat to gain a foothold in the conversation. Telemarketers use this device all the time, as if the rest of us don't know what their phony friendliness is all about.

Margaret wasn't fooled. She tucked her bag up against her body and gripped it closely with her arm. "I don't know what you said to Rafer, but he was ticked off all day and I was the one had to take the flak."

"Really? I'm sorry to hear that. I didn't mean to set him off."

"Everything sets him off since Tom passed away. They worked together for years, long before I hired on."

"I can see why he'd be upset." I was making myself sick with all this conciliatory bullshit, though it seemed to be having the desired effect.

Margaret rolled her eyes. "He'll get over it, I guess,

but I wouldn't advise you to cross paths with him if you can help it."

"I'll avoid him if possible, but I'm only in town for another couple of days and I'm not sure where else to get information."

I was hoping this would prompt an offer of assistance, but Margaret didn't seem to care. She stood there without a word, forcing me to blunder on. "Why don't I just tell you what I need and maybe you can help. Honestly, I'm not looking for any dirt on Tom Newquist. That's not my intention. I've heard he's a great guy and everybody seems real sorry that he's gone."

"Well, that's true," she said, grudgingly.

"I wasn't sure what to make of your boss. I mean, I could tell he was aggravated, but I couldn't figure out what I'd done."

"It's not you in particular. Rafer says Selma's the one stirring up trouble. Says he's sick and tired of her meddling in Tom's affairs."

"It's hardly meddling," I said. "She was married to the man and has a legitimate concern."

"About what?"

"She told me Tom was worried about something. He slept badly. He brooded. She kept hoping he'd confide in her, but he never said a word. She wanted to ask him, but she couldn't bring herself to do it. You know how it is. You've got a subject you want to talk about and you keep trying to find the perfect time to do it. I guess he was prickly and she was reluctant to irritate him. At any rate, before she could broach the subject, he dropped dead, so now she's stuck."

"That still doesn't entitle her to mess around in Tom's business."

"Of course not, but she's troubled by the possibility he died with some burden. She's heartsick she didn't barge in when she had the chance. That's why she's hired me."

"Good luck," Margaret said in a tone that really meant she hoped I'd fall in a hole.

"I don't think my chances are good, but I don't blame her for trying. She's hoping to make amends. What's wrong with that? In her place, you'd do the same thing, wouldn't you?"

Margaret said, "Well." I could see she was having trouble marshaling an argument. She was good at put-downs; not so good when it came to defending her position. I was feeling damp from the effort of telling the truth. Lies are always easier because the only thing you risk is getting caught. Once you stoop to the truth, you're screwed because if the other person isn't buying, you've got nothing left to sell.

Earlene was watching us like a spectator at a tennis match. Her bright blue eyes darted with interest between my face and Margaret's. I really couldn't tell whose side she was on, but I decided to pull her in. "What do you think, Earlene? What would you do in Selma's place?"

"Same thing, I guess. I can see your point." She flicked a look at Margaret. "You said yourself Tom was a bear the last few weeks before he passed." She looked back at me, hooking a thumb in Margaret's direction. "She thought he was going through the change. You know, moody and short-tempered . . ."

"*Earlene*."

"Well, it's the truth."

"Of course, it's true, but that doesn't mean it bears repeating in the ladies' room." This from the woman discussing someone's genital warts.

"Do you have any idea what was bothering him?" I asked.

Margaret was indignant. "I most certainly do not. And I have to tell you I think she'd be better off letting sleeping dogs lie. If he'd wanted her to know, he'd have told her, so it's really none of her concern. Even if he was crabby and hard to get along with, that's hardly a crime."

"But who'd know? Who should I be talking to if not Rafer?"

Earlene raised her hand. "Wouldn't hurt to ask Hatch."

"Would you butt out?" Margaret snapped.

"Who's Hatch?" I asked Earlene.

"Hatch's her husband. He's sitting right out there," she said, pointing toward the bar.

Margaret snorted. "He won't help and I give you odds Wayne won't either. Wayne hasn't worked for Tom in years so what's he know about anything?"

"Hatch worked for Tom?" I said to Margaret.

"Uh-unh. Both him and Wayne are sheriff's deputies, only Wayne covers Whirly Township and Hatch is working days down here."

"It couldn't do any harm," I said.

Margaret thought about it and then frowned. "I don't guess I can stop you, but it's a waste of time if you ask me."

The three of us left the ladies' room together.

"I'll grab my beer and be right back," I said.

I hustled my butt over to the bar to get my things. I figured in my absence Margaret could go to work on her husband, thus advancing my case. I grabbed my beer mug and jacket and moved over to their table, watching as Hatch dutifully scrounged up an extra chair from a table nearby. I went through another round of introductions, trying to seem winsome as I shook hands with both men. "Winsome" is not a quality I normally project. "Did Margaret tell you what I was up to?"

Hatch said, "Yes ma'am." He was a big rangy man with a thatch of blond hair shorn close along the sides. His face was bony, all jaw and cheekbones, with a big bumpy nose. His ears stuck out like handles on a vase.

Earlene's husband, Wayne, took a swig of beer and put the mug down with a tap. He was dark-haired with a receding hairline, the hair itself cut short and combed forward. He had the pretty-boy handsomeness of a small-time thug. He didn't seem to like me. He avoided my eyes, his attention diverting to other parts of the room. Once in a while he tuned into the conversation, but he made it plain he didn't like the idea of discussing Tom with anyone.

Hatch at least *seemed* friendly, so I focused on him. "I understand you knew Tom."

"Everybody knew Tom," he said.

"Can you tell me a little bit about him?"

Hatch regarded me uneasily, shaking his head. "You're not going to get me to say anything bad about the man."

"Absolutely not. I'm hoping to get a sense of who he

was. I never met him myself so I'm operating in the dark. How long did you know him?"

"Little over fifteen years, since way before I joined the sheriff's department. I'd moved up here from Barstow and first thing you know, someone broke into my apartment and took my stereo. Tom was the one showed up when I dialed 9–1–1."

"What was he like?"

"With regard to what?"

"Anything. Was he smart? Was he funny? Was he a hang-loose kind of guy?"

Hatch tilted his head, allowing one shoulder to creep up toward his ear. "I'd say Tom was a good cop, first, last, and always. You just about couldn't separate the man from the job. He was smart, for sure, and he played by the book."

"Someone who didn't bend the rules," I said, repeating the coroner's comment.

"Yeah, right. You know, little things, he might try to give a guy a break, but high-ticket crime, he was a strictly law-and-order type. All this victim stuff you see nowadays cut no ice with him. He believed you're accountable and there's no two ways about it. He took a hard line on that and I think he was right. Small town like this, somebody breaks the law, you might have dated their sister or they lived down the street from you way back when. In Tom's mind, it wasn't personal. He wasn't mean or anything like that. Business was just business and you had to respect him for his attitude."

"Can you give me an example?"

"I can't think of one offhand. What about you,

Wayne? You know what I'm saying. What's the kind of thing Tom did?"

Wayne shook his head. "Hey, Hatch. This is your party. By me."

Hatch scratched at his chin, pulling at the flesh underneath. "Well now, here's one I remember and this is pretty typical I'd say. We had this good ol' boy named Sonny Gelson. Remember him, hon? This was maybe five, six years ago, I guess. He used to live over by Winona in a big old falling-down house." He didn't wait for a response, but I could see Margaret nod as her husband went on. "His wife shot 'im one night by mistake. She thought he was an intruder and pumped a big hole in his chest. About six months before, she'd reported a prowler and Sonny got her a Smith & Wesson. So one night he's out of town and she's home by herself. She hears someone in the downstairs hall, pulls the gun out of a drawer, and pops the guy as he comes in. Problem was the gun misfired and blew up in her hand. Sonny'd packed the reload himself and I guess he'd done it wrong, or that's what it looked like at any rate. Bullet still exited the gun and hit him smack in the chest. I think he died before Judy could even dial 9-1-1. Meantime, Judy's got a hand full of fragments and she's bleeding all over everywhere. See, but now here's the point. Tom got it in his head that this's premeditated murder. He's convinced the whole thing's a setup. So here's Judy Gelson crying her heart out for her terrible mistake. She swears she didn't know it was him. The whole town's up in arms. Everybody out there protesting. DA was going to let her plead out and let it go at that. I doubt she'd have served time because her record was clean. Save the county a ton of money, plus a lot of bad press. Tom just kept digging and pretty soon he comes up with this hefty insurance policy. Turns out Judy had a lover and the two of 'em concocted this plan to get rid of her husband, take the money, and run. She's the one jimmied the cartridge with an overload of fast powder so she'd look like an innocent victim of circumstance herself. Tom's the one nailed her and he'd went *steady* with her once upon a time. She's homecoming queen in high school and they nearly run off together the night of the senior prom. Cut no ice with him and that's the point I'm trying to make."

"What happened to Judy Gelson?"

"She's doing twenty-five to life somewhere. Lover dropped out of sight. In fact, nobody ever figured out who he was. Maybe somebody local with a lot to lose. Tom was always workin' that one, trying to get a line on the guy. It bugged him to see a fellow get away with anything."

"He liked to work old cases?"

"Everybody does. Always the chance you'll crack one and make a name for yourself. Anyway, it's more than that; it's putting paid to an account. 'Closure' they call it nowadays, but it amounts to the same thing."

I glanced at Margaret, saying, "That's all Selma wants."

Hatch shook his head at the mention of her name. "Well, now Selma. She's something else. I wouldn't want to say anything bad about her. Tom was crazy about her, worshiped the ground she walked on, and that's no lie."

Margaret chimed in. "The rest of us find Selma pretty hard to take."

"How so?"

"Oh, you know, she's easily offended, imagines slights where there's none intended. Tom tried his best to reassure her, but it was never enough. You'd run into the two of 'em out in public and he'd always make sure she was included in the conversation, didn't he?" she said, turning to Earlene for confirmation. "I think he knew people didn't like her and he wanted her to look good."

"That's right. He'd sit there and draw her out . . . get her to talking like anybody gave a shit. Everybody liked him and hadn't any use for her."

"So in a way, her insecurity was justified," I said.

Earlene laughed. "Sure, but if she wasn't so self-centered, people might like her better. Selma's convinced the sun rises and sets in her own hineybumper and she had Tom convinced of it, too. He used to jump every time she snapped her fingers. On top of that she's a social climber, acting like she's so much better than the rest of us. In a town this size, we all tend to socialize. You know, go to the same church, join the same country club. Selma has to be there, right out in front. The woman's tireless, I'll give her that. Ask her to do anything and she's got it done just like that."

Earlene's husband, Wayne, had caught my eye more than once in the course of her recital. I thought he was irritated that she was talking to me. Given the fact that Wayne had worked with Tom, I suspected he didn't like his wife being so free with her opinions. He seemed guarded, remote, his eyes pinned on the table while the other three exchanged anecdotes. I couldn't get a fix on the source of his disaffinity. Maybe Rafer'd had a chat with him and made it clear he didn't want any of his deputies to cooperate with me. Or maybe his attitude reflected the habitual reluctance of a cop to share information, even at the level of gossip and personal opinion.

I caught his attention. "What about you, Wayne? Anything you'd care to add?"

He smiled, but more to himself than at me. "Ask me, them three are doing pretty good."

"You agree with their assessment?"

"Basically, I don't see Tom's marriage as any of our business. What him and Selma worked out is between them."

Earlene tossed a crumpled paper napkin in his direction. "You old sourpuss," she said.

"You're not going to get me to respond," he replied airily.

"Oh, loosen up. Honest to Pete. You never liked Selma any better than the rest of us so why not admit it?"

"Say what you want. You're not going to draw me into this."

"Let him be," I said. I was suddenly feeling tired. The combination of tension and smoke-filled air was giving me a headache. I'd asked for general information and that's what I'd received. It was clear no one was going to offer up much more than that. "I think I'll head on back to the motel," I said.

"Don't go away mad. Just go away," Wayne said, smiling.

"Very funny. Ha ha," Earlene said to him.

"We'd best be off, too," Margaret said, glancing at her watch. "Oh, geez. I have to be at work at eight and look what time it is. Eleven forty-five."

Earlene reached for her jacket. "I didn't realize it was that late and we still have to drop you off at your place."

"We can walk. It's not far," Margaret said.

"Don't be silly. It's no trouble. It's right on our way."

The four of them began to gather their belongings, shrugging into their parkas, scraping chairs back as they rose.

"Catch you later," I said.

Various good-bye remarks were made, the yada-yada-yada of superficial social exchange. I watched them depart, and then returned to the bar where I settled my tab. Alice, the orange-haired waitress, was just taking a break. She pulled up a stool beside me and lit a cigarette. Her eyes were rimmed in black eyeliner and she had a fringe of thick dark lashes that had to be false; bright coral lipstick, a swathe of blusher on each cheek. "You a cop?"

"I'm a private investigator."

"Well, that explains," she said, blowing smoke to one side. "I heard you're asking around about Tom Newquist."

"Word travels fast."

"Oh, sure. Town this small there's not much to talk about," she said. "You're barking up the wrong tree with that bunch you were talking to. They're all law enforcement, loyal to their own. You're not going to get anyone to say a bad word about Tom."

"So I discover. You have something to add?"

"Well, I don't know what's been said. I knew him from in here. I knew her somewhat better. I used to run into the two of them at church on occasion."

"I gather she wasn't popular. At least from what I've heard."

"I try not to judge others, but it's hard not to have *some* opinion. Everybody's down on Selma and it seems unfair. I just wish she'd quit worrying about those silly teeth of hers." Alice put a hand to her mouth. "Have you noticed her doing this? Half the time I can hardly hear what's she saying because she's so busy trying to cover up her mouth. Anyway, Tom was great. Don't get me wrong . . . I grant you Selma's abrasive . . . but you know what? He got to look good by comparison. He wasn't confrontational. Tom'd never dream of getting in your face about anything. And why should he? He had Selma to do that. She'd take on anyone. Know what I mean? Let her be the bitch. She's the one takes all the heat. She does the work of the relationship while he gets to be Mr. Good-Guy, Mr. Nice-As-Pie. You see what I'm saying?"

"Absolutely."

"It might have suited them fine, but it doesn't seem right to hold her entirely accountable. I know her type; she's a pussy cat at heart. He could have pinned her ears back. He could have raised a big stink and she'd have backed right off. He didn't have the gumption so why's that her fault? Seems like the blame should attach equally."

"Interesting," I said.

"Well, you know, it's just my reaction. I get sick and tired of hearing everyone trash Selma. Maybe I'm just like her and it cuts too close. Couples come to these agreements about who does what. I'm not saying they sit down and discuss it, but you can see my point. One might be quiet, the other talkative. Or maybe one's outgoing where the other one's shy. Tom was passive—pure and simple—so why blame her for taking over? You'd have done it yourself."

"Selma says he was very preoccupied in the last few weeks. Any idea what it was?"

She paused to consider, drawing on her cigarette. "I never thought much about it, but now you mention it, he didn't seem like himself. Tell you what I'll do. Let me ask around and see if anybody knows anything. It's not like people around here are dishonest or even secretive, but they protect their own."

"You're telling me," I said. I took out a business card and jotted down my home number in Santa Teresa and the motel where I was staying.

Alice smiled. "Cecilia Boden. Now there's a piece of work. If that motel gets to you, you can always come to my place. I got plenty of room."

I smiled in return. "Thanks for your help."

I headed out into the night air. The temperature had dropped and I could see my breath. After the clouds of smoke in the bar, I wondered if I was simply exhaling the accumulation. The parking lot was only half full and the lighting just dim enough to generate uneasiness. I took a moment to scan the area. There was no one in sight, though the line of pine trees on the perimeter could have hidden anyone. I shifted my car keys to my right hand and hunched my handbag over my left shoulder as I moved to the rental car and let myself in.

I slid under the wheel, slammed the car door, and locked it as quickly as possible, listening to the locks flip down with a feeling of satisfaction. The windshield was milky with condensation and I wiped myself a clear patch with my bare hand. I turned the key in the ignition, suddenly alerted by the sullen grinding that indicated a low charge on the battery. I tried again and the engine turned over reluctantly. There was a series of misses and then the engine died. I sat there, projecting a mental movie in which I'd be forced to return to the bar, whistle up assistance, and finally crawl into bed at some absurd hour after god knows what inconvenience.

I caught a flash of headlights in the lane behind me and checked the source in my rearview mirror. A dark panel truck was passing at a slow rate of speed. The driver, in a black ski mask, turned to stare at me. The eye holes in the knit mask were rimmed with white and the opening for the mouth was thickly bordered with red. The driver and I locked eyes, our gazes meeting in the oblong reflection of the rearview mirror. I could feel my skin prickle, the pores puckering with fear. I thought *male*. I thought *white*. But I could have been wrong on both counts.

SEVEN

I could hear the crunch of gravel, a dull popping like distant gunfire. The truck slowed and finally came to a halt. I could hear the engine idling against the still night air. I realized I was holding my breath. I wasn't sure what I'd do if the driver got out and approached my car. After an interminable thirty seconds, the truck moved on while I followed its reflection in my rearview mirror. There was no lettering on the side so I didn't think the vehicle was used for commercial purposes. I turned my head, watching as the panel truck reached the end of the aisle and took a left. There was something unpleasant about being the subject of such scrutiny.

I tried starting my car again. "Come *on*," I said. The engine seemed, if anything, a little less energetic. The panel truck was now passing from right to left along the lane in front of me, the two of us separated by the intervening cars, parked nose to nose with mine. I could see the driver lean forward, the masked face now tilted in my direction. It was the blankness that unnerved me, the shapeless headgear wiping out all features except the eyes and mouth, which stood out in startling relief. Terrorists and bank robbers wore masks like this, not ordinary citizens concerned about frostbite. The panel truck stopped. The black ski mask was fully turned in my direction, the prolonged look intense. I could see that both the eye holes and the mouth hole had been narrowed by big white yarn stitches, with no attempt to disguise the modification. The driver extended a gloved right hand, index finger pointing at me like the barrel of a gun. Two imaginary bullets were fired at me, complete with recoil. I flipped him the bird in return. This brief digital exchange was charged with aggression on his part and defiance on mine. The driver seemed to stiffen and I wondered if I should have kept my snappy metacarpal retort to myself. In Los Angeles, freeway shootings have been motivated by less. For the first time, I worried he might have a real weapon somewhere down by his feet.

I pumped the gas with my foot and turned the key again, uttering a low urgent sound. Miraculously, the engine coughed to life. I put the car in neutral and applied pressure on the accelerator, flipping on the head-lights while I gunned the engine. The arrow on the voltage indicator leaned repeatedly to the right. I flicked my attention to the panel truck, which was just turning out of the lot at the far end. I released the emergency brake and put the car in reverse.

I backed out of the slot, shifted gears, and swung the car into the lane heading in the opposite direction, peering through the dark to see what had happened to the panel truck. I could hear my heart thudding in my head, as if fear had forced the hapless organ up between my ears. I reached the marked exit and eased forward, searching the streets beyond for signs that the panel truck was rounding the block. The street was empty as far as I could see. I patted myself on the chest, a calming gesture designed to comfort and reassure. Nothing had actually happened. Maybe the driver was mistaken, thinking I was an acquaintance and then realizing his error. Someone passing in a panel truck had turned and looked at me, firing symbolically with a pointed index finger and a wiggle of his thumb. I didn't think the incident would make the national news.

It wasn't until I was midway through town that I caught a glimpse of the truck falling into line half a block back. I could see now that one headlight was sitting slightly askew, the beam directed downward, like someone with one crossed eye. I checked in all directions, but I could see no other traffic and no pedestrians. At this late hour, the town of Nota Lake was deserted, stores locked for the night with only an occasional cold interior light aglow. Even the gas station was shut down and cloaked in darkness. The streetlights washed the empty sidewalks with the chilliest of illumination. Stoplights winked silently from green to red and then to green again.

Was this a problem or was it not? I considered my options. My gas gauge showed half a tank. I had plenty of gas to get back to the motel, but I didn't like the idea of someone following me and I didn't want to try to outrun my pursuer if it came to that. Highway 395, leading out to the Nota Lake Cabins, represented one long continuous stretch of darkened road. The few businesses along the highway would be closed for the night, which meant my vulnerability would increase as the countryside around me became less populated. I glanced in the rearview mirror. The panel truck still hung half a block back, matching my speed, a sedate twenty miles an hour. I could feel myself shuddering from some internal chill. I turned on the heater. I was desperate to get warm, desperate for the sight of another human being. Didn't people walk their dogs? Didn't parents dash out for a quart of milk or a croupy child's cough medicine? How about a jogger I could flag down on sight? I wanted the driver of the panel truck to see that I had help.

I turned left at the next street and drove on for three blocks, eyes pinned to the rearview mirror. Within seconds, the panel truck came around the corner behind me and took up its surveillance. I continued west for six blocks and then turned left again. This street paralleled Main, though it was narrower and darker, a quiet residential neighborhood with no houselights showing. Ordinarily, I keep a gun in my briefcase, which is tucked into the well behind the VW's backseat. But this car was a rental and when I'd left Santa Teresa, I was with Dietz. Why did I need a weapon? The only jeopardy I imagined was living in close quarters with an invalid. Given my nature, what scared me was the possibility of emotional claustrophobia, not physical danger.

I was checking the rearview mirror compulsively every couple of seconds. The panel truck was still there, with one headlight focused on the street and one on me. I've taken enough self-defense classes to know that women, by nature, have trouble assessing personal peril. If followed on a darkened street, many of us don't know when to take evasive action. We keep waiting for a sign that our instincts are correct. We're reluctant to make a fuss, just in case we're mistaken about the trouble we're in. We're more concerned about the possibility of embarrassing the guy behind us, preferring to do nothing until we're sure he really means to attack. Ask a woman to scream for help and what you get is a pathetic squeak with no force behind it and no power to dissuade. Oddly, I found myself suffering the same mind-set. Maybe the guy in the panel truck was simply on his way home and I happened to be taking the very path he intended to take all along. Uh-hun, uh-hun. On the other hand, if the driver in the truck was trying to psych me out, I didn't want to give him the satisfaction of any overt reaction.

I refused to speed up. I refused to play tag. I turned left again, driving at a measured rate as the blocks rolled by. Ahead of me, close to the intersection, was the Nota Lake Civic Center with the sheriff's headquarters. Next door was the fire department and next door to that was the police station. I could see the outside lights showing, though I wasn't sure the place was even open this close to midnight. I coasted to a stop and idled the engine with my headlights on. The panel truck rolled up even with my car and the driver turned, as before, to stare. I could have sworn there was a smile showing through the red-rimmed knit mouth. The driver made no other move and, after a tense moment, he drove on. I checked the rear license plate, but it was covered with tape and no identifying numbers showed. The truck began to speed up, turned left at the intersection, and disappeared from sight. I felt my insides turning luminous as adrenaline poured through me.

I waited a full five minutes, though it felt like for

ever. I studied the street on all sides, craning my head to scan the area behind, lest someone approach on foot. I was afraid to shut down my engine, worried I wouldn't be able to get the car started again. I squeezed my hands between my knees, trying to warm my icy fingers. The feeling of apprehension was as palpable as a fever, racking my frame. I caught a glimpse of headlights behind me again and when I checked the rearview mirror, I saw a vehicle come slowly around the corner. I made a sound in my throat and leaned on the horn. A howling blare filled the night. The second vehicle eased up beside me and I could see now that it was James Tennyson, the CHP officer, in his patrol car. He recognized my face and rolled down the window on the driver's side. "You okay?" he mouthed.

I pressed a button on the console and opened the window on the passenger side of my car.

"Something I can help you with?" he asked.

"Someone's been following me. I didn't know what else to do, but come here and honk."

"Hang on," he said. He spotted a parking place across the street and pulled his patrol car over to the stretch of empty curb. He left his vehicle running while he crossed the street. He walked around to my side of the car and hunkered so we could talk face-to-face. "What's the story?"

I explained the situation, trying not to distort or exaggerate. I wasn't sure how to convince him of the alarm I'd felt, but he seemed to accept my account without any attempt to dismiss my panic as foolish or unwarranted. He was in his twenties by my guess and I suspected I'd seen more in the way of personal combat than he had. Still, he was a cop in uniform and the sight of him was reassuring. He was earnest, polite, with that fair unlined face and all the innocence of youth.

"Well, I can see where that'd worry you. It seems creepy to me, too," he said. "Might have been a guy sitting in the bar. Sometimes the fellows around here get kind of weird when they drink. Sounds like he was waiting for you to come out to the parking lot."

"I thought so, too."

"You didn't notice anybody in Tiny's staring at you?"

"Not at all," I said.

"Well, he probably didn't mean any harm, even if he scared you some."

"What about the truck? There couldn't be that many black panel trucks in a town this size."

"I haven't seen it, but I've been cruising the highway south of town. I was passing the intersection when I caught a glimpse of your headlights so I doubled back. Thought you might be having car trouble, but I wasn't sure." He tilted his head in the direction of the police station. "They're locked up for the night. You want me to see you home? I'd be happy to."

"Please," I said.

He escorted me the six miles to the motel, driving ahead of me so I could keep my gaze fixed on the sight of his patrol car. There was no sign of the panel truck. Once at the Nota Lake Cabins, we parked side by side and he walked me to the cabin, waiting while I unlocked the door and flipped on the light inside. I intended to check the premises, but he held out an arm like the captain of the grade school safety patrol. "Let me do this."

"Great. It's all yours," I said.

I make no big deal about these things. I'm a strong, independent woman, not an idiot. I know when it's time to turn the task over to a cop; someone with a gun, a nightstick, a pair of handcuffs, and a paycheck. He did a cursory inspection while I followed close on his heels, feeling like a cartoon character with slightly quaking knees. If a mouse had jumped out, I'd have shrieked like a fool.

He glanced in the closet, behind the bathroom door. He moved the shower curtain aside, got down on his hands and knees and looked under the bed. He didn't seem any more impressed with the place than I'd been. "Never been inside one of these before. I believe I'd take a pass if it came right down to it. Doesn't Ms. Boden believe in heat?"

"I guess not."

He got to his feet and brushed the soot from his knees. "What kind of money does she get for this?"

"Thirty bucks a night."

"That much?" He shook his head with amazement. He made sure the windows were secured. While I waited in the cabin, he made a circuit of the place outside, using his flashlight beam to cut through the dark. He came back to the door. "Looks clear to me."

"Let's hope."

He let his gaze settle on my face. "I can take you somewhere else if you'd prefer. We got motels in the heart of town if you think you'd feel safer. You'd be warmer, too."

I considered it briefly. I was both keyed up and exhausted. Moving at this hour would be a pain in the ass. "This is fine," I said. "I didn't see any sign of the truck on the way out. Maybe it was just a practical joke."

"I wouldn't count on that. World's full of freaks. You don't want to take something like this lightly. You might want to talk to the police in the morning and file a report. Wouldn't hurt to lay the groundwork in case something comes up again."

"Good point. I'll do that."

"You have a flashlight? Why don't you take this tonight and you can return it to me in the morning. I got another in the car. You'll feel better if you have a weapon."

I took the flashlight, hefting the substantial weight of it in my hand. You could really hurt somebody if you whacked 'em up the side of the head. I'd seen scalps laid wide open when the edge hit just right. I felt like asking for his nightstick and his radio, but I didn't want to leave him denuded of equipment.

I held up the flashlight. "Thanks. I'll drop it off to you first thing."

"No hurry."

Once he was gone, I locked the door and then went through the cabin carefully, doing just as he'd done. I made sure the windows were locked, looked under every piece of furniture, in closets, behind curtains. I turned the lights out and let my eyes adjust to the dark, then moved from window to window, eyeing the exterior. The black wasn't absolute. There was a moon up there somewhere, bathing the surrounding woods in a silvery glow. The trunks of the birches and the sycamores shone as pale as ice. The evergreens were dense, shapeless, and compelling against the night landscape. I should have gone to another motel. I regretted the isolation, wishing that I could find myself safely ensconced in one of the big chains—a Hyatt or a Marriott, one with hundreds of identical rooms and numerous in-house security. In my current situation, I had no phone and no immediate neighbors. The rental car was parked at least a hundred yards away, not readily available if I should have to make a hasty exit.

I leaned my forehead against the glass. From out on the highway, I could catch flashes of light as an occasional car sped by, but none seemed to slow and none turned into the motel parking area. Times like this, I longed for a husband or a dog, but I never could decide which would be more trouble in the long run. At least husbands don't bark and tend to start off paper trained.

I remained fully dressed and brushed my teeth in the dark, barely letting the water run as I washed my face. Frequently, I paused, listening to the silence. I took my shoes off, but kept them by the side of the bed within easy reach. I crawled under the covers and propped myself against the pillows, flashlight in hand. Twice, I got up and looked out the windows, but there was nothing to see and eventually I felt calm return.

I didn't sleep well, but in early morning light, I felt better.

I was blessed with a full three minutes of hot water before the pipes began to clank. I walked out to the highway into a morning filled with icy sunlight and air clear as glass. I could smell loam and pine needles. There was no sign of the panel truck. Nobody in a ski mask paused to stare at me. I had breakfast at the Rainbow, taking a certain comfort at the mundane nature of the place. I watched the short-order cook, a young black girl working with remarkable efficiency and concentration.

Afterward, I returned to Selma's.

Her sister-in-law, Phyllis, was in the kitchen. The two of them were working at the breakfast table, which was covered with paperwork. File folders were spread out, lists of names on legal pads with removable tags attached. I gathered they were determining the seating for some country club event, arguing about who to seat by whom for maximum entertainment and minimum conflict.

"Nawp. I wouldn't do that," Phyllis said. "The fellows like each other, but the women don't speak. Don't you remember that business between Ann Carol and Joanna?"

"They're not still mad about that, are they?"

"Sure are."

"Unbelievable."

"Well, trust me. You seat them together, you got a war on your hands. I've seen Joanna throw one of those hard dinner rolls at Ann Carol. She bonked her right in the eye and raised a welt this big."

Selma paused to light a cigarette while she studied the chart. "How about put her at Table 13?"

Phyllis made a rueful face. "I guess that'd do. I mean, it's dull, but not bad. At least Ann Carol wouldn't be subject to an attack by flying yeast bread."

Selma looked up at me. "Morning, Kinsey. What's on your plate today? Are you about finished in there?"

"Almost," I said. I glanced at Phyllis, wondering if this was a subject to be discussed in front of her.

Selma caught my hesitation. "That's fine. Go ahead. You don't have to worry about her. She knows all this."

"I'm drawing a blank. I don't doubt your story. I'm sure Tom was worried about something. Other people have told me he didn't seem like himself. I just can't find any indication of what was troubling him. Really, I'm no better informed now than when I started. It's frustrating."

I could see the disappointment settle across Selma's face.

"It's only been two days," she murmured. Phyllis was frowning slightly, straightening a pile of papers on the table in front of her. I hoped she had something to offer, but she said nothing so I went on.

"Well, that's true," I said. "And there's always the chance something will pop up unexpectedly, but so far there's nothing. I just thought you should know. I can give you a rundown when you have a minute."

"I guess you can only do your best," Selma said. "Coffee's hot if you want some. I left you a mug alongside that little pitcher of milk over there."

I crossed to the coffeemaker and poured myself a cup, taking a quick whiff of the milk before adding it to my coffee. I debated whether to mention the business with the panel truck, but I couldn't see the point. The two of them were already back at work and I didn't want to have to deal with their concern or their speculation. I might net myself a little sympathy, but to what end?

"See you in a bit," I said. The two didn't lift their heads. I shrugged to myself and moved into the den.

I stood in the doorway while I sipped my coffee, staring at the disarray that still littered the room. I'd been working my way through the mess in an orderly fashion, but the result seemed fragmented. Many jobs were half done and those I'd completed hadn't netted me anything in the way of hard data. I'd simply proceeded on the assumption that if Tom Newquist was up to something he had to have left a trace of it somewhere. There were numerous odd lots of paperwork I wasn't sure how to classify. I'd piled much of it on the desk in an arrangement invisible to the naked eye. I was down to the dregs and it was hard to know just where to go from here. I'd lost all enthusiasm for the project, which felt dirty and pointless. I did have six banker's boxes stacked along one wall. Those contained the files that I'd labeled and grouped: previous income tax forms, warranties, insurance policies, property valuations, various utility stubs, telephone bills, and credit card receipts. Still no sign of his field notes, but he might have left them at the station. I made a mental note to check with Rafer on that.

I set my mug on an empty bookshelf, folded together a fresh banker's box, and began to clear Tom's desk. I placed papers in the box with no particular intention except to tidy the space. I was here as an investigator, not as char in residence. Once I cleared the desk, I felt better. For one thing, I could see now that his blotter was covered with scribbles: doodles, telephone numbers, what looked like case numbers, cartoon dogs and cats in various poses, appointments, names and addresses, drawings of cars with flames shooting from the tailpipes. Some of the numerals had been cast in three dimensions, a technique I employed sometimes while I was talking on the phone. Some items of information were boxed in pen; some were outlined and shaded in strokes of different thicknesses. I pored over the whole of it as though it were hieroglyphic, then panned across the surface item by item. The drawings were much like the ones sixth-grade boys seemed to favor in my elementary days—daggers and blood and guns firing fat bullets at somebody's cartoon head. The only repeat item was a length of thick rope fashioned into a hangman's noose. He'd drawn two of those; one with an X'd-out phone number in the center, the second with a series of numbers followed by a question mark. In one corner of the blotter was a hand-drawn calendar for the month of February, the numbers neatly filled in. I did a quick check of the calendar and realized the numbers didn't correspond to February of this year. The first fell on a Sunday, and the last two Saturdays of the month had been X'd out. I paused long enough to make a detailed list of all the telephone and case numbers.

Intrigued, I retrieved the file of telephone records from the past six months, hoping for a match. I was temporarily sidetracked when I spotted seven calls to the 805 area code, which covers Santa Teresa County, as well as Perdido County to the south and San Luis Obispo County to the north of us. One number I recognized as the Perdido County Sheriff's Department. There were six calls to another number spaced roughly two weeks apart. The most recent of these was late January, a few days before his death. On impulse, I picked up the phone and dialed the number. After three rings, a machine clicked on, a woman's voice giving the standard: "Sorry I'm not here right now to receive your call, but if you'll leave your name, number, and a message, I'll be happy to get back to you as soon as I can. Take as long as you need and remember, wait for the beep." Her voice was throaty and mature, but that was the extent of the information I gleaned. I waited for the beep and then thought better of a message, quietly replacing the handset without saying a word. Maybe she was a friend of Selma's. I'd have to ask when I had the chance.

I made a note of the number and went back to work. I tried comparing the numbers on the phone bills with the numbers on the blotter and that netted me a hit. It looked as if someone—I assumed Tom—had completed a call to the number I'd seen X'd out in the center of one noose, though that number had been noted without the 805 area code attached. I tried the number myself and the call was picked up by a live human being. "Gramercy. How may I direct your call?"

"Gramercy?"

"Yes ma'am."

"This is the Gramercy Hotel in downtown Santa Teresa?"

"That's correct."

"Sorry. Wrong number."

I depressed the plunger and disconnected. Well, that was odd. The Gramercy Hotel was a fleabag establishment down on lower State Street. Why would the

Newquists call them? I circled the number in my notes, adding a question mark, and then I went back to my survey of telephone bills. I could find no other number that seemed significant on the face of it. I placed another banker's box on the desk top and continued packing.

At ten, I paused to stretch my legs and did a few squats. I still had the lower cabinets to unload, two of which were enclosed by wide doors spanning the width of the bookshelves. I decided to get the worst of it over with. I got down on my hands and knees and began to pull boxes out of the lefthand side. The storage space was so commodious I had to insert my head and shoulders to reach the far corners. I heaved two boxes into view and then sat there on the floor, going through the contents.

At the top of the second box, I came across two blue big-ring loose-leaf binders that looked promising. Apparently, Tom had photocopies of the bulk of the reports in the sheriff's department case books. This was the log of unsolved crimes kept on active status, though many were years old, copies yellowing. These were the cases detectives reworked any time new information came to light or additional leads came in. I leafed through with interest. This was Nota County crime from the year 1935 to the present. Even reading between the lines, there wasn't much attention paid to the rights of the defendant in the early cases. The notion of "victim's rights" would have seemed a curious concept in 1942. In those days, the victim had the right to redress in a court of law. These days, a trial isn't about guilt or innocence. It's a battle of wits in which competing attorneys, like intellectual gladiators, test their use of rhetoric. The mark of a good defense attorney is his ability to take any given set of facts and recast them in such a light that, *presto change-o*, as if by magic, what appeared to be absolute is turned into a frame-up or some elaborate conspiracy on the part of the police or government. Suddenly, the perpetrator becomes the victim and the deceased is all but forgotten in the process.

"Kinsey?"

I jumped.

Phyllis was standing in the doorway.

"Shit, you scared me," I said. "I didn't hear you come in."

"I'm sorry. I'm just on my way home. Can I talk to you for a minute?"

"Sure. Come on in."

"In private," she added, and then turned on her heel.

EIGHT

I scrambled to my feet and followed her down the hall. Behind us, I could hear Selma chatting with someone on the phone. When we reached the front door, Phyllis opened it and moved out onto the porch. I hesitated and then joined her, stepping to one side as she pulled the door shut behind us. The cold hit like a blast. The sky had turned hazy, with heavy gray clouds sliding down the mountains in the distance. I crossed my arms and kept my feet close together, trying to preserve body heat against the onslaught of nippy weather.

The outfit Phyllis sported was thin cotton and looked more appropriate for a summer barbecue. She wore abbreviated tennis socks, little pom-poms resting on the backs of her walking shoes. No coat or jacket. She spoke in a low tone as if Selma might be hovering on the far side of the door. "There's something I thought I better mention while I had the chance."

"Aren't you cold?" I asked. There she stood with her bare arms in a skimpy cotton blouse, her skirt blowing against her bare legs. I was wearing a long-sleeved turtleneck and jeans and I was still on the verge of lockjaw trying to keep my teeth from chattering.

117

She made a careless gesture, brushing aside the bitter chill. "I'm used to it. Doesn't bother me. This will only take a minute. I should have said something sooner, but I haven't had the chance."

For mid-March, her face seemed remarkably tanned. I had to guess it was from skiing, given that the rest of her was pale. Her face was nicely creased, lines radiating from the corners of her eyes, lines bracketing her mouth. Her nose was long and straight, her teeth very white and even. She looked like the perfect person to have with you when you were down; pleasant and capable without being too earnest.

Out in the yard, a stiff breeze ruffled through the dead grass. I clamped my mouth shut, trying to keep from whining like a dog. I could feel my eyes water from the cold. Soon my nose would start running and me with no hankie. I sniffed, trying to postpone the moment I'd have to use my shirt sleeve. I focused on Phyllis, already chatting away.

"You know Macon joined the sheriff's department because of Tom. The two fellows were always close—despite the difference in their ages—and of course when Tom married Selma, we wished him all the best."

"Aren't there any other jobs in this town? Everyone I've met is in law enforcement."

Phyllis smiled. "We all know each other. We tend to hang out together, like a social club."

"I guess so," I said, mentally begging her to hurry since I was freezing my ass off.

"Tom was a wonderful man. I think you'll find that out when you start asking around."

"So everybody says. In fact, most people seem to prefer him to her," I said.

"Oh, Selma has her good points. Not everybody likes her, but she's all right. I wouldn't say we're friends . . . in fact, we're not even that close, which may seem surprising given the fact we live two doors away . . . but you can see somebody's weaknesses and still like them for their better qualities."

"Absolutely," I said. This was hardly an endorsement, but I understood what she was saying. I felt like making that rolling hand gesture that says *Come on, come on.*

"Selma'd been complaining to me for months about Tom. I guess it's the same thing she told you. Well, in September . . . this was about six months ago . . . Tom and Macon went to a gun show in Los Angeles and I tagged along. Selma wasn't really interested—she had some big event that weekend—so she didn't come with us. Anyway, I happened to see Tom with this *woman* and I remember thinking, uh oh. Know what I mean? Just something about the way they had their heads bent together didn't look right to me. Let's put it this way. This gal was interested. I could tell by the way she looked at him."

I felt a flash of irritation. I couldn't believe she was telling me this. "Phyllis, I wish you'd mentioned this before *now.* I've been in there slogging through that bullshit and what I hear you saying is that Tom's 'problem' didn't have anything to do with paperwork."

"Well, that's just it. I don't really know. I asked Macon about the woman and he said she was a sheriff's investigator over on the coast. Perdido, I believe, though

I could be wrong about that. Anyway, Macon said he'd seen her with Tom on a couple of occasions. He told me to keep my mouth shut and that's what I did, but I felt awful. Selma was planning this big anniversary party at the country club and I kept thinking if Tom was ... well, you know ... if he was *involved* with someone, Selma was going to end up looking like a fool. Honestly, what's humiliating when your husband's having an affair is realizing everybody in the whole town knows about it but you. I don't know if you've ever had the experience yourself—"

"So you told her," I suggested, trying to jump her like a game of checkers. I did conclude from her comments that Macon had subjected her to the very humiliations she was so worried about for Selma.

Phyllis made a face. "Well, no, I didn't. I never worked up my nerve. I hate to defy Macon because he turns into such a bear, but I was debating with myself. I adored Tom and I couldn't decide how much I owed Selma as a sister-in-law. I mean, sometimes friendship takes precedence regardless. On the other hand, you don't always do someone a favor telling something like that. In some ways, it's hostile. That's just the way I see it. At any rate, the next thing I knew, Tom had passed away and Selma was beside herself. I've felt terrible ever since. If I'd told her what I suspected, she could have confronted him right then and put a stop to it."

"You know for a fact he was having an affair?"

"Well, no. That's the point. I thought Selma should be warned, but I didn't have any *proof*. That's why I was so reluctant to speak up. Macon felt like it was none of our business, and with him breathing down my neck I was caught between a rock and hard place."

"Why tell me now?"

"This was the first opportunity I had. When I was listening to you in there, I realized how frustrating this must be from your perspective. I mean, you might turn up evidence if you knew where to look. If he was scr— misbehaving, so to speak—he had to leave *some* trace, unless he's smarter than most men."

The front door burst open and Selma popped her head out. "*There* you are. I thought the two of you'd gone off and left me. What's this all about?"

"We were just jawing," Phyllis said, without missing a beat. "I was on my way home and she was nice enough to walk me out."

"Would you look at her? She's frozen. Let the poor thing come in here and get thawed out, for Pete's sake!"

Gratefully, I scurried into the house while the two of them discussed another work session the next morning. I headed for the kitchen where I washed my hands. I should have considered another woman in the mix. It might explain why Tom's buddies were being so protective of him. It might also explain the six 805 calls to the unidentified woman whose message I'd picked up from her answering machine.

A few minutes later, Selma came in, agitated. "Well, if that doesn't take the cake. I cannot believe it. She was just telling me about a dinner party coming up in the neighborhood, but have I been invited? Of course not," she was saying. "Now I'm a widow, I've been dropped like a hot potato. I know Tom's friends . . . the fellows . . . would include me, but you know how women are; they feel threatened at the thought of a single woman on the loose. When Tom was alive, we were part of a crowd that went everywhere. Cocktail parties, dinners, dances at the club. We were always included in the social scene, but in the weeks since he died I haven't left the house. The first couple of days, of course, everybody pitched in. Casseroles and promises. That's how I think of it. Now, I sit here night after night and the phone hardly rings except for things like this. Scut work, I call it. Good old Selma's always up for a committee. I do and I do. I really knock myself out and what's the point? The women are all too happy to pass off responsibility. Saves them the effort, if you know what I mean."

"But Selma, it's only been six weeks. Maybe people are trying to show their respects, giving you time to grieve."

"I'm sure that's their version," she said tartly.

I made some reply, hoping to get her off the subject. Her view was distorted and I wondered what would happen if she could see herself as others saw her. It was her very grandiosity that offended, not her insecurities. Selma seemed to be unaware of how transparent she was, oblivious to the disdain with which she was regarded for her snobbery.

She seemed to shake off her mood. "Enough of this pity party. It won't change anything. Can I fix you a bite of lunch? I'm heating some soup and I can make us some grilled cheese sandwiches."

"Sounds great," I said. Already I felt guilty accepting her hospitality when I'd sat around listening to other people's withering assessments. I'd told myself it was part of the information I was gathering, but I could have protested the venom with which such opinions had been delivered. By now familiar with the kitchen, I opened the cupboard door and took down soup bowls and plates. "Will Brant be joining us?"

"I doubt it. He's still in his room, probably dead to the world. He goes to the gym three days a week, so he likes to sleep in on the mornings between. Let me go check." She disappeared briefly and returned shaking her head. "He'll be right out," she said. "Why don't you tell me what you've found out so far."

I took out an extra plate and bowl, then opened the silverware drawer and took out soup spoons. While she heated the soup and grilled sandwiches, I filled her in on activities to date, giving her a verbal report of where I'd been and who I'd talked to. My efforts sounded feeble in the telling. Because of what Phyllis had told me, I now had a new avenue to explore, but I was unwilling to mention it when I was only dealing with suspicions. Selma had never even *suggested* the possibility of another woman, and I wasn't going to introduce the subject unless I found some reason to do so.

Brant appeared just as we were sitting down to eat. He was wearing jeans and cowboy boots, his snug white T-shirt emphasizing the effectiveness of his workouts. Selma ladled soup into bowls and cut the sandwiches in half, putting one on each plate.

We began to eat in the kind of silence I found mildly unsettling. "What made you decide to become a paramedic?" I asked.

I had caught Brant with his mouth full. He smiled, embarrassed, signaling the delay while he tucked half the food in his cheek. "I had a couple of friends in the fire department so I took a six-month course. Bandages and driving. I think Tom was hoping I'd join the sheriff's department, but I couldn't see myself doing that. I enjoy what I do. You know, it's always something."

I nodded, still eating. "Is the job what you expected?"

"Sure. Only more fun," he said.

I might have asked him more, but I could see him glance at his watch. He wolfed down the last of his sandwich and crumpled his paper napkin. He pushed back from the table, picking up his half-empty bowl and his plate. He stood at the sink and drank a few mouthfuls of soup before he rinsed his bowl and set it in the dishwasher.

Selma gestured. "I'll get that."

"I got it," he said as he added his sandwich plate. I heard his spoon *chink* in the silverware container just before he snapped the dishwasher shut. He gave his mother's cheek a quick buss. "Will you be here a while?"

"I've got a meeting at the church. What about you?"

"I think I'll drive on down to Independence and see Sherry."

"Will you be back tonight?"

"I wouldn't count on it," he said.

"You drive carefully."

"Twenty-five whole miles. I think I can handle it." He snagged the four remaining cookies from the plate, placing one in his mouth with a grin. "Better make more cookies. This was a short batch," he said. "See you later."

*

Selma left the house after lunch so I didn't have the chance to broach the subject that was beginning to tug at me—a quick trip to Santa Teresa to pick up my car. I'd had the rental for over three weeks and the cost was mounting daily. I'd never imagined an extended stay in Nota Lake so my current wardrobe was limited. I longed to sleep in my own bed even for one night. The issue of the female sheriff's investigator I could dig into once I got home. Anything else of interest here could wait 'til I got back to Nota Lake.

Meanwhile, it was time to have a chat with the Nota Lake Police Department. Given the new lead, I couldn't see how last night's incident could be tied to my investigation, but I thought I should do the smart thing and report it anyway. I left a note for Selma, shrugged on my leather jacket, took my shoulder bag, and headed off.

The Nota Lake Police Department was housed in a plain one-story building with a stucco exterior, a granite entryway, and two wide granite steps. The windows and the plate glass door were framed in aluminum. An arrow under a stick figure in a wheelchair indicated an accessible entrance somewhere to the left. The bushes along the front had been trimmed to window height and from the flagpole both the American and the State of California flags were snapping in the breeze. Six radio antennae had been erected on the roof like a series of upright fishing poles. As with the Nota Lake Fire Department, located next door, this was generic architecture, a strictly functional facility. No tax dollars had been needlessly squandered here.

The interior was consistent with its no-frills decor,

strongly reminiscent of the sheriff's headquarters two doors down: a lowered ceiling of fluorescent panels and acoustical tile, metal file cabinets, wood-grained laminate counters. On the desks, I could see the backs of the two computer monitors and attendant CPUs from which countless electrical cords sprouted like airborne roots.

The desk officer was M. Corbet, a fellow in his forties with a smooth round face, thinning hair, and a tendency to wheeze. "Thiss iss asthma in case you're thinking I'm contagious," he said. "Cold air gets to me and this dry heat doesn't help. Excuse me a second." He had a small inhaler that he placed in his lips, sucking deeply of the mist that would open up his bronchi. He set the inhaler aside with a shake of his head. "Thiss-iss the damndest thing. Never had a problem in my life until a couple years back. Turns out I'm allergic to house dust, animal hair, pollen, and mold. What's a fella supposed to do? Quit breathing altogether is the only cure I know."

"That's a tough one," I said.

"Doctor tells me it's more and more people developing allergies. Says he has this one patient reacts to inside air. Synthetics, chemicals, microbes coming through the heating vents. Poor woman has to tote around an oxygen trolley everywhere she goes. Passes out and falls down the minute she encounters any alien pathogens. Thankfully, I'm not yet as bad off as her, though the chief had to take me off active duty and put me on desk. Anyway, that's my story. Now what can I help you with?"

I gave him my business card, hoping to establish my credibility before I launched into a description of the events involving the driver of the panel truck. Officer Corbet was polite, but I could tell just by looking at him that the issue of someone in a ski mask staring at me real hard wasn't going to qualify as a major case for the Crimes Against Persons unit, which probably consisted solely of him. Lungs awhistle, he took my report, printing the particulars in block letters on the proper form. He placed his hands on the counter, tapping with his fingers as if he was playing a little tune. "I do know someone with a truck like that."

"You do?" I said, surprised.

"Yes ma'am. Sounds like Ercell Riccardi. He lives right around the corner about three doors down. Keeps his truck parked in the drive. I'm surprised you didn't see it on your way over here."

"I didn't come from that direction. I turned right off of Main."

"Well, you might want to have a look. Ercell leaves it sit out any time it's not in use."

"With keys in the ignition?"

"Yes ma'am. It's not like Nota Lake is the auto-theft capital of the world. I think he started doing it maybe five, six years back. We had us a rash of break-ins, bunch of kids busting into cars, smashing windows, taking tape decks, going joyriding. Ercell got tired of replacing the stereo so he 'give up and give in' is how he puts it. Last time his truck was broke into he didn't even bother to file a claim. Said it was driving his rates up and to hell with the whole thing. Now he leaves the truck open, keys in the ignition, and a note on the dash saying, 'Please put back in the drive when you're done.'"

"So people take his truck any time they like?"

"Doesn't happen that often. Occasionally, somebody borrys it, but they always put it back. It's a point of honor with folks and Ercell's a lot happier."

The telephone began to ring and Officer Corbet straightened up. "Anyway, if you think the truck was Ercell's, just give us a call and we'll talk to him. It's not something he'd do, but anybody could have hopped in his vehicle and followed you."

"I'll take a look."

Out on the street again, I shoved my hands in my jacket pockets and headed for the corner. As soon as I turned onto Lone Star, I saw the black panel truck. I approached it with caution, wondering if there were any way I could link this truck to the one I'd seen. I circled the vehicle, leaning close to the headlights. Impossible in daylight to see if the beams were askew. I moved around to the rear and ran a finger across the license plate, scrutinizing the surface where I could see faint traces of adhesive. I stood up and turned to study the house itself. A man was stationed at the window, looking out at me. He stared, scowling. I reversed my steps and returned to my parking spot.

When I reached the rental car, Macon Newquist was waiting, his black-and-white vehicle parked behind mine at the curb. He glanced up at me, catching my eye with a smile. "Hi. How are you? I figured this was your car. How's it going?"

I smiled. "Fine. For a minute, I thought you were giving me a ticket."

"Don't worry about that. In this town, we tend to reserve tickets for people passing through." He crossed his arms and leaned a hip against the side of the rental. "I hope this doesn't seem out of line, but Phyllis mentioned that business about the gun show. I guess she passed along her opinion about the gal Tom was talking to."

I felt my reaction time slow and I calculated my response. Phyllis must have felt guilty about telling me and blabbed the minute she got home. I thought I better cover so I shrugged it aside. "She said something in passing. I really didn't pay that much attention."

"I didn't want you to get the wrong impression."

"No problem."

"Because she attached more to it than was warranted."

"Ah."

"Don't get me wrong. You don't know the ladies in this town. Nothing escapes their notice and when it turns out to be nothing, they make it into something else. The woman Tom was talking to, that was strictly professional."

"Not surprising. Everybody tells me he was good at his job. You know her name?"

"I don't. I never heard it myself. She's a sheriff's investigator. I do know that much because I asked him about it later."

"You happen to know what county?"

He scratched at his chin. "Not offhand. Could be Kern, San Benito, I forget what he said. I could see Phyllis put the hairy eye-ball on the two of them and I didn't want you to be misled. Last thing Selma needs is some kind of gossip about him. All she has is her memories and once those are tainted, what's she got left?"

"I couldn't agree more. Trust me, I'd never be irresponsible about something like that."

"That's good. I'm glad to hear that. People don't like the notion you're using up Tom's money on a wild-goose chase. So what's your timetable on this?"

"That remains to be seen. If you have any ideas, I hope you'll let me know."

Macon shook his head. "I wish I could help, but I realize I'm the wrong one to ask. I know I offered, but this is one of those circumstances where I'm not going to be objective. People admired Tom and I'm not just saying that because I admired him myself. If there was something tacky in his life . . . well, people aren't going to want to know that about him. You take somebody like Margaret's husband. I believe you talked to him at Tiny's. Hatch was a protégé of Tom's, and the other fellow, Wayne, was somebody Tom rescued from a bad foster care situation. See what I mean? You can't run around asking those fellows what Tom was *like*. They don't take to it that well. They'll be polite, but it's not going to sit right."

"I appreciate the warning."

"I wouldn't call it a warning. I don't want to give you the wrong impression. It's just human nature to want to protect the people we care about. All I'm saying is, let's not be hasty and cause trouble for no reason."

"I wouldn't dream of it."

NINE

I went back to the motel, making a brief detour into the Rainbow Cafe, where I picked up a pack of chips and a can of Pepsi. I was eating for comfort, but I couldn't help myself. I hadn't jogged for three weeks and I could feel my ass getting larger with every bite I ate. The young black woman who handled the griddle had paused to follow the weather channel on a small color television at the end of the counter. She was trim and attractive with loopy corkscrew curls jutting out around her head. I saw a frown cross her face when she saw what was coming up. "Hey now. I'm sick of this. Whatever happened to spring?" she asked of no one in particular.

Out in the Pacific, the radar showed the same clustered pattern of color as a CAT scan of the brain, areas of storm activity represented in shades of blue, green, and red. I was hoping to hit the road for home before the bad weather reached the area. March was unpredictable, and a heavy snowstorm could force the mountain passes to close. Nota Lake was technically located out of the reach of such blockades, but the rental car had no chains and I had scant experience driving in hazardous conditions.

Back in the cabin, I finished typing up my notes, translating all the pointless activity into the officious-sounding language of a written report. What ended up on paper didn't add up to anything because I'd neatly omitted the as-yet-unidentified female sheriff's investigator, who may or may not have been interested in Tom Newquist and he in her. San Benito or Kern County, yeah, right, Macon.

At two, I decided to make a trip to the copy shop in town. I locked the cabin behind me and headed for my car. Cecilia must have been peering out the office window because the minute I walked by, she rapped on the glass and made a beckoning motion. She came to the door, holding a piece of paper aloft. Cecilia was so small she must have been forced to buy her clothes in the children's department. Today's outfit consisted of a long red sweatshirt with a teddy bear appliquéd on the front worn over white leggings, with a pair of enormous jogging shoes. Her legs looked as spindly as a colt's, complete with knobby knees. "You had a telephone call. Alice wants you to get in touch. I took the number this time, but in future, she ought to try reaching you at Selma's. I run a motel here, not an answering service."

Her aggrieved tone was irritating and inspired a matching complaint. "Oh, hey, now that I've got you, do you think I could get some heat? The cabin's almost unliveable, close to freezing," I said.

An expression of annoyance flashed across her face. "March first is the cutoff date for heating oil out here. I can't just whistle up delivery because a couple of short-term visitors to the area make a minor fuss." Her tone suggested she'd been beleaguered with grumbles the better part of the day.

"Well, do what you can. I'd hate to have to complain to Selma when she's footing the bill."

Cecilia gave the door a little bang as she withdrew. Good luck to me, getting any other messages. I crossed to the pay phone and stood there, searching for change in the bottom of my handbag. I found a little cache of coins tucked in one corner along with assorted hairs and a ratty tissue. I dropped some money in the slot and dialed. Alice picked up on the fourth ring just about the time I expected her machine to kick in. "Hello?"

"Hello, Alice? Kinsey Millhone. I got your message. Are you at work or home?"

"Home. I'm not due at Tiny's until four. I was in the process of setting my hair. Hang on a sec while I get the curlers out on this side. Ah, better. Nothing like a set of bristles sticking in your ear. Listen, this might not be helpful, but I thought I'd pass it along. The waitress who works counter over at the Rainbow is a good friend of mine. Her name's Nancy. I mentioned Tom and told her what you were up to. She says he came in that night about eight-thirty and left just before closing. You can talk to her yourself if you want."

"Is she the black girl?"

"Nuhn-uhn. That's Barrett, Rafer LaMott's daughter. Nancy doubles as a cashier. Brown hair, forties. I'm sure you've seen her in there because she's seen you."

"What else did she say? Was he alone or with someone?"

"I asked that myself and she says he was alone, at

least as far as she could see. Said he had a cheeseburger and fries, drank some coffee, played some tunes on the jukebox, paid his ticket, and left about nine-thirty, just as she was closing out the register. Like I said, it might not mean anything, but she said she'd never known him to come in at that hour. You know the night he was found, he was out on 395, but he was heading toward the mountains instead of home to his place."

"I remember that," I said. "The coroner mentioned his having eaten a meal. According to Selma, he was in for the night. He didn't even leave a note. By the time she got back from church, he was DOA at the local emergency room. Maybe he got a phone call and went to meet someone."

"Or maybe he just got hungry, hon. Selma's the type who'd make him eat veggies and brown rice. He could have sneaked out for something decent." She laughed at herself. "I always said the food out there would kill you. I'll bet his arteries seized up from all the fat he took in."

"At least we know where he was in the hour just before he died."

"Well, that's hardly news. Nancy says the coroner covered the same ground. Anyways, I told you it wouldn't count for much. I guess that about says it for my detective career."

"You never know. Oh, one more thing as long as I have you on the line. You ever hear rumors about Tom and any other woman?"

She barked out a laugh. "Tom? You gotta be kidding. He was stuffy about sex. Lot of guys, you can tell just by looking they got a problem around dominance. Assgrabbers and pinchers, fellows telling dirty jokes and gawking at your boobs. They wouldn't mind a quick bounce on the front seat of their pickups, but believe me, romance is the fartherest thing from their minds. Tom was always pleasant. I've never known him to flirt and I never heard him make any kind of off-color remark. What makes you ask?"

"I thought he might have been at the Rainbow for a rendezvous."

"Oh, a *rahndez-vous*. That's rich. Listen, if you're fooling around in this town, you'd best meet somewhere else unless you want everyone to know. Why take the risk? If his sister'd showed up, she'd have spotted him first thing. Cecilia's not that fond of Selma, but she'd have told on him anyway. That's how people around here operate. Anything you find out is fair game."

"I take it word's gone out about me."

"You bet."

"What's the consensus? Anybody seem upset?"

"Oh, grumbles here and there. You're picking up notice, but nothing serious that I've heard. Town this size, everybody has an opinion about something—especially fresh blood like yours. Some of the guys were wondering if you're married. I guess they noticed no wedding ring."

"Actually, I took my ring off to have the diamond reset."

"Bullshit."

"No, really. My husband's *huge*. He's always pumped up on steroids so he's touchy as all get out. He'd tear the head off anyone who ever laid a hand on me."

She laughed. "I bet you've never been married a day in your life."

"Alice, you would be surprised."

As predicted, the weather was turning nasty as the front moved in. The morning had been clear, the temperatures in the fifties, but by early afternoon, a thick mass of clouds had accumulated to the north. The sky changed from blue to a uniform white, then to a misty-looking dark gray, which made the day seem as gloomy as a solar eclipse. All the mountain peaks had been erased and the air became dense with a fine, biting spray.

Here's what I did with my afternoon. I drove into town and went to the copy shop, where I made copies of my typewritten report and several cropped five-by-seven photocopy enlargements made of the head shot of Tom Newquist. I dropped the original photograph and the original of my report in Selma's mailbox, drove six blocks over, and left the flashlight inside the storm door on James Tennyson's front porch. And I still had hours to kill before I could decently retire.

In the meantime, I was bored and I wanted to get warm. Nota Lake didn't have a movie theater. Nota Lake didn't have a public library or a bowling alley that I could spot. I went to the lone bookstore and wandered up and down the aisles. The place was small but attractive, and the stock was more than adequate. I picked up two paperbacks, returned to the cabin, crawled under a pile of blankets, and read to my heart's content.

At six, I hunched into my jacket and walked over to the Rainbow through an odd mix of blowing sleet and buffeting rain. I ate a BLT on wheat toast and then chatted idly with Nancy while she rang up my bill. I already knew what she had to say, but I quizzed her nonetheless, making sure Alice had reported accurately. At 6:35, I went back to the cabin, finished the first book, tossed that aside, and reached for the next. At ten o'clock, exhausted from a hard day's work, I got up, brushed my teeth, washed my face, and climbed back in bed, where I fell promptly asleep.

A sound filtered into the tarry dream I was having. I labored upward, slow swimming, my body weighted with dark images and all the leaden drama of sleep. I felt glued to the bed. My eyes opened and I listened, not even sure where I was. Nota Lake crept back into my consciousness, the cabin so cold I might as well have slept outside. What had I heard? I turned my head with great effort. According to the clock, it was 4:14, still pitch black. The tiny scrape of metal on metal . . . not the sound of a key . . . possibly a pick being worked into the door lock. Fear shot through me like a bottle rocket, lighting my insides with a shower of adrenaline. I flung the covers aside. I was still fully dressed, but the chill in the cabin was numbing to both my face and my hands. I swung my legs over the side of the bed, felt for my shoes, and shoved my feet in without bothering to tie the laces.

I stood where I was, tuned now to the silence. Even in the depths of the country with minimal light pollution, I realized the dark wasn't absolute. I could see the blocks of six lighter gray squares that were the windows on three sides. I glanced back at the bed, empty white sheets advertising my departure. Hastily, I arranged the pillows to form a plump body shape, which I covered with my blankets. This always fooled the bad guys. I eased over to the door, trying to pick up the scratchings of my intruder over the pounding of my heart. I felt along the door jamb. There was no security chain so once the lock was jimmied, there was nothing else between me and my night visitor. The cabin, though dark, was beginning to define itself. I surveyed the details in memory, looking for a weapon somewhere among the homely furnishings. Bed, chair, soap, table, shower curtain. On my side of the door, I kept my fingers on the thumblock to prevent its turning. Maybe the guy would assume his skills were rusty or the lock was stiff. On the other side of the door, I could hear a faint chunking across wood chips as my visitor retreated in search of some other means of ingress. I tiptoed to the table and picked up a wooden chair. I returned to the door and eased the top rail under the knob, jamming the legs against the floor. It wouldn't hold for long, but it might slow him down. I took a brief moment to bend down and tie my shoes, unwilling to risk the sound of my laces clicking across the expanse of bare wooden floor. I could hear faint sounds outside as the intruder patiently circled the cabin.

Were the windows locked? I couldn't recall. I moved from window to window, feeling for the shape of the latches. All of them seemed to be secured. A slight parting of the curtains allowed me a thin slice of the exterior. I could see dense Christmas tree shapes, a series of evergreens that dotted the landscape. No traffic on the highway. No lights in neighboring cabins. To the left, I caught movement as someone disappeared around the side of the cabin toward the rear.

I crossed the room in silence, entering the darker confines of the bathroom. I felt for the shower curtain, hanging by a series of rings from a round metal rod. I let my fingers explore the brackets, which were screwed into the wall on either side of the shower stall. Carefully, I lifted the rod from the slots, sliding the curtain off, ring by ring. Once in hand, I realized the rod was useless, too light, too easily bent. I needed a weapon, but what did I have? I glanced at the frosted glass of the bathroom window, which appeared infinitesimally paler than the dark of the wall surrounding it. Framed in the center was the intruder's head and shoulders. He cupped his hands to the glass to afford himself a better look. It must have been frustrating to discover the dark was too dense to penetrate. I stood without moving though I could see his movements outside. A snippet of sound, perhaps the faint scrape of a clawhammer being eased into crack between the frame and the glass.

Feverishly, I reviewed the items in the cabin, hoping to remember something I could use as a weapon. Toilet paper, rug, clothes hangers, ironing board. Iron. I set the curtain rod aside, taking care not to make a sound. I moved to the closet, feeling through the dark until my fingers encountered the ironing board. I raised up on tiptoe and lifted the iron from the shelf above, shielding the contours with my hand so as to avoid banging into anything. I searched for the end of the plug, holding the prongs while I unwrapped the cord. Blindly, I felt for the outlet near the sink, inserted the prongs, and slid the heat lever on the iron as far to the right as it would go. I set the iron upright on the counter. I glanced back at the window. The head-and-shoulders silhouette was no longer visible.

I eased my way across the room to the door, where I leaned closer and pressed my ear to the lock, trying not to disturb the chair. I could hear the key pick slide in again. I could hear the tiny torque wrench join its mate as the two rods of metal crept across the tumblers. Behind me, I could hear a ticking from the bathroom as the iron picked up heat. I'd rammed the setting up to LINEN, a fabric known to wrinkle more easily than human flesh. I longed to feel the weight of the iron in my hand, but I didn't dare yank the plug from the socket just yet. I could feel pain in my chest where the rubbery muscle of my heart slapped the wooden pales of my rib cage. I'd picked many a lock myself and I was well acquainted with the patience required for the task. I'd never known anyone who could use a lockpick wearing gloves, so the chances were he was using his bare hands. From the depths of the lock, I fancied I could hear the pick ease across the tumblers and lift them one by one.

I placed my right hand lightly on the knob. I could feel it turn under my fingers. With the chair still in place, I did a quick tiptoe dance across the room to the bath. I could feel heat radiating from the iron as I pulled the plug from the socket. I wrapped my fingers around the handle and returned to the door, taking up my vigil. My night visitor was now in the process of easing the door open, probably fearful of creaks that might alert me to his presence. I stared at the doorframe, willing him to appear. He pushed. The chair began to inch forward. As stealthily as a spider, his fingers crept around the frame. I lunged, iron extended. I thought my timing was good, but he was quicker than I expected. I made contact, but not before he'd kicked the door in. The chair catapulted past me. I could smell the harsh chemical scent of scorched wool. I pressed the iron into him again and sensed burning flesh this time. He uttered a harsh expletive—not a word but a yelp.

At the same time, he swung and his fist caught me in the face. I staggered backward, off balance. The iron flew out of my hand and clattered heavily across the floor. He was fast. Before I knew what was happening, he'd kicked my feet out from under me. I went down. He had my arm racked up behind me, his knee planted squarely in the middle of my back. His weight made breathing problematic and I knew within minutes I'd black out if he didn't ease up. I couldn't fill my lungs with sufficient air to make a sound. Any movement was excruciating. I could smell stress sweat, but I wasn't sure if it was his or mine.

Now you see? This is precisely the kind of moment I was talking about. There I was, face down on Cecilia Boden's bad braided rug, immobilized by a fellow threatening serious bodily harm. Had I foreseen this sorry development the day I left Carson City, I'd have done something else ... dumped the rental car and flown home, bypassing the notion of employment in Nota Lake. But how was I to know?

Meanwhile, the thug and I were at a temporary impasse while he decided what kind of punishment to inflict. This guy was going to hurt me, there was no doubt of that. He hadn't expected resistance and he was pissed off that I'd put up even so puny a fight as I had. He was supercharged, juiced up on rage, his breathing labored and hoarse. I tried to relax and, at the same time, steal myself for the inevitable. I waited for a bash on the back of the head. I prayed that a pocketknife or semiautomatic didn't appear on his list of preferred weapons. If he yanked my head back, he could slit my throat with one quick swipe of a blade. Time hung suspended in a manner that was almost liberating.

I'm not a big fan of torture. I've always understood that in situations of extreme duress—offered the choice between, say, a hot poker in the eyeball or betraying a friend—I'd rat out my pal. This is one more reason to keep others at a distance, since I clearly can't be trusted to keep a confidence. Under the current circumstances, I surely would have begged for mercy if I'd been capable of speech.

Hostility energizes. Once unleashed, anger is addicting and the high, while bitter, is irresistible. He half-lifted himself away from me and slammed his knee into my rib cage, knocking the breath out of me. He grabbed the index finger of my right hand and in one swift motion snapped it sideways, dislocating the finger at what I later learned was the proximal interphalangeal joint. The sound was like the hollow pop of a raw carrot being snapped in two. I heard myself emit a note of anguish, high pitched and ragged as he reached for the next finger and popped the knuckle sideways in its socket. I could sense that both fingers protruded now in an unnatural relationship to the rest of my hand. He delivered a kick and then I heard his heavy breathing as he stood staring down at me. I closed my eyes, fearful of provoking further attack.

I kept my face down against the rug, sucking in the odor of damp cotton fiber saturated with soot, feeling absurdly grateful when he didn't kick me again. He crossed the cabin in haste. I heard the door bang shut behind him and then the sound of his muffled footsteps as they faded away. In due course, at a distance, I heard a car engine start. I was alive. I was hurt. Time to move, I thought.

I rolled over on my back, cradling my right arm. I could feel my hands tremble and I was making noises in my throat. I'd broken out in a sweat, so much heat coursing through my body that I thought I'd throw up. At the same time, I began to shake. A stress-induced personality had separated herself from the rest of me and hovered in the air so that she could comment on the situation without having to participate in my pain and humiliation.

You really should get help, she suggested. *The injuries won't kill you, but the shock well could. Remember the symptoms? Pulse and breathing become faster. Blood pressure drops. Weakness, lethargy, a little clamminess? Does that ring a bell here?*

I was laboring to breathe, struggling to keep my wits about me while my vision brightened and narrowed. It had been a long time since I'd been hurt and I'd nearly forgotten how it felt to be consumed by suffering. I knew he could have killed me, so I should have been happy this was the worst he'd conjured up. What exhilaration he must have felt. I had been brought low and my attempts at self-defense seemed pathetic in retrospect.

I held my hand against my chest protectively while I eased onto my side and from there to my knees. I pushed upward with left elbow, supporting myself clumsily as I struggled to my feet. I was mewing like a kitten. Tears stung my eyes. I felt abased by the ease with which I'd been felled. I was nothing, a worm he could have crushed underfoot. My cockiness had left me and now belonged to him. I pictured him grinning, even laughing aloud as he sped down the highway. He would shake his fist in the air with joy, reliving my subjugation in much the same way I would in the days to come.

I turned on the overhead light and looked down at my hand. Both my index finger and my insult finger jutted out at thirty-degree angles. I really couldn't feel much, but the sight of it was sickening. I found my bag near the bed. I picked up my jacket and laid it across my shoulders like a shawl. Oddly, the cabin wasn't that disordered. The iron had been flung into the far corner of the room. The wooden chair had been knocked over and the braided rug was askew. Tidy little bun that I am, I righted the chair and flopped the rug back into place, picked the iron up and returned it to the top closet shelf, cord dangling. Now I had only myself to accommodate.

I locked the cabin with effort, using the unaccustomed left hand. I headed toward the motel office. The night was cold and a soft whirl of snow whispered against my face. I drank deeply of the cold, refreshed by the dampness in the air. Out near the road, I could see the glow of the motel vacancy sign, a red neon beacon issuing its invitation to passing motorists. There was no traffic on the highway. None of the other cabins showed any signs of life. Through the office window, I could see a table lamp aglow. I went in. I leaned against the doorframe while I knocked on Cecilia's door. Long minutes passed. Finally, the door opened a crack and Cecilia peered out.

I could hear the mounting roar of a fainting spell rising around my ears. I longed to sit down and put my head down between my knees. I took a deep breath, shaking my head in hopes of clearing it.

Still squinting, she tied the sash of her pink chenille robe as she emerged. "What's this about?" she said, crossly. "What's the matter with you?"

I held up my hand. "I need help."

TEN

Cecilia dialed 9–1–1 and reported the break-in and the subsequent attack. The dispatcher said he'd send an ambulance, but Cecilia assured him she could get me to the hospital in the time it would take the paramedics to arrive. She threw on her sweats, a coat, and running shoes, and put me in her ancient Oldsmobile. To give her credit, she seemed properly concerned about my injury, patting me occasionally and saying things like, "You hang on now. You'll be fine. We're almost there. It's just down the road." She drove with exaggerated care, both hands on the steering wheel, chin lifted so she could see over the rim. Her speed never exceeded forty miles an hour and she solved the problem of which lane to drive in by keeping half the car in each.

I no longer felt pain. Some natural anesthesia had flooded through my system and I was woozy with its effect. I leaned my head back against the seat. She studied me anxiously, no doubt worried I'd barf on the hard-to-clean upholstery fabric.

"You're dead white," she said. She depressed the window control, opening the window halfway so that a wide stream of icy air whipped against my face. The highway was glossy with moisture, snow blowing across the road in diagonal lines. At this hour of the night, there was a comforting silence across the landscape. So far, the snow wasn't sticking, but I could see a powdering of white on tree trunks, an airy accumulation in the dead and weedy fields.

The hospital was long and low, a one-story structure that stretched in a straight line like some endless medical motel. The exterior was a mix of brick and stucco, with a roof of three-tab asphalt shingle. The parking area near the ambulance entrance was virtually deserted. The emergency room was empty, though the few brave souls on duty roused themselves and appeared in due course, one of them a clerk whose name tag read L. LIPPINCOTT. I was guessing *Lucille, Louise, Lillian, Lula*.

Ms. Lippincott's gaze flicked away from the bristling bouquet of digits. "How did you fall?"

"I didn't. I was assaulted," I said and then proceeded to give her an abbreviated account of the attack.

Her facial expression shifted from distaste to skepticism, as though there must be portions of the story I'd neglected to tell. Perhaps she fantasized some bizarre form of self-abuse or S&M practices too nasty to relate.

I sat in a small upholstered chair, reciting my personal data—name, home address, insurance carrier—while she entered the information into her computer. She was in her sixties, a heavy-boned woman with graying hair arranged in perfect wavelets. Her face looked like half the air had leaked out, leaving soft pouches and seams. She wore a nursy-looking pantsuit of waffle-patterned white polyester with large shoulder pads and big white buttons down the front. "Where'd Cecilia disappear to? Wasn't she the one brought you in?"

"I think she's gone off to find a restroom. She was sitting right out there," I said, indicating the waiting area. A new-found talent allowed me to point in two directions simultaneously—index and insult fingers going north-west, ring finger and pinkie steering east-north-east. I tried to avoid the sight, but it was hard to resist.

She made a photocopy of my insurance card, which she set to one side. She entered a print command and documents were generated, none of which I was able to sign with my bunged-up right hand. She made a note to that effect, indicating my acceptance of financial responsibility. She assembled a plastic bracelet bearing my name and hospital ID number and affixed that to my wrist with a device resembling a hole punch.

Chart in hand, she accompanied me through a doorway and showed me a seat in an examining room about the size of a jail cell. She stuck my chart in a slot mounted on the door before she left. "Someone'll be right with you."

The place looked like every other emergency room I'd ever been exposed to: beige speckled floor glossy with wax, making it easy to remove blood and other body fluids; acoustical tile on the ceiling, the better to dampen all the anguished cries and screams. The prevailing smell of rubbing alcohol made me think about needles and I desperately needed to lie down that instant. I set my jacket aside and crawled up on the examining table, where I lay on the crackling paper and stared at the ceiling. I wasn't doing well. I was shivering.

The lights seemed unnaturally bright and the room oscillated. I laid my left arm across my eyes and tried to think about something nice, like sex.

I could hear a low conversation in the corridor and someone came in, picking up my chart from the door. "Miss Millhone?" I heard the click of a ballpoint pen and I opened my eyes.

The ER nurse was black, her name tag identifying her as V. LaMott. She had to be Rafer LaMott's wife, mother to the young woman working as a short-order cook over at the Rainbow Cafe. Was theirs the only African American family in Nota Lake? Like her daughter, V. LaMott was trim, her skin the color of tobacco. Her hair was cropped close, her face devoid of makeup. "I'm Mrs. LaMott. You've met my husband, I believe."

"We spoke briefly."

"Let's see the hand."

I held it up. Something about her mention of Rafer made me think he'd confessed to her fully about his rudeness to me. She looked like the kind of woman who'd have given him a hard time about that. I hoped.

I kept my face averted while she completed her inspection. I could feel myself tense up, but she was careful to make only gingerly contact. There was apparently no nurse's aide on duty so she checked my vital signs herself. She took my temperature with an electronic thermometer that gave nearly instant results and then she held my left arm against her body as she pumped up the blood pressure cuff and took a reading. Her hands were warm while mine felt bloodless. She made notes on my chart.

"What's the *V* stand for?" I asked.

"Victoria. You can call me Vicky if you like. We're not formal around here. Are you on any medication?"

"Birth control pills."

"Any allergies?"

"Not that I know of."

"Have you had a tetanus shot in the last ten years?"

My mind went blank. "I can't remember."

"Let's get that over with," she said.

I could feel the panic mount. "I mean, it's really not necessary. It's not a problem. I have two dislocated fingers, but the skin wasn't broken. See? No cuts, no puncture wounds. I didn't step on a nail."

"I'll be right back."

I felt my heart sink. In my weakened condition, I hadn't thought to lie. I could have told her anything about my medical history. She'd never know the difference and it was my lookout. Lockjaw, big deal. This was all too much. I'm phobic about needles, which is to say I sometimes faint at the very idea of injections and become giddy at the sight of a *S-Y-R-I-N-G-E*. I've been known to pass out when *other* people get shots. In traveling, I would never go to a country that required immunizations. Who wants to spend time in an area where smallpox and cholera still run rampant among the citizens?

· What I hate most in the world are those obscene newscasts where there's sudden minicam coverage of wailing children being stabbed with hypodermics in their sweet, plump little arms. Their expressions of betrayal are enough to make you sick. I could feel the sweat breaking out on my palms. Even lying down I was worried I'd lose consciousness.

She came back in a flash, holding the you-know-what on a little plastic tray like a snack. In my only hope of control, I persuaded her to stick me in the hip instead of my upper arm, though lowering my blue jeans was a trick with one hand.

"I don't like it either," she said. "Shots scare me silly. Here we go."

Stoically, I bore the discomfort, which truly wasn't as bad as I remembered it. Maybe I was maturing. Ha ha ha, she said.

"Shit."

"Sorry. I know it stings."

"It's not that. I just remembered. My last tetanus shot was three years ago. I took a bullet in the arm and they gave me one then."

"Oh, well," she said. She inserted the syringe into a device labeled "sharps" and neatly snapped off the needle, like I might snatch it away and stick myself with it six more times for fun. Ever the professional, I took advantage of the opportunity to quiz her about the Newquists while we waited for the doctor. "I gather Rafer and Tom were good friends," I said, for openers.

"That's right."

"Did the four of you spend much time together?" The answer seemed slow in coming so I offered a prompt. "You might as well be honest. I've heard it all by now. Nobody likes Selma."

Vicky smiled. "We spent time together when we had to. There were occasions when we couldn't avoid her so we made the best of it. Rafer didn't want to make a scene, nor did I for that matter, I swear to god, she once said to me—these are her exact words—'I'd have invited you over, but I thought you'd be more comfortable with your own kind.' I had to bite my tongue. What I wanted to say is 'I sure wouldn't want to hang out with a bunch of white trash like you.' And just to complicate matters, our daughter, Barrett, was going out with her son."

"She must have loved that."

"She could hardly object. She was always so busy acting like she wasn't prejudiced. What a joke. If it wasn't so pitiful it'd have cracked me up. The woman has no education and no intelligence to speak of. Rafer and I both graduated from U.C.L.A. He's got a degree in criminology . . . this was before he applied for the position with the sheriff's department. I've got a B.A. in nursing and an R.N. on top of that."

"Selma knew the kids were dating?"

"Oh, sure. They went steady for years. Tom was crazy about Barrett. I know he felt she was a good influence on Brant."

"Does Brant have a problem?"

"Basically, he's a good person. He was just screwed up back then, like a lot of kids that age. I don't think he ever did drugs, but he drank quite a bit and rebelled every chance he had."

"Why'd they break up?"

"You'd have to ask Barrett. I try not to mess in her business. You want my assessment, I think Brant was too needy and dependent for someone like her. He tended to be all mopey and clinging. This was years ago, of course. He was twenty, at that point. She was just out of high school and didn't seem that interested in getting serious."

Her comments were cut short when the doctor came in. Dr. Price was in his late twenties, thin and boyish, with bright blue eyes, big ears, dark auburn hair, and a pale freckled complexion. I could still see the indentation on his cheek where he'd bunched up his pillow to sleep. I pictured the entire ER staff napping on little cots somewhere. He wore surgical greens and a white lab coat, stethoscope coiled in his pocket like a pet snake. I wondered how he'd ended up at a hospital as small as this. I hoped it wasn't because he was at the bottom of his med school class. He took one look at my fingers and said, "Oh wow! Keen!" I liked his enthusiasm.

We had a chat about my assailant and the job he'd done. He studied my jaw. "He must have clipped you good," he said.

"That's right. I'd forgotten about that. How's it look?"

"Like you put eye shadow in the wrong place. Any other abrasions or contusions? That's doctor talk," he said. "Means little hurt places on your body."

"He kicked me twice in the ribs."

"Let's take a look," he said, pulling up my shirt.

My ribcage on the right side was swiftly turning purple. He listened to my lungs to make sure a rib hadn't been thrust into them on impact. He palpated my right arm, wrist, hand, and fingers, and then proceeded to deliver a quick course on joints, ligaments, tendons, and exactly what happens when someone wrenches them asunder. We trooped into the other room where a rumpled-looking technician took X-rays of both my chest and my hand. I returned to the table and lay down again, feeling thoroughly air-conditioned as the room spun.

When the film had been developed, he invited me into the corridor where he tucked the various views onto the lighted screen. Vicky joined us. We stood there, the three of us, and studied the results. I felt like a colleague called in for consultation on a troublesome case. My ribs were bruised, but not cracked, likely to be sore for days, but requiring no further medical attention. Roentgenographically speaking, the two pesky fingers were completely screwed. I could see that no bones were broken, though Dr. Price did point out two small chips he said my body would reabsorb.

I went back to the table where I reclined again with relief. My butt was still smarting from the sting of the tetanus, so I hardly noticed when the doctor, with a merry whistle, stuck me repeatedly in the joints on both fingers. I'd ceased to care by then. Whatever they did, I was too grossed out to notice. While I stared at the wall, the doctor maneuvered my digits back into their original upright position. He left the room briefly. When I finally dared to look at my hand, I saw that the injured fingers were now fat and reddened. While the fingers would now bend, the knuckles were swollen as though with sudden rheumatoid arthritis. I placed my mouth against the hot, numb flesh like a mother gauging a baby's fever with her lips.

Dr. Price returned with (1) a roll of adhesive tape, (2) a packet of gauze, and (3) a metal splint that looked like a bent Popsicle stick, for which my insurance company would ultimately be charged somewhere in the neighborhood of five hundred dollars. He taped the two fingers together and then affixed them to the ring finger with another wrapping of tape, all supported by the splint. I could sense my premiums going up. Medical insurance is only valid if the benefits are never used. Otherwise, you're rewarded with a cancellation notice or a hefty increase in rates.

I could hear another conference in the hallway and a deputy appeared outside the examining room door. He chatted with Dr. Price and then the doctor departed, leaving me alone with him. This was a fellow I hadn't seen before; a tall skinny kid with a long face, dark hair, dark ragged eyebrows that met in the middle, and shiny metal braces on his teeth. Well, I was filled with confidence.

"Ms. Millhone, I'm Deputy Carey Badger. I understand you had a problem. Can you tell me what happened?"

I said, "Sure," and went through my sad tale of woe again.

With his left hand, he jotted the information in a small spiral-bound notebook, his eyes never leaving my face. His pencil was the size you'd use on a bridge tally, small and thin, the point looking blunt. He might have been a waiter making a little memo to himself . . . tuna on wheat toast, hold the mayo. "Any idea who this fellow was?" he asked.

"Not a clue."

"What about height and weight? Can you give me an estimate?"

"I'd say close to six feet and he must have outweighed

me by a good sixty pounds. I'm one eighteen, which would put him at a hundred and seventy-five or one eighty minimum."

"Anything else? Scars, moles, tattoos?"

"It was pitch black. He wore a ski mask and heavy clothing so I didn't see much of anything. Night before, the same guy followed me out of Tiny's parking lot. I couldn't swear on a stack of Bibles, but I can't believe two different fellows would come after me like that. The first time, he drove a black panel truck with no plate numbers visible. I reported it this morning to the Nota Lake Police."

"Can you tell me anything else about him?"

"He smelled strongly of sweat."

He turned the page, still writing, and then frowned at his notes. "What'd he do the first encounter? Did he accost you on that occasion?"

"He stared and did this," I said, making a little shooting gesture with my left hand. "It doesn't sound like much, but it was meant to intimidate me and it did."

"He didn't talk to you either time?"

"Not a word."

"What about the vehicle he was driving? Was it the same one last night?"

"I didn't see. He must have parked out by the road and walked back to the cabin where I was staying."

"So he must have known which one it was, unless this was random breaking and entering."

I looked at him with interest. "That's true. I hadn't thought of that. I wonder how he found out which cabin I was in. I woke while he was picking the lock.

When that didn't work, he tried the window in the bathroom. After that, he went to work on the door again."

"And after he dislocated your fingers, he took off?"

"Correct. I could hear a car start in the distance, but I have no idea what kind it was. At that point I was focused on pulling myself together to get help."

Deputy Badger made an additional note for himself and then tucked his little book in his pocket with the pencil in the coil of wire. "I guess that's it then. I'll pass this information on to the deputy works days."

There was conversation outside the door and Rafer LaMott appeared. He shook hands with the deputy, who soon excused himself and disappeared down the hall. I could see Rafer's wife out at the nurse's station, her body language suggesting that she was well aware of his presence. I wondered if she'd called him herself. He looked freshly showered and shaved, natty in a pair of tan corduroy trousers and a soft red cashmere vest with a dress shirt under it. His expression was neutral. He put his hands in his pockets, leaning casually against the wall. He looked like an ad in a menswear catalog. "Cecilia was tired so I told her to go on home. As soon as you're finished here, I'll take you anywhere you want."

ELEVEN

It was six A.M. by the time Rafer finally put me in the front seat of his car. The offer of a ride was as close to an apology as I was likely to get. No doubt his true motivation was to quiz me about the current state of my investigation, but I really didn't care. The sun was not officially up and the early morning air was curiously gloomy. I was at a loss where to have him deliver me. I couldn't bear the idea of being in the cabin by myself. I didn't think Selma would be up at this hour and I couldn't believe Cecilia would welcome my further company. As if reading my mind, Rafer said, "Where to?"

"I guess you better drop me at the Rainbow. I can hang out there until I figure out what to do next."

"I'd like to check the cabin. I've got a print tech from Independence coming up at seven, as soon as he gets in. Maybe we'll get lucky and find out your intruder left his prints."

"Perform an exorcism while you're at it. I don't expect a good night's sleep until I'm out of there."

He glanced over at me. "You thinking about going home?"

"I've been thinking about that ever since I arrived."

He was silent for a while, turning his attention to the road. The town was beginning to come to life. Cars passed us, headlights almost unnecessary as the sky began to alter in gradients from steel gray to dove. At one of the intersections, a restaurant called Elmo's was ablaze with light, patrons visible through the windows. I could see heads bent over breakfast plates. A waitress moved from table to table with a coffeepot in each hand, offering refills. Out on the sidewalk, two women in sweatsuits were absorbed in conversation as they jogged. They arrived at the corner as the light turned red and began to run in place. We moved forward again.

Rafer finally spoke up. "Last time I had anything to do with a P.I. guy claimed to be working a missing-persons case. I went to quite a bit of trouble to follow up, taking two days of my time to track his fellow down in another state. Turns out the P.I. lied to me. He was trying to collect on a bad debt. I was pissed."

"I don't blame you," I said. I began to rack my brain, trying to remember if I'd lied to him myself.

"You have a theory about last night's attack?"

"I'm assuming this was the same guy who followed me from Tiny's," I said.

His gaze returned to the road. "I heard about that. Corbet made sure we got a copy of the report. I passed it on to the CHP so they could keep an eye out as well. Anything missing?"

"I didn't even bother to look. I was too busy taking care of this," I said, lifting my hand. "Anyway, I doubt the motive was theft. I think the point was to discourage my investigation."

"Why?"

"You tell me. I guess he feels protective of Tom Newquist. That's the best I can do."

"I'm not convinced this has anything to do with Tom."

"And I can't prove it does so where does that leave us?"

"You could be mistaken, you know. You're single and you're attractive. That makes you a natural target—"

"For what? This wasn't sexually motivated. It was plain old assault and battery. The guy wanted to cause me great bodily harm."

"What else?"

"What else, what? There's nothing else," I said. "Here's a question for you: Where's Tom's notebook? It's missing. No one's seen it since he died."

He shot me a look and then shook his head blankly. I could see him casting back in his mind. "I'm trying to remember when I last saw it. He usually kept it somewhere close, but I know it's not in his desk drawers because we cleaned those out."

"The CHP officer doesn't remember seeing it in the truck. It didn't occur to him to look for it, but it does seem odd. I know it must irritate you that I'm pursuing the point—"

"Look. I was out of line on that. I get huffy about Selma. It has nothing to do with you."

I could feel the distance between us easing. There's nothing as disarming as a concession of that sort. "It may not be relevant in any event," I said. "What's the procedure on reports? Wouldn't most of his notes have already been written up and submitted?"

"Possibly. He kept his own copies of every report in the particular file he was working. The originals are sent to the records section down in Independence. Reports are submitted at regular intervals. Newer officers seem to be better organized about this stuff. Old timers like me and Tom tend to do things when we get around to it."

"Would there be any way to work backward by checking to see what reports were missing?"

"I don't know how you'd do that and it wouldn't tell you much. You'd have no way of knowing where he'd been and who he'd talked to, let alone the content of conversations. It's not uncommon to have a file with a couple of reports missing ... especially if he was working a case and hadn't typed up his notes yet. Besides, all notes wouldn't be incorporated, just the information he judged relevant. You might scribble down a lot of stuff that wouldn't amount to a hill of beans when you get right down to it."

"Suppose he was developing information on a case of his?"

"He probably was. It also might have been a case someone else had worked that he was reworking for some reason."

"Such as?"

Rafer shrugged. "He might have picked up a new lead. Occasionally, there's a case in the works where the information is sensitive ... might be an informant in another state, or something to do with Internal Affairs."

"My point exactly. I mean, what if Tom was privy to something he didn't know how to handle."

"He'd have told me. We talked about everything."

"Suppose it concerned you?"

He made a little move that indicated agitation. "Let's get off this, okay? I'm not saying we can't talk about this further, but let me think about it some."

"One more thing. And don't get all testy on me. Just tell me what you think. Is there any possibility Tom might have been involved with another woman?"

"No."

I laughed. "Try to keep your answer to twenty-five words or less," I said. "Why not?"

"He was a deeply moral man."

"Well, couldn't that explain his brooding? A man with no conscience wouldn't be at war with himself."

"Objection, your honor. Purely speculative."

"But Rafer, something was troubling him. Selma's not the only one who saw that. I don't know if it was personal or professional, but from what I gather, he was truly distressed."

We pulled into the parking area between the Rainbow Cafe and the Nota Lake Cabins. Rafer put the car in park and then opened his door. "Come on. I'll buy you breakfast. I got a daughter works here."

I struggled with the handle and then gave up. I sat while he walked around the car and opened the door on my side. He even offered a helping hand as I emerged. "Thanks. I can see this is going to be a pain."

"It'll be good for you," he said. "Force you to deal with your dependency issues."

"I don't have dependency issues," I said stoutly.

He smiled in response.

He held the cafe door open and I entered ahead of him. The place was bustling, all men, clearly the stopping-off place of early risers, ranchers, cops, and laborers on their way to work. The interior was, as usual, overheated, and smelled of coffee, bacon, sausages, maple syrup, and cigarettes. The brown-haired waitress, Nancy, was taking an order from a table full of fellows in overalls while Barrett, behind the counter, was focused on a griddle spread with pancakes and omelettes in the making. Rafer took the lead and found us an empty booth. As we passed the intervening tables, I could see we were attracting any number of stares. I was guessing the jungle drums had already spread the news about my assailant.

"How'd you end up in Nota Lake?" I asked, as we slid into the seats.

"I started out as a dispatcher for the L.A.P.D., working on my degree at night. Once I graduated, I applied to the academy. I was hired on at San Bernardino, eventually assigned to robbery detail, but when Barrett was born, Vicky started bugging me to leave LA. She was working as an ER nurse at Queen of Angels, and hated the commute. Even on two salaries, we couldn't afford to buy a house in any of the areas we liked. I heard about an opening in the sheriff's department up here. Vick and I drove up one weekend and fell in love with the place. That's been twenty-three years. Tom was already here. He grew up in Bakersfield."

Two tables over, I caught sight of Macon with his gaze fixed on me. He leaned forward, making some comment. The man with him made one of those casual turns, pretending to glance idly around the room when he was really taking aim at me. I picked up a menu, pretending I didn't notice him pretending not to notice me. Margaret's husband, Hatch.

"You know what you want?" Rafer asked. "I do the works myself. I keep trying to reform, but I can't resist."

"I'm with you," I said. "Your daughter's name is Barrett?"

"That was Vick's idea. I'm not sure where she got it, but it seems to fit. The job is temporary, by the way. She's applied to med school. She wants to be a shrink. This allows her to live at home and save her money 'til she goes."

"Where'd she do her undergraduate work? U.C.L.A.?"

"Where else?" he said, smiling. "What about you?"

"I hated school," I said. "I made it through high school by the hair of my chinny-chin-chin, but that's as far as I went. Well, I guess I did three semesters of junior college, but I hated that, too."

"How so? You seem smart."

"I'm too rebellious," I said. "I graduated from police academy, but that was more like boot camp than academia."

"You're a cop?"

"I was. I was rebellious about that, too."

Nancy appeared with a coffee pot in hand. She was in her forties, hair pulled back in a smooth chignon over which she wore a net. She had large brown eyes, a beauty mark high on her right cheek, and the sort of body men seem to have trouble keeping their hands off. She wore a T-shirt, generously cut slacks, and brown oxfords with an inch-thick crêpe sole. "You're out early," she remarked to Rafer. We both pushed our mugs in her direction and she filled them.

"You met Kinsey?"

"Not formally, but I know who she is. I'm Nancy. You talked to Alice about me."

"How are you," I said. "I'd shake hands if I could."

"Yeah, I heard about that. Cecilia stopped by when we were opening the place. She says you took quite a hit. I can see your jaw turning blue."

I put a hand to the place. "I keep forgetting about that. It must look terrific."

"Gives you character," she said. She glanced at Rafer. "What's for breakfast?"

He looked back at the menu. "Well, let's see. I'm trying to keep my cholesterol up so I think I'll have the blueberry pancakes, sausage, couple of scrambled eggs, and coffee."

"Make that two," I said.

"You want orange juice?"

"Oh sure. What the heck?" he said.

"Back in a flash," she said.

I saw Rafer's gaze flicker to the window. "Excuse me. I see Alex. I'll take him on back to the cabin and get him started."

I had to use two hands to hold my coffee mug, given that three fingers on my right hand were taped together like an oven mitt. The doctor had told me I could remove the tape after a day or two, as long as it felt comfortable. He'd given me four painkillers, neatly sealed in a small white envelope. I remembered a similar envelope from my childhood church-going days, when my nickel or dime offering was placed in the collection plate. The plate itself was wood, passed from hand to hand until it reached an usher at the end of the pew. I'd been kicked out of any number of Sunday school classes for reasons I've repressed, but my Aunt Gin, feeling huffy on my behalf, decided I was entitled to go to proper church services. I suppose her intention was to expose me to spiritual admonition. Mostly what I learned was how hard it is to do an accurate visual count of organ pipes.

I glanced out the window, watching Rafer cross the parking pad, heading toward the cabin in the company of a young man carrying a black case, like a doctor's bag. I took a physical inventory, noting the sore ribs on my right side. I didn't think my jaw was swollen, but it was clearly bruised. No teeth missing or loose. I could feel a knot on my butt the size of a silver dollar and I knew from experience it would itch like a son of a bitch for weeks on end.

"Miss Millhone, can I talk to you?"

I looked up. James Tennyson was standing at the table in his tan CHP uniform, complete with all its creaking paraphernalia: nightstick, flashlight, keys, holster, gun, bullets.

"Sure. Have a seat."

He put a hand against his holster, securing his gun as he slid into the booth. I thought he was ill at ease, but I didn't know him well enough to be certain. "I saw Rafer step away from the table and figured you might have a few minutes."

"This is fine. Nice to see you. You got your flashlight back?"

"Yes ma'am. I appreciate your returning it. Jo found

166

it inside the storm door when she went out to get the paper." He pointed at my hand. "I just heard about the fellow coming after you last night. You all right?"

"More or less."

"He meant business."

"I'll survive," I said.

"The reason I came over . . . I didn't even think about this until yesterday. The night Tom died? I was cruising along 395 when I spotted his truck . . . you know, with the hazard lights on. At first, I didn't realize it was him because he was still some distance away, but I intended to stop and see if there was anything I could do. Anyway, there was a woman walking along the road, heading toward town."

"A woman?"

"Yes ma'am. I'm almost sure."

"And she was facing you?"

"That's right, but she veered off about then. This was shortly before I passed so I didn't get a good look at her, just a fleeting impression. She was bundled up pretty good. If it hadn't been for Tom and trying to get help for him, I'd have cruised back in her direction in case she needed help."

"Is it unusual to see someone walking out there?"

"Yes ma'am. At least, I thought it was at the time. This was miles from anywhere and there's very little in the way of houses out there, except for one subdivision. She could have been out for a jog, but she didn't seem dressed for that, and in the dark? I doubt it. Anyway, it struck me as odd. I guess in my mind I was thinking she might have got mad at her boyfriend and taken off

167

on foot. I didn't see another vehicle so I don't think it was a flat tire or anything like that."

"And this was no one you knew?"

"I really couldn't say. It was nobody I recognized under the circumstance. Like I said, I didn't think much about it and later it slipped my mind entirely. I don't even know what made me think of it. Just the fact that you asked."

I thought about it for a moment. "How far away was she from the truck when you saw her?"

"It couldn't have been a quarter of a mile because I could see Tom's hazard lights blinking in the distance."

"Do you think she was *with* him?"

"I suppose it's possible," he said. "If he was having chest pains, she might have been on her way to find help."

"Why not flag you down?"

"Beats me. I don't know what to make of it," he said.

"I'd like to see the spot where Tom's truck was parked," I said. "Could you maybe take me out there later?"

"Sure, I'd be happy to, but the place isn't hard to find. It's maybe a mile in that direction. You look for a couple big boulders near a pine with the top sheared off. Thing was struck by lightning in a big storm last year. Just keep an eye out. You can't miss it. It's on the right-hand side."

"Thanks."

He glanced toward one of the tables near the front of the cafe. "My breakfast is here. You have any more questions, give me a call."

I watched him move away. Hatch and Macon stood together near the cash register, waiting for Nancy to take their money. My conversation with James hadn't gone unnoticed, though both men made a big display of their disinterest. Rafer returned, entering the cafe without the technician, whom I assumed was busy at the cabin with his little brushes and powders. Rafer eased into the seat, saying, "Sorry about that. I told him we'd join him as soon as we finished here."

When we reached the cabin after breakfast, the door was standing open. I could see smudges of powder along the outside edges of the sills. Rafer introduced me to the fingerprint technician, who rolled a set of my prints for elimination purposes. Later, he'd ink a set of Cecilia's prints, along with the prints of any cleaning or maintenance workers. He could have saved himself the trouble. The cabin yielded nothing in the way of evidence: no useful prints on the window glass, nothing on the hardware, no footprints in the damp earth leading to or from the cabin.

The interior seemed dank, the bed still lumpy with the pillows I'd tucked under the pile of blankets. The place was drab. It was cold. The digital clock was blinking, which meant there'd been another power failure. The adrenaline had seeped slowly out of me like gray water down a clogged drain. I felt like crap. A rivulet of revulsion trickled over me and I was embarrassed anew at the inadequacies of my attempt to defend myself. Anxiety whispered at the base of my spine, a feathery reminder of how vulnerable I was. A memory burbled up. I was five years old again, bruised and bloodied after the wreck that killed my parents. I'd forgotten the physical pain because the wrenching emotional loss had always taken precedence.

While Rafer and the tech conferred outside, talking in low tones, I hauled out my duffel and began to pack my things. I went into the bathroom, gathered up my toiletries, and tossed them in the bottom of the bag. I didn't hear Rafer come in, but I was suddenly aware of him standing in the doorway. "You're taking off?" he asked.

"I'd be crazy to stay here."

"I agree with you on that, but I didn't think you were finished with your investigation."

"That remains to be seen."

His gaze rested on me with concern. "You want to talk?"

I looked up at him. "About what? This is a simple job to me, not some moral imperative. I'm getting paid for a piece of work. I guess I have my limits on that score."

"You're going to quit?"

"I didn't say that. I'll talk to Selma first and then we'll see where we go from here."

"Look, I can see you're upset. I'd offer you protection, but I don't have a deputy to spare. We operate on a shoestring—"

"I appreciate the sentiment. I'll let you know what I decide."

"It wouldn't hurt to have help. You know anybody who could pitch in on personal security?"

"Oh, please. Absolutely not. I wouldn't do that. This

is strictly my problem and I'll handle it," I said. "Trust me, I'm not being pig-headed or proud. I hired a body-guard once before, but this is different."

"How so?"

"If that guy meant to kill me, he'd have done it last night."

"Listen, I've been beat up in my day and I know what it can do to you. Screws your head up. You lose your confidence. It's like riding a horse—"

"No, it's not! I've been beaten up before—" I raised a hand, stopping myself with a shake of my head. "Sorry. I didn't meant to snap at you. I know you mean well, but this is mine to deal with. I'm fine. I just don't want to spend another minute in this godforsaken place."

"Well," he said, infusing the single syllable with skep-ticism. He paused, silent, hands in his pockets, rocking back on his heels. I zipped the duffel, picked up my jacket and my handbag, looking around the cabin. The table was still littered with my papers and I'd forgotten about the Smith-Corona, still sitting in its place with the lid half closed. I snapped the cover into place and stuffed papers in a manila envelope that I shoved into an outer pocket of the duffel. Using my left hand, I lifted the typewriter case. "Thanks for the ride and thanks for breakfast."

"I have to get on in to work, but you let me know if there's anything I can do to help."

"You can carry this," I said, passing him the type-writer. He did me one better, carrying both the duffel and the Smith-Corona as he escorted me to the car. I waited until he'd pulled away and then I headed for the office and stuck my head in the door. There was no sign of Cecilia. The usual table lamp was still on, but her door was shut and I imagined her catching up on the sleep she'd lost taking me to the emergency room. I got into my car and pulled out of the parking lot, turning left onto 395.

I kept an eye on the odometer, clocking off a mile and then began to look for the spot where Tom's truck had been parked the night he died. As Tennyson indicated, it wasn't hard to find. Two massive boulders and a towering pine tree with the top missing. I could see the raw white inner wood where the lightning had slashed away at the trunk.

I eased over onto the berm and parked. I got out of the car, draping my heavy leather jacket across my shoulders. There was no traffic at this hour and the morning air was silent. The sky was massed with dark gray, the mountains obscured by mist. Snow had begun to fall; big lacy flakes that settled on my face like a series of kisses. For a moment, I leaned my head back and let the snow touch my tongue.

There was, of course, no remaining trace of vehicles having been parked here six weeks before. If the truck, Tennyson's patrol car, and the ambulance had chewed up the soil and gravel along the shoulder, nature had come afterward and smoothed away any suggestion of events. I did a grid search, my gaze fixed on the barren ground as I walked a linear pattern. I imagined Tom in his pickup, the pain like a knife wedged between his shoulder blades. Nausea, clamminess, the chill sweat of Death forcing him to concentrate. For the time being, I set aside the image of the woman walking down the road. For all I knew, she was a figment of James Tennyson's imagination, some piece of misdirection designed to throw me off. In any investigation, you have to be careful about accepting information without a touch of skepticism. I wasn't sure of his motivation. Maybe, as implied, he was just a genuinely helpful guy who took his job seriously and wanted to apprise me of his recollection. What interested me here was the possibility that Tom had dropped his notebook out the window, or that he'd somehow destroyed the contents in the final moments of his life.

I covered every inch of ground within a radius of a hundred feet. There was no notebook, no pages fluttering in the breeze, no confetti of torn paper, no nook or cranny into which such detritus might have been secreted. I kicked over rocks and dead leaves, set aside fallen branches and dug into crusty patches of snow. It was hard to believe Tom had dragged himself out here to take care of such business. I was operating on the assumption that his field notes were sensitive and that he'd made some effort to secure the confidentiality of the contents. Then again, perhaps not. The notes might not have been relevant.

I returned to my car and turned the key in the ignition, not without struggle. The tape on my right hand made everything slightly awkward and I suspected that the compensatory effort over the next couple of days was going to wear me down. While the injury wasn't major, it was annoying and inconvenient, a constant reminder that I'd suffered at someone's hands. I did a U-turn onto the highway and headed back to Selma's. By ten A.M., I was on the road for home.

TWELVE

Shortly after leaving Nota Lake, I'd thought I caught a glimpse of a county sheriff's cruiser keeping me company from half a mile back. The car was too far away to identify the driver, but the effect was to make me feel I was being ushered across the county line. I kept my eye on the rearview mirror, but the black-and-white maintained a discreet distance. When we reached the junction of 395 and 168, a road sign indicated that it was five miles to Whirly Township, seven miles to Rudd. The patrol car turned off. Whether the escort was deliberate or coincidental, I couldn't be sure. Nor could I determine whether the intention was benign or belligerent. Earlene's husband, Wayne, was the deputy who worked in Whirly Township, so maybe it was only him on his way to work.

After that, the desert landscape sped by in a monotonous repetition of scrub-covered low hills, and I spent the rest of the journey in a haze of road-induced hypnosis. The intervening towns were few—Big Pine, Independence, Lone Pine, Cartago, Olancha—unexpected small enclaves that consisted primarily of gas stations, wooden cottages, coffee shops, perhaps a pizza restaurant or a Frosty Freeze, sometimes still boarded over for the winter. In most towns, there seemed to be more buildings abandoned than were currently in use. The structures were low wood fronts with a Western or Victorian feel to them. In some areas, the commercial businesses seemed to be devoted almost entirely to propane sales and service. An occasional feed store would be tucked in among the cottonwoods and pines. I passed one of those plain motel-style brown-and-yellow churches that made you suspect it would be depressing to believe whatever these people believed.

Between townships, the empty stretches of wilderness picked up. The air felt clear, warming as the road descended from the higher elevations. The snow had disappeared, soft flakes turning into an even softer rain. What should have been a clear, unobstructed view was subdivided by the march of power lines, telephone poles, and oil derricks—the cost of doing business in an otherwise pristine countryside. Out of the raw hills to my left I could see the occasional cinder cone and the dark craggy outcroppings of lava from ancient volcanic activity. Rocks dotted the landscape: green, red, brown, and cream. The area was undercut by two major fault lines—the San Andreas and the Garlock—that in 1872 had generated one of the largest earthquakes in Californian history.

Gradually, I let my thoughts drift back to events I'd left behind. I'd spent an hour at Selma's before I'd departed Nota Lake. So far, given my four days' work, I'd earned a thousand dollars of the fifteen hundred she'd paid me in advance. That meant that I would owe *her* money if I decided to quit . . . which I confess had crossed my mind. My medical insurance would cover the expenses incurred in behalf of my bunged-up hand. She'd been properly upset by what had happened and we'd gone through the predictable litany of horror and remorse. "I feel sick. This is my fault. I got you into this," she'd said.

"Don't be silly, Selma. It isn't *your* fault. If nothing else it gives credence to your hunch about Tom's 'secret,' if you want to call it that."

"But I never dreamed it'd be dangerous."

"Life is dangerous," I said. I was feeling oddly impatient, ready to move on to the job at hand. "Look, we can sit here and commiserate, but I'd much prefer to use the time constructively. I've got a big pile of phone bills. Let's sit down together and see how many numbers you recognize. Any that seem unfamiliar, I can check from Santa Teresa."

Which is what we'd done, eliminating slightly more than three-quarters of the calls listed for the past ten months. Many were Selma's, related to her church work, charity events, and assorted friendships outside the 619 area code. Some of the remaining numbers she'd recognized as business calls, a fact confirmed by judicious use of Tom's Rolodex. I'd placed the entire file of last year's phone bills in my duffel and then I'd gone down to the basement to take a look at the storage boxes I'd seen previously. There, in the dry, overheated space that smelled of ticking furnace and hot paper, a curious order prevailed.

Despite the fact that both Tom's desk and his den upstairs were an ungodly mess, Tom Newquist was systematic, at least where work was concerned. On a shelf to my left was a series of cardboard boxes where he'd placed bundles of field notes going back twenty-five years, including his days at the academy. Once a notebook had been filled, his method was to remove the six-hole lined pages, apply a wrapper showing the inclusive dates, and then secure them with a rubber band. Many times several bundles of notes pertained to the same case and those tended to be packed in separate manila envelopes, again labeled and dated. I could walk my fingers back through his investigations, year after year, without gaps or interruptions. Occasionally, on the outside of an envelope he'd penned a note indicating that a call or teletype had come through regarding the particulars of a case. He would then type an update and include a copy with his notes, indicating the agency making the call, the nature of the inquiry, and the details of his response. He was clearly prepared to substantiate his findings with court testimony where required, on every investigation he'd done since he'd been in Nota Lake. The last of the bundled notes were dated the previous April. Missing were notes from May and June of last year until the time of his death. I had to assume the missing notebook covered the previous ten months. There was no other gap in his records of that magnitude.

I went back upstairs, through the kitchen, and into the garage, where I searched the truck again—more thoroughly than I had the first time around. I even eased onto one shoulder so I could shine a flashlight up under the seats, thinking Tom might have secured his note-book in the springs. There was no sign of it, so essentially I was back to square one. My only conso-lation was knowing I'd left no stone unturned—as far as I could tell. Clearly, I'd overlooked *something* or I'd have his notes in hand.

The rain increased as I drove south. At Rosamond, I found a McDonald's and stopped to use the restroom. I picked up a big cola, a large order of fries, and a QP with cheese. I downed a painkiller while I was at it. Twelve minutes later, I was on the road again. The closer I came to Los Angeles, the more my spirits lifted. I hadn't even realized how depressed I was until my mood began to improve. The rain became my companion, the windshield wipers keeping a steady rhythm as the highway sizzled under my tires. I turned on the radio and let the drone of bad music fill the car.

When I reached Highway 5, I turned north as far as the junction with Highway 126, where I cut west again through Fillmore and Santa Paula. Here the landscape was made up of citrus and avocado groves, the roadway populated with produce stands, beyond which tracts of houses stretched out as far as the eye could see. Route 126 spilled into 101 and I nearly whimpered aloud at the sight of the Pacific. I rolled the window down and tilted my head sideways, letting raindrops blow on my face. The scent of the ocean was dense and sweet. The surf made its relentless approach and retreat, soft pounding at the shoreline, where occasional sea birds race-walked along the hard-packed sand. The water was silken, endless reams of gray taffeta—churning lace at the edge. I'm not fond of mountains, in part because I have so little interest in winter sports, especially those requiring costly equipment. I avoid activities associated with speed, cold, and heights, and any that involve the danger of falling down and breaking significant body parts. As fun as it all sounds, it's never appealed to me. The ocean is another matter, and while I can spend brief periods in land-locked locations, I'm never as happy as I am when close to deep water. Please understand, I don't go *in* the water because there are all manner of biting, stinging, tentacled, pincered, slimy things down there, but I like to *look* at the water and spend time in its immense, ever-changing presence. For one thing, I find it therapeutic to consider all the creatures not devouring me at any given moment.

Thus cheered, I powered through the final few miles into Santa Teresa. I took the Cabana off-ramp and turned left, passing the bird refuge on my right and shortly thereafter, the volleyball courts on the sand at East Beach. By that time, I'd been on the road for five hours, so focused on home that my foot felt as if it was welded to the accelerator. I was exhausted. My neck was stiff. My mouth tasted like hot metal. My bruised fingers were deadened by drugs yet somehow managed to throb with pain. Also, my butt hurt along with everything else.

My neighborhood looked the same, a short residential street a block from the beach: palms, tall pines, wire fences, crooked sidewalks where tree roots had buckled the concrete. Most houses were stucco with aging red-tile roofs. An occasional condominium appeared between single-family dwellings. I found a parking spot across the street from my apartment, once a single-car garage, now a two-story hideaway attached by a sunporch to the house where my landlord lives. This month marked the fifth anniversary of my tenancy and I treasure the space I've come to think of as mine.

It took me two trips to unload the rental car, passing in and out of Henry's squeaking gate. I made a pile on the small covered porch, unlocked the front door, left the typewriter by the desk, went back for my duffel, and hauled it up the spiral stairs. I stripped off my clothes, removed the bandages from my hand, and treated myself to a long hot shower wherein I washed my hair, did a left-handed leg shave, and sang a medley of show tunes with half the lyrics consisting of *dah-dah-dah*. The luxury of being clean and warm was almost more than I could bear. I skipped my flossing for once, did a left-handed toothbrushing, and annointed myself with an inexpensive drugstore cologne that smelled like lilies of the valley. I put on a fresh turtle-neck, a fresh pair of jeans, clean socks, Reeboks, and a touch of lipstick. I checked my reflection in the bath-room mirror. Nah, that looked dumb. I rubbed off the lipstick on a piece of toilet paper and pronounced myself whole. After that, all I had to do was spend approxi-mately twenty minutes trying to get my fingers splinted and retaped. This was going to be ob-*noxious*.

I ducked out my door and splashed across the patio in the rain. Henry's garden was just coming to life again. The weather in Santa Teresa is moderate all year long, but we do enjoy a nearly indiscernible spring in which green shoots nudge through the hard ground as they do every place else. Henry had begun to clear the flower beds where his annuals and a few tomato plants would eventually go. I could smell the wet walkways, bark mulch, and the few narcissus that must have opened in the rain. It was quarter to five and the day was gloomy with approaching twilight, the light a mild gray from the rain clouds overhead.

I peered through the window in Henry's back door while I rapped on the glass. Lights were on and there was evidence he was in the midst of a cooking project. For many years, Henry Pitts earned his living as a commercial baker and now that he's retired, he still loves to cook. He's lean-faced, tanned, and long-legged, a gent with snowy white hair, blue eyes, a beaky nose, and all of his own teeth. At eighty-six, he's blessed with intelligence, high spirits, and prodigious energy. He came into the kitchen from the hallway carrying a stack of the small white terrycloth towels he uses when he cooks. He usually has one tucked in his belt, another resting on his shoulder, and a third that occasionally serves as an oven mitt. He was wearing a navy T-shirt and white shorts, covered by a big baker's apron that extended past his knees. He set the towels on the counter and hurried to unlock the door, his face wreathed in smiles.

"Well, Kinsey. I didn't expect you back today. Come on in. What happened to your hand?"

"Long story. In a minute, I'll give you the abbreviated version."

He stepped aside and I entered, giving him a hug as I passed. On the counter I could see a tall Mason jar of flour, a shorter jar of sugar, two sticks of butter, a tin of baking powder, a carton of eggs, and a bowl of Granny Smith apples; pie tin, rolling pin, grater.

"Something smells wonderful. What's cooking?"

Henry smiled. "A surprise for Rosie's birthday. I've got a noodle pudding in the oven. This is a Hungarian dish I hope you won't ask me to pronounce. I'm also making her a Hungarian apple pie."

"Which birthday?"

"She won't say. Last I heard, she was claiming sixty-six, but I think she's been shaving points for years. She has to be seventy. You'll be joining us, I hope."

"I wouldn't miss it," I said. "I'll have to sneak out and find a gift. What time?"

"I'm not going over 'til six. Sit, sit, sit and I'll fix a pot of tea."

He settled me in his rocking chair and put the kettle on for tea while we filled each other in on events during the weeks I'd been gone. In no particular order, we went through the usual exchange of information: the trip, Dietz's surgery, news from the home front. I laid out the job as succinctly as I could, including the nature of the investigation, the players, and the attack the night before, a process that allowed me to listen to myself. "I have a couple of leads to check. Apparently, Tom was in touch with a local sheriff's investigator, though, at this point, I'm not sure if the contact was personal or professional. The way I heard it, they had their heads bent together and the woman's manner was noticeably flirtatious. Strictly rumor, of course, but it's worth looking into."

"And if that doesn't pan out?"

"Then I'm stumped."

While I finished my tea, Henry put together the pie crust and began to peel and grate apples for the filling. I washed my cup and saucer and set them in his dish rack. "I better whiz out and find a present. Are you dressing for the party?"

"I'm wearing long pants," he said. "I may rustle up a sports coat. You look fine as you are."

As it turned out, Rosie's entire restaurant had been given over to her birthday party. This tacky neighborhood tavern has always been my favorite. In the olden days (five years ago), it was often empty except for a couple of local drunks who showed up daily when it opened and generally had to be carried home. In the past few years, for reasons unknown, the place has become a hangout for various sports teams whose trophies now grace every available surface. Rosie, never famous for her good humor, has nonetheless tolerated this band of testosterone-intoxicated rowdies with unusual restraint. That night, the ruffians were out in full force and in the spirit of the occasion had decorated the restaurant with crêpe paper streamers, helium balloons, and hand-lettered banners that read WAY TO GO ROSIE! There was a huge bouquet of flowers, a keg of bad beer, a stack of pizza boxes, and an enormous birthday cake. Cigarette smoke filled the air, lending the room the soft, hazy glow of an old tintype. The sportsers had seeded the jukebox with high-decibel hits from the 1960s and they'd pushed all the tables back so they could do the twist and the Watusi. Rosie looked on with an indulgent smile. Someone had given her a cone-shaped hat covered with glitter, a strand of elastic under her chin, and a feather sticking out the top. She wore the usual muumuu, this one hot pink with a three-inch ruffle around the low-cut neck. William looked dapper in a dark three-piece suit, white dress shirt, and a navy tie with red polka dots, but there was no sign of anyone else from the neighborhood. Henry and I sat to one side—he in jeans and a denim sports coat, I in jeans and my good tweed blazer—like spectators at a dance contest. I'd spent the better part of an hour at a department store downtown, finally selecting a red silk chemise I thought would tickle her fancy.

We ducked out at ten and scurried home through the rain.

I locked the door behind me and moved through the apartment, marveling at the whole of it: the porthole window in the front door, walls of polished teak and oak, cubbyholes of storage tucked into all the nooks and crannies. I had a sofa bed built into the bay window for guests, two canvas director's chairs, bookshelves, my desk. Up the spiral stairs, in addition to the closet built into one wall, I had pegs for hanging clothes, a double-bed mattress laid on a platform with drawers built into it, and a second bathroom with a sunken tub and a window looking out toward the ocean. I felt as if I were living on a houseboat, adrift on some river, snug and efficient, warm, blessed with light. I was so thrilled to be home I could hardly bear to go to bed. I crawled, naked, under a pile of quilts and listened to the rain tapping on the Plexiglas skylight. I felt absurdly possessive—my pillow, my blanket, my secret hideaway, my home.

The next thing I knew, it was six A.M. I hadn't set my alarm, but I woke automatically, reverting to habit. I tuned into the sound of rain, bypassed the thought of jogging, and went back to sleep again. I roused myself at eight and went through my usual morning ablutions. I had breakfast, read the paper, and then set the type-writer case on the desk top. I paused, making a quick trip upstairs where I retrieved my notes from the duffel. My first chore of the morning would be to return the rental car. That done, I'd take a cab to the office, where I'd put in an appearance and catch up with the latest lawyerly gossip. I still hadn't decided whether to work from the office or home. I'd either stay where I was or bum a ride home from someone at Kingman and Ives.

In the meantime, I thought I'd get my typewriter set up and begin the painful hunt-and-peck addition to my progress report. It wasn't until I opened the typewriter case that I saw what I'd missed in the process of packing to leave Nota Lake. Someone had taken the middle two rows of typewriter keys and twisted the metal into a hopeless clot. Some of the keys had been broken off and some were simply bent sideways like my fingers. I sat down and stared with a sense of bafflement. What was going on?

THIRTEEN

I decided to skip the office and concentrate on running down the few leads I had. In my heart of hearts, I knew perfectly well the trashing of my typewriter had taken place in Nota Lake before I'd left. Nonetheless, the discovery was disconcerting and tainted my sense of security and well-being. Annoyed, I opened my bottom desk drawer and took out the Yellow Pages, flicked through to TYPEWRITERS-REPAIRING, and made calls until I found someone equipped to handle my vintage Smith-Corona. I made a note of the address and told the shop owner I'd be there within the hour.

I took out my notes and found the local numbers I'd cribbed from the surface of Tom Newquist's blotter. When I'd dialed the one number from Tom's den, the call had been picked up by an answering machine. I was operating on the assumption that the woman I'd heard was the same female sheriff's investigator Phyllis claimed she'd seen flirting with Tom. If I could have a talk with her, it might go a long way toward cleaning up my questions. I punched in the number. Once again a machine picked up and the same throaty-voiced woman told me what I could do with myself at the sound of the beep. I left my name, my home and office numbers, and a brief message indicating that I'd like to talk to her about Tom Newquist. Next, I called the Perdido Sheriff's Department, saying: "I wonder if you could help me. I'm trying to get in touch with a sheriff's investigator, a woman. I believe she's in her forties or fifties. I don't have her name, but I think she's employed by the Perdido County Sheriff's Department. Does any of this ring a bell?"

"What division?"

"That's the point. I'm not sure."

The fellow on the phone laughed. "Lady, we've got maybe half a dozen female officers fit that description. You're going to have to be more specific."

"Ah. I was afraid of that," I said. "Well, I guess I'll have to do my homework. Thanks anyway."

"You're entirely welcome."

I sat there, mentally chewing on my pencil. What to do, what to do. I dialed Phyllis Newquist's number in Nota Lake and naturally got an answering machine into which I entrusted the following: "Hi, Phyllis. This is Kinsey. I wonder if you could give me the name of the female sheriff's investigator Tom was in touch with down here. I've got a home telephone number, but it would help if you could find out what her name is. That way, I can try her at work and maybe speed things along. Otherwise, I'm stuck waiting for this woman to call back." Again, I left both my home and office numbers and moved down my mental list.

The second number I'd picked up from Tom's blotter was for the Gramercy Hotel. I thought that one deserved my personal attention. I tucked Tom's photograph in my handbag, grabbed my jacket and an umbrella, and headed out into the rain. My fingers, though bruised and swollen, were not throbbing with pain and for that I was grateful. I used my left hand where I could, fumbling with car keys, transferring items from one hand to the other. The simplest transactions were consequently slowed since the splint on my right hand forced me to proceed by awkward degrees. I made a second trip for the typewriter, which I placed on the front seat.

I dropped off the typewriter, extracting a promise from the repair guy to get it back to me as soon as possible. I returned the rental to the agency's downtown office, completed the financial transactions, and then took a cab back to my apartment. I picked up my car, which—after a series of groans and stutters—finally coughed to life. Progress at last.

I drove into downtown Santa Teresa and left my car in a nearby public parking garage. Umbrella tilted against the rain, I walked one block over and one block down. The Gramercy Hotel was a chunky three-story structure on lower State Street, a residential establishment favored by the homeless when their monthly checks came in. The stucco building was painted the sweet green of a crème de menthe frappé and featured a covered entrance large enough to accommodate six huddled smokers seeking shelter from the rain. A marquee across the front spelled out the hotel rates.

SGL RMS $9.95.   DBL RMS $13.95

DAILY*WEEKLY*MONTHLY

RATES ALSO AVAILABLE ON REQUEST.

A fellow using a plastic garbage bag as a rain cloak greeted me rheumy-eyed as he moved his feet to allow me passage into the lobby. I lowered my umbrella, trying not to stab any of those assembled for their morning libations. It seemed early for package liquor, but maybe that was fruit juice being passed in the brown paper bag.

The hotel must have been considered elegant once upon a time. The floor was green marble with a crooked path of newspapers laid end to end to soak up all the rainy footsteps that criss-crossed the lobby. In places, where the soggy papers had been picked up, I could see that the newsprint had left reverse images of the head-lines and text. Six ornate pilasters divided the gloomy space into sections, each of which sported a blocky green plastic couch. To all appearances, the clientele was discouraged from spending time lounging about on the furniture as a hand-printed sign offered the fol-lowing admonishments:

NO SMOKING

NO SPITTING

NO LOITERING

NO SOLICITING

NO DRINKING ON THE PREMISES

NO FIGHTING

NO PEEING IN THE PLANTERS

Which just about summed up my personal code. I approached the long front desk, located beneath an archway decorated with white plaster scrolls and orna-mental vegetation. The fellow behind the marble counter was leaning forward on his elbows, clearly interested in my intentions. This felt like one more fool's errand, but it was truly the only thing I could think to do at this point.

"I'd like to talk to the manager. Is he here?"

"I guess that's me. I'm Dave Estes. And your name?"

"Kinsey Millhone." I took out my business card and passed it across to him.

He read it with serious attention to each word. He was in his thirties, a cheerful-looking fellow with an open countenance, glasses, a crooked smile, slight overbite, and a hairline that had receded to reveal a long sloping forehead like an expanse of empty seashore when the tide is out. What hair he had was a medium brown and cropped close to his head. He wore a brown jumpsuit with many zippered pockets, like an auto mechanic's. The sleeves were rolled up to reveal muscular forearms.

"What can I help you with?"

I placed the photograph of Tom Newquist on the counter in front of him. "I'm wondering if you happen to have seen this man. He's an investigator for the Nota County Sheriff's Department. His name is Tom—"

"Hold on, hold on," he cut in. He held a hand up to silence me, motioning me to wait a moment, during which time he made the kind of face that precedes a sneeze. He closed his eyes, screwed up his nose, and opened his mouth, panting. His expression cleared and he pointed at me. "Newquist. Tom Newquist."

I was astonished. "That's right. You know him?"

"Well, no, I don't know him, but he was in here."

"When was this?"

"Oh, I'd say June of last year. Probably the first week. I'd say the Fifth if forced to guess."

I was so unprepared for the verification, I couldn't think what to ask next.

Estes was looking at me. "Did something happen to him?"

"He died of a heart attack a few weeks back."

"Hey, too bad. Sorry to hear that. He didn't seem that old."

"He wasn't, but I don't think he took very good care of himself. Can you tell me what brought him in here?"

"Oh, sure. He was looking for some guy who'd just been released from jail. We seem to get a lot of fellows here in that situation. Don't ask me why. Classy place like this. Word must go out that we got good rates, clean rooms, and won't tolerate a lot of nonsense."

"Do you remember the name of the man he was looking for?"

"That's an easy one to remember for other reasons, but I like to test myself anyway. Hang on." He went through the same procedure, face screwed up to show how hard he was working. He paused in his efforts. "You're probably wondering how I do this. I took a course in mnemonics, the art of improving the memory. I spend a lot of time by myself, especially at night when I'm on desk duty. Trick is you come up with these devices, you know—aids and associations—that help fix an item in the mind."

"That's great. I'm impressed."

"Reason I remember the time frame for your Newquist's visit is I started my study just about the time he came in. He was my first practice case. So the name

Newquist? No problem. *New* because the fellow was new to me, right? *Quist* as in question or query. New fellow came in with a question, hence *Newquist*."

"That's good," I said. "What about his first name?"

Estes smiled. "You told me that. I'd forgotten it myself."

"And the other guy? The one he was inquiring about?"

"What did I come up with for that? Let's see. It had something to do with dentists. Oh, yes. His last name was Toth? That's *tooth* with an *O* missing. That was a good one because the fellow had a tooth missing so it all tied together. His first name was Alfie. Dentists connect to doctors. And like at the doctor's, you say 'Ahh' when they stick in that tongue depressor in your mouth? First name began with *A*. So mentally, I go through all the *A* names I can think of. Allen, Arnold, Avery, Alfie. And there you have it."

"So Tom Newquist was here on business."

"That's correct. Trouble is, he missed him. Toth'd been here two weeks, but he moved out June One, shortly before this detective of yours came in."

"Do you have any idea why he was looking for Toth?"

"Said he was developing a lead on a case he was working. I remember that because it was just like the movies. You know, Clint Eastwood comes in, flashing a badge and real serious. All I know is Newquist never had the chance to talk to him because Toth was gone by then."

"Did he leave a forwarding address?"

"Well, no, but I have his ex-wife's address, under

192

'nearest relative not living with you.' That's so we got someone to call if a guy trashes the room or drops dead. It's a hassle trying to figure out what to do with a dead body."

"I can imagine," I said. "Is there any way I could get the ex-wife's name and address?"

"Sure. No problem. This's not confidential information as far as I'm concerned. People check in, I tell 'em the hotel files are open to the authorities. Cops come in asking to see records. I don't insist on a subpoena. That'd be obstruction of justice, in my opinion."

"I'm sure the police appreciate your attitude, but don't the hotel guests object?"

Dave Estes shrugged. "I guess the day I get sued, we'll change the policy. You know, another fellow came in, too. Plainclothes detective. This was earlier, maybe June One. I wasn't working that day or I'd have filed it away in the old noggin," he said with a tap to his temple. "I told Peck he better take the same course I did, but so far I haven't managed to talk him into it."

"Too bad," I said. "So who was this other detective who came in?"

"Can't help you there and that's my point. If Peck took this course, he could recall in detail. Since he didn't; no dice. The slate's blank. End of episode."

"Could I talk to Peck myself?"

"You could, but I can tell you exactly what he's going to say. He remembers this investigator came in—had a warrant and all, but Toth wasn't on the premises. In fact, he checked out later that day so maybe he was worried about the law catching up with him. Detective called back the next morning and Peck gave him the address and telephone number of Toth's ex-wife, same as I would."

"Did you tell Tom Newquist about the other detective?"

"Same way I'm telling you. I figured it must have been a cop he knew."

"What about Toth's ex? Did you tell him how to get in touch with her?"

"Sure did. The woman had a regular parade coming through the door."

"Hasn't anybody suggested you shouldn't be quite so free passing out information?"

"Lady, I'm not the guardian of public safety. Some cop comes in looking for information, I don't want to get in his way."

"What about the warrant? Was that local?"

"Can't answer that. Peck doesn't pay attention to these items the same way I do. He's got the right idea—we're here to cooperate. Place like this, you want the cops on your team. Fight breaks out, you want action when you hit 9–1–1."

"Not to mention help with all the bodies afterward."

"Now you're getting it."

"Could we just back up a minute and see if I got this straight? Alfie Toth was here two weeks, from sometime in the middle of May."

"Right."

"Then a plainclothes detective came in with a warrant for his arrest. Alfie heard about it and, not surprisingly, checked out later that day. The detective called back and Peck told him how to get in touch with Alfie Toth's ex-wife."

"Sure. Peck figured that's where Toth went," Estes said.

"Then around June Fifth, Tom Newquist came in and you passed the same information along to him."

"Hey, I don't show favorites, is my motto. That's why I'm giving it to you. Why say yes to one and no to someone else is the way I look at it."

"You haven't given me anything yet," I said.

He reached for a piece of scratch paper and jotted down a woman's name, address, and telephone number, apparently off the top of his head. He passed it across the counter.

I took the paper, noting at a glance the Perdido address. "Sounds like Alfie Toth was suddenly very popular."

"Yep."

"And you have no idea why?"

"Nope."

"What's Peck's first name?"

"Leland."

"Is he in the phone book if I need to talk to him?"

Estes shook his head. "Number's unlisted. Now *that* I wouldn't give out without getting his permission."

I thought about it for a moment, but couldn't think what other ground I should cover. I could always check with him later if something else occurred to me. "Well. Thanks for the help. You've been very generous and I appreciate that." I reached for my umbrella, shifting my handbag from my right shoulder to my left so I could manage both.

"Don't you want to hear the rest of it?"

I hesitated. "What rest?"

"The guy's dead. Murdered. Some backpacker found his body up near Ten Pines couple months ago. January Thirteen. Reason I remember is it's my great-aunt's birthday. Death. Birth. Doesn't take a wizard to make that connection. I got it locked right in here."

I stared at him, remembering a brief mention of it in the paper. "*That* was Alfie Toth?"

"Yep. Coroner figured he'd been dead six, seven months—since right about the time everybody came looking for him—including the fellow with the warrant and your Tom Newquist. Somebody must have caught up with him. Too bad Peck's never bothered to develop his skills. He might've been the state's star witness."

"To what?"

"Whatever comes up."

I sat in my car, trying to figure out what this meant. Everybody had wanted to talk to Alfie Toth until he turned up dead. I'd have to search back issues of the local newspaper, but as nearly as I remembered, there was precious little information. Decomposed remains had been found in a remote area of the Los Padres National Forest, but I hadn't registered the name. There was no mention of cause of death, but the presumption was of foul play. The police had been stingy with the details, but perhaps they'd told the papers everything they knew. I hadn't been aware of any other reference to the matter and I'd thought no more of it. The Angeles and Los Padres national forests are both dumping grounds for homicide victims, whose corpses one imagines littering the hiking trails like bags of garbage.

I dutifully fired up the VW and drove the eight blocks to the public library, where I turned up the relevant paragraph in a copy of the *Santa Teresa Dispatch* for January 15.

BODY FOUND IN LOS PADRES
THAT OF TRANSIENT

The decomposed remains discovered by a hiker in the Los Padres National Forest January 13 have been identified as a transient, Alfred Toth, 45, according to the Santa Teresa County Sheriff's Department. The body was found Monday in the rugged countryside five miles east of Manzanita Mountain. Detectives identified Toth through dental work after linking the body to a missing-persons report filed by his ex-wife, Perdido resident Olga Toth. The case is being investigated as a homicide. Anyone with information is asked to call Detective Clay Boyd at the Sheriff's Department.

I found a pay phone outside the building, scrounged a couple of coins from the bottom of my handbag, dialed the Santa Teresa County Sheriff's Department, and asked for Detective Boyd.

"Boyd." The tone was flat, professional, all business. All he'd done so far was give me his name and already I knew he wasn't going to be my best friend.

"Hi, my name is Kinsey Millhone," I said, trying not to sound too chirpy. "I'm a local private investigator working on a case that may connect to the death of Alfie Toth."

Pause. "In what way?"

"Well, I'm not sure yet. I'm not asking for confidential information, but could you give me an update? The last mention in the paper was back in January."

Pause. This was like talking to someone on a time delay. I could have sworn he was taking notes. "What's the nature of your interest?"

"Ah. Well, that's tricky to explain. I'm working for the wife—I guess I should make that the widow—of a sheriff's investigator up in Nota Lake. Tom Newquist. Did you know him by any chance?"

"Name doesn't sound familiar."

"He drove down last June to talk to Alfie Toth, but by the time he reached the Gramercy, Toth had moved out. They might have connected later—I'm not sure about that yet—but I'm assuming this was part of an ongoing investigation."

"Uh-unh."

"Do you have any record of Newquist's contacting your department?"

"Hang on." He sounded resigned, a man who couldn't be accused later of thwarting the public's right to know.

He put me on hold. I listened to the mild hissing that signals one's entrance into telephone hyperspace. I sent up a little prayer of thanks that I wasn't being subjected to polka music or John Philip Sousa. Some companies patch you into news broadcasts with the volume pitched too low and you sit there wondering if you're flunking some bizarre hearing test.

Detective Boyd clicked back in. He apparently had the file open on the desk in front of him as I could hear him flipping pages. "You still there," he asked idly.

"I'm here."

"Tom Newquist didn't get in touch with us when he was here, but I do show we've been in communication with Nota Lake."

I said, "Really. I wonder why he didn't let you know he was coming down."

"Gosh, I don't know. That's a stumper," he said blandly.

"If he'd gotten in touch, would there be a note of it?"

"Yes ma'am."

I could see how this was going to go. I was on a fishing expedition and Detective Boyd was responding only to direct questions. Anything I didn't ask, he wasn't going to volunteer. Somehow I had to snag his interest and inspire his cooperation. "Why don't I tell you my problem," I said conversationally. "His widow's convinced her husband was deeply troubled about something."

"Uh-unh."

I could feel my frustration mount. How could this man be so pleasant and so completely obtuse at the same time? I switched gears. "Was Alfie Toth wanted for some crime at the time of his death?"

"Not that I'm aware of. He'd just finished serving time on a conviction for petty theft."

"The desk clerk at the Gramercy says a plainclothes detective came in with a warrant for his arrest."

"Wasn't one of ours."

"You don't show any outstanding warrants?"

"No ma'am, I don't."

"But there must have been *some* connection or Tom Newquist wouldn't have bothered to drive all the way down here."

"I'll tell you what. If this is just a question of satisfying Mrs. Newquist's curiosity, I can't see any reason to share information. Why don't you talk to Nota Lake and see what they have to say. That'd be your best bet."

"Are you telling me you *have* information?"

"I'm telling you I'm not going to reveal the substance of an ongoing investigation to any yahoo who asks. You have knowledge of the facts—something new to contribute—we'd be happy to have you come in."

"Has there been a resolution to the case?"

"Not so far."

"The newspapers indicated that this was being investigated as a homicide."

"That's correct."

"Do you have a suspect?"

"Not at this time. I wouldn't say that, no."

"Any leads?"

"None that I'm willing to tell you about," he said. "You want to make a trip out here, I could maybe have you talk to the watch commander, but as far as giving out information by phone, it ain't gonna fly. I don't mean to cast aspersions, but you could be anyone . . . a journalist."

"God forbid," I said. "Surely you don't think I'm anyone that low."

I could hear him smile. At least he was enjoying

200

himself. He seemed to think about it briefly and then he said, "Let's try this. Why don't you give me your number and if anything comes up I'm at liberty to pass along, I'll be in touch."

"You're entirely too kind."

Detective Boyd laughed. "Have a good day."

FOURTEEN

Olga Toth opened the door to her Perdido condominium wearing a bright yellow outfit that consisted of form-fitting tights and a stretchy cotton tunic, cinched at the waist with a wide white bejeweled plastic belt. The fabric clung to her body like a bandage that couldn't quite conceal the damage time had inflicted on her sixty-year-old flesh. Her knee-high boots looked to be size elevens, white vinyl alligator with a fancy pattern of stitchwork across the instep. She'd had some work done on her face, probably collagen injections given the plumpness of her lips and the slightly lumpy appearance of her cheeks. Her hair was a dry-looking platinum blond, her brown eyes heavily lined, with a startling set of eyebrows drawn in above. I could smell the vermouth on her breath before she said a word.

I'd driven the thirty miles to Perdido in the midst of a drizzling rain, that sort of fine spray that required the constant flip-flop of windshield wipers and the fiercest of concentration. The roadway was slick, the blacktop glistening with a deceptive sheen of water that made driving hazardous. Under ordinary circumstances, I might have delayed the trip for another hour or two, but I was worried the cops would somehow manage to warn Alfie's ex-wife of my interest, urging her to keep her mouth shut if I knocked on her door.

The address I'd been given was just off the beach, a ten-unit complex of two-story frame townhouses within view of the Pacific. Olga's was on the second floor with an exterior stairway and a small sheltered entrance lined with potted plants. The woman who answered the door bell was older than I'd expected and her smile revealed a dazzling array of caps.

"Mrs. Toth?"

She said, "Yes?" Her tone conveyed a natural optimism, as though, having sent in all the forms, having held on to the matching numbers that established her eligibility, she might open the door to someone bearing the keys to her new car or, better yet, that oversized check for several million bucks.

I showed her my card. "Could I talk to you about your ex-husband?"

"Which one?"

"Alfie Toth."

Her smile faded with disappointment, as though there were better ex-husbands to inquire about among her many. "Honey, I'm sorry to be the one to tell you, but he's deceased so if you're here about his unpaid bills, the line forms at the rear."

"This is something else. May I come in?"

"You're not here to serve process," she asked, cautiously.

"Not at all. Honest."

"Because I'm warning you, I put a notice in the paper

the day we separated saying I'm not responsible for debts other than my own."

"Your record's clean as far as I'm concerned."

She studied me, considering, and then stepped back. "No funny business," she warned.

"I'm never funny," I said.

I followed her through the small foyer, watching as she retrieved a martini glass from a small console table. "I was just having a drink in case you're interested."

"I'm fine for now, but thanks."

We entered a living room done entirely in white; trampled-looking, white nylon cut-pile carpeting, white nylon sheers, white leatherette couches, and a white vinyl chair. There was only one lamp turned on and the light coming through the curtains had been subdued by the rain. The room felt damp to me. The glass-and-chrome coffee table bore a large arrangement of white lilies, a pitcher of martini's, several issues of *Architectural Digest*, and a recent issue of *Modern Maturity*. Her eye fell on the latter about the same time mine did. She leaned forward impatiently. "That belongs to a friend. I really hate those things. The minute you turn fifty, the AARP starts hounding you for membership. Not that I'm anywhere close to retirement age," she assured me. She poured herself another drink, adding olives she plucked from a small bowl nearby. She licked her fingertips with enthusiasm. "Olives are the best part," she remarked. Her nails, I noticed, were very long and pink, thick enough to suggest acrylics or poorly done silk overlays.

"What sort of work do you do?" I asked.

She motioned me into a seat at one end of the couch

while she settled at the other end, her arm stretched out along the back. "I'm a cosmetologist and if you don't mind my saying so—"

I held up a hand. "Don't give me beauty tips. I can't handle 'em."

She laughed, an earthy guttural sound that set her breasts ajiggle. "Never hurts to try. You ever get interested in a makeover, you can give me a buzz. I could do wonders with that mop of yours. Now what's this about Alfie? I thought all his problems were over and done with, the poor guy."

I filled her in on the nature of the job I'd been hired to do, thinking that as a widow, she might appreciate Selma Newquist's concern about her husband's mental state in the weeks before he died.

"I remember the name Newquist. He was the one called me a couple weeks after Alfie took off. Said it was important, but it really wasn't urgent, as far as I could tell. I told him Alfie was still around some place and I'd be happy to go looking for him if he'd give me a day or two."

"How long was Alfie here?"

"Two days, maybe three. I don't let any ex of mine stay longer than that. Otherwise, you have fellows camping on your doorstep every time you turn around. They all want the same thing." She lifted her right hand, ticking off the items as she mentioned them. "They want sex, want their laundry done, and a few bucks in their pocket before you send 'em on their way."

"What made Alfie leave the Gramercy?"

"I got the impression he was nervous. I noticed he was jumpy, but he never said why. Alfie was always restless, but I'd say he was looking for a place to hole up. I think he was hoping for the chance to set up permanent residence here, but I wasn't having any. I tried to discourage any long-range plans of his. He was a sweet man, the sweetest. He was twenty years younger than me though you never would have guessed. We were married for eight years. Of course, he was in and out of jail for most of it which is why we lasted as long as we did."

"What was he in jail for?"

She waved the question away. "It was never anything big—bad checks, or petty thievery, or public drunkenness. Sometimes he did worse, which is how he ended up in prison. Nothing violent. No crimes against persons. His problem was he couldn't figure out how to outsmart the system. It wasn't in his nature, so what could you do? You couldn't fault him for being dumb. He was just born that way. He tended to fall into bad company, always taking up with some loser with a harebrained scheme. He was easily dominated. Anybody could lead poor Alfie around by the nose. It all sounded good to him. That's how innocent he was. Most of it ended in disaster, but he never seemed to learn. You had to love that about him. He was good-looking, too, in a goofy sort of way. What he did, he did well, and the rest you might as well write off as a dead loss."

"What was it he did well?"

"He was great in the sack. The man was hung like a donkey and he could fuck all day."

"Ah. And how did you two meet?"

"We met in a bar. This was when I was still doing the singles scene, though I've about given that up. I don't know about you, but these days, I stick to the personal ads. It's a lot more fun. Are you single? You look single."

"Well, I am, but it seems to suit me."

"Oh, I know what you mean. I don't mind living on my own. I have no problem with that. I prefer it, to tell the truth. I just don't know how else to get *laid*."

"You run ads for sex?"

"Well, you don't come right out and say so. That'd be dumb," she remarked. "There's a hundred cute ways to put it. 'Party-Hearty,' 'Girls Just Want to Have Fun,' 'Passionate at Heart Seeks Same.' Use the right terminology and guys get the point."

"But doesn't that make you nervous?"

"What?" she said, her big eyes fixed on me blankly.

"You know, picking up a bed partner through a newspaper ad."

"How else are you going to get 'em? I'm not promiscuous by any stretch, but I've got your normal appetite for these things. Three, four times a week, I get the itch to go lookin' for love." She shimmied in her seat, snapping her fingers to indicate the joys of the bump-and-grind single life, something I'd obviously missed. "Anyway, at the time I met Alfie, I was still cruising the clubs which, believe me, in Perdido really limits your range, not to mention your choices. Looking at Alf, I never guessed his talents would be so impressive. The man never got tired—just kept banging away. I mean, in some ways, it was fortunate he spent so much time in jail." She paused to sip her martini, lifting her eyebrows appreciatively.

I made some bland comment, wondering what might

constitute a proper response to these revelations. "So he was here less than a week last June," I said, trying to steer her back onto neutral ground.

She set the glass on the table. "Something like that. Couldn't have been long, because I met the fellow I'm currently balling at the end of May. Lester didn't take kindly to the idea of Alfie's sleeping on my couch. Men get territorial, especially once they start jumping your bones."

"Where'd he go when he left?"

"Your guess is as good as mine. Last time I saw him he was gathering up his things. Next thing I know, they're asking about his bridgework, trying to identify his body from the crowns on his molars. This was the middle of January so he'd been gone six months."

"Do you think something frightened him into leaving when he did?"

"I didn't think so at the time, but that could have been the case. The cops seemed to think he'd been killed shortly after he took off."

"How'd they pinpoint the time?"

"I asked the same thing, but they wouldn't give me any details."

"Did you identify his body?"

"What was left of it. I'd reported him missing, oh I'd say early September. His parole officer had somehow tracked down my address and telephone number and he was in a tiff because Alfie hadn't been reporting. There he was chewing me out. I told him what he could do with it."

"Why'd you wait so long to call the cops?"

"Don't be silly. Somebody spends as much time as

Alfie did on the wrong side of the law, you don't call the cops just because he hasn't showed his face in two months. He was usually missing, as far as I was concerned. In jail or out of town, on the road . . . who the hell knows? I finally filed a report, but the cops didn't take it seriously until the body showed up at Ten Pines."

"Did the police have a theory about what happened to him?"

She shook her head. "I'll tell you this. He wasn't killed for his money because the man was stone broke."

"You never told me why Newquist was looking for Alfie in the first place."

"That was in regard to a homicide in Nota County. He'd heard Alfie was friends with a fellow whose body was found back in March of last year. I guess they had reason to believe the two were traveling together around the time of this man's death."

"Alfie was a suspect?"

"Oh, honey, the cops will never say that. They think you'll be more cooperative if they tell you they're looking for a potential witness to a crime. In this case, probably true. Alfie was a sissy. He was scared to death of violence. He'd never kill anyone and I'd swear to that on a stack of Bibles."

"How did Tom Newquist find out Alfie was here?"

"The fellow at the hotel told him."

"I mean, in Santa Teresa."

"Oh. I don't know. He never said a word about that. He might have run the name through the computer. Alfie'd just done a little jail time so he'd have popped right up."

"What about the victim? Did Newquist give you the name of the other man?"

"He didn't have to. I knew him through Alfie. Fellow by the name of Ritter. He and Alfie met in prison. This was six years ago at Chino. I forget what Alfie was doing time for at that point, something stupid. Ritter was vicious, a real son of a bitch, but he protected Alfie's backside and they hung around together after they got out. Alfie wanted Ritter to stay here as well, but I said absolutely not. Ritter was a convicted rapist."

"'Ritter,' was the first name or last?"

"Last. His first name was something fruity, maybe Percival. Everybody called him Pinkie."

"What was Alfie's reaction when he heard about Ritter's death?"

"I never had the chance to tell him. I looked all over town for him, but by then he was gone and I figured he took off. As it turns out, he was probably dead within days, at least according to the cops."

"I take it he was good about keeping in touch?"

"The man never went a week without calling to borrow money. He referred to it as his stud fee, but that was just a joke between us. Alfie was proud."

"I'm sure he was," I said.

"I really miss the guy. I mean, Lester's okay, but he can be prissy about certain sexual practices. He's opposed to anything south of the border, if you know what I mean."

"You don't think Lester had anything to do with Alfie's death? He might have been jealous."

"I'm sure he would have been if he'd known, but I never said a word. I told him Alfie was camping out on my couch, but he had no idea we were screwing like bunny rabbits every chance we got. Bend over to tie your shoe, Alfie'd be right on you, the big dumb lug."

"And no one else called or came around looking for him?"

"I was off at work most days so I don't really know what Alfie did with himself, except drink, play the ponies, and watch the soaps on TV. He liked to shop. He dressed sharp so that's where a lot of his money went. Why the credit card companies kept sending him plastic is beyond my comprehension. He filed bankruptcy twice. Anyway, he might have had friends. He usually did. Like I said, he was a sweet guy. You know, horny, but kind."

"He sounds like a nice man," I murmured, hoping God wouldn't strike me dead.

"Well, he was. He wasn't quarrelsome or hard to get along with. He never got in bar fights or said a cross word to anyone. He was just a big dumb Joe with a hard-on," she said, voice wavering. "Seems like, any more, people don't get killed for a reason. It's just something that happens. Alfie was a bumpkin and he didn't always show good sense. Someone could have killed him for the fun of it."

I drove back to Santa Teresa, trying not to think much about the information I'd gleaned. I let thoughts wash over me without trying to put them in order or make any sense of them. I was getting closer to something. I just wasn't sure what it was. One thing seemed certain:

Tom Newquist was on the same track and maybe what he'd found caused him untold distress.

I reached my apartment shortly after three o'clock. The rain had passed for the moment, but the sky was darkly overcast and the streets were still wet. I bypassed the puddles, my furled umbrella tucked under my arm, moving through the gate with a sense of relief at being home. I unlocked my door and flipped on the lights. By then, my hand was beginning to ache mildly and I was tired of coping with the splint. I shed my jacket, went into the kitchenette for water, and took some pain medication. I perched on a stool and removed the gauze wrap from my fingers. I tossed the splint but left the tape in place. The gesture was symbolic, but it cheered me up.

I checked the answering machine, which showed one message. I pressed Replay and heard Tom's contact at the sheriff's department, who'd left me one sentence. "Colleen Sellers here, home until five if you're still interested."

I tried her number. She picked up quickly, almost as though she'd been waiting for the call. Her "Hello" was careful. No infusion of warmth or friendliness.

"This is Kinsey Millhone, returning your call," I said. "Is this Colleen?"

"Yes. Your message said you wanted to get in touch with me regarding Tom Newquist."

"That's right. I appreciate your getting back to me. Actually, this is awkward. I'm assuming you've heard that he passed away." I hate the phrase *passed away* when what you really mean is *died*, but I thought I should practise a little delicacy.

"So I heard."

That was as much as she gave me so I was forced to plunge right on. "Well, the reason I called . . . I'm a private investigator here in town . . ."

"I know who you are. I checked it out."

"Well, good. That saves me an explanation. Anyway, for reasons too complicated to go into, I've been hired by his widow to see if I can find out what was going on the last two months of his life."

"Why?"

"Why?"

"Why is it too complicated to go into?"

"Is there any way we can do this in person?" I asked.

There was a momentary pause, during which I heard an intake of breath that led me to believe she was smoking. "We could meet someplace," she said.

"That would be good. You live in Perdido? I'd be happy to drive down, if you like, or . . ."

"I live in Santa Teresa, not that far from you."

"That's great. Much better. You just let me know when and where."

Again, the pause while she processed. "How about the kiddy park across from Emile's in five minutes."

"See you there," I said, but she was gone by then.

I spotted her from a distance, sitting on one of the swings in a yellow slicker with the hood up. She had swiveled the seat sideways, the chains forming a twisted X at chest height. When she lifted her feet, the chains came unwound, swiveling her feet first in one direction and then another. She tipped back, holding herself in position with her toes. She pushed off. I watched her straighten her legs in a pumping motion that boosted her higher and higher. I thought my approach would interrupt her play, but she continued swinging, her expression somber, her gaze fixed on me.

"Watch this!" she said and at the height of her forward arc she let herself fly out of the swing. She sailed briefly and then landed in the sand, feet together, her arms raised above her head as though as the end of a dismount.

"Bravo."

"Can you do that?"

"Sure."

"Let's see."

Geez, the things I'll do in the line of duty, I thought. I'm a shameless suck-up when it comes to information. I took her place on the swing, backing up as she had until I was standing on tiptoe. I pushed off, holding on to the chains. I leaned back as I straightened my legs and then pumped back, leaning forward, continuing in a rocking motion as the trajectory of the swing increased. I went higher and higher. At the top of the swing, I released myself and flew forward as she had. I couldn't quite stick the landing and was forced to take a tiny side step for balance.

"Not bad. It takes practice," she said charitably. "Why don't we walk? You got your bumbershoot?"

"It's not raining."

She pushed her hood back and looked up. "It will before long. Here. You can share mine."

She put up her umbrella, a wide black canopy above our heads as we walked. The two of us held the shank,

214

forced to walk shoulder to shoulder. Up close, she smelled of cigarettes, but she didn't ever light one in my presence. I placed her in her late forties, with a square face, oversized glasses set in square red frames, and shoulder-length blond hair. Her eyes were a warm brown, her wide mouth pushing into a series of creases when she smiled. She was large-boned and tall with a shoe size that probably compelled her to shop out of catalogs.

"You don't work today?" I asked.

"I'm taking a leave of absence."

"Mind if I ask why?"

"You can ask anything you want. Believe me, I'm experienced at avoiding answers when the questions don't suit. I turn fifty this coming June. I'm not worried about aging, but it does make you take a long hard look at your life. Suddenly, things don't make sense. I don't know what I'm doing or why I'm doing it."

"You have family in town?"

"Not any more. I grew up in Indiana, right outside Evansville. My parents are both gone . . . my dad since 1976, my mom just last year. I had two brothers and a sister. One of my brothers, the one who lived here, was diagnosed with a rare form of leukemia and he was dead in six months. My other brother was killed in a boating accident when he was twelve. My sister died in her early twenties of a botched abortion. It's a very strange sensation to be out on the front lines alone."

"You have any kids?"

She shook her head. "Nope, and that's another thing I question. I mean, it's way too late now, but I wonder about that. Not that I ever wanted children. I know myself well enough to know I'd be a lousy mom, but at this stage of my life, I wonder if I should have done it differently. What about you? You have kids?"

"No. I've been married and divorced twice, both times in my twenties. At that point, I wasn't ready to have children. I wasn't even ready for marriage, but how did I know? My current lifestyle seems to preclude domesticity so it's just as well."

"Know what I regret? I wish now I'd listened more closely to family stories. Or maybe I wish I had someone to pass 'em on to. All that verbal history out the window. I worry about what's going to happen to the family photograph albums once I'm gone. They'll be thrown in the garbage . . . all those aunts and uncles down the tubes. Junk stores, you can sometimes buy them, old black-and-white snapshots with the crinkly edges. The white-frame house, the vegetable garden with the sagging wire fence, the family dog, looking solemn," she said. Her voice dropped away and then she changed the subject briskly. "What'd you do to your hand?"

"A fellow dislocated my fingers. You should have seen them . . . pointing sideways. Made me sick," I said.

We strolled on for a bit. To the right of us, a low wall separated the sidewalk from the sand on the far side. There must have been two hundred yards of beach before the surf kicked in; all of this looking drab in current weather conditions. "How are we doing so far?" I asked.

"In what respect?"

"I assume you're sizing me up, trying to figure out how much you want to tell."

"Yes, I am," she said. "Tom confided in me and I take that seriously. I mean, even if he's dead, why would I betray his trust?"

"That's up to you. Maybe this is unfinished business and you have an opportunity to see it through for him."

"This is not about Tom. This is about his wife," she said.

"You could look at it that way."

"Why should I help her?"

"Simple compassion. She's entitled to peace of mind."

"Aren't we all?" she said. "I never met the woman and probably wouldn't like her even if I did, so I don't give a shit about her peace of mind."

"What about your own?"

"That's my concern."

That was as much as I got out of her. By the time we'd walked as far as the wharf, the rain was beginning to pick up again. "I think I'll peel off here. I'm a block down in that direction. If you decide you have more to tell me, why don't you get in touch."

"I'll think about that."

"I could use the help," I said.

I trotted toward home under a steadily increasing drizzle that matted my hair. What was it with these people? What a bunch of anal-retentives. I decided it was time to quit horsing around. I ducked into the apartment long enough to run a towel through my hair, grab my handbag and umbrella, and lock up again. I retrieved my car and drove the ten blocks to Santa Teresa Hospital.

FIFTEEN

I caught Dr. Yee on his way to the parking lot. I'd left the VW in a ninety-minute spot at the curb across from the hospital emergency room and I was circling the building, intending to enter by way of the main lobby. Dr. Yee had emerged from a side door and was preparing to cross the street to the parking garage. I called his name and he turned. I waved and he waited until I'd reached his side.

Santa Teresa County still utilizes a sheriff-coroner system, in which the sheriff, as an elected official, is also in charge of the coroner's office. The actual autopsy work is done by various forensic pathologists under contract to the county, working in conjunction with the coroner's investigators. Steven Yee was in his forties, a third-generation Chinese American, with a passion for French cooking.

"You looking for me?" He was easily six feet tall, slender and handsome, with a smooth round face. His hair was a straight glossy black streaked with exotic bands of white that he wore combed straight back.

"I'm glad I caught you. Are you on your way home?

I need about fifteen minutes of your time, if you can spare it."

He glanced at his watch. "I'm not due at the restaurant for another hour," he said.

"I heard about that. You have a second career."

He smiled with pleasure, shrugging modestly. "Well, the money's not great, but I make enough here. It's restful to chop leeks instead of . . . other things."

"At least you're skilled with a boning knife," I said.

He laughed. "Believe me, nobody trims meat as meticulously as I do. You ought to come in some night. I'll treat you to a meal that'll make you weep for the pure pleasure."

"I could use that," I said. "You know me and Quarter Pounders with cheese."

"So what's up? Is this work?"

"I'm looking for information about a man named Alfie Toth. Are you familiar with the case?"

"Should be. I did the post," he said. He hooked a thumb in the direction of the building. "Come on back to my office. I'll show you what we have."

"This is great," I said happily, as I followed him. "I understand Toth's death may be related to a suspected homicide in Nota Lake. One of the sheriff's investigators there was working on the case when he died of a heart attack a few weeks back. His name was Tom Newquist. Did he get in touch with you?"

"I know the name, but he didn't contact me directly. I spoke to the Nota Lake coroner by phone and he mentioned him. What's your connection? Is this an insurance claim?"

"I don't work for CF these days. I've got an office in Lonnie Kingman's law firm on Capillo."

"What happened to CF?"

"They fired my sorry butt, which is fine with me," I said. "It was time for a change so now I'm doing mostly freelance work. Newquist's widow hired me. She says her husband was stressed out and she wants me to find out why. Nota Lake law enforcement's been very tight-lipped on the subject and the cops here aren't much better."

"I'll bet."

When we reached the elevator, he punched the Down button and we chatted idly of other matters as we descended into the bowels of the building.

Dr. Yee's office was a small bare box down the hall from the morgue. The ante-room was lined with beige filing cabinets, the office itself barely large enough for his big rolltop desk, his swivel chair, and a plain wooden chair for guests. His medical books had been moved to the shelves of a freestanding bookcase and the top of his desk was now reserved for a neat row of French cookbooks, trussed on either side by a large jar of murky formalin in which floated something I didn't care to inspect. He was using a gel breast implant as a paperweight, securing a pile of loose notes. "Hang on a second and I'll pull the file," he said. "Have a seat."

The chair was stacked with medical journals so I perched on the edge, grateful Dr. Yee was willing to trust me. Dr. Yee was never careless with information, but he wasn't as paranoid as the police detectives. He returned with a file folder and a manila envelope and took his seat in the swivel chair, tossing both on the desk beside me.

"Are those the photographs? Can I see?"

"Sure, but they won't tell you much." He reached for the envelope and extracted a set of color photographs, eight-by-ten prints showing various views of the scene where Alfie Toth had been found. The terrain was clearly rugged: boulders, chaparral, an ancient live oak. "Toth was identified through his skeletal remains, largely dental work. Percy Ritter's body in Nota Lake was found in much the same circumstances; same MO and a similar remote locale. In both cases, it took a while before anyone stumbled across the remains."

I paused, staring at one close-up view with perplexity, not quite sure what I was looking at; probably the lower half of Alfie Toth's body crumpled on the ground. The pelvic bones appeared to be still joined, but the femur, tibia, and fibulas were tangled together in a heap, like bleached kindling. The haphazard skeletal assortment looked like a Halloween decoration badly in need of assembly.

Dr. Yee was saying, "Ritter's mummified body was found fully clothed with various personal items in his pockets . . . expired California driver's license, credit cards. Identification was confirmed by his fingerprints, which had to be reconstructed. Must have been dry out there because bacterial growth and putrefaction are halted when the body moisture diminishes below fifty percent. Ritter's flesh was as stiff as leather, but Kirchner managed to retrieve all but the right-hand thumb and ring finger. Ritter'd had his prints in the system since 1972. What a bad ass. Real scum."

"I didn't know you could salvage prints like that."

He shrugged. "You sometimes have to sever the fingers first. To rehydrate, you can soak 'em in a three percent lye solution or a one percent solution of Eastman Kodak Photo-Flo 200 for a day or two. Another method is to use successive alcohol solutions, starting at ninety percent and gradually decreasing. With Ritter, the first presumption was of suicide, though Kirchner said he had big doubts and the county sheriff did, too. Keep in mind, there wasn't any suicide note at the scene, but there was also no environmental disorder and no signs of trauma on the body. No fractured hyoid to suggest cervical compression, no evidence of knife wounds, skull fractures, gunshot—"

"In other words, no signs of foul play."

"Right. Which is not to say he couldn't have been subdued in some way. Same thing with Toth, except there was no personal ID. Sheriff's department went back through months' worth of missing-persons reports, contacting relatives. They made the initial match that way."

"So what are we looking at?" I asked, turning the photograph so he could see.

"To all appearances, both guys tied a rope around a boulder, put a noose around their necks, pushed the rock through the Y of a tree limb, and hung themselves. It wasn't until later that the similarities came to light."

I stared at him. "That's odd." I glanced down at a photograph, in which I could now see the crisscross of rope circling the circumference of a rock about the size of a large watermelon. Toth's torso and extremities had separated, falling in a tumble on one side of the tree while the upper half of his body, pulled by the weight of the boulder, had fallen on the other still attached by the length of rope.

"Nothing remarkable about the rope, in case you're wondering. Garden variety clothes line available at any supermarket or hardware store," he said. Dr. Yee watched my face. "Not to be racist about it, but the method's more compatible with an Asian sensibility. Some dude out in Nota County, how'd it even occur to him? And then a second one here? I mean, it's possible Toth heard about his pal's alleged suicide and imitated his methodology, but even so, it seems off. As far as I know, the Nota Lake cops kept the specifics to themselves. That was information only shared between agencies."

"Really. If Alfie Toth wanted to kill himself, you'd think he'd blow his brains out; something simple and straightforward, more in keeping with his lifestyle."

Dr. Yee shifted back in his chair with a squeak. "A more plausible explanation is that both victims were killed by the same party. The reason the cops are so paranoid is to avoid all the kooks and the copycats. Someone ups and confesses, you don't want anyone other than the killer in possession of the details. So far the papers haven't gotten wind of it. They know a body was found here, but that's about the extent of it. I'm not sure reporters have put two and two together with the deceased in Nota Lake. That didn't get any play here."

"What's the estimated time of death for Ritter?"

"Oh, he'd been there five years from Kirchner's estimate. A gasoline receipt among his effects was dated

April 1981. Gas station attendant remembers the two of them."

"Quite a gap between deaths," I said. "Have you ever run across a methodology like this?"

"Only in a textbook. That's what makes it curious. Take a look at this." He reached backward and pulled a thin oversized volume from the bottom shelf. "Tomio Watanabe's *Atlas of Legal Medicine*. This was first published in 'sixty-eight, printed in Japan, so it's hard to find these days." He flipped the pages open to a section on hangings and turned the book so I could see. The photographs were of Japanese suicide victims, apparently supplied by various police headquarters and medical examiners' offices in Japan. One young woman had wedged her neck in the V of a tree, which effectively compressed her carotid and vertebral arteries. Another woman had made a double loop of long rope, which she wound around her neck and then put her feet through, achieving strangulation by ligature. In the method Dr. Yee'd referred to, a man tied a rope around a stone, which he placed on a chair. He'd wrapped the same rope around his neck, sat with his back to the chair back, and then tilted the chair forward so the stone rolled off the seat and strangled him. I studied the photographs on adjoining pages, which depicted in graphic detail the ingenuity employed by human beings in extinguishing their lives. In every case, I was looking at the face of despair. I stared at the floor for a moment, running the scenario through my head like a piece of film. "There's no way two men on opposite sides of California would have independently devised the same method."

"Probably not," he said. "Though, given the fact

they were friends, it's possible they overheard someone describe the technique. If you're intent on suicide, the beauty of it is once you topple the boulder through the fork in the tree, there's no way back. Also, death is reasonably quick; not instantaneous, but you'd lose consciousness within a minute or less."

"And these are the only two deaths of this kind that you know of?"

"That's right. I don't think this is serial, but the two have to be connected."

"How'd you hear about Ritter's death?"

"Through Newquist. He'd known about Ritter since his body was discovered back in March of this past year. When a backpacker came across Toth, he reported it to the local sheriff's department and they contacted Nota Lake because of the similar MO."

"Isn't there a chance Toth killed his friend Ritter, hoping to make it look like suicide instead of murder, and then ended up killing himself the same way? There'd be a certain irony in that."

"It's possible," he said dubiously, "but what's your picture? Toth commits a murder and five years pass before he finds himself overwhelmed with guilt?"

"Doesn't make much sense, does it?" I said, in response to his tone. "I talked to his ex-wife and from what she said, he wasn't behaving like a man who was terminally depressed." I checked my watch. It was close to 4:45. "Anyway, I better let you go. I appreciate the information. This has been a big help."

"My pleasure."

*

225

When I got home at five o'clock, Henry's kitchen lights were on and I found him sitting at his kitchen table with a file box in front of him. I tapped on the glass and he motioned me in. "Help yourself to a cup of tea. I just made a pot."

"Thanks." I took a clean mug from the dish rack and poured myself a cup of tea, then sat at the kitchen table watching Henry work.

"These are rebate coupons. A new passion of mine in case you're wondering," he said. Henry had always been enthusiastic about saving money, sitting down daily with the local paper to clip and sort coupons in preparation for his shopping trips.

"Can I help?"

"You can file while I cut," he said. He passed me a pile of proof of purchase seals, which I could see were separated according to the company offering to refund a portion of the price. He was saying, "Short's Drugs has started a Receipt Savers Rebate Club, which allows you to collect your rebates and send them in all at once. There's no point in trying to get fifty cents back when it costs you nearly thirty-five cents for stamps."

"I can't believe the time you put in on this," I remarked as I filed. Over-the-counter diet remedies, detergent, soap, mouthwash.

"Some are products I use anyway so who can resist? Look at this one. Free toothpaste. Makes your smile extra white it says."

"Your smile's already white."

"Suppose I end up preferring the taste of this one. There's no harm in trying something new," he said. "Here's one for shampoo. You get one free if you buy before April First. Only one per customer and I've got mine already, so I kept this for you if you're interested."

"Thanks. You do this in addition to the store coupons?"

"Well, yes, but this takes a lot more patience. Sometimes it takes as long as two to three months, but then you get a nice big check. Fifteen bucks once. Like found money. You'd be surprised how quickly it adds up."

"I'll bet." I took a sip of my tea.

Henry passed me another ragged pile of clippings. "When you finish that batch, you can start on these."

"I don't mean to sound petty," I said, bringing the conversation around to my concerns, "but honestly, Rosie paid more attention to those rowdies than she did to us last night. It didn't hurt my feelings so much as piss me off."

Henry seemed to smile to himself. "Aren't you over-stating your case?"

"Well, it may be too strong a term, but you get my point. Henry, how much children's aspirin do you take these days? I counted fifteen of these."

"I donate the extras to charity. Speaking of pain relievers, how's your hand?"

"Good. Much better. It hardly hurts," I said. "I take it Rosie's attitude doesn't bother you."

"Rosie's Rosie. She's never going to change. If it bugs you, tell her. Don't complain to me."

"Oh right. I see. You want me to take the point."

"Battle of the Titans. I'd like to see that," he remarked.

*

At six, I left Henry's, stopping by my apartment to pick up my umbrella and a jacket. Once again, the rain had eased off, but the cold saturated the air, making me grateful to step into the tavern. Rosie's was quiet, the air scented with the pungent smell of cauliflower, onions, garlic, bacon, and simmering beef. There were two patrons sitting in a booth, but I could see they'd been served. The occasional clink of flatware on china was the only sound I heard.

Rosie was sitting at the bar by herself, absorbed in the evening paper, which was open in front of her. A small television set was turned on at the far end of the bar, the sound muted. There was no sign of William and I realized if I was going to catch her, this would be my only chance. I could feel my heart thump. My bravery seldom extends to interactions of this kind. I pulled out the stool next to hers and perched. "Something smells good."

"Lot of somethings," she said. "I got William fixing deep-fried cauliflower with sour cream sauce. Also hot pickled beef, and beef tongue with tomato sauce."

"My favorite," I said dryly.

Behind us, the door opened and a foursome came in, admitting a rush of cold air before the door banged shut again. Rosie eased down off her stool and moved across the room to greet them, playing hostess for once. The door opened again and Colleen Sellers was suddenly standing in the entrance. What was *she* doing here? So much for my confrontation with Rosie. Maybe Colleen had decided to give me some help.

*

"I don't even know what I'm doing here," she said, glumly. Her blond hair drooped with the damp and her glasses had fogged over from the heat in the place.

"Talking about Tom."

"I guess."

"You want to tell me the rest of it?"

"There's nothing much to tell."

We were seated in the back booth I usually claim as my own. I'd poured her a glass of wine that was now sitting in front of her untouched. She removed her glasses, holding them by the frames while she pulled a paper napkin from the dispenser and cleaned the lenses in a way that made me worry she was scratching them. Without the glasses, she looked vulnerable, the misery palpable in the air between us.

"When did you first meet him?"

"At a conference up in Redding a year ago. He was there by himself. I never did meet his wife. She didn't like to come with him, or at least that's what I heard. I gathered she was a bit of a pain in the ass. Not that he ever admitted it, but other people said as much. I don't know what her gig was. He always spoke of her like she was some kind of goddess." She pushed her hair back from her face and tucked it behind her ears in a style that wasn't flattering. She put on her glasses again and I could see smears on the lenses.

"Did you meet by chance or by design?"

Colleen rolled her eyes and a weary smile played around her mouth. "I can see where you're headed, but okay . . . I'll bite. I knew he was going to be there and I looked him up. How's that?"

I smiled back at her. "You want to tell it your way?"

"I'd appreciate that," she said dryly. "Until the conference in Redding, I only dealt with him by phone. He sounded terrific so naturally, I wanted to meet him in person. We hit it off right away, chatting about various cases we'd worked, at least the interesting ones. You know how it is, trading professional tales. We got talking department politics, his experiences versus mine, the usual stuff."

"I don't mean to sound accusatory, but someone seemed to think the two of you were very chummy."

"Chummy?"

"That you were flirtatious. I'm just telling you what I heard."

"There's no law against flirting. Tom was a doll. I never knew a man yet who couldn't use a little boost to his ego, especially at our age. My god. Who the hell's telling you this stuff? Someone trying to make trouble, I can tell you that."

"How well did you know him?"

"I only saw him twice. No, correction. I saw him three times. It was all work at first, starting with the case he was on."

"What case was that?"

"County sheriff up in Nota Lake found an apparent suicide in the desert, an ex-con named Ritter, who'd hung himself from a branch of a California white oak. Identification was confirmed through his fingerprints and Tom tracked him back as far as his release from Chino in the spring of 'eighty-one. Ritter had family in this area; Perdido to be precise. He talked to them by phone and they told him Ritter'd been traveling with a pal."

"Alfie Toth," I supplied. I was curious to hear her version, but I didn't want her to think I was completely ignorant of the facts.

"How'd you hear about him?" she asked.

"Hey, I have my sources just like you have yours. I know Tom drove down here in June to look for him."

"That's right. I was the one got a line on the guy. Toth had been arrested here on a minor charge. I called Tom and he said he'd be down within a day. This was mid-April. I told him I'd be happy to make the contact, but he preferred doing it himself. I guess he got caught up in work and it was June by the time he made it down here. By then, Toth was gone."

"So Tom never talked to him?"

"Not that I know of. As it turned out, Toth's body was the one found in January of this year. The minute the ID was made, I called Tom. The MO was the same for both Ritter and Toth and that was worrisome. The two deaths had to be related, but it was tough to determine what the motivation might have been."

"From what I hear, the murders were separated by a five-year time gap. You have a theory about that?"

I could see her mouth pull down and she wagged her head to convey her ambivalence. "This was one time when Tom and I didn't agree on anything. It could have been a double-cross . . . you know, a bank heist or burglary with Ritter and his sidekick betraying an accomplice. Fellow catches up with them and kills Ritter on the spot. Then it takes another five years to hunt down his pal, Toth."

"What was Tom's idea?"

"Well, he thought Toth might have been a witness to

Ritter's murder. Something happens in the mountains and Pinkie Ritter dies. Toth manages to get away and eventually the killer catches up with him."

I said, "Or maybe Alvin Toth killed Ritter and someone else came along and avenged Ritter's death."

She smiled briefly. "As a matter of fact, I suggested that myself, but Tom was convinced the perpetrator was the same in both cases."

I thought about Dr. Yee's assessment, which was the same as Tom's. "It would help if I knew how to get in touch with Ritter's family."

"I can give you the phone number. I don't have it with me, but I could call you later if you like."

"That'd be great. One other thing. I know this is none of my business, but were you in love with Tom? Because that's what I'm picking up, reading between the lines," I said.

Her body language altered and I could see her debate with herself about how much to reveal. "Tom was loyal as a dog, completely devoted to his wife, which he let me know right off the bat. Ain't that always the way? All the good men are married."

"So they say."

"But I'll tell you something. We had real chemistry between us. It's the first time I ever understood the term *soul mate*. You know what I mean? We were soul mates. No kidding. It was like finding myself in this other guise ... my spiritual counterpart ... and that was heady stuff. We'd be in a room together with five or six hundred other people and I always knew where he was. It was like tentacles stretching all the way across the auditorium. I wouldn't even have to look for him. The bond was that strong. There wasn't anything I couldn't say to him. And laugh? God, we laughed."

"You go to bed with him?" I asked, casually.

A blush began to saturate Colleen's cheeks. "No, but I would have. Hell, I was so crazy about him I broached the subject myself. I was shameless. I was wanton. I'd have taken him on any basis . . . just to be with him once." She shook her head. "He wouldn't do it, and you know why? He was honorable. Decent. Can you imagine the gall of it in this day and age? Tom was an honorable man. He made a promise to be faithful and he meant it. That's one of the things I admired most about him."

"Maybe it's just as well. He wouldn't have been good at deceit even if he'd been willing to try."

"So I've told myself."

"You miss him," I said.

"I've cried every day since I heard about his death. I never even had the chance to say goodbye to him."

"It must be tough."

"Awful. It's just awful. I miss him more than I missed my own mother when she died. So maybe if I'd slept with him, I'd have had to kill myself or something. Maybe the loss and the pain would have been imposs-ible to bear."

"You might have had less respect for him if he'd given in."

"That's a risk I'd have taken, given half a chance."

"At any rate, I'm sorry for your pain."

"No sorrier than I am. I'm never going to find another guy like him. So what can you do? You soldier on. At least his wife has the luxury to mourn in public. Is she taking it hard?"

"That's why she hired me, trying to find relief."

Colleen looked away from me casually, trying to conceal her interest. "What's she like?"

I thought for a moment, trying to be fair. "Generous with her time. Terribly insecure. Efficient. She smokes. Sort of hard-looking, platinum blond hair teased out to here. She has slightly gaudy taste and she's crazy about her son, Brant. This was Tom's stepson."

"Do you like her? Is she nice?"

"People claim she's neurotic, but I do like the woman. A few don't, but that's true of all of us. There's always someone who thinks we're dogshit."

"Did she love him?"

"Very much, I'd say. It was probably a good marriage ... maybe not perfect, but it worked. She doesn't like the idea of his dying with unfinished business."

"Back to that," she said.

"I'd do the same for you if you hired me to find answers."

Colleen's gaze came back to mine. "You thought it was me. That we were having an affair."

"It crossed my mind."

"If I'd had an affair with him, would you have told his wife the truth?"

"No. What purpose would it serve?"

"Right." She was silent for a moment.

"Do you know why Tom was so distressed?" I asked.

"I might."

"Why so protective?"

"It's not up to me to ease her mind," she said. "Who's easing mine?"

I held my hands up in surrender. "I'm just asking the question. You have to do as you see fit."

"I have to go," she said abruptly, gathering up her coat. "I'll call you later with the phone number for Ritter's daughter."

I held a finger up. "Hang on. I just remembered. I have something for you if you're interested." I reached into the outer zippered compartment of my shoulder bag and pulled out one of the black-and-white photographs of Tom at the April banquet. "I had these done up in case I needed 'em. You might like to have something to remember him by."

She took the picture without comment, a slight smile playing across her mouth as she studied it.

I said, "I never met him myself, but I thought it captured him."

She looked up at me with tears rimming her eyes. "Thank you."

SIXTEEN

When I returned from my run the next morning, there was a message from Colleen Sellers on my answering machine, giving me the name and Perdido address of a woman named Dolores Ruggles, one of Pinkie Ritter's daughters. As this represented the only lead I had, I gassed up the VW and headed south on 101 as soon as I was showered and dressed.

On my left, I could see fields under cultivation, the newly planted rows secured by layers of plastic sheeting as slick and gray as ice. Steep hills, rough with low-growing vegetation, began to crowd up against the highway. On my right, the bleak Pacific Ocean thundered against the shore. Surfers in black wetsuits waited on rocking boards like a scattered flock of sea birds. The rains had moved on, but the sky was still white with a ceiling of sluggish clouds and the air was thick with the mingled scents of brine and recent precipitation. Snow would be falling in the high Sierras near Nota Lake.

I took the Leeward off-ramp and made two left turns, crossing over the freeway again in search of the street where Dolores Ruggles lived. The neighborhood was a warren of low stucco structures, narrow streets intersecting one another repeatedly. The house was a plain box, sitting in a plain treeless yard with scarcely a bush or a tuft of grass to break up the monotonous flat look of the place. The porch consisted of a slab of concrete with one step leading up to the front door and a small cap of roofing to protect you as you rang the bell, which I did. The door was veneer with long sharp splinters of wood missing from the bottom edge. It looked like a dog had been chewing on the threshold. .

The man who opened the door was drying his hands on a towel tucked into the waist of his trousers. He was easily in his sixties, maybe five-foot-eight, with a coarsely lined face and a thinning head of gray-white hair the color of wood ash. His eyes were hazel, his brows a tangle of wiry black and gray. "Keep your shirt on," he said, irritably.

"Sorry. I thought the bell was broken. I wasn't even sure anyone was home. I'm looking for Dolores Ruggles."

"Who the hell are you?"

I handed him my card, watching his lips move while he read my name. "I'm a private investigator," I said.

"I can see that. It says right here. Now we got that established, what do you want with Dolores? She's busy at the moment and doesn't want to be disturbed."

"I need some information. Maybe you can help me and we can spare her the imposition. I'm here about her father."

"The little shithead was murdered."

"I'm aware of that."

"Then what's it to you?"

"I'm trying to find out what happened."

"What difference does it make? The man is D-E-A-D dead and not soon enough to suit my taste. I've spent years coping with all the damage he did."

"Could I come in?"

He stared at me. "Help yourself," he said abruptly and turned on his heel, leaving me to follow. I scurried after him, taking a quick mental photograph as we passed through the living room. Not to sound sexist, but the room looked as if it had been designed by a man. The floors were bare hardwood, stained dark. I noted a tired couch and a sagging upholstered chair, both shrouded by heavy woven Indian-print rugs. I thought the coffee table was antiqued, but I could see as I passed the only patina was dust. The walls were lined with books: upright, sideways, slanting, stacked, packed two deep on some shelves, three deep on others. The accumulation of magazines, newspapers, junk mail, and catalogs suggested a suffocating indifference to tidiness.

"I'm doing dishes out here," he said, as he moved into the kitchen. "Grab a towel and you can pitch in. You might as well be useful as long as you're picking my brain. By the way, I'm Homer, Dolores's husband. Mr. Ruggles to you."

His tone had shifted from outright rudeness to something gruff, but not unpleasant. I could see he'd been rather good-looking in his day; not wildly handsome, but something better—a man with a certain amount of character and an appealing air. His skin was darkly tanned and heavily speckled with sun damage, as if he'd spent all his life toiling in the fields. His shirt was an earth brown with an elaborately embroidered yoke done in threads of gold and black. He wore cowboy boots that I suspected were intended to add a couple of inches to his height.

By the time I reached the kitchen, he'd turned on the water again and he was already back at work, washing plates and glassware. "Towel's in there," he said, nodding at the drawer to his immediate left. I took out a clean dish towel and reached for a plate still hot from the rinse water. "You can stack those on the kitchen table. I'll put 'em up when we're done."

I glanced at the table. "Uhm, Mr. Ruggles, the table needs to be wiped. Do you have a sponge?"

Homer turned and gave me a look. "This is a telling trait of yours, isn't it?"

"Oh, sure," I said.

"Skip the Mr. Ruggles bit. It sounds absurd."

"Yes, sir."

That netted me half a smile. He wrung out the cloth and tossed it in my direction with a shake of his head. I wiped off the table top, setting several items aside: newspaper; salt-and-pepper shakers shaped like the Wolf and Little Red Riding Hood; a clutch of pill bottles with Dolores's name plastered on them, along with various warning labels. Whatever she was taking, she was supposed to avoid alcohol, excessive exposure to sunlight, and the operation of heavy machinery. I wondered if this referred to cars, tractors, or Amtrak locomotives. When I'd finished, I handed him the rag and then picked up the dish towel and resumed wiping the plate.

"So what's the deal?" he said belatedly. "What's your

interest in Pinkie Ritter? Nice girl like you should be ashamed."

"I didn't know anything about him until yesterday. I've been tracking down a friend of his, who may have been . . . Could we just skip this part? It's almost too tricky to explain."

"You're talking Alfie Toth."

"Thank you. That's right. Everybody seems to know about him."

"Yeah, well, Alfie was a birdbrain. Women thought he was attractive, but I couldn't see it myself. How can you think some guy's handsome when you know he's dim? To my way of thinking, it spoils the whole effect. I think he hung out with my father-in-law for protection, which just goes to show you how dumb he was."

"You knew Alfie was dead?"

"You bet. The police told us about it when his body turned up. They came around asking the same question you probably want answered, which is what's the connection and who did what to whom? I'll give you the same answer I gave them. I don't know."

"What's the story on Pinkie? I take it you didn't think much of him."

"That's a gross understatement. I really hated his guts. Whoever killed Pinkie saved me life in prison. Pinkie had six kids—three sons and three daughters— and mistreated every one of them from the day they were born 'til they got big enough to fight back. Nowadays there's all this talk of abuse, but Pinkie did the real thing. He punched them, burned them, made 'em drink vinegar and hot sauce for talking back to him. He locked them in closets, set them out in the cold. He screwed 'em, starved 'em, threatened them. He hit 'em with belts, boards, metal pipes, sticks, hairbrushes, fists. Pinkie was the meanest son of a bitch I ever met and that's goin' some."

"Didn't anybody intervene?"

"People tried. Lot of people blew the whistle on him. Trick was trying to prove it. Teachers, guidance counselors, next-door neighbors. Sometimes Children's Services managed to take the kids away from him and foster them out. Judge always gave 'em back." He shook his head. "Pinkie knew how the game was played. He kept a clean house—the kids saw to that—and he did like to cook—that was his specialty. It's what he did for a living when he wasn't breaking their heads or breaking the law. Social workers came around and everything looked fine. Kids knew better than to open their mouths. Dolores says she can remember the six of them lined up in the living room, answering questions just as nice as you please. Pinkie wouldn't be in the room, but he was always somewhere close. Kids knew better than to rat on him or they'd be dead by dark. They'd stand there and lie. Said social workers knew, but couldn't get anything on him without their assistance. Only thing saved 'em was his getting thrown in jail."

"What about his wife? Where was she all this time?"

"Dolores thinks he killed her though it couldn't be proved. He claims she ran off with some barfly and was never heard from again. Dolores says she remembers as a kid waking up in the dead of night. Pinkie was out in the woods behind the house with a power saw. Lantern on the ground throwing these big shadows up against the trees. Moths fluttering around the light. She still has nightmares about that. She was the baby in the family, six years old at the time. I think the oldest was fifteen. She went out there next day. The ground was all turned, probably to hide the blood. She still remembers the smell—like a package of chicken when it's gone funny and has to be thrown out. Mom was never seen nor heard from again."

"Pinkie sounds like a very nasty piece of work."

"The worst."

"So anybody could have killed him, including one of his kids. Is that what you're saying?"

"That would cover it," he said. "Of course, by the time he died, they were out from under his control. The rest of the kids had scattered to hell and gone. Couple of 'em still in California, though we don't see 'em all that much." Homer finished the last dish and turned the water off. I continued drying silverware while he put away the clean plates.

"When did you see him last?"

"Five years ago in March. The minute he got out of Chino, he headed straight up here, arrived on the Twenty-fifth and stayed a week."

"Good memory," I remarked.

"The cops asked me about that so I looked it up. How I pinpointed the date is I withdrew five hundred bucks from a bank account the day Pinkie left. I counted backward from that and the date stuck in my mind. Anything else you want to quiz me about?"

"I didn't mean to interrupt. Go on."

"Dolores was the only kid of his still living in the area so naturally, he felt she owed him room and board for as long as he liked."

242

"She agreed to that?"

"Of course."

"Didn't you object?"

"I did, but that was an argument I couldn't win. She felt guilty. She's a hell of a gal and what she's endured, believe me, you don't want to know—but the upshot is, she's anxious to please, easily manipulated—especially when it came to him. She wanted that man's love. Don't ask me to explain, given what she suffered. He was still Daddy to her and she couldn't turn him away. He was just like he always was: demanding, critical. He refused to lift a finger, expecting her to wait on him hand and foot. I finally got fed up and told him to clear out. Pinkie says, 'Fine, no problem. I won't stay where I'm not wanted. To hell with you,' he says. He was sore as a boil and feeling much put upon, but I was damned if I'd back down."

"Toth was with him at the time?"

"Off and on. I think Alfie's ex-wife lived in town somewhere. He mooched off her when he wasn't here mooching off us."

"And the two left together?"

"As far as I know. At least, that was the plan."

"And where were they headed?"

"Los Angeles. You piece it together later and it turns out they stole a car in Los Angeles and drove up to Lake Tahoe."

"What about Pinkie's parole officer? Wasn't he supposed to report in?"

"Hey, you're talking a career criminal. Following the rules wasn't exactly his strong suit. Who the hell knows how he got away with it? Same with Toth."

"You think someone could have been after them?"

"I wouldn't know," he said. "Pinkie didn't act like he was worried. Why? You think someone might have been trailing them?"

"It's possible," I said.

"Yeah, well it's also possible Pinkie overstepped his bounds for once. He was one of those little guys, chip on his shoulder and feisty as all get out. I can't say that about Alfie. He seemed harmless. Pinkie's another matter. Whoever killed Pinkie should get a medal, in my opinion. And don't quote me. Dolores gets upset if she hears me talkin' like that. I notice I'm doing all the talking."

"I appreciate that."

"This is good. I appreciate your appreciation. Now it's your turn. What's a private investigator doing in the middle of a homicide investigation? Last I heard they didn't have a suspect so you can't be working for the public defender's office."

Given his cooperation, I thought he was entitled to an explanation. I filled him in on the situation, beginning with Selma Newquist and ending with Colleen Sellers. The only thing I omitted were details of the two killings. He didn't seem curious about specifics and I wouldn't have revealed the information for all the money in the world. In the meantime, on an almost subliminal level, I could hear an odd series of voices from another room. At first, I thought the sound was coming from a radio, or television set, but the phrases were repeated, the tone lifeless and mechanical. Homer heard it, too, and his gaze caught mine. He tilted his head in the direction of the short hallway that seemed to lead into a back bedroom. "Dolores's back there. You want to talk to her?"

"If you think it's okay."

"She can handle it," he said. "Give me a second and I'll tell her what's going on. She might have something to add."

He moved down the hall to the door, tapping once before he entered. As he eased through the opening, I felt a moment's unease. Here I was in a strange house in the company of a man I'd never laid eyes on before. I had taken him at face value, trusting him on instinct though I wasn't sure why. Really, I only had his word for it that Dolores was in the other room. I had one of those flash fantasies of him emerging from the bedroom with a butcher knife in hand. Fortunately, life, even for a private eye, is seldom this interesting. The door opened again and Homer motioned me in.

At first sight, I thought Dolores Ruggles couldn't have been a day over twenty-five. Later, I found out that she was twenty-eight, which still seemed too young to be married to a man Homer's age. Slim, petite, she sat at a workbench in a room filled with Barbie dolls. Floor to ceiling, wall to wall, dressed in an astonishing array of styles, these bland plastic women were decked out in miniature sun dresses, evening clothes, suits, furs, shorts, capes, pedal pushers, bathing suits, baby doll pajamas, sheaths—each outfit complete with appropriate accessories. There was a whole row of Barbie brides, though I'd never thought of her as married. The row below showed twenty Barbies uniformed as flight attendants and nurses, which must have represented the entire gambit of career options available to her. Some of the dolls were still in their boxes and some were freestanding, affixed to round plastic mounts. There was a row of seated Barbies—black, Hispanic, blonde, brunette—their long perfect legs extended like a chorus line, all shoeless, their unblemished limbs ending in nearly pointed toes. Their arms were long and impossibly smooth. Their necks must have contained extra vertebrae to support the weight of their tousled manes of hair. I confess I found myself at a loss for words. Homer leaned against the open door, watching for my reaction.

I could tell something was expected of me so I said, "Amazing," in what I hoped was a properly respectful tone.

Homer laughed. "I thought you'd like that. I don't know a woman alive who can resist a room full of dolls."

I said, "Ah."

Dolores glanced at me shyly. She had a doll in her lap, not a Barbie to all appearances, but some other type. With a little hammer and an X-acto knife, she was cutting open its stomach. There was a box of identical little plastic girls, sexless, unmarred, standing close together with their chests pierced in a pattern of holes like those old-fashioned radio speakers. Beside them, there was a box of little girls' heads, eyes demurely closed, a smile turning up the corners of each set of perfect lips. "Chatty Cathys," she said. "It's a new hobby. I fix their voices so they can talk again."

"That's great."

Homer said, "I'll leave you girls to your own devices. You have a lot you want to talk about."

He closed me into the room with her, as pleased with himself as a parent introducing two new best friends to each other. Clearly, he hadn't guessed my unfortunate history with surrogate children. My first, a Betsy Wetsy, if she'd survived, would have had to enter therapy at some point in her life. At age six, I thought it was a bore to be constantly feeding her those tiny bottles of water and it annoyed me no end every time she peed in my lap. Once I figured out it was the water, I quit feeding her altogether and then I used her as the pedestrian I ran over with my trike. This was my definition of motherly love and probably explains why I'm not a parent today.

"How many Barbies do you have?" I asked, feigning enthusiasm for the little proto-women.

"A little over two thousand. That's the star of my collection, a number one Barbie still in her original package. The seal's been broken, but she's in near-mint condition. I'm afraid to tell you what I paid," she said. Her speech was uninflected, her manner without affect. She made little eye contact, addressing most of her comments to the doll as she worked. "Homer's always been very supportive."

"I can see that," I said.

"I'm a bit of a purist. A lot of collectors are interested in others in the line—you know, Francie, Tuttie and Todd, Jamie, Skipper, Christie, Cara, Casey, Buffy. I never cared for them myself. And certainly not Ken. Did you have a Barbie as a kid?"

"I can't say I did," I said. I picked one up and examined her. "She looks like she's suffering from some sort of eating disorder, doesn't she? What prompted you to get into Chatty Cathys? That seems far afield for a Barbie purist."

"Most of the Chatties aren't mine. I'm repairing them for a friend who runs a business doing this. It's not as far-fetched as it seems. Chatty Cathy was introduced in 1960, the year after Barbie. Chatty Cathy was more realistic—freckles, buck teeth, little pot belly—this in addition to her ability to speak. Even with Barbie, 1967 to 1973 is known as the Talking Era, which includes the Twist 'n' Turn dolls. Few people realize that."

"I know I didn't," I said. "What's that thing?"

"That's the little three-inch vinyl record of Cathy's sayings. When you pull the string, it activates a spring that makes that little rubber belt drive the turntable. The early versions of the doll had eleven sayings, but that was increased to eighteen. Odd thing about Chatties is that no two look alike. Of course, they were mass-produced, but they all seem to be different. It's almost creepy in some ways. Anyway, I'm sure you didn't drive all the way down here to talk about dolls. You're interested in my father."

"Homer filled me in, but I'd like to hear your version. I understand he and Alfie Toth spent some time with you just after they were released from Chino."

"That's right. Pops was feeling sorry for himself because none of the other kids wanted anything to do with him. He tried to spend a night with my brother, Clint—he lives down in Inglewood by the L.A. airport. Clint's still bitter about Pops. He refused to let him in, but he told him he could sleep in the toolshed if he wanted to. Pops was furious, of course, so he left in a huff, but not before he broke into Clint's house. Him and Alfie waited 'til Clint was gone, stole his cash, and busted up all his furniture."

"That must have been a big hit. Did Clint report it to the police?"

Dolores seemed startled, the first real reaction I'd seen. "Why would he do that?"

"I've heard there was a plainclothes detective trying to serve a warrant against Toth around the time of his death. I'm wondering if it dated back to that same incident."

Dolores shook her head. "I'm sure not. Clint would never do a thing like that. He might not want Pops in his house, but he'd never snitch on him. It's odd, but when my sister Mame called—this was just about a year ago—to say they'd found his body, I started laughing so hard I peed my pants. Homer had to call the doctor when it turned out I couldn't quit. Doctor gave me a shot to calm me down. He said it was hysteria, but it was actually relief. We hadn't heard from him for five years by then so I guess I was waiting for the other shoe to drop."

"Why do you think he went from Clint's to Lake Tahoe?"

"My sister lives up there. Or one of them, at any rate. Not in Lake Tahoe exactly, but that vicinity."

"Really? I've been curious what prompted him to travel in that direction."

"I don't think Mame's husband was any happier to see him than Homer was."

"How long was he with her?"

"A week or so. Mame told me later him and Alfie

went off to go fishing and that's the last anyone ever saw Pops as far as I know."

"Do you think I could talk to her? I'm sure the police have covered this ground, but it would be helpful to me."

"Oh, sure. She isn't hard to find. She works as a clerk in the sheriff's department up there."

"Up there where?"

"Nota Lake. Her name is Margaret, but everybody in the family calls her Mame."

SEVENTEEN

When I got home, Henry was in the backyard, kneeling in the flower bed. I crossed the lawn, pausing to watch him at work. He was aware of my presence, but seemed content with the quiet. He wore a white T-shirt and farmer's pants with padded knees. His feet were bare, long, and bony, the high arches very white against the faded grass. The air was sweet and mild. Even with the noon sun directly overhead, the temperature was moderate. I could already see crocuses and hyacinths coming up in clusters beside the garage. I sat down on a wooden lawn chair while he turned the soil with a hand trowel. The earth was soft and damp, worms recoiling from the intrusion when his efforts disturbed them. His rose bushes were barren sticks, bristling with thorns, the occasional leaf bud suggesting that spring was on its way. The lawn, which had been dormant much of the winter, was beginning to waken with the encouragement of recent rains. I could see a haze of green where the new blades were beginning to push up through the brown. "People tend to associate autumn with death, but spring always seems a lot closer to me," he remarked.

"Why's that?"

"There's no deep philosophical significance. Somehow in my history, a lot of people I love have ended up dying this time of year. Maybe they yearn to look out the window and see new leaves on the trees. It's a time of hope and that might be enough if you're on your way out; allows you to let go, knowing the world is moving on as it always has."

"I have to go back to Nota Lake," I said.

"When?"

"Sometime next week. I'd like to hang out here long enough to get my hand back in working order."

"Why go at all?"

"I have to talk to someone."

"Can't you do that by phone?"

"It's too easy for people to tell lies on the phone. I like to see faces," I said. I was silent, listening to the homely chucking of his trowel in the dirt. I pulled my legs up and wrapped my arms around my knees. "Remember in the old days when we talked about vibes?"

I could see Henry smile. "You have bad vibes?"

"The worst." I held up my right hand and tried flexing the fingers, which were still so swollen and stiff I could barely make a fist.

"Don't go. You don't have anything to prove."

"Of course I do, Henry. I'm a girl. We're always having to prove something."

"Like what?"

"That we're tough. That we're as good as the guys, which I'm happy to report is not that hard."

"If it's true, why do you have to prove it?"

"Comes with the turf. Just because we believe it, doesn't mean guys do."

"Who cares about men? Don't be macha."

"I can't help it. Anyway, this isn't about pride. This is about mental health. I can't afford to let some guy intimidate me like that. Trust me, somewhere up in Nota Lake he's laughing his ass off, thinking he's run me out of town."

"The Code of the West. A girl's gotta do what a girl's gotta do."

"It feels bad. The whole thing. I don't remember feeling this much dread. That son of a bitch *hurt* me. I hate giving him the opportunity to do it again."

"At least your tetanus shot's up to date."

"Yeah, and my butt still hurts. I got a knot on my hip the size of a hard-boiled egg."

"So what worries you?"

"What worries me is I got my fingers dislocated before I knew jack-shit. Now that I'm getting closer, what's the guy going to do? You think he'll go down without trying to take me with him?"

"Phone's ringing," he remarked.

"God, Henry. How can you hear that? You're eighty-six years old."

"Three rings."

I was off the chair and halfway across the yard by then. I left my door open and caught the phone on the fly, just as the machine kicked in. I pressed STOP, effectively cutting off the message. "Hello, hello, hello."

"Kinsey, is that you? I thought this was your machine."

"Hi, Selma. You lucked out. I was out in the yard."

"I'm sorry to have to bother you."

"Not a problem. What's up?"

"Someone's been searching Tom's study. I know this sounds odd, but I'm sure someone came in here and moved the items on his desk. It's not like the room was trashed, but something's off. I can't see that anything's missing and I don't know how I'd prove it even if there was."

"How'd they get in?"

She hesitated. "I was only gone for an hour, maybe slightly more. I hardly ever lock the door for short periods like that."

"What makes you so sure someone was there?"

"I can't explain. I'd been sitting in Tom's den earlier, before I went out. I was feeling depressed and it seemed like a comfort just to sit in his chair. You know how it is when you think about things. You're aware of your surroundings because your gaze tends to wander while your mind is elsewhere. I guess I was realizing how much work you'd done. Anyway, when I got home, I set my handbag on the kitchen table and went back to the car. I'd picked up some boxes to finish packing Tom's books. The minute I walked into his den I could see the difference."

"You haven't had any visitors?"

"Oh, please. You know how people have been treating me. I might as well hang out a sign . . . 'Town siren. Straying husbands apply here.'"

"What about Brant? How do you know he wasn't in there looking for something on Tom's desk?"

"I asked him, but he was at Sherry's until a few

minutes ago. I had him check the perimeter, but there's no sign of forced entry."

"Who'd bother to force entrance with all the doors unlocked?" I said. "Can Brant tell if anything's missing?"

"He's in the same boat I'm in. It's certainly nothing obvious, if it's anything at all. Whoever it was seemed to work with great care. It was only coincidental that I'd been in there this morning or I don't think I'd have noticed. Do you think I should call the sheriff's office?"

"Yeah, you better do that," I said. "Later, if it turns out something's been stolen, you can follow up."

"That's what Brant said." There was a tiny pause while she changed tacks, her voice assuming a faintly injured tone. "I must say, I've been upset about your lack of communication. I've been waiting to hear from you."

"Sorry, but I haven't had the chance. I was going to call you in a bit," I said. I noticed how defensive I sounded in response to her reproof.

"Now that I have you on the line, could you tell me what's happening? I assume you're still working even if you haven't kept in touch."

"Of course." I controlled my desire to bristle and I filled her in on my activities the past day and a half, sidestepping the personal aspects of Tom's relationship with Colleen Sellers. Telling a partial truth is much harder than an outright lie. Here I was, trying to protect her, while she was chiding me for neglect. Talk about ungrateful. I was tempted to tell all, but I repressed the urge. I kept my tone of voice professional, while my inner kid hollered *Up yours*. "Tom came down here in

June as part of an investigation. Do you remember the occasion? He was probably gone overnight."

"Yes," she said, slowly. "It was two days. What's the relevance?"

"There was a homicide down here Tom felt was connected to some skeletal remains found in Nota County last spring."

"I know the case you're referring to. He didn't say much about it, but I know it bothered him. What about it?"

"Well, if we're talking about an active homicide investigation, I don't have the authority. I'm a private investigator, which is the equivalent of doing freelance research. I can't, even on your say-so, stick my nose into police business."

"I don't see why not. Surely, there's no law against asking questions."

"I *have* asked questions and I'm telling you what I found. Tom was stressed out about matters that had nothing to do with you."

"Why didn't he tell me what it was, if that's true?"

"You were the one who said he played things close to his chest, especially when it came to work."

"Well yes, but if this is strictly professional, then why would someone go to all the trouble to search the house?"

"Maybe the department needed his notes or his files or a telephone number or a missing report. It could be anything," I said, rattling off the possibilities as quickly as they occurred to me.

"Why didn't they call and ask?"

"How do I know? Maybe they were in a hurry and

you weren't home," I said, exasperated. It all sounded lame, but she was backing me into corners and it was annoying me no end.

"Kinsey, I am paying you to get to the bottom of this. If I'd known you weren't going to help, I could have used that fifteen hundred dollars to get my teeth capped."

"I'm doing what I can! What do you want from me?" I said.

"Well, you needn't take *that* attitude. A week ago, you were cooperative. Now all I'm hearing are excuses."

I had to bite my tongue. I had to talk in very distinct, clipped syllables to keep from screaming at her. I took a deep breath. "Look, I have one lead left. As soon as I get up there, I'll be happy to check it out, but if this is sheriff's department business, then it's out of my hands."

There was one of those silences that sounded like it contained an exclamation point. "If you don't want to finish the job, why don't you come right out and say so?"

"I'm not saying that."

"Then when are you coming back?"

"I'm not sure yet. Next week. Maybe Tuesday."

"Next *week*?" she said. "What's wrong with today? If you got in your car now, you could be here in six hours."

"What's the big hurry? This has been going on for weeks."

"Well, for one thing, you still owe me five hundred dollars' worth of work. For that kind of money, I would think you'd want to get here as soon as possible."

"Selma, I'm not going to sit here and argue about this. I'll do what I can."

"Wonderful. What time shall I expect you?"

"I have no idea."

"Surely, you can give me *some* idea when you might arrive. I have other obligations. I'll be gone all day tomorrow. I go to ten o'clock service and then spend some time with my cousin down in Big Pine. I can't sit around waiting for you to show up any time it suits. Besides, if you're coming, I'll need to make arrangements."

"I'll call when I get there, but I'm not going to stay at the Nota Lake Cabins. I hate that place and I won't be put in that position. It's too remote and it's dangerous."

"Fine," she said, promptly. "You can stay here at the house with me."

"I wouldn't dream of imposing. I'll find another motel so there won't be any inconvenience for either one of us."

"It's no inconvenience. I could use the company. Brant thinks it's high time he moved back to his place. He's already in the process of packing up. The guest room is always ready. I insist. I'll have supper waiting and no arguments about that, please."

"We'll talk about it when I get there," I said, trying to conceal my irritation. I was rapidly reassessing my opinion of the woman, ready to cast my vote with her legions of detractors. This was a side of her I hadn't seen before and I was churning with indignation. Of course, I noticed I'd already started revising my mental timetable, preparing to hit the road as soon as possible. Having consented, in effect, I now found myself wanting to get it over with. I shortened the fare-thee-wells, trying to get her off the phone while I could.

The minute I replaced the receiver, I picked it up again and placed a call to Colleen Sellers. While the interminable ringing of her line went on, I could feel my impatience mount. "Come on, come on. Be there..."

"Hello?"

"Colleen, it's Kinsey here."

"What can I do for you?"

She didn't sound that thrilled to hear from me, but I was through pussy-footing around. "I just spent thirty minutes with Pinkie Ritter's daughter Dolores and her husband. Turns out Pinkie has another daughter in Nota Lake, which is why he and Alfie went up there in the first place."

"And?"

"This is someone I've met, a woman named Margaret who works for the sheriff's department as a clerk. I'm going to have to go back up there and talk to her again, but I can't go without knowing what I'm up against."

"Why call me? I can't help."

"Yes, you can..."

"Kinsey, I don't know anything about this and frankly, I'm annoyed you keep pressing the point."

"Well, *frankly*, I guess I'll just have to risk your irritation. What's the matter with you, Colleen?"

"Does it ever occur to you that I might find this painful? I mean, I'm sorry as hell for Selma, but she's not the only one who's suffered a loss. I was in love with him, too, and I don't appreciate your constantly picking at the wound."

"Oh, really. Well, it's interesting that you should say

so because you want to know what I think is going on? I think it pisses you off that you never had any power or any control in that relationship. Tom may have taken the moral high ground, acting from his lofty-sounding principles, but the fact is he left you with nothing and this is your payback."

"That's not true."

"Try again," I said.

"What's to pay back? He never did anything to me."

"Tom was a tease. He was willing to flirt, but he was quick to draw lines you couldn't cross. He could afford to enjoy your attention because it didn't cost him a thing. He accepted the tribute without taking any risks, which meant he got to feel virtuous while you were left like a kid with your nose pressed to the glass. You could see what you wanted, but you weren't allowed to touch. And now you're thinking that's the best you'll ever have, which is *really* bullshit because you didn't have anything. All this talk about pain is an attempt to sanctify a big, fat, emotional zero." I knew I was only ragging on her because Selma had ragged on me, but it felt good nonetheless. Later, I'd feel guilty for being such a bitch, but for now it seemed like the only way to get what I wanted.

She was silent for a moment. I could hear the intake of cigarette smoke, followed by the exhale of her breath. "Maybe."

"Maybe, my ass. It's the truth," I said. "Everybody sees him as noble, but I think he was supremely egotistical. How honorable was he when he never had the courage to tell his wife?"

"Tell her what?"

"That he was tempted to be unfaithful because of his attraction to you. He didn't act on his feelings, but it's no bloody wonder she ended up feeling insecure. And what did it net you? You're still hung up on him and you may never get yourself off the hook."

"Look, you really don't know what you're talking about so let's skip all the homegrown psychology. Tell me what you want and get it over with."

"You have to level with me."

"Why?"

"Because my life may depend on it," I snapped. "Come on, Colleen. You're a professional. You know better. You sit there doling out little tidbits of information, hanging on to the crumbs because it's all you have. This is serious damn shit. If Tom were in your position, do you think he'd withhold information in a situation like this?"

She inhaled again. "Probably not." Grudgingly.

"Then let's get on with it. If you know what's going on, for god's sake, let's have it."

She seemed to hesitate. "Tom was facing a moral crisis. I was the easy part, but I wasn't all of it."

"What do you mean, you were the easy part?"

"I'm not sure how to explain. I think he could do the right thing with me and it was a comfort to him. That situation made sense while the other problem he was facing was more complicated."

"You're just guessing at this or do you know for a fact?"

"Well, Tom never came out and said so, but he did allude to the issue. Something about not knowing how to reconcile his head and his gut."

"In regard to what?"

"He felt responsible for Toth's murder."

"He felt *responsible*? How come?"

"A breach of confidentiality."

"As in what? I don't get it."

"Toth's whereabouts," she said. "I gave him the address and phone number of the Gramercy. Tom thought someone used the information to track Toth down and kill him. It was driving him crazy to think the man might have died because of his carelessness."

I felt myself blinking at the phone, trying to make sense of what she'd said. "But Selma tells me Tom was always tight-lipped. That was one of her complaints. He never talked about anything, especially when it came to his work."

"It wasn't *talk* at all. He thought someone took an unauthorized look at his notes."

"But his notebook is missing."

"Well, it wasn't back then."

"Who did he suspect? Did he ever mention a name?"

"Someone he worked with. And that's my guess, by the way, not something he said to me directly. Why else would it bother him if it wasn't someone betraying the department?"

I felt myself grow still. I flashed on the officers I'd met in Nota Lake: Rafer LaMott; Tom's brother Macon; Hatch Brine; James Tennyson; Earlene's husband, Wayne. Even Deputy Carey Badger who'd taken my report on the night of the assault. The list seemed to go on and on and all of them were connected with the Nota Lake Sheriff's Department or the CHP. At the back of my mind, I'd been flirting with a possibility I'd scarcely dared to admit. What I'd been harboring was the suspicion that my attacker had been trained at a police academy. I'd been resisting the notion, but I could feel it begin to take root in my imagination. He'd taken me down with an efficiency I'd been taught once upon a time myself. Whether he was currently employed in some branch of law enforcement, I couldn't be sure, but the very idea left me feeling cold. "Are you telling me one of Tom's colleagues was involved in a double homicide?"

"I think that was his suspicion and it was tearing him apart. Again, this wasn't something he said. This is my best guess."

This time I was silent for a moment. "I should have seen that. How stupid of me. Shit."

"What will you do now?"

"Beats the hell out of me. What would you suggest?"

"Why not talk to someone in Internal Affairs?"

"And say what? I'm certainly willing to give them anything I have, but at this point, it's all speculation, isn't it?"

"Well, yes. I guess that's one reason I didn't call myself. I've got nothing concrete. Maybe if you talk to Pinkie's daughter up there, it will clarify the situation."

"Meanwhile alerting the guy that I'm breathing down his neck," I said.

"But you can't do this on your own."

"Who'm I gonna call? The Nota Lake Sheriff's Department?"

"I'm not sure I'd do that," she said, laughing for once.

"Yeah, well if I figure it out, I'll let you know," I

said. "Any other comments or advice while we're on the subject?"

She thought about it briefly. "Well, one thing . . . though you may have already thought about this. It must have been general knowledge Tom was working on this case, so once he dropped dead, the guy must have thought he was home free."

"And now I come along. Bad break," I said. "Of course, the guy can't be sure how much information Tom passed to his superiors."

"Exactly. If it's not in his reports, it might still be in circulation somewhere, especially with his notes gone. You'd better hope you get to 'em before someone else does."

"Maybe the guy already has them in his possession."

"Then why's he afraid of you? You're only dangerous if you have the notes," she said.

I thought about the search of Tom's den. "You're right."

"I'd proceed with care."

"Trust me," I said. "One more question while I have you on the line. Were you ever in Nota Lake yourself?"

"Are you kidding? Tom was too nervous to see me there."

I replaced the receiver, distracted. My anxiety level was rising ominously, like a toilet on the verge of overflowing. The fear was like something damp and heavy sinking into my bones. I have a thing about authority figures, specifically police officers in uniform, probably dating from that first encounter while I was trapped in the wreckage of my parents' VW at the age of five. I can still remember the horror and the relief of being rescued by those big guys with their guns and night-sticks. Still, the sense of jeopardy and pain also attached to that image. At five, I wasn't capable of separating the two. In terms of confusion and loss, what I'd experienced was irrevocably bound up with the sight of men in uniform. As a child, I'd been taught the police were my pals, people to turn to if you were lost or afraid. At the same time, I knew police had the power to put you in jail, which made them fearful to contemplate if you were sometimes as "bad" as I was. In retrospect, I can see that I'd applied to the police academy, in part, to ally myself with the very folks I feared. Being on the side of the law was, no doubt, my attempt to cope with that old anxiety. Most of the officers I'd known since had been decent, caring people, which made it all the more alarming to think that one might have crossed the line. I couldn't think when anything had frightened me quite as much as the idea of going up against this guy, but what could I do? If I quit this one, then what? The next time I got scared, was I going to quit that job, too?

I went up the spiral stairs and dutifully started shoving items in my duffel.

EIGHTEEN

The ocean was white with fog, the horizon fading into milk a hundred yards offshore. The sun behind clouds created a harsh, nearly blinding light. Colors seemed flattened by the haze, which lent a chill to the air. A quick check of the weather channel before I'd departed showed heavy precipitation in the area of California where I was headed and within the first twenty-five miles, I could already begin to sense the shift.

I took Highway 126 through Santa Paula and Fillmore until I ran into Highway 5, where I doglegged over to Highway 14. I drove through canyon country— balding, brown hills, tufted with chapparel, as wrinkled and hairy as elephants. Power lines marched across the folds of the earth while the highway spun six lanes of concrete through the cuts and crevices. Residential developments had sprung up everywhere, the ridges dotted with tract houses so that the natural rock formations looked strangely out of place. There was evidence of construction still in progress—earth movers, concrete mixers, temporary equipment yards enclosed in wire fencing in which heavy machinery was being housed for the duration. An occasional Porta-Potty occupied the wide aisle between lanes of the freeway. The land was the color of dry dirt and dried grass. Trees were few and didn't seem to assert much of a presence out here.

By the time I'd passed Edwards Air Force Base, driving in a straight line north, the sky was gray. The clouds collected in ascending layers that blocked out the fading sun overhead. The drizzle that began to fall looked more like a fine vapor sheeting through the air. Misty-looking communities appeared in the distance, flat and small, laid out in a grid, like an outpost on the moon. Closer to the road, there would be an occasional outbuilding, left over from god knows what decade. The desert, while unforgiving, nevertheless tolerates man-made structures, which remain—lopsided, with broken windows, roofs collapsing—long after the inhabitants have died or moved on. I could see the entire expanse of rain-swept plains to the rim of hushed buff-colored mountains. The telephone poles, extending into the horizon ahead of me, could have served as a lesson in perspective. Behind the barren, pointed hills, rugged granite out-croppings grew darker as the rain increased. Gradually, the road moved into the foothills. The mountains beyond them were imposing. Nothing marred the featureless, pale surface—no trees, no grass, no mark of human passage. At higher elevations, I could see vegetation where low-hanging clouds provided sufficient moisture to support growth.

I'd tucked my semiautomatic in the duffel. The gun experts, Dietz among them, were quick to scoff at the little Davis, but it was a handgun I knew and it felt far more familiar to me than the Heckler and Koch, a more recent acquisition. Given the condition of my bunged-up fingers, I doubted I'd be capable of pulling the trigger in any event, but the gun was a comfort in my current apprehensive state.

Little by little, I was giving up my initial irritation with Selma. As with anything else, once a process is under way, there's no point in railing against the Fates. I regretted that I hadn't had time to contact Leland Peck, the clerk at the Gramercy Hotel. I'd taken his co-worker's word that he had nothing to report. Any good investigator knows better. I should have taken the trouble to look him up so I could quiz him about his recollections of the plainclothes detective with the warrant for Toth's arrest.

In the meantime, secure in my ignorance of events to come, I thought idly of the night ahead. I truly hate being a guest in someone's home. The bed seldom suits me. The blankets are usually skimpy. The pillows are flat or made out of hard rubber that smells of half-deflated basketballs. The toilet refuses to flush fully or the handle gets stuck or the paper runs out so that you're forced to search all the cabinets looking for the ever so cunningly hidden supply. Worst of all, you have to "make nice" at all hours. I don't want someone across the table from me while I'm eating my breakfast. I don't want to share the newspaper and I don't want to talk to anyone at the end of the day. If I were interested in that shit, I'd be married again by now and put a perma-nent end to all the peace and quiet.

By the time I arrived in Nota Lake at 6:45, night had settled on the landscape and the weather was truly nasty. The drizzle had intensified into a stinging sleet. My windshield wipers labored, collecting slush in an arc that nearly filled my windshield. My guess was the people of Nota Lake, like others in perpetually cold climates, had strategies for coping with the shifting character of snow. From my limited experience, the freezing rain seemed extremely hazardous, making the roadway as slick as a skating rink. In moments, I could feel the vehicle slide sideways and I slowed to a snail's pace. At the road's edge, the dead grass had stiffened, collecting feathery drifts of whirling snow. Selma had bullied me into having supper with her. I'm easily influenced in food matters, having been conditioned these past years by Rosie's culinary imperiousness. When ordered about by any woman with a certain autocratic tone, I do as I'm told, largely helpless to resist.

I parked out in front of Selma's, snagged my duffel, and hurried to the front porch, head bent, shoulders hunched as though to avoid the combination of blowing rain and biting snow. I knocked politely, shifting impatiently from foot to foot until she opened the door. We exchanged the customary chitchat as I stepped into the foyer and dried my feet on a rag rug. I shrugged off my leather jacket and eased out of my shoes, conscious of the pristine carpet. The house was toasty warm, hazy from the cigarette smoke sealed into the winterproofed rooms. I shivered with belated relief at being out of the cold. I padded after Selma, who showed me to the guest room. "Take whatever time you need to freshen up and get settled. I cleared some space in the closet and emptied a drawer for your things. I'll be out in the kitchen putting the finishing touches on supper. You know your way around, but don't hesitate to holler if you need anything."

"Thanks."

Once the door closed behind me, I surveyed the room with dismay. The carpet here was hot pink, a cut-pile cotton shag. There was a four-poster bed with a canopy and a puffy, quilted spread of pink-and-white checked gingham. The same fabric continued in the dust ruffle and ruffled pillow shams, stacked three deep. A collection of six quilted teddy bears was grouped together in a window seat. The wallpaper was pink-and-white stripes with a floral border across the top. There was an old-fashioned vanity table with a padded seat and a pink-and-white ruffled skirt. Everything was trimmed in oversized white rickrack. The guest bath was an extension of this jaunty decorative theme, complete with a crocheted cozy for the extra roll of toilet paper. The room smelled as though it had been closed up for some time and the heat here seemed more intense than in the rest of the house. I could feel myself start to hyperventilate with the craving for fresh air.

I crossed to the window, like a hot prowl thief trying to escape. I managed to inch up the sash, only to be faced with a seriously constructed double-glazed storm window. I worked at the latches until I loosened all of them. I gave the storm window a push and it fell promptly out of the frame and dropped into the bushes below. *Oops.* I stuck my head through the gap and let the blessed sleet blow across my face. The storm window had landed just beyond my grasp so I left it where it was, resting in the junipers. I lowered the sash again and adjusted the ruffled curtains so the missing storm window wasn't evident. At least, at bedtime, I could sleep in a properly refrigerated atmosphere.

Selma had urged me to freshen up and I used her advice to stall my return to the kitchen. I peed, washed my hands, and brushed my teeth, happy to occupy my time with these homely ablutions. I stood in the bathroom and stared at myself in the mirror, wondering if I'd ever develop an interest in the painful process of plucking my eyebrows. Not likely. My jaw was still bruised and I paused to admire the ever-changing hue. Then I stood in the bedroom and did a quick visual scan. I removed my handgun from the duffel and hid it between the mattress and the box springs near the head of the bed. This would fool no one, but it would allow me to keep the gun close. I didn't think it would be wise to pack a rod in this town, especially without the proper permit. Finally, there was nothing for it but to take a deep breath and present myself at the supper table.

Selma seemed subdued. Her attitude surprised me, given the fact that she'd gotten her way. I was back in Nota Lake, staying at her house, which was the last thing I wanted. "I kept everything simple. I hope you don't mind," she said.

"This is fine," I said.

She took a moment to stub out her cigarette, blowing the final stream of smoke to one side. This, for a smoker, constitutes etiquette. We pulled out our chairs and took seats at the kitchen table.

Given my usual diet, a home-cooked meal of any kind is an extraordinary treat. Or so I thought before I was faced with the one she'd prepared. This was the menu: iced tea with Sweet 'N Low already mixed in, a green Jell-O square with fruit cocktail and an internal ribbon of Miracle Whip, iceberg lettuce with bottled dressing the color of a sunset. For the main course, instant mashed potatoes with margarine and a stout slice of meatloaf, swimming in diluted cream of mushroom soup. As I ate, my fork exposed a couple of pockets of dried mashed potato flakes. The meatloaf was strongly reminiscent of something served at the Perdido County Jail, where there was an entire (much-dreaded) punishment referred to as being "on meatloaf." On meatloaf means an inmate is placed on a diet of meatloaf and two slices of squishy white bread twice a day, with only drinking water from the faucet. The meatloaf, a six-inch patty made of turkey, kidney beans, and other protein-rich filler, is served on something nominally known as gravy. Every third day the law mandates that the inmate has to be served three square meals for one day, then back to meatloaf. By comparison to Selma's version, a simple QP with cheese came off looking like a gourmet feast. Especially since I knew for a fact she didn't feed Brant this way.

Selma was quiet throughout the meal and I didn't have much to contribute. I felt like one of those married couples you see out in restaurants—not looking at each other, not bothering to say a word. The minute we'd finished eating, she lit up another cigarette so I wouldn't miss a minute of the tars and noxious gases wafting across the table. "Would you like coffee or dessert? I have a nice coconut cream pie in the freezer. It won't take a minute to thaw. I can pop it in the microwave."

"Golly, I'm full. This was great."

"Are you cold? I saw you shiver. I can turn the heat up if you like."

"No, no. Really. I'm toasty warm. This was wonderful."

She tapped her cigarette ash on the edge of her plate. "I didn't ask you about your fingers."

I held up my right hand. "They're a little stiff yet, but better."

"Well, that's good. Now that you're back, what's the plan?"

"I was just thinking about that," I said. "I'm not sure what to make of this and I don't want it going any further, but I think I have a line on what was bothering Tom."

"Really?"

"After we spoke this morning, I made another phone call. Without going into any detail . . ." I paused. "I'm not even sure how to tell you this. It seems awkward."

"For heaven's sake. Just say it."

"It looks like Tom suspected a fellow officer in that double homicide he was investigating."

Selma looked at me, blinking, while she absorbed the information. She took a deep drag of her cigarette and blew out a sharp stream of smoke. "I don't believe it."

"I know it sounds incredible, but stop and think about it for a minute. Tom was trying to establish the link between the two victims, right?"

"Yes."

"Well, apparently he believed one of his colleagues lifted Alfie Toth's address from his field notes. Toth was murdered shortly afterward. Toth was always on the move, but he'd just gotten out of jail and he was living temporarily in a fleabag hotel. This was the first time anyone had managed to pin him down to one location.

273

No one else in Nota Lake knew where Alfie Toth was hanging out except him."

"What makes you so sure? He might have mentioned it to someone. Or someone else might have come up with the information independently," she said.

"You're right about that. The point is, Tom must have gone crazy thinking he played a role in Alfie's death. Worse yet, suspecting someone in the department had a hand in it."

"But you don't really *know*," she said. "This is just a guess on your part."

"How are we ever going to *know* anything unless someone 'fesses up? And that seems unlikely. I mean, so far this 'someone' has gotten away with it."

"Who told you this?"

"Don't worry about that. It was someone with the sheriff's department. A confidential source."

"Confidential, my foot. You're making a serious allegation."

"You think I don't know that? Of course I am," I said. "Look, I don't like the idea any better than you do. That's why I came back, to pin it down."

"And if you can't?"

"Then, frankly, I'm out of ideas. There is one possibility. Pinkie Ritter's daughter, Margaret . . ."

Selma frowned. "That's right. I'd forgotten their relationship. The connection seems odd, what with her working for Tom."

"Nota Lake's a small town. The woman has to work somewhere, so why not the sheriff's department? Everybody else seems to work there," I pointed out.

"Why didn't she speak up when you were here before?"

"I didn't know about Ritter until yesterday."

"I think you better talk to Rafer."

"I think it's best to keep him out of this for now." I caught the odd look that crossed her face. "What?"

She hesitated. "I ran into him this afternoon and told him you'd be back this evening."

I felt my eyes roll in despair and I longed to bang my head on the table top just one time for emphasis. "I wish you'd kept quiet. It's hard enough as it is. Everybody here knows everybody else's business."

She waved aside my objection like a pesky horsefly sailing through the smoke-filled air. "Don't be silly. He was Tom's best friend. What will you do?"

"I'll talk to Margaret tonight and see what she knows," I said. "After that, my only option is to go back to Santa Teresa and confer with the sheriff's department there."

"And tell them what? You don't have much."

"I don't have *anything*," I said. "Unless something develops, I'm at a dead loss."

"I see. Then I suppose that's it." Selma stubbed out her cigarette and got up without another word. She began to clear the dinner dishes, moving from the table to the sink.

"Let me help you with that," I said, getting up to assist.

"Don't trouble." Her tone of voice was frosty, her manner withdrawn.

I began to gather up plates and silverware, moving to the sink where she was already scraping leftover

Jell-O into the garbage disposal. She ran water across a plate, opened the door to the dishwasher, and placed it in the lower rack. The silence was uncomfortable and the clattering of plates contained a note of agitation.

"Is something on your mind?" I asked.

"I hope I didn't make a mistake in hiring you."

I glanced at her sharply. "I never offered you a guarantee. No responsible P.I. could make a promise like that. Sometimes the information simply isn't there," I said.

"That's not what I meant."

"Then what were you referring to?"

"I never even asked you for references."

"A little late at this point. You want to talk to some of my past employers, I'll make up a list."

She was silent again. I was having trouble tracking the change in her demeanor. Maybe she thought I was giving up. "I'm not saying I'll quit," I said.

"I understand. You're saying you're out of your league."

"You want to go up against the cops? Personally, I've got more sense."

She banged a plate down so hard it broke down the middle into two equal pieces. "My husband *died*."

"I know that. I'm sorry."

"No, you're not. Nobody gives a shit what I've gone through."

"Selma, you hired me to do this and I'm doing it. Yes, I'm out of my league. So was Tom, for that matter. Look what happened to him. It fuckin' broke his heart."

She stood at the sink, letting the hot water run while her shoulders shook. Tears coursed along her cheeks. I stood there for a moment, wondering what to do. It seemed clear she'd go on weeping until I acted sincerely moved. I patted her awkwardly, making little murmurings. I pictured Tom doing much the same thing in his life, probably in this very spot. Water gurgled down the drain while the tears poured down her face. Finally, I couldn't stand it. I reached over and turned off the water. Live through enough droughts, you hate to see the waste. Where originally her grief had seemed genuine, I now suspected the emotion was being hauled out for effect. At long last, with much blowing and peeking at her nose products, she pulled herself together. We finished up the dishes and Selma retreated to her room, emerging shortly afterward in her nightie and robe, intending to make herself a glass of hot milk and get in bed. I fled the house as soon as it was decently possible. Nothing like being around a self-appointed invalid to make you feel hard-hearted.

Margaret and Hatch lived close to the center of town on Second Street. I'd called from Selma's before I left the house. I'd scarcely identified myself when she cut in, saying, "Dolores said you came to see her. What's this about?"

In light of her father's murder, the answer seemed obvious. "I'm trying to figure out what happened to your father," I said. "I wondered if it'd be possible to talk to you tonight. Is this a bad time for you?"

She'd seemed nonplussed at my request, conceding with reluctance. I couldn't understand her attitude, but I wrote it off to my imagination. After all, the subject had to be upsetting, especially in light of his past abusiveness. Twice she put a palm across the mouthpiece and conferred with someone in the background. My assumption was that it was Hatch, but she made no specific reference to him.

The drive over was uneventful, despite the treacherous roads and the continuous sleet. There was no accumulation of snow so far, but the pavement was glistening and my tires tended to sing every time I hit a slippery patch. I had to use the brakes judiciously, pumping gently from half a block back when I saw the stoplights ahead of me change. Paranoid as I was at that point, I did note the close proximity of the Brine's house to the parking lot at Tiny's Tavern where I'd been accosted. Once Wayne and Earlene dropped the Brines off at home, Hatch could easily have doubled back. I found myself scouring the streets for sight of a black panel truck, but of course saw nothing.

I entered a tract of brick ranch houses maybe fifteen years old, judging from the maturity of the landscaping. Tree trunks were now sturdy, maybe eight inches in diameter, and the foundation plantings had long ago crept over the windowsills. I slowed when I spotted the house number. The Brines had two cars and a pickup truck parked in or near the drive. I found a parking spot two doors down and sat at the curb wondering if there was a party in progress. I turned in my seat and studied the house. There were dim lights in front, brighter lights around the side and toward the portion of the rear that I could see from my vantage point. This was Saturday night. She hadn't mentioned a Tupperware party or Bible study, nor had she suggested I come at some other time. Maybe they were having friends in to watch a little network television. I debated with myself. I didn't like the idea of walking into a social gathering, especially since I could always talk to her tomorrow. On the other hand, she'd said I could come and meeting with her tonight would delay my return to Selma's. I still had a key to her place and the plan was for me to let myself in the front door whenever I got back that night. The car became noticeably colder the longer I sat. The neighborhood was quiet with little traffic and no one visible on foot. Someone peeking out the windows would think I'd come to case the joint.

I got out of the car and locked the doors. The sidewalks must have been warmer than the streets. Snowflakes melted instantly, leaving shallow pools in lieu of icy patches. The trees in the yard were some deciduous variety, caught by surprise with tiny green buds in sight. March in this area must have been a constant series of nature pranks. I knocked on the door, hoping I wasn't walking in on a naughty lingerie party. Maybe that's why she'd invited me, in hopes I'd purchase a drawerful of underpants to replace all my tatty ones.

Margaret opened the door wearing blue jeans and a thick, red sweater with a Nordic design across the front; snowflakes and reindeer. She wore clunky calf-high suede boots with a sheepskin lining that must have felt warm on a night like this. With her black hair and oval glasses, she looked like a teenager hired to babysit. "Hi. Come on in."

"Thanks. I hope I'm not interrupting. I saw cars in the drive."

"Hatch's poker night. The boys are in the den," she said, hooking a thumb toward the rear. "I'm on kitchen detail. We can talk out there."

Like Selma's house, this one smelled as if it had been sealed for the winter, the rubber gaskets on the storm windows insuring the accumulation of smoke and cooking smells. The wall-to-wall carpet was a burnt orange high-low, the walls in the living room painted a shade of café au lait. The eight-foot sofa was a chocolate brown with two black canvas butterfly chairs arranged on either side of the coffee table. "You didn't have any trouble finding the place?" she asked.

"Not at all," I said. "You prefer Margaret or Mame? I know Dolores refers to you as Mame."

"Either one is fine. Suit yourself."

I followed her to the kitchen at the end of the hall. She was in the process of preparing food, platters of cold cuts on the long wood-grained Formica counter. There were bowls of chips, two containers of some kind of dip made with sour cream, and a mixture of nuts and Chex cereals tossed with butter and garlic powder. I know this because all the ingredients were still in plain view. "If you'll help me move these snacks to the dining room, we can get 'em out of the way and we can talk."

"Sure thing."

She picked up two bowls and shoved the swinging door open with a hip, holding it for me while I moved through with the tray of sliced cheeses and processed meats. Of course, it was all so unwholesome I was immediately hungry, but my appetite didn't last long. Through an archway to my left, I saw Hatch and his five buddies sitting on metal folding chairs at the poker table in the den. There were countless beer bottles and beer mugs in evidence, cigarettes, ashtrays, poker chips, dollar bills, coins, bowls of peanuts. To a man, the entire gathering turned to look at me. I recognized Wayne, James Tennyson and Brant; the other two fellows I'd never seen before. Hatch made a comment and James laughed. Brant raised his hand in greeting. Margaret paid little attention to the lot of them, but the chill from the room was unmistakable.

I placed bowls on the table and moved back to the kitchen, trying to behave as though unaffected by their presence. Here's the truth about my life. Just about any jeopardy I encounter in adulthood I experienced first in elementary school. Guys making private jokes have struck me as sinister since I was forced to pass the sixth-grade boys every morning on my way to "kinney garden." Even then, I knew no good could come of such assemblages and I avoid them where possible.

I picked up a platter from the kitchen counter and intercepted Margaret as she reached the swinging door. "Why don't I pass these to you and you can put them on the table," I said, feigning helpfulness. In truth, I couldn't bear subjecting myself to that collective stare.

She took the platter without comment, holding the door open with her hip. "You might want to open a couple more beers. There's some on the bottom shelf of the refrigerator out on the utility porch."

I found six bottles of beer and the beer flip and made myself useful removing caps. Once we'd assembled the eats, Margaret pulled the swinging door shut and sighed with relief. "Lucky they don't play more than once a month," she said. "I told Hatch they should rotate, but he likes to have 'em here. Usually Earlene tags along with Wayne and helps me set up, but she's coming down with a cold and I told her to stay home. Shit . . . excuse my language . . . I forgot to put out the paper plates. I'll be right back." She snatched up a giant package of flimsy paper plates and moved toward the dining room. "You want anything to eat, you can help yourself," she said. As I was still burping meatloaf, I thought it wise to decline.

She came back to the kitchen and tossed the cellophane packaging in the trash, then turned and leaned against the counter, crossing her arms in front. "What can I help you with?" The question suggested cooperation, but her manner was all business.

"I'm just wondering what you can tell me about his last visit. I'm assuming he and Alfie Toth came to the area to see you that spring."

"That's right," she said. As though to distract herself, she began to screw lids on the pickle jars, stowing mustard and mayonnaise back in the refrigerator. "I hope you don't think this is disrespectful, but my father was a loser and we all knew that. Truthfully, I was happiest when he was in jail. He always seemed to cause trouble."

"Was he a problem on this visit?"

"Of course. Mostly chasing women. Like any woman here was that hard up," she said.

"From what little I know, I never pictured him as a ladies' man."

"He wasn't, but he'd just gotten out of jail and he was itching to get laid. He'd be at Tiny's at four, the minute the doors opened. Once he started drinking, he'd hit on anyone who crossed his path. He thought he was irresistible and he'd be angry and combative when his ham-handed flirtations didn't net him what he wanted."

"Anybody in particular?"

Margaret shrugged. "A waitress at the Rainbow and one at Tiny's. Alice, the one with red hair."

"I know her," I said.

"That's all he talked about, how horny he was. *Poon-tang*, he called it. I was embarrassed. I mean, what kind of talk is that coming from your dad? He couldn't have been more obnoxious. He got in fights. He borrowed money. He dinged the truck. People around here won't tolerate behavior like that. It drove Hatch insane so, of course, the two of us were fighting. Hatch wanted them out of here and I can't say I blamed him. What are you going to do though, your own dad? I could hardly ask him to leave. He'd been here less than a week."

"So what finally happened?"

"We sent him and Alfie off on a fishing trip. Anything to get them out from underfoot for a couple of days. Hatch lent 'em a couple of fishing rods he never did get back. He was p.o.'d about that. Anyway, I don't know what happened, but something must have gone wrong. Next morning, Alfie showed up and said they'd decided to take off and he'd come for their things."

"Where was your father?"

"Alfie told us Daddy was waiting for him and he had to get a move on or Pinkie'd be furious with him. I didn't think anything about it. I mean, it did sound like him. He was always trying to get Alfie to fetch and carry for him."

"Did Tom know all this?"

"I told him in March when Daddy's remains turned up. Once the body was identified, Tom notified me and I passed the news on to the rest of the family. Before that, as far as I knew, Dad was fine."

"Didn't it strike you as odd that no one in the family ever heard from him once he supposedly left here?"

"Why should it? Bad news travels fast. We always figured if something happened to him, someone would be in touch. Police or a hospital. He always carried ID. Besides, we heard from Alfie now and then. I guess the two of them split up, or that's the impression he gave."

"Why did he call?"

Margaret shrugged. "Beats me. Just to see how we were doing is what he said."

"Did he ever ask about your dad?"

"Well, yes, but it wasn't like he really wanted to get in touch. You know how it is. How's your dad? . . . What do you hear from him? . . . And that sort of thing."

"So he was wondering if Pinkie ever showed up again. Is that it?"

"I guess. Finally, he stopped calling and we lost touch with him."

"Maybe he realized Pinkie wasn't ever going to put in an appearance."

"That's what Tom said. He thought Daddy might have been murdered the very day Alfie left, though there was never any way to prove it. One thing they found was a gas receipt he'd tucked in his pocket. That was dated the day before. Him and Alfie filled up the tank on their way to the lake. You think Alfie knew something?"

"Almost certainly," I said.

"Maybe the two of them quarreled."

"It's always possible," I said. "Judging from his behavior, he was either trying to create the impression that Pinkie was alive, or he really wasn't sure himself. The last time you saw him . . . when he stopped by to pick up their belongings . . . did he seem okay to you?"

"Like what?"

"He wasn't nervous or in a hurry?"

"He was in a hurry for sure, but no more than he'd be with Daddy waiting."

"Any signs he'd been in a scuffle?"

"Nothing that I noticed. There wasn't any dirt or scratches."

"How did they plan to travel? Bus, train, plane? Hitchhiking?"

"They must have gone by bus. I mean, that was my assumption because the truck was left over at the Greyhound station. Hatch spotted it in the parking lot later that same day," she said.

NINETEEN

By the time I left Margaret's, it was close to nine-thirty. I unlocked the VW and slid under the wheel, sticking the key in the ignition. A car approached and as it pulled up alongside, I could see that it was Macon, driving a black-and-white. Even through the car window I could tell he was better dressed for the cold than I was. I was wearing my brown leather bomber jacket, but was short the gloves, scarf, and cap. I rolled down my window. His car idled, static from the radio filling the air. The temperature had dropped. I blew on my fingers briefly and then turned the key in the ignition, firing up the VW just to get the engine warm. I adjusted the heat, which in a VW consists of moving one lever from OFF to ON. "What's up?" I asked.

"I'm on tonight anyway so I thought I might as well follow you home. I talked to Selma a little while ago and she told me what was going on. I'm glad you came back. She was worried you'd abandon ship."

"Believe me, I was tempted. I'd rather be at home," I said.

"I remember this Pinkie Ritter business. Ornery son of a gun. Was Margaret any help?"

"About what you'd expect," I said, evading the issue. "I'm heading over to Tiny's. She says he hustled one of the waitresses so I'll see what she says. It might not mean anything, but I could pick up additional information. Maybe a jealous husband or a boyfriend was dealing out paybacks. You have any other suggestions?"

"Not offhand. You seem to be doing pretty good," Macon said, but he didn't sound convinced. "Why don't you let me ask around and see what I can find out. Seems like the fewer people who know what you're after the better."

"My sentiments exactly. Anyway, I better get a move on before I freeze."

Macon glanced at his watch. "How long will this take?"

"Not that long. Thirty minutes at best. I'm not even sure Alice works Saturdays. I'm assuming she does."

"Why don't I follow you as far as the parking lot? I can swing back at ten and follow you to Selma's. If the woman isn't working, have a Coke or something until I show up."

"I'd appreciate that. Thanks."

I rolled up the window and put the car in gear. Macon pulled out first, waiting for me to do a U-turn so I could follow him. With the boys entrenched in their poker game inside, I was feeling safer than I had all day.

The parking lot at Tiny's was packed with cars, RVs, and pickup trucks with camper shells. I tucked the VW into a small gap at the end of the last row. Macon waited, watching me cross two aisles, passing through the shadowy spaces between vehicles. Once I was at the rear entrance, I turned and waved to him and he took off with a little toot of his horn. I checked my watch. 10:05. I had until 10:30 which should give me plenty of time.

Saturday night at Tiny's was a rowdy affair; two alternating live bands, line dancing, contests, whooping, hollering, and much thumping of cowboy boots on the wooden dance floor. There were six waitresses working in a steady progression from the bar to the crowded tables. I spotted Alice with her gaudy orange hair half a room away and I pushed my way through the jostling three-deep bystanders ringing the room. I had to yell to make myself heard. She got the message and pointed toward the ladies' room. I watched her deliver a sloshing pitcher of beer and six tequila shooters, then collect a fistful of bills that she folded and pushed down the front of her shirt. She angled in my direction, taking orders as she came. The two of us burst into the empty ladies' room and pushed the door shut. The quiet was remarkable, the noise in the tavern reduced by more than half.

"Sorry to drag you away," I said.

"Are you kidding? I'm thrilled. This is hell on earth. It's like this most weekends and the tips are shit." She opened the first stall door and stepped just inside. She took a pack of cigarettes out of her apron pocket. "Keep an eye out for me, would you? I'm not supposed to stop for a smoke, but I can't help myself." She shook a cigarette free and fired it up in no time. She inhaled deeply, with a moan of pleasure and relief. "Lord, that's good. What are you doing here? I thought you went home to wherever it is."

"I left. Now I'm back."

"That was quick."

"Yeah, well I know a lot more now than I did two days ago."

"That's good. More power to you. I hear you're investigating a murder. Margaret Brine's father, or that's the word."

"It's slightly more complicated, but that's about it. As a matter of fact, I was just at her place, asking about his last visit."

Alice snorted. "What a horse's ass he was. He hustled my butt off, the randy little shit. I pinned his ears back, but he was hard to shake."

"Who else did he hustle? Anyone in particular? Margaret tells me he was horny as all get out—"

Alice held up a hand. "Mind if I interrupt for a sec? Something I should mention before you go on."

I hesitated, alerted by something in her tone. "Sure."

Alice studied the tip of her lighted cigarette. "I don't know how to say this, but people around here seem to be concerned about you."

"Why? What'd I do?"

"That's what everybody's asking. Grapevine has it you're into drugs."

"I am not! How ridiculous. That's ludicrous," I said.

"Also, you shot a couple of fellows in cold blood a while back."

"*I* did?" I said, laughing in startlement. "Where'd you hear *that*?"

"You never killed anyone?"

I felt my smile start to fade. "Well, yes, but that was self-defense. Both were killers, coming after me—"

Alice cut in. "Look, I didn't get the details and I

don't really give a shit. I'm willing to believe you, but folks around here take a dim view of it. We don't like the idea of somebody coming in here starting trouble. We take care of our own."

"Alice, I promise. I've never shot anyone without provocation. The idea's repugnant. I swear. Where did this come from?"

"Who knows? This is something I picked up earlier. I overheard the fellows talking."

"This was tonight?"

"And yesterday some, too. This was shortly after you left. I guess someone did some digging and came up with the facts."

"*Facts?*"

"Yeah. One guy you killed was hiding in a garbage can—"

"That's bullshit. He wasn't hiding, *I* was."

"Well, maybe *that's* what I heard. You were lying in wait, which somebody pointed out was pretty cowardly. Word is, the most recent incident was three years back. It was in the Santa Teresa papers. Someone saw a copy of the article."

"I don't believe this. What article?"

Alice drew on her cigarette, regarding me with skepticism. "You weren't involved in a shoot-out in some lawyer's office?"

"The guy was trying to *kill* me. I just told you that. Talk to the cops if you don't want to take my word for it."

"Don't get so defensive. I'm telling you for your own good. I might've done the same thing if I'd been in your place, but this is redneck country. Folks here close ranks. You better watch your step is all I'm saying."

"Somebody's trying to discredit me. That's what this is about," I said, hotly.

"Hey, it's not up to me. I don't give a damn. You can whack anyone you want. There's times *I'd* do it myself, given half a chance," she said. "The point is, people are getting pissed. I thought I should warn you before it went too far."

"I appreciate that. I wish you could tell me where it's coming from."

Alice shrugged. "That's the way it is in small towns."

"If you remember where the story originated, will you let me know?"

"Sure thing. In the meantime, I'd avoid crossing paths with the cops if I were you."

I felt a pang of anxiety, like an icicle puncturing my chest wall. "What makes you say that?"

"Tom was a cop. They're mad as hell."

Alice dropped the lighted cigarette in the toilet with a spat and then she flushed the butt away, waving at the air as if she could clear the smoke with a swishing hand. "You want anything else?"

I shook my head, not trusting myself to speak.

I waited at the side exit, my hands in my pockets though the chill I felt was internally generated. I kept my mind on other things, defending against a mounting surge of uneasiness. Maybe this was why Macon was suddenly being so protective.

The night sky was overcast, and where the air should

have been crystalline, a ground fog began to drift across the darkened parking lot. Two couples left together. One of the women was blind-drunk, laughing boisterously as she staggered across the icy tarmac. Her date had his arm across her shoulders and she leaned against him for support. She stopped in her tracks, held her hand up like a traffic cop, and then turned away to be sick. The other woman leaped backward, shrieking in protest. The ill woman lingered, holding on to a parked car 'til she was done and could move on.

The foursome reached their vehicle and piled in, though the sick woman sat sideways with her head hanging out the door for a good five minutes before they were finally able to pull away. I searched the empty rows of cars, checking the dark. The music from the bar behind me was reduced to a series of dull, repetitive thumps. I caught a flash of light and saw a car pull in. I stepped back into the shadows until I was assured it was Macon in his black-and-white. He pulled up beside me and sat there with his engine running. I moved forward, walking around the front of the patrol car to the window on the driver's side. He rolled it down as I approached.

"How'd it go?" he asked. I could hear the racket of his car radio dispatcher talking to someone else. He turned the volume down.

I put a hand on the door. "Alice tells me there's a rumor going around that I'm some sort of dope-crazed vigilante."

He looked off to one side. He stirred restlessly, tapping the steering wheel with his gloved hand. "Don't worry about gossip. Everybody talks in this town."

"Then you heard it, too?"

"Nobody pays any attention to that stuff."

"Not true. Someone went to the trouble to do a background check."

"And got what? It's all bullshit. I don't believe a word of it."

Which meant he'd heard the same stories everyone else had been treated to. "I better see you home. I got a call to check out."

I got in my car and he followed me as far as Selma's driveway, his engine idling while I crossed the front lawn.

Selma had left the porch light on and my key turned easily in the lock. I waved from the doorway and he took off. I slipped out of my wet shoes and carried them down the hall to the guest room. The house was quiet, not even the murmur of a television set to suggest Selma was awake.

I slipped into the guest room and closed the door behind me. She'd turned on a bed table lamp and the room was washed in cheery pink. On the nightstand, she'd left me a plate of homemade chocolate chip cookies secured in plastic wrap. I ate two, savoring the flavors of butter and vanilla. I ate two more to be polite before I stripped off my jacket. Apparently, Selma was not in the habit of turning down the furnace at night and the room felt close with heat. I crossed to the window, pushed the curtains aside, and raised the sash. Frigid air poured through the gap left by the storm window, still resting against the bushes three feet down.

I stared out at the portion of the street that I could see. A car passed at a slow speed and I pulled back out of sight, wondering if the occupants had spotted me. I hated being in Nota Lake. I hated being an outsider, the target of local gossip that misrepresented my actions. I hated my suspicions. The thought of a uniform was beginning to make me salivate like a dog subjected to some odd form of Pavlovian conditioning. Where once the badge and the nightstick had been symbols of personal safety, I now found myself picturing them with trepidation, as if stung by electric shocks. If I was right about the guy's connection to law enforcement, then his was the badge of authority and what was I? Some little pipsqueak P.I. with a prissy sense of justice. Talk about a mismatch.

Why couldn't I just hop in my car and barrel home tonight? I needed to be in a place where people cared for me. For a moment, the pull was overpowering. If I left within the hour, I could be in Santa Teresa by four A.M. I pictured my snug platform bed with its blue-and-white quilt, stars visible through the Plexiglas dome overhead. Surely, the sky there would be clear and the air would smell like the Pacific thundering close by. I visualized the morning. Henry would bake cinnamon rolls and we'd have breakfast together. Later I could help him in the yard, where he'd kneel at his flower beds, the pale soles of his feet like something cast in plaster of Paris. I stepped away from the window, effectively breaking the spell. The only road home is through the forest, I thought.

Within minutes, I'd peeled off my clothes and pulled on the oversized T-shirt I was using as a gown. Usually I sleep nude, but in someone else's house, it pays to be prepared in case of fire. I washed my face and brushed my teeth with the usual difficulty. I returned to the bedroom and circled restlessly. The bookshelves were filled with knick-knacks. There was not so much as a magazine in view and I'd forgotten to bring a book this time. I was too wired for sleep. I took the file from the duffel and got into bed, adjusting the reading lamp so I could review the notes I'd typed. The only item that leaped out at me was James Tennyson's report of the woman walking down the road the night Tom died. According to his account, she was approaching from the direction of Tom's truck and she veered off into the woods when she caught sight of his patrol car. Was he lying about that? Had he invented the woman in an attempt to throw me off? He hadn't struck me as devious, but the touch would have been nice since it suggested Tom had been in the woman's company when he was stricken with his fatal heart attack. I wondered what kind of woman would have walked off and left him in the throes of death. Perhaps someone who couldn't afford to be seen with him. Knowing what I knew of him, I didn't believe he was having an affair, so if the woman existed, why conceal her presence? I knew he'd been at the Rainbow Cafe at some unaccustomed hour.

What was interesting was that James had told me about this alleged female as an addendum to his original comments. I tend to be suspicious of elaborations. Eyewitness reports are notoriously unreliable. The story changes each time it's told, modified for every passing audience; amplified, embellished, until the final version is a twisted variation of the truth. Certainly, the memory is capable of playing tricks. Images can be camouflaged by emotion, popping into view later when the mental film is rewound. Conversely, people sometimes swear to have seen things that were never there at all. For the second time, I wondered if Tom had gone to the Rainbow Cafe to meet someone. I'd asked Nancy about it once, but it might be time to press.

I set my notes aside and doused the lights. The mattress was soft and seemed to list to one side. The sheets had a satin finish that felt slick to the touch and generated little traction to offset my tendency to slide. The quilted spread was puffy, filled with down. I lay there and basted in my own body heat. In testimony to my constitution, I fell asleep at once.

I woke to the distant sound of the phone ringing in the kitchen. I thought the answering machine would pick up, but on the eighth persistent *ding-a-ling*, I flung off the covers and trotted down the hall in my T-shirt and underpants. There was no sign of Selma and the machine had been turned off. I lifted the receiver. "Newquists' residence."

Someone breathed in my ear and then hung up.

I replaced the receiver and stood there for a moment. Often, someone calling a wrong number will dial the same number twice, convinced the error is yours for not being who they wanted. The silence extended. I reactivated the answering machine, and then checked Selma's appointment calendar, posted on the refrigerator door. There was nothing marked, but this was Sunday and I remembered her mentioning a visit to a cousin down in Big Pine after church. The dish rack was empty. I opened the dishwasher. I could see that she'd eaten breakfast, rinsed her plate and coffee cup, and left them in the machine, which was otherwise empty. The interior walls of the dishwasher exuded a residual heat and I assumed she'd done a load of dishes first thing this morning before she'd left. The coffee machine was on. The glass carafe held four cups of coffee that smelled as if it had sat too long. I poured myself a mug, adding sufficient milk to offset the scorched flavor.

I padded back to the guest room, where I brushed my teeth, showered, and dressed, sipping coffee while I girded my loins. I didn't look forward to another day in this town, but there was nothing for it except to get the job done. Like a dutiful guest, I made my bed, ate the remaining three cookies to fortify myself, and returned the empty coffee mug and plate to the kitchen, where I tucked both in the dishwasher, following Selma's good example. I grabbed my leather jacket and my shoulder bag, locked the house behind me, and went out to the car. Phyllis was pulling into her driveway two doors down. I waved, convinced she'd spotted me, but she kept her eyes averted and I was left, feeling foolish, with the smile on my lips. I got in the car, forcing myself to focus on the job at hand. The gas gauge was close to E and since I was heading toward the Rainbow, I stopped for gas on my way out of town.

I pulled up to the full-serve pump and turned the engine off, reaching into my bag to find my wallet and gasoline credit card. I glanced over at the office windows where I could see two attendants in coveralls chatting together by the cash register. Both turned to look at my

VW and then resumed their conversation. There were no other cars at the pumps. I waited, but neither came forward to assist me. I turned on the engine and gave the car horn a sharp toot. I waited two minutes more. No action at all. This was annoying. I had places to go and didn't want to sit here all day, waiting for a lousy tank of gas. I opened the car door and stepped out, peering across the top of the car to the open bay. The two attendants were no longer visible. Irritated, I slammed the car door and moved toward the office, which had been deserted.

"Hello?"

Nothing.

"Could I get some service out here?"

No one.

I went back to the car where I waited another minute. Maybe the two lads had inexplicably quit work or had been devoured by extraterrestrials hiding in the gents'. I started the engine and honked sharply, a display of impatience that netted nothing in the way of help. Finally, I pulled out with a little chirp of my tires to demonstrate my agitation. I slid into the flow of traffic on the main street and drove six blocks before I spotted another station. Hahaha, thought I. So much for the competition. I had no credit card for this rival brand, but I could afford to pay cash. Filling a VW never amounts to that much. I pulled into the second station, doing much as I had before. I turned the engine off, checked my wallet for cash. There was a car at the adjacent pump and the attendant was in the process of removing the nozzle from the tank. He glanced at me briefly and then I saw the alteration in his gaze.

I said, "Hi. How're you?"

He took the other woman's credit card and disappeared into the office, returning moments later with her receipt on a tray. She signed and took her copy. The two chatted for a moment and then she pulled out. The attendant went back to the office and that was the last I saw of him. What was going on? I checked myself with care, wondering if I'd been rendered invisible in my sleep.

I stared at the office window and then checked for another service station within range. I could see an off-brand station three doors down. Even with my gauge showing empty, I knew my trusty VW could soldier on for many miles yet, given the mileage I got. Still, I was reluctant to squander the last of a tank of gas looking for a place to buy the next tank of gas. I started my engine, put the car in gear, drove out of that gas station, and into the one two hundred yards away.

This time I saw an attendant in the service bay and I pulled in there first. Let's get this out in the open, whatever it was. I leaned over and rolled down the window on the passenger side. Pleasantly, I said, "Hi. Are you open for business?"

His blank stare sparked a moment of uneasiness. What was wrong with him?

I tried a smile that didn't feel right, but was the best I could manage. "Do you speak English? *Habla Inglés?*" Or something to that effect.

His return smile was slow and malevolent. "Yeah, lady, I do. Now why don't you get the fuck out of here? You want service in this town, you're out of luck."

"Sorry," I said. I shifted my gaze, keeping my expression neutral as I drove out of the station and turned right at the first street. Under my jacket, the sweat was soaking through the back of my shirt.

TWENTY

Once out of sight, I pulled over and parked on a side street to assess my situation. The word had clearly gone out, but I wasn't sure whether these guys were cueing off my car or my personal description. I removed my leather bomber jacket and tossed it in the backseat, then rooted through the assorted garments I keep for just such emergencies. I donned a plain red sweatshirt, a pair of sunglasses, and a Dodgers baseball cap. I got out, opened the trunk, and took out the five-gallon gasoline can I keep in there. I locked the car and hiked over to the main street where I headed for a service station I hadn't tried so far.

I bypassed the office and went straight to the service bay, where a cursing mechanic was struggling to loosen a stubborn lug nut on a flat tire. I checked the sign posted by the door that said MECHANIC ON DUTY with the guy's name ED BOONE on a plastic plaque inserted in the slot. I moved out of the bay and sidled up to the office where I poked my head in the door. The attendant was maybe nineteen, with a bleach-blond crew cut and green-painted fingernails, his attentions focused on the glossy pages of a pornographic magazine.

301

"Uncle Eddy told me I could fill this. My pickup ran out of gas about a block from here. This is mine, by the way," I said, holding up the can. I didn't want the fellow claiming later that I'd stolen it. Given my current reputation as a stone-cold killer, the theft of a gasoline can would have been right in character. I fancied I saw a flicker of uncertainty cross his face, but I went about my business like I owned the place.

I walked to the self-serve pump, giving him a sidelong glance to see if he was on the telephone. He stared through the plate glass window, watching me without expression as I filled the container. The total was $7.45. I returned to the office and handed him a ten, which he tucked in his pocket without offering change. His gaze dropped to his magazine again as I walked off. Nice to know that regardless of how low you sink, someone's always willing to make a profit at your expense. I returned to my car, where I emptied the five gallons of gasoline into my tank. I returned the can to the trunk and took off with the gauge now sitting at the halfway mark.

My heart was beating as though I'd run a race and perhaps I had. Apparently, my actions would be observed and curtailed wherever possible from here on. Never had I felt quite so alienated from my surroundings. I was already on unfamiliar turf and in subtle and not-so-subtle ways, I depended on the ordinary day-to-day pleasantries for my sense of well-being. Now I was being shunned and the process was scaring the shit out of me. Scouring the moving traffic, I realized my pale blue VW was highly visible among all the pickups, campers, utility vehicles, horse vans, and 4×4s.

Six miles out of town, I pulled into the gravel apron of the Rainbow Cafe, angling around to the left where I backed into a parking spot on the far side of the big garbage bins. I sat for a moment, trying to get "centered," as Californians say. I've no idea what the term means, but in my present circumstance, it seemed applicable. If I was being banished from the tribe, I better make sure I had a grip on my "self" before I went any further. I took a couple of deep breaths and got out. The morning was overcast, the mountains looming in the distance like an accumulation of thunder clouds. Down here, where large tracts of land stretched out empty and desolate, the wind whistled along the surface, chilling everything in its path. Snow flurries, like dust motes, hung in the icy air.

Crossing the gravel parking area, I felt extraordinarily conspicuous. I glanced at the cafe windows and could have sworn I saw two customers stare at me and then avert their eyes. A chill went through me, all the ancient power of ostracism by the clan. I imagined church services in progress, the Catholics and the Baptists and the Lutherans all singing hymns and giving thanks, attentive to their respective sermons. Afterward, the Nota Lake devout would crowd into the local restaurants, still dressed in their Sunday best and eager for lunch. I said a little prayer of my own as I pushed through the door.

The cafe was sparsely occupied. I did a quick visual sweep. James Tennyson was sitting at the counter with a cup of coffee. He wore jeans, the newspaper open in front of him. Close at hand were an empty water glass and a crumpled blue-and-black Alka-Seltzer packet.

There was no sign of his wife, Jo, or his baby, whose name escaped me. Rafer's daughter, Barrett, with her back to me, was working the grill. She wore a big white apron over jeans and a T-shirt. A white chef's toque concealed her springy, fly-away hair. Deftly, she wielded her spatula, rolling sausage links, flipping a quartet of pancakes. While I watched, she moved the steaming food to a pair of waiting plates. Nancy picked up the order and delivered it to the couple sitting by the window. Rafer and Vicky LaMott sat in the booth midway down the line of empty tables. They'd finished eating and I could see that Vicky was in the process of collecting her handbag and overcoat. James looked baggy-eyed and drawn. He caught sight of me and nodded, his manner a perfect blend of good manners and restraint. His fair-skinned good looks were only slightly marred by what I imagined was a hangover. I headed for a booth in the far corner, murmuring a greeting to Rafer and Vicky as I breezed by. I was afraid to wait for a response lest they cut me dead. I sat down and positioned myself so I could keep an eye on the door.

Nancy caught my attention. She seemed distracted, but not unfriendly, crossing toward the counter to pick up a side of oatmeal. "I'll be with you in just a minute. You want coffee?"

"I'd love some." Apparently, she wasn't a party to the social boycott. Alice, the night before, had been friendly as well . . . at least to the point of warning me about the freeze coming up. Maybe it was just the guys who were shutting me out; not a comforting thought. It was a man, after all, who'd dislocated my fingers only three days earlier. I found myself rubbing the joints, noticing for the first time that the swelling and the bruises gave them the appearance of exotic, barely ripe bananas. I turned my crockery mug upright in anticipation of the coffee, noting that the fingers still refused to bend properly. It felt like the skin had stiffened, preventing flexion.

While I waited for service, I studied James in profile, wondering about his contact with Pinkie Ritter and Alfie Toth. As a CHP officer, he would have been removed from any sheriff's department action, but he might have exploited his friendships with the deputies to glean information about the homicide investigation. He was certainly first at the scene the night Tom died, giving him the perfect opportunity to lift Tom's notes. I was still toying with the possibility that he invented the walking woman, though his motive remained opaque. It wasn't Colleen. She'd assured me she'd never visited the area, a claim I tended to believe. Tom had too much to lose if he were seen with her. Besides, if she'd been in the truck, she wouldn't have deserted him.

The LaMotts emerged from their booth, hunching into overcoats in preparation for their departure. Vicky crossed to the counter to chat with Barrett while Rafer moved to the register and paid the check. As usual, Nancy did double duty, setting her coffee pot aside to take his twenty and make change. James rose at the same time, leaving his money on the counter beside his plate. He and Rafer exchanged a few words and I saw Rafer glance my way. James pulled on his jacket and left the restaurant without a backward look. Vicky joined her husband, who must have told her to go out and wait for him in the car. She nodded and then busied herself with her gloves and knit cap. I wasn't sure if she was ignoring me or not.

Once she was gone, Rafer ambled in my direction, his hands in his coat pockets, a red cashmere scarf wrapped around his neck. The coat was beautifully cut, a dark chocolate brown setting off the color of his skin. The man did dress well.

"Hello, Detective LaMott," I said.

"Rafer," he corrected. "How's the hand?"

"Still attached to my arm." I held my fingers up, wiggling them as though the gesture didn't hurt.

"Mind if I sit down?"

I indicated the place across from me and he slid into the booth. He seemed ill-at-ease, but his expression was sympathetic and his hazel eyes showed disquiet, not the coldness or hostility I'd half-expected. "I had a long talk with some Santa Teresa fellows about you."

I felt my heart start to thump. "Really. Who?"

"Coroner, couple cops. Homicide detective named Jonah Robb," he said. He put one elbow on the table, tapping with his index finger while he stared out across the room.

"Ah. Tracking down the stories going around about me."

His gaze slid back to mine. "That's right. I might as well tell you, from the perspective of the sheriff's department, you're okay, but I've heard rumbles I don't like and I'm concerned."

"I'm not all that comfortable myself, but I don't see any way around it. Responding to rumors only makes you look guilty and defensive. I know because I tried it and got nowhere."

He stirred restlessly. He turned in the seat until he was facing me squarely, his hands laced in front of him. His voice dropped a notch. "Listen, I know about your suspicions. Why don't you tell me what you have and I'll do what I can to help."

I said, "Great," wondering why I didn't sound more sincere and enthusiastic. I thought about it briefly, experiencing a frisson of uneasiness. "I'll tell you what concerns me at the moment. A plainclothes detective— or someone posing as one—showed up at a fleabag hotel in Santa Teresa with a warrant for Toth's arrest. The Santa Teresa Sheriff's Department has no record of an outstanding warrant anywhere in the system, so the paper was probably bogus, but I don't have a way to check that because I don't have access to the computer."

"I can run that," he said smoothly. "What else?"

I found myself choosing my words with care. "I think the guy was a phoney, too. He might have been a cop, but I think he misrepresented himself."

"What name did he give?"

"I asked about that, but the clerk I talked to wasn't on the desk that day and he claims the other fellow didn't get a name."

"You think it was someone in our department," he said, making it a statement, not a question.

"Possibly."

"Based on what?"

"Well, doesn't the timing seem a tiny bit coincidental?"

"How so?"

"Tom wanted to talk to Toth in connection with Pinkie Ritter's death. The other guy got there first and that was the end of poor old Alfie. Tom was a basket case starting in mid-January when Toth's body turned up, right?"

"That's Selma's claim." Rafer's manner was now guarded and he started tapping, the tip of his index finger drumming a rapid series of beats. Maybe he was sending me a message in Morse code.

"So isn't it possible this is what Tom was brooding about? I mean, what else could it be?"

"Tom was a consummate professional for thirty-five years. He was the investigating officer in a homicide matter that I would say, yes, captured his interest, but no, did not in any way cause him to lie awake at night and bite his nails. Of course he thought about his work, but it didn't cause his heart attack. The idea's absurd."

"If he was under a great deal of stress, couldn't that have been a contributing factor?"

"Why would Toth's death cause him any stress at all? This was his *job*. He never even met the man, as far as I know."

"He felt responsible."

"For what?"

"Toth's murder. Tom believed someone gained access to his notebook where he'd jotted down Toth's temporary address and the phone number at the Gramercy."

"How do you know what Tom *believed*?"

"Because that's what he confided to another sheriff's investigator."

"Colleen Sellers."

"That's right."

"And Tom told her this?"

"Well, not explicitly. But that's how the killer could have found Toth and murdered him," I said.

"You still haven't said why you suspect someone from our department."

"I'll broaden the claim. Let's say, someone in law enforcement."

"You're fishing."

"Who else had access to his notes?"

"Everyone," he said. "His wife, his son, Brant. Half the time, the house was unlocked. Add his cleaning lady, the yard man, his next-door neighbor, the guy across the street. None of them are involved in law enforcement, but any one of them could have opened his front door and walked right in. And what makes you so sure it wasn't someone in Santa Teresa? The leak didn't necessarily come from this end."

I stared at him. "You're right," I said. He had a point.

The tapping stopped and his manner softened. "Why don't you back off and let us handle this?"

"Handle what?"

"We haven't been entirely idle. We're developing a lead."

"I'm glad to hear that. About bloody time. I hate to think I'm the only one out here with my ass on the line."

"Cut the sarcasm and don't push. Not your job."

"Are you saying you have a line on Alfie's killer?"

"I'm saying you'd be smart to go home and let us take it from here."

"What about Selma?"

309

"She knows better than to interfere with an official investigation. So do you."

I tried Selma's line. "There's no law against asking questions."

"That depends on who you ask." He glanced at his watch. "I got Vick in the car and we're late for church," he said. He got up and adjusted his coat, taking his leather gloves from one pocket. I watched him smooth them into place and thought, inexplicably, of his early morning arrival at the emergency room; freshly showered and shaven, nattily dressed, wide awake. He looked down at me. "Did anyone ever fill you in on local history?"

"Cecilia did."

He went on talking as if I hadn't spoken. "Bunch of convicts were shipped to the colonies from England. These were hardened criminals, literally branded for the heinousness of their behavior."

"The 'nota' of Nota Lake," I supplied dutifully.

"That's right. The worst of 'em came west and settled in these mountains. What you're dealing with now are their descendants. You want to watch your step."

I laughed, uneasily. "What, this is like a Western? I'm being warned off? I have to be out of town by sundown?"

"Not a warning, a suggestion. For your own good," he said.

I watched him leave the restaurant and realized how dry my mouth had become. I had that feeling I used to get before the first day of school, a low-level dread that acted as an appetite suppressant. Breakfast didn't sound like such a hot idea. The place had cleared out. The couple by the window were getting up to leave. I saw them pay their check, Barrett taking over the cash register while Nancy hurried in my direction with a coffee pot and menu, all apologies. She handed me the menu. "Sorry it took me so long, but I was brewing a new pot and I could see you and Rafer had your heads together," she said. She filled my mug with hot coffee. "You have any idea what you want to eat? I don't mean to rush you. Take your time. I just don't want to hold you up, you've been so patient."

"I'm not hungry," I said. "Why don't I move to the counter so we can talk?"

"Sure thing."

I picked up my mug and reached for the silverware.

"I'll get that," she said. She took the menu and the flatware, moving to the counter where she set a place for me between the griddle and the cash register. Barrett was in the process of cleaning the grill with a flat-edged spatula. Bacon fat and browned particles of pancake and sausage were being pushed into the well. Nancy rinsed a rag and twisted out the excess water, wiping the counter clean. "Alice says you've been asking about Pinkie Ritter."

"You remember him?"

"Every woman in Nota Lake remembers him," she said, tartly.

"Did he ever bother you?"

"Meaning what, unwanted sexual advances? He attacked me one night when I got off work. He waited in the parking lot and grabbed me by the neck as I was getting in my car. I kicked his ass up between his shoulder blades and that was the last of that. He was convicted of rape twice and that's just the times he was caught."

"Did you report it?"

"What for? I took care of it myself. What's the law going to do, come along afterwards and smack his hand?"

Barrett had now come over to the small sink just below the counter in front of us and she was in the process of rinsing plates and arranging them in the rack for the industrial dishwasher I assumed was in the rear. She had her father's light eyes and she made no secret of the fact that she was listening to Nancy's tale and enjoying her attitude.

I caught her attention. "Did he ever come on to you?"

"Uhn-uhn. No way," she said, a blush creeping up her cheeks. "I was close to jailbait at that point, barely eighteen years old. He knew better than to mess with me."

I turned to Nancy. "What about other women? Anyone in particular? Earlene or Phyllis?"

Nancy shook her head. "Not that I heard, but that doesn't mean he didn't try. Guy like that goes after anyone who seems weak."

"Could I ask you about something else?"

"Sure."

"The night Tom Newquist died, he was in here earlier, wasn't he?"

"That's right. He came in about nine o'clock. Ordered a cheeseburger and fries, sat around and smoked cigarettes, like he was killing time. Occasionally he'd look at his watch. I couldn't figure it out. He never came in at that hour. I figured he was meeting someone, but she never showed up."

"Why do you say 'she'? Couldn't it have been a man?"

Nancy seemed surprised at the idea. "I never thought about that. I just assumed."

"Did he mention anyone by name?"

"No."

"Did he use the telephone?"

She shook her head with some uncertainty and then turned to Barrett with a quizzical look. "You remember if Tom Newquist used the phone that night?"

"Not that I saw."

Again, I directed a question to Barrett. "Did you get the impression he was here to meet someone?"

Barrett shrugged. "I guess."

Nancy spoke up again. "You know what I think it was? He was freshly shaved. I remember remarking about his cologne or his aftershave. He looked sharp, like he'd gussied himself up. He wouldn't do that if he were here to meet some guy."

"You agree with that?" I asked Barrett.

"He did look nice, now you mention it," she said. "I noticed that myself."

"Did he seem annoyed or upset, like he'd been stood up?"

"Not a bit of it," Nancy said. "Nine-thirty, got up, paid his check, and went out to his truck. I never saw him afterwards. I did closing that night so I was stuck in here. Did you see him out there?"

"In the parking lot? Not me."

"You must have. You took off shortly before he did."

Barrett thought about it, frowning slightly before she shook her head. "Maybe he was parked around back."

"Where were you parked that night?" I asked.

"Nowhere. I didn't have a car. My dad was picking me up."

"She lives just over there on the other side of that subdivision, but her folks don't like her walking home at night. They're real protective, especially her dad."

Barrett smiled, her dark skin underlined with the pink of her embarrassment. "I could be a preacher's daughter. That'd be worse."

We chatted on for a while. The place began to fill with the early church service crowd and I was clearly in the way. I was also hoping to avoid further confrontation with any irate citizens. I hunched into my jacket and went out to the car. Since the parking spot I'd found was around to the rear, I didn't think I was visible to passing vehicles. I didn't have the nerve to drive into town just yet. I couldn't bear the idea of wandering around on my own, risking rudeness and rejection on the basis of floating rumors. People in the cafe had been fine so maybe it was just the service station attendants who'd passed a vote of no confidence.

I saw Macon Newquist pull off the highway and into the parking lot in a pickup truck. He was dressed in a suit that looked as unnatural on him as a bunny costume. I knew if he saw me, he'd start pumping me for information. I torqued myself around, reaching for my briefcase as though otherwise occupied. Along with my case notes, I'd tucked in the packets of index cards. I waited until he disappeared into the cafe before I got out of the car and locked it. I took my briefcase with me as I crunched along the berm to the Nota Lake Cabins.

Out front, the red Vacancy sign was lighted. The office lobby was unlocked and there was a flat plastic clockface hanging on the doorknob with the hands pointing to 11:30. The sign said BACK IN A JIFFY. I went in, crossing to the half-door that opened onto the empty office. "Cecilia? Are you here?"

There was no answer.

I was tempted, as usual, by the sight of all those seductive-looking desk drawers. The Rolodex and the file cabinets fairly begged to be searched, but I couldn't for the life of me think what purpose it would serve. I sat down in the upholstered chair and opened a pack of index cards. I began to read through my notes, transferring one piece of information to each card with a borrowed ballpoint pen. In some ways, this was busy-work. I could feel productive and efficient while sheltered from public scrutiny. Transcribing my notes had the further advantage of diverting my attention from the state of discomfort in which I found myself. Whereas last night I longed for home, I couldn't picture turning tail and running on the basis of Rafer's veiled "suggestion" about my personal safety. So what was I doing? Trying to satisfy myself that I'd done what I could. The deal I made with myself was to keep following leads until the trail ran out. If I came up against a blank wall, then I could return home with a clear conscience. In the meantime, I had a job and I was intent on doing it. Yeah, right, you chickenshit, I thought.

I went through a pack and a half of index cards without any startling revelations. I shuffled them twice and laid them out like a hand of solitaire, scanning row after row for telling details. For instance, I'd made a note that Cecilia'd told me she got home around ten o'clock the night Tom died. She said she'd seen the ambulance, but had no idea it had been summoned for her brother. Could she have seen the woman walking down the road? It occurred to me the woman might have been staying at the Nota Lake Cabins, in which case her stroll might not have had anything to do with Tom. Worth asking, at any rate, just to eliminate the issue.

TWENTY-ONE

Cecilia was late getting back. Instead of returning at 11:30, it was closer to 12:15 when she finally walked in the door. She was dressed for church in a baggy blue tweed suit with bumble bee scatter pins on the lapel. The white blouse underneath featured a frothy burst of lace at the neck. She expressed no surprise when she saw me and in my paranoid state, I imagined my presence had been reported in advance. She opened the half-door to the office, closed it behind her, put her handbag on the desk, and turned to look at me. "Now. What can I do for you? I hear you're staying at Selma's so it can't be a room you've come to ask about."

"I'm still working on this business of Tom's death."

"Seven weeks ago tomorrow. Hard to take it in," she said.

"Do you happen to remember who was staying here that weekend?"

"At the motel? That's easy." She reached for the registration ledger, licked her index finger, and began to page back through the weeks. March became February as she reversed the days. The week of February 1 appeared. She ran a finger down the list of names. "A party of skiers, maybe six of 'em in two cabins. I gave 'em Hemlock and Spruce, as far away from the office as I could make it because I knew they'd get to partying. That type always do. I remember them toting in more cases of beer than they had luggage. Complained a lot, too. Water pressure, heat. Nothing suited them," she said, shooting me a look.

"Anyone else? Any single women?"

"Meaning what?"

"Not meaning anything, Cecilia," I said, patiently. "I'm following up on the CHP report. Tennyson says he saw a woman walking down the road. She may have been a figment of his imagination. It's possible she had nothing to do with Tom. It would be helpful to find her so I'm hoping against hope she was staying here that night. That way you could tell me how to get in touch with her."

She checked the register again. "Nope. Married couple from Los Angeles. Or so they claimed. Only saw that pair when they crawled out of bed to take meals. And one other family with a couple of kids. Wife was in a wheelchair so I doubt he saw her."

"What about you? When you came back from the movies, was there anyone on the road? This would have been between ten and ten-thirty."

Cecilia seemed to give it some thought and then shook her head. "The only thing I remember is someone using the phone out there. I try to discourage strangers stopping off to make calls; tromping up and down the porch stairs, ripping pages from the telephone book. Handset's been stolen twice. This is private property."

"I thought the pay phone was public."

"Not as far as I'm concerned. That's strictly for motel customers. One of the amenities," she said. "Anyway, I could see the Rainbow was closed and the outside lights were off. I poked my head out, but it was only Barrett calling her dad to pick her up. I offered her a lift, but she said he was already on his way."

"You have any idea if Rafer had picked up on the 9-1-1 dispatch?"

"You mean, the ambulance for Tom? Probably," she said. "Or James might have called him, knowing they were such good friends." She closed the ledger. "Now, I hope you'll excuse me. I have someone joining me for Sunday lunch."

"Sure. No problem. I appreciate your help."

I tucked my papers in the briefcase, gathered up the index cards, put a rubber band around them, and dropped them in there, too. I shrugged into my jacket, grabbed my handbag and the briefcase, and returned to my car at the Rainbow. So here's the question I asked myself: If Barrett left work at nine-thirty, why did it take her thirty to forty minutes to call her dad? I sat in the car, watching the clouds gather in a dark gray sky, watching the light dim down to a twilight state. It was only one o'clock in the afternoon, but the dark was so pervasive that the photosensor on Cecilia's exterior lights popped to life. Snow began to fall, big airy flakes settling on the windshield like a layer of soap suds. I waited, watching the rear of the Rainbow Cafe.

By two-thirty, the lunch crowd was all but gone. I sat with the inborn patience of the cat watching for a lizard to reappear from the crevice between two rocks. At 2:44, the back door opened and Barrett came out, wearing her apron and her chef's toque and carrying a large plastic garbage bag intended for the trash bin to my left. I rolled down the window. "Hi, Barrett. You have a minute?"

She dumped the garbage bag and moved closer. I leaned over and unlocked the passenger door, pushing it open a crack. "Hop in. You'll freeze to death out there."

She made no move. "I thought you were gone."

"I was visiting Cecilia. What time do you get off work?"

"Not for hours."

"Why don't you take a break? I'd like to talk to you."

She hesitated, looking toward the Rainbow. "I'm really not supposed to, but it's okay for just a minute." She got in the car, slammed the door, and crossed her bare arms against the cold. I'd have run the engine for the heat, but I didn't want to waste the gas and I was hoping her discomfort would motivate her to tell me what I wanted to know.

"Your dad says you're on your way to med school."

"I haven't been accepted yet," she said.

"Where're you thinking to go?"

"Did you want something in particular? Because Nancy doesn't know I'm out here and I really don't have a coffee break until closer to three."

"I should get to the point, now you mention it," I said. I could feel a fib start to form. For me, it's the same sensation as a sneeze in the making, that wonderful reaction of the autonomic nervous system when something tickles my nose. "I was curious about something." Please note, she didn't ask what. "Wasn't it you Tom Newquist was here to meet that night?"

"Why would he do that?"

"I have no idea. That's why I'm asking you," I said.

She must have done some acting at one point; maybe high school, the senior play, not the lead. She made a show of frowning, then shook her head in bafflement. "I don't think so," she said, as though racking her brain.

"I have to tell you, he made a note on his desk calendar. He wrote *Barrett* plain as day."

"He did?"

"I ran across it today, which is why I was asking earlier who he was here to meet. I was hoping you'd be honest, but you dropped the ball," I said. "I would have let it pass, but then the story was confirmed, so here I am. You want to tell me how it went?"

"Confirmed?"

"As in verified," I said.

"Who confirmed it?"

"Cecilia."

"It wasn't anything," she said.

"Well, great. Cough it up, in that case. I'd like to hear."

"We just talked a few minutes and then he started feeling bad."

"What'd you talk about?"

"Just stuff. We were chatting about my dad. I mean, it was nothing in particular. Just idle conversation. Me and Brant used to go steady and he was asking about the breakup. He always felt bad that we didn't hang in together. I knew he was leading up to something, but I didn't know what. Then, he started feeling sick. I could see the color drain from his face and he started sweating. I was scared."

"Did he say he was in pain?"

She nodded, her voice wavering when she spoke. "He was clutching his chest and his breathing was all raspy. I said I'd go back to the motel and get some help and he said, fine, do that. He told me to lock the truck door and not mention our meeting to anyone. He was real emphatic about that, made me *promise*. Otherwise, I might have told you when you asked the first time." She fumbled in her uniform pocket and found a tissue. She swiped at her eyes and blew her nose.

I waited until she was calmer before I went on. "Did he say anything else?"

She took a deep breath. "Stay off the road if any cars came along. He didn't want anyone to know I'd been talking to him."

"Why?"

"He didn't want to put me in any danger, was what he said."

"He didn't say from whom?"

"He didn't mention anyone by name," she said.

"What else?"

"That's everything."

"He didn't give you his notebook for safekeeping?" She shook her head mutely.

"Are you sure?"

"Positive."

"I thought he gave you the little black book where he kept his field notes."

"Well, he didn't."

"Barrett, tell the truth. Please, please, please? Pretty

please with sugar on it? Trust me, I won't say a word to anyone about your having it."

"I'm telling you the truth."

I shook my head. "I hate to contradict you, but Tom always kept it with him and yet nobody's seen it since he died."

"So?"

"So everybody's been assuming he was by himself that night. Now it turns out you were in his truck. Where else could it be? He was anxious to protect the notebook so he must have given it to you. That's the only way it adds up. If you can think of another explanation, I'd love to hear it."

The silence was exquisite. I let it drag on a bit without breathing another word.

"I went for help."

"I'm sure you did," I said. "The CHP officer saw you on the road. What about the notebook?"

Barrett looked out the window. "You don't have any proof," she said, faintly.

"Well, yeah, I know. I mean, except for the fact that Cecilia saw you on the motel porch that night," I said. "She says your dad came and picked you up, which is what you said yourself. You just fudged a tiny bit about the sequence of events. I can't *prove* you have the notebook, but it stands to reason."

Nancy poked her head out of the Rainbow's back door. Barrett opened the door and leaned out, calling, "I'll be right there!" Nancy nodded and waved.

"So where's the notebook?"

"In my purse," she said, glumly.

"Could you give it to me?"

"What's so important about the notes?"

"He was investigating two murders so I'm assuming his notes are somehow relevant. Did you read them yourself?"

"Well, yeah, but it's just a bunch of interviews and stuff. Lots of dates and abbreviations. It's no big deal."

"Then why does it matter if you pass it on to me?"

"He told me to hide it 'til he could decide what to do with it."

"He didn't know he would die."

"What a bummer," she said.

"Look, if you'll give it to me now, I'll make a copy first thing tomorrow and give it back to you."

After an agonizing moment, she said, "All right."

She got out of the car on her side and I got out on mine, locking the doors quickly before I followed her in. She kept her handbag in the storage room to the left of the kitchen door. Barrett took the notebook out of her bag and passed it to me. She seemed irritated that I'd managed to outmaneuver her somehow. "The other thing he said was the key's on his desk," she said.

"The key's in his desk?"

"That's what he told me. He said it twice."

"In or on?"

"On, I think. I have to go."

"Thanks. You're a doll." I put my finger to my lips. "Top secret. Not a word to anyone."

"Shit. Then why did I tell you?"

Nancy stuck her head in the kitchen door. "Oh, Kinsey. You're here. Brant's on the phone," she said.

I went out into the cafe proper, which was virtually

deserted. The receiver was face down on the counter by the register. "Brant, is that you?"

He said, "Hi, Kinsey."

"Where are you? How'd you know I was here?"

"I'm at Mom's. I drove past the Rainbow a while ago and saw your car parked out back. I just wanted to check and make sure you're okay."

"I'm fine. Is your mother home yet?"

"She won't get back 'til close to nine," he said. "You need something?"

"Not really. If you have a way to call her, would you let her know I got it?"

"Got what?"

I curled my fingers around the mouthpiece, feeling like a character in a spy movie. "The notebook."

"How'd you manage that?"

"I'll explain later. I'll be home in a few minutes. Can you wait?"

"Not really. I just stopped by for some stuff I'll be taking to Sherry's later."

"You work weekends?"

"Not usually," he said. "I'm filling in for someone and hoping to run some errands first. We'll talk tomorrow."

"Right. I'll see you then," I said.

I let myself into Selma's house and headed out to the kitchen. The house was dim, silent, insufferably warm. Everything was much as I'd left it, except for a plastic-wrapped plate of brownies with chocolate frosting sitting on the counter with a note attached: HELP YOUR-SELF. The condensation on the wrap suggested it had been refrigerated or frozen until recently. Brant must have assumed the note was meant for him because a plate and fork, showing telltale traces of chocolate, were sitting on the table at the place he occupied. I was sorry I'd missed him. We could have put our heads together.

I went into Tom's study and sat down in his swivel chair. I turned on his desk light and started going through the notebook. The cover was a pebbly black leather, soft with wear, the corners bent. I took the obvious route, starting at the first page—dated June 1—and working through to the last, which was dated February 1, two days before he died. Here, at last, were the ten months' worth of missing notes. The scribbles, on thin-lined paper, covered all the miscellaneous cases he'd been working on during that period. Each was identified by a case number in the margin to the left, and included complaints, crime-scene investigations, names, addresses, and phone numbers of witnesses. In a series of nearly indecipherable abbreviations, I could trace the course of successive interviews on any given matter; Tom's notes to himself, his case references, the comments and questions that cropped up as he proceeded. There, in something close to hieroglyphics, I read about the discovery of Pinkie's body, the findings of the coroner, Trey Kirchner . . . whom Tom referred to as III. Any recurring name Tom generally reduced to its first letter. I found references to R and B, which I assumed were Rafer and Tom's boss, Sheriff Bob Staffer. By copious squints and leaps of imagination, I could see that he'd worked backward from Pinkie's death to his incarceration in Chino and his friendship with Alfie Toth, a fact confirmed by MB, Margaret Brine at NLSD,

Nota Lake Sheriff's Department. *CS* I took to refer to Colleen Sellers, sometimes referred to as *C*, who'd called to report Alfie Toth's jail time in *ST*. I found the summary of his trip to Santa Teresa in June, including dates, times, mileage, and expenditures for food and lodging. As I'd learned earlier, he'd talked to Dave Estes at the Gramercy on 6–5. Later, he'd talked to Olga Toth, her address and phone number neatly noted. By the time *CS* called again to report the discovery of Toth's remains, Tom's notes had become cursory. Where previously he'd been meticulous about detailing the contents of conversations, he was suddenly circumspect, reverting I suspected to a code of some kind. The last page of notes contained only some numbers—8, 12, 1, 11, and 26 writ large, and underlined with an exclamation point and question mark. Even the punctuation suggested a disbelief most emphatic. I sat and stared at the numbers until they danced on the page.

I got up and went to the kitchen, where I paced the floor. I poured myself some water from the tap and I drank it, making the most satisfactory gulping sounds. I put the glass in the dishwasher and then in a fit of tidiness, added Brant's fork and his plate. I let my brain off the hook, tending to idle occupations while I picked at the riddle. What the hell did the numbers 8, 12, 1, 11, and 26 signify? A date? The combination to a safe? I thought about Tom's telling Barrett about the "key" in or on his desk. I'd been working at his desk for a week and hadn't seen any key that I remembered. What kind of key? The key to what? It's not as though his notebook had a tiny lock like a teenager's diary.

I went back to the den and sat down at his desk,

immediately searching through his drawers again. Maybe he had a lock box. Maybe he had a home safe. Maybe he had a storage cupboard secured by a small combination lock. How many bags full of garbage had I thrown out this past week? How could I be sure I hadn't tossed the key he was referring to? I felt a wave of panic at the idea that I'd thrown out something crucial to his purposes and critical to mine.

One by one, I emptied the contents of each drawer, then removed the drawer itself, checking the back panel and the bottom. I got down on my hands and knees and peered at the underside of the desk, feeling along the sides in case a key had been taped in place. In the drawer with his handcuffs and nightstick, I came across his flashlight and used that as I felt along the drawer rails, tilted his swivel chair back to check the underside of the seat. Did he mean the key, as "a thing that explains or solves something else," or a literal key, as an instrument or device to open a lock? I put the drawers back together and moved everything off the top. I ran a finger across his blotter, looking for a repetition of the numbers among the notes he'd scribbled. The numbers were there—8, 12, 1, 11, 26—appearing in the center of a noose. They were written twice more, once with a pen line encircling it and once in a box with a shaded border done in pencil. What if I'd discarded the critical information? Had the trash been picked up? I was working hard to suppress the nagging worry I felt. I was in a white-hot sweat. The house, as usual, felt like an oven. I crossed to the window and lifted the sash. I loosened the catches on the storm window and pushed the glass out unceremoniously, watching with satisfaction as the window dropped to the ground below. I swallowed mouthfuls of fresh air, hoping to quell my anxiety.

I sat down at the desk again and shook my head. I cleared my mind of emotion, thinking back through the work I'd done earlier in the week. I didn't remember a key, but if I'd seen one I knew I would never have discarded it. If I hadn't found the key yet, there was still the chance that I'd uncover it somewhere. So. The point was to keep searching, as calmly and thoroughly as possible. Again, I went through each drawer, looking carefully at the contents. I checked each item in Tom's file folders, looked in envelopes, opened boxes of paper clips and staples, peered at pens, rulers, labels, tape. Maybe the key was a saying or a phrase that would make everything else clear. At the back of my mind, I kept returning to the notion that the numbers were a code of some kind. I'd never heard any mention of Tom's having worked in Intelligence so if I was right, the code was probably something simple and easily accessible.

On or in his desk.

I found a piece of paper and wrote out the alphabet in sequence, attaching the numbers 1 through 26 underneath. If the numbers 8, 12, 1, 11 and 26 were simple letter substitutions, then the name or initials would be *HLAKZ*. Which meant what? Nothing on the face of it. *Something-Los Angeles-Something-Something?* Didn't suggest anything to me. I tried the same sequence backward, letting *A* correspond with the number 26, *B* correspond with 25, and so forth until I reached the number 1, which I assumed represented *Z*. If this were the case, then the numbers 8, 12, 1, 11, 26 would spell out *SOZPA*. Another puzzlement. What the hell was this? A name? My frustration level mounted at a pace with my confusion.

8, 12, 1, 11, 26. Months of the year? August, December, January, November? Then what did the 26 denote? And why out of order? Was I supposed to add? Subtract? Sound out the words phonetically like a vanity license plate? I repeated them aloud. "Eight. Twelve. One. Eleven. Twenty-six." This meant nothing. If the numbers represented letters and this was a word, then all I knew for sure was that the five letters were different . . . with no repetitions. Someone's name? I thought about Nota Lake and how many people I'd met here who had five-letter first names. Brant, Macon, Hatch, Wayne. James Tennyson. Rafer. I looked at the exclamation point and the question mark. *!?* Which said what? Consternation? Dismay?

I realized I was famished . . . a manifestation of my anxiety no doubt. Waiting for Barrett in the cafe parking lot, I'd skipped lunch altogether and this was the price I paid. It was now four-fifteen. I went back to the kitchen in search of sustenance. I was so hungry and so befuddled, my brain cells felt like they'd quit holding hands. I looked in Selma's refrigerator, greeted by plastic-wrapped leftovers from last night's dinner. Not memorable to begin with and certainly not worth re-eating. I checked the bread drawer. No crackers. I checked the cupboards. No peanut butter. What kind of household did she run? I glanced at her note and in the absence of wholesome foodstuffs, I allowed myself to lift a corner of the plastic wrap and help myself to several brownies. The texture was off—a bit dry for my taste—but the icing was nice and gooey, only a faint chemical taste suggesting she'd used a boxed mix. Anyone who'd eat Miracle Whip would eat that shit, I thought. This was not Selma's best effort by a long stretch, but I figured my days consuming her cooking were just about over. I drank some milk from the carton, figuring to save a glass.

Thus fortified, I was prepared to tackle the problem. I went back to Tom's swivel chair and swiveled. What if 8, 12, 1, 11, and 26 were page numbers, referring to the notes themselves? I tried that approach, but the contents of the pages seemed in no way related, sharing no visible common elements and no designated page numbers. The afternoon was stretching toward evening and I was getting nowhere. I went back to the original premise. Selma had hired me to find out why Tom was distressed. I slouched down on my spine and leaned my head on the back of the chair. Why was Tom brooding, Kinsey asked herself? I rocked, allowing myself to ruminate at my leisure. If someone he knew had violated his privacy, reading his notes and using the information to get to Alfie Toth to kill him, that would certainly do the trick. But why would Hatch's involvement . . . or James's or Waynes's . . . have generated a moment's uneasiness or hesitation. Tom played by the rules. I'd been told over and over, he was strictly a law-and-order type. If he'd suspected any one of them, he'd have acted at once. Wouldn't he? Why would he not? It wouldn't have meant anything to him if Wayne had violated the sanctity of his field notes. My gaze dropped to the blotter. I pushed a stack of files aside. Down in the right-hand corner, Tom had drawn a grid, penning in the days of the month of February, the year unspecified. The First fell on a Sunday, the Twenty-eighth on a Saturday. The last two Saturdays of the month—the Twenty-first and the Twenty-eighth—were crossed out. Was the year 1908? 1912, 1901, 1911 or 1926? I got up and went to the bookshelf, where I took down a copy of his almanac. I thumbed to the index and found the page numbers for a perpetual calendar. In a table to the left the years between 1800 and 2063 were listed in order. Beside each year was a number corresponding to a numbered template, representing all the variations in the way the months could be laid out. Calendar number one was a year in which January 1 fell on a Sunday; February 1 fell on a Wednesday; and each month thereafter was depicted. Calendar number two represented any and all years in which January 1 fell on a Monday; February 1 fell on Thursday; and so forth. If you wanted to know the day of the month for a particular date—say, March 5, 1966—you simply checked the master list for the year 1966, beside which appeared the number seven. Moving to Calendar number seven, you could see that March 5 fell on a Saturday.

I flipped on the desk light and studied the series of calendar pages, looking at the Februaries laid out like the one he'd drawn. Calendar number five was like that. February 1 fell on a Sunday and the Twenty-eighth fell on the last Saturday of the month. Calendar number twelve was similar except there were twenty-nine days instead of twenty-eight. I checked the years that corresponded, starting with 1900. 1903 was such a year, but not 1908 and not 1912. In 1914, the First fell on a Sunday and the Twenty-eighth on the last Saturday, but the same wasn't true of 1926. 1925, 1931, 1942, 1953, 1959, 1970, 1981, 1987, 1998. Why were these particular Februaries important? The year couldn't be relevant, could it? And why had he crossed out the last two Saturdays of that month? I thought about it for a minute. Eliminating those two Saturdays cut the number of days from twenty-eight to twenty-six—the number of letters in the alphabet. I tried that approach, lining up the letters with the days of the month. The answer was still *HLAKZ*.

Still rocking in his desk chair, I swiveled toward the window. It was nearly five-thirty, fully dark outside. Cold air still spilled through the gap where I'd raised the window. I could almost discern the waves of household heat pouring out in exchange. The room was decidedly chilly. I leaned forward and closed the window, staring at my reflection in the smoke-clouded glass. What the hell did those numbers mean? I could feel a draft from somewhere. Was there a draft coming down the chimney? Curious, I got up and moved out of the den. I walked along the front hall to the living room where I turned on the table lamps. The drapes were wavering as though pushed by an unseen hand. I peered up the chimney and flipped the flue to the shut position. I checked the perimeter doors. The front door was closed and locked, as was the back door, and the door to the garage. That wasn't it. I poked my head into Selma's bedroom. All was undisturbed yet the draft was such that the curtains rippled in the windows. I proceeded down the hall. All the windows in Brant's old bedroom were closed.

I stopped where I was. The door to my room was ajar. Had I left it that way? I pushed it open with apprehension. Curtains flapped and fluttered. The room was a shambles. There were jagged shards of glass on the carpet. The window, which I'd oh-so-carefully locked, had been shattered by a hammer that someone had left on the floor. Pebbles of glass the size of rocksalt were spread out across the sill like discarded diamonds. The sash had been pushed up, probably from the outside. Someone had clearly entered. I moved to the bed and slid my hand between the box spring and mattress. My gun was missing.

TWENTY-TWO

I glanced at my watch. 5:36. I walked back to the kitchen prepared to dial 9-1-1. I hesitated, my hand on the receiver. Who was I going to call? Rafer? Brant? Tom's brother, Macon? I wasn't sure I trusted any one of them. I stood there, trying to determine whom I could confide in at this point. A chill went through me. Surely, there wasn't anybody in the house *with* me. I hadn't gone to the guest room since I'd returned to the house early in the afternoon so the intruder had probably been here and departed long before I showed up. Ordinarily, I'd have gone to my room to drop my jacket. After the day I'd had, I might have showered or napped—anything to perk myself up and restore my confidence—but I'd been intent on Tom's notes and I'd gone directly to his den. I felt disembodied, my mind having been separated from my flesh by the harrowing sensation of fear.

The phone shrilled with extraordinary loudness, setting off a surge of nausea. I jumped, nerves raw, my reflexes responding sharply, almost to the point of pain. I snatched up the receiver before it had ceased to ring. "Hello?"

335

"Hey, Kinsey. Brant here. Is my mom home yet?" He sounded young and carefree, relaxed, unconcerned.

My stomach churned in response. "You need to come home," I said. My voice seemed to be coming from a curious distance.

He must have been alerted by my tone because his shifted. "Why? What's going on?"

"Someone's broken in. There's glass on the bedroom floor and my gun is gone."

"Where's Mom?"

"I don't know. Yes. Wait. At your cousin's in Big Pine. I'm here alone," I said.

"Stay where you are. I'll be right there."

He hung up.

I replaced the receiver. I turned and leaned my back up against the wall, making little mewling sounds. A town full of cowboys and someone was coming after me. I held my hands out in front of me. I could see my fingers tremble, the recently dislocated digits looking all puffy and useless. My gun had been stolen. I had to have a weapon, some way to defend myself against the coming onslaught. I started opening the kitchen drawers, one after the other, in search of a knife. One drawer flew off its rails and banged against my thigh, spilling out its contents. Utensils jangled together, tumbling to the floor at my feet. I could feel the tears stinging my lids. I gathered a fistful of items and tossed them back in the drawer, but I couldn't seem to get it mounted on its track again. I banged it on the counter top so hard a metal spatula bounced and flew out. I left the drawer where it was. I found a steak knife, some generic brand that looked like a giveaway in a box of detergent. The overhead light glinted off its surface. I could see the bevel on the blade. What good would a serrated steak knife do against a speeding bullet?

Hours seemed to go by.

I could hear the second hand on the kitchen clock tick each passing second in turn.

Outside, I heard the squeal of brakes, and then a car door slammed shut. I turned and stared at the front door. What if it was someone else? What if it was them? The door flew open and I could see Brant in his civilian clothes. He moved toward me with all the comforting bulk of a battleship. I put a hand out and he took it.

"Jesus, you look awful. How'd the guy get in?"

I pointed to my room and then found myself following as he moved purposefully down the hall in that direction. His assessment was brief, the most cursory of glances. He turned away from the guest room and toured the rest of the house methodically, looking in every closet, every nook and cranny. He went down to the basement. I waited at the top of the stairs, one hand plucking at the other. My injured fingers held a particular fascination for me—clumsy and swollen. Where was my gun? How could I defend myself when I'd left the knife on the counter?

Brant returned to the kitchen. I followed him like a duckling. I could tell by his tone he was trying to control himself. Something in his manner conveyed the seriousness of the situation. "Did he get the notebook?"

I found myself grinding my teeth. "Who?"

"The guy who broke in," he said sharply.

"It was in my bag," I said. "Is that what he was after?"

"Of course," Brant said. "I can't think why else he'd risk it. Tell me exactly what you did today. What time did you leave and how long were you gone?"

I felt burbling and incoherent, spilling out the story of my rebuff, the refusal of the gas station attendants to do business with me, my subsequent stop at the Rainbow to talk to Nancy. I told him I'd run into Rafer and Vick, that I'd talked to Cecilia and Barrett. My brain was moving at twice the speed of my lips, making me feel sluggish and stupid. Brant, god bless him, seemed to follow the staccato pace of the narrative, filling in the blanks when an occasional word came up missing. What was wrong with me? I knew I'd felt like this before—this scared—this powerless—this out of it . . .

Brant was staring at me. "You actually talked to him?"

What was he talking about? "Who?" I sounded like an owl.

"Rafer."

What had I asked? What had he said before this? What did Rafer have to do with anything? "What?"

"Rafer. At the Rainbow."

"Yes. I ran into him at the Rainbow."

"I know that. You told me. I'm asking you if you talked to him," he said, with exaggerated patience.

"Sure."

"You *talked* to him?!" His voice had risen with alarm. I could see the question mark and the exclamation point hurtling through the air at me. "I brought him up to date," I said. My voice was delayed, like something in an echo chamber. Words in balloons bumped together above my head, images like projectiles flying off in all directions.

"I told you to wait 'til I could check it out. Who do you think started all the rumors?"

"Who?"

Brant took me by the shoulders and gave me a little shake. He seemed angry, his fingers biting into my shoulders. "Kinsey, wake up and pay attention. This is serious," he said.

"You're not saying it was him?"

"Of *course*, it was him. Who else could it be? Think about it, dummy."

"Think about what?" I asked, confused. The immediacy of his discomposure was contagious. I was relying on him for help, but his anxiety was pushing mine into the danger zone.

His voice pounded on, pleading and cajoling, wheedling. "You told Mom it was someone in law enforcement. Do you honestly think my father would have lost even one night's sleep if it was anyone but Rafer? Rafer was his best friend. The two of them had worked together for years and years. Dad thought Rafer was one of the finest cops who ever lived. Now he finds out he killed two guys? Jeez. He must have shit himself when he understood what was going on. Didn't he write this down? Isn't this in his notes?"

His words were like streamers, blowing above his head.

I heard snapping, like flags. "The notes are in code. I can't read them."

"Where? Can you show me? Maybe I can crack it."

"In there. You think he was on the verge of talking to Internal Affairs?"

"Of course! The decision couldn't have been easy, but even as loyal as he was to Rafer, the department came first. He must have been praying for a way out, hoping he was wrong."

My brain worked lickety-cut. It was my mouth that fumbled, thoughts crashing against my teeth like rocks. I had to clamp my jaw shut, barely moving my lips. "I talked to Barrett. She was with Tom in the truck just before he died," I said.

"What did they talk about? Why did he do that?"

"Something. I can't remember."

"Didn't you press her for answers? You had the girl right there in the palm of your hand," he said. His words appeared in the air, written in big capital letters.

"Quit yelling."

"I'm not yelling. What's the matter with you?"

"Barrett never said a word about Rafer." I remembered then. She did say Tom had asked about her father.

"Why would she? She doesn't know you from Adam. She's not going to confide. She wouldn't tell you something like that. Her own father? For god's sake, she'd have to be nuts," he shrilled.

"But why give me the notes? Wouldn't she assume they'd be incriminating?"

"Barrett doesn't have a clue. She has no idea."

"How do you know what he did?"

"Because I can add," he said, exasperated. "I put two and two together. Listen, Tom met with Barrett. He was probably trying to find out about Rafer's whereabouts when Pinkie was murdered. Same with Alfie Toth. He saw the connection. He was worried someone in the department would get wind of his suspicions, didn't you say that? Someone had already ripped him off for the information about Toth. Who do you think it was? *Rafer.*"

"Rafer," I said. I was nodding. I could see what he was saying. I'd been thinking the same thing. Tom's friendship with Rafer was such that he'd think long and hard before he turned him in to the authorities, betraying their friendship. A conflict of that magnitude would have caused him extreme distress. My brain was clicking and buzzing. *Click, click, click.* Rafer. It was like a pinball game. Thoughts ricocheted around, setting off bells, bouncing against the rails. I thought about the clerk at the Gramercy. Why didn't he tell me the phony plainclothes detective was black? You'd think he'd remember something so obvious. My mind kept veering. I couldn't hold a thought in one place and follow it to its conclusion. *Click, click.* Like pool balls. The cue ball would break and all the other balls on the table would fly off in separate directions. I wished I'd talked to Leland Peck before I left Santa Teresa. I was feeling very weird. So anxious. Sound fading in and out. I could see it undulate through space, sentences like surfers cresting on the waves of air.

Brant was still talking. He seemed to be speaking gibberish, but it all made a peculiar sense. "Pinkie went after Barrett. She was hiking in the mountains and stumbled across their fishing camp."

On and on he went, creating word pictures so vivid I thought it was happening to me.

"Barrett was assaulted. He put a gun to her head.

She was raped. She was attacked and sexually abused. Pinkie sodomized and hurt her. He forced her to perform unspeakable acts. Alfie did nothing—offered her no assistance—ran off, leaving her to Pinkie's mercy. Barrett came back hysterical, in a state of shock. Rafer went after Pinkie and took him down. He strung him up, hung him from the limb of a tree and let him die slowly for what he had done to her. He would have killed Alfie, too, but Alfie escaped and blew town. Rafer thought he was safe all these years and then Pinkie's body turned up and Dad found the link between the two men. He drove all the way to Santa Teresa to talk to him, but Rafer got there first. He hung Toth the same way he hung Pinkie." Brant was looking at me earnestly. "What's wrong with your eyes?"

"My eyes?" Once he mentioned it, I realized my field of vision had begun to oscillate, images sliding side to side, like bad camera work. I felt giddy, as if I was on the verge of fainting. I sat down. I put my head between my knees, a roaring in my ears.

"Are you okay?"

"Fine." Lights seemed to pulsate and sounds came and went. I couldn't keep it straight. I knew what he was saying, but I couldn't make the words stand still. I saw Rafer with the noose. I saw him tighten it on Pinkie's neck. I saw him hang Alfie in the wilderness. I felt his rage and his pain for what they'd done to his only daughter. I said, "How do you know all this?"

"Because Barrett told me when it happened. Jesus, Kinsey. That's why I broke up with her. I was twenty years old. I couldn't handle it," he said, anguished.

"I'm sorry. I'm sorry," I said, but immediately forgot

who was more deserving of my pity—Barrett for being raped, Brant for not having the maturity to deal with it.

Brant's tone became accusatory. "You're loaded. I don't believe it. What the hell are you high on?"

"I'm high?" Of course. Daniel playing the piano. My ex-husband. So beautiful. Eyes like an angel, a halo of golden curls and how I'd loved him. He'd given me acid once without telling me and I watched the floor recede into the mouth of hell.

Brant's head came up. "What's that?" he hissed.

"What?"

"I heard something." His agitation washed over me. His fear was infectious, as swift as an airborne virus. I could smell corruption and death. I'd been in situations like this before.

"Hang on." Brant strode down the hall. I saw him look out of the small ornamental window in the front door. He pulled back abruptly and then gestured urgently in my direction. "A car cruised by with its lights doused. He's parked across the street about six doors down. You have a gun?"

"I told you someone stole it. Whoever broke in. I don't have a gun. What's happening?"

"Rafer," he said, grimly. He crossed to the drawer in his mother's kitchen desk where she did her menu planning. He pulled out a gun and thrust it in my hand. "Here. Take this."

I stood and stared at it with bewilderment. "Thanks," I whispered. The gun was a basic police revolver, Smith & Wesson. I'd nearly bought one like it once, .357 Magnum, four-inch barrel, checkered walnut stocks. I studied the grooves in the stock. Some of them were so deep, I couldn't see to the bottom.

"Rafer will come in with guns blazing," Brant was saying. "No deals. He's told everyone that you're a killer, that you do drugs, and here you are stoned on something."

"I didn't do anything," I said, mouth dry. The brownies. I was higher than he knew. I racked back through my memory, classes at the police academy, my years in uniform on the street, trying to remember symptoms; phencyclidines, stimulants, hallucinogens, sedative-hypnotics, narcotics. What had I ingested? Confusion, paranoia, slurred speech, nystagmus. I could see the columns marching across the pages of the text. PCP vocabulary. Rocket Fuel, DOA, KJ, Super Joint, Mint Weed, Gorilla Biscuits. I was out of my brain on speed.

"You found him out. He'll have to kill you. We'll have to shoot it out," Brant said.

"Don't leave me. You talk to him. I can get away," I burbled.

"He's thought of that. He'll have help. Probably Macon and Hatch. They both hate you. We better get down to business."

When Brant peeled off his outer jacket, I smelled stress sweat, the scent as acrid and piercing as ammonia. I glanced at his hands. Given any visual field, the eye tends to stray to the one different item in a ground of like items. Even bombed, I caught sight of a blemish on his right wrist, a dark patch ... a tattoo or a birthmark ... shaped like the prow of a ship. The blot stood out like a brand on the clean white surface of his skin. Sizzling, my brain zapped through the possibilities: scar, hickey, smudge, scab. I was slow on the uptake. I looked back and then I saw it for what it was. The mark was a burn. The healing discoloration was a match for the tip of the ticking hot iron I'd pressed on him. Adrenaline rushed through me. Something close to euphoria filled my flesh and bones. My mind made an odd leap to something else altogether. I'd been struggling to break the code with logic and analysis when the answer was really one of spatial relationships. Vertical, not horizontal. That's how the numbers worked. Up and down instead of back and forth across the lines.

I put the gun on the kitchen table. "I'll be right back," I said. With extraordinary effort, I propelled myself into Tom's den, hand to the wall to steady my yawning gait. 8, 12, 1, 11, and 26. I sat down at his desk and looked at the calendar Tom had drawn. I could see the month of February, twenty-eight days penned in with the First falling on a Sunday and the last two Saturdays, the Twenty-first and the Twenty-eighth, crossed out, leaving twenty-six numbers. I'd suspected the code was simple. If Tom encrypted his notes, he had to have an uncomplicated means by which to convert letters to numbers.

I found a pencil. I turned to the calendar grid that he'd drawn on the corner of his blotter. I wrote the letters of the alphabet, inserting one letter per day, using vertical rows this time. If my theory was correct, then the code would confirm what I already knew: 8 would represent the letter *B*. The number 12 would stand in for the letter *R*. The number 1 would be *A*, and 11 would represent an *N*, and the 26 would be *T*.

B-R-A-N-T.

Brant.

I could feel a laugh billow up. I was stuck in the house with him. He would have had easy access to his father's notes. The search of the den—the broken window—both had been a cover, suggesting to the rest of us that someone from the outside had entered the house in hopes of finding the notes. It wasn't Barrett at all. Pinkie hadn't raped and sodomized Barrett. It was Brant he'd humiliated and degraded.

"What are you doing?"

I jumped. Brant was standing in the doorway. I was standing in horseshit up to my underpants. The sight of him wavered, shimmering, image moving side to side. I couldn't think of a way to answer. Nystagmus. Something in brownies, possibly PCP. Aggression, paranoia. I was smarter than him. Oh, much smarter. I was smarter than anyone that day.

"What are you looking at?"

"Tom's notes."

"Why?"

"I can't make heads or tails of them. The code."

He stared at me. I could tell he was trying to determine if what I'd said was true. I kept my mind empty. I don't think I'd ever seen him looking so lean and young and handsome. Death is like that, a lover whose embrace you sink into without warning. Instead of flight or resistance, voluptuous surrender. He held out his hand. "I'll take the notes."

I passed the notebook across to him, picturing the Smith & Wesson. Where had I heard about a gun like that before? I could feel my brain crackling, thoughts popping like kernels banging against the lid of a popcorn pan. There was no way in the world he would give me a gun unless he intended to see that I was killed with it. Rafer LaMott wasn't outside and neither was anybody else. This was a charade, setting me up in some way. I envisioned the scene—the two of us skulking through the house, ostensibly waiting for an attack that would never come. Brant could shoot me anytime he chose, claiming later he'd mistaken me for an intruder, claiming self-defense, claiming I was stoned out of my gourd, which I was. Even as the thought formed, I felt the drugs kick up a notch. I could feel myself expanding. I could outsmart him. He was strong, but I had more experience than he did. I knew more about him than he knew about me. I'd been a cop once. I knew everything he knew, plus some.

"Is the car still out there?" I asked.

Brant dropped back into his fantasy. He moved to the window and put his face close the the glass, peering off to the right. "Down half a block. You can barely see it from here."

"I think we should turn the lights out. I don't like standing here in plain view."

He studied me for a second, picturing the house black as pitch. "You're right. Hit the switch. I'll take care of all the other lights in the house."

"Good." I turned the den light out. I waited until I heard him moving down the hall toward the front. Then I eased to the window, flipped the lock, and pushed the sash up about six inches. I dropped down to the floor, felt my way across the room to the cabinet, and slid myself feet-first into the space beneath the bookshelves.

Birth in reverse. I was hidden from view. Moments went by, the house becoming darker by the minute as lamps were being switched off in every room Brant entered.

"Kinsey?" Brant was back.

Silence.

I heard him come to the den. He must have stood in the doorway, allowing his eyes to adjust to the black. He crossed to the window, bumping into cardboard boxes. I heard him force the window open and look out. I was gone. There was no sign of me running across the grass. "Shit!" He slammed the window shut and said, "Shit, shit, *shit!*" He must have had a gun because I heard him rack one into the chamber.

He left the den, hollering my name as he went. Now he was mad. Now he didn't care if I knew he was coming. I pulled myself out of the cabinet, hanging on to the shelf as I staggered to my feet. I crossed to the desk and opened the bottom drawer as quietly as possible. I took out Tom's handcuffs and tucked them in my back pocket. I could feel myself swell with power. I was suddenly larger than life, far beyond fear, luminous with fury. As I turned right out of the den into the darkness of the hallway, I could see him moving ahead of me, his body mass blacker than the charcoal light surrounding him. I began to run, picking up speed, my Reeboks making no sound on the carpet. Brant sensed my presence, turning as I lifted myself into the air. I snapped a hard front kick to his solar plexus, taking him down with one pop. I heard his gun thump dully against the wall, banging against wood as it flew out of his hand. I kicked him again, catching him squarely on the side of the head. I scrambled to my feet and stood over him. I could have crushed his skull, but as a *courtesy*, I refrained from doing so. I pulled the handcuffs from my pocket. I grabbed the fingers of his right hand and bent them backward, encouraging compliance. I lay the cuff on his right wrist and snapped downward, smiling grimly to myself as the swinging arm of the cuff locked in place. I put my left foot on the back of his neck while I yanked his right arm behind him and I grabbed for his left. I would have stomped down on his face, pulverizing his nose if he'd so much as whimpered. He was out cold. I double-locked both handcuffs in place. All of this without hesitation. All of this in the dark.

The light in the kitchen was snapped on. Selma appeared in the doorway, still wearing her fur coat. She stood as still as a soldier and took in the sight before her. Brant was now moaning. Blood was pouring from his nose and he was struggling for breath. "Mom, watch out. She's stoned," he croaked.

Selma backed into the kitchen. I was moving away from her down the corridor, looking for Brant's gun when she showed up again, this time with the Smith & Wesson in her right hand. I had no idea where Brant's gun had gone. I remembered the telltale thump at the end of its airborne journey.

"Stop right there," she said. She was now holding the gun with two hands, arms extended stiffly at shoulder height. I went about my business, ignoring her little drama. She had no way of knowing I'd been sanctified by Angel Dust. I was higher than a kite on PCP, methamphetamines, whatever it was—some amazing mix of excitation and immortality. The unpleasant side effects were now gone and I was detached from all feeling, secure in the sense that I would prevail over this bitch and anyone else who came after me.

"You're not going to take my son away from me."

As much as anything, I was annoyed with her. "I told you to forget it. You should have left well enough alone. Now you've not only lost Tom, you've lost Brant as well," I said, conversationally. I got down on my hands and knees and felt under the chair. Where the hell was Brant's gun?

"You are completely mistaken. I haven't lost Brant at all," she said. "Now get up right this minute! Do as I say!"

"Blow it out your ass, Selma. Do you see Brant's gun? I heard it bang against the wall. It's gotta be here somewhere."

"I'm warning you. I'll count to three and then I'm going to shoot you."

"You do that," I said. I moved into the dining room, convinced the gun had somehow become wedged under the hutch, the centerpiece in Selma's entire set of handsome, formal, glossy dark wood furniture. I placed my shoulder against the floor, reaching under the hutch as far as the length of my arm. It was in this awkward position—me spread-eagled on my stomach, Brant handcuffed and moaning in the hall, Selma angling herself into position to blow my head off if she could manage it—that I chanced to look up at her, watching in slow-motion amazement as she screwed up her face, closed her eyes, turned her head, and squeezed the trigger. There was a bright flash and a loud bang. The bullet exited the barrel at a lethal velocity. The normal football-shaped muzzle flash out the front of the gun and the vertical fan-shaped flashes at the cylinder gap seemed to be enhanced, a dazzling yellow. Brant had apparently packed the first cartridge with an overload of fast powder. I thought I knew now who Judy Gelson's lover was the night she blew a hole in her husband's chest. The chamber and the top strap ruptured. The blast unlatched the cylinder and drove it out to the left side of the gun. The brass cartridge case shredded and tiny bits of brass peppered Selma's hands, flakes of unburned powder peppering her face as well. Simultaneously, as though by magic, all the glass in the cabinet doors, including the crystal goblets and the bone china plates, exploded like fireworks and formed a glittering starburst of falling glass and debris.

"Fuck. That was great. You should try that again," I said.

Selma was weeping as I walked to the phone and dialed 9–1–1.

EPILOGUE

Later, the Nota County Sheriff gave me permission to read the file on the Ritter/Toth murders. Rafer and I sat down together and by comparing Tom's notes with other reports submitted in the case, we managed to piece together the course of Tom's investigation. The irony, of course, was that the evidence he'd collected was not only spotty, but entirely circumstantial. None of it was sufficient to result in an arrest, let alone a conviction. Tom realized Brant had committed double murder and he knew it was something he couldn't keep to himself for long. Revealing the truth would destroy his marriage. Concealing the truth would destroy everything else he valued. Tom had died in silence, and if Selma had been content to leave it there, the case might have died, too.

Brant is currently out on bail on a charge of attempted murder for what he did to me. Selma's hired a fancy-pants attorney who (naturally) advised him to plead not guilty. I suspect if we get to court this same attorney will find a way to blame the whole thing on me. That's the way justice seems to work these days.

In the meantime, Selma's house is on the market and

she's leaving Nota Lake. The town is unforgiving and the people there never liked her anyway. I guess what it all boils down to is a lesson in personal insecurity and low self-esteem. If I'd been clairvoyant—if I'd been capable of seeing all of these events in advance—I'd have told her to have her teeth capped instead of hiring me. She'd have been better off that way.

Respectfully submitted,
Kinsey Millhone